THE FINAL JIHAD

When the "best of the worst" finally come for us!

MARTIN KEATING

LOGICAL FIGMENTS BOOKS – LOS ANGELES

LOGICAL FIGMENTS BOOKS
a division of Logical Figments, Inc.
557 Norwich Drive
Los Angeles, CA 90048

Copyright © 1996 by Martin Keating

Library of Congress Catalog Card Number: 96-76572

ISBN: 0-9647048-1-1

First Logical Figments Books hardcover printing July 1996

10 9 8 7 6 5 4 3 2 1

Printed in the U.S.A.

*To Captain Barney Martin (Ret.), my uncle and hero,
upon whose life this book is based.
His contacts at the helm of the U.S. Navy's
counterespionage operations introduced me to
the foreign intelligence community worldwide, which, in turn,
opened many doors—some quite dangerous—into
governments within governments and into the boiling
infrastructure of fanatical terrorist organizations.*

*To my brother Frank Keating, whose achievements and
capabilities led him to become the governor of Oklahoma
only three months before the worst terrorist attack
on American soil. Frank's positions in the Treasury
and Justice departments provided me valuable
introductions to operatives within the FBI, the Secret
Service, the ATF, U.S. Customs, and the Pentagon.*

To my many partners around the "circle of color"
who continually risk their lives for the
enlightenment of our deepest hunger.
Special thanks to K Kim*** (Sr. and Jr.)
for the teachings and nurturing of your instructors;
to Alexandrov for deicing the nest and melting
the snow in the darkness of the winter glacier;
and a rose to ESTANKA for the records.

To my comrades here mining for an
everlasting treasure of plasma; and, of course, to Col. Said
for your tingling fingers. Your brothers and sisters hold
the key to the irrigation of our farmland.

ANGELS OF DEATH

When the Soviet Union imploded, a lot of people figured the long nightmare was finally over. However, no one at the FBI felt that way. We knew that the former KGB hard-liners still controlled billions of dollars in gold in Zurich and could keep their cause alive by financing and directing scores of militants and terrorist-for-hire groups around the world. If they ever completed the loop by establishing a terrorist base here in America, they could tear us apart in a month.

Corley Brand
Chief, Counterterrorism Section
Federal Bureau of Investigation

Las Colinas Hotel and Conference Center, Irving, Texas
Monday, December 28, 4:59 a.m.

"Jack, I have touched the face of Death. *Please!* I've got to show you what I've found . . . before it's too late."

Those were Reuben Gentry's exact words, over the telephone . . . just after midnight.

Jack Stroud rubbed an open hand across his unshaven face and stared at the bedside alarm clock. The hotel room was cool and quiet, the setting for a good night's sleep under normal circumstances. He took a deep breath and wondered how many times in the intervening hours his brain had replayed his father-in-law's puzzling message. Twenty? Hell, it could just as easily have been fifty. So far, his attempts to fathom the cryptic telephone call had been in vain.

It had been Reuben's voice, all right, but what really haunted Jack was the uncharacteristic emotion that had oozed from the older man's delivery. It was pure fear—palpable, malignant. He'd attempted to extract from the prominent television evangelist the reason for his anxiety, but Reuben wouldn't yield. At least not over the phone. "For God's sake, Jack," the voice had moaned, "I have to meet with you today!"

Jack focused and saw that the time displayed by the red LED digits of the clock was exactly 5:00 a.m. He yawned and realized he'd been lost in thought for most of an hour. Before that, he'd slept fitfully. As he contemplated the glowing numbers, he remembered that the alarm would sound in forty minutes. Reuben's flight would arrive in four hours.

"I'll miss you," Laura Stroud whispered.

Jack turned in the semidarkness. "Did I wake you?"

His wife rolled to her side and propped herself on an elbow. The blanket and top sheet barely covered her breasts. The night-light in the hallway cast a soft glow across her attractive face. She shook her head. "Couldn't sleep. I've been thinking about Dad's call."

Jack sighed. "So have I." He didn't want to add to her concerns, so he decided not to tell her his own misgivings.

She brushed away a lock of hair and looked into his eyes. "I'm worried, Jack."

"Come here." He slid his hand under her waist and invited her with a tug toward his side of the bed. "We'll only be apart for a day." He hoped she'd accept his no-problem demeanor. He tried to keep his attitude neutral. He couldn't . . . wouldn't . . . tell her that her father's call reminded him of the unsettling late-night alerts he'd received while he was with the Naval Investigative Service, when he'd had to disappear for weeks. No, he prayed, the old man simply had a problem at the college, probably all blown out of proportion. But his instincts told him otherwise.

Laura shifted closer. Her arms encircled his neck.

"Jack, listen to me." Her tone was sober. "There must be something terribly wrong. Otherwise, Dad wouldn't think of interrupting our plans. Tell me again, how'd he sound?"

Jack tried to maintain his noncommittal façade. "Oh, you know your Dad. He's a master at hiding his true intentions when he wants to." He kissed the tip of her nose. "Don't worry. Whatever it is, he and I can straighten things out in short order." Jack had learned long ago to turn off any disturbing thoughts about the old evangelist. Laura was always quick to pick up on negatives where her family was involved, especially those about her father. He smiled. "But it's nice to know he thinks enough of me to ask for my help."

"No, Jack," she declared firmly, "it sounded too much like the old days. You know what I mean. And I won't have it. We're a family now, and I won't allow you to be taken away from me again."

Jack drew her closer and advanced an inquiring hand up her back and across her shoulders. He welcomed his own physical stirrings, undiminished over the years.

"Know what?" His open palm descended and found a bare breast. He circled and erected her nipple with the tip of his finger. "I'll work my usual wonders on your dad, then I'll be on a plane to join you." He embraced her and savored the exquisite sensations of their naked bodies, pressed together under the covers.

"Jack?" Laura's voice remained firm, but he knew she only wanted his assurance.

"I promise."

She tilted her head away from him and displayed the little-girl pout he could never resist.

"Will you promise to work your wonders on *me* afterwards?"

He returned a grin and pressed his lips to her ear. "Does the lady want *another* preview?"

Laura moaned and traced her fingernails in figure eights across his shoulders. Her hips moved in response to his need. After all this time, she could still surprise him with her sexual abandon. When Jack had told friends he was marrying the daughter of a famous television evangelist, they'd had definite opinions. "Preachers' daughters have iceboxes between their legs, so you'd better check the merchandise before you buy," some had advised. But others joked, "They're in heat, man. Those deprived broads are sexual explosions waiting to happen. They want it bad." Laura was the best of all worlds—cool and ladylike in public, yet warm and affectionate at home with him and their children. And strongly sexed with him in private. Jack considered himself a very lucky man.

In a fluid and erotic ritual perfected by years of their passion for each other, they caressed and maneuvered for the delicious moment. Laura's breath was short in anticipation as Jack positioned himself. Then, propelled by his ever-renewing longing to be one with her, he thrust deeply and banished all intrusions of the outside world. They knew each other so well that their primal movements smoothly produced the sensations that escalated them upward toward the ultimate pinnacle. Finally they reached and, for a second, were poised together at the top . . . before they gasped and cascaded downward and were consumed by the pleasure of their love.

For uncounted minutes they remained blissfully removed from reality, a touch here, a knowing stroke there. Then, with a lingering, grateful kiss, Jack withdrew and lay next to her in the shared afterglow. Laura turned toward him and cuddled into his arms. Her breathing was easy.

Jack touched the back of her neck and repeated his smoothing of her skin. How incredibly fortunate he was, he thought. He didn't know what he would ever do without her. He wished he didn't have to stay behind today.

Laura opened her eyes and smiled. "I love you, Jack," she whispered. "More than I could ever tell you."

Dallas–Fort Worth International Airport
6:05 a.m.

Special Agent Scott Collister pressed his face against the cold glass of the deserted departure lounge and squinted into the darkness. Outside, under the focused brilliance of the sodium-vapor lamps, the supersonic transport looked like a fragile bird of prey trapped in the shadow of a Lufthansa A340 Airbus. Shorter, and with a wingspan less than half that of its wide-bodied cousin, the sleek titanium dart crouched in the frosty predawn quiet. From his warm, carpeted observation post, Collister saw that the SST's characteristic nose pointed directly at him. It looked inquisitive—almost alive.

Three and a half miles to the south, a maroon Cutlass turned onto International Parkway and headed for the airport. As it approached the lighted toll plaza, the car maneuvered behind an American Airlines crew van and slowed. At the gate, a woman pulled a ticket from the automatic dispenser. The two men with her stared at the road ahead.

Traffic was sparse. As soon as the car passed into the void beyond the control area, the two men stripped off dark jumpsuits, revealing the beige-and-orange jackets and uniforms of Lone Star Flight Kitchens. They folded their coveralls and stowed them in black garbage bags. The man in front unzipped a small plastic case and took out two laminated identification cards. He examined them for a moment, then handed one to the man in back. Each clipped an ID to the left pocket of his jacket. The men opened larger rectangular kits and counted. They nodded to each other.

"We're here," the woman said as the car neared the south parking lot.

The man in front closed his kit. His companion looked at his watch and did the same. The woman turned the car toward the service exit.

Collister stepped away from the window. He pushed back his cuff to recheck the time. As the winter sunrise approached the North Texas plains, he knew the elaborate ground-servicing preparations were about to begin. Caterers would arrive in the twenty-degree darkness, tens of thousands of pounds of fuel would be forced up into the thin wings, and the sophisticated systems of the $100 million supersonic marvel would be electronically awakened for its flight from Dallas–Fort Worth to Washington, D.C., and Paris. By 8:10 a.m., 101 passengers and eight crew members would be on board AirParis's Flight 002, and Collister could close his investigation. It would be good to get back to more customary matters, he thought. He looked around the empty waiting room and made his way to a row of seats closest to the Jetway.

6:50 a.m.

"Hurry your ass, Annie," the dispatcher shouted after her.

The command was a continuation of the blue joke he had just told, and the three men on the loading dock roared once again. The chunky woman locked the last food-service pallet into the truck and slammed the door. She turned and wagged a finger at them.

"Don't forget," she retorted with mock sternness, "the early bird gets the worm." Her breath condensed into puffs and accented her chiding gesture.

The men loved it—and her—and they waved as she climbed into the right side of the bulky vehicle. Doug Galloway started the engine, pulled on the lights, and drove out from the dock. Annie had been riding shotgun like this for nearly six years. Doug was her new driver.

"How 'bout stopping up here a ways for some of that champagne and caviar?" he suggested, jerking his thumb over his shoulder at their cargo.

"Goddamn, man," Annie replied, "if I ever started in, I'd never stop."

Doug looked sideways and laughed as she rubbed her large middle.

When the truck neared the security checkpoint for ground vehicles using DFW's inner taxiway system, he leaned forward. "Will ya look at that?" The headlights framed two Lone Star employees standing in the middle of the pavement, waving their arms.

"What in the hell are *they* doing out here?" Doug braked and rolled down his window as the truck stopped. "You fellas lose your horse or something?" he offered with a grin. The bullet tore out his upper teeth and blew away the right side of his skull. His body twisted and fell against Annie. His eyes stared toward the floor. Annie opened her mouth in horror and struggled to release her seat belt. Two more muffled shots sealed the screams in her throat.

Las Colinas Hotel and Conference Center, Irving, Texas
6:56 a.m.

Jack Stroud contemplated his wife as they rode down the lighted glass elevator inside the hotel. Laura gripped the polished railing and looked out at the rapidly ascending lobby. Her pale saffron shearling coat was open, revealing an ivory cashmere turtleneck with matching ivory pants. An Hermès scarf of bronze and gold paisley cascaded over her shoulders. Her diamond-cluster wedding ring sparkled in a tableau of oranges and yellows as she tightened and released her hold on the railing. She was as striking today, Jack concluded, as when they first met. Laura felt his attention and smiled back.

The elevator came to a smooth stop at the first floor, and the doors opened. Laura touched her husband's arm as she turned to leave. She sighed.

"I wish their anniversary were a day later."

Jack, trim and two inches taller than six feet, looked down and saw that the illumination from the top of the elevator reflected softly from her auburn hair.

"Darling, why don't you go with me tomorrow?" He followed her out of the elevator. "It won't take a minute to change your reservations. The McVeys will understand."

Laura stepped across the lobby. "No, one of us should be there."

Jack remembered the evening in Pensacola when he'd stood inside the crowded country-club ballroom with his back to a cold Gulf of Mexico and raised his champagne glass to Linda and Tom McVey, the new bride and groom. As best man—proud in his Navy lieutenant's dress-blue dinner jacket with black tie, miniature medals, and gold cummerbund—Jack had tried to propose an unforgettable toast for the occasion. Predictably, however, he'd long forgotten the immortal lines he'd delivered . . . with one exception. He'd promised to be with the McVeys on their anniversary every five years, to celebrate in person.

Incredibly, Jack thought, tomorrow would be their thirtieth.

Over the years, the Strouds and the McVeys had traveled and laughed together across three continents and, at times, seemed almost to be members of one another's families. Linda and Tom moved to Zurich eighteen months after Laura and Jack left Washington for Tulsa, but the two couples and their children had reunited at least once a year since. Of course, Jack and Tom had kept their agreement not to reveal the secrets of their Don Juan bachelor days together. Better for everyone that way. As fellow "spooks," secrecy was second nature.

Laura looked back at Jack. "I suppose twenty-four hours isn't forever," she concluded. "Besides," she teased with a toss of her head, "they'd prefer to see *me* anyway."

Jack grabbed her arm. "Is that so, smarty-pants?" He winked at her. "Well, don't *you* forget our New Year's Eve date."

Laura kissed in his direction. She fully intended to make December 31st, *their* wedding anniversary, the most romantic evening they'd ever spent together. She took Jack's hand and held it tightly as they walked across the already-crowded atrium toward the cashier. A hundred early-morning guests and travelers arriving from red-eye flights bustled through the entrances of the hotel and hurried between the front desk and the bank of glass elevators that whisked up the side of the open interior of the eighteen-story building. The atmosphere of activity belied the cold stillness of the December morning.

A twenty-foot Christmas tree dominated a display at the center of the large room. The plastic evergreen had been scented with pine spray and decorated with dozens of gold-colored globes that twinkled in the reflected light of a thousand miniature electric bulbs. Gaily decorated boxes of various sizes and shapes were arrayed around its base, and a life-size Santa

Claus, hands on hips, beamed his approval from one side. Laura glanced at the scene, but Jack noticed her eyes seemed to focus beyond it.

"Mom, tell him to quit being such a fucking sexist shit and make him give me back my fifty dollars." Rachel, one of the Strouds' sixteen-year-old twins, bolted from the all-night newsstand ahead of her brother. The cold fury in her aquamarine eyes matched her shrill delivery. "And don't tell me to wait. I want it *now*."

"I do *not* owe her the money," Jeff defended himself as he loped up behind his sister. He reached into his pocket and shrugged. "Besides, the fifty's already in francs, and she can have it when she gets to Switzerland." He drew out the crisp bills and counted them with confidence.

"If the money's hers," Laura snapped, "give it to her!"

Jeff's mouth fell open in disbelief. He couldn't believe his mother was serious.

"But it's not *fair*," he pleaded. He took a step backwards and dropped his arms in supplication. "She lent it to me for a week."

"Jeff!" Laura's stare was adamant.

Rachel plucked the Swiss currency out of her brother's hand. "Just because you and Mom get to leave first doesn't mean you're special," she chided in her best singsong manner.

"And, *you,* young lady," Laura shook her finger at her daughter. "I'm not going to tell you again. I do *not* want to hear that word any more, what you called your brother. Do you understand?"

"*What* word?" Rachel's face was angelic. " 'Sexist'?"

"You know what I mean!"

Rachel sighed loudly and turned toward the entrance of the hotel.

"Well?" Laura glared after her.

"*Yes,* mother." Her over-the-shoulder response was heavy with teenage exasperation. Laura watched Rachel rejoin her brother.

"And they think they've grown up," Laura remarked as the twins resumed an animated conversation. "One thing's for sure, though." She hesitated before continuing the observation. "I'm the shortest one in the family."

"And unquestionably the prettiest," Jack added quickly. She looked up and accepted his kiss.

A few minutes after seven, the Strouds boarded the courtesy bus for the ride to the airport. The twins were first in line and sat right behind the driver. Jack and Laura took seats in the last row. Jack put his arm around his wife. He knew her uneasiness lay just beneath the surface. He turned and looked out the rear window. The eastern sky was just beginning to show its promise. He crossed his fingers.

Dallas–Fort Worth International Airport
Monday, December 28, 7:05 a.m.

Led by fifty-three-year-old Captain Adrien Toussaint, the three-member AirParis flight deck crew arrived at Operations on the lower level of Terminal 2W. First Officer Claude Lemierre and Second Officer Yves Charron followed through a buzzer-lock door crosshatched in yellow and black and marked "Restricted Zone."

"OPS" was a four-room complex of AirParis's administration, flight planning, maintenance, medical, and passenger service. There were twenty-six Texas-based employees at full complement, with their data boards, PCs, and desks arranged around the large gray Unisys computer that was connected by satellite with the headquarters mainframe system at Orly. The facility was a microcosm of the airline itself, with weather analysts, baggage and cargo handlers, schedulers, maintenance specialists, gate agents, an executive in charge, and, twice a day, flight crews. Since AirParis had only one daily trip each way at Dallas–Fort Worth, the two six-hour periods of peak activity began at 5:00 a.m., a little more than three hours before the departure of Flight 002, and at 5:00 p.m., exactly three hours before the arrival of Flight 001, the airline's SST from Paris and Washington, D.C. The eastbound flight this last Monday of the year was scheduled to be full. OPS was crowded, the atmosphere frenetic.

"Hey, Skipper," a familiar voice boomed over the background clatter as the three pilots placed their luggage and flight cases against the wall.

Lemierre looked at the captain and groaned. "Too early in the morning for me to chat with 'Mr. Sunshine.' " With Charron in tow, the first officer took leave for duties elsewhere in the room.

Toussaint turned and grinned at the eager face of Ted Panally, the airline's local dispatcher. He had known this rotund character for two decades, half of which had been when the loyal and overworked Panally ran Braniff's DFW operations during that airline's tough on-again, off-again times. Toussaint appreciated Panally's professionalism—not to mention his sense of humor.

"Just as I told 'em before you arrived." Panally gestured with an unlit cigar. "You'll merely sit on your derrière again today while the rest of us will be busting ours. You button pushers have forgotten how to fly."

Toussaint sighed and began to object, but Panally adroitly changed the subject to the weather. He directed the captain's attention to a stack of computer-generated charts on one of the posting tables.

"There's only an expanding low dropping south of Greenland toward Newfoundland." Panally drew his pencil across the top of the first chart. It left a faint trail on the thin paper. "You might go right over its center, but at sixty grand you'll never even notice." He peeled off the sheet and pointed to another one, a color satellite photo with superimposed meteorological symbols. "There's nothing between here and Dulles. Just the old 'severe clear' all the way." Panally put the well-chewed cigar back in his mouth. "I think you'll be happiest at thirty-three until about a hundred miles southwest of Memphis." He tapped his pencil at the northeastern corner of Arkansas. "Right there, the winds will favor you up at forty-one."

Toussaint picked up the weather printouts and nodded. After looking at their planned route, he surveyed a bank of video terminals. He punched a keyboard for the winds-aloft forecasts for four locations en route. When the screen came up, Toussaint saw that the data from the stations confirmed his dispatcher's interpretation. He frowned and folded the two computer sheets.

"I hate to say this, Théodore." The captain's tone was serious. He slipped the papers into the inside pocket of his uniform jacket.

Panally moved in closer. "What?"

"You are so right." Toussaint straightened his tie and looked over his shoulder. "I will have to, as you say . . . merely sit on my butt today."

Panally feigned a kick to the captain's behind.

Toussaint laughed and reached for his pen. "That's one small step for the Frenchman," he proclaimed. With a flourish, he signed the authorization to file the primary IFR flight plan as programmed in the company's computer. Within seconds, the three FAA Air Route Traffic Control Centers along the way to Washington would have 002's flight profile for the first segment of its journey to Europe.

"You take care of yourself, Captain," Panally said as Toussaint stood back and tucked his pen into his pocket. "Ol' buddy, you're the best in the business."

Toussaint raised his eyebrows at the unexpected compliment. He turned toward Panally.

"Monsieur, we at AirParis . . . " he pressed the fingers of his right hand together at his mouth and sprang them open, " . . . are the *epitome* of excellence." He put his arm around the smiling Texan. "Au revoir, my friend. I'll see you next week." Toussaint then aimed his index finger at Panally's cigar. "And don't light that thing while I'm gone."

"No, siree, Skipper," the big man answered with a salute and a smile. "It's been eight years, New Year's Eve."

Signaling to his entourage, the captain headed for the door and the SST beyond.

7:20 a.m.

Jacques Dubois, AirParis's DFW station manager, wasn't really surprised at the large number of reporters and security personnel who were already positioned around the departure lounge for Gate 67-A. Flight 002 was the most prestigious run for what many seasoned travelers had already begun calling the most attentive airline in the world, and Dubois was used to handling the logistics for world-class passengers. Today would be no different. As he looked around in satisfaction at the elaborate holiday wreaths, he unconsciously smoothed the front of his uniform jacket. He felt the golden AirParis pin on his chest. All was in Gallic readiness, everything appropriate for the occasion.

"Mornin', chief," came a pert voice to his side. It belonged to Claudine, his twenty-six-year-old French jeune fille–turned–true Texan gate agent, who had been on duty since seven o'clock. The drawl she had worked to perfect was heavy. She blinked her new eyelashes at him.

"When will the treasury secretary arrive?" an NBC-TV correspondent yelled before Dubois could acknowledge Claudine.

"The flight departs in less than an hour," Dubois responded with an exaggerated nod to the questioner.

The man persisted. "Will he be boarded privately, or can we ask him a few questions first?"

"All I know is we will depart on time."

"All right, pal, but will he have a statement for us, or will we have to sit tight until the conference tomorrow in Paris?"

Dubois didn't reply. The reporter turned and shook his head at the others. They'd probably have to wait.

Attracted by the aroma of freshly brewed coffee, Dubois made his way to the special service unit AirParis provided its SST guests. At least Claudine hadn't become too American to make coffee, he noted. Dubois poured the hot liquid from a silver carafe into one of the Limoges cups that the airline proudly featured. As he stirred in thick cream, he could see that the Secret

Service briefing was about to begin. Dubois raised the china to his lips and cautiously drew off the surface of the steaming beverage. He hoped there wouldn't be any embarrassing security episodes this morning. It seemed that every time a beefy cop got overzealous with a passenger, there was a newspaper photographer at the ready. And the AirParis logo was always prominently framed in the picture. Dubois had a collection of the offending prints, all sent to him with "fond regards" from marketing in Paris. He took another careful sip of his coffee and strode toward the briefing.

7:23 a.m.

The beige-and-orange catering truck approached the lighted security station at the airport's fenced southern perimeter. It nosed to a stop at an electrically operated chain-link gate, and the driver lowered his window and looked toward the cubicle. A uniformed inspection officer slid open the glass. He recognized the Lone Star logo.

"Hey, when are you guys going to get into your new kitchens so you won't have to haul ass from the sticks all the time?"

"First of March," the driver replied with a shrug. He handed over two ID cards, which the security man took and held together for examination. The officer then looked at the two men. They matched their pictures, although their faces appeared pasty-brown in the bright artificial lighting. Both had short black hair and seemed to be in their late twenties. The clean-shaven driver glanced around and adjusted his tie. His passenger rubbed an index finger back and forth against a thick mustache and kept his gaze on the road ahead.

The guard extended an open hand. "670?"

The driver looked startled. "What?"

"Your Form 670. The new airport access pass." He snapped his fingers. "C'mon."

"Oh . . . that." The driver reached under the front seat. He brought up a plastic case and opened it. He found the document and handed it out the window.

The security man read the laser-printed descriptions of the driver and his assistant.

"Hey, wait a minute." He looked across at the men. They stared back. "Where's Annie? And her regular driver?"

"Sick. Called in last night with the runs or something."

"Both?"

The driver nodded. "The boss is really pissed. She's never missed a day in years."

"Well, no one told me about it, and there's a lot of extra security up there this morning. I'd better check this out."

As the officer closed the window and picked up the telephone, the driver slipped his hand inside his jacket. The guard keyed in the special four-digit airport number for Lone Star Flight Kitchens. The line returned only static, then went dead. He pushed the window open again.

"Goddamn phone's screwed up. Construction, I guess. Anyway, you guys must be OK. I can smell the food all the way in here." He reached out. "Here's your stuff back. And your special security badges. Y'all be good."

The driver withdrew his hand from his jacket, took the materials in silence, and looked out the windshield. As the gate opened, he rolled up the window and pressed the accelerator. The truck jerked ahead and proceeded north on the wide taxiway.

The security man slid the cubicle window shut and watched the taillights of the truck through a thin coating of ice on the glass. After a moment, he picked up the telephone and punched in the Lone Star number again. Once more, static. He then tried the number for another catering company. It rang. As he waited for someone to answer, he saw that the truck's taillights had merged into the radiance of the massive airport complex.

"Morning, Dobbs House." The connection was crystal clear. The officer clicked off without saying anything. He looked to the north again.

The driver was careful to keep within the white lines for ground service vehicles. Three minutes later, the truck steered onto the apron for Terminal 2W. It passed along the starboard side of the glistening SST, closed to within a few feet of the aircraft's forward galley access door, and stopped. The driver secured the emergency brake and pressed the "ramp ready" button. Both men stepped out, walked toward the back, and pulled on work gloves.

"Open your cargo."

A heavyset man approached in a half jog from underneath the plane's wing. His breath trailed in silvery wisps in the lighted coldness. He gestured to a gold cloth badge sewn to his insulated jacket.

"Airport police."

The two men stopped. "Everything's . . . sealed," the driver offered as he faced the officer. "State law, you know."

The policeman halted five feet from the men. "*Federal* law says you'll open your cargo." He crossed his arms. "Now!"

The driver grumbled, then nodded to his companion, who unlatched the rear door of the truck and yanked it open.

"Let me see every other canister," the officer ordered. "Put them here in a row."

The men hesitated. A radio crackled. "Two Seven, do you read?"

The officer retrieved a portable transceiver from his jacket pocket and brought it to his mouth. "Affirmative."

"OK, we're observing your inspection from two positions."

The two men looked at each other and began unloading the selected metal canisters. "The company isn't going to like it if something's ruined by this," the driver protested as he lugged a container toward the policeman. "Couple of these are supposed to stay real hot."

The officer pointed. "Open this, this, and that one. Forget the rest."

The men broke paper seals and opened the containers. When the inspection revealed only liquor, linen, dry ice, and butter, the airport policeman cleared the men to continue.

"Two Seven's secure," he radioed and tucked the transceiver back into his jacket. He adjusted the ear flaps of his patrol cap and turned toward the caterers.

"Sorry for the trouble, but you know the rules."

Neither man responded.

When the policeman walked away, the driver and his companion reloaded the canisters. They climbed onto the forward platform at the top of the truck and engaged the "raise" handle. The platform and the entire body of the truck whined upward on hydraulic legs and mated with the aircraft's galley access door. The driver pressed the SST's handle-release button and grabbed and twisted the aluminum-alloy bar. As the door opened, a rush of warm air escaped from the cabin.

"Bonjour," a petite flight attendant greeted the two men cheerfully. They stared at her without speaking.

"*Quels drôles types!*" she sniffed before turning to prepare for the boarding of the passengers. The flight attendant gave one more glance at the caterers. They were already unloading the truck.

There were nine canisters to be stowed and one to be activated. Their work required eleven minutes.

7:35 a.m.

Jack and Laura Stroud left the AirParis ticket counter after checking five pieces of luggage through to Zurich. Laura walked with her arm around her husband's waist. Her mind was obviously elsewhere.

"A penny for your thoughts?" Jack knew, but he had to ask anyway. She didn't reply. He kissed her soft hair. Reuben Gentry's message had disturbed both of them, Laura more than him. Reuben was her father, after all. In one sense, Jack didn't much care what the old man had to say. He'd kept his anger in check for Laura's sake, but he intended to read the riot act to the evangelist when they got together. By interrupting their trip, Reuben was again showing who was in charge in the family. As usual, Jack was paying for Reuben's ego.

"Why now, Jack?" Laura questioned without looking up at him. "What could be so important that we have to change our vacation plans? Couldn't he have told you over the telephone?"

Jack wanted to agree with her out loud, but didn't. He shook his head. "Darling, I'm sure your father wouldn't ask me to stay behind for a frivolous reason." He squeezed her hand and wondered if there really was a valid reason this time. Once more Jack thought about giving up the work he was doing for Reuben. In truth, it hadn't been what he had expected. There were just too many emotional conflicts. Jack promised himself he'd talk it over with his wife when he joined her tomorrow.

Laura stopped and looked up into his eyes. There were tears in hers. "I'm afraid, Jack."

Jack drew her to him. He inhaled deeply and detected a hint of Shalimar, his favorite perfume. He was exactly a foot taller when they were in their stocking feet. Or better yet, he thought, their bare feet. Right now, her heels narrowed the difference. The physical stirrings, which had been extinguished so sublimely only hours earlier, washed again as a glow from his groin. He felt her respond, and he kissed her before she could say anything.

"Oh, gross!" Rachel's voice pierced their spell. "Do you have to do that in public?"

"You senior citizens ought to be ashamed of yourselves," Jeff tossed at them as he passed.

"M.Y.O.B., you . . . you . . . children," Laura called out with a smile.

Jeff rolled his eyes in mock resignation at his mother's pronouncement. Jack kissed his wife again before they resumed their walk to the gate.

"Dad's never kept anything from us before," Laura posed. "What's he planning for you? For us?" She turned toward him. "Why wouldn't he be more specific?"

"Maybe he didn't want to be overheard," Jack suggested. Maybe, he reflected to himself, it concerns that worthless brother of hers. Possibly another of Norman's power tantrums. Jack couldn't remember more than a handful of times since he'd married into this unusual family when he'd been able to have anything approaching a civil conversation with the little son of a bitch. It was hard to believe that Norman came from the same stock as Laura. But then, what could Reuben have meant about touching "the face of Death"? Maybe it really was something serious. Jack forced a smile and hoped his voice matched.

"I'll call you tonight with all the details. Then I'll be on a flight to join you."

Laura tightened her grip on his hand. "I need you, Jack, far more than he does."

The security check at 67-A was thorough. "Special guest," the officer offered in explanation as he asked Laura to remove the necklace with the gold St. Christopher medal that Jack had given her upon their engagement. Rather than putting it back on after it was inspected, Laura pressed the medallion into her husband's hand.

Jack knew that Reuben would have preached an entire sermon about "Popish Catholic symbols" if he'd known the religious significance of the medal. It amused him to slip such things into "the family." He was glad that Laura understood and respected his Roman Catholic upbringing. Jack might have done some work for the ministry, but he was certainly no convert.

"Here," Laura insisted, "I want you safe." Jack started to say something, but didn't. He looked at the inscription on the back of the medallion—"To protect you for me wherever you may be"—and closed his fingers over it.

7:45 a.m.

"Bonjour, ladies and gentlemen," Jacques Dubois held the microphone to his lips and began. "AirParis proudly announces the departure of Flight 002 to Washington-Dulles, with continuing service to Paris-Orly." His accent was just right for the occasion. He pretended he didn't notice the looks of approval from a few in the departure lounge who appreciated the lilt of his Par-EE Oar-LEE. He continued his announcement. "All passengers may now board." He smiled and gestured with a flourish toward the door to the Jetway. "Please have your boarding passes ready for the flight attendant. Bon voyage! We wish you a very enjoyable trip." Dubois repeated the announcement in French for the three couples returning to Chartres. They nodded their thanks and moved toward the plane.

Laura wanted to stay until everyone else had gone ahead, but two uniformed policemen saw her boarding pass and motioned her toward the plane. *Their* passenger would be last. She grabbed Jack's hand and squeezed it.

"Call me?" Her face reflected her misgivings.

"The phone will be ringing when you walk into your room," Jack promised.

Jeff patted his sister on the back with a gentleness that spurred her to kiss his cheek.

"Hey," he grumbled, "I'm still mad at you about the money." He turned and followed his mother down the boarding ramp.

Jack and Rachel watched as mother and son were quickly surrounded by other passengers pressing into the Jetway. Jack saw Jeff's last wave. He raised his arm in return.

"Over here, Daddy."

Rachel had already positioned herself at a new vantage point to watch the departure. Jack smiled. He always found it charming that teenagers in the South and Southwest, even grown women, called their fathers "Daddy." In relaxed moments, Reuben was still "Daddy" to Laura. It was more personal than "Father," which his parents had expected from him. He was pleased that his almost-grown daughter felt comfortable with the regional tradition. He hoped she'd never give it up.

When Jack moved to stand beside his daughter at the window, he noticed a man at the frosted glass a few feet away who turned and seemed to study the people in the gate area with a suspicious gaze. The man's overcoat and suit jacket were open. Of course, Jack thought, more security. For that VIP. The scene reminded him of the endless pursuits of spies and felons during his tours of duty with naval intelligence and the Naval Investigative Service. Years of working with wily Reuben Gentry might have extracted their emotional toll from Jack but, thank God, the heavy-drinking and exhausting cloak-and-dagger days held no attraction for him anymore.

"All passengers should be on board," came the final call.

Jack shook his head as the announcement faded. He'd always thought that particular statement sounded ridiculous. Those to whom it was directed shouldn't be able to hear it, and if you were a passenger who could hear it, were you supposed to run toward the gate, give up, or what? He scanned the boarding area to see who that last passenger was going to be. The cameras and reporters were ready. He wondered if he'd recognize him.

"Mr. Stroud?"

The voice came from his left. Jack turned to see a man's eyes locked with his. Then he saw the identification credentials.

"Special Agent Collister, FBI. You and your daughter will please come with me."

Iselin, New Jersey
Monday, December 28, shortly after sunrise

It had been an hour since the two men had left their stolen Amtrak mini-van at the abandoned warehouse. In silence, they'd balanced a heavy rectangular object down the concrete steps of the ragged embankment to the dual tracks below. They moved it along the northbound rails of the right of way. Once outside the chilled glow of the lighted parking lot, one of them nodded. They lowered their burden to the ground and peeled off bands of restraining tape. The men opened their parcel lengthwise and fitted baffles into place to secure the shape. They then lifted the object and fitted it over the track. Each took a position on an opposite side and kicked locking pins against the rails. One man stooped to the molded assembly and drew out a short antenna, which he rotated upward until it extended above the plane of the track. They looked over their work for a moment before walking back to the steps. The camouflaged mold was virtually indistinguishable from the rails and the concrete ties. The men returned to the van.

Train Number 100, the first weekday-morning Metroliner on the 225-mile, two-hour-and-fifty-minute New York run, had pulled out of Washington, D.C.'s Union Station on time at six sharp. Today the all-reserved streamliner was packed with 423 of its usual assortment of wintertime riders. Half were regular corporate and government commuters to Philadelphia and New York, together with savvy business people and vacationing outsiders who wanted to make the Northeast circuit without having to suffer the ordeal of the perennially congested airports. The other half included college students—many clothed in smugness and blue jeans—traveling between home and friends and the snowbound resorts of Vermont and New Hampshire. Sitting among their elders and wearing bravely expectant expressions were the unaccompanied children, nearly half a hundred this morning, most shuttling between divorced parents, each little one to be shared for a holiday with somebody at the other end of an unraveled union.

Two girls, sisters eight and ten, sat holding hands and waited for their inevitable delivery. Military men in uniform punched one another and told off-color stories at inappropriate volumes, while others, similarly attired, stared out the windows in silence.

The café car was already crowded with noisy passengers who jostled to obtain their coffee-and-sweet-roll infusions from two harried attendants. A loud man waved a twenty-dollar offering aloft in hopes of securing faster service. He was ignored. One couple sat in a booth and grinned at each other, celebrating a week's wedding anniversary by sharing a glazed doughnut. The man flicked at a piece of sugarcoating on his wife's chin, then pressed the tip of his finger against her smile.

With a shudder, No. 100 felt the percussion of a speeding southbound freight and began slowing for its mandatory 6:10 stop at New Carrollton, Maryland. As the train slid alongside the narrow platform, a handful of passengers noticed a couple waiting with their five children. The instant the doors opened, the father shooed at his stairstep brood.

"Hurry up! Ya wanna *walk* to grandma's?" He had to repeat his exhortation before they all scurried aboard. With a jangle of a warning buzzer in each car, the Metroliner rolled forward and began accelerating. Two minutes later, it held at 90 miles per hour.

The passenger cars rocked back and forth ever so slightly on the seamless rails as No. 100 coursed northward through the gentle hills of central Maryland. The train ran parallel to mile-long stretches of four-lane highways carrying cars of gawking youngsters who irrevocably committed themselves to becoming locomotive engineers when they grew up. Thirty miles north of Washington, the Metroliner roared through a valley of approach-light stanchions along the west side of the Baltimore-Washington International Airport and aimed for the heart of Baltimore, less than ten minutes away.

"Ball-mer!" the conductor called out over the public address system. The train showed no signs yet of slowing. "Two minutes to Ball-mer." He sounded quite secure with the regionalism of his pronunciation. He then added the company's mandatory tag line, "Thank you for riding Amtrak's Metroliner."

No. 100 braked and decelerated and entered the artificial darkness of underground Baltimore. The solid metal wheels clanked and jarred over switches and intersections and radiated the cacophony of bumps upward to the passengers. As the Metroliner picked its way through the maze of tracks, passengers rose in the lighted cars and held onto overhead racks and referred to their wristwatches: 6:32 a.m. The train jerked once ... twice ...

then stopped. Three minutes later, No. 100 was moving again. Northeast, toward Wilmington and Philadelphia.

As the Metroliner raced along the northern shore of a blustery and choppy Chesapeake Bay near Aberdeen, Maryland, the first glow of the new day appeared. At Wilmington, Delaware, thirty-five miles later, the sun broke above a cloudless horizon and reflected from the dustings of frost on trees and rooftops. The train coursed onward along the Delaware River and entered the industrial environs of Philadelphia.

"Two minutes to Philll-adelphia," the conductor called out. "Two minutes. Thirtieth Street Station. Philll-adelphia." One could almost hear his smile through the cadence. "And thank you for riding Amtrak's Metroliner."

No. 100 slowed and came to a stop at the downtown Philadelphia station. Again, after three minutes, the buzzer, a slight jerking motion, and the train was once more on its way, now only ninety miles from its ultimate destination. The sun was well above the barren trees to the east. The two little sisters moved closer to each other. They sensed that their trip to their father's was almost over, and they whispered questions about their new stepmother.

The train centered and balanced across a steel passageway over the Delaware River, then roared into the flatness of New Jersey. There were to be no more stops until No. 100 arrived at Newark, in the western shadows of the spires of New York City. Business types in custom-tailored suits adjusted their reclining chairs and looked out at the scene-a-second world. Most were familiar with this dash across the Garden State, and it provided them with the last uninterrupted time to prepare for the maneuvers of the day. Some of those in pinstripes talked and planned with one another across the aisle. They'd be in midtown Manhattan before nine o'clock, and, even though it was the week between Christmas and New Year's, this was the ideal time to get a head start on their competitors.

Southwest of New Brunswick, as Train No. 100 passed over U.S. 1 and streaked onward for Iselin and Newark, attendants began closing and locking the steel cabinets of the snack bar. A coffee customer returned a half-consumed cup of the black liquid, long since cold. The family of seven from New Carrollton faced one another in the club seating at the end of one of the coaches. Their voices overlapped. The youngest, a boy of six, smudged the window with his nose and forehead and made trainlike sounds against the glass.

Twenty-four miles from Pennsylvania Station, the electric locomotive and seven passenger cars streaked toward Iselin's Metropark station at 104 miles an hour. No. 100 was cleared to pass through at full speed. As the train was within seconds of the Metropark platform, the engineer caught a reflection of something on the roadbed. He cursed and grabbed for the emergency brake. He never reached it.

The wheels of the Metroliner's engine thundered over the grooved switch and slammed to the right. The entire train followed. The locomotive yawed and skipped sideways across the local commuter tracks and headed for the passengers standing on the platform. Less than fifty yards from the exposed Metropark station, the 200-ton locomotive began tumbling. Hundreds of trapped commuters screamed and clawed for escape as the interconnected metallic monster bounced and rolled toward them. A few froze and watched as the unavoidable nightmare hurled to engulf them. When the train hit, its explosive impact uprooted the massive concrete and steel platform, crushing its flailing occupants.

The violence of the collision with the station punctured and shredded the stainless steel skin of the Metroliner's passenger cars. Disjointed remains tumbled over the platform, screeching as they spewed and mashed their human contents. Transmission towers supporting 275,000-volt lines buckled into the maelstrom, and dozens of severed wires writhed and sparked and electrocuted fleeing survivors. Chunks of hot metal flamed and bounced away from the disintegrating locomotive and seared into automobiles waiting in a bumper-to-bumper line of traffic two hundred yards from the derailment. The cars exploded and burned while their broiling occupants attempted to wriggle free. A nearby gasoline storage facility erupted in a geyser of liquid fire as its aboveground lines were severed by the spreading holocaust. Sheets of burning fuel poured from the remains of the steel tanks and slapped across curbs and consumed fleeing dogs before setting fire to powder-dry storefronts. A city transit bus swerved to avoid colliding with a disconnected wheel assembly from the locomotive. The directionless object careened obliquely past the vehicle and carved out the ground floor of a brick building on the opposite side of the suburban street before it jerked to a smoky stop in an alley. The occupants of the bus screamed and jumped out and ran for their lives as a foot-high river of burning gasoline poured toward them.

Everlasting minutes later, the horror was spent. Moans rose with the stench from two square blocks of burning metal and wood, tissue and bone as the once-proud Metroliner came to its final resting place.

Rising pillars of black smoke boiled upward into the quiet morning sky. They were clearly visible at the Linden municipal airport, five miles away, as a man spoke into the public telephone before he and his companion boarded a waiting business jet.

"Tell him the train made its unscheduled stop, right on time."

Dallas–Fort Worth International Airport
7:59 a.m.

Jack and Rachel followed the tall FBI agent through the main concourse of Terminal 2W. He set a brisk pace. Jack could only raise his eyebrows and shake his head when Rachel asked where they were going. They passed the ticket counters for Lufthansa and British Airways and stopped abruptly at a door marked "Private Lounge." The door was unlocked from inside and pulled open by a man who looked as if he might be an FBI agent also.

"I'm Special Agent Stewart Alley," the second man greeted Jack and his daughter as they entered. "Mr. Stroud. Rachel. Please come in." Alley closed the door and motioned to the arrangement of furniture. "It's not home, but it's comfortable."

Jack looked around the gray-carpeted, thirty-by-thirty room. It was windowless and appointed with a scuffed brown Naugahyde couch and four upholstered chairs in a corner. There was a portable refrigerator and a coffee brewer on a metal table next to the couch. A stack of plastic cups was grouped with a jar of nondairy creamer and a bowl stuffed with the red, white, and blue packets of Sweet'N Low, sugar, and Equal. A black telephone hung on a sidewall. There were three rows of recessed overhead lights. Rachel looked at her father.

"It's all right, sweetie." Jack nodded toward the couch.

"Coffee? Juice?" Alley inquired of his visitors.

Both shook their heads. The two agents took chairs facing Jack and his daughter.

"Mr. Stroud." Alley leaned forward and clasped his hands together. "We need your help."

Jack had a feeling he knew what the men were looking for. Something told him the FBI was interested in the matters that were developing at the ministry in Tulsa. If so, Reuben's cryptic message on the telephone might be as ominous as it sounded. Then again, they might want to talk about something that jackass Norman had done.

Alley stared at him. "You're related to the evangelist Reuben Gentry, aren't you?"

"I'm his son-in-law." Jack sighed. "Has he done something wrong?"

Alley looked at Collister, then moved forward in his chair. "May I call you Jack?"

"Please do."

"Jack, twice over the past six weeks, Doctor Gentry expressed concerns to the United States Attorney in Tulsa about possible criminal activities involving his ministry."

Jack frowned. He hadn't expected this. Why the hell hadn't Reuben mentioned criminal activities before?

Alley continued. "He said you were one of the few people he could trust. Has he told you about his statements to the U.S. Attorney?"

Jack shook his head. Then he thought about Rachel. He didn't want her to hear any sordid tales involving her grandfather . . . or her Uncle Norman, for that matter.

"Perhaps one of you can take my daughter for a Coke while we discuss this," he suggested.

"No, Daddy," Rachel insisted. "I want to stay with you." She gripped his hand tightly.

Jack hesitated. "Well, if these gentlemen think it's all right . . . "

The FBI men looked at each other and nodded. Alley went on. "What do you know about any problems Gentry might be having?"

Jack leaned back and rubbed his face. "I think I'll take that cup of coffee if it's still available."

"Just made it before you arrived." Alley stepped to the metal table. "Black?"

"Please."

As the FBI agent poured the hot liquid, he cocked his head. "Rachel, how about some apple or grape juice?"

The teenager sat stoically with her coat in her lap. "No, thank you."

Alley picked up the full cup and handed it over carefully. For a few seconds, Jack contemplated the surface of the steaming beverage. No reason not to talk, he thought. Besides, what I know—together with whatever the FBI's learned—might help me with Reuben this morning. He looked at the two men.

"Reuben appointed me trustee of Tulsa Bible College when I moved to Oklahoma after retiring from the Navy. I'd just been named president of U.S. Simulation Systems—we build flight simulators. I really had a less-than-positive attitude about evangelists. Considered them all con artists." He glanced apologetically at Rachel, but she was staring at the floor. "That is, until I married Laura and got to know her dad." Jack started to say that while the old man wasn't a clone of Billy Graham, he wasn't the worst in his field either. Because of his daughter's presence, he didn't add the editorial. "So I took the post as trustee. Anyway, we've had the usual, garden-variety monthly board meetings." Jack sipped at the hot coffee. "Oh, we've had our so-called crises. Student attire was one. A couple of drinking incidents. Nothing cataclysmic." He blew across the top of the cup. "Tulsa Bible College and the Reuben Gentry Ministries are two separate entities. One serves the other, and it's sometimes hard to make the distinction, but they're not linked in a legal sense. The media sometimes say the ministry is the PR arm of the school." He smiled. "Probably is. Anyway, I've recently become involved on the ministry side, as a consultant. Basically because of the new financial situation. That's what I thought you wanted to talk to me about."

"*New* financial situation?" Both agents looked interested.

"Yes, there've been some dramatic changes," Jack replied. "As you probably know, during the late '80s all television ministries suffered declines in contributions—mainly because of the Bakker and Swaggart scandals. In our own backyard, Oral Roberts didn't help any with his $8 million, 'God-will-call-me-home' ransom appeal and his other pleas of desperation. The whole world of televangelism was hit hard."

Alley's eyes fixed on Jack. "Was Gentry's ministry badly hurt?"

"Yes, at first."

"How badly?" Both agents watched him.

"Well, I don't recall the exact amount, but his ministry lost about half of its monthly income by late '87, early '88. It was devastating. As I remember, Reuben had to lay off more than four hundred employees almost immediately. Another three hundred or so went within a year. And that was out of an original total of about 1,300 people, so it was a major reduction. Lasted for years. Then, about twelve months ago, things improved. Almost overnight." Jack was silent for a moment before he added, "But Reuben seemed more troubled than ever."

Alley crossed his arms. "Do you know why?"

"No. At first he didn't talk to anyone. He came to me the middle of last month and asked me to get involved with the business side of his ministry. Tulsa Bible College was doing well, so I wasn't spending a lot of time being a trustee. I was willing to be of further service to him. You know, for the good of the family and all." Jack smiled. "He told me he could probably trust a Catholic boy who was now 'one of us.' "

Alley raised his eyebrows. "He never mentioned any concerns about criminal activities?"

Jack shook his head. "Reuben was pretty vague with explanations. I got the feeling there was something out of focus and that he knew more than he wanted to reveal. Maybe he didn't have any proof." Jack tugged at his tie. "Maybe he needed independent confirmation."

Alley leaned forward and placed his hands on his knees. "So what have you learned?"

"Only that his financial matters turned around, and quickly." Jack cleared his throat. "Nothing more."

"Jack," Collister interjected, "we're here because Doctor Gentry became very specific late yesterday. He told our office in Tulsa that his ministry was the target of a blackmail and extortion scheme. He said he feared for his life. Do you know anything about that?"

Jack looked at Collister, then at Alley. "Reuben's pretty dramatic in his speech, but he did call me at the hotel early this morning. He told me he'd touched the face of Death."

"What?"

"He said he'd 'touched the face of Death.' He didn't explain what he meant, but I've never heard him talk like that before. And I've never known him to sound fearful. Putting the words and emotions together . . . yes, I suppose you could conclude . . . "

"How about his relationship with his son?" Collister stared at Jack.

Jack rubbed his hands together. "It's been . . . strained." He didn't volunteer his personal suppositions.

Collister leaned toward him. "To tell you the truth, our people in Tulsa think there's something to the blackmail and extortion matter. Something big. No hard facts yet, just allegations. You're on the inside. Gentry trusts you. Are you telling us everything?"

Jack drew himself to the edge of the couch. "Reuben asked me to postpone the start of my vacation so he could tell me about something in person. Perhaps it's this blackmail and extortion threat." Jack looked at his watch, then at both FBI agents. "He's flying down from Tulsa right now. Why don't we all meet together?"

"Good idea." Collister stood up. "What's his flight? I'll have him brought here."

Jack reached inside his jacket and pulled out an AirParis ticket envelope. He looked at his penciled notes.

"American 348. Arrives at 9:01."

Collister walked to the telephone. He picked up the receiver and punched in a number.

8:07 a.m.

"Just like the old days at Braniff, flying the Concorde from Texas, eh, Capitaine?" Second Officer Charron had noticed Toussaint's distant gaze as the flight-deck crew completed the 106-question pretaxi checklist and waited for push-back clearance. Toussaint acknowledged with a bob of his head.

"Oui."

The cockpit fell silent as each man escaped to the past for a moment. Toussaint remembered the day when AirParis negotiated two Concordes away from Air France—before anyone really knew what would happen to commercial aviation in Europe after the privatization and merger pressures. Once the deal became better understood in business circles, AirParis was a first-class competitor to Air France on the North Atlantic; two of its best air-planes were refitted at Toulouse with state-of-the-art engines and avionics and renamed Aurora, for the Roman goddess of dawn. The dawn of a new age.

"We've made money since Day One," Toussaint mused out loud. "Maybe brilliant marketing . . . but maybe a little magic, too." He smiled. Toussaint was proud that passengers were drawn to the airline. *His* airline, he thought, and today's departure would be another "moment" to experience.

8:08 a.m.

Jeff watched as the attractive flight attendants advanced through the cabin, checking seat belts and securing overhead compartments in prepa-ration for departure. Their movements were deliberate and smooth, and they smiled as they passed. Laura watched her son.

"Pretty, aren't they?"

"What? Oh, yeah." He blushed and looked out the window.

Laura wanted to touch his hair. It was hard to believe that it had been almost seventeen years since they learned they'd have twins. She remem-bered feeling God was making up to them for her miscarriage five years ear-lier. Today Jeff and Rachel were everything Laura had prayed for. The twins now had driver's licenses, and they were undoubtedly the most active juniors at Indian Springs Preparatory School. They were only eighteen months from college. Laura swallowed hard. College. Where had the time gone?

It seemed only yesterday that she was a skinny, scared Okie who'd gotten a job in Senator Grady Haskell's office after the old pol himself had invited her to come to Washington following her graduation from Tulsa Bible College.

"People just seem to like you, honey," the populist senator had told her during the second interview. "And that's the first step for success in anything. I'd be delighted if you'd join me." He'd emphasized the "delighted" with a slap on his knee. Haskell had been the commencement speaker at the college her junior year, and she was mesmerized by his conviction that a country with talented people and the will to go to the moon could do any-thing. She, too, believed that with all her heart, and she wanted to follow him back to Capitol Hill right after the ceremony.

Being asked to join the staff of the new chairman of the Senate Finance Committee was a heady, almost out-of-place opportunity for the daughter of a charismatic Pentecostal minister. She had expected her career to be a quiet, behind-the-scenes role in her father's life. Many of her school friends doubted the wisdom of her decision to serve in the secular world. Of course, they'd meant she'd surely be corrupted and lost in the diabolical whirlpool of politics. A few had chosen not to speak to her since the day she accepted the job.

Jack had walked into her life at a formal White House reception for the Soviet ambassador. He had returned from duty in Moscow three months earlier, and he poured a ladle of punch into her glass before she realized he was next to her.

"Anyone who has such a faraway look needs to talk about it."

She turned at the sound of his voice and looked into the warm eyes of her soul mate.

8:10 a.m.

"We're going!" Jeff saw the gate agent deliver some papers to a flight attendant and wave into the cockpit.

Laura felt the thump as the main door of the SST was pulled shut and sealed. She leaned over and looked through the window.

"Can't see them, Mom," Jeff observed. "Only our plane's reflection in the glass."

"Well, I hope they can see us."

Laura touched her fingertips to her lips and blew a kiss.

8:14 a.m.

As Flight 002 received its final boarding and weight calculations and ramp release, Second Officer Charron began the engine-start sequence. Lemierre adjusted his headset and pressed the push-to-talk button on the control yoke.

"Good morning, Ground, AirParis Zero Zero Two with Information Echo and our clearance. Ready to push and taxi."

"AirParis 002, roger. Cleared for push-back, taxi to Three-Six-Right, via the Inner."

The driver below heard the same information and pressed the accelerator. The tow tractor began to move, and the 370,000-pound SST was slowly rolled backwards. Once the plane was positioned with its nose facing south, the tractor braked to a smooth stop, and the tow bar was removed. The ramp agent walked to the underside of the forward fuselage and disconnected his intercom link with the pilots. With a curt salute, he motioned the SST on its way. In the cockpit, the glowing electronic displays on the instrument panel showed that the four Olympus-D engines were at idle. Toussaint released the brakes and advanced the throttles one notch. The aircraft began to move under its own power.

It took slightly more than four minutes for the SST to reach the turn toward Runway 36R. Lemierre changed frequencies to the tower and received instructions to taxi into position and hold. The silver airliner, trimmed in blue and gold, maneuvered onto the runway and rolled to a stop. Toussaint held the brakes with the tips of his shoes and turned to his crew.

"Ready, messieurs?"

Both men scanned their instruments and nodded.

"AirParis Zero Zero Two, cleared for takeoff," came the transmission from the tower.

The captain looked out at the more than two miles of runway that lay ahead. He flexed his fingers and gripped the control yoke.

"Allons!"

Toussaint released the brakes and advanced the throttles to the preset position on the center quadrant. The engines spooled up and began consuming fuel at the rate of 1,300 pounds a minute.

First Officer Lemierre adjusted the boom microphone closer to his mouth.

"Zero Zero Two's rolling."

8:20 a.m.

Collister was standing next to the telephone when it rang.

"Yes? *What?* When?"

The FBI agent replaced the receiver and stood facing the wall. Then he turned and looked at Jack.

"Reuben Gentry suffered a stroke about two hours ago. He's in critical condition."

Rachel put her hand to her mouth.

"Oh, Lord," Jack exclaimed as he put his arm around his daughter. "Has my wife's flight left yet?"

As each engine came up to 41,000 pounds of thrust, everyone aboard the SST was pressed backward by the acceleration. At fifteen seconds into the roll, the aircraft was traveling at 115 miles per hour. A slight oscillation developed as the gear thumped faster over the frozen expansion joints of the concrete. Forty seconds after brake release, Toussaint pulled back on the control yoke and rotated the nose upward. The ground fell away, and Flight 002 lifted off at a speed of nearly 200 feet per second. Through the right-side windows, the bright yellow rays of the early sun intruded over the terminals and hotels of the airport and bathed the interior of the aircraft. Passengers at windows on the opposite side saw in the distant haze the fading grays of the retreating night.

Departure Control turned 002 toward the northeast and cleared it to 17,000 feet. As the aircraft passed through 1,500 feet, Charron switched off the afterburners and adjusted the throttles to a lower setting for noise abatement over sensitive north Dallas. Toussaint pressed the nose angle down and trimmed the SST to maintain the temporary speed limit of 250 knots. Once they climbed to 10,000 feet above the city, the captain pushed the throttles forward again and raised the flexible nose, which had been drooped for takeoff. Their speed increased to 300 knots.

Thirty-five miles northeast of DFW, Fort Worth Center cleared Flight 002 onto J-42, its assigned jet route, and, initially, to Flight Level 330. The throttles were advanced once more, and the aircraft knifed upward through the cold, peach dawn. Flight 002 would not go supersonic on its two-hour trip to Washington. However, early that afternoon, shortly after it left northern New York State at Flight Level 410 and passed over Montreal on its Great Circle route toward the European evening, Flight 002 was scheduled to accelerate to 1,430 miles an hour.

Jeff looked out the port side and imagined himself an astronaut leaving an alien planet. As they passed through a thin deck of ice crystals, he was piercing a layer of frozen methane.

Twenty-three minutes after takeoff, the SST nosed over gently in the frigid atmosphere and leveled at 33,000 feet. As they prepared for the elaborate brunch, cabin attendants chatted with passengers. Hand-cut crystal bowls of grapes and trays of canapés and cheeses—Camembert, Brie, Pont l'Evêque—and Russian Sevruga caviar and pâté de foie gras were served on damask tablecloths with two champagnes, all as a prologue. Later there would be médaillons de boeuf and crêpes aux bananes and a myriad of French wines.

Laura looked at her son and smiled. "Hungry?"

"Yeah!"

She bit her lip. He looked so much like Jack. Jeff didn't resist when she took his hand and squeezed it.

On board AirParis 002
8:46 a.m.

"Zero Zero Two, Dispatch."

First Officer Lemierre frowned. He had been studying the Jeppesen high-altitude aeronautical chart for their assigned route when the call came in on a discrete frequency from their DFW base. He laid the navigation sheet aside and straightened his headset.

"Go ahead, Ted."

"Airport police report there may be a bomb aboard your aircraft. I repeat: There *may* be a bomb aboard your aircraft. Police found the bodies of two catering company employees who were to have serviced 002. A security guard said two men entered the airport in a Lone Star Flight Kitchens truck. Your aircraft was the only one they serviced. Over."

The three flight deck professionals looked at one other.

"Nom de Dieu!" Charron swore.

The captain keyed his microphone. "This is Toussaint. Do you know what kind of a bomb it is?" There was no alarm in his voice.

"We can't verify that there *is* a bomb, Skipper," Panally replied, "but that's what security assumes. No idea what kind it might be."

"OK, we'll get back with you."

Toussaint pointed at Lemierre. "Tell Memphis Center what's going on and get vectors to the nearest airport. Military, if possible. We're declaring an emergency." He set the SST's transponder at 7700, the international aircraft distress code. "You've got it," he directed as he turned the controls over to the first officer. Lemierre reached over his shoulder and donned an oxygen mask. The captain released his seat harness and stood up.

"I'm going back to have a look."

Toussaint opened the cockpit door and started down the narrow aisle. His expression was unperturbed.

"Captain, do you have a minute?" Treasury Secretary David Rowland reached for his hand.

Out of the corner of his eye, Toussaint saw a flight attendant in the forward galley. He started for her.

"Antoinette, *non!*"

Her last mortal act was twisting the timer dial. As the cordite relay tripped, the four kilos of plastique became a microsun, instantaneously eliminating half of the right side of the fuselage and vaporizing the cabin within eleven feet of the epicenter. In the cockpit, First Officer Lemierre tightened his grip on the control yoke as the SST lurched and filled with a thick fog. He attempted to steady the plane, but the controls were inoperative.

The effects of the breakup were irreversible. The aircraft yawed to the right into the nearly supersonic slipstream. Pieces of the fuselage had already impacted the right wing and the vertical tail section. As the plane continued its clockwise spin, another explosion occurred, this time from the starboard fuel cells, severing the entire right wing. The speeding residue of Flight 002 yielded to the inevitable, and the remaining integrity of the aircraft was lost. One hundred and nine lives blinked out 6.25 miles above sea level. Shards of titanium shot outward in spirals and reflected the light of the rising sun.

Hebron, Arkansas
8:51 a.m.

Oliver Marshall patted his dogs, shut the storm door of his southwest Arkansas farmhouse, and started for the chicken coop. He looked up through the cold fog and saw a dim sun above the murky eastern horizon. As he shuffled onward, the first sound hit him, like a distant cannon. He looked up again. Suddenly there were two suns in the grayness, one still to the east but the other nearly overhead. The second grew to a brighter intensity than the first; then it was gone. He stood and stared. A second report slapped him and reverberated through the woods below. As he strained to penetrate the fog, materials began impacting around him, and a kerosene mist seared his eyes.

Marshall ran for his house.

As Delta's Flight 667 climbed northward on its short, 240-mile run, Rachel anchored her elbow against the narrow armrest and rested her chin in the palm of her hand. She stared out the window at the golden-white sun and wondered what her mother and brother were doing at this exact moment. Probably stuffing themselves with good food, she concluded. She envied them.

"Coffee?" It was the same flight attendant who had checked their boarding passes. She smiled at Jack and inclined her head toward the metal carafe she was holding.

"Please," he nodded.

Jack watched as the woman kept the stream of scalding liquid centered until the cup was full. She extended the tray toward him, and he reached for the cup.

"Sugar? Cream?"

Jack shook his head.

"May I have some orange juice?" Rachel raised her eyebrows in anticipation. The woman smiled.

"Coming right up."

Jack sank back and retrieved his concerns. He stared at the blue-over-red triangles of the airline's logo, then brought the cup to his lips. Just what in *hell* was going on in Tulsa? All that new money for the ministry . . . then the blackmail and extortion threats. Reuben talked about death; now he's had a stroke.

"Do Mom and Jeff know about Grampa?" Rachel's inquisitive expression stole his attention.

"I don't know, sweetie. But someone will tell them in Washington, or Paris." He put his arm around his daughter. He wasn't sure if he wanted to comfort her or himself.

"Aren't they nearly in Washington?" she asked.

Jack looked at his watch. "Not yet. About another hour."

The flight attendant delivered the orange juice. Rachel turned back to the window and her thoughts. Jack returned to his own disconcerting questions. He tried the coffee again. When he'd called from Dallas, Norman's responses were enigmatic. Not that they usually weren't.

"I just heard about your father," Jack had reported. "Is there anything I can do?"

"Jack? Jack Stroud?"

"Yes, Norman. How is he?"

"Shit, Jack, you're supposed to be on a plane to Paris. Has it left yet?"

"Look, God damn it," Jack responded with exasperation, "something came up." He thought it advisable to skip the details. "Laura took the flight with Jeff. Rachel and I are supposed to leave tomorrow. Now, what about your father?"

"Can you still catch your plane, Jack? I mean, there's nothing anyone can do here. Reuben simply had a stroke. He's unconscious."

"How bad is it, Norman?" Jack tried to suppress his frustration. The line was silent for a moment.

"What?"

"What do the doctors say, for Christ's sake?" Jack was furious at the slow pace at which Norman yielded the information. Conversation with his brother-in-law was always an uphill climb.

"Uh . . . recovery might take a long time. Like, months."

"Damn it, Norman, what happened?"

"Well, uh, he was fine, just fine until after dinner last night when he said he, uh, felt weak." Norman sounded as if he was making it up as he went. "Or . . . dizzy. Yeah, dizzy. Then he passed out."

"Where is he now?"

Norman didn't answer for a few seconds, and Jack started to repeat the question.

"Here . . . at Bible College Hospital," he finally replied in a low voice. "Jack, there's nothing you can do, believe me."

"I'm coming home."

"No, Jack, you go on." Norman's voice was edgy. "I mean, there's really no reason to interrupt your vacation. Everything's under control here. You can take my word for it."

"I'll be there in a couple of hours." Jack cut off his brother-in-law's protests by hanging up. What was that son of a bitch trying to hide?

"Magazine?" The flight attendant balanced a dozen periodicals in her arms.

"Do you have today's paper?"

"I'm sure I do." She thumbed down and handed over a copy of *The Dallas Morning News.*

Jack looked at the headlines. PRESIDENT DEPLORES RENEWED MIDDLE EAST VIOLENCE, CALLS AGAIN FOR SYRIAN COOPERATION IN ELIMINATING REMAINING TERRORIST TRAINING CAMPS IN LEBANON.

What would become of the Reuben Gentry Ministries if Norman gained control? Jack stared over the top of the newspaper. An absolute catastrophe! And God knows the little bastard had tried. Fortunately, the ministry's board would see that it would never happen. They'd been better at keeping him at bay than the board had at the college. Jack refocused on the front page and felt somewhat better.

NASA READIES NEWEST SHUTTLE AND DEEP-SPACE SATELLITE LAUNCH.

But Reuben was the key. Unlike the Tulsa Bible College board, the ministry's was Reuben's own creation. It relied on him completely for its direction. If Gentry couldn't function because of a stroke, the ministry could become a house of cards.

Jack remembered he hadn't learned about Reuben's son until a full month after he met Laura. They were on their way to Tulsa to announce their engagement to her parents when she initially broached the subject of her brother. At first, Jack thought it was a simple case of his not listening. Surely she'd said something to him about Norman earlier, but with all of the commotion following their love-at-first-sight encounter, he probably just didn't remember. Jack had been apprehensive about meeting Reuben and Lillian Gentry, but after Laura's convoluted explanation of her only sibling, he decided that meeting her parents would be a piece of cake by comparison. And it was.

Norman was 5-feet-8, obese, and twenty years old at the time, half a decade younger than his sister. A junior at Tulsa Bible College, he had only a few friends, whom Laura charitably referred to as "geeks." A rumor made the rounds at the school each fall that he was adopted and possibly gay. In most ways, Norman and Laura were opposites. She was well liked; he wasn't. She was good looking; he wasn't. And where she attempted to get along, Norman was always committed to getting his way. Nothing had changed over the years. Today he was even more overweight and nonathletic. His light brown hair was now thinner, his face still a greasy milk-white that displayed the effects of a long-running bout with acne.

Reuben's successor? Jack shuddered and opened the newspaper.

FOUR U.S. TRADE REPRESENTATIVES KILLED IN MONTERREY CAR BOMB ATTACK; FLF WARNS AMERICAN INTERESTS WORLDWIDE.

Jack skipped through the paper, then tucked it into the seat-back pocket and folded his arms. Nothing but the usual heartening news, he thought.

"Ladies and gentlemen, Captain Bolton has illuminated the fasten-seat-belt sign in preparation for our landing. Please check to see that your seat belts are securely fastened."

Jack turned toward his daughter. "Buckle up, sweetie. After we check on Grampa, we'll see about joining Mom and Jeff."

Rachel smiled. He took her hand.

Thirteen miles south of the Tulsa airport, the McDonnell Douglas MD-88 banked smoothly and aligned itself with the active runway. The plane nosed over gently, and the landing gear rumbled out.

"Please see that your seat backs and tray tables are in their full-upright-and-locked position," the flight attendant's voice continued. "We'll be landing in about two minutes."

Washington, D.C.
Midmorning

"Jesus H. Christ, lady!"

Transportation Secretary Bradford Nielsen fell back against the plush leather of the rear seat and clenched his teeth as he watched a portly woman in a silver BMW finally pull away from the curb. He formed a fist with his right hand and slammed it down on the padded armrest. His driver looked in the rearview mirror and winced.

"Some of us can't wait until the Second Coming," Nielsen yelled at the departing woman, who was in no danger of hearing him. She had consumed an eternity extracting her keys and getting situated inside her automobile before she started its engine and slowly eased into the traffic.

"Thank God she didn't have another biddy with her. I could be here until Easter!"

Nielsen's car had circled the block in Georgetown three times looking for a parking space. He'd seen the woman standing at her car on their first pass for a spot. His short ration of patience ran out on their second circuit.

"Goddamned M Street's always like this," he railed as he leaned forward and gripped the top of the front seat. "Especially after Christmas, when everyone's returning dumb presents."

That's exactly what Nielsen planned to do with the two shirts his sister had given him.

"Hell, she knows I never wear orange or green," he snarled as his driver positioned the black Continental outside Arthur's for Men. "But she keeps giving crap, so I keep returning crap."

Once his driver had stopped the car at the curb, Nielsen slid out of the backseat and stepped onto the crowded sidewalk.

"Stay right here," he ordered as he slammed the door. His driver grimaced. The man had no intention of leaving.

Nielsen waited for an opening in the press of pedestrians. The winter sun produced only the appearance of warmth. He placed the offending package under his arm, rubbed his bare hands together, and pushed forward. His first thought was of this morning's Metroliner accident in New Jersey. "Just what we need," he muttered for his own benefit, "a major disaster to screw up everything on rails between here and Boston."

The initial report had been called into his office at 8:32, ten minutes after the tragedy. Nielsen spent most of the next hour on the telephone with subordinates who would be immediately involved in the aftermath. The appropriate members of the National Transportation Safety Board's "Go Team" were alerted at 8:34 and had already left for the site. As a courtesy, the independent NTSB would deliver a preliminary "eyes-only" summary of the accident to the Department of Transportation by midafternoon.

Nielsen's mind jumped to the forthcoming special DOT budget hearings. He was especially wary of Congress's disgust with the recent restrictions on airline operations, especially in the Northeast Corridor. God damn it, where was all their concern when he'd asked for more money for a genuine modernization plan? The procedures those ignoramuses on the Hill established back in the '80s for the FAA's new air-traffic control computers only bought crap and billion-dollar cost overruns. They wouldn't provide new personnel or fund new procedures, either. Now the SOBs got delayed over Poughkeepsie, and they were pissed. Maybe this train thing would get them off their leaden asses.

As Nielsen reached for the doorknob of the exclusive shop, he felt a sting in his lower left thigh, and he spun around. A man with a cane mumbled something and quickly merged with the shoppers along the busy street. Nielsen reached down and rubbed his leg.

"*Mister* Secretary," the proprietor exulted as Nielsen entered the store. "I hope you had a very merry Christmas. You know, your sweet sister was in last week, and I'll bet ... "

"Arthur, could I use your restroom?"

"Oh ... certainly, sir. Behind that counter."

Nielsen proceeded in the direction Arthur had pointed. Once inside the stall, he lowered his trousers and bent around to find the irritation. It was already a reddish spot just above the back of his left knee, and it looked like a spider bite. Nielsen touched it. It hurt, and it made him mad.

That clumsy son of a bitch, he thought. He pulled up his pants and went to tend to his original business of surrendering the obnoxious shirts.

On the return drive to the Department of Transportation's building on Seventh Street, Nielsen rubbed the affected area on the back of his leg. He could already feel the outline of a dime-size bump through the worsted wool of his suit. So many impolite people, he groused. Where in the hell was their Christmas spirit? And that asshole didn't even stop to see if he'd hurt me. The cellular telephone rang. He reached for the handset mounted on the back of the front seat.

"Yeah?"

It was a patch through his office from the Federal Aviation Administration. Nielsen frowned as the administrator delivered his message in a staccato tone.

"Forty minutes ago in Arkansas and no survivors?" He shook his head at the confirmation. "Damn! Listen, I'll be back in my office in ten minutes. You *be* there."

His driver nodded to the uniformed security guards at the gate and pulled into the Secretary's private parking space. Nielsen stepped out and walked gingerly into the building. The muscles in his leg were stiffening.

"Mr. Secretary, there're three calls already from the White House. All in the past five minutes, sir." Sarah, his secretary, somehow single-handedly made sure that he was at the right place at the right time. She usually made it look easy. Today she was harried. She scurried around her desk and tapped at her notes. "Then there're the NTSB and Treasury calls—two from the Secret Service separately—not to mention the ones from the media. WRC wants a live remote for their 11:55 NBC-network break."

Sarah was on automatic.

"The FAA administrator will be here shortly, as you asked, sir. Are you still going to have your noon luncheon with the Amtrak board? I mean, I don't know if you'll have time."

"Thank you, dear." Nielsen waved her off and shuffled into his paneled office. As he sat down, the room seemed to keep moving, and a feeling of nausea nearly overwhelmed him. He reached for the intercom.

"Sarah, I feel . . . terrible," he panted. "Call a doctor."

The agony in his voice propelled his secretary into his office. She gasped at the sight. Nielsen was holding onto the edge of his desk and was taking unsteady steps toward the couch against the opposite wall. His eyes were half closed. Sarah ran forward, seized him around the waist, and guided him the remaining distance. He made gargling sounds in a struggle to breathe.

Within minutes, a government physician assigned to the Transportation Department arrived and found Nielsen with a rapid pulse and an ashen face, and barely breathing. He took the Secretary's temperature: 103°F. Moments later, Nielsen lapsed into unconsciousness.

"We've got to get him to a hospital immediately," the doctor yelled. "This is an emergency. He's going into shock."

Almost as soon as Sarah went for her telephone to place a call to George Washington University Hospital, the atmosphere in the office gave way to frenzy. Members of Nielsen's immediate staff ran in. Assistant Secretaries stood next to typists and gawked helplessly. Sarah's carefully orchestrated atmosphere of stability descended into chaos as the word spread throughout the building and more employees crowded in. After she ordered an ambulance, she tried to clear the area, but no one responded. She pushed her way through the worried onlookers. To her horror, she saw that the physician was frantically performing cardiopulmonary resuscitation on Nielsen.

"I think I'm losing him," the doctor groaned. "Shit, I'm losing him."

The doctor pounded on Nielsen's chest again. Then he stopped and stared at the limp form underneath him. Sarah's immediate reaction was to grab the doctor and shove him aside. He's hurting the Secretary, she thought.

The exhausted physician sighed and sank back on his heels.

"He's gone."

Tulsa
10:06 a.m.

As they deplaned, Jack spotted Norman lurking behind three bodyguards, the pudgy man's eyes darting from passenger to passenger. Norman pointed and whispered something to the hefty security men. They moved toward Jack and his daughter.

"How did you hear about Reuben?" Norman's voice was higher than usual, almost tinny, as he fell into the procession.

"I called his office," Jack replied matter-of-factly. "Your dad asked me to stay behind to discuss some matters with him. He'd planned to fly to Dallas this morning, and I wanted to confirm his arrival time." Jack decided to remain civil toward his brother-in-law. "How's your wife taking this?"

"Bunny? Uh, well, she ... " Norman stepped faster and moved alongside. He changed the subject. "What'd Reuben want to talk about?"

Jack ignored the question. It galled him that Norman always called his father "Reuben."

41

Norman matched the aggressive gait.

"You can't help him now, Jack. Reuben's dead."

Jack staggered to a stop. *"What?"*

Norman fidgeted with his diamond pinkie ring. "Happened about an hour ago. The doctors say it was a massive cerebral hemorrhage. He never felt a thing." Norman admired his manicure. "Boy, this is a real blow to the ministry."

Jack stared at him, incredulous. "I've got to find a phone," he finally responded. "I have to intercept Laura in Washington."

As they passed a broad concession area, Rachel noticed a group of travelers watching a television set. She slowed and saw it was a bulletin on CNN.

"Rachel!" Jack motioned her to follow.

"Daddy, look. . . . "

Jack turned and went to get her. As he walked up behind his daughter, Jack heard part of the announcement: "The president will ask for a complete investigation of the two disasters. The unexplained crash this morning of the AirParis DFW-to-Washington supersonic transport claimed the lives of all on board, including Treasury Secretary David Rowland, who was en route to a special meeting of the European finance ministers in Paris."

The television report continued with the first live pictures from the crash scene—a burning swath in central Arkansas and the pieces of bodies found. Rachel turned toward her father and screamed. Jack grabbed her and held her tightly as he stared numbly at the screen. No, it couldn't be. The commentator went on, "In the New Jersey accident earlier today, an Amtrak Metroliner . . . "

Someone noticed the reaction of the man and the girl and turned off the set.

J. Edgar Hoover Building, Washington, D.C.
Monday, December 28, Noon

Jerry Reynolds, deputy director of the Federal Bureau of Investigation, headed for the emergency meeting he'd called for FBI division heads, their assistants, selected section chiefs, and other appropriate personnel. He withdrew notes from his jacket and strode through the held-open doors of the auditorium. William Colquitt, assistant director for the National Security Division; Corley Brand, chief of the Counterterrorism Section; and three of Reynolds's aides followed and took seats at the side of the stage.

The deputy director looked at his watch, then at the clock on the rear wall. He was ten minutes late. "Please be seated," he ordered into the microphone as he laid out his notes and gripped the edges of the podium. Reynolds scanned the faces in his audience and began.

"Transportation Secretary Bradford Nielsen died suddenly in his office about an hour ago." The FBI personnel looked at one another. No one spoke. "Information concerning his death is sketchy. There'll be an autopsy at Bethesda today." Reynolds paused. "The director and I were at the White House when we learned about Secretary Nielsen. We had gone to brief the president about the AirParis SST crash and the death of Treasury Secretary Rowland." There were only occasional coughs in the room.

"Ladies and gentlemen, there is a strong indication that sabotage was the cause of the airliner accident. We've received numerous reports of suspicious activities surrounding the flight." Reynolds referred to his notes. "The Dallas–Fort Worth airport police and the Tarrant County Sheriff's Department have now confirmed the killings of two caterers there. Their bodies were discovered in a culvert. Two as-of-yet-unknown individuals serviced Flight 002. About an hour ago, a late-model Oldsmobile was found abandoned inside the DFW airport property. It was not authorized to be where it was, and our people are going over it now. Clothing was found in plastic bags in its trunk. We haven't yet located the Lone Star catering truck that was commandeered. I expect a more detailed report momentarily."

Reynolds took a sip of water from a glass next to the podium and continued.

"Three agents from our Little Rock field office are on their way to the crash site, about an hour and a half's drive, and six members of our disaster team are flying there from Dulles with the National Transportation Safety Board's 'Go Team.' They should be at the location by early afternoon."

The only sounds in the auditorium now were the scratchings of pens and pencils.

"Because two members of the Cabinet died in incidents at about the same time and under suspicious circumstances, it is the director's decision that the two events be linked for purposes of our investigation. These separate actions may be—I repeat, *may* be—part of a terrorist conspiracy against the United States."

Some of those assembled leaned back and considered the consequences. A few saw a connection to the Oklahoma City bombing and to other more recent actions by "homegrown" terrorists. Others remembered the World Trade Center bombing and the hundreds of threats that followed. Several wondered if today's tragedies could be the ultimate fulfillment of the ominous promises made by the worst of the foreign militants over the past year.

"The president and Deputy Treasury Secretary Margaret Burnell have agreed that Secret Service protection should be provided to the Constitutional line of succession and all members of the Cabinet, effectively immediately. In addition, the Service will coordinate protective intelligence with the security agencies of Congress and the Supreme Court."

Many in the room laid aside their pens and pencils and watched the deputy director.

"Ladies and gentlemen," he folded his notes and concluded, "absent any evidence to the contrary, you are hereby instructed to regard these actions as subversive and directed against the integrity of the government of the United States. Responsibility for monitoring this situation has been transferred to the Strategic Information Operations Center. All further reports will come through SIOC and," he nodded toward Corley Brand, "the Counterterrorism Section. You have a summary of the events as we know them, and you're instructed to give priority to this matter in your various departments."

Reynolds took off his glasses and rubbed the bridge of his nose. "The Disaster Team supervisors and the lab people will meet here immediately after this briefing." He spoke in a lowered voice. "You will be kept informed of all developments. Thank you."

Most in attendance stood and walked quietly for the exits. A group of men and women in the back of the room came forward and sat down.

Fairview, Arkansas
1:14 p.m.

Numerous columns of smoke rose into the winter stillness from a swath of blackened terrain. It began with a trail of metallic confetti just outside Hebron, 80 miles southwest of Little Rock, and it continued northeastward across the Ouachita River and extended across State Highway 7 between Fairview and Sparkman. Aircraft slivers and tufts of clothing and flesh smoldered among the occasional spires of the tall pines. The largest recognizable piece of the SST was the vertical stabilizer section of the tail. Its stylized "AirParis" logo could be read from a thousand yards.

Two deputy sheriffs were the first authorities to arrive on the scene. Area residents had reported thunderous booms and pieces of burning metal falling from the foggy sky. As the lawmen brought their car to a stop at a burning patch of highway, they saw the smoky devastation across rolling farmland to the southwest. They radioed their find to headquarters, then blocked the highway to the inevitable curiosity seekers who would follow. Units of the Arkansas State Police arrived next and were quick to seal off connecting roads to the area. The regional office of the National Transportation Safety Board at Fort Worth issued instructions that no unauthorized persons were to be allowed within a mile of the swath, under penalty of arrest by local authorities. The FAA immediately instituted a ban on low-altitude flights, and the governor taped television and radio messages asking citizens to cooperate by staying away.

Regardless of the pleas, within the hour traffic on nearby Interstate 30 was heavier than on a Fourth of July weekend. Helicopters from television stations as far away as Fort Smith and Memphis swooped in to provide a closer look for their viewers. Some souvenir-seeking local residents walked through the burned-out area before the belatedly mobilized National Guard reached the site and warned them away. A few with sticks continued to root among the macabre human shreddings, even in the presence of the armed troops. One drifter was arrested as he wrenched gold crowns from a severed lower jaw while he asked a guardsman where the best bodies were. Another individual had to be forced at gunpoint to relinquish the clasped hands of a man and a little girl. When he was turned over to the sheriff's department, he marveled that the polish on the child's fingernails was still bright and fresh looking.

The FBI and NTSB teams landed at Little Rock's Adams Field just after noon and were taken to the scene in all-terrain vehicles, preceded by a state police escort. Once the two teams arrived at the command post at the eastern fringe of the disaster, they met with the Little Rock FBI agents and the other authorities. Five NTSB section investigators—Structures, Systems, Power Plants, Recorders, and Witnesses—were on the scene. Five others—Maintenance Records, Operations, Weather, Human Factors, and Air-Traffic Control—were on their way to Dallas, where they would meet with representatives of AirParis, the FAA, and the National Weather Service. Three AirParis maintenance specialists were scheduled to arrive from France in a chartered jet later in the evening. They would bring copies of all data relevant to the airworthiness and operation of the SST. Without being told, the Washington investigators knew there were no survivors. No one on the ground had been killed.

"Is the area secure?" the NTSB team chief asked, looking around.

"It is now," a state policeman responded. "Our men and members of the Arkansas National Guard are being stationed along the perimeter, about every thousand yards. There were a handful of trespassers. Couple arrests. Don't think they obscured anything."

"Good. Please don't move a thing. Our first priority is to locate the flight data and cockpit voice recorders. They'll help us to determine the probable cause of the accident. They're painted a luminescent orange, and they should be found in or near the tail section of the aircraft, if it survived the impact."

"It's about a quarter of a mile from here," one of the FBI men called out. "A TV station reported seeing it."

The NTSB chief nodded. "And we'll need your assistance in photographing, tagging, and recording all relevant debris, including human remains. We'll get the bodies out first. Or what's left of them. Any questions?" There were none.

"OK, we'll be in radio contact at all times. Let's go."

Tulsa
1:55 p.m.

Jack stared into the courtyard of the comfortable house he'd shared with Laura and their children. He'd refused a tranquilizer from Leland Marks, their family physician.

"I don't want any feelings covered up right now, Lee," he'd answered as he waved away the medication. "I want to remember just how Laura and Jeff looked when I last saw them." He cleared his throat and closed his eyes. "That last moment, when they boarded, I didn't even tell them that I loved them."

"They knew," Dr. Marks replied. He touched Jack on the arm, then left to join the others who had come to comfort and console. Board members from Tulsa Bible College, employees of U.S. Simulation Systems, neighbors, students and faculty from Indian Springs Preparatory School, and other friends of the Strouds gathered elsewhere in the house. Members of Jack's immediate family were on their way from out of town. Rachel had been given a sedative and was asleep in her room.

Jack was numb. Laura had really wanted to stay behind, but she went because of his promise thirty years before. *His* promise! Tears welled as he pictured her in the doorway of the boarding ramp just hours ago. She'd looked so vulnerable. Then Jack saw Jeff, with his inimitable smile, as he'd turned and waved before he left with his mother. Jeff was Jack's very own image and likeness, and he'd told his dad a hundred times how proud he was to be his son. Now both of them—his precious wife and his beloved son—were gone forever. And Reuben. Reuben, too!

For the first time, Jack's mind began to comprehend the magnitude of the events of the day. He caught his breath. He had wanted to go to Arkansas, to attempt somehow to be close, maybe to experience something about the last day his wife and son existed on earth. But everyone had dissuaded him. There's nothing left, they'd told him. Leland Marks had been insistent. "You must remember them as they were." Jack had been similarly persuaded not to visit the funeral home where they had taken Reuben's body.

Suddenly he felt as if his body was possessed by ants, hundreds of them, crawling throughout his arteries. Jack wanted to act, to do something. But when he walked into his study and closed the door, he knew that more than anything else he needed to be alone because, just possibly, there was something he'd missed . . . some tie with Laura that would keep her from slipping into eternity. Like a thunderbolt, it flashed through his mind. In a surge of energy, Jack dug into his pants pockets, then sought out his suit coat. He grabbed his overcoat and found the St. Christopher. He sat and cupped the medal in his hand, silently smoothing the engraved inscription with his fingers. He'd ordered the gold piece from Tiffany's and had presented it to Laura with her engagement ring. His face contorted, and he fell against the chair and let harsh sobs overtake him.

For over an hour, Jack was aware of voices from the hall and kitchen as more neighbors and associates arrived to express their shock and sympathy. However, no one disturbed him in his initial moments of reconciliation with the enormity of the tragedy. He heard people say they would return tomorrow or the day after. He remembered that Leland Marks had reported that both the memorial service for Laura and Jeff and Reuben's funeral had been set for Thursday afternoon.

Jack thought he'd slept. Some length of time had passed without his feeling the continuing agony. He hadn't watched the clock, so he wasn't sure. He rose and went to the bookcases that lined one wall of the room. The memories of the past were all there. He picked up his graduation picture from Sacred Heart High School in Leawood, Kansas, where he'd been an all-state end on the Crusader football team and co-captain of the Catholic school's debate team. Jack examined the faces. Many of them were still familiar, even after nearly four decades. He put the picture back, next to the newspaper photo of Congressman Warren Garvey shaking Jack's hand after notifying him of his appointment to the United States Naval Academy. He smiled. There were his parents standing in the background with looks of pride that would radiate from the photograph for as long as it existed. He touched the next one, the traditional caps-in-the-air photo taken when he'd finished sixteenth in his class at Annapolis. Then his attention fell upon a picture of himself in Boca Raton, taken the next year. That was when he married Susie Chambers, his childhood sweetheart. She was killed in a boating accident in the Gulf of Mexico on her birthday six months later. Jack had never forgiven himself for that, because he had gotten drunk at a party earlier and had to stay behind. Susie couldn't swim, and she just went under when no one was looking.

He leaned over, and tears came again. There were the beaming faces in Tulsa when Laura and he were married, barely three months after they met. It was a fantasy courtship, one that constituted the core of romance novels, and no one doubted that it was a marriage made in heaven. There were eight hundred at the "restricted" service in the new chapel at Tulsa Bible College, and 1,500 more at the country-club reception later. Reuben and Lillian Gentry's little girl, their only daughter, drew the attention of the politically, the socially, and the religiously significant throughout the country. As she grew up, Laura had been seen by millions on Reuben's television crusades, and many who had believed in her father accepted her as their own. When she was married, they, too, cried and wished her Godspeed with her handsome new husband. Reuben had soft-pedaled Jack's Catholicism during those days, especially to the media. Jack had been so crazy in love that it hadn't mattered. All he cared about was Laura and the time they could spend together.

There was the honeymoon picture he'd taken at dawn from their hotel balcony in Paris, with the Eiffel Tower in the background. He reached for the gilded frame. The suffused light revealed a lithe beauty who coyly returned the attentions of her photographer. With their love they had warmed the elegant three-room suite at the small Raphaël, just off the Etoile. The beginning of their marriage was everything Jack could have hoped for. They sailed the Seine in the touristy *bâteau-mouche* and ate from the culinary riches offered by the City of Light and, hand in hand, laughed and kissed along the walkways for lovers in the Bois de Boulogne. He stared at the photograph for a full minute.

Jack reached to the back of a bookcase and drew out a framed newspaper obituary. It was during a dreary week in February, five years after their marriage, when the world looked through the one-way window of television and again fell in love with Laura as the devoted daughter, three months pregnant with their twins, attended to her dying mother in the last days of her valiant struggle with ovarian cancer.

Jack also remembered that time as an on-again-off-again trial. Reuben was the plaintiff, Jack the defendant. Having a televangelist as a father-in-law was something he couldn't have prepared for, and Jack often reflected on the substantial differences between his and Laura's family. But he'd stayed. There had really been no doubt. Nothing could tear him from Laura. Nothing . . . until now.

Jack wiped his eyes and smiled at the first picture of their twins, Jeffrey and Rachel, who were born in Arlington shortly after he had been appointed head of the counterterrorism section of the Naval Investigative Service. Now Laura and Jeff were gone. "I promise you, darling. . . . " He reached up to touch the photograph.

"Daddy?"

Rachel stood in the doorway, her hair matted from sleep. He saw that she was crying. Clutched in her left hand, wrinkled and wet from tears, was the Swiss money she had taken from her twin brother only hours earlier. Thank God, Jack thought, for their long-standing policy of separating the children when the family traveled on different flights. Otherwise he'd have lost Rachel, too.

"Oh, Daddy, *Daddy,*" she moaned as she ran into his arms. "I was so mean to him."

Jack held his daughter and cried with her.

Elsewhere, a voice whispered into a telephone. "The girl's with him now."

"Keep monitoring. Let me know if he leaves the house."

Near Baalbek, Lebanon
7:23 p.m.

It had been slightly more than two hours since the early winter sunset allowed the temperature to fall in the inland Bekaa Valley of eastern Lebanon. Augmented by a light north wind, it now dropped as quickly as the darkness. At three degrees Celsius, local thermometers were closing in on freezing.

Six kilometers south of the busy village of Baalbek and its Roman temple ruins, in the gentle trough on the lower slopes of the Al Jabal Ash Sharqi range dividing Lebanon from Syria, a nondescript camp lay camouflaged against the sandy terrain. It had been an abandoned army facility, but it was now double-patrolled. A fresh detachment of soldiers wearing helmet-mounted night-vision goggles referred to their timepieces and scampered out to position themselves along the sterile zone surrounding seven one-story buildings. Inside the second-largest structure, six men shifted awkwardly under an overhead rack of clear bulbs at the front of the room and were subjected to the scrutiny of their olive-skinned trainers.

"You have received our best," the Asian leader started as he paced the floor. The stubby fingers of his hands, clasped behind his back, manipulated a short riding crop. He stopped and snapped the crop against his trousers.

"Now you *are* our best."

Five other North Koreans, partially illuminated by the bright lights, watched in silence. Four of them sucked on unfiltered Turkish cigarettes and nodded their agreement.

The leader approached the trainees.

"You now depart for the last step in your education." He embraced each man and spoke through a thin smile. "Soon you will be teachers yourselves."

It was a simple commencement ceremony, but the celebration would wait until they employed what they had learned. By helicopter, the six men would now scale the modest mountains nearby and, within thirty minutes, be in Damascus, forty-nine kilometers away. Then to Vienna and Frankfurt ... and beyond. Their final honing would occur nearly half a world away.

Lester Graham stood next to the refrigerator, pulled off his leather hunting gloves, and let them plop to the wrinkled linoleum floor. The impact disturbed a latticework of dust in the corner of the small kitchen. From a hip pocket he drew out a soiled handkerchief and blew his nose. This hadn't been the best morning for him, starting with the frozen pipes. He'd attempted to wash up after an hour of crawling under the house to get the water flowing again. That's when he discovered that the pilot light on the water heater was out.

Graham brought his left hand to his mouth and chewed across his thumbnail with little bites. He regularly manicured himself this way, but an earlier effort had been less than perfect, and the nail's ragged edge had hung up in the lining of his glove when he'd attempted to slip it on. He touched an inspecting tongue to his work, then chewed once more at a raised spot. He ran his index finger across the nail's edge and pursed his lips in satisfaction.

"Darn fingernail could hold up an army," he muttered as he stooped for the gloves.

Graham looked out the storm door of his three-room house while he thrust his left hand into the glove. It went in smoothly this time. Outside, shrubbery along the concrete sidewalk shook in the frigid gusts of the north wind. He put on the other glove and fumbled at the large plastic zipper of his insulated coat before it caught in its track. He drew the closure up to his neck. He then picked up his woolen knit cap and pulled it on to just below his ears. With his chin, he nudged a thick scarf a little further down into the opening of his jacket.

He lowered a double-barrel 12-gauge shotgun from its rack and inserted two shells. The remaining contents of a box of ammunition were already distributed evenly in the four pockets of his jacket. He secured the butt of the weapon against his right armpit, ready for a quick response. Graham was finally set for the rigors of the twenty-degree outdoors. He intended to pick off a couple of fat cottontails today. Might be lucky enough to flush a covey of quail while he was at it, he thought. Or maybe even be able to spot one of those mysterious neighbors of his.

Graham opened the storm door, pushed against the rickety screen of the frame house, and stepped out into the cold and windy morning. He ran a gloved finger under the headband of his cap for a precise fit and looked around the straw-colored terrain. It was flat except for a slight rise toward a grove of scrub oak trees to the west. He raised his face and sniffed at the air. There was a hint of smoke from a grassland fire somewhere. His boots clumped down the naked cinder blocks and along the concrete sidewalk toward the north. He crossed the frozen ruts of his driveway and entered the field that ran to the old Cummings property.

His own half-mile-wide tract extended nearly a mile north and south along the county road. Twenty-six miles south of Tulsa as the crow flies, he used to say. He had built his house on the northeast quadrant. In all, he had 306 acres, most of which he'd dedicated to soybeans the previous summer. Before that, he'd leased the acreage for grazing. He would have owned the full half-section, but an oil company wouldn't part with fourteen acres at the bottom corner. Said they'd be building a pumping station or something. But that was years ago, when the oil industry was in one of its frenzies. He thought again of old man Cummings.

"Kinda miss the old fart."

He smiled at the memory of his friend. "Took 'em months to come for him, but they never laid a hand on him." Cummings promised they wouldn't evict him, taxes or no taxes. He probably thought they'd never come. But they did, all right. He'd let go with that .410 of his just as they drove up.

"Hell of a greeting to find him coating the kitchen cabinets."

Graham winced and imagined the lawmen's faces when they found that their quarry had escaped, in a manner of speaking.

It was spooky watching that house afterwards. Sat there empty for years without changing, like it was waiting for the old man to come back. Graham had sometimes wondered if Cummings hadn't returned after all. On more than one occasion, after midnight, he could have sworn he'd seen a light through the front window.

As he trudged onward, all that interrupted the horizon were clumps of stubble from last year's harvest—good ground trash that could hide plump quail on this crisp morning. Graham sensed the other life here, beneath his feet. This area was crisscrossed by underground pipelines, some up to three feet in diameter, carrying crude oil to Oklahoma refineries in Cushing and Tulsa and finished products from Texas to markets north and east. The oil business had always been a hardscrabble life, he reflected, a peak-and-valley industry where former millionaires hawked real estate a day or so after the banks shuttered their companies. But they peddled, or whatever, and proudly, because they knew they'd be back someday. Funny thing about it. In the next upturn in the cycle, they usually were.

Graham's Uncle Royce had been one of those who'd had it all and lost it. At the peak, Royce's family had lived on a four-square-mile horse farm, fenced and cross-fenced by lengths of white-painted pipe. The drive to the front door of the high-columned mansion was nearly a quarter mile. There were hills and woods and fishing holes—a hundred places where a boy could hide out and play make-believe, which Graham did every time he came up from Texas to visit. Sometimes he sat with Chestnut, the mongrel who reigned over the place, and stroked her coat while he pictured himself among the faraway scenes that the clouds revealed. He took the dog along on his fanciful travels most of the time. But all of that was more than fifty-five years ago.

Fifty-five *years?*

His father had enlisted immediately after Pearl Harbor. The old man had apparently been so angry at the Japanese that he'd quickly been able to convince a coterie of co-workers to join him in a sort of personal crusade. Mad Texans, they'd all marched away together. All but one returned. Graham's dad died in a 1942 training accident in California, before he was able to fire a single bullet at the enemy. The trips to his uncle's ended, and Graham went to work to help feed the family . . . his mother, his sister, and himself. He'd often thought about the days when he'd just sat and looked and fantasized. He frequently promised himself that he'd return to this place where he'd left his dreams. And, thankfully, he had.

The property had been sold many times over the years. The original house was gone, a victim of a lightning strike in the mid-sixties, but most of the white drill-pipe fencing remained. Seeing the place for the first time after so many years gave him goose bumps. The Clabber Girl shield on the fence along the highway was still there, though rusted over. Like other country boys, Graham had had a secret love affair with that pretty metal visage. He scraped at the rust to renew the acquaintance, but she hadn't waited for him.

Graham bought the frontage property first, then some of the interior acreage of the farm. He built his simple residence on less than an eighth of the hallowed ground of the past, and he tried to turn back the clock. But, in truth . . .

He stopped with a jerk. Reality replaced the reverie. Less than fifty feet ahead lay the adjacent property. Graham grew apprehensive as he remembered the recent events.

The Cummings property had been purchased a couple of years ago by some out-of-town folks who kept tightly to themselves. One afternoon, just after they moved in, Graham saw two men in coveralls walking briskly from their house toward the highway, about a quarter of a mile to the east. But by the time he'd gotten outside in an attempt to give them a neighborly welcome, they had yanked up their roadside mailbox and returned with it to the house. He hadn't really tried to meet them since. Not that they'd given him a lot of opportunities, either. Anytime he thought he'd made eye contact, the people looked away—or through him as if he weren't there. It was apparent they didn't like outsiders. Graham hadn't forced the issue.

The new people started construction of a large metal barn a year ago last spring and had it finished by the first freeze. It wasn't really a barn in the usual sense. Rather, it was a flat, two-story building, more like a big equipment storage facility. Maybe three hundred feet or so square. When they took out the building permit, they called the place "indoor tennis courts." Graham had checked at the courthouse himself. He was sure it was the largest such structure in Okmulgee County. He was curious where all the players were going to come from. Many of the folks at the courthouse said they'd never even met a tennis player. "Why, when them tennis shows come on TV," the county clerk had confided with a giggle, "I just flip that dial."

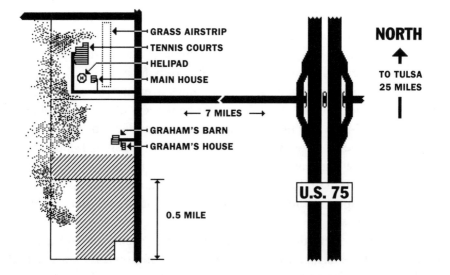

Throughout the previous year and a half, Graham witnessed the comings and goings of vehicles. Lots of them. A hundred different times, and mostly at night, after eleven. Vans and station wagons. Later he saw buses. Forty-five-foot road cruisers. The first ones woke him up early in the morning a year ago Thanksgiving. Must be coming from the south on the county road, he figured. He had gotten up and pulled on his coveralls in the dark and left his house to see. There were three buses the first time. He could tell by the light of the moon that they'd stopped in a single file next to the main house. Small beams, probably mini-flashlights, probed here and there around the tires. Then all was dark again. The diesel engines revved up, and the buses drove around to the back of the new metal building. Two more buses arrived the next afternoon. He saw they were an army-drab brown, with smoked windows. A few nights later, after midnight, all five left the compound. They returned a week later. Again, after a couple of days, they left. Late at night. This procedure was repeated at least a dozen times over a seven-week period. Graham hadn't seen more than three buses since then. He didn't think any of the people coming and going at the old Cummings place were there for tennis.

As he reached the fence, the puttering sound of a small airplane caught his attention. He cocked his head and squinted. The little craft swooped left, then right, in the slate-gray morning sky. It remained a couple of thousand feet in the air while it performed additional banking and power maneuvers.

"Goddamned student pilots," he swore under his breath. "How many times do I have to warn them people?"

The trainees from a Tulsa airport were always using this area for their practice lessons. *Abusing,* Graham thought, was a better way to put it. What especially annoyed him were the low-level turns about a point, as they called them, and right over his land, usually picking his house as their "point." He'd spoken with the Southwest School of Aviation enough to know the proper terminology, and they'd heard from him so many times that they'd posted warnings all over the campus for students to avoid his property as a practice area. But this morning another kid was struggling through the motions of becoming a pilot. And, damn it, precisely where he shouldn't be.

As Graham watched in disgust, the single-engine plane suddenly looked unsteady. It seemed to slow and shake. First it plunged, then it leveled off. Graham cupped his hand behind his ear. There was no engine sound. The red-and-cream Cessna 152 trainer came into closer view, turned away, then banked back silently. It was obvious the pilot was in trouble and was going to have to make an emergency landing. In the clear winter sky, the small plane slipped and turned and knifed downward and aimed right for Graham's land. It didn't require more than a minute for the aircraft to be just above his barn and pointed north for the broad expanse of his neighbor's property. As the plane approached the perimeter fence where Graham stood, it straightened out and ballooned upward. He ducked. It barely cleared him and the barbed wire and glided toward touchdown. With a severe bounce, and another, it settled onto the level field beyond and shook as it decelerated. Finally it stopped. The left-side door popped open, and the pilot stepped onto the hard turf. He looked unhurt as he surveyed his predicament.

Graham remained in a crouch and wondered where the dark green van had come from. It was next to the plane within seconds. Three men in coveralls jumped out and ran toward the pilot. They seized him by the arms and legs and forced him inside the van, which lurched ahead and disappeared through an opening in the barn. Within seconds, a flatbed truck drove out from the same door of the metal building. As Graham stared, it stopped next to the small airplane. Two men emerged and started removing equipment from the back of the vehicle. He heard a gasoline engine being pulled to life, and he realized that one of the men was wielding a chain saw. The man approached the empty aircraft. With a throwing motion, he directed the roaring device into the metal of the left wing where it joined the fuselage. The little plane shook on its spindly landing gear as the saw sliced into the main spars. They gave way with sharp cracks, and, tip first, the severed wing clanged to the hard earth. The man walked around and did the same thing to the right wing. It was separated as quickly as the first. He then began cutting at the fuselage, and he continued until there were only abbreviated slices of the metal structure strewn on the ground. The two men piled the pieces onto the back of the truck. When they drove away, twenty-five minutes after the hapless pilot had sought out the strip for survival, there was nothing remaining of his intrusion.

Something told Graham this was not the time to attract attention by firing a shotgun. He stepped backward a dozen or so feet before he turned for his house. As he bolted, a covey of quail lifted off to his left. The scattering of the birds was noticed only by a man with binoculars who watched from the upstairs window of the old Cummings place.

Tulsa
9:35 a.m.

Jack searched the ceiling of his bedroom for a full minute before his mind permitted the events of the previous day to wash into his consciousness. He caught his breath at their enormity. The first emotion that filtered through was a sense of total, irrevocable loss. In an attempt to isolate and nullify the horror, Jack pictured Laura standing before him, smiling. He waited for her to speak, but she didn't. The vision was replaced by a feeling of utter hopelessness. He closed his eyes again and prayed for the Almighty to temper the sharpness of reality. Then he recalled the arrival the night before of his brother Edgar and Edgar's wife Jenny. Ed, the middle son, was two years younger than Arthur and two years older than Jack. Their sister, Anne, had been born the day Jack entered kindergarten. Ed and Jenny flew in from Chicago and arrived just after dinner. Art and Fran were to be here this morning. As was Anne.

Thinking of Ed made the moment somewhat easier. Ed had always been the family cheerleader, and it was important for him to arrive first and arrange the sense of acceptance of the way things were. He was good at that.

With the sluggishness of a man twenty years older, Jack peeled back the comforter and the sheets and stepped out of bed and into his slippers. As he stood and wrapped himself in his robe, he thought of his parents. He shook his head. It'd be nice if he could lean on them today. He headed for the bathroom.

"Mr. Stroud?" His housekeeper's voice filtered through the veneer of his thoughts. Jack had dressed and was just slipping into his loafers. God, Flora. He imagined how distressed she must be. He'd have to talk to her, to reassure her. He reached for his cardigan and looked toward the door.

"Please, Flora, come in."

"Your brother's here, sir." Flora wiped at her eyes, then hid the hand-kerchief behind her back.

"Oh, Flora." He walked toward her and embraced her tightly. She felt so little in his arms. He and Laura and the twins had depended on this woman.

"I couldn't make it without you."

The door opened further. "Jack?"

"Ed!" Jack motioned for his brother to enter. Flora stepped back and brought the handkerchief to her face again.

"We'll talk later," Jack assured the woman. "I promise." She bit her lip and quickly went for the door.

Ed moved toward his brother. In silence, they embraced. The Strouds had never been an expressive family, but the present circumstances allowed the emotions of the heart to overwhelm the checkmate of the brain. Both men cried.

J. Edgar Hoover Building, Washington, D.C.
12:44 p.m.

The message arrived twice. It was received first by the FBI's Strategic Information Operations Center, via satellite, as an encrypted summary of a longer document from the Bureau's new legal attaché office in Berlin. Later, two armed State Department couriers presented themselves downstairs and handed over the complete text of the communication, which had been delivered by government jet, nonstop, in a special diplomatic pouch.

Three men hurried down the main corridor of the Criminal Investigative Division floor in the middle of the headquarters building on Pennsylvania Avenue. Deputy Director Jerry Reynolds was followed by Corley Brand, chief of the Counterterrorism Section, and Paul Simpson, an intelligence research specialist in the Terrorist Research and Analytical Center. They stopped at the unmarked entrance to SIOC. Reynolds picked up a handset and punched in the current hour's access code.

"Lew, we're here," he announced after the verification tone sounded. He hung up and waited.

With a whine, a worm-drive motor was activated, and the foot-thick bank-vault door of the secured blockhouse slowly swung open. Lewis Bittker, SIOC's chief, greeted the three visitors with a terse "It's been verified."

The men entered the eight-room fortification of steel walls and bulletproof glass partitions and followed Bittker to the conference room. An agent wearing a stainless-steel 10mm handgun in a shoulder holster actuated the closing of the heavy door.

To the left were two cavernous bunkers containing tiers of video monitoring screens, which flickered with their color displays of data from a hundred thousand sources around the world. Digital pictures of maps and drawings filled the oversize screens along one of the walls. Television sets captured and held pictures from the major U.S. broadcast and cable networks, as well as from the BBC and all other international communications services, while agents and technicians sat and listened through headsets and silently followed their assigned events. There was only the occasional whisper of orders into microphones and the muffled sound of warm air passing through heat registers along the wall. The men walked into the conference room. No one sat down. Bittker began.

"The initial transmission, in English, was delivered to me immediately after the message was received and decoded." He handed a sheet to Reynolds. It had originated from the *Bundesnachrichtendienst*, the German foreign intelligence service. Reynolds read it out loud.

"BND HAS CONFIRMED EXISTENCE OF NEW EXTREMIST ORGANI-

ZATION, THE 'BROTHERHOOD OF THE ULTIMATE IJIMA.' APPARENT ORIGIN MIDDLE EASTERN. OPERATIVE FLOW PATTERN FROM LEBANON THROUGH CENTRAL GERMANY TO NORTH AMERICA ESTABLISHED AT LEAST SEVEN MONTHS AGO. EVIDENCE INDICATES GROUP WELL FINANCED.

"IN CONVERSATION INTERCEPTED 1723 HOURS LOCAL TIME 28 DECEMBER, UNIDENTIFIED GROUP MEMBER UNDER SURVEILLANCE AT WIESBADEN CALLED PUBLIC TELEPHONE AT FRANKFURT AIRPORT HOTEL. IN ARABIC, ENTIRE MESSAGE WAS, 'THE FINAL JIHAD HAS BEGUN. THE FIRST WOUNDS HAVE BEEN INFLICTED. GO SEVER THE HEAD OF THE PHARAOH AND COMPLETE THE CLEANSING. THE BROTHERHOOD IS WITH YOU. ALLAH AKBAR.' "

Reynolds whistled. "North America, and seven months ago. Anything else?"

Bittker shook his head. "Not yet. Apparently nothing turned up when the BND checked at the Frankfurt airport. It was a telephone in the lobby of the Hotel Rhein-Main."

" 'Go sever the head of the pharaoh'?" Brand questioned.

Reynolds glanced back at the paper. After a moment, he spoke without looking up.

"SIOC was specifically designed to monitor two separate incidents of major consequence, a half-dozen at most, in the event of multiple threats. We came close to shorting out the system during Desert Storm—not to mention the aftermath of the World Trade Center and Oklahoma City bombings. We've got yesterday's domestic actions, resulting in the deaths of two Cabinet members under extremely suspicious circumstances. We're monitoring the FLF's rapid upsurge in Mexico. Now this."

The deputy director made eye contact with each man.

"Gentlemen, at this rate and if this message means what I think it does, SIOC could be overloaded within seventy-two hours."

Tulsa
3:09 p.m.

"Please don't let me go, Jack!"

Laura's terrified face was inches away. Her mouth gaped, and her eyes darted back and forth. "Dear God, I don't want to die!" Suddenly her outstretched hands waved before him, and he attempted to reach for them. But his reactions were outrageously sluggish, as if time were winding down. She screamed again. "Jack, save me!" He commanded his body to respond. His arms extended slowly, awkwardly. Then came the blast, and his beloved's face was illuminated in iridescence. Jack watched in horror as Laura was pulled away from him into a boiling vortex.

"Laura!" he panted. He sat upright in bed, his heart racing. He drew a hand across his sweat-drenched face. "Laura?"

Albuquerque, New Mexico
Early evening

The man withdrew the rental car's lighter and pressed its glowing tip to his cigarette. He sucked, and the tobacco ignited into brightness that reflected across his gaunt face. He exhaled through the open window. He leaned down, pushed the lighter into its receptacle, and glanced at the timer on the front seat. 7:08 p.m. He reached into the backseat and grabbed his overcoat. The mountain night was cold; he'd need more than a windbreaker. He stepped out of the car and put on the coat and buttoned it. He took another pull on the cigarette. As he waited, he moved his arms in broad circles and flexed his fingers.

An hour earlier, he had merged his car with the traffic on Interstate 40 as it crossed the Rio Grande on the west side of Albuquerque. Six miles further, he'd exited and headed south on a county road. Within a minute he was out of sight of the lights of the bustling highway. The place he had chosen was less than three miles ahead. He recognized it and slowed the car. A rutted path continued westward. He set the parking lights and drove another fifty yards. He swung the car onto a clear area and stopped.

The man looked to the east. The lights of the city extended in a bright chain from north to south. Due east, he could make out the alternating green-and-white rotating beacon of Albuquerque International Airport. Above and beyond it, spaced at regular intervals, were the landing lights of approaching aircraft. He was on the extended centerline of the airport's main east-west runway—precisely 9.8 miles from the departure end of Two-Six. The man picked up a portable transceiver from the front seat of the car and turned it on. Its illuminated window displayed the frequency for Albuquerque Ground Control. The flight was scheduled to depart the gate at 7:10 p.m. The man increased the volume of the radio.

"Are we really gonna get to throw snowballs on a mountain and then swim in the ocean?" The pretty thirteen-year-old looked up from her wheelchair. "All on the same afternoon?"

"You betcha, sweetheart." Tony Hidalgo squatted down next to the teenage quadriplegic and patted her shoulder. He looked at her hand-lettered name tag. "I absolutely guarantee it, Shawna." Hidalgo rose slightly and kissed her forehead. "And if you want to know a secret ... " He puffed up his chest. "Afterwards, I'm going to arrange the biggest luau for you in the history of Hawaii. I mean food like you've never seen. You'll think you died and went to heaven." He ruffled her hair and laughed. "I'm telling you, sweetie pie, don't you sleep for a second on this trip. You might miss something."

The girl drew in his every word. She closed her eyes and visualized his promises. He saw on her lips the smile of a true believer. He left to deliver a similar message to the other young travelers.

Last year, he'd taken them to Walt Disney World. As usual, the trip was the talk of the town. This year, two hundred and thirty-one disabled and disadvantaged kids, and their thirty-seven escorts, were going to spend a week on the pink sands of the Big Island's Mauna Kea Royal Pacific, compliments of New Mexico's most prominent car dealer and, in the opinion of many residents of the Land of Enchantment, its most generous citizen. Hidalgo had again chartered a Lockheed L-1011 from TWA for his quarter-of-a-million-dollar mission of love. The aircraft had arrived from St. Louis at 4:56 p.m. As the eleven-member crew stepped into the lighted VIP reception area, the local media crowded around.

"Will you be staying and playing with the kids on the beach?"

The captain grinned. "You betcha," he promised. The other crew members nodded their agreement.

"Are you going to be appearing on the 'Tonight' show, too?"

"If we can't," a beaming flight attendant replied, "we'll certainly be watching."

As the nation looked on and identified with this oasis of kindness, the pilots and flight attendants couldn't help becoming as excited as their young passengers.

"Albuquerque Ground, this is TWA 4115 Heavy. Ready to push back."

The man looked at the timer. 7:10 p.m. He dropped his cigarette and stepped on it.

"TWA 4115 Heavy, Albuquerque Ground. Ramp uncontrolled, push your discretion. Taxi to Two-Six."

"Roger."

The man entered the tower frequency into his transceiver and laid the radio on the front seat. He walked to the rear of the car, opened the trunk, and seized the handle of a long metal case. He pulled the container upright and flipped the clasps. The weak light of the trunk outlined the launcher of a small heat-seeking missile. He hoisted the weapon to his shoulder and returned to the driver's side of the car.

"American 1087, maintain runway heading, cleared for take-off."

The man could hear the radio transmissions clearly from twenty feet. He looked at the timer again, then activated the electronic circuitry of the launcher. A row of small red bulbs blinked on, three at a time.

The lights of a Boeing 757 rose rapidly above those of the airport and climbed in the man's direction. The American jet continued upward and passed nearly a mile overhead. The man followed it in his sights, developing the proper arc of movement.

The expected clearance came a few seconds later.

"TWA 4115 Heavy, maintain runway heading, cleared for takeoff."

"Roger, runway heading, and we're cleared to go. TWA 4115 Heavy."

The man adjusted the weapon on his right shoulder and peered into the sight. Even though he could not yet make out the form of the departing plane, which had started to roll along the 13,375-foot runway nearly ten miles away, his earlier calculations told him that the L-1011 would be directly overhead in three minutes and twenty-two seconds. As he peered through the glass lens, the lights of the jumbo jet became visible. They rose slowly above the airport and climbed toward him. The sensors within the launcher remained silent. The TWA jet continued its climb. The man followed it in a gradually increasing angle. He extended his right index finger, then carefully wrapped it around the trigger. The system was fully armed. With an audible growling sound, the sensors now locked on.

The L-1011 flew directly overhead and continued westward. When it passed slightly beyond the zenith, the man squeezed the trigger. With a roar, the Stinger disappeared into the darkness. The man lowered the launcher and looked up. The white exhaust of the missile had burned an impression into his night vision. He blinked and could barely make out the navigation lights of the chartered aircraft. Suddenly there was a small flash of light high in the sky. Then, almost immediately, an all-consuming fireball boiled outward. Sounds of the massive explosion pounded the ground seconds later, causing the sandy soil to vibrate. The man watched as hundreds of red and white streamers spewed forth and fell in wide arcs. The plane's large fuselage tumbled forward separately before it began its final descent. From its spiraling trajectory, the man knew the missile had severed the left wing. It had zeroed in on the exhaust of the number-one engine and had probably been four feet inside the underslung Rolls Royce power plant before it detonated.

In the brilliance of the falling conflagration, the man returned the launcher to its case in the trunk. Fiery debris continued to impact nearby as he started the car's engine. He didn't pull on the headlights. He noticed he didn't need them tonight.

En route, Washington Dulles to Albuquerque
Wednesday, December 30, 1:06 a.m.

The cabin of the chartered Citation was quiet at 43,000 feet. It was also dark, with one exception. Corley Brand's overhead lamp bore down on a slew of papers. He picked up the top sheet. The Bureau's Terrorist Research and Analytical Center in Washington had written it in 1987 but modified it following the tragedies in Oklahoma and New York, coupled with incontrovertible evidence of the insidious strengthening of former Soviet hard-liners and their minions worldwide. As far as Brand was concerned, it was still the best statement of the continuing possibility. When he considered the past two days, something told him this message dealt with probability.

> *The United States, because of its size, open society and borders, and involvement in the global political arena, is vulnerable to international terrorist criminal activity. Potential support networks are already in place across the nation, and certain international groups have the motivation to commit attacks as a statement against U.S. foreign policy, out of hatred for particular ethnic and exile groups in residence here, or in retribution for the undermining and collapse of the Soviet Union and other repressive regimes. The recent incidents of sabotage involving American citizens, particularly that in Oklahoma City on April 19, 1995, cannot be allowed to distract the U.S. counterterrorism program from the even greater threat of international-source activities, the precursor of which was the bombing of the World Trade Center in New York City. The possibility of well-financed international terrorists committing a series of major acts in the United States continues to grow and is of significant concern to the Bureau.*

Brand set the page aside and pulled out the German communiqué.
So it's the "Brotherhood of the Ultimate Ijima," he pondered, and it's had something going for seven months between Lebanon and North America. Well financed, too. He had a gut sense that he was in for a lot of

sleepless nights. Brand cupped his hand to his mouth to cover a yawn and looked around the dim interior of the small jet. His three companions, forensic specialists with the FBI's Disaster Team, were asleep. In spite of a bracing bleed of fresh air that funneled from above, he hooked the ballpoint into his shirt pocket and yielded to the hour. Might be my last snooze for a while, he decided as he laid the papers into his briefcase. He reached for the overhead panel, twisted the vent closed, and punched off the light.

Brand reclined the leather seat and looked outside from his pressurized vantage point. The frigid atmosphere was smooth. A waning moon toward the western horizon brought out the uniform whiteness of a solid cloud layer far below. The only sounds in the cabin were the reassuring hums of the two Garrett turbofans and the hiss of the slipstream.

Brand crossed his arms and took a deep breath. He closed his eyes and contemplated the irony of life and wondered if he had somehow caused all of this. When he joined the Bureau, twenty-plus years earlier, he had done so with the cocksure belief that the FBI would always be better than any challenge. But the reality had been that the harder he worked, the better the bad guys seemed to become. Now that he was on top of the Counterterrorism Section, all hell was breaking loose around the country. Some sort of a perverted cause-and-effect relationship?

Brand opened his eyes and stared out the window again. He looked up at the stars. Where was that celestial point of reference? Ah, there it was, in the middle of the southern sky. Brand instantly recognized the reliable fix, Orion—the Great Hunter, with his star-studded belt. It was an old friend, as it had been since his Boy Scout days in Michigan. He remembered Orion because he had proudly identified it on his own, from an astronomy book he'd received one Christmas. He believed there was always something soothing about studying the heavens, for regardless of the consternations here on earth, the constellations never seemed to be perturbed.

There was a lesson for him in that, Brand concluded, as his thoughts merged with the gentle sounds of the cabin. What do the French say? *Plus ça change. . . .*

His breathing became slow and regular.

What else did that message say? The "Final Jihad" has begun? And that other expression? Oh, yes. "Allah akbar." Brand prayed that God was not only great . . . but still on his side.

FBI Office, Tulsa
10:39 a.m.

"Neil Wirick on one, sir."

Tom Bentley tossed his suit jacket over the arm of the sofa as he strode for his desk. As newly appointed supervisory senior resident agent of the FBI's Tulsa office, Bentley had looked forward to the relatively placid waters of northeastern Oklahoma. He sat down and picked up the telephone.

"Neil?"

Wirick started right in. "Tom, you spoken with Gentry's son-in-law yet?"

Bentley couldn't mistake the gravelly voice and move-ahead style of the new special agent in charge of the FBI's Dallas office.

"Nope," he replied. "Will tomorrow."

Bentley had worked for this bald, bullet-shaped lawman during the spring and summer of 1988, while the Bureau prepared for the Republican national convention. That's when the New Orleans police had dubbed Wirick "Kojak without the warm personality." Since then, the two FBI men had stayed in touch regularly. Today's call, however, exceeded the average. It was their third conversation this week.

"Out of courtesy," Bentley continued, "we're still planning to wait until after Gentry's funeral and the memorial service for Stroud's wife and son before we talk with him. Is there something more than Monday's airport interview and the notes you sent up?"

"Nothing to change your plans," the Dallas SAC returned. "But there are some things you ought to know about his military background. By the way, I'm faxing this data to you as soon as I hang up. From now on, you'll be getting all of it directly from Washington."

Wirick started reading. "While he was a lieutenant commander in the Navy, Stroud attended the Defense Intelligence School. Did damn well, apparently, and was accepted by the Office of Naval Intelligence. He completed ONI's six-month course in basic intelligence work and their nine-month course in the Russian language, plus an abbreviated program in Arabic. He was sent to Moscow in 1972, as assistant naval attaché and the naval attaché for air. Two years later, he returned to the States . . . to the Pentagon. Then, in 1978, he joined the Naval Investigative Service, and he was appointed head of the NIS counterterrorism section twenty-four months later. His beat was the Middle East. He retired from the Navy in 1983 and became a consultant to Flight Safety International. They build aircraft flight simulators for the airlines and the military. Made quite a name for himself there and, apparently, some good money on their stock options. He moved to Tulsa a couple of years later to become president of United States Simulation Systems, Inc., a Flight Safety competitor."

"Sounds like a talented son of a bitch. Any black marks?"

Wirick laughed. "Big reputation as a lady's man. Porked anything in a skirt, according to this. That is, until he married his second wife. Also, a lot of bartenders around the world owed their livelihood to him. Worked hard, but played hard, too. Couple of bar brawls years ago in Norfolk one weekend. No charges or anything like that. Anyway, he's solid, clever, and experienced and ought to be a real asset. I don't know why you get all the breaks."

"Oh, get back to your nap!" Bentley barked. He grinned and hung up. Out the window to his left lay south Tulsa. In the distance, he saw the spires of Tulsa Bible College.

Tulsa
Noon

"Flora, please come sit with us." Jack leaned forward in his chair, his hardly touched apple dumpling on the dining room table in front of him. "We need to talk."

Rachel gazed at her own untouched dessert, her face a blank. She was as closed to him as she had been for two days now, Jack thought. It was as if she blamed him for what had happened.

"Come on, Flora. Never mind the dishes." Jack watched as the round-bodied little housekeeper hesitantly slipped into a place at the end of the table.

"You're part of our family. Rachel and I are going to need you more than ever." He noticed that his daughter didn't raise her eyes. Rachel started to get up.

"Don't leave yet, Rach. It's time we had a family chat."

"I need to be excused, Daddy."

"Sweetie, please, this isn't a time to shut me out. We both hurt." He glanced at Flora. "We *all* hurt. Maybe we can help each other make it through this terrible time."

Flora rose slowly and moved to stand behind Rachel. She put her hands on the teenager's shoulders. "Yes," she whispered, "we must all be comforting each other."

Rachel stared at the table. A tear slid from the corner of her eye.

"I don't think I can stand it, Daddy. Why'd you let them go . . . and leave us like this?"

Jack shuddered. Oh, God, she *does* blame me for their deaths, but then, I blame myself as well. Why *did* I let them go?

Flora leaned over and hugged Rachel. "Your father didn't know what would happen, Miss Rachel. He loved your mother and your brother more than life itself."

Jack felt as if he had been turned to stone. His hands rolled into a fist. He wanted to hit something, or someone. He forced his hands to uncurl, and he placed them on the table, one on each side of his dessert plate. He glanced at Rachel, but she still wouldn't look at him. He felt a wave of disappointment. How could he break through the shield she'd raised against him? He inhaled deeply. They'd have time. He looked back at Flora.

"Flora, I just want to reassure you. You still have your place here. We desperately need you . . . especially now."

Rachel turned and nodded to Flora. She was agreeing with him, Jack realized. Maybe she really didn't blame him. He sighed. Even if she didn't think her father had sent her mother and her twin brother to their deaths, her father continued to blame himself.

"Rachel, Flora. They'll find the people who blew up that plane." He put his clenched fist on the table and pounded it, once, twice, and again. "They'll *find* them, all right." After his outburst, he was silent for a few seconds. "No . . . damn it . . . *I'm* going to find them."

Frankfurt-am-Main Airport
1:07 p.m.

The TWA departure lounge was too warm. Ahmed Pasha placed his black alligator briefcase on a chair and removed his overcoat. Typical German overreaction to the season, he sniffed, as he laid the heavy garment over his arm and retrieved the polished briefcase. He wasn't used to such bulky outerwear anyway, since he was fortunate enough to remain in Egypt most winters. Yet it was a nice perk of his seniority to get away like this once in a while. He spotted an empty seat closer to the plane and walked toward it.

Pasha was the Cairo chief of the Anti-Terrorism Group of the International Criminal Police Organization. He had started at Interpol in Egypt just before the 1967 War with Israel, and he'd worked his way around the world—Bonn, Asunción, Canberra, New Delhi—then back to Cairo ten years ago. For his efforts, three countries had honored him with their highest civilian citations. Twice he'd received the Legion of Merit from his own country, once from President Anwar Sadat for his work in uncovering the cell of Soviet-sponsored terrorists that had carried out numerous assassination attempts on political candidates, and the second time from President Hosni Mubarak when he'd helped defuse two Libyan-sponsored hijacking incidents at Port Said. It was rumored that he would receive a third Legion of Merit because of his work exposing and expelling henchmen of Saddam Hussein who had come to destroy the High Dam at Aswan.

Today was the beginning of a trip to recount officially some of those experiences at a weeklong conference on terrorism at Washington University in St. Louis, sponsored by the International Association of Chiefs of Police. Pasha was to be a featured speaker on Monday.

Immediately after he sat down, he noticed the face. Fifteen feet away, a slim man held open a copy of the *Frankfurter Allgemeine Zeitung* and stared at him over its top. A second after eye contact was established, the man broke the gaze and said something to a companion. The second man made a slow assessment of the room and fixed his eyes on Pasha. The first man's face was hidden by his raised newspaper.

Pasha was *certain* he knew that man. His basic instincts, honed by years of training to be observant, confirmed that he had had contact with him, somewhere. And he sensed it wasn't good. He extracted a leather pocket diary from his suit coat. Pencil poised, he looked through the double-glass window at the Boeing 767 being readied for departure. Out of the corner of his eye, Pasha appraised the man who had just laid aside the newspaper. Medium build, moustache, black hair, and the shadow of a heavy beard. He looked to be in his mid-thirties. Definitely Middle Eastern.

"Ladies and gentlemen," a woman's voice came over the lounge's public address system, "may I have your attention. We are ready to board TWA's Flight 741 to St. Louis. We will be boarding by rows."

As the announcement continued, the man across the way stood up. His companion and four other men, all about the same age, rose in unison. Pasha's sense of unease grew at the sight of the six of them together.

"Passengers with seats in rows twenty-six and higher should now board."

People began moving toward the airliner. A group of chattering Germans stood and blocked his view temporarily. After a moment he looked again, but the man and his group had boarded.

"Rows eighteen through twenty-four, please."

Pasha started for the plane. That face continued to haunt him.

"Twenty-four two," the flight attendant at the door spoke cheerfully and motioned Pasha toward the rear of the aircraft. "It's the aisle seat of row twenty-four, to your right." He smiled and started looking for the man again.

"Hey, waitress, when can I have a drink?" An inebriated man ahead stuffed his coat into an overhead bin and looked shakily at a woman in uniform.

"Soon as we're airborne, sir. And I'll try to be more than just a waitress."

The man frowned at her explanation and slid downward into his seat.

Pasha reached 24-2 and began to stow his carryons. He felt watched as he folded his overcoat and pressed it into an available space overhead.

He pulled off his suit jacket and saw the man again, four rows aft and in the middle of the aircraft, staring at him. Pasha squeezed into the narrow chair. There was no one at the window seat. He preferred the aisle position for his long legs. He hoped he'd be lucky and not have a seatmate. He checked the time. 1:25. They were already five minutes late. The instant he made his observation, he heard the doors being closed and secured. Pasha raised the armrest between his seat and the one next to the window. Good. He'd have plenty of room for the long journey. He struggled again with his memory in an attempt to match the man's face with past experiences. Nothing clicked.

The red-striped white airliner lumbered onto Runway Seven-Left and began its takeoff roll. Thirty-three seconds later, the twin-engine wide-body lifted off into the frigid afternoon air of central Germany and began a gentle roll toward the great circle route to St. Louis, an even nine hours away. As the plane ascended through 10,000 feet, the lead flight attendant announced that the beverage and luncheon service would begin momentarily. Afterwards, she promised the latest James Bond movie thriller, in both English and German sound tracks.

"Cocktail?" A blonde flight attendant peeled off a paper napkin in anticipation of his request. There was a hint of a German accent to her voice.

"Soda with lime, please."

"Perrier?"

"That would be fine."

The main cabin service began at the conclusion of the second round of drinks. Flight attendants moved bulky Singl-Serv carts into the two aisles from the center galley. The attractive woman was back. As she placed a spinach-and-mushroom salad before him, she looked at the service unit and launched her recitation.

"Chicken Tikka Kebab, Salisbury Steak Mushroom Zinfandel, or Chicken Breast Cape Cod?"

What words can conceal, Pasha thought. "I'll have the chicken breast."

The flight attendant positioned the steaming entrée on his tray table. He picked up a plastic packet of salad dressing and twisted at the corner. That's when it hit him.

"Bism Allah!" he swore under his breath. Kuttab! Abu Kuttab! Pasha's heart pounded. It had been fifteen years since he had last seen that face.

Now Pasha remembered. Kuttab was an organizer of the group that commanded the unit of Lieutenant Khaled Ahmed Shawky al Islambouli in Cairo on October 6, 1981. They'd killed President Sadat as he smiled and waved from his carpeted reviewing stand. Taking the places of regulars in an antitank gun crew in a military parade, Kuttab's four men in army uniforms had jumped from a passing truck and attacked the reviewing stand with grenades and automatic firearms. Many in the Muslim world believed it was in the service of Allah to eliminate the defiler of Islam who had been corrupted by Western ways and who forfeited his right to live and govern by his abominable agreement with Israel at Camp David.

Kuttab had somehow slipped through the tight net that the authorities cast over Cairo following the assassination. Pasha had traced him through Athens to Belgrade before he lost him. Kuttab was believed to have joined Soviet-sponsored terrorist training forces in the Crimea. His hand was evident in a dozen murderous incidents since, but he had never again appeared in public, until now. Pasha turned his head carefully and looked over his shoulder. Surgery on Kuttab's nose, it appeared, but there was no change whatsoever in those fearsome eyes. And he's right behind me. Almost like my prisoner. What incredible luck!

Pasha hurried through lunch while his mind attempted to fashion the best way to take the terrorist into custody. He sipped at his cup of tea and considered possible scenarios as the cabin was darkened for the movie. Pasha set aside his tea and pushed himself upward from his seat. He walked forward to the center galley.

"Pardon me." He interrupted two flight attendants who were finishing the cleanup after lunch. Both turned and smiled. One's name tag read "Carolyn." Pasha reached inside his shirt pocket and extracted his identification. He held the credentials under a small spotlight at the side of the stainless-steel tabletop. "I'm with Interpol, and I'd appreciate your help."

Carolyn peered at the picture. "What can we do for you, Mr. Pasha?"

"I think I recognize someone back there, but I'd like to check his name."

"Where's he seated?" The woman picked up a computer printout of the passenger manifest.

Pasha glanced down the aisle. "I'm in row twenty-four, and he's four further back. In the middle seat."

The flight attendant ran her finger down the listing. At row twenty-eight, she moved to the middle seat in the middle row. "There he is, seat 28-5. 'El-Asail.' First initial 'S.' Ring a bell?"

Pasha thought for a few seconds. "No, but thank you anyway." He started to return to his seat. Then he had an idea.

"Uh, Carolyn, is there a telephone on board?"

"Yes, sir, six in every other row." She made a face and sighed. "But our satellite uplink is inoperative today, and we won't be in range of a ground station for another five hours. Would you like for me to let you know when that happens?"

Pasha stood with his arms crossed. He tapped his right index finger against his lips. Should he inform the captain? No, he'd wait. After all, Kuttab wouldn't be getting off before then. "Please. It's most important." He walked back and sat down.

"El-Asail, is it now?" he spoke under his breath. Then he smiled, adjusted the seat, and fitted on the one-size-fits-all plastic-and-rubber headset. "Well, Mister . . . 'El-Asail,' just wait until I tell U.S. Immigration who you *really* are." With his right thumb Pasha selected the movie channel and settled back.

3:18 p.m.

"Ladies and gentlemen," a male voice crackled over the public address system, "this is Captain Brunckhorst."

Passengers stretched and listened.

"We've begun our descent into the St. Louis area. We're currently over southern Michigan, just about to cross the Indiana border. Those of you on the right side of the aircraft have an excellent view of Chicago and Lake Michigan. Those on the left, if you look carefully toward the horizon, you can make out the grid of Indianapolis, about 100 miles away. We're twenty-five minutes from landing. I'll be turning on the fasten-seat-belt sign in ten or fifteen minutes, so you might want to make that last trip to the lavatory before then."

The pilot clicked off but was back a few seconds later.

"You also might check over your customs declaration form. And if you're not a U.S. citizen, don't forget to fill out the immigration card."

The occupant of seat 28-5 withdrew a ballpoint pen from his shirt pocket and rolled it in his fingers. He stood up and stepped into the aisle. He held the pen in his left hand and began a slow walk toward the front. Four rows ahead, he paused for a second next to a passenger, then continued walking. He opened the door of the lavatory and went in. Before he pulled the door shut, he glanced down the aisle, in the direction of his seat. The pre-landing activity in the cabin continued. No one looked at him.

Flight 741's scheduled arrival time at St. Louis's Lambert International was 3:55 p.m. The heavy jet touched down twelve minutes ahead of schedule. As the last passengers deplaned, a flight attendant noticed that one man remained in his seat. She walked toward him. He appeared to be sleeping.

"Omigosh, it's the man who wanted to use the phone. I forgot, and I guess he fell asleep." She leaned over him. "Sir?"

There was no reaction.

"Time to wake up, sir. We're here." She touched his shoulder. The man didn't move. She leaned closer and saw a wide crimson stain on his collar. Then she noticed that blood had dried in a rivulet from his right ear.

"Bonnie, come here." Her voice was shrill. "And have the gate agent call a paramedic."

Two other flight attendants rushed to her side. One placed her fingers against the man's neck.

"My God, Carolyn, he's dead."

Lambert–Saint Louis International Airport
Wednesday, December 30, 4:12 p.m.

"Salim Abu El-Asail?"

The Immigration and Naturalization Service agent read the name on the Form I-94 Arrival/Departure Record and looked at the grainy picture on the Syrian passport. A slender man scuffed at a cigarette butt on the concrete floor and looked up. He stroked his moustache with the fingers of his left hand and nodded.

"Yes, I am a student." His English was only slightly accented. "F-1 visa. There're six of us together."

The INS inspector looked over the three lines of passengers and spotted the others.

"Little old to be a student, aren't you?" he asked as he swiveled the computer terminal around and punched in the man's visa number.

"Airplane power plant. Four of us. And couple of pilots. At Southwest School of Aviation in Tulsa, Oklahoma."

Two green bars appeared on the screen, along with the man's itinerary.

The INS man eyed the traveler. "Why are you here so early? School probably doesn't start for a week or so."

"We want to get a head start so we will do very well."

The inspector studied the man for another moment. "Sure." He extended the documents and motioned the Syrian forward. "Customs is next."

The man walked to a baggage carousel, where he picked up two scuffed suitcases and took a position in the line marked "U.S. Customs— All Passengers." At the desk, he lifted his luggage onto a steel countertop. A woman took his completed form.

"Do you have anything to declare?"

"No."

Without saying anything, the customs officer flipped the latches of the larger suitcase. She lifted the cheap leather top and looked inside at a haphazard collection of casual clothes and toilet articles. She watched the man as she felt along the sides of the suitcase and pressed her fingers into the corners. The agent closed the top and jerked her thumb toward the doors to America.

"Next."

Tulsa
5:00 p.m.

It was supposed to have been another quiet nap, a respite from the obscenity of the past two days. But the nightmare continued. Jack saw his precious Laura again. He had to tell her he wouldn't give up without exacting revenge. She stared as he gesticulated frantically. The words wouldn't come out. He awakened, covered in sweat.

Houston
8:15 p.m.

The annual party at Sessions had started, as usual, a week early. Tonight's bash was the next-to-final link in the beautiful people's celebration of another successful year—personally, financially, and in all other ways in which they competed with each other. Young business professionals, their aspirants and sycophants, packed the glitzy facility off Westheimer near the posh Galleria shopping center and the exclusive homes of River Oaks.

Gold and glass, the karat and crystal kind, were conspicuous throughout the modern five-story building. Spotlights and moving tracks of illumination crisscrossed the ceiling of the atrium. Forty feet below was the center of attraction, a 10,000-square-foot translucent dance floor in the shape of a croissant that was lighted from below. A panoply of colors changed beneath the dancers in rolls and stabs of light. Couples made their way to the center down wide, carpeted aisles from polished rosewood tables and steel-and-leather chairs, arranged on multitiered levels and staggered decks accessed by glass-enclosed elevators and spiral staircases. The back wall was covered by an original oriental tapestry, which portrayed in magnificent grandeur the arrival of Marco Polo. The main bar stood at the base and was illuminated principally by the lighted backdrop of the priceless work of art. Eleven bartenders filled orders along the hundred-foot length of the wide and polished ribbon of wood, as half a thousand guests celebrated the close of one of their best years ever. Amorous patrons in the curved booths flirted and made whispered arrangements for later assignations over the cellular telephones provided. The night pulsed with sex and money, and the beautiful people created a synergism felt by all in attendance.

One man shook his head as a stylish young woman maneuvered her teal-green Jaguar Vanden Plas Majestic alongside the curb in front. The tanned blonde turned off the engine of the sedan, stepped out, and smoothed her designer gown. As she locked the car, she smiled at party-goers on their way inside. The lights of the entrance reflected warmly from the Jaguar's oyster finish.

"Sorry, miss." An off-duty police officer came from the foyer of the disco. "Can't park there." He pointed at the forty-five feet of red paint on the curb. "Fire zone."

"Oh, be a sweetie and don't notice," she pleaded with a hurt expression and an exaggerated drawl. "For just a minute. I have to give my address to someone inside. He's the most gorgeous hunk I've ever seen. A teeny-weeny minute?" She giggled and hurried toward the entrance.

"All right, ma'am." The policeman compromised with a smile. "You've got sixty seconds." He tapped his watch. "And I'm counting."

The woman winked at him and entered the disco. She made her way along the crowded wall of those observing libidinous pairings from a safe distance and moved in the direction of the stairs leading to the restrooms below. She surveyed the packed room, then descended and walked toward an exit sign above a door at the end of a corridor. She pushed it open and quickly climbed the steps to the alley. She continued onward to a car waiting in the shadows.

"Nine seconds, Rima," a man's accented voice spoke as she got in. "Cutting it awfully close." The car pulled out into the light traffic of the side street.

The officer glanced at his watch and frowned. He had given the woman nearly two extra minutes. He looked in at the contoured seats and the hand-polished burl elm trimming of the luxury automobile and shook his head.

"She'll just have to get that 'hunk' to pay this." He withdrew a book of traffic tickets from his jacket pocket, flipped the pages to a fresh citation, and pulled out his pen. Before he could touch its point to the paper, his face was fused to the back of his skull by the hexogen and butane explosion. In a microsecond, what was left of his body vanished into molecular debris.

The fireball blew through the outside glass of the disco like spherical lightning and seared through the wooden partitions inside. A hundred laughing and teasing and drunken revelers were consumed in the incandescence. Those behind a stone wall, sixty feet inside, had the luxury of confronting their fate for barely more than the blink of an eye before the force of the explosion slapped the wall over them and sprayed away their remains in a mist of flesh.

Three seconds after the detonation, the upper floors of the building collapsed, and the outer walls yawed and fell inwards, forming a seal over the burning, the dying, and the dead. One remaining corner of the edifice ruptured and spit out a column of flaming and writhing figures, who raised their limbs in slow motion and pirouetted before dissolving into pools of fire.

In all, 291 human beings ceased to exist in a minute's time. Seventy more would succumb within two days. For a lifetime, another hundred or so would stroke at conspicuous grafts of nerveless skin and never forget.

Beggs, Oklahoma
9:36 p.m.

Lester Graham waited until the van eased into the metal barn and the door was lowered before he stepped out of his darkened kitchen into the blackness of the overcast winter night. He had watched from his north window as a night patrol was conducted along the perimeter of the old Cummings property. It appeared that at least two men made a motorized circuit, stopping every fifty yards or so and directing a strong light to either side of the van. Most of the adjacent land was rough and rutted and covered by the remains of summer weeds, and the van made it around the entire tract in a half hour. As Graham waited and listened, he thought the men could have made it faster, but they were thorough in their rounds.

Graham figured he could make his way along the familiar terrain tonight without using the new Eveready he toted in his jacket. But he was glad it was there, just in case. A pair of inexpensive binoculars dangled from a plastic strap around his neck. As he stood and peered across the dark acreage, he was aware of occasional vehicles traversing the county road.

"Well, whatcha waitin' for, old man?" he goaded himself under his breath.

He started for the fence at a lanky gait. Moving like this reminded him of his boyhood days when he'd stalked deer—good forward progress without much sound. It was a skill he could employ at night because of his intimate knowledge of his, and their, property. As he neared the fence, he stopped and stared into the darkness. His eyes were acclimated now, and he hoped to detect movement by looking at different points on the adjacent property. A glance at an angle might reveal something through his peripheral vision.

After nearly four minutes of waiting, there were no new sights or sounds, so Graham walked the remaining ten feet to the fence at a careful pace and felt for one of the wooden posts. He found it and touched the barbed wire at one side to locate a safe place to put his foot. He was about to propel himself over when the mournful call of an owl echoed cleanly off his barn. He caught his breath and stepped back as he sensed his growing uneasiness. He looked across at the other property again. For some reason, something just didn't seem right. But that, he told himself, was why he was here in the first place. He squinted. The house and the nearby metal barn were to his left. The property's east-west access road lay some 100 yards ahead. He decided to proceed along the fence, keeping on his side for the time being.

As Graham started to his left in a modified crouch, he noticed the wind. It was light and out of the north. He was glad of that, for if they had any watchdogs, he just might not be detected. He continued paralleling the property line on the south side of his neighbor's and was able to approach within a couple of hundred yards of the main house. There was no outside illumination, although Graham could see lights coming through the shades of two downstairs windows. Suddenly there was a third source of light when the front door of the house opened. He sank to his haunches and raised the binoculars. A man wearing a suit and tie seemed to be looking in the direction of the main highway. The man studied his watch, then went back inside and closed the door. Graham remained in his huddled position. He looked to the right. There was no traffic on the highway.

He rose carefully and resumed his westward trek along the fence. All of a sudden, something in the ground just across the fence caught his attention. Glancing alternately from the house to the object, Graham observed what looked like a partially buried metal box, about five feet square and two feet high, camouflaged with berms and shrubbery. He turned his head in a quiet reconnaissance. Then, with a practiced pivot from a fence post, Graham swung over the barbed wire and was on his neighbors' land for the first time.

He could hear the unearthly hum well before he came upon the box. Once next to it, he sank to his knees and reached out. His fingers contacted the metal, and he sensed the energy flowing inside. Slowly he felt along the top and detected a raised surface. Using his hand as a shield, he pointed the Eveready at what he had found and held down its "intermittent on" button. The stenciled lettering read "CAUTION: 33kV." Graham turned off the flashlight.

"Thirty-three thousand volts?" His voice broke. "What in tarnation do they need that kind of power for? And why didn't I notice this sucker before?"

As he sat back on his heels in thought, he saw the sentry. Just in time. The man moved along the side of the house. He turned on a powerful light and pointed it in Graham's direction. The brilliance of the beam cut a broad back-and-forth swath. Graham fell to the ground and scrambled behind the electrical box as the beam hit. It held for a second, then resumed its sweep to his right. Then it went out. From the corner of his eye, he saw four white lights flicker on and form the corners of a square on the ground in back of the house. The lights grew in intensity. Then he heard the thup-thup-thup of a helicopter coming in low from the east. There were no lights on the craft, not even the standard red rotating beacon. It approached along the driveway and hovered above the four lights, then descended slowly to the ground. Graham thought he saw two men emerge and jog to the house. The helicopter's engine continued to run. There might even have been three men, he figured. Graham raised his head above the electrical unit and looked in the direction of the sentry. That man was gone, too. He wished he'd kept him in sight while the helicopter landed, for he wasn't sure now if the man had gone back inside or was walking around nearby. He remained in place and watched the area where the man had stood.

With more hope than assurance, Graham opted to continue. He rose to a crouch and moved further along the south side of the property. The road wrapped around the place where the helicopter had landed and went to the back of the metal building. He skirted the edge of a tight grouping of scrub oaks and gazed to the north. There was a small parking lot and a utility-like structure at the back. Graham slipped behind one of the bigger trees and looked through his binoculars again. There was a wide, two-part door to the building next to the utility structure. He thought it best to stay in the wooded area and venture further to the north. When he got to a spot opposite the back of the building, he heard voices coming from inside. Then he heard loud metal-on-metal sounds at the doors, as if someone was unlocking them. Graham made sure he was well hidden behind a tree trunk as the doors swung open.

A low-slung, battery-powered tractor emerged, pulling a cart with three rows of cylindrical containers. As the tractor and cart rolled into the parking lot, Graham could see inside the building. There were two men at the doorway. Both were in khaki uniforms and wore sidearms. Beyond them was another large open door to a vast room. He noticed that the centerpiece of the room was a white, boxlike object, some twenty feet long and ten feet wide and high, with steps down the back. It stood on what appeared to be six hydraulic legs. There were bundles of colored hoses and wires of varied sizes coming out of it and going across the floor and into a wall. The room had several windows, and rows of lights flashed on and off on a mounted panel. Graham wasn't too sophisticated, but he knew a high-tech place when he saw one. He'd toured some of the control rooms at area refineries, and this place was certainly equal to those.

The tractor and cart continued down the paved driveway toward the helicopter. Graham looked back at the lighted area. Two men in business suits and overcoats entered the large room from a side entrance. They were accompanied by two others in white coveralls. The four stood at the base of the box and talked animatedly. Within minutes, the tractor returned to the back entrance of the metal building, its trailing cart empty. Graham then heard the sound of the helicopter as it lifted off and climbed away. As the tractor drove inside the building, he noticed something else. Lining the side wall of the room, next to where the hoses were connected, were upright rolls of some sort of shiny fence wire. Before he could be more definite, the guards pulled the doors closed.

Graham waited until the sounds inside receded before he looked toward his return route. Moving catlike from his hiding place, he retraced his path to the point where he had crossed the fence. He looked back. The house was completely dark. As he stepped quietly over onto his property, a dog barked plaintively in the distance. It was a usual nocturnal sound for the area. Somehow it seemed strangely out of place tonight.

Tom Bentley handed over the letter. "What do you make of this?" Special Agent Don Evans took the single sheet of paper and remained standing.

Evans was Tulsa's only African-American agent. His path from middle-class Indianapolis had taken him straight north to Notre Dame, where he achieved a 3.6 as a history major and held his own as a running back on the football field. Upon graduation, he joined the Indianapolis police department and settled in for a career in local law enforcement. The day he made sergeant, however, Evans received his letter of acceptance from Notre Dame's law school and left home for good. It was on the campus at South Bend, in his third year, that he met his first FBI agent, a fellow black Hoosier who'd come recruiting for America's premier law enforcement agency. Evans liked the possibilities and the promised prestige, and he made application. Less than two months later, he was at Quantico for training. Afterwards it was on to Des Moines, then here a year ago. Evans's specialty was internal security; in other words, he told acquaintances, he was a spy. In some parts of the country, a black man was either noticed and watched carefully, or simply ignored. In Tulsa, no one paid any attention to him. He figured that wasn't the greatest of personal compliments, maybe it was even racist, but it certainly helped his work.

The message was typewritten, single-spaced, on eggshell onionskin. The paper made a crinkling sound as Evans shifted it in his hands. He noticed that several of the old typewriter's keys had struck out of position, e's above and s's below the baseline. The writer had listed exact deposit figures in seven foreign banks and estimated deposits, with high and low ranges, in two others. All accounts were labeled "Secret." Evans tallied the totals.

"Fifteen, maybe $20 million," he answered without looking up.

"At least," Bentley grunted.

Evans raised his eyebrows. "No return address?"

"Nope. Mailed from the main post office downtown." Bentley leaned back. "But Washington was able to learn that at least two of those accounts *do* exist, and in the Gentry ministry's name. We haven't gone for a court order yet to verify the balances. Might take a while for that."

The supervisory senior resident agent rose from his chair and looked across the desk.

"Don, old man Gentry died before he could deliver some sort of message to his son-in-law. Supposedly something very important. But we just might be lucky." He pointed to the letter. "Someone else out there might know what the minister wanted to say." He came around and put his hand on Evans's shoulder.

"When you get with Stroud after the ceremonies this afternoon, be careful. A hidden twenty-plus million dollars is usually pretty well defended."

Tulsa Bible College
1:30 p.m.

Reuben Gentry's funeral took place in the glass-and-steel Chapel of Jesus at the center of his beloved Tulsa Bible College. Although the spacious edifice could seat 4,300, many more thousands of followers had heeded his son's television call to attend in person. "Come and sanctify the ministry of this great man who has gone home to God," Norman had exhorted a worldwide audience. A memorial service for Gentry's daughter and grandson was scheduled for later in the afternoon.

The procession of mourners wound throughout the campus. Most had driven for a day or more to say farewell to their inspirational leader. Reuben Gentry had given them hope when their days were darkest, promising God's blessings in return for their personal sacrifices, including their contributions. The cars and campers and motor homes bore license tags from as far away as Alaska and Nova Scotia. They arrived, too, by air, many by pleading for a temporary increase in credit card limits to make the trip. The banks had granted their requests easily, for they knew that these customers possessed a code of ethics that would compel them to trim other expenditures in favor of their obligations on behalf of the Lord. Dozens of chartered buses pulled into the parking lots and released grandmothers and handymen whose only contact with the prominent minister had been their hands pressed against their television screens, touching his. By being there, they would demonstrate to the Lord that Brother Gentry had been a good steward and should be accepted quickly into the Kingdom of Heaven. They endured the cold winds with unwavering pride. This was where they belonged.

Tulsa Bible College, or "TBC" as everyone called it, was a collection of thirty-four buildings on 400 acres in a valley twelve miles south-southeast of downtown Tulsa. Founded by Reuben Gentry in 1954 and housed for more than twenty years in a succession of temporary quarters around the city, the college at the edge of the Arkansas River was the largest evangelical institution in the world. For more than a decade, TBC had been considered the finest and best-funded training center of its kind in America.

The campus initially consisted of 655 acres of rich river-bottom land that had been cultivated for vegetables since the 1930s. Until Gentry's plan created a new use for the area in 1969, Tulsans had come here to pick corn, beans, potatoes, and tomatoes from fields tended by commercial growers. Gentry loved the scenic expanse of the property. "God will bring forth a great school of the Gospel on this fertile land," he had proclaimed to the world at the groundbreaking. "It is anointed soil."

TBC had developed quietly but methodically. Today, with 20,300 students in one location, the school surpassed the enrollments of most of the other private universities in America. Harvard at its peak hosted only 19,000.

The architects originally presented a plethora of traditional styles for the evangelist and the board of trustees to consider, but Gentry had known from the beginning exactly what he wanted: a modernist campus, with distinctive and intriguing structures. "It will inspire us for our work ahead . . . the twenty-first century and beyond," he had promised the local press. However, in their first public rift, Norman had attacked his father's plans, arguing that they were ridiculous and would make the ministry a laughingstock, especially to those who already held it in low esteem. After months of vitriolic skirmishing, the evangelist prevailed upon the independent board to adopt an uncommon appearance for TBC. "We are the ministry of a new era," he had proclaimed. "We must have a home that reflects that role."

Gentry never forgave his son for deriding the architecture. Norman's incessant references to the glittering college as "God's Disneyland" or "Lego U" or, worse, "Six Flags Over Jesus" hurt the senior evangelist deeply. Their relationship was never the same again.

Televised crusades to raise money for the construction effort began in 1970, and within two years, $39 million had been committed by thousands of contributors around the world. By then, Gentry had four weekly hour-long television shows in the United States and Canada. His Toronto-based Canadian Broadcasting Company show, entitled "Today's Jesus," remained first against the competition for months. By 1974, Gentry's television audience had soared to 47 million, and collections climbed to an average of $100,000 each business day.

TBC opened its new campus in the fall of 1976 with an initial enrollment of 1,300 enthusiastic and committed young people who were carefully chosen for their attractive appearance as well as for their ability to pay. The lame, the halt, and the blind, together with the pimpled and the fat—unless they were wealthy—were gently turned away.

Reuben Gentry's vision from God was to reach every human being on the face of the earth with the Gospel of Jesus Christ. He felt that God had honored his determination by giving him the sales skills and financial tools necessary to reap a harvest of souls unprecedented in any generation. There were annual foreign crusades and seventeen overseas missions, and, at the end of 1994, Gentry announced that TBC would build its European counterpart in Belgium. He understood the truth that people needed great challenges and new vistas to lift them above their mundane existences. He intended to continue providing both.

Regardless of their embarrassment, the more sophisticated citizens of Tulsa had to concede that this local attraction had never produced a scandal to sully the city's image. Even so, they felt that the potential was always there, given the nature of this most unconventional business.

Tulsans grew accustomed to seeing the ministry's fleet of seventeen white Lincoln Town Cars, which they dubbed the "sacred cows," making their ministerial runs throughout the community. Gentry's was a chauffeur-driven, seven-passenger version with smoked windows, gold-plated wire wheel covers, two cellular telephones, and a personalized license plate bearing the exhortation, PRAISE. Today the luxury automobiles coursed between the airport and the chapel door, carrying Gentry's most generous contributors to his funeral.

The TBC choir began the ceremony with two selections Reuben Gentry himself had written, "Hold My Hand as I Follow Thee, Lord" and "It's a Heavenly View." Those inside and the 9,000 in the adjacent gymnasium wiped their tears and sang along. Millions more cried with them in homes across the land. The white casket at the base of the sanctuary was closed.

Jack and his daughter occupied the first two seats in the first row of mourners. Jack wore the midnight-blue worsted wool suit Laura had proudly presented to him at their family's Christmas Eve dinner just a week before. He touched the smooth material of the sleeve and bit his lip. Rachel wore a short, azure-blue wool jersey skirt with a matching quilted blazer, over a stark-white tailored blouse. She fidgeted with her charm bracelet. Her fingers found and held the tiny golden horse that her grandfather had given her on her sixteenth birthday. It represented the Arabian that Reuben had promised her for the coming spring.

Seated immediately behind the Strouds were Linda and Tom McVey, who had arrived from Zurich only hours earlier. Both touched handkerchiefs to their eyes and wanted to reach across to the shaken man and his daughter. But they resolved to wait until a more private moment when they could better express their feelings about such incomprehensible losses.

At precisely 1:50 p.m., Norman, in his scarlet-trimmed black robe, rose and walked to the pulpit and looked over the congregation. For nearly a minute, he let their silence prepare their hearts for his message. His wife, Bunny, sat demurely to his left on the stage. She wore a Calvin Klein black wool-crepe double-breasted jacket and short draped skirt. Her champagne blond hair was pulled back into a tight French knot. There was no jewelry other than her diamond wedding ring. She held a small alligator-covered Bible in her lap. Her dark hose and classic pumps completed her uncharacteristically conservative appearance. For the ceremony, she had toned down her makeup with beige eye shadow and a touch of red lipstick. Her only concession to her usual flashiness was her polish. A bright red enamel, Signal Flare, covered her long nails.

Norman ran his tongue across his full upper lip, then brought his hands to his chest. He clenched his fists together. "Brothers and sisters," he began, "I bring a personal message to you from Jesus Christ." The audience shuffled in anticipation of the revelation. He raised his arms to heaven and shouted, "Reuben Gentry is *alive.*"

Cries of "Hallelujah!" filled the chapel.

"I say to you," he boomed with his eyes cast upward, "Reuben Gentry is alive with *Jesus.*"

The chapel erupted in pandemonium. Norman grinned and nodded as hundreds stood and hugged one another. They screamed their agreement and extended their arms above their heads. Bunny remained seated. She watched her husband impassively.

"Reuben Gentry's alive with *Jesus,*" he repeated. His voice could barely be heard above the cries of acquiescence. It was almost two minutes before he could continue.

"But, brothers and sisters," he said in a lowered voice, "Reuben Gentry's ministry on earth . . . is . . . in . . . trouble."

Norman watched as the audience quieted and sat back down.

"Brothers and sisters, we are in *desperate* trouble." All were now silent. "And I am afraid." Norman wrung his hands, then clasped them together again against his chest. "The yoke of Satan has been tightened around the neck of this ministry, and I am afraid the worst is about to happen. I fear for myself, but, more importantly . . . " He pointed toward the worshipers and singled out members one by one. "I fear for *you*. *You* are the personal targets of Satan."

The audience shifted nervously.

"This morning, brothers and sisters, I asked Jesus for our deliverance from the domination of Satan and freedom from the evils of this world. And do you know what Jesus told me?"

"Tell us, Brother Norman," a few cried out. "Tell us!"

"Jesus said, 'Yes!' "

The audience stood again and started applauding.

"Jesus said 'Yes!' to you and to me. Praise Jesus!" he shouted. The audience was in a frenzy.

"Praise Jesus!" he intoned once more.

The congregation swayed and waved their outstretched arms. "Praise Jesus!" they returned in one voice.

Norman's face was flushed with emotion as he continued. "You and I are not alone . . . *now*." The cheering grew even louder. "We have Jesus with us . . . *now*." The audience wanted more. "We will conquer the forces of evil . . . *now*." The response was deafening as Norman raised his fist into the air. "Praise Jesus!" he shouted.

"Praise Jesus!" four thousand voices echoed.

"Jesus wants us to begin today. You and I must take a fresh stand, today. You and I must make ourselves heard, today. You and I must root out the evildoers, today." He directed the back of his hand across his soaking face and wiped it against his waist. "We must march forth and rid the earth forever of those who would rip our faith from our breasts and trample it into the dust. We must eliminate the abortionists, the pornographers, the secular humanists, and the others who would steal our bond with Jesus. For the purveyors of the filth and the lies of Satan, there can be no hiding."

His message was hypnotic, and the congregation screamed their assent and punctuated his words with frequent amens.

"I say that the books which lead God's people astray must be destroyed."

"Amen," they moaned.

"I say to you, the abominable abortion clinics of death across this land must be eliminated forever."

"Amen," came the chorus. "Amen."

"I say, brothers and sisters, the politicians who are not responsive to the ways of the Lord must be defeated and disgraced, and the world must be made to conform to the literal teachings of the Bible."

"Amen, amen!" the response rolled in waves.

"That's what Jesus is telling us to do today. And that's what we *will* do!"

"Praise Jesus!" they called out with renewed fervor.

"But, brothers and sisters," he lowered his voice and warned with a wagging finger, "there will be a heavy price to pay."

A pall descended over the congregation, and hundreds of bodies swayed in silence.

"Doing Jesus' work will not be easy. You and I will have to purify ourselves against the temptations of Satan. We will have to risk losing the friendship of those with little or no faith. They may hate us. They may persecute us."

Norman paused for effect.

"They may even try to *kill* us." Heads nodded in understanding.

"But we will prevail, because *Jesus* will prevail."

A righteous cheer broke out, and fists shook in the air.

"So, today," he continued, "as we yield our beloved leader to Jesus, we begin a new fight . . . the glorious cleansing of this great nation of ours. Then, praise Jesus, the world!"

The congregation erupted. Norman held out his arms.

"This Sunday we begin our Christian Cavalcade to Seattle. There, and in six cities along the way, I will preach the new message Jesus has revealed to me. I will warn people of the grave times facing us in our fight against the evils of Satan. But I will also tell them that while it might be a struggle to the death with the Devil's forces, we're secure in the knowledge that Jesus is personally involved with us. It's His cause. Praise Jesus!"

The audience rose and shouted in unison.

"Praise Jesus!" they cried out as one.

Norman beamed his approval and bowed. He placed his sweat-drenched forehead on the pulpit, and he remained in that position as the room pulsed with emotion. Finally he stood erect and gestured to the choir. The eighty-five young men and women began singing "Lead Us to the Promised Land," and Norman walked down to his father's casket and laid his hands on it. Only a scattering among the frenzied were any longer aware of the composed man and the young woman in the front row.

3:30 p.m.

The memorial for Laura and Jeff was a private affair in the school's Prayer Room, adjacent to the Chapel of Jesus. Three rows of fresh flowers and plants, gifts of remembrance from mourners of the deceased mother and her son, lined and scented the front of the smaller room. Their silent presence augmented the solemnity—and the sadness—of the occasion.

The ceremony was conducted by TBC's silver-haired chaplain, Dr. James Roth. Jack and Rachel sat together in the front row, while other family members, relatives, and close friends remained at a respectful distance behind. Rachel's eyes were red from grief. She looked toward her lap and twisted her handkerchief. Jack stared ahead. Norman and Bunny arrived late and sat alone in the last pew. Norman, in a dark suit, beamed and winked at those he recognized, or thought he did. Bunny hadn't changed from what she wore to her father-in-law's funeral. Dr. Roth, an imposing figure at 6-feet-3, entered from the side and walked to the podium. After a moment with his head bowed, he looked out at the grieving congregation.

"For reasons known only to Himself, Almighty God has allowed Laura Gentry Stroud and Jeffrey Arnold Stroud to be taken from us."

Rachel sobbed.

"We were not asked, nor were we given a reason why. We do know, directly from the words of Jesus Christ while he walked on this earth, that God's home is a glorious place which is reserved for His people as their reward for their faith in Him. Laura and Jeff had such faith. I'm certain they are now safe with Him."

Rachel closed her eyes and held her hand over her mouth and leaned against her father. Jack felt the convulsions that racked her body. Today's acknowledgment of the triple loss was nearly overwhelming for him, too. He wondered if his daughter could cope with her heavy burden . . . and forgive him. But, he resolved, he'd always be here for her.

"God knows our anguish at this loss," Dr. Roth went on, "and, while it might seem impossible to believe so soon after their leaving us, He will give us strength to accept it and to anticipate our own being with Him, when it is our time to be called home. Death is not the end of anything, but the beginning of everything. We have trouble seeing that, especially when we lose such precious human beings as Laura and Jeff. God understands and will give us the capacity to accept what has happened."

Dr. Roth paused and took a deep breath.

"We shared many happy moments with Laura and Jeff, and we'll cherish those memories forever. In our time of grief, I ask that we think of the smiling faces of those two children of God who are now at peace with the Lord."

He looked around the room, then made eye contact with Jack and Rachel.

"Please bow your heads. Almighty God, help us accept your will in allowing Laura and Jeff Stroud to be called home. Let us know in our hearts that they are happy with you, and will be forever, and give us the understanding that what you ordained at the creation of the world will allow us to be reunited with them someday in heaven. Bless Jack Stroud and his daughter, Rachel, in their hour of sadness. Bestow upon them your peace and watch over them as they proceed with their lives. Amen."

He stepped back from the podium.

Jack and Rachel remained in their seats as the others got up and filed out. Dr. Roth walked over to them.

"I want you both to know that my thoughts and prayers will be with you every day." He took their hands. "Your tragedy is mine." Dr. Roth looked into Jack's eyes. "I know that today would have been your wedding anniversary. Jack, God knows it, too. May He bless you always."

Jack could only nod. He felt little from the minister's words. Then father and daughter rose and walked toward the back of the chapel. Jack kept his arm around Rachel. She was sobbing.

As they passed through the vestibule, a short man in his late fifties approached rapidly from a dark corner. His brown overcoat was buttoned, and a wide cashmere scarf was coiled about his neck. A pulled-down fedora shrouded his face. He held out his hand toward Jack.

"Mr. Stroud," he whispered as he pressed a piece of paper into Jack's palm, "you are in great danger." His voice was heavily accented.

Before Jack could reply, the man slipped away. Jack looked at the folded onionskin in his hand. He opened it. His stomach clenched as he read the typed message: "Another attempt will be made on your life. You will be contacted soon."

J. Edgar Hoover Building, Washington, D.C.
4:35 p.m.

The director of the FBI sat motionless as the toxicologist from the Bureau's Scientific Analysis Laboratory began his report.

"After the autopsy was performed on Secretary Nielsen at Bethesda, Dr. Paul Staggs, the chief pathologist there, called and reported that the cause of death was still unknown. The Secretary's white blood count had been nearly off the graph at 34,000 per cubic centimeter, the highest reading they'd ever seen, short of leukemia. The normal range is between 4,000 and 10,000. However, there were no anomalies discovered by the standard toxicological tests that could account for the elevated reading. They then X-rayed an apparently infected place on the Secretary's thigh and discovered a puncture wound containing an embedded metallic object less than two millimeters in diameter. It was extracted and found to be a cylinder. They sent it to us for detailed examination."

The toxicologist cleared his throat and went on.

"Employing high-resolution microscopic analysis, we found that the cylinder was hollow with two outlets, one on each end. There was a residue of paraffin on the rims of both holes. An irrigation of the inside of the cylinder and a sample of attached tissue yielded a substance that we examined by spectrography and discovered to be ricin."

The director broke his silence and leaned forward in his chair.

"Ricin? A man tried to smuggle 130 grams of the stuff from Alaska into Canada back in '93. As I remember, he killed himself in jail before he could be tried."

The specialist continued. "Ricin's a protein derivative of the castor-oil plant, one of the five most toxic compounds on earth. It's 6,000 times more deadly than cyanide. One gram can kill 40,000 people. The Secretary's body heat melted the paraffin seals, releasing the ricin into his system. We also suspect that it was combined with an anaerobic bacteria that created fulminating gangrene. He didn't have a chance."

"You're saying Nielsen was deliberately poisoned?"

"Yes, sir, but here's the interesting part. During the Cold War, ricin was manufactured in Czechoslovakia and Hungary. For the past three or four years, we've traced it to clandestine labs at Mizdah, south of Tripoli in Libya, and at a couple of places in the Bekaa Valley of Lebanon." The toxicologist fixed his gaze on the director. "And when we ran a spectrographic analysis of the cylinder itself, it turned out to be 88% platinum and 12% iridium."

"So?"

"That combination of metals, sir, used to be the classic calling card of the old KGB."

Tulsa
Thursday, December 31, 6:10 p.m.

Aleksandr Voronov stood at the frosted upstairs window of his one-bedroom apartment and felt fear take possession. The sensation coursed out of an almost-forgotten inner sanctum and passed down his extremities. He'd been sure he'd never have to experience such terror again. Voronov stared at his trembling hands for a moment before thrusting them into the pockets of his coat, hoping that putting them out of sight would steady them. He raised his head and looked out at the campus of Tulsa Bible College. Who would have thought those monsters would surface here?

It had not really been that many years since the events at No. 51 Nevsky Prospekt in what was still called Leningrad. But he had treated it like a lifetime ago, forever sealed. Now it all came back quickly and clearly, the appropriate pictures to accompany his growing nausea.

He well remembered that night, in that terrifying era shortly before the Soviet Union disintegrated, sweating as he peered across the living area of his cramped flat. A floor lamp in the corner of the room produced a yellow haze through the musty newspapers taped around its top, and he could barely recognize the faces of those seated before him. They had arrived singly over the previous half hour. Most lived in adjacent concrete high-rises in the monolithic residential complex and had to walk only a few minutes in the bitter night of minus 10°C. The smell of dinner's cabbage mixed with the body odors of the dozen men. Voronov stroked his beard and began.

"They are searching for us."

The whispers stopped, and eleven pairs of eyes focused on the older man.

"Socialism is dead, but before it is buried, others will die in its name." He added deliberately, "We will probably be among the first."

The men were silent.

"You have come at considerable personal risk." He held up a copy of *Izvestia*. "In spite of superficial changes, certain leaders of the Party warn that 'political' assemblies of more than three persons could be considered anti-Soviet agitation. They will accuse us of that."

He looked over the front page of the newspaper.

"Thousands of our citizens have been beaten and arrested at unlawful gatherings in the Republics, and the Ministry of Health has reaffirmed the legitimacy of rehabilitation 'treatments' at the psychiatric hospitals for these crimes."

He laid the newspaper aside.

"Yet the world is blind to all of this. When Mikhail Gorbachev began undermining the Party structure in 1986, it meant the beginning of a nightmare for us." He continued, "For a dying bear kills even its own."

No one stirred as Voronov paused and lit a dark cigarette. He inhaled deeply and held its acrid smoke in his lungs. Each man knew that tonight was probably their last meeting together. They had been known as the Leningrad Group, but the new reality meant that any subsequent contacts would have to take place as they had in earlier years, before *glasnost:* one-on-one in the Summer Garden or along the Dvortsovaya Embankment of the Neva River. Their evening sessions with the graduate students at Leningrad State University had ended more than a month ago when police had blocked their entrance. The outside world was sightless now, mesmerized by Gorbachev. It never heard of that encounter, nor of the many others involving the KGB's black hand. Even if it had, it wouldn't have believed it.

Voronov exhaled and propped the smoldering cigarette in an ashtray. He cleared his throat again. "It was a calculated risk for the *nomenklatura* to elevate Gorbachev to General Secretary." He sighed. "Do nothing, and the country would disintegrate from within. Or hope that Gorbachev could win concessions from the West, in order to buy time. But now that he's embarked on a course that could get away from him, it's no longer if, but when. In the meantime, they'll pick us off, one by one."

"Gorbachev is a fraud!" a voice called out from the side of the room. A balding man with a goatee jumped up and punctuated his feelings with a pointed finger. "It's all an act, a trick to expose us and the others. There are no changes. There is no 'new reality.' He's fooled everyone. We should never have taken him seriously!"

"Shut up, Gorelkin!" A man stood up in the back. "Gorbachev's no actor. He's the first realist in the Politburo. But we keep telling him that Ligachev and Yazov will turn on him when they get the opportunity. Proposing European or American supervision of agriculture in the Ukraine might do it, but his insane Baltic Accords idea will be the last straw. Everything will unravel then." Most of the men nodded.

"When we wrote our letter to the CPSU in 1986," Voronov resumed, "we knew we were stepping beyond the boundary. When we said the Party had lost its raison d'être, that it was drowning in its own Marxist gibberish, it was too much for the conservatives." He paused and looked around the room. "Now, while they may let Gorbachev go for a while, they'll attempt to draw us out and to liquidate us during his so-called program of *perestroika*. It will be clean. No one will notice. Then, one way or another, the darkness will come once again."

Voronov held up an edition of *Komsomolskaya Pravda*.

"Mark my words, gentlemen. It will soon say something like, 'The newly constituted Politburo will reestablish political and social order with the assistance of our patriotic military, and the strengthened Komitet Gosudarstvennoy Bezopasnosti will eliminate all anti-Soviet dissident and revisionist movements. These times are similar to the troubled ones of the late 1920s, which yielded only to the firm hand of Josef Stalin.' "

The fears of the earlier days returned to the hearts of the men in Voronov's flat. Even though they knew the KGB had had copies of their studies and reports from the very beginning, they'd felt that the immediate times were inappropriate for heavy-handed action and that they were too prominent for the usual automatic retribution of arrest and imprisonment. Further, the group had disseminated *Svoboda,* its monthly periodical, among members of the Western media, which had reported the contents widely. Many of the members had been interviewed on Soviet and Western television and were considered Russian celebrities throughout the world.

"We must now become strangers to each other, and we must keep our hopes to ourselves until it is safe to meet again. Otherwise . . . "

A pounding on Voronov's door had interrupted his address.

Voronov was released by the KGB from his solitary cell six months later, after a direct petition to Gorbachev from Amnesty International. That investigation had been instigated by Reuben Gentry himself, who had admired the Russian's outspokenness in favor of massive changes in his country's attitude toward religious and political freedom. Gentry asked Voronov to come to Tulsa for a series of appearances, which he was able to do after the Berlin Wall fell. He proudly emigrated to America nine months later and accepted the newly created position of professor of political philosophy at TBC.

Tonight, Voronov felt trapped in a ghastly time warp. The death of the Soviet Union was supposed to have ended the KGB's power forever. Now the nightmare was continuing, this time for everybody. He hoped he could find a way to get back with Gentry's son-in-law—to tell him about the transplanted horrors—before those people could put both of them away for good. He hoped, too, that sending the letter to the authorities had been the right thing to do. If something bad were to happen to him, there'd be someone to follow up, to ask the right questions.

Denver
6:24 p.m.

"Hurry up, Dad."

Monica Pritchard stood at the foot of the spiral staircase of their Cherry Hills home and blew across a newly painted fingernail. "We've got to eat *right now*. Jody'll be here in thirty minutes."

"Coming, coming."

Grant Pritchard fiddled with his bow tie. He held its unresolved ends with one hand and started down the steps.

"Does anyone around here know how to tie one of these damn things?"

"I thought the mayor could do everything," his daughter taunted as he came into view. She tightened the cap of the nail polish and laid the bottle on the front table. He descended and stepped past her.

"Only at City Hall," he replied with a wink.

Catching up with him, she put her arm around his shoulder and matched his gait as they walked toward the dining room.

He grimaced. "Please don't smear any of that stuff on my shirt, Monica."

She ignored the warning and got right to the point. "Hey, Pops, I know you won't mind if I take the car afterwards. Jody and I plan ... " Her father made an elaborate stopping effort. He glanced obliquely at her sheepish face.

"Two seventeen-year-olds out cruising after midnight? On New Year's Eve?" He turned again for the dining room and rolled his head. "Nope."

"Oh, come on, Dad. We're just going to his place for a little while. You know, popcorn and a movie."

"Aren't his parents in Aspen?"

Monica was silent for a few steps. "Yeah, but his grandmother's here."

"N.U.A."

"OK, Dad." Monica put the palm of her hand on her hip. "What does *that* mean?"

Pritchard smiled in her direction. "No . . . Use . . . Asking."

"Dad!"

"I'll tell you what." He pointed his index finger toward the floor. "You can watch the movie over here after we all get back." His decision left her pouting in the hall.

"Willy called." Ginger Pritchard kissed her husband on the cheek and took charge of the tie tying. "He'll pick us up at 7:15."

Pritchard laughed. "The one single, solitary benefit of being head honcho . . . a chauffeur in a Chrysler driving us to the city party on New Year's Eve."

"Come on, everyone," Ginger called. "Dinner's ready." She looked toward the figure in the hall. "You too, Monica."

The doorbell rang.

"I'll get it." Fourteen-year-old Shelley scampered to the front. "I know who it is." She fumbled with an out-of-place lock of hair and bent toward the door.

"Who *is* it?"

"It's meee, Rodney."

Shelley scrunched up her shoulders in glee and reached for the door-knob.

"Dinner, Shel," Ginger prodded her daughter.

"Moth-er."

A minute later, Shelley paraded her date into the dining room. She beamed.

"Here's Rodney, everyone."

Rodney tugged at the sleeves of his suit coat and nodded to the assembled family. He was obviously uncomfortable being out of uniform. His usual attire was a pair of bleached Levis and his Denver Broncos sweatshirt, and his usual haunt was their kitchen.

"My, don't you look nice, Rodney." Ginger knew her cheery expression of approval wouldn't be completely appreciated. He forced a smile and shrugged.

Pritchard looked at the clock. "Hey, gang, we only have forty-five minutes."

The members of his coterie collected at their appropriate places at the dining-room table and sat down. Pritchard placed his hands together and bowed his head. "Dear God, please bless this meal and those of us who have gathered together to share it in Your Name. Watch over us during the new year. Amen."

The doorbell rang again.

"Now, who could *that* be?" Ginger looked to her left. "Monica?" She raised an eyebrow. "Is that Jody? I thought he wouldn't be here until seven."

Her elder daughter slipped out of her chair. "Well, that's what he said." She scurried to the front hall and called through the thick door. "Yes?" She didn't bother to look through the peephole, anticipating Jody's familiar voice.

"Flowers, ma'am."

"He sent me a corsage!"

Monica unlocked the door and pulled it partially open. With an explosive force, the door slammed against her face, nearly breaking her nose and throwing her backwards into the hallway. She opened her mouth to scream as she fell across the coat rack and onto the floor, but nothing came out. Three men wearing military fatigues, black leather jackets, and pull-over ski masks pounded into the Pritchard house. Each carried a silencer-equipped 9mm Uzi in combat-ready posture. The last man took a position over the prostrate girl.

The two other men bolted into the dining room. "Don't move," a gravelly-voiced man shouted. He swept his weapon in a neck-high arc. Shelley grabbed at the tablecloth and started screaming. One of the gunmen leveled his weapon at her. "Shut your goddamn face." The second man circled around the table and slapped a gloved hand against her mouth. He yanked her upright against the back of her chair. Pritchard jumped up at the assault on his daughter.

"Freeze!" the first man yelled. The muzzle of his gun smashed against the mayor's right ear and knocked him back into his chair.

"What the hell do you want?" Pritchard thundered as he cupped his lacerated ear. Blood oozed around his fingers.

The first man leaned closer.

"Shut your mouth, asshole."

"Don't kill us," Ginger moaned from the other end of the table. "Please, no. . . ."

"You. Get up!" the third man ordered Monica. He motioned the girl toward the table with a jerk of his gun. She struggled to her feet and held a hand over her bloodied nose.

"Everyone sit up in your chairs."

The first man positioned himself in the corner of the dining room and swung his gun back and forth. "Say anything, *anything,* and I'll slice your head off." His glower bore into the eyes of each of the five individuals. When he was sure they understood, he nodded to his cohorts. They pulled large rolls of silverized duct tape from their jackets and withdrew nine-inch serrated steel combat knives from leg sheaths. The two men started with the mayor and his wife. Each man extracted a length of the rubbery tape and slapped the end against the legs of the Pritchards. They continued overlapping the tape until the elder Pritchards were tightly secured to their chairs. They did the same to the three teenagers.

Seven and a half minutes from the time the intruders burst into the house, the four Pritchards and their guest were wrapped to their necks in cocoons of duct tape. The two men then went around the table and forced Ping-Pong balls into the mouths of their victims and slapped foot-long lengths of tape across their faces to hold the plastic balls in place. They extracted prepared rayon nooses from a case and laid one over the head of everyone but the mayor. They tightened the nooses and connected the four individuals together so that no one could move more than a foot backwards without pulling over the others and asphyxiating them. Finally the men secured Pritchard to the table with additional strips of tape. One man pushed at the tightly wrapped mayor and grinned at the man in the corner.

"He ain't goin' nowhere."

The first man walked up behind Pritchard and seized a clump of his hair. In almost slow motion, he pulled the mayor's head back. The man slipped his hand inside his jacket and drew out two large construction nails. He placed the tip of one against the right side of the mayor's neck. With a grunt, he slammed his gloved palm against the flat end of the nail. The projectile plowed through the mayor's carotid artery. Blood jetted out and splattered over the man's hand. Pritchard jerked and twisted against the restraints, and a deep moaning rumble came from his chest. The hooded man quickly did the same to the left side of Pritchard's neck.

The mayor's wife shook in terror before she fainted and fell against the table. Monica's eyes filled with tears, then rolled upward as unconsciousness banished her from the scene. The two fourteen-year-olds bucked against their restraints and gargled in their vomit.

Tulsa
8:46 p.m.

When he returned home, Jack saw the blinking light of the telephone recorder. One message was from a man who said that Laura's death was punishment for Jack's sins. He left no callback. Another caller quoted Jesus' words from John 8:51: "Verily, verily, I say unto you, If a man keep my saying, he shall never see death." Most of the messages were from friends who had called to express their condolences. Jack wrote down all the names and numbers and put the list on his desk, to call later.

The doorbell rang. Jack heard Flora's footsteps in the hall as she went to answer.

"Yes?" she called through the door.

"Prescription, ma'am," came the muffled reply. Jack heard the front door being opened.

"From Dr. Marks."

A few seconds later, his housekeeper appeared at Jack's door. Her face bore a look of solicitation and concern. Flora had been with the Strouds ever since they'd moved to Tulsa. A proud Señora Flora Hernandez viuda de Cuyás had just arrived from San Antonio to enroll her son at TBC. It had been her fondest wish for years to see her only child embark upon his college education under the auspices of a man she fairly worshiped. She was a recent widow of a Mexican craftsman who had immigrated to the United States in order to pursue his gift of cabinetmaking, and she had followed Reuben Gentry from her living room ever since his earliest days on television. When she arrived in Tulsa, she immediately fell in love with the lakes and the soft rolling features of the Ozark foothills, and Reuben had hugged her and suggested that she consider staying and helping his daughter raise her two little children. Of course she'd stay. How could she refuse?

"Thanks, Flora."

Jack took the package and unwrapped it in the doorway. He stared at the plastic container and shook his head. "I told Lee I didn't want anything." The label read: "Jack Stroud. Xanax, 0.5 mg. Take one every six hours, as needed for anxiety. Leland F. Marks, M.D." Jack opened the bottle with his thumb and looked at the peach-colored tablets. He tapped two of the oval-shaped pills into his palm. I'm just not ready to relax, he thought. It wasn't until he'd put the tablets back and replaced the cap that he saw the hand-printed message on the receipt: "Follow these instructions before you take these." Jack sat down on the couch and read the rest of the message. "Please meet me in fifteen minutes at the public parking lot on the south side of the 71st Street Bridge, off Riverside Drive."

Jack frowned and looked at his wristwatch. "Lee Marks wants to see me? At a parking lot?" He sat in the darkness for a minute and listened to the sounds of the evening. Finally curiosity propelled him, and he got up.

Jack drove out of his quiet neighborhood and headed toward the rendezvous four miles away. Suddenly an unaccustomed sense of foreboding seized him.

"Something doesn't compute. Reminds me of the old NIS days, with their endless surprises." He checked off the recent events. "The guy who gave me the note at church didn't seem to be a crackpot, and whoever wrote that message on the receipt went to some trouble to get it to me." He was silent for a moment. "So here I am, former intelligence whizbang, probably driving right into a goddamn trap."

Jack proceeded north on Lewis Avenue and turned left onto 71st Street. The bridge lay less than a mile ahead.

The Magic Empire Parking Esplanade had been built by the city a decade earlier. The lot covered nearly twenty-five acres, and it was accessible by two wide entry points on each of its four sides. Jack entered from the north end. He drove past a raised gate and across the paved and lighted expanse. There were no other cars. Jack slowed his automobile and stopped about 100 yards inside the perimeter. He pushed the light switch to the parking mode and waited.

A few vehicles traversed Riverside Drive to the west. An occasional burst of fireworks popped across the northeast Oklahoma night. Jack looked at his watch. 9:33. In his rear-vision mirror he noticed that a car had turned into the lot behind him. It drove toward him. He saw a Tulsa Parking Authority shield on its door. The car circled and approached from his left front. It came within two feet and stopped. Jack lowered his window.

"Problem?" a uniformed city employee asked. The black man looked to be in his early thirties.

Jack smiled. "No, I just needed to get away for a while."

The other man peered across. "Lot's closed, sir. How long do you plan to stay?"

"Oh, half an hour. Maybe less. If it's all right, that is."

"May I see some identification?"

Jack began to think the man suspected him of being involved in a drug deal. That's all he'd need now.

"Sure." He reached inside his jacket. "Here's my driver's license." He handed it over.

The man took the laminated document, examined it, and gave it back.

"Mr. Stroud, I'm not a Parking Authority employee. I'm Don Evans, special agent with the FBI." He held open his credentials. Jack shook his head at the unexpected turn of events. The agent continued. "I'm sorry to get you away from your house at a time of such a personal tragedy, but it's extremely important that I talk to you now. I couldn't risk being overheard."

Jack squinted. "You think my phone's tapped?"

The FBI man went on. "You know from your meeting with our agents in Dallas that serious criminal allegations have been raised concerning the ministry of Reuben Gentry."

Jack looked at the agent and nodded. Evans pressed ahead.

"Even though Dr. Gentry's deceased, we're more interested than ever in this matter because of the additional information we've received."

"Oh?" Jack watched the agent closely.

"Our office got an anonymous letter today from someone who's apparently inside the ministry. It contained detailed information about the organization's financial affairs and listed dates and amounts of large bank deposits in France, Mexico, and elsewhere over the past eighteen months. According to the letter, this money was not deposited in the ministry's U.S. bank accounts. From what we've been able to confirm, the letter appears to be genuine."

Jack raised his eyebrows. "I've never heard of any foreign bank accounts. There *were* to be some, once the new school was started in Belgium. What do you want me to . . . ?"

"Mr. Stroud, you're Gentry's son-in-law, a trustee of Tulsa Bible College, and his recently appointed consultant to the ministry. See what you can find out about the foreign money and report to us as soon as you have something. I'll be your contact. Until we have a handle on what's going on, please tell no one—absolutely no one—about the FBI's interest."

"But what about this 'grave danger' I'm supposed to be in, and the 'another-attempt-on-my-life' matter?"

"I don't know what you're talking about."

"Wasn't it your man who gave me the note in the Prayer Room this afternoon?"

"No, sir. Our message with your prescription tonight was the first contact we've had with you since Dallas."

Jack described the messenger and his message.

"Has anyone contacted you yet?"

"No."

The agent didn't say anything for a few seconds.

"OK, if someone does get in touch, please call me immediately. Use a public telephone. Here's my business card. I'll get right back with you."

Jack looked at the card. It read, "Jones Brothers Chimney Sweeps. A. Jones, Proprietor."

Evans pointed. "Our people answer that number twenty-four hours a day."

The FBI man rolled up the window of his car and drove away.

The White House
Thursday, December 31, 10:20 p.m.

The president spun around in his chair and confronted his CIA chief.

"Barney, you damn well better have something. I don't need to remind you the whole country's up in arms, and the media's screaming for explanations. Not to mention what our friends at the other end of Pennsylvania Avenue are saying. It's ten times worse than the first day after Oklahoma City."

The lanky intelligence director pulled himself forward in his chair and adjusted his half-moon spectacles.

"Mr. President, there's nothing to add." He patted a leather briefing manual in his lap and inclined his head in the direction of the FBI director seated next to him. "This is definitely his ball game. Again."

The president opened his copy of the report. "You're sure?"

"Yes, sir. As I told you before I came over from Langley, according to our listening posts, as of an hour ago, there's no indication whatsoever of foreign involvement." He shook his head. "No, we've concluded that the events of the past few days have been wholly domestic in origin. We have no jurisdiction."

The president looked at the sixty-one-year-old FBI chief. "Do you agree?"

"Not at all."

"Why not?"

The director crossed his arms and nodded toward the CIA chief. "I'll match my domestic ears to his foreign ones any day. And all the meaningful data we're getting on these outbreaks is coming from overseas."

"Explain," the president demanded.

"First of all, our lab people have concluded that the AirParis crash was a case of sabotage. The CIA agrees with us on that. But where the bomb came from and who directed the action are, at best, open questions right now."

The director reached into his attaché case and extracted a folder. He flipped to a metal tab attached to one of the sheets. He opened the document and continued.

"The plastic explosive used, Gellex-4, was undoubtedly placed on the plane in this country, but we know it's an imported product. We track what little is brought in legally and where it goes. As far as we can determine, this is the first time Gellex-4 has been used here for terrorist activities. This is the really bad stuff. Ammonium nitrate is child's play by comparison. We think it was brought in by the very people who used it."

The president rested his elbows on the desk and clasped his hands together.

"But you don't have any proof."

"No, sir. Not yet. However," the director emphasized with a raised finger, "the German foreign intelligence service, the BND, informed us the day before yesterday that they're onto a new Middle Eastern group called the 'Brotherhood of the Ultimate Ijima,' which, they say, has some sort of infiltration pattern going between Lebanon and North America."

The president raised an eyebrow. "Ultimate what?"

" 'Ijima.' In Arabic it means 'unity of the faithful.' It's, uh, something like a cult."

"And what do they mean by 'infiltration pattern'?"

The FBI director shook his head. "The Germans aren't sure. That's one of the terms they've overheard. Also, we don't know exactly what the group's target might be. Of course, we're assuming it's the United States."

"So how are you connecting that with the airliner?"

The FBI man flipped through the pages of his report.

"The Germans intercepted a telephone conversation last Monday evening. Someone called a public telephone at a Frankfurt airport hotel and gave someone else quite a send-off." He referred to the report. "Here it is. 'The Final Jihad has begun. The first wounds have been inflicted. Go sever the head of the pharaoh and complete the cleansing.' "

"Meaning?"

"The AirParis flight exploded Monday morning at 8:51 Central Standard Time. That's 3:51 p.m. in Frankfurt. The first official confirmation of the crash aired at 10:07 Central time, which is 5:07 p.m. in Frankfurt. That caller in Germany told someone at the airport hotel 'the first wounds have been inflicted' just sixteen minutes later. Too close to be coincidental, I'd say."

"No, it's *pure* coincidence," the CIA director snapped. "You certainly can't ... "

"I can't prove a connection? You're right. At least not yet. But it's my job to oversee the effort to analyze every potential shred of evidence. And we're definitely interested in what the Germans have uncovered. It's ominous, and the Bureau isn't about to ignore it."

The president stared at the FBI director. "And Nielsen?"

"Murdered, sir. Poison injected into his leg. Ricin, an old KGB technique."

"Go on."

"It apparently came from one of the new Libyan or Lebanese labs. That's where it's all manufactured now. If it's Lebanese, it could be connected with that new group I just mentioned." He nodded toward his compatriot. "We're working together on the matter."

"Yes, Mr. President, we're looking into it," the CIA director confirmed. "We'll get a report from an operative in each of those areas in . . . " He paused and considered his watch. "About twelve hours. But . . . " he smiled in the direction of his counterpart, "I wouldn't get excited. People anywhere in the world can buy ricin. Even U.S. terrorists."

"And what about the plane crash in New Mexico on Tuesday and the disco bombing in Houston last night?"

The FBI chief leaned back and smoothed at his salt-and-pepper hair. He sighed.

"The best we have right now is that the L-1011 was hit by a surface-to-air missile just after its departure from Albuquerque. Probably shoulder-launched. The media's still calling it an engine explosion, but the NTSB will set the record straight tomorrow afternoon. They're having a news conference on it."

"Do we know who's responsible?"

The director sat up straight. "No, but we're pulling all the stops. Every potential informant is being interrogated. I will say that a couple of our people are absolutely convinced that the missile was one of the 1,000-plus Stingers missing from Afghanistan. Their best guess is that a third of these contraband weapons are now in America."

The president exhaled audibly. "And Houston?"

"ATF says it was a car bomb. Compressed petroleum gas, in combination with another explosive agent, similar to those employed in Northern Ireland and the Middle East. Seven in Israel alone since '95. Never used here before, though."

The chief executive leaned forward and clasped his hands. "Anything else?"

Both shook their heads.

"Still looks like a conspiracy, doesn't it?"

The visitors looked at one another, then back at the president.

The FBI director nodded his head. "A high likelihood, yes. Both Secretaries were killed within hours of each other, by sophisticated methods. Hardly a coincidence. At least that's what our people think. The missile attack on the airliner Tuesday was thoroughly professional, better than anything that's been attempted before. And as for Houston, we're not sure it's connected. But, yes, it all seems to add up to something."

"I agree," the CIA director remarked. "Except for the source."

The president rotated his chair so that he faced the bulletproof windows of the Oval Office. He sat in silence for a minute. Then he spoke with his back to the two men.

"As you know, on Monday I arranged for Secret Service protection and coordination for the top echelon of the three branches of government. That's been carried out, and so far the media hasn't made an issue of it. I hope to hell they won't. At least not for a while."

He swiveled back around.

"What else is lurking out there, gentlemen?"

The FBI director took a deep breath.

"We've turned up some additional information, sir. About an hour ago."

"Which is?"

"Our informants in Mexico City tell us they have reason to believe there's probably more to come. They don't know what, but they've tapped into a virulently anti-American cell with Marxist-Maoist roots. Can't be sure there's any connection with what's been happening, but they've heard about something being planned called 'Lux.' "

"Like the soap?"

The FBI director shook his head.

"No, sir. It's Latin, for 'light.' "

Overland Park, Kansas
11:48 p.m.

The governor himself had snipped the entrance ribbon with giant golden scissors at its grand opening on the Fourth of July. There stood the Sunflower, a $1.9 billion offering to the shoppers of mid-America. It was the nation's largest single-site marketplace, seven stories of stores and cinemas and fountains in the middle of walkways and gardens and topped by a massive bubble-top roof that allowed the sun and stars to contribute to the illusion of an opulent oasis in the midst of the great outdoors.

And the rides. Interspersed with the walkways and escalators were trams and trains and moving sidewalks that transported both buyers and the just-curious to and around the displays of more than six hundred merchants. The favorite mode of introduction to this plethora of products and services for most first-time visitors was the Window Shopper, a spacious monorail that departed from the front entrance twice every hour. It coursed in and through the stores and shops up and down the center's multitiered building. The Shopper required twenty-five minutes to tour everything on its route. As the train moved through tunnels in the walls and openings between floors, riders looked up and through aisles laden with the magnificence of the world. The trip cost five dollars, but that was an inexpensive and sensible investment by thousands each day, for many specials were announced to monorail passengers only. Merchants frequently boarded the train and distributed discount coupons, which could be used for immediate and real savings, and the shopping center chose lucky riders throughout the day for even more largess. Some shrieked as smiling young women peeled from stacks of ten-dollar bills; others nearly fainted when they were announced as the winners of diamond jewelry or $1,000 gift certificates. Automobiles and vacations were occasional grand prizes for surprised in-house travelers.

Large anchor-tenant department stores were interspersed with cozy soap and shampoo shops with their scratch-and-sniff samples. The center presented establishments with footwear for any and every need, fashion boutiques, and places that sold leather goods, tobacco, and art. Books and orchids were available next to corn dogs, French wines, and three computer-simulated golf driving ranges. One could order Broadway tickets and receive instant confirmation and a charge against a major credit card, or punch in a selection for scuba or snorkeling off the Great Barrier Reef of Australia. Holographic and 3-D cinemas drew crowds the clock around. A hundred thousand people a day came to the Sunflower, southwest of metropolitan Kansas City. It had become the biggest new attraction in America.

Tonight, New Year's Eve, the indoor party of the century was under way, and tens of thousands of revelers packed the concourses in anticipation of the heady atmosphere of bands, booze, and banquets. Few paid any attention to the uniformed workmen lugging in last-minute food supplies at the center's sixteen entrances. Families and couples and singles alike streamed along the walkways and bounced to the cacophony of the six musical groups playing in the center atrium, while restaurants served the hungry and thirsty with their usual attention to quality, which had earned most of them stars in the gustatory rating books. As midnight grew near, party hats and horns by the thousands were distributed by grateful merchants, and the masses pressed toward the hub of activity on the levels surrounding the music makers at the core. A large lighted cylinder with its red, white, and blue neon striping stood atop a six-story pole, ready for its sixty-second midnight descent and the inexorable transformation to a new beginning.

As the last sands filtered through the neck of one store's large plastic hourglass in the background, the bandleaders motioned to one another in preparation of their coordinated effort at "Auld Lang Syne." The chorus of thousands of voices became louder and was punctuated by shouts and the bleating sounds of kazoos and other noisemakers, which would accompany the organized melody. With a flash and a roar from the crowd, the neon sentinel was illuminated, notifying everyone that January was but a minute away. The cries from the multitude as the ball made its first movement toward the floor masked the sound of the initial explosion. The subsequent series of unanticipated staccato blasts was heard by everyone.

At each of the sixteen entrances to the shopping complex, the blinding incandescence of phosphorus sesquisulfide detonations thundered outward in sheets of sticky fire at a thousand feet per second. Immense walls of white-hot gobs shot through the corridors and smashed into the pressed masses, searing through and igniting their clothing and flesh. Dozens of rows of the suddenly mortally wounded were propelled forward like fiery dominoes. Within ten seconds of the first eruption, more than five thousand human beings had expired in agony, their bodies, or what was left of them, pitted and disfigured with smoldering craters. Another five seconds produced five thousand more cadavers, each bearing the scars of an unspeakable death by the crematory fire. Seventeen seconds into the abomination, the remaining crowds were transformed by the sights and stench into maddened herds, screaming and clawing insanely against the unyielding walls for deliverance from the satanic inferno. By the time the first of nine alarms was called in to area fire departments ninety seconds later, 11,178 individuals had ceased to exist.

Tulsa
Midnight

Jack slipped into his daughter's room. He stood at the edge of her bed and looked down at her as she slept. Her arms clasped a long-ignored doll, Snoopy. She was so precious to him, and he whispered a vow.

"I'll get those bastards, Rachel." His jaw tightened, and he spoke through clenched teeth. "I promise you that."

Private Airstrip, Panama City, Florida
Midnight

The ringing of a telephone reverberated across the metal hangar. It signaled a second time.

"*Sí?*"

"Bird season has begun. Good hunting."

The man replaced the receiver and gave a thumbs-up gesture to two men next to a Sabreliner. They nodded and started loading their cargo into the small jet.

12

Even though the large video display screens across the top portion of the two situation rooms had been cleared and segregated thirty minutes earlier, in anticipation of a major addition to the FBI's monitoring effort, the Bureau's Strategic Information Operations Center didn't officially become involved in the investigation of the bombing of the Sunflower outside Kansas City until 1:41 a.m. Still, this was less than forty-five minutes after the first explosion occurred at the huge shopping center. Such response would be considered a record for SIOC's engagement under ordinary circumstances. But this last week of the year had turned out to be anything but ordinary.

When Lewis Bittker, SIOC's chief, walked into his Rockville condominium at 12:45 in the morning, he thought there wasn't much room for a New Year's Eve celebration when one's world was going into overload. For what he knew were a host of good reasons, he hadn't been able to get himself slowed down for sleep—even after his usual shot of cold Maalox.

He stood in the doorway of his study and contemplated the electronic row of seven twenty-inch Sony color monitors that the FBI had installed when he'd taken over command of SIOC. Four of the television sets were always tuned to the major commercial networks, one displayed CNN's "Headline News," and the other two showed selected data from SIOC. All of the sets were turned on but silent. Bittker reached for the *TV Guide* on the table inside the door and headed for his bedroom and his big-screen Panasonic. He flipped through the magazine's selections and figured there wouldn't be much of interest on television at this hour. Most of the viewing audience was out partying, so there'd be a lot of diet and exercise infomercials. He pulled out and arranged two pillows on his bed and turned on Washington's Channel 7. It featured a live picture from a crowded New York City party where obviously drunken people were weaving and singing and blowing horns and other noisemakers at the camera. Bittker sat down and lay back against the pillows. He was about to change to a cable channel for a movie when a panel with the network's logo flashed on the screen.

"We interrupt our regularly scheduled programming to bring you the following bulletin from ABC News."

Bittker glanced at his watch. Its digital numbers showed 1:06 a.m. The screen filled with flames of a massive fire.

"Shit!" He jerked up and stared.

"A series of explosions erupted minutes ago at a mammoth shopping center complex outside Kansas City, Missouri. Initial reports are that upwards of thirty thousand people attending a New Year's Eve party may be trapped. We have no estimate yet of deaths or injuries, but officials on the scene say both totals will be very high. Witnesses outside the center report that the explosions appeared to have occurred simultaneously at many entrances."

The picture cut to a local newsman standing in a parking lot a block from the blazing center. It was hard to see the features of the man's face because of the intensity of the fires behind him.

Bittker didn't move as the reporter relayed the horrifying facts: a dozen or more explosions of some kind and thousands—thousands, the man repeated—thought dead, and no one yet claiming responsibility for what clearly appeared to be an intentional act. From the magnitude of the story, Bittker knew his SIOC team would have to carve out yet another niche in the already crowded field of crises. His secure telephone rang. He knew the call was from his department. He picked up the unit.

"Yes, I'm watching it now. Give it space. I'll be there in thirty minutes."

As he rode downtown, Bittker reviewed SIOC's structure and staffing. He was glad he wouldn't have to request more people to cover the new crisis. He had already slightly overstaffed the center for the previous events, so he would be able to allocate three specialists to the Kansas City situation right away.

"But if this keeps up," he thought out loud, "the next emergencies will have to take a number and wait their turn." He sighed in frustration. "Jee-sus Christ!"

The onslaught was unprecedented, and Bittker wondered what America would be like after another week of this. There was something in the air that was vastly different from the days after the New York and Oklahoma attacks, when everyone thought they were going to see Middle Eastern terrorists lurking everywhere. One word crossed his mind: anarchy. He picked up the car's cellular telephone. An FBI operator answered.

"This is Bittker. Get me Corley Brand. He's in Albuquerque. I think he's at the Hyatt."

Bittker looked at his watch. It indicated that the new year was ninety-five minutes old. But it was still last year out in New Mexico. He heard the connection being made, then the hotel operator ringing the room. Brand's telephone sounded three times.

"Yo?"

Bittker recognized the inflection.

"Corley, it's Lew. We've got another major one."

"I know. It's on every channel. I was just about to call you."

"I'm almost at the office now. We're running out of staging room. This'll push us to our limits. It's worse than anything we've ever had before."

"Two things," Brand replied. "First, I'm going to catch the earliest flight out of here for Kansas City. I think there's a Southwest around dawn. Second, I want you to consider something seriously."

"Go."

"How would you orchestrate SIOC in the event these incidents are directly related?"

"Which ones?"

"All of them, damn it! The Metroliner, the SST, the thing out here. Now the shopping center. Suppose this was one big, coordinated effort."

"Brand, you're hallucinating."

"Listen to me, Lew. They definitely have one thing in common."

"Which is?"

"What they're doing to the country."

Tulsa
6:13 a.m.

It was almost time to get up. Jack moved his hand to the adjacent space in the bed. The area was empty and cold. And last night was to have been so special with her. He closed his eyes. Finally he reached for the light, pulled himself to a sitting position, and listened to an uncommonly quiet house. There was usually at least a creak among the supports or a thump from the furnace. But there wasn't even the moan of a winter wind this morning. He looked at the clock again. It glowed back: 6:14. He reached over and disabled its alarm, which was a minute from sounding. No need to wake up the household. He hoped Rachel had been able to sleep the entire night.

Reluctantly, Jack extended his legs over the edge of the bed. He positioned his feet above his slippers and stood up into them and moved toward the window. He held back the curtain with one hand and lifted a miniblind.

Snow. At least half a foot of it, he guessed by looking at what had accumulated on a nearby birdbath. And it was still coming down in large, silent flakes.

He headed for the bathroom and thought again about his daughter. He couldn't let her slip back into her silence and separation from him. He stopped and closed his eyes and sighed. She meant everything to him. And he had so much to do.

McLean, Virginia
7:20 a.m.

"More than ten thousand murdered last night!"

House Speaker Homer Jenkins jerked away from *The Washington Post* and threw a teaspoon into the kitchen sink. It splashed into his used cereal bowl and sprayed soapy water on his new silk Christmas robe.

"Shit!"

He grabbed a towel and tamped at a large wet spot. "Happy Fuckin' New Year, Homer." Jenkins tossed the towel aside and picked up his cup. He strode for the telephone.

"All hell's broken loose in Congress over these goddamn incidents, and the president's keeping me in the dark. Again."

Not that the chief executive hadn't used lots of words in his so-called briefings at the White House the previous Monday and Tuesday, Jenkins muttered to himself. Over an hour each time, but all form and little substance. I wonder what sort of inane pap he'll come up with to explain last night's shopping center inferno. And maybe he'll insist a lone band of hippies did in the Denver mayor.

"Oh, but Homer, there's no connection," he mocked the president's voice. "They're all coincidences."

He grabbed the receiver from the wall unit.

"I'm sick and tired of this evasive crap."

Even though it was a holiday, Jenkins had gotten up early with the intention of talking with the president before the media started in for the fourth straight day. He swallowed a mouthful of the tepid coffee and punched in the number for the White House. The operator rang Brian O'Shaunessey's office.

"I'm sorry, Mr. Speaker," the chief of staff replied with an air of condescension, "but the president's still asleep. After all, it *is* New Year's, sir. Besides, the news conference and his meetings with you contained all that's known at this time."

Jenkins could sense the smirk on O'Shaunessey's face.

"Goddamn it, Brian, screw the news conference. What about the shopping center? I know he's sitting on a big story now. First, two Cabinet members wiped out, hundreds ground up in a train wreck, the poor little kids on that plane, Houston, then the assassination of Grant Pritchard in Denver. Now Kansas City! We've never had anything like this before."

"Sir, purely isolated incidents, and ... "

"Isolated incidents, my ass! It's a fucking avalanche."

"Oh, now ... "

"You little son of a bitch. Secret Service as thick as fleas in summer, and the president says it's only 'precautionary.' Precautionary for what?"

"Sir, I don't ... "

"Listen to me, O'Shaunessey. Something's going on, your boss is covering it up, and I *demand* to know what it is."

"I'm really sorry, sir," the president's aide cooed. "I really am."

"Oh, go to hell!" Jenkins slammed the receiver into its holder. "You little bastard."

Soon as we're back in session, he swore to himself, I'm going to get to the bottom of this if I have to haul every single FBI and CIA spook up to the Hill by the short hairs. It'd be worse than their worst PR nightmares. Waco, Ruby Ridge, and Aldrich Ames will be orgasms in comparison. He dropped into a chair and stared at the ceiling.

"I'm going to put an end to his hide-and-seek bullshit once and for all. No president's going to brush Homer Jenkins aside."

Through the window, he saw two Secret Service agents in their car, looking back at him. He gave them the finger.

Cape Canaveral
8:15 a.m.

Seventy-two hours earlier the Space Shuttle *Encounter* had been rolled out from the Vehicle Assembly Building, where it had been joined to its solid rocket boosters and external fuel tank. The combined 2,300-ton vehicle now stood 184 feet tall at Launch Complex 39A in preparation for its five-day voyage. This would be the third mission for the newest shuttle. *The New York Times* had billed today's launch as "America's most spectacular New Year's celebration." The president and members of Congress would be in attendance.

The NASA media briefing began on time. Deputy Administrator Donald Westbrook smiled at familiar faces as he walked toward the podium. More than three hundred accredited reporters crowded into the main auditorium. The tanned former Olympic champion runner and decorated

Vietnam veteran was a favorite. He had been a spokesman for the space agency since the *Challenger* disaster in 1986, when he'd argued eloquently for complete disclosure to the American people and won the admiration of the presidential commission investigating the tragedy. In his interaction with reporters, Westbrook intuitively understood the demands of their editors and program producers, and he made sure they had everything they needed or, at least, everything he could give them. Most had never heard him say, "No comment."

"Good morning, ladies and gentlemen." Westbrook added his usual greeting on launch day. "Hope you enjoyed our sumptuous breakfast buffet. The champagne was my idea." He feigned surprise at the groans from those who had partaken again of NASA's simple offering of coffee and doughnuts. He put his hands in his pockets and waited for them to sit down.

"Welcome to Kennedy Space Center."

He looked at the news release.

"Flight commander Bob Andries and pilot "Buzz" Stewart are commanding a team of three astronomers and one astrophysicist. All six, as you probably know, are veterans of earlier shuttle launches. They're scheduled to board *Encounter* shortly after two o'clock this afternoon to prepare the orbiter for its 4:16 liftoff. Any questions?"

Dozens of arms waved in the air. The deputy administrator pointed to a young woman. She stood up.

"Mr. Westbrook, can you give us a few more details about the scientific purpose of this mission?"

"Certainly. At an orbital altitude of 370 miles, *Encounter* will send two of our Jet Propulsion Laboratory probes, Sentinels I and II, toward the center of the Milky Way, which is 30,000 light years from Earth in the direction of the constellation Sagittarius. They cost $2.8 billion, together. They each weigh 26,990 pounds with their boosters, and we hope they'll provide radio and optical analysis of conditions toward the core of our galaxy, which many astronomers believe contains a massive black hole."

He paused and looked at his notes.

"The Sentinels are not actually intended to reach the center of the galaxy. Rather, they're designed to detect, within twenty-five years of their release, evidence, if any, of the presumed black hole. The designers believe the probes will probably collide with the debris of other star systems and be destroyed within two centuries. Even then, they will have covered less than one one-hundredth of the distance to the center of the Milky Way."

"Don?"

Westbrook acknowledged a network television correspondent in the second row. The man rose.

"There is speculation that the shuttle will also launch one of the Pentagon's newest KH-12 reconnaissance satellites. What can you tell us about that?"

The deputy administrator grinned. "I've heard that, too, Randy. No, this is purely a scientific mission. Somebody's been reading too many spy novels." Many of the reporters laughed.

"I beg your pardon," the man persisted. "There's a scheduled communications blackout on the seventh and eighth orbits early tomorrow morning, local time. That's typical of a military mission."

The audience shifted as the briefing took on a new tone.

Westbrook stared at the questioner before he answered. His voice was on edge. "The blackout is nominal for the period immediately preceding the ejection of the probes. Their launch is a special, precision maneuver, and there is no need for distracting communications at that time. Any other questions?"

"Yeah, one more." It was the same man. "The controllers' flight profile itinerary, which I obtained this morning, still shows your JPL payload deployment on the twenty-sixth orbit. That's more than a day after the blackout."

"Well, that's been changed!" Westbrook snapped as he seized his notes. "I think our news release is complete. That'll be all." He walked from the stage.

Bridge of the Americas, Juárez, Mexico
8:50 a.m.

The dark-green Buick station wagon pulled into line and approached the U.S. Customs inspection plaza. There were only a few cars ahead. On an average weekday, more than 100,000 Mexicans crossed here to work in the United States. The driver checked his watch. He noted that each vehicle clearance this morning was taking less than half a minute.

"Happy New Year." The Customs agent looked in and smiled at the well-dressed family. The muscular driver grinned back.

"Where were you born, sir?"

"The good ol' U. S. of A.," the man replied with a Texas accent. "San Antonio. All of us."

"How long have you been out of the country?"

The man turned to his right. "Uh, honey, how long we been down there in Acapulco?"

The Customs agent noticed that the brunette woman tensed and shifted in her seat.

"Six days?" She seemed hesitant. The boy and girl in the back glanced back and forth between the Customs inspector and the front seat. They appeared to be six or seven years old.

"Yeah," the man answered loudly. "Six great days at the Hacienda Real."

"My, that's a long drive. Acapulco's a good two days each way."

The man frowned. "Oh? Oh, yeah. Ten days out of the country, then."

"Do you have anything to declare?"

"Uh, we bought a few trinkets. You know, straw hats and a shirt or two. Like this one." He patted his chest and grinned again. "Nothin' else."

"Please drive to the marked parking zone at the building on your right."

"What? Are you holdin' us for something?"

"Sir, please do as I say."

As the car pulled away, the Customs agent went inside the booth and picked up the telephone. "I think these are our people."

Three men stepped out of the brick building when the station wagon stopped in front. They identified themselves to the driver. "FBI. Please get out of your car."

The man glared at the agent at his window. "Fuck you!" He twisted the steering wheel and jammed the accelerator to the floor. Two of the agents crouched and drew their pistols.

"Don't shoot! Don't shoot!" the third agent shouted.

Five hundred yards ahead, in El Paso, four cars blocked the street. As the station wagon roared toward them, a Border Patrol officer waved his arms. The car swerved and attempted to go around. It jumped the curb and smashed into the wall of a building. Two uniformed agents ran to the wrecked vehicle. Steam jetted from under the hood, and the children moaned. One agent opened a rear door and lifted out the boy. The driver raised his bloodied head from the steering wheel and groaned something.

"What'd you say?" the second agent asked as he leaned toward the injured man.

"I said, fuck you!"

The driver groped beneath the steering column and touched two wires together. The fireball consumed a quarter of a block.

Tulsa Bible College
10:16 a.m.

The snowfall persisted at a stable rate, while the temperature continued to drop. The local television weathermen were unanimous in their forecasts of another four to six inches during the day.

Jack stopped by Rachel's room.

"I'm going to TBC for a little while. Will you be OK?" He raised a hand to touch her shoulder, but she flinched. He let his hand drop. "Now, you and Flora look after each other. Don't let any strangers in."

Rachel lifted her eyes. "Do I *have* to stay home?" She let him touch her this time.

"Please do. I don't want to take any chances." He squatted down next to her. "You and Flora can keep each other company, can't you? I won't be long." He embraced her. "Don't forget that your cousins will be here this afternoon."

"Daddy?"

"Yes, sweetie?"

Rachel hesitated. "Please be careful."

Jack stroked her hair. "I promise."

He left at ten o'clock. It usually took him five or six minutes to drive to TBC. Today, even though it was a holiday, he allowed twenty. Before he left, he'd called his brothers and sister to remind them to be at his house later that afternoon. He was looking forward to time with Rachel, his other family members, and Linda and Tom McVey before they returned to Europe.

Jack drove slowly through the glazed streets. Cars had been abandoned in snowbanks along the way. "Okies have never gotten used to this kind of weather," he reflected aloud as he passed a man waving a warning of a ditched automobile ahead.

He entered the campus from the north side and drove to the empty lot behind the ministry's administration building. Tulsa Bible College occupied most of the land at 121st Street and South Yale. The Reuben Gentry Ministries were concentrated in three buildings that stood between the Chapel of Jesus and the Arkansas River. Jack parked in an area recently cleared by TBC's lone snowplow. He was thankful that someone had thought the ministry's business might have to be carried out in spite of the holiday.

He unlocked the main door of the five-story building and entered the dark foyer. The building's heat was maintained at 50°F during the holidays. He decided to walk up the three flights to the well-appointed office Reuben had insisted Jack have for his role as special consultant. He opened the door to his reception area, turned on the lights, and walked in. He shivered. The room was colder than the hallway. The phrase "cold as death" hovered in his consciousness. Jack found a portable heater, plugged it in next to his desk, and flipped the switch.

An IBM computer workstation stood to the right of his chair. The console was connected to the school's mainframe system. Jack sat down and turned on the master switch. He closed his eyes and breathed deeply as the machine and the laser printer hummed to life. He could smell the recently polished wood of his office's furniture. The screen flashed once, then illuminated completely. At the blinking question-mark prompt, he entered his personal identification code.

INVALID USER.

Jack frowned. He repeated the access protocol and waited.

INVALID USER.

Invalid user? What was going on here? Jack knew a third failed attempt would refuse him access for twenty-four hours. Security would ask a lot of questions, too. He sat back to contemplate his next move. Apparently the access process had been changed. And in the last day or so. Why hadn't he been informed? He tapped his fingers against the cold desktop and stared at the screen. An idea hit him. The ministry's PC network!

TBC had its mainframe computer, which was used by all departments of the school, but the Reuben Gentry Ministries had its own independent network of personal computers linked together inside the main office. Maybe, just maybe, Norman had used it for his private files. And that might be where the strange financial information was. Jack crossed his fingers. Norman's office was down the hall. There was an outside chance he could get into the little bastard's files from right here. With a little more luck, he could even guess Norman's password. And there wouldn't be any automatic cutoff after three tries. That particular bit of security had been talked about but never implemented.

Jack drew up the "RGM-TEL" icon and hit the return key. The interoffice communication system paused, then displayed a menu. He selected the fourteenth item, GENTRY, N. Jack requested entry.

PASSWORD?

Jack tapped in "Norman."

INVALID PASSWORD. TRY AGAIN.

"Norman Gentry."

INVALID PASSWORD. TRY AGAIN.

Jack wondered where Norman's mind was when the jerk had made up his latest password. He tried the easy ones first . . . the ministry's name, the school's name, city, state, Norman's personal office telephone number, his unlisted one. Nothing. Jack then thought about people. He remembered that hackers usually guessed correctly when they tried to break into amateurs' systems using family names. How about starting with his perplexing sister-in-law? He typed in "Bunny."

WELCOME TO RGM-TEL, NORMAN.

Bingo.

The new screen listed everything Norman had entered and currently maintained, from "Abortion" to "Zionism." There were more than two hundred categories. Near the middle was "Money." Jack selected it. When it came up, he chose "Contributions." There was only one listing, "$10,000 Club," which showed the heavy hitters who had given to the ministry as a result of Norman's latest plea. There were thirty-three names and addresses from around the country. Nothing stood out. Jack scrolled up and tried "Banks." As he waited for the data to appear, he wondered why Norman hadn't placed it under "Money." Nothing there either, other than the names and addresses of the ministry's principal financial institutions in the U.S., which Jack already knew about. "Giving," another heading apparently out of place, turned out to be the draft of the speech for Norman's major television appearance, which was scheduled for Seattle on the seventeenth.

Would he have put anything really confidential on his computer in the first place?

Jack tried again. Under "Friends" he found two categories, "Friends of RGM" and "Others." He chose the latter. It was a list of organizations. Two of them were immediately conspicuous: Banco de México and Banque Nationale de Paris.

"Incredible," Jack exclaimed. There were also seven other foreign banks. Jack requested the Banco de México file. A chronology of dates and deposits filled the screen.

"Christ Almighty, there must be 5 million in U.S. dollars on this page alone," he whispered. There were two more pages. Jack copied the information to his machine's hard disk and went to the data on the French bank. It showed a total of 12 million francs on deposit. He copied that information also. Over the next twenty minutes, Jack looked at and copied the data on the other bank accounts. There were 1.2 million Swiss francs at Credit Suisse in Zurich, DM 975,000 at Frankfurt's Deutsche Bank, and nearly a million English pounds at Barclays in London.

"Probably 20 to 21 million dollars all told." He whistled. "Where's this money coming from? Better yet, why?" He shook his head. "I've got to get back home and try to sort this out."

He punched the print button and waited while the laser printer produced nine pages. As he gathered them together, he thought about the hard disk where he had stored this critical information.

"Better make a copy, just in case." He went back to the computer and inserted a fresh floppy disk. He made the copy and tucked the disk into his pocket. He returned to his car at 11:35.

His hand trembled as he started the ignition. His heart was racing. It had been a long time since he had been this eager to solve a puzzle. As he drove off the campus, he noticed a TBC security car parked near the entrance. It appeared to be empty.

Once Jack's car was a block away, a man inside the campus vehicle sat up and keyed a transmitter.

"He's off the property."

"Come to my office at once," a voice responded. "We may have to act faster than planned."

13

The White House
Friday, January 1, 10:30 a.m.

Secret Service agent Timothy Vance pushed open the northwest door of the Oval Office from the outside and nodded. The president held a telephone in one hand and raised his other in acknowledgment to the security man.

"No, Mister Speaker," the chief executive continued, "I am *not* covering up anything." He stood and shook his head.

"Not true. No, sir. Look, Homer, I've got the NSC waiting for me. I'll let you and the rest of the leadership know as soon as we have better information." He paused. "Yes, that's a promise. Oh, and I'm sorry about how you were treated this morning. I've already talked to Brian, and ... Right. Goodbye." He replaced the telephone and held it down for a moment, as if it might jump back up on its own.

"Don't call us, we'll call you," he said to no one in particular. He withdrew a pen from the set on his desk.

"One more second, Tim."

He made a mark in his personal appointment book, replaced the pen, and slid the narrow leather diary into the inside pocket of his suit coat. He walked to the door and followed his escort down the carpeted hall.

"I want to meet that guy who said the presidency was too much for any one mortal," he remarked as they stepped past staff offices in the West Wing. Vance looked over his shoulder. The president muttered, "He deserves a Nobel Prize for sheer insight."

"At least you don't have to do windows," the Secret Service agent offered.

The president shook his head. "Another few days like these and I'll wish that were my full-time job."

The two men stopped at the doorway to the Cabinet Room, and the president accepted a thick briefing manual from an aide.

"So, Jim, are we all set for tomorrow morning?"

"Yes, sir," the young man replied. "Eleven o'clock."

The president looked over the yellow summary sheet that was

clipped to the outside of the binder. He nodded as he read. "All right, I want to make a television statement about the shopping center later this afternoon, but only after the shuttle launch. Has Kevin issued anything more than the one-liner?"

"No, sir."

"Well, tell him to put out a release with a little more substance at the same time he announces that my statement will be forthcoming."

The young man nodded.

The president turned and entered the room. He wasn't wearing his usual smile.

"Good morning, everyone."

The vice president and the secretaries of State and Defense stood at the mahogany conference table. Behind them was the president's national security advisor, Alan Kaufmann. Deputy Treasury Secretary Margaret Burnell, the attorney general, the FBI and CIA directors, and the chairman of the joint chiefs had been asked to attend, and they stood against the doors opening toward the Rose Garden. Copies of newspapers from Washington, Baltimore, Philadelphia, New York, and Boston lay on an adjacent table.

"Good morning, Mr. President," they replied, almost in unison.

The chief executive gestured toward the brown leather chairs. "Please." He took his place at the table's middle position. The others sat down on both sides and across from him. In front of each place was a fresh legal pad, a sharpened pencil, and a flat pewter ashtray. The president didn't smoke, and he frowned on anyone who did. He had even had the ashtrays removed on two occasions, but the White House Historical Association returned them quickly, respectfully pleading that they were important memorabilia dating back to the administration of William Howard Taft, when the Cabinet Room was built. Besides, the meticulous society members had commented, they were not just ashtrays. Today the president's antique supported his water carafe.

"Thank you for attending this emergency meeting of the National Security Council," he began. He looked around the room. Even though it was a holiday, no one had chosen to break NSC protocol by dressing informally. The seriousness of the growing national crisis would have dictated business attire in any event.

The president poured a glass of ice water, then pulled off the paper clip and separated the summary from the briefing book. "Thank heavens it's a new year." He took a swallow of water and cleared his throat.

"After yesterday's horror in Kansas City, let's pray the past keeps its nightmares," the vice president volunteered.

The president made eye contact, one by one, with those gathered around the table.

"These have been the most difficult days I've faced since assuming office. I know you've been under similar pressures." The president took out a red pen. "What is extremely disturbing is the fact that there may be a pattern to these tragedies. Let's review them."

He shook his head at the first entry.

"Item One: The terrible Sunflower shopping center bombing last night." He turned toward the director. "What does the FBI have on that?"

"Mr. President, over eleven thousand dead, best estimate."

Two men in the room groaned as if they had been hit physically. The others sat in silence. The FBI chief read from a printout.

"No leads yet but, apparently, numerous phosphorus explosives—the lab guesses phosphorus with a potassium chlorate oxidizer, which is really bad stuff—were placed at the entrances to the shopping center and detonated simultaneously at midnight. Two security guards talked with one man who was standing at the back of an unmarked van, unloading what he said were supplies for a restaurant. They didn't ask for his identification, but they did get a tag number. We're checking it out right now. Our personnel and the Alcohol, Tobacco, and Firearms people are still on the scene. I'll have a better idea of where we stand this afternoon."

The president shifted and faced the acting head of the Treasury Department. "Margaret, what *is* the latest from the ATF?"

The deputy secretary inclined her head toward the FBI director. "ATF personnel, working with the FBI, have determined that at least two but probably three radio-triggered explosive units were placed at each of the sixteen entrances to the shopping center. Based upon interviews with witnesses, the explosions apparently occurred simultaneously. They produced an immediate and complete seal, which then seared inward from the entrances at close to the speed of sound and at a temperature of at least five thousand degrees Fahrenheit. Without a doubt, it was the largest cremation of living human beings since Nagasaki."

There was no sound in the Cabinet Room. A few shook their heads at the enormity of the event.

"I don't need to tell you the country's in shock," the president stated. "No one's claimed responsibility yet?" He glanced back and forth between the FBI chief and the deputy Treasury secretary. Both shook their heads.

"So, just like the others . . . nobody's talking." The president looked back at his sheet. "Well, I'm going to make a special statement later this afternoon. Get me anything that might help. Leads, interviews with witnesses, anything." The two officials made notes and nodded. The president resumed.

"Item Two: According to current intelligence, both Treasury Secretary David Rowland and Transportation Secretary Bradford Nielsen were killed last Monday by terrorists. We're looking into the developing evidence that both acts could have been foreign-sponsored."

Most of those around the table were now writing. The president continued.

"The CIA has just presented me with information that one of two groups, both apparently operating out of Mexico, might have been involved in the SST bombing. The first one is a pro-Syrian cell called *Estrella Fugaz*. That's Spanish for 'Shooting Star.' The second is a pro-Iranian cadre, the FLF. In English, they call themselves the 'Final Liberation Front.'"

The president turned toward the FBI leader. "What have you come up with concerning the explosives on the AirParis flight?"

The director tapped his pencil on his notes. "We've pulled all the stops at the lab, and we've identified traces of Gellex-4 on some of the debris. That's a foreign-made plastique that is extremely powerful. We've also found minute amounts of nitroglycerin and nitrocellulose. Those could be an indication of cordite, which might have been used in the detonation. Not enough pieces of the puzzle yet. But we're expediting everything."

The president reached for his water glass again. "And Brad Nielsen?"

"Yes, sir. Secretary Nielsen's death resulted from a poison known as ricin, which was injected into his leg by a sophisticated delivery system perfected by the former KGB decades ago. Over the past few years, we've been aware of the production of ricin in both Libya and the Middle East. But as far as we know, no groups other than the KGB and its old Bulgarian comrades have ever utilized that particular method."

The president looked around the table. "We don't yet know if the killing of the two Secretaries is part of a conspiracy against the United States, but we're operating under the assumption that it is."

He made another mark on the sheet.

"Item Three: As you're aware, Monday's Metroliner disaster was caused by sabotage. According to the NTSB's preliminary report, it took at least two men to position that switching unit over the rails. It was radio-controlled by someone who waited for the Metroliner. Five earlier trains, all freights, passed over the mold without incident. However, we don't have any reason yet to connect this tragedy with the others."

The chief executive turned the page.

"Item Four: I was informed last night that the chartered airliner crash at Albuquerque on Tuesday was caused by a portable surface-to-air missile. There were no meaningful leads at the time. Is that still the case?"

"Still the case," the director confirmed. "As soon as I get back to my office, I'll see if the NTSB has anything else for their news conference today."

The president laid his summary on the table. "All right, then there's Wednesday's catastrophe in Houston, the car bombing of the disco. Again no leads?" He turned to the FBI chief, who shook his head.

"No, other than the fact that the explosive was the same kind typically employed in the Middle East over the past five years. Propane or butane, most probably with another ingredient. We can't make a connection yet with any of the other events."

The president found the next entry.

"Item Six: The FBI director and I were informed just before we came to this meeting that less than an hour ago in El Paso, four FBI and two Border Patrol agents were killed when terrorists entering from Mexico detonated a bomb in their car. They were apparently posing as husband and wife. Two children with them were also killed."

The vice president thumped his fist into the table without saying anything. His face was a study in frustration. The president referred to his notes.

"The FBI had been tipped off about an attempt by one of the Mexican terrorist groups to bring in a substantial quantity of Gellex-4 at El Paso. There was another vehicle under observation at the time, but it turned away from the border and drove back into Juárez."

The FBI director raised his index finger. "Mr. President, may I add something to that?"

"Please do."

"We haven't had time to analyze the debris from the car's explosion, but we were told by one of our informants that the couple loaded Gellex-4 into their station wagon near El Porvenir, which is just across the Rio Grande, sixty to seventy-five miles southeast of El Paso."

The FBI chief clasped his hands together and worked his thumbs in circles.

"Gellex-4 is what we understand the FLF cell down there has obtained and stocked. We think the couple was bringing it in for redistribution, but we have no idea of their intended destination. An earlier shipment apparently made it across the border and onto the SST. Generally, the amounts per shipment are far too large for a one-time use. An automobile can carry enough Gellex-4 for a thousand bombs."

Everyone stared at the director. The president's voice broke the spell.

"In addition to this immediate link to Mexico, we're also very concerned over the intensification of activity during the past six months connecting the Middle East, Germany, Mexico, and the United States. Regardless of the new peace accords, there is a renewal of terrorist training under way again in Lebanon, involving practice attacks on airports, urban settings, and other sites typical of a well-developed country. It appears more secretive than ever before."

"May I make a comment on that?"

The president nodded to the CIA director.

"These new groups, sir, specifically the ones in the Bekaa Valley, are organizing and training with a rapidity that continues to surprise our specialists. There is now every indication that a couple of these entities are committed to employing whatever means necessary to sponsor new attacks against American interests anywhere in the world, and as soon as possible. They've been working with seasoned ex-KGB hard-liners who are masters of terrorism. Some of their operatives have been traced to bases in Pakistan, which we funded in the '80s for strikes against the Soviets in Afghanistan. We don't have anyone on the inside yet. It's an extremely worrisome situation."

The CIA chief tapped his fingers on the table.

"As I told you earlier, Mr. President, our informants in Lebanon have uncovered Syrian and Iranian ties to the two Mexican groups. I have to admit we're having a change of heart."

"About?"

"About the probable source of what's been going on around the country. From our intelligence-gathering perspective, what we've gotten over the past twelve hours amounts to an embarrassment of riches. We're coming to believe that at least some of the terrorist acts in the United States may indeed have a Middle East nexus. And far more significant than what—or who—was behind the bombing of the World Trade Center."

"The basis of your conclusion, Barney?"

"I don't have that yet, sir. We're still assembling the mosaic." He rubbed his forehead. "Tomorrow . . . maybe Sunday."

"FBI?"

The director faced the chief executive.

"As I briefed you last evening, we received a transmission from our legal attaché in Berlin on Tuesday. It contained the text of a telephone conversation that had been intercepted by the BND, the German foreign intelligence service. Apparently a member of a new terrorist group, the 'Brotherhood of the Ultimate Ijima,' called someone at a public telephone at the Frankfurt airport. This was his entire message: 'The Final Jihad has begun. The first wounds have been inflicted. Go sever the head of the pharaoh and complete the cleansing. The Brotherhood is with you. Allah akbar.' "

"What do you make of it?"

"Well, what bothers us is that the telephone call was made only a few minutes after the AirParis flight was brought down. Plus, the Germans report that this new group is well financed and has established some sort of regular logistical flow between Lebanon through Germany to North America. And they say it was started at least seven months ago."

"What's this 'logistical flow'?"

"They've generated intelligence indicating that both men and materiel have moved from the Bekaa Valley of Lebanon to Germany. As far as they know, the personnel, on three or four separate occasions, arrived in Frankfurt from either Damascus or Cairo. The Germans have not been able to identify the individuals yet, but they're working on it. Especially the last group, which supposedly came through this week. They should have some match-ups for us within twenty-four hours."

The president gripped his hands together.

"And where might these men and materiel be going?"

The FBI director shook his head. "We don't know yet. Maybe Mexico. Maybe here. We've pulled all the stops to find out."

The president sat back in his chair and stared at the ceiling. "Do they know where this 'Brotherhood' is based?"

"No, sir."

The chief executive grimaced. He paused, then looked down at his summary. "Well, under the circumstances, we've been a little slow getting this next matter taken care of, but early tomorrow the space shuttle will deploy a 41,000-pound, enhanced KH-12 'real-time' imaging reconnaissance satellite, under the direction of the National Reconnaissance Office. It's a $640 million piece of equipment that has been under expedited development at Lockheed's Advanced Development Projects facility at Burbank for nearly two years."

He held his summary sheet closer.

"Once it's placed in an orbit slightly over two hundred miles and at an inclination of thirty-four degrees from the equator, we'll be able to monitor the new coded microwave transmissions between Teheran and Damascus and the Syrians' new communications installation at Az Zabadani, both ground-to-ground and downlink-to-satellite. We'll even be able to intercept their erratic millisecond optical signals. The NRO is confident we can decipher all messages within fifty minutes of transmission. Also, with the KH-12's 'dash-3' Indigo Lacross radar system, we'll be able to locate and follow missile and troop movements of any size over there, even at night and during bad weather. We'll be able to monitor everything going on in the Bekaa Valley. Even under the worst conditions or with interference, the resolution will be smaller than three centimeters, about an inch wide."

The president paused for a few seconds.

"I hope we're not gaining all of this capability to spy on the barn after the proverbial horse was stolen." He then turned to a man in uniform.

"Jerry, what do you have to add to all of this?"

Admiral Gerald Chapman turned in his chair. "Really nothing, Mr. President."

The chairman of the joint chiefs pulled himself toward his notes on the table.

"We've had the usual commerce in the Gulf of Mexico, and nothing out of the ordinary in the Caribbean, Central America, or along Mexico's Gulf or Pacific coasts. After your call yesterday, I asked for summaries from the service intelligence agencies, but nothing stands out. Nothing has come from any of our other sources either. Those Mexican groups are staying underground. We're not seeing them in overt activities."

"Art?"

Secretary of State Arthur Cromwell shook his head.

"All's quiet, Mr. President. Officially, that is. Our Damascus embassy has been trying to reinterpret the data it's sent us over the past month. Our contacts in the countryside, along the border between Syria and Lebanon, haven't been able to pick up any details of merit. We receive the regular Israeli briefings from the Mossad concerning the ongoing training operations in Lebanon, but it's the same sort of intelligence we've been getting for half a dozen years, even through the Iraqi situation. These new efforts must be really closed operations. And nothing suspicious to report on a Mexican effort."

"And Defense?"

The president had saved Stephen McConnell for last. The former science teacher and business entrepreneur had first served for two years as DOD's deputy secretary and was widely respected for his imaginative approach to the nation's post–Cold War defense planning. His insights were usually borne out. The sandy-haired McConnell folded his arms across his chest.

"This may be it, Mr. President. I have no proof yet. But call it a reliable gut source."

The chief executive peered over his glasses. "*What* may be it?"

McConnell leaned across the table.

"Consider this. During the early '80s the Soviets shifted troops all over Eastern Europe and redeployed weapons systems regularly, but we didn't panic. However, when one of our commercial airliners was hijacked or a bistro was bombed by terrorists near a base in Wiesbaden, we as a nation came positively unglued. It was headlines for days. Pan Am 103? Everyone saw quicksand everywhere. Then the war with Baghdad, the World Trade Center, Oklahoma City, and the other bombings. Not to mention the Hamas attacks and the escalating Korean situation. Second verse, same as the first. A lesson not lost on someone."

"Go on," the president encouraged with a nod of his head.

The defense secretary rubbed his open palms together. "Terrorists, especially those festering in the Middle East, aren't stupid. The militants hate us in their gut. They've seen what really gets our attention. I've always said that someday . . . "

"Someday what?" the president snapped.

"Someday, sir, they'll catch on and play the terrorism card for all it's worth. Not overseas, . . . " he stabbed the table with his index finger, "but *big* time right here at home, where we're most vulnerable. And I think that's precisely what they're doing now. Look at what's happening around the country today. It's working. Damn it, we're coming apart."

No one spoke. All eyes were on McConnell. The DOD secretary continued, "For over two centuries, we've had a psychological Maginot Line around the United States. It's been our comfort zone. But we knew that if someone ever got inside, with a massive assault, they'd destroy our national confidence. We were lucky after the Iraqi war . . . and even after New York and Oklahoma City. Anyway, I always figured it wouldn't take them more than a month to do incalculable damage to the spirit of America, if they did it right. Well, sir, give 'em three more weeks, and we'll have anarchy on Main Street in every town."

The president shook his head. "Sandy, we've had the terrorist incidents in this country as you've described, and we survived."

"But we've faced nothing like this week, Mr. President. Or what's coming."

There wasn't a sound in the room as McConnell turned in his chair and faced the chief executive.

"Sir, we haven't seen anything yet. It'd be bad enough if they were coming in, striking, then returning home. No, they're going to test us to our limits, to the fullest, because they've come to stay. This isn't a skirmish with one little Middle Eastern country. And forget the homegrown 'camouflage crowd.' Call it World War III, or whatever what you want, but the American Armageddon has begun."

No one moved. McConnell took a deep breath.

"I'd stake my reputation on it. Analyzing all of this 'logistical flow' data from the Middle East through Germany is a fucking waste of time, pardon my French. We need to go door-knocking in Dubuque. We'll find them sooner."

The president stared at the defense secretary. "Well, I can't buy that." He picked up his summary and tapped the bottom of the paper against the table. "Matter of fact, I won't. For the past fifty years, we've watched the rise and fall of various groups in the Middle East. We've been repeatedly threatened by surrogates of the Iranians and the Syrians; more recently, the Iraqis and the North Koreans. Some of these groups were terrifyingly dangerous, but none of them has ever been able to put it all together. We've suffered a handful of attacks from them, all right, but nothing causing more than relatively minor problems. Maybe certain individuals have slipped in for a particular mission, but . . ."

"That's just my point, sir," McConnell interjected. "If someone . . ."

The president held up his hand. "No more." He looked at the others, then spoke calmly. "Much of this information is classified. I'm going to sit on it as long as I can, until we have better explanations. As you know, the media's all over me, screaming 'cover-up,' and now they're waiting for a statement on the shopping center. I'll give them that."

He stared at McConnell again. "But I'll have to have hard facts before I tell the nation that all of this is a monstrous conspiracy operating in our midst. Coincidences and a good imagination do not constitute facts, Sandy. I need proof! Besides, the FBI's done a beyond-the-call-of-duty job in keeping us insulated from such a possibility. They're awfully good at what they do."

The president forced a smile.

"I've asked for television time at eleven in the morning to report on the whole situation. Kevin Howard has announced that my address will cover all the incidents. He's stressed that it'll be a thorough report to the nation. I'll try to make it as reassuring as I can. As I said before, I'll make a statement about the Kansas City bombing later today. In the meantime, we can't afford to be alarmists."

The defense secretary shook his head in frustration.

The president picked up the nearly empty glass of water and sat back in his chair. He turned the vessel slowly in his hands.

"I'm going down to the Cape for the launching of the shuttle this afternoon. Maybe *Encounter* will lift some spirits and make my speeches tonight and tomorrow a little easier."

Tulsa
10:43 a.m.

Tom Bentley picked up the kitchen telephone after the first ring. His glass of fresh orange juice was in his other hand. Neil Wirick was back, an even forty-eight hours after his last call. Wirick immediately started his recitation.

"Add this to your bio for Mr. Jack Stroud."

"Hold it," Bentley interrupted the Dallas FBI head. "I thought you said I'd be getting everything direct from Washington."

"Oh, you will, you will," Wirick replied with a hint of exasperation. "Damn it, Tom, this is unofficial anyway."

Bentley sat down at the kitchen table and set his glass aside. He reached for a pencil.

"All right, I'm ready."

Wirick sounded excited. "Remember I said that Stroud was named supervisor of the counterterrorism section of the Naval Investigative Service sixteen years ago? Well, that's when Corley Brand was placed in charge of our own Counterterrorism Section. I just found out they're old friends. Worked together on a couple of joint investigations."

"So far, so good."

"Get this," the Dallas SAC continued. "Brand says the guy was the best of the best at investigations. Had, *has* one of the best analytical minds he's ever encountered. Tenacious, a real pro. He says we couldn't have anyone better on the inside for this one." Wirick was silent for a moment. "Tom, Jack Stroud might be our ace in the hole up there."

"I'll take all the help I can get," Bentley reflected. "One of my agents, Don Evans, contacted Stroud last night and asked for his assistance in unraveling some of the Gentry ministry's mysterious accounting information we just learned about. Anything else?"

"No, except Happy New Year."

"Yeah, same to you."

Bentley replaced the handset. He picked up his orange juice.

Ace in the hole? he thought. Let's hope.

Café de la Ciudad, Juárez
Friday, January 1, Early Afternoon

The four men in khaki jumpsuits finished tacos de pollo con chorizo. One glanced around at the adjacent tables of the one-room restaurant. They were empty. He slapped away a pesky fly and turned back to the group.

"I'm telling you not to worry," he growled in a low voice. "It was pure coincidence they were spotted. No one saw us. There's nothing left to connect us anyway." He drained the last of his beer and set the bottle in the middle of the grease-coated table.

"But they can tell what kind of explosive it was."

The first man belched and shrugged. "So what? Gellex's everywhere. Highways, construction sites. Nothing special about it."

"Let's go," another man ordered as he put on his dark glasses and grabbed his jacket. "We have less than two hours to be at the crossing. They won't wait."

Frontenac, Missouri
2:30 p.m.

A woman in her late twenties opened the door of the apartment. One of the two men outside stepped forward.

"Miss Arthurs?"

"No, I'm Sandy Wade, her roommate. You're the FBI?"

"Yes, ma'am." Both opened credentials.

"Carolyn's expecting you." The woman smiled. "Please come in."

The agents followed her through a hallway and into a holiday-decorated living room.

"Let me have your coats," she offered.

Both agents slipped out of their overcoats and handed them over. Because of the brightly burning logs in the fireplace, the room felt warmer than it really was. A skinny Christmas tree stood next to the opposite wall. It bore evidence of hours of loving attention, with silver reflective bulbs, candy canes, and tinsel shrouding red and green lights that twinkled on and off.

"I just hate the thought of putting all this away," the woman sighed as she came back in. "We spent a lot of time on it." She escorted the men to an oversize white couch in front of the fireplace.

"Sorry to keep you gentlemen waiting."

A taller, slightly older woman entered and held out her hand. "I'm Carolyn Arthurs. I was upstairs on the phone, making sure Sandy and I aren't on call tomorrow." She smiled. "They've screwed us up before. Please sit down."

Her roommate excused herself as the FBI men took out notepads.

"Miss Arthurs, I'm Jim Jennings. This is Lou Howerton. Thanks for letting us come over this afternoon."

She clasped her hands nervously. "It was just awful."

"You were the flight attendant who discovered the body on last Wednesday's Flight 741 from Frankfurt?"

"Yes, sir. As I told the police, I knew he was dead as soon as I saw the blood on his collar."

"We'd like to know what he said to you."

The flight attendant tugged at her skirt and swallowed. "Well, I was working main cabin, where he was." She looked at Jennings. "I don't remember much about him until he came into the galley during the movie. He seemed really considerate, the way he acted."

"How do you mean?"

"He said he was sorry for interrupting our cleanup after lunch. Most passengers don't ever apologize, or thank us, for anything. Anyway, he asked me who was sitting in a certain seat, and I found out and told him."

"Exactly how did he ask the question?"

"He said he thought he recognized someone on the airplane. I checked our manifest. You know, a computer printout. I gave him the name."

"Did he indicate he knew the individual?"

"No. Well, I don't know. He . . . he kind of frowned, like he might have known the man, but the name was wrong."

Howerton referred to his pad. "Miss Arthurs, we understand the manifest identified the occupant of seat 28-5 as 'S. El-Asail.' Is that correct?"

"Yes, it was 'E-L' hyphen 'A-S-A-I-L.' I'll never forget it."

"Would you describe him, please?"

The woman paused. "Hey, what about his passport? Can't you get a description from it, like from Immigration and Naturalization?"

"Yes, ma'am. We've already done that, but we want to match your description with the INS report."

"Well, the man was in his early or mid-thirties, and short. Maybe five-five, five-six, and he looked like he fitted his name. Middle Eastern . . . that area. You know, olive skin, moustache, a fairly heavy beard. Or it would have been, if he hadn't shaved it off. Anyway, short black hair, longer-than-usual sideburns. And there was a scar on his hand. I noticed it when he reached for the Coke he'd requested."

Jennings took over again. "Tell us about the scar."

"He reached over with his right hand, and the scar looked like it might have started on the underside, toward his palm. It came up and over and ran parallel to his thumb, back to near his wrist. I'd say it was a good four inches long. It didn't look new."

Both men scribbled on their notepads. The woman leaned toward them.

"Do you know where he went after he got off here?"

The FBI men ignored her question and stood up. Jennings smiled and tucked his notepad away. "You've been very helpful, Miss Arthurs."

"Do you think he killed that guy?"

"We'll get back with you if we have any more questions."

During their drive back downtown, the two agents relayed their findings on their cellular telephone and asked for the latest on the six men who had transferred at St. Louis.

"No trail," their office answered.

"Have we confirmed they made their connection to Tulsa?"

"They made it all right," came the reply. "Bound for the Southwest School of Aviation down there."

"And?"

"The TWA plane arrived on time. The six were on it, but the flight school says they never showed up on campus."

Panama City, Florida
2:55 p.m.

The overhead door of the hangar creaked and rose into its housing, and a small tractor drove inside. The driver stopped in front of the Sabreliner, got out, and attached a tow bar to the jet's nose gear. The two pilots in the cockpit nodded at him. The driver put the tractor into reverse. The Sabreliner started to roll. Its number-one engine was already turning.

The jet taxied away and proceeded to the end of the narrow strip. Without waiting, it turned onto the runway and began its takeoff. It lifted into the humid air of the afternoon and banked toward the southeast.

Cape Canaveral
3:04 p.m.

ABC-TV estimated that over a million people had positioned themselves in cars and boats on the roads and lagoons and other viewing areas around Merritt Island. Including the presidential entourage, there would be another two thousand witnesses to the launch from the VIP bleachers. Live television would beam the event to hundreds of millions around the world. One announcer assured viewers that the launch would be shown on a split screen so it wouldn't interfere with the afternoon's bowl games.

An hour earlier, the six astronauts had shaken hands with the handover/ingress team and had entered the crew compartment of *Encounter*. They had taken their positions, four on the flight deck and two on the middeck. One hundred and forty-three thousand gallons of liquid oxygen, at a temperature of minus 297°F, had been forced into the external tank. The filling of 383,000 gallons of liquid hydrogen was now being completed.

Andries and Stewart removed the Velcro-backed cue cards from the flight-data file and attached them to the instrument panel.

"*Encounter*, this is Launch Control. Radio check on Channel 2. Over."

Andries keyed his microphone. "Roger, Launch Control. Loud and clear."

The same communications check was conducted with Mission Control at the Johnson Spaceflight Center in Houston. The astronauts continued their preflight checklist.

"*Encounter*, ready abort advisory check."

The light on the panel in front of Andries illuminated, dimmed, then went out.

"Check satisfactory," the flight commander reported.

The side hatch was closed at 3:06 p.m.

"Side hatch closed and secure, gentlemen."

"Roger, copy."

Panama City, Florida
3:25 p.m.

The departure controller acknowledged the new blip on his screen.

"Sabreliner Three Zero Seven Seven Alpha, radar contact, fly heading 150, join the Panama City 103-degree radial, on course. Climb and maintain Flight Level 330."

"Roger all that. Seven Seven Alpha."

A commuter flight inbound to Panama City was descending through six thousand when the departing Sabreliner was called out as traffic.

"Metro 1039, traffic two o'clock, three miles, a Sabreliner climbing through three thousand. It'll pass below you on your starboard side."

"Metro 1039, we're lookin'."

Thirty seconds later, the Metro first officer spotted the silver jet, abeam and slightly below.

"Tallyho the Air Force, three o'clock."

"Ah, it's not Air Force. But, roger, 1039."

"Hey, man, if he's not one of our fly boys, why's he's got the Air Force insignia and 'U.S. AIR FORCE' on the fuselage?"

"Metro 1039, say again?"

"Approach, if that's not an Air Force Sabreliner, I need an eye exam."

The controller punched a button that opened a landline with nearby Tyndall Air Force Base.

"Tyndall, this is Panama City Tracon. We've got a departing Sabreliner, reportedly with Air Force markings, heading for the Cape. But it's not filed as Air Force. Do you know anything about it?"

The Tyndall controller checked for a moment. "Negative. What's his call?"

"3077 Alpha."

"Where'd he come out of?"

"A private airport northeast of here. Picked up his IFR clearance in the air."

"OK, let me get back with you." He clicked off.

Less than three minutes later, Tyndall was back. "There's no such aircraft registered with the Air Force."

Tulsa
Friday, January 1, Midafternoon

A persistent wind buffeted the parked Street Department sand truck. Snow grains tapped against the windshield of the yellow vehicle and melted. An occasional sweep of the wipers cleared the moisture from the glass. Inside, two men sat in silence. The driver fingered the handle of a leather carrying case and surveyed the deserted residential street. The other man tapped a cellular telephone against his leg.

Jack watched the departing guests from his front door. He waited until the chatting aunts, uncles, cousins, and the McVeys were inside their cars before he waved one more time and went back inside. Their presence meant so much to him. He was glad they'd be around for a while longer. As he walked toward the kitchen, his daughter blew past him and struggled into her coat.

"Hey, where are *you* going?"

"The hotel, then a movie," Rachel replied. "Aunt Anne invited me. She said it's our secret. I'm going to pick her up, and I'm late."

"But she just left. Why didn't you go with . . . " Jack rolled his eyes as he caught on to the plan. "Of course, the car. She doesn't have one, and you have an underused driver's license. How silly of me." He grinned and helped her with her coat. "OK, have a good time, but don't drive the way you run through the house."

Rachel looked at her father as she grabbed the doorknob. "I promise. See you in a couple of hours. Love ya." He tossed back an errant lock of his steel-flecked hair. Her smile was like sunshine on his face.

In the kitchen, Jack accepted a cup of fresh coffee from Flora, who remained silent, almost sullen. Then he headed down the hall toward his study.

Jack leaned over his rosewood desk and considered the computer data from Norman's files. He shook his head at the nine pages of single-spaced information and sat down. He pulled himself toward his desk and picked up the first sheet.

"What in the hell is that little pervert up to?"

Jack stared at the paper. It was labeled "Barclays," and it showed thirty-six entries. The deposit dates were every ten days or so over the past year. Jack ran his finger down the columns. The initial monthly totals were small, $1,600 to $8,400 in their U.S. equivalents. The most recent ones were £5,500, £6,500, and £10,000.

"Unbelievable."

He thumbed through the other pages and calculated that, starting six months earlier, the monthly averages for all the deposits had climbed to nearly $1.5 million. A million and a half every thirty days? *"Damn,* where's it coming from?" He looked out the window of his study. Better yet, why?

Jack was familiar with most of the traditional sources of the funds reflected in the ministry's American bank accounts. They were small contributors whose donations were carefully logged so they could be contacted later for more. But these foreign accounts, and amounts, had been kept from him.

"And who sent this information to the FBI?"

His telephone sounded. Jack reached over.

"Hello?"

"Mr. Stroud?"

"Yes."

"Hi, how are you doing today?" The caller continued without waiting for an answer. "I'm with the Oklahoma Center for the Homeless. You know there're a lot of people around town who don't have . . . "

"Oh, I'm sorry," Jack interrupted him. "I already give to a number of charities. But thank you for calling." He replaced the receiver and stood up. Hate to do that, but enough is enough. He looked out at his snowy lawn. The telephone rang again. Jack frowned and turned to pick up the receiver.

"Mr. Stroud?" It was the same voice.

"Yes, and I told you, *no!"* Jack bent forward and slammed the phone down in its cradle. The glass expanse behind him exploded, and shards sprayed the room as a bullet ripped across his scalp. Jack toppled over his desk and lost consciousness.

Central Florida
3:29 p.m.

"Sabreliner 3077A, this is Jacksonville Center. Over."

"Go, Jacksonville."

"Are you Air Force?"

"Affirmative. At least we will be once the techs in Florida put in the new avionics. Got the plane from Customs a couple of weeks ago."

"Seven Seven Alpha, then why aren't you filed as Air Force?"

"Uh, regs, you know. We're not supposed to file as military until we're on line with the new equipment. So we just used the old numbers."

The controller looked up from his screen.

"Now what?"

His supervisor kept chewing his gum. "I'd better run a fast check with Oke City."

The emergency telephone number for the Federal Aviation Administration in Oklahoma City rang twice. Within seconds, a woman drew up the registration information for 3077A.

"November Three Zero Seven Seven Alpha . . . first registered May 23, 1985. Original owner, CNE Technologies of Framingham, Massachusetts. Sold to Arturo Sánchez y Vega of Monterrey, Mexico, on March 7, 1990. He's owned it since. Home base, El Paso."

"Nothing about any ownership by the U.S. Customs Service?"

"No, sir. That would be recorded here."

The supervisor thanked the woman and disconnected. He immediately punched in the number for Tyndall Air Force Base.

"Give me the base commander, please."

Once the secretary was on the line, the supervisor identified himself and the nature of the call. She put him through.

"You're sure the plane's got our markings?" the commander asked.

"Yes, sir. And if they're not Air Force, just who are they?"

"That, 'Mister FAA,' we definitely intend to find out."

St. Francis Hospital, Tulsa
Midafternoon

Jack regained consciousness as the ambulance rolled from his driveway. He struggled against the restraints and focused his eyes. A uniformed paramedic patted his shoulder.

"Relax, man. You're lucky to be alive."

Jack's head ached.

"Got a nice new part in your hair, though."

Jack could hear the alternating pulse of the siren. It sounded surrealistic through the padded insulation of the ambulance. He attempted to ask a question, but his words were muffled by a mask on his face.

"Oxygen, sir." The technician shook his head. "Don't talk. You'll be just fine."

Jack looked up and noticed an IV bag swaying on a metal support. He closed his eyes.

The ambulance slipped and shuddered through the grooves in the icy streets. Its side-to-side motions caused Jack to grimace. Within minutes the vehicle braked and pulled into the emergency receiving area of St. Francis Hospital. The paramedic opened the doors from the inside and jumped out. The driver came around and released the stretcher, and the two men pulled it out. Jack kept his eyes shut during the jarring motions.

"Trauma Room Two. Take him to Trauma Room Two," a woman's voice yelled from inside the hospital.

Jack sensed the bright overhead lights of the emergency room, and he smelled the pungent odor of disinfectants. He squeezed open a look. Nurses and orderlies stared at him.

"Mr. Stroud?" A younger man's face came into view. He smiled. "I'm Dr. Paul Cunningham. You've received a gunshot wound to the head. But you're very fortunate. The paramedics report that the bullet only grazed the top of your skull. Your EKG and vital signs are normal. We'll need to take some blood and an X-ray. Then we'll fix you up." The physician took Jack's hand and squeezed it.

Two men lifted Jack onto a cold stainless-steel examination table. A portable X-ray unit was wheeled alongside, and a technician positioned the machine against Jack's head and took a series of pictures. A nurse prepped his arm and inserted a needle. Dr. Cunningham leaned over and carefully peeled off the bandages. He probed at the wound for a minute. Jack winced.

"Well, Mr. Stroud, I think you'll get out of this with a few stitches . . . and, of course, a headache."

Jack smiled but kept his eyes closed. Dr. Cunningham began to suture. The intravenous analgesic had done its work. Jack felt no pain as his scalp was sewn back together.

"I don't see anything critical," the physician commented when he finished. "But it *is* a five-inch laceration. You were knocked out and suffered a severe concussion. I'm going to admit you for observation. A day or so, OK?"

Jack slowly opened his eyes. "Sure."

"Who's your personal physician?"

Jack forced the sluggish reply through his dry mouth. "Leland Marks."

"I'll get in touch with him. But before we take you to your room, there's someone who wants to see you." Dr. Cunningham stepped aside.

"Daddy?"

"Oh, precious." Jack reached for his daughter with his free arm. Rachel approached hesitantly and leaned over him. There were tears in her eyes. She lowered her head to his chest and tucked her arms around his waist.

"Daddy, I don't want you to die," she cried. "Not you, *too.*"

Jack immediately thought of what her horror must have been. "Oh, no, sweetie. I'm not going to die." He held her tightly. "I'll be out of here tomorrow." He looked behind her and saw two policemen. "Are you here by yourself?"

"No, everyone's in the waiting room. Uncle Arthur and Aunt Fran, and Uncle Edgar and Aunt Jenny, and Aunt Anne. Flora called the hotel, and she's here, too, but they wouldn't let anyone come in."

Jack took a deep breath. If someone wanted to kill him, they might want to kill his daughter, too. Maybe even his brothers and sister and their families.

"You go home and stay there. Don't leave without my permission. Understand?"

Rachel nodded, then started to say something. The doctor touched her shoulder.

"That's all for now, young lady."

Rachel kissed her father and turned to wave before she disappeared down the hall. She looked so much like Laura. He felt a peculiar, paradoxical ache in his soul . . . half joy, half sorrow.

"Sir?" The two policemen moved forward.

Dr. Cunningham intervened and shook his head. "Sorry, not here. You can question him for a few minutes in his room."

"Your goddamned imbecile drivers took him to St. Francis, where we'll have one fucking hell of a time getting to him before he tells everything to the police."

"For Christ's sake, the dispatcher ordered them to St. Francis!"

"Since when did they start following orders? And you only winged the sonofabitch. A clear, no-nonsense shot, in broad daylight, and you didn't make it."

"Oh, back off. We'll get him. Anyway, they got the papers out of his house, so it'll only be his word against yours."

Aboard Air Force One
3:31 p.m.

The president stared out the window of his private quarters as the blue-and-white Boeing 747-200 slowed and began its descent. It passed directly over Daytona Beach, seventy miles north of Patrick Air Force Base. He tightened his seat belt. "I was in tall clover with the polls and the media a week ago." He watched a few dozen boats traversing the Intracoastal Waterway. "Now the whole country's turned upside down."

"Sir, are you going to say something to them?" Press Secretary Kevin Howard stood in the doorway.

The president looked up. "About Kansas City?" He nodded. "After the launch. But just the statement."

"The networks are reporting that the shuttle's official mission is only a cover. Are you going to address that?"

"No."

Howard grimaced. "Well, they're really digging into me on that one."

"Kevin, I'm only going to deal with the shopping center. No questions from the media afterward. They'd want to talk about everything, and I wouldn't know what the hell to say."

The press secretary looked toward the ceiling and pulled the door shut.

The heavy aircraft banked and descended toward the runway at Patrick. The landing gear rumbled down, and Air Force One settled onto the concrete. As the 747 decelerated, the president gripped the padded armrests and gazed at the nearby swells on the slate-gray Atlantic. Three Coast Guard patrol boats bobbed offshore.

"Time's running out on me, boys," he spoke under his breath as he unfastened his seat belt. He gathered his NASA briefing papers. "I need some good news. You'd better make this a beautiful launch."

The jumbo jet turned off the runway and taxied slowly to the ramp. It came to a stop in front of the operations building, and a stairway was driven to the forward door. The red carpet was already in place. Over a thousand Air Force personnel and their dependents stood in the warm breeze of the sunny afternoon and waved American flags. As the president stepped out, the band struck up "Hail to the Chief." He smiled and filled his lungs with the salty air.

Central Florida
3:42 p.m.

Two single-seat F-16E Fighting Falcon interceptors of the 56th Tactical Fighter Wing lifted off together from MacDill AFB, six miles south of Tampa. Each was armed with two AIM-9R infrared-guided Sidewinder air-to-air missiles and a 20mm Gatling gun. As the sleek fighters, twenty-six feet apart, roared into the late afternoon sky on their afterburners, the weapons controller at MacDill passed along the latest appraisal from an E-2C Hawkeye command-and-control aircraft over the Gulf of Mexico off central Florida.

"Scorpion Three-One, the bogey is level at Angels 33 over Cross City, bearing three-four-eight degrees and one-zero-zero nautical miles. It's maintaining a heading of one-two-two degrees. Jacksonville Center has just reported that it's no longer responding to transmissions. Over."

After a few seconds, the reply was a laconic, "Roger. Three-One."

The Air Force pilots were under orders to force the Sabreliner to land at MacDill. It was not to be allowed within fifty miles of Cape Canaveral.

Forty miles from the target, the pulse-Doppler radar systems of both F-16s located and locked on the Sabreliner as it approached Ocala.

"Good contact," the flight leader radioed to his wingman. "We'll execute an over-and-under cutoff from his two o'clock position."

The F-16s quickly made the formation adjustment. At slightly over five hundred knots, they were now less than two minutes from visual contact. Both pilots watched the converging blip on their screens. They slowed to three hundred knots.

"Tallyho the bogey!" the flight leader called out.

From a mile out, the Sabreliner looked like a toy airplane. An instant later, they had passed it.

"If they didn't see us, they're blind."

As they circled to come up behind, the flight leader transmitted on 127.45 MHz, the VHF frequency Jacksonville Center was using to try to communicate with the jet.

"Sabreliner 3077A, this is the United States Air Force. You have been intercepted. You are to comply with our instructions. Do you read?"

There was no response.

The two fighters came up on either side of the Sabreliner. The Air Force markings on its fuselage were unmistakable. The flight leader pulled ahead and positioned himself a hundred feet in front and to the left of the intercepted jet. His wingman remained on the right side and slightly behind.

"Sabreliner 77A. You are to divert to MacDill Air Force Base. You will follow me. Do you read?"

The Air Force pilot could see the pilots of the Sabreliner. Both were looking at him. Neither made any gesture of acknowledgment. The radio remained silent.

"Check 121.5 and 243.0," the leader instructed his wingman. "Maybe they're on one of the emergency frequencies."

Still nothing.

The flight leader rocked his wings as a signal. "Sabreliner 77A, you have been intercepted. Follow me."

The Sabreliner continued without acknowledging.

"No joy on the signal," the leader transmitted.

Suddenly the Sabreliner pulled into a near-vertical climb. The maneuver caught the Air Force pilots by surprise.

"Shit!" the wingman exclaimed.

Both started to climb in pursuit when the Sabreliner streaked past them in a dive. They pushed their aircraft down and accelerated.

"Hostile aircraft! Repeat, hostile!" the leader radioed. "Close in and prepare to fire warning shots."

The Sabreliner had dropped more than 10,000 feet, and its speed was approaching the sound barrier. The three airplanes were now sixty-five miles from the Cape.

"Closer! Closer!" the flight leader yelled to his wingman. "We've got less than two minutes to stop him."

The Sabreliner continued its dive. At 12,000 feet above the ground, it leveled and began a roll to the left. Then it became inverted. The fighters closed to within a thousand yards, and the leader pressed the switch and fired a five-second burst from his cannon. The warning bullets streaked by the fleeing jet. The Sabreliner rolled upright and pulled into a steep climb.

"Missile locked on!" the flight leader yelled as he heard a growling tone in his headset. The target was centered in the fluorescent green heads-up display projection on his canopy. He pressed a button on his control yoke. A nine-foot-long Sidewinder whooshed from its wingtip mount. Almost immediately, pieces of burning material tumbled past the pursuing fighters.

"Is he hit?" the wingman called out.

"Flares! He's launched flares!"

The heat-seeking Sidewinder homed in on one of the diversionary blazes and missed the Sabreliner by a quarter mile. Both fighters pulled up in a climbing pursuit.

"Can you get him?"

The flight leader's question went unanswered as his wingman launched both Sidewinders.

State of Chihuahua, Mexico
Midafternoon

Two sentries crouched in the cracks of the sandy bluff above the Río Grande at El Porvenir and peered through their binoculars. A brisk wind whistled through the wide valley and stirred up irregular eddies of sand. The men continued staring into Texas as four others walked up behind them.

"Clear, radius of ten kilometers," one of the observers called out. "One hour. No patrols." He sank back on his heels and glanced at his watch. "Pickup in five."

The other lookout kept his vigil.

"Aircraft!"

In the cold and cloudless azure sky, a small silver airplane came into view a mile to the east. It banked slowly and flew north, staying away from Mexican airspace. The fading sound of its engine was barely perceptible above the shrill wind.

"Not Border Patrol."

The observer with the wristwatch stood up. "Probably real estate people, looking at property near Esperanza." He checked the time, then pointed toward the river.

"Now!"

The four men ran down the incline and waded across the shallow depths. On the other side, they boarded a waiting Jeep Wagoneer.

Cape Canaveral
3:43 p.m.

Commentators in the network and cable television booths overlooking the launch area continued briefing their global audiences. Invited astronauts, engineers, and other experts provided background "color."

"The six *Encounter* astronauts boarded the shuttle nearly an hour and a half ago," the ABC science reporter recapped. "They earlier enjoyed a leisurely lunch of roast beef sandwiches on French rolls, potato chips, fresh fruit salad, and chocolate ice cream, with cookies and milk."

The CNN woman provided more insight.

"Flight Commander Robert Charles Andries is a Navy captain with a master's degree in aeronautical engineering from Penn State. He's a five-time veteran of shuttle launches, and he commanded the last Discovery mission. He and his wife, Susan, live in Clear Lake City, Texas, and they have three children." Family snapshots on the screen accompanied her presentation of Andries's bio.

"Pilot B. Z., for Byron Zachary, Stewart is a lieutenant colonel in the United States Air Force. 'Buzz' has an M.S. degree in aerospace engineering from the University of Colorado. He was the pilot of last May's Atlantis mission, his first flight in the orbiter. He and Michelle have four children and also live near the Johnson Spaceflight Center at Clear Lake City."

The CNN report continued with more photographs.

"There are two Mission Specialists aboard *Encounter,* Catherine F. Gorney and Rodney I. Allen. Katy Gorney is a lieutenant commander in the United States Navy, with a Ph.D. in astrophysics from MIT. She is married, lives in Newton, Massachusetts, and has one child. Rodney Allen, of Alexandria, Virginia, is a lieutenant colonel in the Air Force. He earned a doctorate in astronomy from the University of Michigan. Colonel Allen is not married.

"Astronauts Gorney and Allen spent fifty-three days last year orbiting the earth in *Atlantis,* a record for the shuttle program. These two mission specialists will launch the Sentinel probes.

"The two payload specialists are Howland 'Hal' Messer and Margaret Simmons, both civilian employees of Jet Propulsion Laboratory in Pasadena, California. Messer has his master's in engineering science from Florida State, and Simmons graduated from the University of Texas at Austin, where she earned her master's degree in aerospace engineering. Messer and Simmons played a role in the planning and assembly of the probes. Both made two rides each in *Discovery.*"

The CNN commentator looked at a monitor to her right.

"And, ladies and gentlemen, here comes the president."

3:56 p.m.

Nine motorcycle police escorts led the president's motorcade from Patrick Air Force Base to the VIP viewing area three miles from Launch Complex 39A and *Encounter.* As the seven-car procession rolled to a stop in front of the main bleachers, five members of the Secret Service's Presidential Protective Division jumped from their trailing GMC Suburban van and surrounded the elongated black Cadillac. The men took positions in front and at the four quadrants, their backs to the car. Raymond Shaffer, chief of the Secret Service's White House detail, stepped from the limousine and looked around. After a deliberate visual reconnoiter, he transmitted a message, then opened the right rear door. The president emerged and buttoned his jacket. He waved and walked to shake hands with the NASA administrator and members of the astronauts' families. With a gesture toward the microphone, the administrator invited him to say a few words. The chief executive turned first for an admiring look at the shuttle, then walked for the podium.

Suddenly the president bounded to his left. The Secret Service tore ahead and attempted to reestablish a secure perimeter. The president jogged to a rope line and began shaking hands with a row of excited Boy Scouts and adult leaders. Their troop had won NASA's first prize in its high-profile name-the-new-shuttle contest. They'd had to wait until its third launch, because their school was in session when *Encounter* made its first two trips. Family members and other supporters of the boys pressed in behind to greet the president.

The Secret Service had a policy that it attempted to enforce without exception: The president was to resist gripping the hands of well-wishers when he delved into crowds. At the most, he could touch people's hands, then move on quickly. Since a determined wacko, or worse, could pull the chief executive into the crowd and out of the perimeter of protection, "pressing the flesh" had a very limited definition in the Secret Service dictionary.

As the president proceeded along the line of admirers, one scout leader grabbed his hand and held on enthusiastically. He pumped it up and down with fervor. The Secret Service moved in on the offensive. One agent leaned forward slightly. With the back of his hand, he delivered a stinging slap against the man's testicles. The scout leader abruptly dropped the president's hand and stood mute for a second. As the procession moved on, the man started waving again, weakly. The Secret Service had determined long ago that few such individuals ever realized what had happened.

The president held the microphone and looked across at the hopeful faces. A noisy group of reporters started in.

"Sir, what are you going to do about the shopping center tragedy? Is it true that international terrorists are responsible for the attacks of the past week? Will you . . . ?"

"Ladies and gentlemen," the chief executive ignored the questions and began. "In less than twenty minutes, six of our finest space professionals will lift off on a historic voyage—that of sending mankind's first listening devices toward the very heart of our Milky Way galaxy."

"Why are you refusing to answer?" one correspondent yelled. The president went on.

"In our continual quest to learn more about the immense universe, and our place in it, this launch will be another of many missions of mankind outside the solar system. It's a gallant effort, and all of us can be proud of our astronauts who are representing not only Americans but all inhabitants of this home planet we affectionately call Earth."

"What's your response to Homer Jenkins's charge of a cover-up?"

The president concluded, "May Almighty God be with our astronauts."

"*Encounter,* this is Launch Control. Clocks started again after the programmed ten-minute hold. We're T minus nineteen and counting."

"Roger, Control."

On his keyboard, Flight Commander Andries punched the OPS-1 flight program into one of the five onboard computers. He reached over and reset the ERR LOG switch and looked up at CRT-1, the cathode-ray screen in front of him, for evidence of any guidance-navigation or control-system faults. None were indicated. Andries then entered "SPEC 9 9 PRO" into the computer, and *Encounter's* launch trajectory was immediately displayed on CRT 2, to his right.

"Launch Control, this is *Encounter,*" he transmitted. "Flight plan has been loaded. We're now loading it into the BFS. Over."

"Roger, *Encounter,* we copy."

As the two pilots entered the flight plan into the backup flight system, a second abort check was conducted by Mission Control.

"Looking good," Andries acknowledged after the ABORT light illuminated, dimmed, and went out three separate times. "Another smooth countdown, you guys. At this rate, we won't even ruffle a feather on one of those wild eagles out there." He turned toward Stewart. "Can't get any easier than this." Andries reached into the top pocket of his flight suit and withdrew a credit card–size photograph. He looked at the color representations of his wife and three children and fixed his eyes on their smiling faces. "This mission's for you."

Stewart got his attention with a raised hand. His partner's fingers were crossed. Andries grinned and returned the picture to his pocket.

The three aircraft streaked toward the launch complex. At 5,600 feet and less than twenty miles from the Cape, the Sabreliner banked to the left and aimed directly for the exposed shuttle.

"Get him!" the wingman's voice crackled. "Damn it, sir, you've got to get him!"

The sweating flight leader maneuvered his F-16 within a thousand yards of the Sabreliner and centered the target on the canopy display. He pressed the launch button for his remaining Sidewinder.

"Take this, you son of a bitch!"

Seconds passed. Nothing.

He pressed again. And again.

"Jesus Christ! It won't fire!"

The flight leader forced the throttle ahead. As his F-16 screamed past the left side of the Sabreliner, he glared at the two pilots inside and stabbed the rudder pedal to the right. "See you in hell, assholes." The nose of his fighter tore into the port side of the Sabreliner and ripped away a section of the fuselage behind the wing. The impaled jet yawed to the left, and the

Air Force leader fired his cannon directly into its exposed belly. The explosion obliterated both aircraft.

"*Encounter,* you're 'go' for launch."
"Roger, Control. Event timer started."

As the fireball boiled outward, chunks of debris smashed into the trailing F-16, sending it spinning out of control. The burning remains of the Sabreliner and the lead F-16 exited beneath the expanding orange-and-black cloud and cascaded toward the earth at nearly five hundred miles an hour. A quarter mile behind, the crippled F-16 erupted in flames and spiraled down in a separate trajectory. The second Air Force pilot ejected as his fighter tumbled through a thousand feet.

The flaming pieces of the first two planes fell and slammed into thousands of spectators along Indian River and Merritt Island and along both sides of Highway 402 north of the Vehicle Assembly Building. The booms of the impacting debris only partially masked the screams of terror. The disabled F-16 spun onward, producing an unearthly whistling sound as it careened toward the ground.

"Cover and evacuate!"
The crisp order from the shift leader in the GMC van snapped through the molded earpieces of twenty-four Secret Service men and women. Two agents grabbed the president from his observation box and started him toward the limousine. Two others immediately moved ahead and formed the front half of a protective diamond-shaped wedge. The president looked quizzically at his security men.

"Emergency, sir," one replied as he pushed firmly against the president's back. "Move!"

"We've got the Principal," the second agent spoke under his breath as the four rushed the chief executive toward the boxy, armor-plated vehicle. A special UHF transmitter picked up his words from the vibrations in his skull.

"Exit south," a voice returned. "Expedite!"

The abort light on the console flashed on, and a frantic message came from Launch Control. "Emergency abort! Evacuate! Evacuate!" The command pierced the calm on the flight deck. "Master Alarm!"

"Say again?" Andries couldn't believe his ears.

"Abort! Bob, get out *now!*"

"Abort! Let's go!" Andries yelled into his helmet microphone and released his harness. Stewart did the same and looked over his shoulder at mission specialists Gorney and Allen. They were already out of their seats and scrambling for the access ladder. Payload specialists Messer and Simmons, on the mid-deck, had already disengaged themselves from their restraints and were at the hatch. They opened the heavy circular door and pressed it outward.

The orbiter's crew access arm, programmed to retract within seconds, was still positioned against *Encounter,* and the six astronauts bounded across it into the White Room. They ran to the far wall of the enclosure and threw open the door of the emergency exit system. Five metal baskets, each attached to a slidewire from the fixed service structure to the entrance of an underground bunker 1,200 feet away, hung in readiness.

Andries stabbed his hand toward the cages. "Get in!"

Two astronauts boarded each basket. They released the brakes and careened downward. Andries and Stewart were the last to swing away from the tower. As they plunged from the poised shuttle, Andries looked to his left and saw the conflagration rolling out of the sky toward them. It was less than a thousand yards away. The baskets whisked into the landing zone and were yanked to a stop by arresting nets. The six astronauts jumped out and ran for the bunker. They had been out of *Encounter* for forty-seven seconds.

The burning F-16 hit the ground at the base of the launch complex in a flat spin and broke into three fiery parts. The largest, the fuselage, skipped ahead and began tumbling end over end toward the shuttle. Its white-hot remains bounced upward and slammed into the right solid rocket booster, puncturing it and igniting the rubbery propellant of the fifteen-story missile at a half-dozen points. A million pounds of aluminum-powder fuel and ammonium-perchlorate oxidizer flamed into life. Fire jetted out of the side and the nozzle of the SRB. It grew in intensity and began to rock the entire 4.6-million-pound shuttle combination.

In a slow-motion effect, *Encounter* shifted, hesitated, then fell ponderously into the steel girders of the main service structure. As it collapsed, the massive external fuel tank buckled and ruptured, and a fireball from the igniting liquid hydrogen engulfed the launch area.

At the monitors in the protective bunker, the astronauts looked on in shock. The rest of the world watched in horror.

Cape Canaveral
Saturday, January 2, 5:40 a.m.

American and foreign television remained with the disaster throughout the night. National Public Radio, the BBC, and the Voice of America presented special five-minute summaries from Kennedy Space Center on the half hour, while the wire services poured out continuous updates. An Associated Press writer sat with his laptop computer in the back of the NASA press room and tapped out the latest dispatch.

1-2, 05:42 ET >>>URGENT

HUNDREDS DIE, PRESIDENT SAFE IN FLORIDA CATASTROPHE

(COMPLETE WRITETHRU, UPDATING THROUGHOUT)

CAPE CANAVERAL, FLA. (AP) - AT LEAST 742 SPECTATORS DIED AND 1,300 OTHERS WERE INJURED YESTERDAY AFTERNOON AT THE KENNEDY SPACE CENTER WHEN A U.S. AIR FORCE F-16 JET FIGHTER AND AN UNIDENTIFIED PLANE COLLIDED AND FELL INTO CROWDS AWAITING THE LIFTOFF OF THE SPACE SHUTTLE ENCOUNTER. THE PRESIDENT AND A DOZEN MEMBERS OF THE HOUSE AND SENATE WERE SEATED IN A VIP VIEWING AREA NEARBY BUT ESCAPED INJURY.

ENCOUNTER'S SIX ASTRONAUTS EVACUATED SAFELY SECONDS BEFORE A SEPARATE AIR FORCE JET CRASHED IN FLAMES AT THE BASE OF THE LAUNCH TOWER AND SENT FIERY DEBRIS INTO THE SPACE SHUTTLE, IGNITING ONE OF ITS SOLID ROCKET BOOSTERS. THE $2.9 BILLION SHUTTLE AND ITS $2.8 BILLION CARGO WERE DESTROYED IN THE RESULTING EXPLOSION.

The AP reporter grimaced at what he had written. "Hey, CNN. How far away did they end up taking the injured?"

His compatriot across the aisle looked up from a stack of photographs.

"Orlando. Melbourne, too, according to Westbrook. A lot of criticals with second- and third-degree burns and impact wounds."

HUNDREDS OF THE INJURED, MANY IN CRITICAL CONDITION, WERE ADMITTED TO HOSPITALS AS FAR AWAY AS FIFTY MILES. MOST INJURIES WERE REPORTED TO BE BURNS AND PUNCTURE WOUNDS.

THE DISASTER OCCURRED AT 4:07 P.M. EASTERN STANDARD TIME, NINE MINUTES PRIOR TO THE SCHEDULED LIFTOFF OF THE SHUTTLE. ACCORDING TO EYEWITNESSES, TWO AIR FORCE JETS WERE PURSUING AN AIRCRAFT THAT HAD INTRUDED INTO THE RESTRICTED ZONE OF THE SPACE COMPLEX. IT IS NOT YET KNOWN WHY THE THIRD PLANE WAS IN THE VICINITY OF CAPE CANAVERAL. SOURCES SAY THAT INTERCEPTION OF RADIO TRANSMISSIONS BETWEEN THE AIR FORCE JETS AND FEDERAL AVIATION ADMINISTRATION CONTROLLERS INDICATED THAT THE UNIDENTIFIED AIRCRAFT DID NOT RESPOND TO ORDERS TO STAY AWAY FROM THE AREA.

The AP man picked up a map. He positioned his thumb on Merritt Island and rotated his forefinger to the Cape.

THE COLLISION OF THE TWO PLANES OCCURRED OVER MERRITT ISLAND, FOUR MILES FROM LAUNCH COMPLEX 39A. THE DEBRIS FELL INTO CROWDS, ESTIMATED AT 100,000 PEOPLE, INSIDE THE PERIMETER OF KENNEDY SPACE CENTER.

THE PRESIDENT, NASA ADMINISTRATOR RICHARD C. MOORE, FLORIDA SENATOR AND MRS. CARLTON LEE, AND FLORIDA CONGRESSMAN ARCHIE DEL VECCHIO WERE HURRIED FROM THEIR SEATS AS THE FALLING AIRCRAFT CAME INTO VIEW. THERE WAS LITTLE OR NO ADVANCE WARNING OF THE IMPENDING CATASTROPHE.

THE PRESIDENT WAS RUSHED TO PATRICK AIR FORCE BASE, WHERE HE BOARDED AIR FORCE ONE FOR THE RETURN FLIGHT TO WASHINGTON. WHITE HOUSE PRESS SECRETARY KEVIN HOWARD SAID THE PRESIDENT WOULD ADDRESS THE NATION ABOUT THE DISASTER AT 11:00 EST THIS MORNING.

The writer repeated the conclusion that had gone out over the wires earlier.

HOMER JENKINS, SPEAKER OF THE HOUSE OF REPRESENTATIVES, ANNOUNCED THAT THERE WOULD BE AN IMMEDIATE CONGRESSIONAL INVESTIGATION OF THE FLORIDA TRAGEDY.

"THIS IS ANOTHER TERRIFYING ATTACK AGAINST AMERICA, AND WE'RE GOING TO FIND OUT WHO'S BEHIND THESE ACTS."

JENKINS CALLED ON THE PRESIDENT TO TELL EVERYTHING HE KNOWS ABOUT THE PERSONS OR GROUPS RESPONSIBLE FOR THE RECENT OUTBREAKS OF TERRORISM ACROSS THE LAND.

"THIRTEEN THOUSAND LIVES HAVE BEEN SNUFFED OUT AND 8 BILLION DOLLARS IN PROPERTY DAMAGE SUFFERED IN THESE VICIOUS INCIDENTS OVER THE PAST WEEK." JENKINS ADDED, "THERE'S A MAJOR CONSPIRACY AGAINST THE UNITED STATES, AND THE AMERI-

CAN PEOPLE HAVE A RIGHT TO KNOW WHAT OUR PRESIDENT IS GOING TO DO ABOUT IT."

5:47 a.m.

Through the telephoto lens of the remote NASA camera, the television picture was shaky. From a distance of two thousand yards, it showed an artificially lighted landscape of destruction. Columns of water continued to pour from twelve-inch pipes and hoses onto the smoldering wreckage of *Encounter* and Launch Complex 39A. Figures in protective suits moved along the edge of the unearthly scene, stopping occasionally to pick at congealed remains.

The automatic camera panned jerkily across the ghostly devastation. Viewers saw little recognizable in the tangled metal. According to a spokesman for the space agency, most of the remains of the shuttle were "tightly commingled with the collapsed and blackened gantry and were consigned to weeks of anonymity before investigators could separate one from the other." Miraculously, the shuttle's left solid rocket booster had fallen away from the conflagration and had not ignited. It lay to the east of the ruins, its nose pointing out to sea . . . in the direction it was to have taken *Encounter*.

Two television networks ran amateur videotapes of the aerial collision that had produced the disaster. One, obtained from a spectator at Titusville, Florida, clearly showed the two pursuing fighters advancing on the Sabreliner. Another tape showed the lead F-16 nosing into the fleeing jet. ABC presented graphic computer reconstructions of the flight paths of the three planes, starting over Sanford, twenty miles north of Orlando.

CNN replayed the previous night's New York interview with the cockpit crew of a USAir Boeing 737. Their Flight 1168 had taken off from Orlando for LaGuardia minutes before the tragedy and had narrowly avoided a midair collision with one of the Air Force planes.

"Sir, you are . . . ?" The reporter held the microphone out to the shorter of the two men. There were four stripes on his epaulets.

"I'm Captain Riley Lambert, and this is First Officer Steven Dyer."

"And would you gentlemen please tell us what happened?"

Captain Lambert spoke first.

"We had just departed Orlando International and were northbound, climbing through 10,000 feet. I'd say we were about eighteen miles northeast of the airport when ATC—uh, that's air traffic control—told us we had traffic, with Air Force pursuit, at our ten o'clock position and ten miles away. I was flying the aircraft on that leg, and First Officer Dyer asked ATC for an altitude readout on the traffic. They reported that there were three planes involved and that they were continuing to change altitude. Their last confirmed altitude was 15,400 and descending. Steve and I started looking for the traffic at that time. I asked him to check with ATC about a possible vector to avoid any conflict. We were told the traffic would probably pass below us and remain at least five nautical miles away."

"And that's when all hell broke loose," First Officer Dyer interjected.

The reporter shifted the microphone to the second pilot. "What do you mean?"

"First," Dyer replied, "ATC warned us that the aircraft were making erratic course changes and their altitudes were not stabilized at all. I asked for their latest transponder readouts. I believe they were down to 9,350 feet, but climbing rapidly again. Then I spotted what looked like a corporate jet being chased by an F-16. Both were about a half mile ahead of us and at our altitude. All of a sudden I saw the other F-16 coming right at us, and I yelled, 'Dive!' Captain Lambert reacted instantly, and we barely slipped under the fighter. It couldn't have missed us by more than twenty feet." The first officer shook his head. "I don't know why the F-16 didn't take the top off our vertical stabilizer as he went over us. Anyway, we still had the fasten-seat-belt sign on, so, fortunately, no one was wandering around the cabin."

"Did you see the collision between the two planes?"

Captain Lambert leaned toward the microphone.

"Yes, we did. About thirty seconds later."

"Did you see the shuttle explode?"

Lambert nodded.

"The whole Cape lit up when it happened. The burst looked like the sun was rising out of the earth. We even felt the shock wave at 23,000 feet."

Libyan television reported that the accident was caused by Air Force pilots who flew through an established airway and collided with an innocent plane. In his latest summary for CNN's "World Report," the Tripoli correspondent at Cape Canaveral mocked accounts that the private plane was in restricted airspace. He reiterated his government's position that the tragedy was entirely the fault of the "incompetent" United States Air Force.

Shortly before dawn, NASA announced that a news conference would be held after the president's scheduled address to the nation.

St. Francis Hospital, Tulsa
7:04 a.m.

"Morning, Father." The nurse at the third-floor desk smiled at the tall, athletic-looking man with the Roman collar. She thought she detected Aqua Velva, an aftershave scent she hadn't encountered in years. "May I help you?"

He smiled back. "Yes, I'd like to see a parishioner of mine. Name's Stroud."

She noticed that his speech was clipped and precise, too much so for him to be from Oklahoma. British, perhaps. The nurse looked down at her patient record sheet and frowned. "Oh, I'm afraid that's going to be a bit difficult, Father. He's to have no outside visitors for a while."

"Hmm." The priest paused for a moment. "That's what they told me downstairs. Well, would you be so kind as to give me his room number? We'd like to send him some flowers, and the Altar Guild ladies *do* want to fix him a few goodies." He lowered his head and winked at her. "You know, candy and cookies. Please?"

The nurse hesitated. "I thought he was connected with Reuben Gentry's ministry. I mean, wasn't his wife Gentry's daughter?"

"You're so right, my dear. He *is* Gentry's son-in-law. Or was. But born and raised a Catholic." He gave her a look of complicity. "I don't believe his religious affiliation is allowed to be common knowledge."

The nurse took a deep breath and nodded. "I see."

"You'll keep Mr. Stroud's secret, won't you?"

"Certainly, Father."

"You wouldn't happen to be a Catholic yourself?"

The nurse beamed. "Why, yes, I am."

"Well, you know how we like to minister to our wandering sheep. Now, could you tell me his room number, dear lady?" The priest smiled and tapped his raised finger against his lips. "I won't tell a soul."

"I guess it's all right," the nurse responded. "He's in 335."

"Bless you."

The priest walked for the elevator and punched the "down" button. When the doors opened, he stepped in. He stopped on the second floor and went quickly to Room 235. The stairwell was twenty feet away. He entered it and sprinted up one flight, back into the quiet corridor of the third floor. Without looking toward the nurse's station, the priest moved deliberately to Room 335, which was marked by a "No Visitors" placard. He pressed against the door handle.

He opened the door, closed it quietly, and stood inside, listening. The room was dark. He reached into his jacket pocket with his right hand. Suddenly the overhead lights flashed on.

"Who the hell are *you?*" a voice demanded.

The priest stared at a big uniformed policeman sitting in the corner of the otherwise empty room. He pulled his hand from his jacket.

"Uh, I must have the wrong place." He turned and dashed out.

"Stop!"

The officer jumped up and ran for the door. The priest was already in the stairwell. The policeman pulled a portable transmitter to his mouth as the sound of footsteps faded down the stairs.

The Pentagon
9:32 a.m.

Defense Secretary Stephen McConnell walked into the reception area of his third-floor office on the "E" ring. The chairman of the Joint Chiefs of Staff, Admiral Gerald Chapman, the chiefs of staff of the Air Force and Army, the chief of Naval Operations, and the commandant of the Marines were waiting. They followed him into his spacious office.

"Please be seated," he indicated.

McConnell smoothed his hair and sat down himself. "We have to have this situation summarized and delivered to the White House within the hour." He introduced the JCS chairman with a wave of his arm. "Admiral Chapman."

The fifty-seven-year-old military leader stood and opened a brown leather sheath. He withdrew a sheet of paper and laid the carrying case on his chair. He pulled his reading glasses to the tip of his nose and began to paraphrase from the report.

"The basic facts are that a North American Rockwell Sabreliner, laden with explosives, successfully evaded interception by two Air Force F-16s out of MacDill and was terminated only after the pursuing flight leader intentionally collided with the unidentified aircraft less than four miles from the space shuttle. The resulting explosion killed the Air Force pilot and those in the Sabreliner, damaged the trailing F-16, and produced falling debris that killed a thousand-plus spectators. The crash of the second fighter destroyed the shuttle." The JCS chief removed his glasses.

"Mr. Secretary, we'll have a complete reconstruction and analysis of the accident within twenty-four hours."

"All right, but what about the NRO recon satellite that was also destroyed?"

Chapman took a deep breath and exhaled. "Sir, the KH-12 can't be replaced for ten weeks, at the earliest. Lockheed will have to build a completely new radar system. The rest they'll be able to fashion together with cannibalized parts from other satellites under development. NASA's going to be out of the orbiter business for a minimum of ninety days, probably more, but we can prepare for a Delta launch at Vandenberg by 19 March. That's simply the best we can do."

McConnell shook his head and leaned forward in his chair.

"Not good enough, Admiral. Look at this." The defense secretary picked up a file from his open briefcase and held it toward Chapman. "The CIA has come around to the FBI's position about the training source of these terrorist acts. From what they just got from their operatives in Lebanon, they now believe either an Iranian- or a Syrian-backed group, maybe even the Iraqis, could well be involved in yesterday's attack on the shuttle, as well as three other significant terrorist attacks of the past week. Possibly even the aircraft downing at Albuquerque and the shopping center torching."

McConnell hit the desk with his palm and stood up. "Gentlemen, we may have a genuine war on our hands right here at home, and if it has any relationship whatsoever with the crazies in the Middle East, we *must* have that intelligence capability as soon as possible." He looked directly at General Daniel Novak, the Air Force chief of staff. "That's still one of the responsibilities of the Air Force's Space Division, isn't it?" The frustration in McConnell's voice was palpable.

"Yes, sir, it is," Novak answered quickly. "Unfortunately, Mr. Secretary, as you know, because of the photographic resolution problems uncovered during the Iraqi war, we've gone back to the drawing board on some of this orbital hardware. I'll run the request-to-expedite back through. It may be possible to take ten to fourteen days off the assembly time, but I couldn't imagine much more than that."

McConnell started pacing. "This is national defense turned inside out. We *must* be able to access the new military transmissions between Teheran and Damascus, especially those going through the fiber-optic networks to those training centers in the Bekaa Valley. *If* that's where it's all coming from." He stopped and faced Admiral Chapman. "Still nothing out of the ordinary in the Caribbean? Any ingress or egress patterns associated with these terrorist acts?"

"No, sir. Nor in the Atlantic or in Mexico," the JCS chairman responded. "It's either a very well hidden operation, or it's not there at all. And there's nothing from satellite or radar. We're concluding it's just not there."

The defense secretary stood with his hands on his hips. Finally he exhaled loudly.

"Well, that's just great . . . the worst good-news-bad-news scenario possible. 'The good news, Mr. President, is there are no terrorists coming into the United States; the bad news is they're already here.'" He stabbed his index finger into the tab of his intercom. "Have our guests arrived?"

"Yes, sir," came the reply.

"Well, damn it, send them in."

McConnell thrust his hands into the pockets of his suit coat and looked at the military chiefs. No one moved. His office door swung open. The uniformed men rose, and the Secretary introduced the newcomers.

"You know the attorney general and the director of the FBI."

The two men entered and nodded their greetings. They shook hands with the Secretary of Defense and looked for a place to sit.

"We only have forty-two minutes to put this together," McConnell said in exasperation as he looked at his watch. "Please begin."

The attorney general gestured to the FBI director, who remained standing and began his report.

"We've just briefed the president on the legal, national security, and related implications of the immediate situation. This is the gist of what we told him." He nodded toward McConnell. "It's our opinion that an organized cadre of professionals, probably backed by international interests, is responsible for the four recent major acts of terrorism in this country: the Amtrak Metroliner derailment on December 28, the sabotage later that morning of the AirParis SST which killed Treasury Secretary Rowland, the killing of Transportation Secretary Nielsen, also last Monday, and the destruction of the space shuttle yesterday, an act we're treating as an attempt to assassinate the president. Our Counterterrorism Section is proceeding under the assumption that this group is operating out of a base somewhere within the United States."

McConnell shook his head. "Talk about déjà vu."

"Sir?" The director looked toward the Secretary.

McConnell nodded at the military men. "We were just talking about that possibility."

"But it's only their working opinion," the FBI director continued, "based on what they've put together so far. They like to take the most aggressive stance commensurate with the facts and the logical extensions of those facts." He shook his head. "They haven't convinced me yet, because they don't have a 'smoking gun.' But they make a good point, and it may prove to be prophetic. I've encouraged them to pursue it."

The defense secretary raised his eyebrows. "What's causing them to make that assumption?"

The FBI chief counted on two fingers. "One, there's the commonality in the types of targets—high profile for maximum political effect—and, two, it takes a lot of logistical coordination to carry out what they've done. Our Counterterrorism Section chief feels that's only possible if it's coming from an established source within the U.S. I've asked him about the variety of explosives used, but he doesn't see that as a negative. Could be planned to make it look like there are numerous, unconnected groups."

McConnell pushed himself back in the chair.

"Well, it makes all the sense in the world to *me*. This is what I've been worrying about for years. Having terrorists here is one thing; having their base here is quite another."

The director made eye contact with each man in the room. "Gentlemen, if there is one cohesive group, whether or not it's based domestically, and it's launched a concerted attack against the United States, then the downing of the chartered jetliner Tuesday night and the bombing of the shopping center on New Year's Eve would likely be its doing also."

He went on.

"This morning, an expedited laboratory check by our materials analysis people of the debris at Cape Canaveral showed that the probable cause of the explosion that destroyed the renegade Sabreliner was the detonation of a plastique explosive known as Gellex-4. From photographs of the fireball, we calculate that the plane carried at least seventy-five kilos of the Gellex. That would have completely leveled the Murrah Building in Oklahoma City, or, for that matter, the World Trade Center. This is the same explosive that blew up the SST last Monday and a station wagon under surveillance at El Paso yesterday morning, and it's a close, but stronger, cousin to Semtex, the explosive that brought down the Pan Am jumbo several years ago over Lockerbie, Scotland."

The FBI director walked in a tight circuit in front of McConnell's desk. He clasped his hands behind his back.

"Gellex-4 is not manufactured in the United States. We track what little is imported legally. A less powerful compound, Gellex-2, is used widely on construction sites around the country. But someone's bringing in—or *has* brought in—large quantities of the 'dash-4' product, apparently repackaging it here, and directing it at domestic targets. Finding out who that 'someone' is is the most important task the Bureau has ever undertaken."

He paused for a moment.

"We do know that Gellex-4 is the preferred explosive of some of the groups in Syria and Lebanon, it's shown up in the hands of the Final Liberation Front in Mexico, and we've received word from German foreign intelligence that one Middle Eastern organization has begun some sort of mission involving America. There may be a relationship between what the Germans are uncovering and what's going on here. It may be a supply route. We're working as fast as we can to find out."

McConnell queried the FBI chief. "If someone really could and did consolidate certain splinter groups in the Middle East, then trained them, and established and funded a base of some kind within the United States to carry out a series of attacks on American facilities and institutions, including the government, there'd be no trail, such as bank robberies for financing, and no one would have to claim responsibility. The acts would speak for themselves by causing the desired effects. Right?"

The director thought for a second, then nodded. "That'd be the worst-case scenario, yes."

McConnell concluded his questioning. "And we'd have a monumental change in the terrorism equation and an overwhelming challenge to the stability and permanence of our way of life, wouldn't we?"

The FBI leader stood at the edge of the Secretary's desk. "Yes, sir," he answered, "it would be the ultimate threat." After a pause, he went on. "Let me say that we've worried about this possibility at the Bureau for at least twenty-five years. The problem for the terror masters in the Middle East hasn't been a shortage of willing people. That part of the world is a cauldron full of zealots who hate us and everything we stand for. They've just never been able to get their act together over here. Not that Hamas and others haven't tried. Anyway, we've always thought that if cooler heads could structure the operation and harness, train, and finance the killers, it could definitely work. And it would tear this country apart."

The FBI director paused and looked at McConnell, then at each of the other men.

"In summary, the FBI is of the opinion that this is the most serious internal threat ever faced by the United States. It has been assigned our highest priority."

The White House
10:57 a.m.

"Three minutes, Mr. President."

Samuel Taylor, the floor director, tapped the plastic crown of his wristwatch and looked toward the main doorway of the basement television studio. The air temperature of the tightly insulated room was maintained at 65°F to protect the sensitive electronic equipment, but the atmosphere was rapidly growing damp in the presence of the extra guests. The director adjusted his headset and called for the activation of a second dehumidifier.

The chief executive stepped into the room and acknowledged with a raised index finger. "One second, Sam." His briefing of the Congressional leadership had run longer than expected. He reached for his chief of staff's shoulder with his other hand. "McConnell and Chapman?" His grip was bony firm.

"With the AG, sir," O'Shaunessey reported. "Their car's on Seventeenth."

The president stared into his aide's eyes. "Cutting it awfully close, Brian."

"They'll be at the southwest entrance momentarily, sir." O'Shaunessey cleared his throat. "I understand they're rewriting on the way."

"Rewriting? Brian, if there's anything new ... " The president's voice trailed off as he noticed the men and women seated along the rear wall. Their chairs were positioned just outside the perimeter of the studio lights. He held out his hand in their direction.

"Thank you for being with me for this."

Two members of the National Security Council stood. The others nodded. All of them had come down from the briefing ahead of the president. Homer Jenkins rose and approached. He started talking from five feet away.

"You're out of excuses, Mr. President. I've got to level with the American people. They won't be too happy with you when I finish."

The chief executive looked over his shoulder as the House Speaker came alongside. They walked to the lighted area together.

"You're all heart, Homer."

"Look, I'll cut the bullshit. The nation's fracturin', and you're fiddlin'."

The president stopped and punched Jenkins in the chest with his finger.

"Get off my back, damn it! You know everything I know. Until we can locate and seize these people, I'd appreciate at least a shadow of support from you."

The president turned and walked away, leaving the Speaker standing by himself. Jenkins hadn't expected such a strong reaction, especially in front of his peers. He watched as a very irritated chief executive walked the remaining feet to a bare wooden desk at the focus of the lighting.

"All right, you want support. I'll give you support." Jenkins patted his watch. "Twenty-four hours, sir. I'll keep my mouth shut for twenty-four hours."

The president put his hands on the top of the midnight-blue leather chair. He gripped it so tightly his knuckles turned white. Jenkins returned to his seat at the back of the room.

The floor director walked into the lighted area and pointed to the digital clock mounted on one of the cameras.

"Comin' up on two minutes."

The chief executive moved the chair away from the desk and sat down. To his left was the blue banner of the presidential flag. In the position of honor to his right stood the flag of the United States of America. Both were trimmed with golden yellow fringe, cord, and tassels. Matched antique gold-plated eagles proudly extended their wings atop the two standards. A royal blue backdrop covered the wall behind.

"Brian?" The president squinted to one side of the glare.

"They're in the building, sir."

The heat of the intense lamps brought beads of perspiration through the pancake makeup on the president's forehead. He raised his hand as a shield.

"Sam, is it all on the TelePrompTer?"

The director studied his notes. "Yes, sir. Everything up to whatever Secretary McConnell's bringing."

The president tapped the top of the desk.

A voice came over the intercom. "Minute-thirty, everyone."

The door at the side of the room was pushed open, and the defense secretary entered, followed by the chairman of the joint chiefs, the attorney general, and the FBI director. Stephen McConnell walked briskly toward the front. He shook his head and handed over a sheet of paper.

"No changes. It's as bad as we thought. Be weeks before we can launch a replacement satellite. DOD's not seeing any trans-border supply movements to match up with what's been going on, so we're inclined to concur with the FBI's counterterrorism people that it's an internal U.S. base." He stepped back and stuffed his hands into his jacket pockets.

"Thirty seconds." The floor director's voice conveyed the urgency of the countdown.

The president looked at the typed information and winced.

"Sandy, I just can't go along with this U.S.-base idea. It's pure speculation, and I'd need to have concrete proof before I could ever go public with it. These terrorist actions are probably one-time events, by groups that have already slipped out of the country. You and the FBI aren't able to see anything else coming in because there *isn't* anything else. They've finished. They've gone."

The defense secretary shook his head. "I think you're dead wrong, Mr. President."

"Ten seconds, everyone."

McConnell moved away. The president looked up into the lens of the silent camera. The director raised his arm in readiness for the start of the telecast.

Beggs, Oklahoma
Saturday, January 2, 10:00 a.m.

"Wait here."

The driver secured the emergency brake of the Wagoneer and stepped out. He pulled up his jacket collar, looked to both sides, and walked into the office of a small motel. Within two minutes he returned to the vehicle. He snapped his fingers at the three sleepy occupants.

"They're ready for us."

The Wagoneer jerked ahead and accelerated onto U.S. 75 for the short run to the turnoff. The men sat up and yawned and stretched as the van exited for the county road and the last seven miles. Minutes later, it bounded onto the ranch property. The driver had seen a pinpoint green laser signal from the house for the last mile. The men held onto the plastic seats and armrests as the Wagoneer bounced and decelerated.

The vehicle drove to the rear of the metal building and skidded to a stop.

"OK, this is it," he yelled. His three passengers got out and shook the stiffness from their limbs. The driver pointed. "Go with him." A uniformed guard stood in the doorway. The men walked toward the building.

"And get some real rest," the driver called after them. "It won't be long now."

10:05 a.m.

"My fellow Americans," the chief executive had begun with a firm voice. "It is traditional at this time for me to reflect on the past year and to wish you everything good during the coming twelve months."

An elderly couple stood behind the motel's worn wooden counter and gazed at a black-and-white Zenith on a metal stand across the small room that served as their lobby. Out of the corner of his eye, the man watched the Wagoneer disappear over the hill to the north. He positioned a plastic wastebasket with his foot and spat a mouthful of Red Man into a brown pool. He reached for the woman's hand. "Betcha they're going up to the old Cummings place. Didn't look like local people to me."

"However," the president continued, "over the past few days, a series of shocking and unprovoked attacks has occurred against our nation and our people. These were criminal acts, and they were unprecedented in magnitude." He paused before continuing. "Today it is my responsibility to tell you that the evil of international terrorism has returned to America with a vengeance."

An estimated 190 million Americans and a billion and a half others overseas watched in silence as the president recounted the events of the previous week. Airliners and cruise ships around the globe carried his message to their captive audiences. Even prisons were stilled as inmates took in the chronicle of death and destruction. Members of the armed services worldwide wondered where the next twenty-four hours would take them.

The president went on.

"Well-organized criminals have again spanned the wide oceans to wreak their horrors upon innocent victims across this country."

St. Francis Hospital, Tulsa
10:23 a.m.

The telephone rang. Jack frowned at the shrill interruption. It rang again. He thumbed down the volume of the television with the remote control unit and shifted in his bed. He picked up the receiver and lay back against the pillow.

"Yes?"

"Jack?"

He closed his eyes. It was Norman. He really didn't need this call.

"Jack, I tried to reach you last night, but they wouldn't let any calls through. And you're not in the same room. Are you all right?"

"I'm fine, Norman."

"Yeah, but they moved you again, Jack."

"Don't worry about it."

"But I want to come by before I leave tomorrow. You know I'm leaving tomorrow, don't you?"

Jack drew a deep breath. "The 'Cavalcade.' "

"Yeah, that's right. But I want to see you tonight, Jack. After all, I'm really worried about you."

"Thanks."

"But I don't have your room number."

Jack was at the outer limits of his patience.

"You'll have to get it downstairs. I might be in a different room. They've got me sequestered, with very limited access."

"Really? Who does? The police? Have you talked with them yet?"

"Norman, I'm really wiped out."

"Mr. Stroud?" A heavyset nurse stepped into his room. "Sir, it's time for your medication."

"Pill time, Norman. Gotta go." Jack hung up and sighed. "I now have a distinct pain in my ass to go with my headache."

The nurse smirked at his complaint and presented him with a small paper cup. Jack picked out the two capsules by feel and drank from the glass of water she had taken from his bedside table. The woman fixed her attention on the television set. "Isn't that awful?"

Jack found the remote unit and increased the volume. The president was assuring that the full force of the United States government would be employed to root out the terrorist elements, wherever they might be.

"U.S. security agencies are working to locate these individuals and to prevent any further such diabolical acts. This new and ghastly outbreak of terrorism is a direct, personal threat to you, to me, and to those we love. I will keep you fully advised. God bless us all."

The screen switched to a display of the presidential seal; then a network commentator began to speak. Jack pushed the mute button on the remote control. There was a knock on the door as it opened.

"Don Evans, Jack. May I come in?"

Jack recognized the face of the FBI agent he'd met in the parking lot two days earlier. They had spoken by telephone an hour and a half ago.

"Please do."

The nurse helped him sit up. Evans entered the room. A second man, half a foot taller, followed. Both men pulled off their gloves. Evans made the introduction.

"Jack, this is Special Agent Charles Carmichael."

Carmichael stepped forward and extended his hand. "Charlie, Mr. Stroud."

"And it's Jack, Charlie. Have a seat, gentlemen."

The agents drew padded hospital chairs alongside the bed and sat down. The nurse cleared Jack's bedside tray and departed. As she did so, two burly Tulsa police officers stepped inside the room and crossed their arms. They were members of the elite Special Protective Division who had newly issued orders to be present whenever Jack had a visitor, regardless of who it was. Anyone requesting admittance to his room had to be identified at the main desk downstairs and patted down by two other uniformed policemen, who maintained a twenty-four-hour vigil at a table outside. Hospital personnel, including physicians and nurses, were no longer exempt.

On the silent television screen, a NASA spokesman pointed to a sequence chart detailing the previous day's calamity.

"There were no loose papers on your desk," Evans began. "Our people checked the room twice. They were thorough."

Jack looked into the agent's eyes. "The printouts were all there, Don. Nine pages and single-spaced. I was reviewing them when I was shot."

"Well, everything's gone now."

"What about Flora? Maybe she moved them."

Evans sat back in his chair and extended his legs.

"No such luck. Your housekeeper said when she heard the front window shatter, she ran into your study. You were sprawled over your desk, unconscious. There was blood and broken glass everywhere. She picked up your desk phone and called 911 and then your daughter. She thinks she remembers seeing some papers on your desk, but she doesn't remember how many. There was just too much debris everywhere. Anyway, she didn't clean anything up until after the police left. And they didn't report seeing any papers at all."

Jack maneuvered himself into a better position. "There's *one* way to get them back." He looked at the men. "I made a copy of the information. It's on a floppy disk . . . if it's still there."

"Where?" Both agents leaned toward him.

"I was going to store the disk in my safe, but I was too interested in reviewing the papers first. So I laid it on the bookshelf behind my desk."

"Out in the open?"

Jack nodded. "On the second shelf."

Evans pointed to his associate. "Charlie, go out to his house. Call me as soon as you find it."

The second agent nodded and tapped his wristwatch. "Give me thirty minutes."

11:01 a.m.

"Fantastic, Charlie! Take it to the office right now and run a printout."

Evans put down the telephone and grinned at Jack. "It was still there next to your desk. Man, you must be living right after all."

Jack cocked his head. "*Next* to my desk?"

"Yeah. In the bookshelf. Where you said."

"No, Don, I said the disk was on the small bookshelf *behind* my desk. The one against the front window."

"Shit." Evans grabbed the telephone again. He punched in the number for the cellular unit in Carmichael's car. There was no answer. He immediately called the FBI's Tulsa office.

"Helen? Don Evans. Signal Carmichael on his beeper and have him call me at St. Francis. Jack Stroud's room. Fast!"

"Don?"

Evans put his hand over the mouthpiece and looked over.

Jack spoke deliberately. "When you met me in the parking lot the other night, I got the feeling you thought my telephone might be tapped. Did Carmichael call you from my house?"

Evans rolled his eyes and pounded the table with his fist.

"Son of a *bitch!*"

11:04 a.m.

"I'm on my way to the office. What's up?"

Evans nearly yelled into the telephone. "Charlie, you got the wrong disk! The one we want is on the bookshelf *behind* his desk. You have the one from the bookshelf *beside* his desk."

"Shit. Well, I'll just go back. I'm only about a mile away."

"Did you use Stroud's house phone to call me?"

"Yeah, the one on his desk."

"Charlie, somebody else might know about the disk now. Be damned careful."

"Wilco."

Carmichael fitted the cellular handset into its cradle, pulled into a Texaco station, and looked for an opening in the traffic. He accelerated through a turn and headed back. He didn't notice the car that made a U-turn behind him.

As he reached Stroud's street, Carmichael saw a dark Honda parked in front of Jack's house. He stopped his car thirty yards away and ran for the porch. Flora opened the door.

"FBI again, ma'am," he spoke in a low voice. "Is someone else here?"

"Uh-huh. It's a Father Arnold, sir. He brought some things for Mr. Stroud."

Carmichael burst past the housekeeper and pulled out his pistol, holding it down with both hands in the braced-ready position. He looked around the silent hallway and moved to the door of Jack's study. A priest was standing inside at the desk. Carmichael targeted his weapon on the man's back.

"FBI! Put your hands on the desk."

The priest turned and grinned. "My, my. What's this all about?"

Carmichael advanced. "I said, hands on the desk." His front sight was on the man's heart.

"You!" Another man's voice came almost immediately from the doorway. Carmichael spun around and saw a snub-nosed revolver pointed at his face. "Put your gun—and the disk—on the desk. Very carefully."

The smiling priest drew a revolver from his suit coat and motioned Carmichael to comply. The agent laid his gun down and stood back.

"I said the disk, too, asshole."

Carmichael reached into his overcoat and brought out the disk.

"On the desk!"

Carmichael placed the disk next to his weapon. The priest grabbed both and pushed them into his jacket pocket.

"And now you're coming with us," the priest announced. He tossed a set of plastic police handcuffs to the second man.

"Put these on him. We'll take him in my trunk."

"And that woman?" the other man asked as he secured the FBI agent's hands.

The priest laughed. "A waste of a bullet. Everything will be over soon anyway."

Flora had scampered for the safety of the kitchen when the FBI agent ran past her and pulled out his gun. She slipped inside a large broom closet and tried to hear what was being said. She waited for a minute after the footsteps faded before she cracked open the door. When she heard the engines of two cars start, she ran for the telephone and punched 911. After making the call, she raced up to Rachel's room.

Evans grabbed the telephone. "Yes, Helen. *What?*" He closed his eyes. "All right, I'm on my way out there." He hung up and looked at Jack.

"Your housekeeper just reported that two men took Carmichael away at gunpoint. One of them was dressed as a priest. Description sounds like the same guy who tried to get to you here."

He looked at the uniformed policemen.

"Don't let *anyone* in this room, other than his doctor, until I say so. Understand?"

The two officers nodded. Evans grabbed his overcoat and started for the door.

"Jack, I'll see that you have all the protection you need, including U.S. marshals. We'll probably move you to another room again. Right now, I'm going out to your house."

"What about my daughter?"

Evans thrust his arm into a coat sleeve.

"Your housekeeper said Rachel's OK. Hid in a closet when she heard the noises downstairs. We'll cover her, too."

J. Edgar Hoover Building, Washington, D.C.
12:40 p.m.

Corley Brand picked up the folder containing the preliminary FBI laboratory memo on the autopsy of Interpol's Ahmed Pasha. The full medical report was on its way from Barnes Hospital in St. Louis. He opened the document and scanned the highlights.

"Pasha, A. Cause of death: massive intracranial catastrophe. Death was instantaneous. Metallic remains discovered from samples removed at autopsy indicate probability that invasive projectile penetrated tympanic membrane and lodged in brain stem, at the pons, where it exploded."

Brand shook his head as he read on.

"Initial conclusions: handheld weapon, probably resembling ballpoint pen or automatic pencil, placed next to ear canal of subject and discharged. Gas cylinder in weapon propelled hollow, dartlike mini-blasting cap containing trinitrophenol and probably detonated by internal fuse. Standard speed of expanding wave caused by usual picric acid explosion: 14,500 m.p.h. Devastation complete but virtually soundless due to containment by skull."

"Good Christ!" Brand laid the folder on the countertop. "The man's brain was nothing more than boiling jelly after that thing went off." He headed back to his office.

St. Francis Hospital, Tulsa
1:13 p.m.

Don Evans rushed back into Jack's room.

"They definitely got Carmichael. We're doing prints at your house now. Probably won't find anything, though. Your housekeeper said the so-called priest wore gloves. We figure the other man did, too. But we got the right disk and had it printed out. Nine pages, just as you said."

"Rachel?"

"She's just fine. Scared, but who wouldn't be?"

"I need to get home, to be with her, to ..."

"I know. We're trying to get your doctor to release you."

Evans sat down and pulled the sheets out of a manila envelope. He handed them over to Jack.

"Same ones?"

Jack looked at the first page, then the second. He flipped through the remainder and nodded.

"Same ones."

Evans collected the documents and put them back in the envelope. "OK, maybe we can now start to assemble this mosaic. I have a feeling we're on the tip of the proverbial iceberg. I think it's time for us to put our heads together."

The FBI agent smiled and reached over and shook Jack's hand.

"Navy Captain Stroud, sir, you're back in the investigation business."

Jack thought about his wife and son, then his daughter. He was enraged at what had happened. He held onto Evans's hand and stared into the FBI man's eyes.

"I'll get those bastards, Don," he spoke in a cold monotone. "Whoever, wherever . . . they're mine."

Tulsa Bible College
Sunday, January 3, 10:00 a.m.

"We go with the blessings of Jesus," Norman intoned in a low voice. The microphone transmitted his whisper to the bundled multitudes gathered on the snow-packed parking lot to witness and support the departure of the nine-bus caravan. He paused. In an attempt to emulate the finest of his peers, he then repeated his opening statement, this time in a booming voice and adding the "ah" syllable to nearly every other word, giving his sentence a resonant delivery worthy of any televangelist.

"We go-ah with the blessings-ah of Jesus-ah." He beamed and continued. "And we go-ah with the knowledge-ah that we are carrying out that great mission-ah that Reuben Gentry possessed as a vision from God-ah."

The four hundred or so who shielded themselves from the unrelenting morning wind across the white landscape felt secure in the warmth of his words and the glow of their faith. Reuben's heir would go forth today unto a world of evil, carrying his clear message of repentance and forgiveness. His Christian Cavalcade would wind its way toward the north and northwest, answering the call of a shaken nation. It would minister to the sick and the sinful and would culminate in a majestic gathering of the faithful in Seattle on January 17, where 50,000 supplicants would sing and be chastised and then be dispersed to their homes and hamlets with their renewed message of an avenging God who had a score to settle with the sinners of the land. And everyone in the crowd this morning knew in their hearts that most Americans had strayed from the straight and severe path known to those who followed the Gentry ministry as the only way to save the country. This trip had been planned for a year and a half, and it was now dedicated to the memory of their beloved Reuben Gentry, who had been called home so suddenly by his Creator. They wept and waved and promised to watch each of Norman's televised performances in the seven blessed cities.

The engines of the nine Road Cruisers were running. Their diesel exhausts puffed out continuous billows of condensation, which disappeared quickly in the moisture-starved atmosphere. Stern-faced drivers in tan uniforms adjusted their hats and dark glasses and scanned the dials one more time. This would be a minutely choreographed affair from its departure until the caravan returned, four thousand miles and three weeks later. Norman was expecting a perfect performance from everyone involved. Nothing had better go wrong, he'd warned the staff. One driver directed his breath across an RPM gauge and wiped away a smudge with his cuff.

With a rolling sequence of depressed accelerators, the buses signaled to the faithful their imminent departure. Norman blew kisses to a group of little boys and slipped inside the second bus. His driver sealed the door and waited for the cue from the lead vehicle. All nine drivers wore headsets that connected them with one another. More importantly, they were plugged in to the security detail in the lead bus. The chief of security called for a final report from each driver. One by one, the men informed him of their state of readiness. After the ninth checked in, they were cleared to depart. "Go!" the chief's command echoed in nine sets of ears. The first driver released the air brakes, and the twenty-two-ton vehicle moved ahead. One by one the buses rolled forward.

As his luxuriously appointed vehicle pulled away, Norman threw his coat aside and slouched into a white leather sofa in the main salon. He lay back against the expensive covering and smacked his lips.

"Bring me something to drink," he ordered without raising his voice.

His private steward placed a double bourbon and Coke into a recessed circle on the burled-wood side bar. Norman drew the glass to his mouth and sucked greedily at the liquid. After a minute, he belched.

"Do you always have to do that?"

Bunny emerged from the bedroom. She wore a gold lamé lounging gown, and she was filing her long fingernails.

Norman grinned at his wife's reaction. "Come give baby a kiss," he taunted with pursed lips.

Bunny waved him away in disgust.

He began to laugh. "Worrying where my mouth's been?" He laughed even louder.

"Norman?" The driver looked over his shoulder. "Shut up!"

Seattle, Washington
Midmorning

The cabbie twisted the radio dial and hit the dashboard with the palm of his right hand.

"Nothin' but all them damn religious programs."

He steered the car from the airport road onto Interstate 5 and headed downtown in the light Sunday-morning traffic.

"You folks mind if I turn this thing off?"

"Whatever," a young man responded as he pulled the pretty woman closer in the backseat and kissed her. "We weren't listening anyway."

The cabbie looked up into the rearview mirror.

"Where'd you guys come in from?"

"Vancouver, B.C. We were just married."

"Oh, yeah?" The driver smiled.

The cab merged into the northbound lanes of the freeway. The couple seemed oblivious to their surroundings.

"Staying here for your honeymoon?"

After a moment, the man answered. "For a few days."

The cabbie heard the woman giggle. He turned his head to the right. "Well, we got a lot to see around here. Even in winter." He laughed. "Not that you guys want to see a lot, but Seattle's a real nice place . . . for anything."

The cab continued toward downtown and exited at the Kingdome. It proceeded onward through a nearly deserted city street and pulled in alongside the Seattle International Hotel. The driver glanced over his shoulder.

"Here we are, folks. Your own 'honeymoon hotel.' "

The young man pushed open the door and helped his bride out into the cool morning air. They beamed at each other as the driver jogged around and extracted their luggage from the trunk.

"Hey, I just thought of something," the cabbie announced as he balanced their three bags. "You guys are lucky you won't be around here in a couple of weeks."

"Why's that?" the woman asked as she kissed her new husband again.

"Well, there's going to be a major convention at this hotel for one of those big television evangelists. There'll be thousands of religious kooks in town for it."

"Oh, really?" The man's arm held the woman's waist.

The cab driver smiled and lugged their suitcases to the entrance. "Have a great stay."

"Thank you." The man's voice was a monotone. "We definitely intend to."

St. Francis Hospital, Tulsa
12:20 p.m.

Jack opened the drawer in the bedside table and picked up his watch. Mass was probably over. His brothers and their families, his sister, and the McVeys would be in for a last visit before they left for the airport. They'd been given nearly an hour by the FBI. He'd asked for them to bring Rachel and Flora with them. Who could say when they'd all be back together again? He put down the watch and pushed the drawer shut. He leaned back against the pillow and reflected.

There was Arthur, the eldest and solid at fifty-nine years old. Always the most serious of the Strouds. His career in corporate law had never been in doubt. Even during grade school, he'd organized everything and everyone. Jack laughed as he remembered. Today, Arthur was a pinstriped soldier in a Wall Street firm. Still marching successfully, somewhere. Then came Edgar, who was fifty-seven and head of his own public relations firm in Chicago. He was the most emotive of the whole lot. Jack had a thousand good memories of their times together. Jack, at fifty-five, was next in line. Then there was Anne, their forty-nine-year-old "baby." Divorced, without children, she painted seascapes from La Jolla to Malibu. Anne was a close second to Ed as the repository of the family's feelings. Maybe Rachel had felt safe enough with her Aunt Anne to open up to her. He hoped she had.

Jack heard the thumping of foot traffic. A policeman opened the door and motioned in Art and Fran, their two married sons and their wives and their single daughter. Then came Ed and Jenny with their two married daughters and their husbands, followed by Anne. Finally he saw Flora, then Rachel, who moved immediately to his bedside.

Jack kissed his daughter and squeezed her hand. "You OK?" She nodded slightly. Jack looked around expectantly. "Weren't Tom and Linda with you?"

Ed frowned. "They were right behind us." As Jack's brother turned, the door opened again. Two additional police officers appeared and made cutting motions with their index fingers across their necks. Jack held up his hand to silence the simultaneous conversations in the room. "Everybody, please. These officers would like to say something."

The family members looked at the policemen and became quiet.

"Folks, I'm sorry," one of the officers said as he moved closer to Jack. "But you're all going to have to leave. Right now."

Jack sat up in his bed. "What's this all about? They just got here. We were told . . . "

The other policeman pointed toward the door.

"Now!"

J. Edgar Hoover Building, Washington, D.C.
1:00 p.m.

The vivid blue background on the overhead screen yielded to the satellite transmission at 1800 Coordinated Universal Time, 7:00 p.m. in

Berlin. Legal attaché Michael Kinney's face flashed on. Through an ear-piece, he could hear his FBI compatriots in Washington, but he couldn't see them. It was a cardinal rule of the Bureau that no outgoing pictures of agents be transmitted from headquarters. Names were another thing.

The deputy director started the meeting.

"Mike, this is Jerry Reynolds."

Reynolds nodded around the table of the conference room, first at the assistant director for the Criminal Division and the assistant director for the National Security Division, then at the chief of the Counterterror-ism Section and the chief of SIOC.

"I'm with Doug Redding, Bill Colquitt, Corley Brand, and Lew Bittker."

Kinney smiled at the camera. "Afternoon, gentlemen."

Reynolds pressed ahead. "We have your written reports, but let's start with the message you picked up last Tuesday from the BND. Then take us through what you've learned since. I want all of us on the same wave-length."

"OK."

Kinney looked at the reference materials on his desk. "I sent you a summary of the German dispatch as soon as I received it on the twenty-ninth. It was after eight in the evening, but I was able to reach Horst Giebler of the BND before I left the office. He's in charge of their Middle East desk, and he offered me everything they had on this new group, the 'Brotherhood of the Ultimate Ijima.' "

Kinney shuffled his notes.

"Over the years, the Germans have built a great network of contacts throughout the Middle East—really going back to the days of the Second World War. We've plugged in on occasion. So have the CIA, the Israelis, the British, and others."

He squinted at a line.

"It was the Israelis who put top intelligence priority on Lebanon twenty years ago. They were the ones who discovered in the '70s that the North Koreans were helping train Palestinian terrorist groups there. And they kicked the gooks all the way back to Pyongyang in the early '80s. Then, later, when the Syrians let the Iranians establish large training bases in the Bekaa Valley for their Hezbollah, Party of God Shi'ite group, the North Koreans came back and reestablished their training relationship with these and some of the other extremist organizations."

The men in Washington made notations alongside their typed sum-maries. Kinney looked into the camera.

"This is what's interesting. Over the past thirty-six to forty-eight months, the BND has monitored a splintering of some of these groups into two distinct camps: the militantly religious and a surprisingly fast development of economic "hired guns." It really accelerated when we went after Iraq. Originally, as you're well aware, the most effective terrorist groups were state-sponsored entities that pursued primarily religious causes. Then, back in the early and mid-'80s, a handful of countries started recruiting mostly nonreligious groups, as terrorists for hire. That's what we've seen with Abu Nidal, Jamil Nasir, Ahmed Jibril and his Popular Front for the Liberation of Palestine—General Command, Abu Abbas, and the other shadowy figures who've been responsible for most of the major anti-Western attacks in Europe and the Middle East over the past decade. Plus the half-dozen incursions we've seen in the States over the past four or five years, with the possible exception of the World Trade Center bombing. These people, both camps, despise anything Western, and they're cold-blooded killers who keep getting better at their craft. But whether they act from a religious orientation or an economic one, in the end virtually all are beholden to the highest bidder for their financial support."

"Mike," Reynolds interjected. "Is that when this 'Brotherhood' originated?"

"Yes, we think so. According to the BND, there was a further fracturing of some of the 'economic' terrorists into virulently anti-American cells. The so-called Brotherhood of the Ultimate Ijima is apparently one of the new cells."

"Where's it being trained?"

"It was being trained in the Bekaa Valley of Lebanon."

"Was?"

"Jerry, their camp was completely abandoned last Tuesday or Wednesday."

The FBI men looked at one another. Reynolds sat back in his chair.

"Mike, the BND dispatch said the group was well financed. Who's supporting it?"

"Not sure, but they found North Koreans all over the place ten days ago."

"They're not financial backers. Just trainers. What's the significance of the statement that the group's been active for seven months between Lebanon and North America?"

Kinney nodded.

"The BND has an informant in the town of Baalbek, in the Bekaa Valley, who reported that, for some seven months, one of the training camps in the area has been preparing teams for service in North America. Usually the training there has been for European assignments. This is the first time they've heard of groups being groomed specifically for overseas work. The BND learned that on the twenty-sixth. The intercepted call was on the twenty-eighth. Maybe the two are related. They don't know, since there was no telling who the recipient of the call was. The summary is that the BND thinks we're looking at a new terrorist-for-hire group, possibly one of the worst offshoots, probably trained or being trained by the North Koreans, paid for or otherwise supported by God only knows, and suited for activity in North America. Which means, in all likelihood, the United States."

"What's next for the Germans?" Reynolds queried.

"They've got two more informants down there," Kinney responded, "attempting to get a fix on who's who in the operation. They've been inside another heavily guarded camp south of Baalbek. I understand we're still trying to get satellite pictures. Is that right?"

Reynolds nodded. "True, but the new KH-12 that was supposed to pinpoint and intercept communications over there was destroyed in the *Encounter* explosion. The NSA's done some reprogramming and repositioning of one of the older satellites that had been used to monitor the area during the war with Iraq. But it isn't completely suitable for the job, and it won't be operational for another couple of days, at the earliest. I hope the BND can interview their insiders pretty soon."

"Jerry, they're supposed to meet them in Damascus on Wednesday."

"Not sooner?"

"Nope. Activities at the second base are tightly orchestrated. The informants are on a cycle that allows them to be away only once a month. Next Wednesday's it."

"Wish it could be sooner, Mike," Reynolds reflected. "Matter of fact, with all that's going on over here, I wish it were weeks ago."

Tulsa Port of Catoosa
6:23 p.m.

If ever there was a typical winter's night, Oklahoma Highway Patrol trooper J. D. Caldwell concluded, this was it. He looked out the windshield of his parked patrol car. Ice pellets that had fallen earlier rimmed the glass of the Ford LTD. He moved a toothpick around with his tongue and surveyed the snowy surroundings once again.

Caldwell was working the three-to-eleven shift on county patrol. In the waning light of the short day, he had made two abbreviated circuits of the state highway that used to be U.S. 66, fifty-mile forays from Tulsa to Vinita and back again, in search of speeders and drunk drivers. So far, only six citations for speeding, one drunk, and no warnings. That was usual for the old highway at the end of a long holiday weekend. Most long-distance travelers were returning home on the nearby turnpike, and the troopers over there would have their hands full.

The report of an abandoned car had come through as he circled to the northwest of the Tulsa Port of Catoosa. Within minutes, he'd found the vehicle hidden under a grove of trees, twenty feet off the lightly traveled highway. It was a late-model Toyota Supra, silver, with current Texas tags. Caldwell copied down the license number on his dash-mounted notepad and lifted the microphone from its mount.

"HQ, this is Unit 270. I'm on the Port Road with a 10-28 and 10-29 on an abandoned vehicle."

He shook his head. Damn codes! Why can't I just ask who owns it and if it's stolen?

"Unit 270, sorry. Computer's down temporarily."

Caldwell made a face and peered out the windshield again. He grabbed his flashlight and reached for the door handle. Almost immediately, he noticed headlights approaching rapidly. One of the lamps was intermittent, the other steady. He watched as a truck roared past, swirling puffs of road-side snow in his direction. One of the truck's rear lights was also flashing on and off. Caldwell tossed the flashlight aside and started the engine.

"This Toyota can wait."

He reached for the headlights and stepped on the accelerator. The truck was about a quarter-mile ahead as his cruiser centered on the road and began the pursuit. A mile later, his car pulled to within twenty yards of the truck. Just what he thought, a one-ton "box." Caldwell looked at his speedometer. Right at fifty-five. Suddenly the flickering ahead ceased, and the truck's rear lamp burned a solid red. The trooper started to slow for a turnaround when the irregular flashing began again.

"OK, buddy, you got a problem." Caldwell flipped on his overhead pursuit lights. "Let's correct it."

His car and the truck slowed in tandem and pulled onto the shoulder. As he braked, Caldwell maneuvered so that his headlights shone against the back of the truck. He frowned. There were green diamond placards on the rear door that read "Nitrogen." Caldwell set his emergency brake and got out. He saw the driver's face in the outside mirror.

"Back here, please," he called and motioned. On the opposite side of the truck, another man stared from the passenger mirror. The driver opened the door of the cab and stepped down. A pullover knit cap sat high on his head.

"Were we speeding?" the man asked as he trudged to the rear of the truck.

Caldwell gripped his ticket pad with his left hand. He held a flashlight under his left arm. "Driver's license, registration, insurance verification, and bill of lading."

The driver stopped and put his hands on his hips. "You say . . . what?"

"I say, your driver's license, your vehicle registration, your insurance verification form, and your bill of lading." Caldwell glared at the man. "That's what I say." This was the time to nip that bit of cuteness in the bud, he thought.

The driver stared back. Then he raised his arms and turned. "OK, OK, you're the boss." He returned to the darkened cab and spoke something to his passenger. After a moment, the other man's arm extended through the open window. The driver reached up and accepted a wad of papers and ambled back toward Caldwell. He thrust them out to the trooper.

Caldwell took the documents and looked them over. He handed them back.

"That's three of the four. How about the registration for the truck?"

"Jesus Christ!" the man objected. "I've got an old draft card. Do you want that, too?"

"No, sir. Just what the law requires."

The driver fumbled for a minute in his coat pocket, then offered a folded certificate.

Caldwell examined it and wrote down the name and address for "Holway Imports."

"What's all this for? Or are you the only one askin' the questions?"

Caldwell handed back the form. "Nope, routine. You've got a bad light." He put on his best smile. "Matter of fact, two of 'em."

The man wasn't amused. "You mean to tell me I had to go through all this just to find out I've got bum lights?"

"Yes, sir." Caldwell walked forward briskly. The driver kicked at a frozen rut of soil and followed reluctantly. The trooper pointed a gloved finger. "Right one, both front and rear. Probably only a loose connection."

The driver trudged up next to the trooper. "Yeah . . . well, thanks a shit load. We'll stop at a gas station later and get them fixed."

"Why don't we see what we can do here?" Only Caldwell appreciated his cheery tone. "Might take only a few minutes."

The driver clearly didn't like the idea. "Look, officer, we're kinda in a hurry."

Caldwell ignored him. "I think if you'll check, you'll find it's just loose." He gestured. "Go ahead."

The man cursed and removed his glove. He bent over and felt at the edges of the front headlight. He looked back. "OK, it's loose."

Caldwell motioned him to proceed.

The driver muttered something under his breath. He pushed the bulb into its socket and tapped it a few times. The beam was now steady.

"All right, that's that," the man barked.

"Now the rear one," Caldwell responded with a smile.

"What?"

"Sir, both your right-side lights were flickering. So that's one down and one to go."

The driver blew out a chestful of air and tucked his hands into his heavy jacket. He followed the trooper around back. Caldwell looked over the rear light's housing. The bulb wasn't loose.

"We'll have to get inside to fix this one," he said after a few second's study. "There's no way we can do it from the outside." By this time the other man had joined them.

"What's holding us up?"

"Have to open the back," Caldwell observed. "Looks like a loose wire."

The second man stared at the trooper. "Are you serious?"

"He's serious," the driver grumbled. "Open it."

The second man leaned toward his partner. "We're already late, you know."

"I know, I know."

"They won't like it if we're late."

The driver glared at his passenger. "Just open the goddamn door!"

The man shrugged and fumbled at a metal ring on his belt. He located a key and inserted it, and the lock popped up with a click. The driver grabbed the handle and forced the door upwards, glaring at the trooper. "We'll take it from here."

Caldwell stood his ground and shone his light into the cavity of the truck. Inside, on wooden pallets, were eighteen stacked cylinders, in a four-three-four-three-four pattern. The word "Nitrogen" was stenciled on a paper label affixed across the top of each cylinder. Caldwell noticed that one of the superimposed signs on the tanks had been dislodged. Underneath it, in black paint, were the letters "RDX."

"Hey, you!" The driver's brusque tone caught Caldwell off guard. "It's over here . . . if you're going to hang around." The man pointed. "Under this covering."

Caldwell directed his light to the inside corner of the truck's interior.

The second man lifted a mat. Two wires lay parallel to the floor of the truck. One had twisted free.

"No big deal," the driver concluded as he pried up the loose wire and peered at its ragged end. He secured it with a few quick twists, and the rear lamp came on. "See, that does it."

Caldwell looked at the men. "What *is* this stuff, anyway, and where're you going with it?"

The driver began to laugh. "You know something, you beat all. We've done everything according to the bills of lading. Six runs so far today. Do they pay *you* extra for hassles?"

Caldwell frowned. The man went on.

"Look, we're pulling shipments from the port to the Sinclair and Sun refineries. But tonight, it's 'Not ours, take it to them,' then the other place says something's mislabeled. 'Nope, it's theirs.' Officer, we don't really give a shit. We just wish they'd decide."

The trooper peered at them. Finally he nodded. "OK, button it up." He motioned them to close the back of the truck. "You're free to go."

The two men locked the rear door and walked to the front.

"Thank you *so* much for your help," the driver called over his shoulder as he climbed into the cab. "This state couldn't survive without your exceptional dedication to duty."

Caldwell grinned and walked back to his car as the truck's engine started. Within a minute, its taillights narrowed into a red dot. He got inside his cruiser and sat back against the seat. He reached over, picked up his clipboard, and wrote down "RDX."

Beggs, Oklahoma
6:55 p.m.

Lester Graham pulled on his work clothes and waited until the last vestiges of the day's light faded. He planned to take another look at the structures up north, particularly the big metal one. Up close, from *their* side of the fence. He figured it was time to learn all he could about his neighbors. He was as familiar with the adjacent property as he was with his own, so he felt comfortable setting out in the darkness. He found his flashlight and checked its beam against a wall. No binoculars needed this time. He'd be close enough in person. He put on his coat and hat and lowered the earflaps.

The January night was still, the air rock-solid at ten degrees below freezing. Graham's eyes burned as he stepped across his frozen, snow-covered acreage. He made it to the fence in just under twelve minutes. There were no lights on the land across the way. He paused for a moment before crossing over.

"Stay with me, Lady Luck."

Graham carefully lifted himself over the barbed wire and stood in the silence. Almost immediately, a flash of light came from the house. He couldn't tell if it had been directed outside. He stood frozen in position for a minute and stared into the darkness. Then he began advancing. He'd gone fewer than fifty yards when he saw alternating red and white lights, like some sort of a code, coming from the top of the house. He watched for the lights to repeat, but they didn't. And they didn't seem to be pointed at him. Graham moved again, with exaggerated steps. After a dozen yards, he stopped and strained for sounds. There were only whispers of the wind. Suddenly blinding lights framed him.

"Freeze!" a raspy voice bellowed.

Graham gasped. He sensed there were more than two men, and very close. He held up his hands as a shield against the intense floods. "Just doin' a little night walkin'," he attempted in a shaky voice. Where in the hell had they come from? He heard the sound of footsteps crunching toward him in the snow. He pointed in the direction of his house, hoping his gesture wouldn't be misinterpreted as other than friendly.

"I'm ... I'm your neighbor."

"Shut your fucking face!"

Someone pulled Graham's arms behind his back and attached a tight plastic cuff.

"Move!" A hand pushed him forward.

As they approached the front porch of the house, bright perimeter lights went on. A man dressed in black and wielding a pistol opened the front door. Graham was shoved inside.

A thin man in his mid-thirties sat at a desk in the middle of the room. He wore a turtleneck, jeans, and a gold wristwatch. Graham was jerked to a stop. The man looked up.

"Good evening, Mr. Graham." A tight smile formed on his lips. "We've been expecting you."

"You don't understand, sir," the farmer started in his most sociable voice. He pointed in the direction of his house. "I'm your neighbor from next door." His face bore a look of hope. "I just ... "

"Get him downstairs," the man snapped.

A hand pushed against Graham's back and propelled him onward. "Hey, listen," he tried to object, but he was forced out of the room before the rest of the words came.

7:40 p.m.

"We're ready."

Four men sat in the front row of a small studio as the lights dimmed. The screen of the big Sony showed the sword and shield of the old Komitet Gosudarstvennoy Bezopasnosti. It held for a minute before the KGB video began. The grainy black-and-white images were unequivocal.

An overweight man wearing a leather mask stood next to a bed. He was naked. His penis was half erect. There was no audio. A boy who looked about seven years old lay on the bed facing the camera, his arms restrained behind his back. He, too, was naked. A taut rope under his arms and across his chest was secured to the headboard. His legs were spread and tied to the bedposts. The terror in his eyes was evident, even at the skewed camera angle.

The man advanced upon his tethered prey and stood before his face. The boy was screaming. The man reached between his victim's legs with his left hand and began to fondle him. The boy's eyes closed. Within a half minute, vomit gushed from the youngster's mouth. The man fell across the bed, pulled off the leather hood, and started laughing. It was Norman Gentry. Then the picture went blank.

The tape continued. Norman was dressed and seated at a bare table. The camera closed in on his face. He ran a hand across his sweating forehead. The sound cracked on. "Of course, we wish to do nothing which might impair your father's ministry," a voice spoke in accented English. "That is, unless you choose not to see the obvious implications of these unfortunate incidents."

As the lights came up in the studio, one of the men stood. He turned and faced his guests.

"There is more, but these two vignettes were all it took."

"Very professional," one of the visitors replied. "Now if we can just keep him under control for another seventeen days."

The first man smiled.

"Don't worry, our best people will be with him every minute."

INTO LUCIFER'S DEN

The nine-headed Hydra, which had
ravaged the country, now waited for
Hercules. The middle head of the
serpentine monster was immortal,
and the others sprouted two for each
one Hercules cut off.

from **The Labors of Hercules**

St. Francis Hospital, Tulsa
Monday, January 4, 2:25 a.m.

"After you, Dr. Tressler."

FBI Special Agent Don Evans figured his lowered voice would carry halfway to the nurse's station, a hundred feet away. He held the door open, looked down the dark corridor, and high-signed the two policemen. Evans wrinkled his nose. The odor of disinfectant meant that the hallway had only recently been prepared for the night. When his charge padded past him into the new room, the agent gripped the curved metal handle and pulled the door shut with a thump. Light from a wall unit illuminated the immediate area of the bed. Two corners of the small room were deeply shadowed. Evans stepped forward and loosened his tie.

"Keep your fingers crossed, Jack. This should be your last move until you check out tomorrow." He slipped out of his overcoat.

"Tomorrow, is it?" Jack sat down on the chair in front of the bed. "And 'Dr. Tressler'?" He touched the edge of the bandage on his head and watched as Evans folded his coat. "OK, what's going on?"

The FBI agent swung the other chair around and sat down.

"My mother's maiden name."

"You know what I mean!" Jack checked his watch. "It's only been fourteen hours since you moved my family and friends out and changed my room a second time. Here we go again, and in the middle of the night. And what about Rachel? Hell, I was supposed to be out of here and with her on Saturday. Yesterday at the latest."

Evans studied Jack for a few seconds. "Rachel's fine. Worried about you, naturally, but let's call the delay in your release and this move an excess of caution."

Jack crossed his arms. "For what?"

The agent shrugged. "Well, with the attempt on your life last Friday, then the second try Saturday by that so-called priest, and Carmichael's being taken from your house, probably involving the same man, we're goosy about your safety." Evans leaned forward. "Can't blame us, can you?"

"Don't bullshit me, Don. You forget that I used to be in charge of games like this myself when I was with the NIS. I ordered people into protective custody all the time, but I never shifted anyone after the first move unless it was absolutely necessary. I wouldn't risk exposure just for the sake of action." Jack leaned toward the FBI man. "You guys act like you're really spooked. You moved me again yesterday—more than twelve hours after they grabbed Charlie. Now you've moved me a third time. Something else happened, didn't it?"

Evans took a deep breath and exhaled. "Didn't want to say anything until we had more to report, but, yes, it looks that way."

Jack felt pressure across his head wound. "All right, tell me about it."

Evans leaned over the back of the chair. "Remember how late your lunch was yesterday?"

Jack nodded. "Not a screw-up in the kitchen?"

Evans shook his head. "A maintenance worker found two women employees in a linen storage area, bound and gagged. They just happened to be the two who were to have served the meals on your floor."

"You concluded from that there was going to be another attack on me?"

Evans shrugged his shoulders. "We thought it was strange that no one took their places. Maybe they got scared off. Maybe they'll be back. Give us a break, Jack! You're in someone's sights, and we're a little jumpy. We're going to have a discussion about your security later today. Right now you're better off here. You're cordoned off, with a protected perimeter."

Jack squinted. "And you're going to scheme up *more* protection for me?"

"Damned right, we are!"

"I want to go home, Don. I'm useless here. Can't you understand that?"

Evans blew into his cupped hands. "We may want to move you and your daughter to a safe house."

"Oh no, you don't." Jack stood up abruptly and waved his hand at the agent. "No way, José. Marshals are fine, but if I'm going to be a part of the team, I'm not going to be taken out of circulation. No, sir." He chopped at the back of the chair with his open hand. "The horrors of the past week have ripped Rachel in ways it'll take years to heal, if ever. Nope. I'm going to try for sanity, hers and mine, and that means a home atmosphere. Period."

"But it would only be temporary." Evans's voice betrayed his surprise at Jack's reaction. "Until we figure out who's after you and why."

Jack pointed at the agent's face. "Don't talk to *me* about threats and what should be done about them." He started pacing. "I've been marked for assassination and chased before—by the venerable Department V of the once-almighty KGB, no less—and I haven't forgotten my training." He stopped at the door and turned around. "I've started to make headway at the ministry. I dug out that financial information for you, didn't I? Well, I'm ready to go back for more. There and elsewhere. I want to go home. I've got to be right in the middle of things. It's the least I can do for Reuben's memory." He put his hands into his robe pockets and paused. "For Laura and Jeff, too."

"How about for Jack?"

Jack shrugged. "Yeah, for me, too."

Evans tried for a compromise. "Safe house . . . nights only?"

Jack shook his head as he walked back to the edge of the bed. "Sorry, Don."

The pockmarked face of a uniformed Tulsa police officer appeared at the door.

"Mr. Stroud?"

Jack motioned. "Come in."

A second officer followed and pulled the door shut. Both policemen positioned themselves shoulder to shoulder. The first man tucked his hands into his insulated jacket.

"Sir, I'm Sergeant Gene Harjo." His prominent cheekbones and earth-brown skin color matched his Indian name, and his Oklahoma twang was heavy. "And this here," he indicated, "is Corporal Bruce Lundgren. We'll be outside. Just wanted you to know we're on duty."

"Thanks, gentlemen," Jack acknowledged, and the policemen started to leave.

"Oh, one thing."

The men stopped and turned. "Sir?"

Jack smiled. "You won't have to chase me down again. The Feds promise this was my last kidnapping."

Both men looked at Evans, grinned, and returned to the corridor.

The FBI man stood and picked up his overcoat. "Well, I'd better go." He shook the coat open and draped it over his arm.

Jack grabbed the agent by the shoulder as they walked for the door.

"Thanks for the offer of extra protection, Don. I just can't hide."

Evans stopped. "I understand." He punched his index finger into Jack's middle. "Get some sleep, Captain. I'll get the wheels rolling so you can be back with your daughter. At home, too. Might take a day or so, but I'll make it happen."

The agent said something to one of the policemen outside, then stepped into the darkness of the corridor. When the footfalls indicated that Evans had turned the far corner, Jack pushed the door shut and walked back to bed. He untied the belt of his robe and peered at the digital thermostat on the wall. It indicated an even sixty-four degrees.

"Sixty-four?" He made a face. "Hell, if I died, I wouldn't spoil for a week."

Jack felt along the bottom of the plastic box for the selector wheel, but it had been removed. He laid his robe over the bed and stood in the cool silence, rubbing his arms. The memories returned, and his shoulders sagged. It had been only a week, almost to the hour, since he had held Laura that last time, when everything had seemed so right. He tightened his lips and looked out the window of the hospital room. If I died right now, he thought, I could be with her. He immediately reconsidered. No . . . if only I could reach across the void and take her hand, Jeff's too, and just go home.

Jack pulled the sheet back and sat down in the middle of the hard bed. He withdrew his feet from the slippers and, in one motion, swung his legs up and extended them between the sheets. He opened a yellow woolen blanket at the foot of the bed and drew it over the top sheet. He spread his robe as another line of defense against the cold and clicked off the light. In the darkness, Jack settled back on the foam pillow. He extended his feet and touched the cold base of the bed. He inched himself up so the blanket and robe draped over his size twelves. He relaxed again, then considered that if he were home, he'd be bounding up to Rachel's room to check on her. His thumb found the clasp of his watch, and he freed it from his wrist. He leaned over and felt for the bedside drawer.

The only sound in the room was a steady background hiss, a white noise that emanated from the heating vents. He clasped his hands behind his head and stared at the ceiling. He wondered if he would ever be able to sleep peacefully again. Or would he have to wait until that final, unending night?

He saw Jeff, and he bit his lip. His son's face was radiant, with that warm smile and those eyes that conveyed the love and admiration the young man had had for his father. "Son," Jack spoke hesitantly and reached out with one hand to touch him, "I love you so much." The tears came again. The connection lasted nearly a minute. He didn't fight its departure. This is the way God wants it to be, he told himself. He made the sign of the cross.

He took a deep breath and wondered how long acceptance would take. When does anyone really know he's aligned with reality again? He concluded that the past would always be a significant part of the present. But it can't keep hurting as much. Surely it can't.

Gusts of a north wind vibrated the window frame of his room and sought admittance. The metal weatherstripping moaned back its protest.

Jack closed his eyes and thought again about Reuben Gentry's words of a week ago. He remembered one sentence in particular, and he repeated it aloud. "I have touched the face of Death." Those words remained as tantalizing—and as ominous—as when he had first heard them. Implications fanned across his consciousness, but nothing Jack had ever experienced offered an answer. The sentence had to be a key, he thought. Maybe *the* key. But to what? He rolled onto his side and looked out the window again. Those foreign bank accounts didn't seem to be enough by themselves to justify the depths of Reuben's fears. Hell, Jack realized with a start, here I am in the hospital because someone wants *me* to touch the face of Death. Then he remembered the rest of Reuben's message: "I've got to show you what I've found ... before it's too late." Reuben died before he could reveal whatever it was he'd discovered. Jack placed that fact in the middle of his consciousness, right next to Reuben's initial statement. He still wasn't able to bring anything into focus.

" 'Before it's too late,' " he repeated, as if speaking Reuben's words might snap everything together. But the mystery remained as obdurate as ever.

"It's there, somewhere. *Some*where."

Weariness finally took possession. Jack tried to suppress a yawn but couldn't. He closed his eyes. Exhaustion won over the curiosity of his mind, and he slept.

Kansas City, Missouri
9:00 a.m.

The nine hand-polished Road Cruisers of the Christian Cavalcade had snaked into the vacant parking lot of the Kansas City Coliseum at 3:20 the previous afternoon. The gleaming convoy coursed to the southeast corner of the expanse adjacent to the back of the city's newest downtown convention headquarters, the Kansas City Renaissance Hotel.

Two circular spires of silverized glass, thirty-six stories each, the 1,200-room, five-star facility was filling with supporters of the Reuben Gentry Ministries, who prayerfully awaited the arrival of their beloved messenger, Norman, and the start of his Mid-America Camp Meeting on Tuesday. In light of the recent horrors, these bewildered people, and other thousands still on their way, desperately looked forward to the inspiration of the words of Reuben's son. Their fears would be calmed only when they could hear directly from the Lord's representative.

A few believers were on hand when the buses air-braked and hissed to a stop in the cold rays of the winter afternoon. On the five-hour trip from

Tulsa, Norman had guzzled a double bourbon and Coke every thirty minutes and was snoring loudly by the time the buses reached their halfway point at Carthage, Missouri, just north of Joplin. In the lead vehicle, the security chief had been kept informed of Norman's condition as the liquor did its work. He radioed the routine order to disguise the corpulent minister before they arrived, and the steward in the second bus went about his practiced work laying out the oversize fur cap and zippered jumpsuit. Once the caravan stopped in Kansas City, a group of six men, likewise dressed, emerged from other buses and stepped into Norman's $700,000 vehicle.

The driver stood inside the front door and waved his hand toward the inert figure on the leather couch, as if he were repelling a noxious insect.

"Get that son of a bitch out of here ... fast! And make damn sure the hat covers his face."

Two minutes later, a disinterested observer would have seen only uniformed attendants, wrapped for the weather and scurrying about, supporting each other and carrying luggage into the hotel.

It was the typical protocol whenever Norman was on the road. The minister was hustled to his room and placed in bed, where he would have fifteen hours to sleep it off. Afterwards, a stout masseur on his personal staff would pummel away any remaining effects of the alcohol in a half hour of frenzied chopping and kneading. Even if Norman hadn't had the luxury of a long recovery period, the immediate and visible effects on his body of the vigorous massage would be enough to mask the drinking, for a few hours at least.

To complete the pretense, Bunny didn't step from their bus for another ten minutes. When she did, she smiled and waved at groupings of the faithful. She held her leather-and-fur overcoat closed and followed her driver inside the hotel. Members of their staff continued to unload the big buses.

The ministry's two advance groups leapfrogged one another from city to city, making ready the television broadcasts in each locale. The Blue Team preceded Norman to Kansas City by forty-eight hours, and it would leave for Albuquerque immediately after the 120-minute telecast tomorrow. The Red Team was already in Denver for Thursday's production. The teams would continue on, alternately, to Phoenix, Los Angeles, San Francisco, and Seattle.

All seventy-seven members of the regular traveling troupe, including the orchestra and singers, counselors, ushers, pitchmen, and tape and book salesmen, were staying at the expensive Renaissance. Norman always said that the ministry's many contributors of wrinkled dollar bills and their Social Security checks would want nothing less than first-class accommodations for their representatives on earth of an all-providing God. Especially in these troubled times. He'd learned at least *one* thing from his old man.

Norman's news conference was scheduled a bare seventy-five yards from the charred remains of the billion-dollar-plus Sunflower at Overland Park, fifteen miles from downtown Kansas City on Interstate 35. At 8:50 a.m., two of the ministry's distinctive buses rolled into the east-side parking area of the bedroom community's once-proud shopping complex. For effect, they circled the blackened ruins of the huge center before maneuvering through the waving crowds awaiting Norman and Bunny. The first bus contained the security chief, a stocky ex-Army C.I.D., and his five men who carried special FM transmitters to enable them to remain in constant contact with each other. In the second vehicle, the minister and his wife looked out the smoked windows of their palatial home on wheels and waved back. The buses came to a smooth stop next to a small stand of metal bleachers, which had been erected by the Blue Team before dawn. Members of the local police—four uniformed officers and two plainclothesmen—mingled with the crowd.

Wearing dark glasses and fortified by a succession of cups of strong coffee, Norman sprayed another puff of cinnamon Binaca into his mouth and bounded out to the cheers of the faithful. He planted his polished Guccis just outside the bus and raised his arms dramatically in the direction of the ruins of the shopping center. Video and still cameras in the hands of admirers and members of the media whirred and clicked and recorded the arrival of the surviving son of one of America's most famous televangelists to the place where more than 11,000 men, women, and children had died barely three days earlier. The smell of burned wood and plastic from the devastation still lingered. Copious quantities of powerful disinfectants had cleansed most of the stench of broiled flesh. Occasionally, however, the putrid combination of dissimilar odors wafted across the loyal believers.

Norman brought his hands together in a prayerful pose. Half of his eighteen-karat gold Rolex President peeked above his left cuff, and the forty-six diamonds in its bezel twinkled chromatically in the morning sunlight. The crowd fell silent while he communicated with the Lord. After a minute, Norman raised his head and swung his right arm grandly in the direction of the bus, and Bunny emerged smiling. The followers started clapping again, and isolated whistles erupted as the lithe blond pranced toward her husband. The two, hand in hand, ascended the steps of the bleachers and walked to the center, where a podium and sprouts of microphones from area radio and television stations stood ready. Norman bobbed his head in feigned recognition of a dozen or so who had crowded in the closest.

"God bless you, dear folks, for coming out today," he proclaimed. "It's so good to see old friends."

Hundreds of others squeezed in behind. Norman waited until they were tightly packed. He solemnly looked out once again at the massive ruins across the way.

"My brothers and sisters," his voice boomed across the lot in his best ministerial style, "as I stand here and survey the horror that has befallen you, I am commanded by Almighty God Himself to proclaim to you today . . . His awful message." He gripped the edges of the podium and looked into their worried faces. A baby's shrill cry unexpectedly broke the silence. Its mother hushed and rocked the infant until it quieted.

"This . . . morning," Norman spoke with deliberate pauses, as if the words were being divinely revealed to him, one by one, "I . . . must tell you, dear friends, that we . . . are witnessing . . . God's wrath . . . for an *evil America.*" Even though most had expected his tirade, gasps erupted from the wide-eyed audience as Norman railed on. A few individuals raised their arms toward heaven in hopeful supplication.

Norman pointed over their heads toward the destroyed shopping center. "And *that,*" he shouted, "is only the beginning of His response!"

Couples held on to each other and bowed their heads in shame. Others moaned and prayed aloud. Many older children pressed their hands over their mouths at the terrifying thought that the ancient prophecies of the Bible were suddenly becoming very real. Norman adjusted his dark glasses and went on.

"Brothers and sisters," he shook his head slowly and announced, "we have selfishly forsaken His ways, His holy Commandments, and now He has decided to punish us for the evil in our hearts." Norman paused briefly. The only sound was traffic passing on the nearby interstate.

"We are witnessing the beginning of an era of terrible plagues, which will sweep across this sinful land, as the Holy Book has promised." None of the faithful needed to be reminded of the other disasters around the country that precisely fitted the minister's description of God's many—and justified—punishments.

Reporters scribbled furiously as Norman continued his recitation of the coming doom and devastation.

"Make no mistake about it," he moved on gravely, "God *knows* how to set the world straight." He pulled out a small leather-bound Bible and held it high for all to see. "He has wiped out entire peoples for their sinfulness. And now," Norman lowered the Bible and patted it with reverence, "He is moving against America for our willful and continuing transgressions against His laws." Norman shook his finger in double time. "He has warned us many times, but we have not listened." He raised his eyebrows and noted their readiness.

"You want examples?"

"Please, Brother Norman," they pleaded. "Please tell us."

Norman relished their unanimous, and predictable, response. He licked his lips and shook his finger again. "Do you remember 1963, when the Godless Supreme Court banned prayer in our schools?"

"Yes, oh, yes," came acknowledgments from the faithful.

"Well, President Kennedy was shot dead just months later!"

There was a collective gasp.

"Then, because of our accelerating evil, God allowed this glorious land of ours to sink into the horrors of the Vietnam War. He saw to it that our once-innocent boys brought back drugs and sexual diseases to undermine our nation. But did we listen?" People shook their heads in anticipation of his answer. "Oh . . . no. We kept pursuing our materialistic ways, and we remained indifferent to Him. So He sent more warnings." The crowd was completely his.

"When He allowed the so-called 'youth' revolution, with its hippies and other moral vermin, to threaten the overthrow of our government, we remained deaf. Well," Norman moved ahead slowly, "Senator Bobby Kennedy was assassinated, and Martin Luther King, Jr., was assassinated. Do you remember those days? Do you? *Do* you?"

A hundred voices moaned their acquiescence as his message burned into their hearts.

"We didn't learn, so God allowed the families of America to disintegrate, until, today, one out of every two sacred marriages ends in divorce. But we still didn't heed His Word. So He sent the epidemics of cocaine addiction, alcoholism, runaway teenage pregnancy, AIDS, and other foul venereal diseases to infect and kill our loved ones."

As Norman continued his chronicle of horrors, even some cynical members of the media frowned and wondered if there wasn't indeed a cause-and-effect relationship to the events.

"When the Supreme Court legalized murdering babies in 1973, it meant the beginning of the killing of millions of the innocent. Evil men and women throughout America began selfishly ripping the forming flesh of His little ones from the warmth and security of their mothers' wombs. Tiny human beings were sucked out and torn apart and discarded with raw sewage." His audience swayed numbly. Norman rolled his eyes upwards. His pronunciation became deliberate. "Well, now, my brothers and sisters, *God has had it.* He is going to see that we reap what we have sown."

Norman paused and leaned over the podium. He extended his arms toward them. They stared back as one.

"My beloved friends," he pleaded, "gather your families and friends and bring them to our magnificent Mid-America Camp Meeting at the Coliseum tomorrow morning at ten o'clock. Will you do that?"

"Oh, yes, Brother Norman," many cried. "We love God." Others looked heavenward and prayed. Most promised, "We'll be there!"

Norman pulled out a handkerchief and rubbed it against his mouth. "I'm going to reveal to you then how you can survive His wrath." He pointed toward the remains of the Sunflower. "Look at what happened to that beautiful center." The crowd turned and stared. Some whispered prayers. He waited until most were facing him again before he concluded. "As you now depart, remember that Almighty God has the power to do the same to the rest of America." He looked upward and held the pose as he spoke. "God has told me that His punishment for our sins is just beginning."

The immobilized gathering took to their very souls his message of a vengeful Creator and pledged themselves to be in attendance at Tuesday's camp meeting. As they shuffled toward their cars, Norman bowed his head. The security chief keyed his FM transmitter, and the engines of the two buses turned over and roared into readiness.

Troop B Headquarters, Oklahoma Highway Patrol, Tulsa 10:05 a.m.

"J. D. Caldwell?"

The questioner in the pinstriped suit was conspicuously out of place among the beefy uniformed lawmen who moved purposefully into and out of the bunkerlike building off Interstate 44, which served as the headquarters of the Oklahoma Highway Patrol for most of the northeastern part of the state. A large OHP patrolman stood up, stepped forward, and removed his Smokey-Bear campaign hat. His well-starched dark brown shirt bore a shiny gold badge, and his trousers were creased razor sharp. The trooper's heavy brogues were polished to a military sheen. A pair of Ray-Bans was tucked into his chest pocket. He was chewing on a toothpick.

"I'm Trooper Caldwell."

The agent held out his hand. "Gary Duvall, FBI." Caldwell returned the grip firmly. Duvall inclined his head toward the man next to him. "This is Roy Meeker, with the Bureau of Alcohol, Tobacco, and Firearms."

The trooper nodded and shook hands with the second visitor.

Duvall looked around the busy facility. "Could we have a little privacy?"

Caldwell swung his hat toward an empty office. "We do most of our interrogatin' in there," he advised through his toothpick.

"Fine," Duvall replied and immediately headed for the room off to the side.

The two other men followed him into the windowless cubicle. Meeker was last, and he closed the door. They sat in chairs arranged in a semicircle in front of a wooden desk with a black telephone. The room reeked of cheap furniture polish, with the stale hint of cigarettes. Duvall opened his pocket spiral notepad to a paper-clipped page and looked up.

"Trooper, we'd like to ask you about your report of last night."

Caldwell raised an eyebrow.

"Your supervisor called us first thing this morning." The FBI agent went on. "He used to be with the ATF, and the shipment caught his eye."

Caldwell shifted the toothpick in his mouth. "The truck on the port road?"

"Right. It was carrying RDX?" Duvall kept his eyes on the patrolman and waited for confirmation.

Caldwell frowned. "Sir?"

"You reported that you saw eighteen cylinders, at least one of which was labeled RDX."

"Uh, yeah." He hesitated. "Whatever that is."

Meeker leaned forward.

"Trooper Caldwell, RDX is a trade name for the chemical compound cyclo-trimethylene-trinitramine. It's one of the most dangerous explosives ever developed. Came out of the Second World War. It's also known as Cyclonite and Hexogen. RDX, in *any* quantity, doesn't belong in Tulsa, Oklahoma."

Caldwell pulled the toothpick from his mouth and stretched out his long legs. He whistled softly. "And I was within ten feet of it."

Duvall leaned closer. "How big were the cylinders?"

The trooper looked at the ceiling. "Can't rightly say." He put the toothpick back in his mouth. "I only looked at the tanks for a few seconds."

"Try to remember. It's extremely important."

Caldwell sat up in his chair and looked at Duvall. "Well, they were larger than the usual commercial stuff, like oxygen, acetylene . . . those things. I'd guess they were about eighteen inches across, and, since the truck was about fifteen feet long . . . " Meeker started shaking his head as Caldwell calculated. "Probably eighteen inches by seven or eight feet."

"Jesus Christ!" Meeker rolled his eyes. He turned toward Duvall. "At normal pressure, and if those cylinders were full, I'd say they had enough destructive power to blow up ten city blocks."

"*Shee*-it." Caldwell's toothpick dropped from his mouth.

"Do you know where they were going?" Duvall stared at the trooper. The patrolman fumbled inside his shirt pocket for a new toothpick.

"Well, uh, as I put in my report, they said they were taking the stuff to the two refineries here. Sinclair and Sun."

"God *damn* it, Caldwell," Meeker snapped. "No refinery in the world would want RDX within fifty miles!" Then he caught himself. "Sorry, but RDX is devastating. And in those quantities . . . "

Duvall took over again. "Do you recall anything else they said? Any other clues?"

Caldwell shook his head slowly. "No, sir." Then his expression brightened. "Now, wait just a minute. There was one thing I forgot to write down."

"Yes?" The two government agents spoke at the same time.

"Well, as I walked alongside the truck, back to their rear light, I noticed a telephone number on the side panel. It was partially painted over. Didn't seem important at the time."

"Do you remember what the number was?" Duvall was half out of his chair.

"Yep. It was 205-0582."

"Are you sure about that?"

"Well, the two of us, that's my wife Ladonna and me, we got married on May 5, 1982. You know, two people, then oh-five, oh-five, eighty-two. Interesting coincidence, isn't it?"

Duvall grabbed for the telephone on the desk.

"Keep your fingers crossed, trooper. If we're lucky, a whole lot of people might be celebrating your wedding anniversary with you."

Lester Graham sat on the foam-rubber mattress with its stained, scratchy army blanket and surveyed his restrictive quarters. The windowless basement was a wood-paneled cubicle of about fifteen feet square with a high ceiling. The floor was cold concrete, partially covered from the door to five feet from the rear wall by a loose piece of gray carpeting that curled up at the edges. Graham remembered the room as one of the original parts of old man Cummings's house. The only light came from a lone bulb dangling from a cord at the center of the room, which was operated by a switch next to the door. The privacy enclosure around the toilet in the corner had been removed, leaving the solitary ceramic bowl exposed. A well-stained sink with one faucet—for cold water—hung from the wall nearby. Occasional blasts of warm air made fluttering sounds as they jetted through the twisted and loose vanes of an opening above his bed. The strong smell of mold and urine irritated Graham's nose.

There weren't many basements in Oklahoma, he mused. But most of those that existed were built as shelters—"fraidy holes," they were called in the heart of Tornado Alley. Usually the below-ground hiding places around here were outside, separate from the houses. But Cummings had always been the consummate worrywart. He never wanted to risk getting caught by a twister while he ran across his property as the menacing clouds boiled up from the southwest. So he'd excavated a basement when he built his house, and outfitted it with some of the upstairs comforts: a throw rug, table, chairs, and a floor lamp. Over the years, he'd begun to utilize one side of the room to store canned goods and fruits from his meager garden.

The underground room served on more than one occasion for Cummings's infamous card tournaments for the males of the area. They always played Pitch, a diversionary staple of the oil patch. One never knew just when the gaming spirit would move the old man to schedule a few rounds. But when he did, the event would run for an evening or two, always late, until the wives would come to break it up. The women didn't wield rolling pins, but they might as well have. Nothing could sting as much as some of their tongue lashings. Eventually, however, in the spirit of contributing to the marital harmony of his neighbors, Cummings had called a halt to the fun and fellowship. Graham nodded and grinned at the memories. Yep, those were the days.

He thought again about the size of the room. Fifteen by fifteen? It had seemed much larger when they'd played cards here. Then he remembered. Cummings had partitioned the basement about a year before he died, when the old man decided to make a separate storage room for the canned goods. Graham looked over his shoulder at the new wall and wondered what the other room now contained.

When they'd pushed him inside the previous night, they'd untied his hands and taken away his flashlight, coat, and hat. But they'd let him keep his wristwatch. It now indicated a few minutes after noon. Suddenly he heard noises outside the heavy door. Scraping sounds again, like a metal gate being moved back. Then the door was unlocked.

Earlier, at breakfast, a bearded, muscular man in his fifties had opened the door and held out a bowl of watery oatmeal and a metal cup of black coffee. Both were lukewarm. Graham always drank his coffee with cream and sugar, and he'd asked for both, but the man pulled the door shut and locked it as soon as the meal, such as it was, was handed over.

"Stand back," a voice ordered this time as the door opened again. Graham remained on his bed. Just outside and to the right of the door frame was the edge of what appeared to be a heavy screen door. But the screen wasn't the usual thin shield against flies and mosquitoes. Graham peered at it as a new man entered carrying a plastic tray. At first, what he saw didn't register. Then, all of a sudden, a chill shook him. Unless he was wrong, that was the same wire he'd seen inside the large metal building, all coiled up against one of the walls. Now that he was up close, Graham had no doubt about what it was. Razor wire!

He had gotten a personal demonstration of the stuff at the Okmulgee County Fair a few years back when a salesman at a booth demonstrated it. The man had called it the ultimate protection against poachers and had pointed to a section that was coiled between two fence posts. "Take a good look, pardner," he'd urged. "But don't get too close." Graham leaned closer anyway. The wire was about a quarter of an inch wide and paper thin. He'd reached out before the salesman could react. The man's "No!" and Graham's hand hit at the same time. All the farmer did was to touch the wire lightly with his open palm. He hadn't used any pressure at all. But when his reflexes bounced his hand back, he saw a thin line of blood across his skin. He hadn't felt a thing. "See what I mean?" The man tossed him a wet rag. "A fella's likely to lose his fixtures if he walks into that."

"Here," the voice barked. Graham snapped to. This man was younger than the individual who'd brought breakfast, but he, too, was well built, and he wore a black T-shirt and faded jeans. Graham took the tray and made a face at the thin sandwich and glass of water. The brawny man turned for the door. Graham noticed that an armed guard stood outside in the hallway, his pistol drawn.

"Hey, buddy," he found himself asking, "when can I go home?" Without answering, the man slammed the door and locked it. He heard the scraping sounds again.

"Bunch of jerks," he muttered.

Graham lifted the top layer of the dry white bread and wrinkled his nose at the three limp slices of chicken. There was some sort of pasty brown mustard in spotty patches on the bread. He sniffed at it. The sandwich smelled better than it looked. He was hungry, so he lifted the offering to his mouth.

J. Edgar Hoover Building, Washington, D.C.
1:56 p.m.

It had turned out just as Deputy Director Jerry Reynolds had feared, although he found scant comfort in the fact that it took seven days instead of three to overload the system. The Strategic Information Operations Center was now reeling from the multiple crises that had erupted around the country.

Both of SIOC's main monitoring rooms were jammed with FBI agents and analysts attempting to make sense of the rush of events that had begun barely a week earlier, when the AirParis supersonic transport was blasted out of the sky over Arkansas. Additional space in three adjacent offices outside the secured facility had been appropriated for SIOC use. By midnight, another thirty agents would arrive from New York, Richmond, and Pittsburgh to man the new observation positions.

The atmosphere was frenetic, and Reynolds feared it was just the beginning of a massive coordination effort by the Bureau that would confirm his earlier warnings to the director that the FBI was unprepared for a widespread outbreak of terrorism. What had happened before this past week could have been announced by that broadcast warning, "This is only a test." They'd learned some lessons, all right, but they hadn't lost that self-assured feeling that America was off-limits for the big time. The quick apprehension of the World Trade Center and Oklahoma City bombers had only fueled false confidence at the Bureau. Today, however, any remaining smugness had dissipated.

"Colquitt, Redding, Turner," he barked into the intercom. "Meeting in the conference room in five." At his side, Corley Brand, chief of the FBI's Counterterrorism Section, finished reading a faxed memo. Reynolds watched as Brand started shaking his head.

"Now what?"

Brand handed it over. "From Tom Bentley. Hell, Jerry, another front's opening up."

Reynolds scanned the transmission from the supervisory senior resident agent in Tulsa. "*That* much RDX?" He whistled. "Damn!"

"Mr. Brand?" An assistant approached with another sheet of paper. "More from Tulsa."

Brand took the new document and held it so both he and Reynolds could read it at the same time.

"HAVE LOCATED ORIGINAL OWNER OF TRUCK THAT CARRIED RDX. VEHICLE RECENTLY SOLD TO 'CHRIST'S BELIEVERS,' DORMANT SUBSIDIARY OF TULSA-BASED REUBEN GENTRY MINISTRIES, INC. AGENT EVANS WILL REINTERVIEW JACK STROUD, HOSPITALIZED BROTHER-IN-LAW OF EVANGELIST NORMAN GENTRY. MORE ASAP. BENTLEY."

"The Gentry Ministries? Again?" Brand pondered out loud. "First it's the blackmail and extortion matter. Then the senior evangelist dies. The strange bank accounts. Carmichael's kidnapped at Stroud's on Saturday. Now this. All in a week. And old Jack's sitting right in the middle of it."

"You used to work with Stroud, didn't you?"

"Sure did. And I'm going to give him a call. He may turn out to be very helpful."

"Mr. Reynolds?" A shirtsleeved technician wearing a headset pointed to a telephone. "Line seven. Bentley in Tulsa."

"Jesus Christ, that place is on a roll." Reynolds sat down at the telephone console. Most of the thirty-six buttons were flashing on hold. He picked up the receiver and punched line seven. "Tom, we got your two faxes, and . . . "

Bentley interrupted. "Jerry, here's the latest on the truck."

"The RDX shipment?"

"Yeah. The director's office at the Tulsa port confirmed about a half hour ago that an outfit called Holway Imports signed for five shipments over the past three weeks. All of the manifests read 'nitrogen.' And the same truck picked up each shipment. The latest was the one last night, which the Oklahoma Highway Patrol intercepted."

"Oh, great . . . it's *five* shipments now." Reynolds said it loud enough for Brand to hear.

Bentley continued. "Four of the cargoes were inspected by the port police. Those cylinders were clearly marked 'nitrogen.' Stenciled on the tanks. We don't know why that fifth shipment had paper labels."

Reynolds rubbed at his chin. "Well, I'll wager all five shipments were RDX. Someone just screwed up labeling that last one. Maybe they were in a hurry. What about Customs?"

"Jerry, the stuff apparently came in from Mexico as containerized cargo and cleared at New Orleans. Customs there tells us what they saw was all labeled nitrogen. I understand they bled off some of it, and it *was* nitrogen."

"Did it come in five separate shipments?"

"I think so."

Reynolds was silent for a moment. "Tom, when we had to check Customs records at New Orleans last August, I talked with their Strategic Investigations Division here. Do you know how much of that containerized cargo they actually inspect at New Orleans?"

"I've heard around half."

"Try three percent."

"Oh, just great," Bentley returned. "OK, Jerry, I've got one for you: We can't find that outfit called Holway Imports. Doesn't exist, at least according to the Oklahoma Secretary of State. And no trace of the truck either. We're going to pursue this with Jack Stroud."

"All right." Reynolds made a notation on a telephone pad. "Corley's going to talk with Stroud later, too." He started to hang up.

"Oh, what's the latest on Carmichael?"

"Absolutely nothing. It was a professional job. We've spent part of two days at Stroud's home. No prints, fibers, or anything. Charlie wasn't even able to leave any clues for us. So it must have been fast and smooth. We did get a good description of the two men from Stroud's housekeeper, but there are no leads yet."

"OK. Keep me advised." Reynolds replaced the handset. He turned in his chair and faced Brand.

"I want a complete review of everything we know, from the SST to the recent stuff in Tulsa, and I want it by seven in the morning. I'm going to schedule a meeting here with the director for an hour later."

The counterterrorism section chief looked at the digital clock on the opposite wall.

Reynolds eyed the clock also. "I know . . . never enough time, right?"

"What?" Then Brand shook his head. "Oh, no problem. I'll have a preliminary summary ready by seven tonight."

Reynolds peered at his subordinate. "Uh-oh, I see those wheels turning. You think something's coming together, don't you?"

"Who knows?" Brand smiled. "But things are getting curiouser and curiouser."

Phoenix
2:37 p.m.

The Maricopa County Independent School District released the fleet of orange buses in staggered shifts, beginning at noon. All 233 vehicles had been overhauled and readied over the holidays and were to be in place at their assigned positions around the city by 2:15 p.m. in order to transport students home this first day of school after the holidays.

Camelback Elementary's ten buses idled outside the administration building as the dismissal bell clanged. Earlier in the morning, they had been given a special, unannounced safety check by three state inspectors. Now, even though it was an unusually cool afternoon, the drivers had the doors open in anticipation of the hordes to come out of the buildings.

An average of thirty-six children sought out and sat down in each of the numbered vehicles. They laughed and poked one another and shuffled in their seats as the buses closed their doors and rolled away. The drivers turned onto the side streets of the middle-class neighborhood and anticipated nothing more than the usual babble of freed-from-school youths during the hour-long circuits before they returned to the central facility.

Bus No. 76 had made its second stop when a third-grader retrieving a dropped crayon made a discovery. "Hey, look, you guys," he called from the floor to his companions. "A hidden bomb!"

The driver heard the characterization and wasn't amused. He watched the commotion in his rearview mirror as other children joined the boy on the floor.

"Sit down, everyone," he yelled over his shoulder. "We're not supposed to be moving while anyone's out of his seat."

"But it's a real bomb, Mr. Tolliver. Come here."

The driver angrily braked to a stop and unfastened his seat belt. "Where's a bomb?" He swung out of his seat and started back.

At exactly 2:41 p.m., digital timers triggered carbon-steel canisters under two seats of each of the ten buses. One cylinder was strategically placed close to the front door, and the other was located near the rear emergency exit. In the fifteen-inch tubes, iron-saturated water jetted into compartments of highly reactive methyl isocyanate, and the virulent chemical reactions began with a strong hiss. Yellowish-white gas began puffing and spewing through the perforations in the containers within two seconds of the triggering injection. The thermal decomposition of the methyl isocyanate yielded the additional deadly byproducts of hydrogen cyanide and carbon monoxide.

The spread of the gas was so fast and pervasive that no driver was able to open the door of his bus in time. Within ninety seconds, the concentration of the gas in each bus exceeded 4,000 milligrams per cubic meter of air, more than ten times the lethal dose. Two buses immediately careened off the street and slammed into trees. Children writhed and held their faces in agony as the toxic gas seared into their eyes and noses. They frothed at the mouth and grabbed and fell across one another in asphyxiating convulsions as the poison did its efficient work.

By 2:50 p.m., 365 children and nine bus drivers were dead. There were only five survivors of the terror: one driver and four of his young passengers, a boy and three girls. They escaped through a smashed windshield when their bus crossed the centerline and crashed into a moving van.

St. Francis Hospital, Tulsa
7:14 p.m.

The telephone on the bedside table rang twice before Jack could move from the chair in the corner to the bedside table. He'd learned earlier that the hookup in his new room wasn't a direct line. Ever since Saturday, the FBI had arranged for his incoming calls to be routed through the hospital operators for screening. There was a list of approved callers, most of whom were family members. Since his out-of-town relatives had left the previous day, and Rachel was now on her way to the hospital, he wondered who the caller might be.

"Mr. Stroud?" a man's voice asked.

"Yes?"

"Sorry to hear you're in the hospital, sir. This is Fred Johnson, down at Sears. Do you still want the Lady Kenmore?"

Jack cocked his head. "I beg your pardon?"

"The washer you talked about before Christmas? It came in last week. Or do you want to think about it and call me back? I'm at Woodland Hills. We're open until nine."

Jack nodded. "Good idea, Mr. Johnson. Yes, let me think about it." He hung up.

"Business or just a social call?" he said aloud as he reached for his robe. That guy hadn't pulled that line since their D.C. days together. Jack stopped at the door and tapped twice.

A policeman stuck his head inside. "Sir?"

"I've got to make a call on a secure phone." Jack tied the belt of his robe.

"OK." The officer pointed. "Room across the hall is ours. The phone's a direct outside line. It's clean." The uniformed man glanced down the empty corridor and motioned him to go ahead. "You'll have privacy in there, too."

Jack entered the room and closed the door. The curtains were drawn, and there was a cot on one side of the cubicle and a couch on the other. A metal table next to the couch bore a standard black telephone. He picked up the receiver. Just what in the hell is his number, anyway? He turned toward the window and thought for a moment. Used to call it all the time. "Well, when in doubt . . . " He punched in 1-202-555-1212.

"Directory assistance." The woman's voice was as clear as if she were downstairs.

"Washington, D.C."

"Yes, sir, go ahead."

"FBI headquarters, please."

There was a pause. "Please hold for the number."

Jack listened to the recorded information, then depressed the button on the telephone and called 1-202-324-3000. The connection was made almost instantly.

"Good evening. FBI."

"Corley Brand, please."

The line was silent for a few seconds. Jack then heard a ringing tone. It sounded again.

"Counterterrorism Section. Comisky."

"Corley Brand, please. Jack Stroud calling."

The man put him on hold, and Jack thought about his own programmed reaction to Brand's method of contact. His friend had called him the previous Wednesday, openly, before the service for Laura and Jeff. Prior to that, they hadn't talked for six months.

"Brand."

"Corley, it's Jack. I almost called you by name when you pulled your Sears routine. I'm on a secure line now."

"I gambled you'd remember."

Jack grinned and shifted against the back of the chair. "What's up?"

"I have a meeting in the morning with the director. I'm going to tell him what I'm going to tell you now."

Jack looked over his shoulder. The door to the room remained closed. "Go ahead."

"What I'm about to say is the result of a confluence of hard facts and all my years of training. I'll tell you right now there's no clear line separating the two, but just hear me out."

The FBI man had Jack's full attention. They had met years ago on a case in New York, and Jack had instantly liked this bundle of uncanny insight disguised as a lanky, mild-mannered investigator. At that time, the FBI had wanted to remove one of the Tass reporters from his post at the United Nations, but the man, actually a high-ranking Soviet KGB officer with diplomatic immunity, had suddenly started playing it straight. Brand knew that the man's past curiosity had included the U.S. Navy's submarine base at New London, Connecticut, so he'd called the Naval Investigative Service and gotten Jack.

Let's try a "dangle," Jack remembered suggesting. That was a ploy in which a supposedly cash-short and desperate sailor would "accidentally" cross the path of a spy who was more than willing to pay for classified information. It took three months to set up the encounter and to ingratiate a chief petty officer to the Russian. The exchange was to be a technical operating manual used for one of the new miniaturized radar systems in return for $2,000, hardly a thousandth of its real value to Moscow. The dangle ensnared the KGB spook, who was quickly and quietly deported, and Jack and Brand developed a genuine friendship out of the initial mutual respect of one professional for another.

"Jack, I think someone in that organization you married into is directly involved with this national outbreak of terrorism."

Jack made a fist but said nothing as Brand went on.

"Last night's discovery of the explosives by the Oklahoma Highway Patrol was the deciding factor for me."

Finally, in Jack's mind, form began to emerge from the ethers of the past week. Don Evans had mentioned the truck earlier in the day, but it hadn't triggered anything. Now something was definitely coming forth. He knew he had to force it out. Regardless.

"What else do you have, Corley?" He was gaining control of his ideas.

"Jack, I think *you* were the primary target of the bombing of Laura's flight, not Treasury Secretary Rowland, as is officially believed."

Jack closed his eyes and leaned back against the chair. He nodded. What the old man meant was so obvious, but he couldn't hear him then.

"And you're probably still in their sights," Brand kept talking, "even though we suspect the latest attempt against you was called off at the last minute. Ironically, your life might have been spared because of your discovery of the foreign bank accounts. They know we have the information now, so maybe they're going to leave you alone. But don't count on it. On the other hand . . . "

"Corley," Jack interrupted, "listen to me."

"I'm listening."

" 'Before it's too late.' "

"What?"

"That's *it,* Corley. That's what Reuben said. He really meant it when he said he feared for his life. I heard him. It was the same thing he told the U.S. Attorney, but I didn't understand. I thought he was only talking about the ministry, which had always *been* his life."

"Would you cut me in on your reasoning?"

"Corley, I've got to get his body exhumed."

"Reuben's?"

"He knew he was going to be killed."

"You think Reuben was murdered?"

"Damn right, and he knew who his murderer was. He'd touched his face, Corley. That's exactly what he meant."

"Why the hell didn't he just tell you, Jack? Simply name the guy. I mean, that was quite a melodramatic conversation. If you're right, that is."

"Oh, I'm right, Corley. Right down the centerline."

Brand recognized Jack's tone of voice. He knew that in Stroud's mind, the chase had already begun. The FBI agent tried anyway.

"Well, damn it, remember your own bandaged head. You're getting out of there tomorrow, and the U.S. marshals will be protecting you twenty-four hours a day. Rachel, too. For God's sake, Jack, let the marshals do their jobs. Don't outrun them, trying to be a fucking hero. Let's get to the bottom of this together . . . when you're feeling better. Okay? Did you hear that? *Together.*"

"Yeah." Jack's voice sounded as if he were already somewhere else.

Brand listened for a clue. "You still there, Jack? *Jack?*"

"Still here, Corley. But not for long."

J. Edgar Hoover Building, Washington, D.C.
Tuesday, January 5, 6:11 a.m.

The metal coffee unit on the scuffed countertop surged and dripped through its third performance of the early morning. Corley Brand held his monogrammed cup with both hands and stood with his back against the wall of the kitchenette, stifling a yawn as he waited for the machine to finish. This was his fourth trip to the trough. The hot stream of aromatic black liquid began to slow. Brand blinked and focused his eyes on the clock above the door. His meeting with Deputy Director Jerry Reynolds was three-quarters of an hour away. He thought it always seemed that the length of the old percolator's brewing cycle was in inverse proportion to the amount of time available before a critical meeting.

Brand needed one more serving of the stimulant to ensure full alertness for the session with the second in command, especially after the revolving-door visit to his bedroom last night. Or, rather, this morning. He had finally gotten to his Crystal City apartment at 12:15, and into bed shortly after one. There was barely enough time to get to sleep before the alarm sounded at three. Brand had flashed his FBI building access-identification pass at the guard downstairs seventy-five minutes later. Four of his counterterrorism subordinates were already in their offices when he stepped off the elevator on the National Security Division floor.

The coffee unit finally produced only sporadic drips, and Brand pulled out the full carafe and poured a mugful. A few tardy drops of the freshly brewed liquid dropped from the filter and danced across the hot plate for a second before they evaporated, leaving an acrid odor of burned coffee that would linger in the kitchenette most of the day. He stabbed the stainless-steel community spoon into the sugar bowl and dumped a full scoop into his cup. He stirred the sweetener through several revolutions and thought again about his forthcoming meeting. Then he thought about Jack Stroud.

"If we're right about all of this, ol' boy, you're going to be one busy son of a gun."

He took a tentative sip of the beverage and pronounced it acceptable. Now, if he could just have the same luck completing the conclusions of his revised summary—and, more importantly, selling them to Reynolds and the director. He headed back to his office.

WRC-TV, Washington, D.C.
7:00 a.m.

Homer Jenkins fidgeted in the swivel chair. He squeezed and released the padded armrests and watched a sweep-hand clock on the side wall. His face was puffy red. The floor director noticed the House Speaker's emotional state and motioned for additional makeup.

Jenkins waved away the offer. "No more of that shit. I want everyone to see how pissed off I am." The floor director held up his hand and stopped a woman with a kit.

"I gave the president twenty-four hours on Saturday," Jenkins went on, mostly to himself. "It's now been *three days,* and he still hasn't gotten a handle on this insanity. Well, just let me turn up the political heat a notch or two and singe that blue-serge fanny of his. . . . "

"Willard in thirty," a disembodied voice announced over the speakers. The nationally recognized weatherman pulled on his fur cap and kidded with a secretary as he headed for the door and his Washington remote in the snow. On a monitor positioned between two television cameras, the network feed showed the wrap-up of a story featuring a Greek Orthodox family's preparation for Epiphany. The live picture then came from the Rockefeller Center studios, and a woman, seated at a desk, started talking. The sound of her voice merged with last-minute commands from the Washington floor staff. Almost immediately, the picture on the screen split in two. The woman in New York was shown on the left side, and the rotund weatherman, wearing a sprig of holly on his overcoat lapel, mugged on the right. Lighted behind him on the studio grounds outside was the desired winter scene of snow-covered trees and shrubs. As Willard talked, his breath condensed in oblong wisps, which he playfully fanned away. A color photograph of an emaciated bald man, celebrating his hundredth birthday with a toothless smile, appeared on the screen. The elderly gentleman received the obligatory compliment on his good looks, and Willard's best wishes.

"Forty-five seconds."

A young NBC-TV network reporter slipped into a chair opposite the House leader. He adjusted his fitted earpiece and smiled at the notorious politician, who fingered his bow tie.

"Morning, Mr. Speaker."

Jenkins nodded perfunctorily and maintained his agitated movements. The floor director listened to something from the control booth. He pressed his earpiece tighter and stepped onto the raised stage. "Mr. Speaker, we need another audio level on you, please."

"You want *what?*" The older man looked up and glared. "What in the hell is it now?"

"That's perfect, sir." The floor director held up his hand. "You just gave it to us." He stepped back and slipped into the dark coolness and relative anonymity of the cavernous room where a dozen employees and congressional aides waited for the telecast to begin.

Most Americans had learned of the horror of the previous day, in which 365 innocent schoolchildren were asphyxiated in Phoenix. Added abruptly to the list of seemingly runaway intentional disasters, this latest affront to America stretched the emotional resilience of many to the breaking point. Everyone at WRC this morning was ready for Homer Jenkins's promised onslaught against a "criminally temporizing" administration.

The House Speaker was scheduled to be a revolving-door guest on other television and radio networks all day. Americans screamed for a response to the nightmare while resolute action was still possible. The coach might be paralyzed on the sidelines, but quarterback Jenkins wasn't going to let his team lose by default.

The reporter maneuvered his chest microphone a little higher on his tie and laid out the scenario for the House Speaker. "New York will do the intro, sir, then hand it to me. I'll ask you three or four open-ended questions. We're scheduled for four and a half minutes. But we can have five and a half, if we need the extra sixty seconds."

The crusty old man rubbed his hands together.

"Son," he snarled, "you'd better book that extra time *right* now."

J. Edgar Hoover Building, Washington, D.C.
8:00 a.m.

Warm, humidified air blew solidly through the wall registers of the narrow conference room of the Strategic Information Operations Center. Six FBI supervisors sat in shirtsleeves at the heavy mahogany table and underlined and updated their briefing materials. Video monitors along one of the walls silently displayed the worldwide areas of interest being staked out by the specialists stationed inside the SIOC bunker. This morning all but one of the screens presented domestic U.S. scenes.

Jerry Reynolds sat at the end of the table and scribbled notes in the margins of his papers. For most of the past hour, he and Brand had reviewed the out-of-control terrorist situation across America.

The deputy director glanced around the room. Each man had a copy of the classified status report that detailed the series of unprecedented attacks. Reynolds had originally called this meeting to review the events and to coordinate the efforts to put a stop to the national madness. But that was yesterday afternoon, before Phoenix. And before the president ordered the Bureau to produce something—anything—within forty-eight hours. Reynolds noticed the time just as the director walked in. He stood up. The others did likewise.

The tall leader of the FBI moved to his usual place at the table and reached for the stapled document. Without looking up, he flipped through its ten pages and motioned for the men to be seated. As they took their places, the director settled into his chair and made eye contact with each one of them in turn. Then he spoke.

"Playtime's over."

Several of the men winced in frustration. The director noticed their reaction. He added, "That's what the president told me last night." The qualifier didn't make anyone feel better.

Reynolds peeled back the cover page of the report and nodded to the FBI's counterterrorism chief. "All right, Corley, let's go."

Brand stood up and looked first at the summary, then at the director.

"I've prepared a chronological list of the incidents of the past eight days, beginning with 28 December and running through last midnight. It's the first part of the report. I'd like to go over it with you, sir, and everyone else here, so we're parallel in our understanding of the crisis. I had an executive summary as an introduction, but I decided last night to make that my oral conclusion. Because of some new information."

"Singular, Corley?" The director peered at Brand.

"I beg your pardon?"

" 'Crisis'? Not 'crises'?"

"Yes, sir. That's the way I see it. One source, one goal. Makes for one crisis. But you're getting ahead of me."

"Hardly," the FBI leader responded. "For a few days you were all alone with that conclusion. Now I understand you've got converts." He looked at Reynolds and the five others. "All right. I'm open-minded. I want appropriate comments as we go. The president wants everything possible for his NSC meeting in the morning. I don't care if you have a hunch or if you've heard a rumor. Nothing's insignificant anymore."

Each man indicated with a nod that he understood. The director signaled Brand to continue.

"Thank you, sir," he replied. "Here are the incidents and our latest intelligence." He read from the report. "A week ago yesterday, two unidentified men killed two caterers at the Dallas–Fort Worth airport and loaded nine metal canisters aboard an AirParis SST. The plane blew up over southwestern Arkansas seventy-five minutes later, killing all on board, including Treasury Secretary David Rowland. We now know they used Gellex-4, probably as much as five kilos to get the kind of destructive effect they achieved from the placement in the galley. The quantity was at least twice that necessary to bring down the jet. We believe there was a third person involved who drove them to the airport in an Oldsmobile Cutlass. The car was found too far away for the men to have left it there themselves. There were no latent prints on the catering truck or on the car. Also, telephone lines into the Lone Star catering firm were deliberately cut. All those involved escaped. We've interviewed a security guard and an airport policeman. We have descriptions of the two men, but we've drawn blanks all around."

One of the section chiefs stopped writing. "Corley, didn't anyone else—airport security, FAA people in the tower—see those individuals?"

Brand shook his head. "No, they apparently got away in the dark. And with all the morning rush-hour highway and airline traffic, there's no telling whether they were picked up or caught a flight. The airport authority's been installing new sensors and security monitoring cameras around the field, but the only units operating that day were near the cargo areas on the west and northeast sides of DFW."

He turned the page and resumed.

"At about the same time that morning, Amtrak's Train No. 100 was deliberately derailed at Iselin, New Jersey. Based on the weight of the molded switch that had been placed over the track—240 pounds—we're assuming that at least two individuals were involved. It was a Lucite composite that was nearly transparent. We've never seen anything like it before. Anyway, someone went to a lot of trouble to measure the roadbed and to construct a device that would be effective in derailing that train only. The switch was triggered by radio, so someone stayed behind to activate it. We're still checking to see if anyone on board would have been a likely target. So far, nothing."

"Damn right we've never seen anything like it before."

Loren Turner, the FBI's assistant director, Laboratory Division, pushed himself away from the table and flipped a pencil into the air in cartwheel fashion. He grabbed but missed, and the pencil hit the table on its eraser, bounced once, then settled and rolled rapidly toward the other side. He slapped it to a stop. "That wasn't any vo-tech project." Turner picked up the pencil. "It took precision engineering to mate the Lucite with the steel moving parts in such a way that the unit would survive five or six heavy freights before it was needed. Whoever assembled it even protected the radio in a recessed section on the side facing the oncoming trains. When the signal activated the switch, the radio itself spring-popped into position on the inside of the right rail. At that location, there was no way it could survive the impact from the Metroliner's wheels, and that's exactly what they wanted. We have the pieces, all right, but learning who built the radio from its shape or structure is out of the question." He tapped the pencil against the table. "It was professional all the way. From construction to destruction."

Brand noted Turner's comments in the margin of his copy. "Anything more, Loren?" The assistant director shook his head.

Brand picked up his report and continued. "The third incident that day was the attack on DOT Secretary Nielsen in Georgetown. One person probably injected the poison into his leg, although he might have had an accomplice to help him get away."

Another man raised his hand. "Any connecting theme with the other attacks?"

Brand shook his head. "Right now, only that it happened on the same day. But it was a style of murder used by Soviet-bloc operatives during the Cold War."

He flipped another page.

"The next attack took place the following day, Tuesday, when someone brought down the L-1011 charter outside Albuquerque. From an examination of the wreckage, we know that a Stinger missile was used. It was probably one of hundreds taken out of Afghanistan." He observed his subdued audience. "There was virtually nothing of the left wing of the TriStar at the main wreckage site. From where the wing's debris was found, and from our own tests, it's our conclusion that the missile homed in on the number-one engine. The rest of the aircraft disintegrated upon impact with the ground. Gentlemen, if these incidents are connected, individuals involved in the first three attacks could have made it to New Mexico in time. But there are no leads yet."

"Corley?" Jerry Reynolds rubbed his chin. "Give us the latest on those Stingers. Specifically, what we have on how many are missing and where they might be."

Brand laid the open report face down on the table and crossed his arms.

"The best intelligence we have is that some 1,400 of the surface-to-air missiles, with launchers, either disappeared from mujahadin camps or were otherwise unaccounted for during the 1985–1995 decade. Probably seven hundred or so fell into the hands of the Soviet-backed Afghan government, and a few of those were used against supply planes aiding the resistance from Pakistan. But the majority of the seven hundred undoubtedly crossed the border, going north with the retreating Soviet troops. We've learned that nearly four hundred were supplied to Saddam Hussein before the Soviets stopped military aid shipments, although, for some reason, he didn't use them against us. Of the other seven hundred, possibly as many as five hundred are in the hands of terrorist organizations worldwide. We and Customs have made two dozen separate intercepts in the United States, and we've confiscated nearly a hundred of them so far. We're now saying that at least three hundred Stingers are illegally in this country today. Some—keep your fingers crossed, maybe as many as a hundred—are in the hands of reclusive underground collectors. A few are being held by right-wing soldiers of fortune. However, domestically, there are probably two hundred Stingers in the absolute worst hands." He paused. "I guess, after Albuquerque, I should say . . . 199."

"What are we getting from the Secret Service?" The director pushed himself away from the table. "The presidential protective boys have got to be changing their underwear a lot these days, just thinking about the possibilities."

"I talked with Ray Shaffer again late yesterday," Brand responded. "They've laid in the most sophisticated electronic equipment for jamming and deflection, but the Stinger is a simple, no-frills heat-seeker. Air Force One is as vulnerable as a Piper Cub during takeoffs and landings. At altitude, of course, they can dump a hundred high-temperature flares to draw missiles, but it doesn't work well near the ground. They're really worried."

"So where *are* the missing Stingers?" the director asked.

Brand shook his head. "I've never seen anything like it. We're squeezing our usual informants and listening posts. We've pulled all the stops. Usually something surfaces. Not this time."

"But you have your ideas."

"Yes, sir." Brand held up his hand. "In just a second." He went on. "We're now adding the death of Ahmed Pasha, the Cairo Interpol agent who was killed on the Frankfurt–St. Louis flight last Wednesday. The autopsy showed he died from an injection of an explosive dart into his brain, through his right ear. That's a well-honed method used by two pro-Syrian organizations. The weapon was probably disguised to look like a ballpoint pen. Sometimes the point even contains enough ink to fool a spot check. There were six Middle Eastern men traveling as a group of F-1 students. Pasha apparently became curious about one of them, according to an interview the St. Louis field office conducted with one of the flight attendants. All six men disappeared in Tulsa later Wednesday."

Brand leaned over and picked up his coffee mug. He frowned at the cold liquid and put the mug back. He turned a page.

"Next comes the destruction of the Houston disco on the evening of 30 December. It was a car bomb, employing RDX. Again, that's a method frequently used by Syrian extremists. One witness who left the place a couple of minutes before it blew up said she saw a police officer talking with a young blond woman next to the car that exploded. That's all we have."

Brand turned to the next page.

"There was another killing, a professional job, which qualifies as a terrorist action from our standpoint." He looked up. "The brutal murder of the mayor of Denver last Thursday."

Dennis Bevens, Deputy Assistant Director, National Security Division, laid down his pencil and clasped his hands together. "Corley, as I remember it, the media referred to that as just a gruesome killing. It might be helpful if you tell us what makes you classify it otherwise."

"Effects." Brand nodded toward Bevens. "In order to decide whether or not such a murder qualifies as a terrorist act, for our purposes, we look at the effects, or what we think were the intended effects. In Mayor Pritchard's case, he was a prominent politician. His murder affected a much larger community than the immediate family. All citizens felt the impact of his death, whether or not they lived in Denver. The attack was destabilizing, and it made the point that virtually anyone can be a victim." Brand referred to his report and continued. "It was the classic demoralizing murder. There *is* a possible connection between that incident and the space shuttle attack, which I'll mention in a minute."

He lifted another page of the summary.

"The New Year's Eve destruction of the shopping center outside Kansas City required from twenty-five to fifty operatives to carry it off. Coordination of the placement of the phosphorus explosives at the many entrances to that place was almost to the second, so it required a sophisticated, timed effort by a fairly large group."

Brand went on. "On January first, we intercepted a car trying to enter El Paso from Mexico. The driver set off an explosion that killed him, a woman with him, four of our men, and two INS agents. And two innocent kids they were using as a cover. Gellex-4 again. A lot of it. We think they were bringing it in for later use."

Two of the men at the table shook their heads.

"Then comes the *Encounter* disaster. We've tracked the Sabreliner back to its Mexican owner, who, it turns out, doesn't exist. At least not in the name on the aircraft registration statement. Now, here's the interesting coincidence: We've learned from the FAA that the Sabreliner flew from Denver to Panama City, Florida, on the thirty-first. Why it was in Denver that day we don't know, but it departed for Florida less than an hour after the mayor was killed."

Brand checked his notes.

"Plus, the pilots' names on their IFR flight plan were phonies."

He paused, then continued. "The plane didn't have Air Force markings until it left the private airstrip near Panama City for the Cape. Our people have been to that place. It's a small metal hangar that was leased for a week, for cash, and it's been cleaned out. The owner, who lives in Macon, Georgia, handled the transaction over the telephone. He said the money was mailed to him in a plain envelope from Panama City. Because of his unusual business modus operandi, the DEA's going to keep an eye on the hangar for a while. And on him."

"A lucky break, Corley," Bill Colquitt observed. As assistant director for the National Security Division, Colquitt was over Bevens, Brand's immediate boss. He tugged at his earlobe. "You know, those pilots could have flown low, VFR, and avoided filing a flight plan altogether. We'd never have known about their trip if they'd done that."

Brand nodded. "We're looking into the weather en route. They may have had to go high that night." He turned to the last page.

"Then there was the gassing of the schoolchildren yesterday in Phoenix. The first reports lead us to believe that two or three so-called 'state vehicle inspectors' probably placed the methyl isocyanate cylinders in the ten buses at a school garage at noon. Those men have disappeared."

"Did anyone see this morning's *Post* story on the survivors?" The director reached for the newspaper and read a portion of the article.

"The lucky five will spend a minimum of six weeks in the hospital, where doctors will struggle to save their sight. All will vomit, defecate, and urinate involuntarily for days and will scream around the clock from seared lungs. The long-term effects will be on their immune and reproductive systems. Even with superior treatment, it is feared the girls will never be able to bear children. If by some miracle they can, their babies will likely be grossly deformed."

No one spoke. After a moment, Brand flipped his page over and placed the summary on the table.

"Over the past eight days, 13,000 people in the United States have died at the hands of terrorists."

"God *damn!*" the director exclaimed through clenched teeth. "And the country's coming apart at the seams."

Brand remained standing. "Direct property loss, close to $8 billion, with uncounted billions in liability claims for the loss of human life. Our best guess is that all of these criminal acts were carried out by a maximum of eighty individuals. Possibly even by as few as fifty."

He looked over his audience. The men stared at their summaries. It was time for him to connect the dots.

"Gentlemen, I've spent twenty years studying terrorism." He started pacing. "I've lived it. I get up with it in the morning, and I go to bed at night thinking about it. I've come to know the mind of the terrorist. In a psychological sense, I've almost become one myself." He drew a deep breath and faced the director. "I've come to two conclusions. I've already expressed the first, which is that one single, elite international terrorist organization—the absolute best of the worst—has set up the American base we've feared for years." Brand made a mental note that most around the table nodded with him.

"What I haven't said before is that I think I know where that base is."

The FBI director leaned back in his chair. "All right, Corley, you're the best in the business. 'Creative,' 'scrupulously thorough,' and 'invariably correct' all aptly describe you." He tapped the armrests impatiently. "Spell it out. If you convince me, I'll give it to the president with both barrels."

The counterterrorism section chief walked to the white board on the side wall. He picked up a red marker, pulled off the plastic cap, and wrote the numeral "1" at the top left corner of the board.

"Watch this." He continued to write. As he did so, he maintained a brisk narrative.

"On 30 December, at least one of six men, traveling together on Syrian passports, was under surveillance by an Interpol agent on a TWA flight to the United States. That agent was later killed by someone on the flight. All six individuals disappeared hours later in Tulsa."

He faced his audience and fitted the cap over the end of the marker.

"The Germans have all the facts we do, and they're running them through their Kommissar cross-referencing system. When we receive something from them, we hope to get a positive identification from a flight attendant who says she'll never forget the suspect's face. Or the scar on his hand."

Brand opened the marker again and turned back to the board.

"Second, there was an attack, by rifle, and as many as three subsequent attempts on the life of a consultant to the Reuben Gentry Ministries. Tulsa again, gentlemen. That man is Jack Stroud. I used to work with him when he was at the NIS."

"I remember Stroud," Loren Turner spoke while he wrote. "Navy. The double sabotage case at Norfolk." He put down his pen. "You've kept in touch with him?"

Brand looked over his shoulder and nodded.

"Now look at this." He started writing again. "There are some very interesting coincidences involving Stroud. He lost his wife and son in the SST crash, and the truck discovered carrying the RDX on Sunday was owned by a subsidiary of the ministry. Stroud's father-in-law was none other than evangelist Reuben Gentry himself. Then, don't forget, Gentry reported suspicious activities to the U.S. Attorney's office in Tulsa before he died on 28 December. The older man said he feared attempts at blackmail, extortion, and even one on his life."

Those seated around the table copied down the information.

"Later, following an anonymous tip to our Tulsa office, Stroud discovered data indicating that the ministry has been receiving secret, and massive, funds. From where and why? No idea yet."

The director stopped taking notes and tapped the point of his gold pen at the corner of the report. The counterterrorism chief moved on.

"As you know, one of our Tulsa agents assigned to the Gentry case was kidnapped at gunpoint on Saturday. In Stroud's home, no less."

The director laid down his pen and clasped his hands.

"I talked with Stroud last night," Brand continued. "Based on all that's happened to him, he thinks Gentry was murdered. And he thinks the old man knew his own killer. Stroud's going for an exhumation order. This is just one more arrow pointing at the ministry."

Jerry Reynolds got the director's attention.

"Sir, we've been in almost continuous contact with Tom Bentley, our SSRA in Tulsa. Ron Oliver, the SAC in Oklahoma City, is proposing the formation of a special task force in Tulsa. They're bringing the appropriate parties together tomorrow afternoon. Based on the compilation of information, and what they end up suspecting, they'll be going for a search warrant. Possibly as early as Friday."

The director watched Reynolds. Finally he looked at Brand.

"That's it?"

Brand nodded. The director shook his head.

"Sorry, Corley, it's not enough. Oh, you make a good case that something very real and possibly very wrong is going on in Tulsa. At the Gentry ministry, no less. I'm all for the task force, leading to a search warrant, to find out. But," he rapped his pen against the surface of the table in metronome fashion, "you . . . just . . . don't . . . have . . . the smoking gun. What you've presented here may be the beginning of something that will lead to it, but you don't have it yet. And, much as I'd like to, I can't tell the president we're absolutely sure we've located the source. Because we're not."

Brand couldn't hide his disappointment.

The FBI chief raised his eyebrows. "Remember what happened during the Watergate affair? Nixon held on, agonizing week by agonizing week. Why? No smoking gun, that's why. When the president was finally forced to release the last of the tapes . . . *voilà!* The smoking gun, and it was all over."

Brand couldn't argue with the director's logic. From a purely legal standpoint, the key part of the evidence was indeed still missing.

"Find that smoking gun, Corley. As fast as you can."

Brand crossed his arms. "I intend to, sir."

The director rose and started for the door. As he came alongside, he put his hand on the section chief's shoulder.

"If you're confident you're on the right track, Corley, you have my support to stay the course."

St. Francis Hospital, Tulsa
8:40 a.m.

Jack had considered taking a nap after breakfast, but he couldn't. He was too eager. This was the day he was finally scheduled to be released. At the FBI's request—security, they'd stressed repeatedly—he had been held over an additional forty-eight hours. Now it was time to go home to be with Rachel, threats or no threats. And time to start unraveling an enigma.

With a perfunctory knock on the door, Dr. Paul Cunningham entered and walked toward Jack's bed.

"Good morning!" The physician smiled and flipped open a medical report. "Ready to get out of here?"

"Have been for days." Jack sat up. "I thought you'd forgotten about me."

Dr. Cunningham glanced over the hospital data.

"I've talked with a Mr. Evans of the FBI who wants to visit with you before you leave." The doctor looked at his watch. "He said he'd be here around ten. So, unless he has a problem, you ought to be home for lunch. In the meantime, let's change your dressing."

Dr. Cunningham turned as a nurse carrying a small metal tray came into the room.

"Just put it here on the table, Miss Singletary."

Jack was immediately struck by the beauty of the woman in white who moved smoothly toward his bed. He had definitely never seen *her* before. She appeared to be about thirty or thirty-five, five and a half feet tall, and, it was irresistibly obvious, most appropriately proportioned. Her caramel-colored hair curled softly from beneath a starched cap, and her face displayed the remains of a tan. She smiled at him as she laid the supply tray next to his bed. Her jade-green eyes held contact with his an instant longer than was purely professional.

Dr. Cunningham interrupted the momentary spell by peeling back the two bandages on Jack's skull. Jack's face twisted. "That . . . I felt."

"Sorry. The adhesive stuck a little tighter than usual." The physician pressed his fingers around the shaved portion of Jack's head. "I see you've been eating your Wheaties. Feels OK. Another six weeks and even your barber won't be able to tell."

Dr. Cunningham swabbed a disinfectant liquid over the wounded area and studied the sutures. "Everything looks just fine, Mr. Stroud. Your stitches can be removed in another three or four days. By Dr. Marks, if you wish."

"Leland says I'm in capable hands," Jack offered. "But I think I'll let him do something for me."

Dr. Cunningham reached for a new bandage.

"The damage was only a bit more than skin deep, so I'm going to cover it with two glorified Band-Aids. Once the stitches are removed, you won't require any more dressing. Other than maybe a hat, for your ego, until your hair grows back."

"Good thing it's winter," Jack replied. "I might look almost normal in the damn thing."

The physician pressed the sterile patches into position, then peeled off and cut four strips of medical tape to hold the covering in place.

"Well, that should hold you until the weekend." He plunked the scissors into the stainless-steel tray. "You're a lucky man, Mr. Stroud. Another quarter inch and it would have been quite another story."

Jack accepted Dr. Cunningham's hand and shook it. "Thanks for everything."

He watched as the nurse smoothly folded the materials together on the tray and followed the physician out of the room. He thought he saw her hesitate before she pulled the door shut. Jack stared at the door for a moment after she disappeared.

Fifteen thousand adherents filed down the steep steps of the spacious, oval-shaped downtown hall and found their places as the Gentry Singers in their white suits and sequined gowns joyfully rendered their grand introductory medley. The orchestra was positioned at the side of the large stage, and it provided exquisite accompaniment to the ten men and ten women who exuberantly projected their upbeat hymns.

Fifteen minutes after ten, the spotlights dramatically winked out, one by one. The singers moved to the back of the stage in the fading light and began humming one of the ministry's Christian marching tunes. The audience knew this was the sign that the long-awaited camp meeting was about to begin. New beams of focused brightness began crisscrossing the darkened auditorium from parapets high above. When the orchestra started playing one of Reuben Gentry's rousing favorites, "Make Way for the Lord!" cheers erupted from the thousands who jumped up and started clapping and singing along. They stomped their feet and raised their arms and swayed in preparation for the anticipated entrance of Gentry's beloved son and his beautiful wife. As the melody faded, the lights swept around the frenzied room, and an announcer's voice cascaded from the massive speakers throughout the hall.

"Ladies and gentlemen," the man proudly boomed, "Norman and Bunny!"

To the screams of the thousands, the orchestra pounded out "When the Saints Go Marching In." The audience rose and waved and yelled with the rhythm. Their voices reverberated from the walls and magnified the effect.

"Oh, when the saints . . . " They gyrated and bellowed along.

"Go marching in . . . "

"Oh, when the saints go marching in . . . "

"I want to be in that number . . . " Thousands of arms waved in the resounding mayhem. "When the saints go marching in."

"Oh, when the saints . . . " "Yea, yea!" they cried out.

"Go marching in . . . " "Yea, Lord!"

"Oh when the saints go marching in . . . " "God forgive us!"

"I want to be in that number . . . " "Norman, show us!"

When the saints go marching in . . . "

A thunderous reception built as the interior lighting flashed on and off, encouraging the casting away of all restraint.

A full five minutes later, at the end of the third frenzied refrain, an intense spotlight focused on the center of a powder-blue backdrop. Norman and Bunny emerged and trotted to the middle of the stage. With uplifted arms and waves to various parts of the vast room, they encouraged the pandemonium to continue. Finally the music softened and the crowd quieted, and, at Norman's signal, a tall, well-dressed man stepped to the microphone and reminded the listeners of their duty to give until it hurt. An army of eager young men and women raced to their places in the aisles, up and down throughout the building. The volunteers quickly reached even the furthest member of the assembly. Everyone had the chance to give to God's work—and they did. When buckets filled, new ones were immediately brought into play. The man then pointed to Norman and Bunny, the orchestra boomed forth once more, and hysteria reigned again.

Norman was dressed in a high-style, double-breasted Italian suit, which was as white as anything ever worn by a virginal bride. This was his traditional public image, the quintessential exhibitionism of his craft, and it was accented by a man-size purple orchid on one of his wide lapels. His diamond pinkie ring flashed like a tiny sparkler. At his side, Bunny was stunning in a bishop's-purple silk suit, its sleeves tightly gathered at the shoulders to deliver a fashionable puffy look as they extended to her elbows. Amethyst earrings peeked from the soft curls of her champagne blond hair when she turned her head, and they complemented an oversize amethyst ring that sparkled in the glare and led enraptured onlookers to notice the pink polish that covered her long fingernails. The dazzling effect was completed by her purple eelskin closed-toe shoes with three-inch heels. She, too, wore an orchid, smaller and alabaster white with a deep purple center.

For ten minutes the volley continued, verse after tearfully repeated verse. Finally, after six full encores, the orchestra's sounds faded, and the faithful sat down. The spirit of the Lord now filled every heart in the auditorium.

"Brothers and sisters . . . "

Norman motioned for quiet, but even in their seats they were too excited to subside.

"Hallelujah, Brother Norman!" the screams poured toward the stage.

"Brothers . . . and . . . sisters!" he boomed and beamed and bowed. It took another five minutes before the celebratory welcome ended. Bunny moved to a chair at the rear of the stage.

"We," Norman started as the multitude quieted, "have brought *Jesus* with us!"

The audience erupted once again. Hundreds jumped up and waved their arms, their eyes closed in the sacred presence of the Lord. The frenzied demonstration went on for another minute and a half.

Norman removed the microphone from its pedestal and walked back and forth in the tight spotlight. He waited until he could be heard.

"And Jesus has a message for *you!*"

The thousands screamed again, then collected themselves and watched with tear-stained faces. Most of the audience sat down, ready for his words from on high.

"Brothers and sisters, Almighty God, in all of His power and glory and wisdom, wants me to tell you this morning . . . that He is *punishing* America." Whispers and moans rose throughout the massive hall. He shook his finger at them.

"Now, you listen carefully."

The receptive thousands wondered which awful prophecy was being fulfilled.

"Almighty God is angry with His country, and He has already begun extracting His terrible retribution. And He is going to continue with these punishments until we change our ways."

Norman peered through the brightness of the lights into the faces of the true believers and repeated his message of the previous day when he had visited the remains of the Sunflower. The crowd cowered at the implications.

He rolled on.

"Today my message from Almighty God is that if we want Him to stop the reprisals against this great land of ours, we must stop all abortions, everywhere, and for any reason. Period."

"Oh, yes, we must," came the screams.

"Abortion is murder, pure and simple!"

"Praise God, *yes!*"

Norman walked to one side of the stage. A five-foot metal easel was covered by a black cloth. He pretended to struggle with the covering, heightening the tension. Suddenly it gave way, revealing a large color photograph of an aborted fetus. The crowd gasped at the sight of the purple torso against a white background. The severed and mutilated legs and arms lay next to its body.

"This," he pointed and railed to the horrified crowd, "is what the secular humanists want more of."

"Oh, no, Brother Norman," hundreds cried out in unison. "No!"

He presented another grotesque picture. "This little baby was injected with poisonous saline solution and sucked from the safety and sanctity of his mother's womb. He writhed in his death throes on a cold steel table before he was thrown into the trash and hauled to the city dump."

The visual horrors brought forth a background wail from the gathering.

The third picture was of a metal bin filled with the bloody remains of abortion. Tiny arms seemed to reach out for deliverance.

"This, my brothers and sisters, is the product of just one morning's effort at a killing clinic."

The effect on the crowd was visceral. Norman wiped his ample lips and continued.

"Millions of babies have gone to their deaths . . . more human beings than Hitler ever killed. We *have* to go after those clinics. They're worse than Auschwitz and the other efficient chambers of death of that horrible era."

"We'll stop them, Brother Norman. We'll even die if we have to!"

"These murderers must be hunted down like Nazi war criminals. They must be brought to justice for their crimes against humanity. They must be punished. Any doctor who performs an abortion should be convicted of first-degree murder . . . along with every willing and knowing accessory." Norman brought a handkerchief to his soaking forehead. "Abortion is destroying our society. If we don't take immediate action, Almighty God will continue His devastation."

"We will follow you, Brother. We're ready to do God's work!"

"God is punishing America for its sins, and He will do more until we get the message."

Norman continued with further examples of the evils of abortion.

"It's bad enough that unmarried women are sexually active, but when they use abortion for birth control, God screams for revenge. These selfish women would rather murder their own children than go through with their pregnancies and give up their babies for adoption. I tell you that any woman who truly opens herself to God will come to see that abortion is one of the ultimate sins." He leaned forward. "And if she doesn't learn her lesson, she deserves the same thing she inflicts on her innocent baby."

"Yes, let her die," his wide-eyed disciples screamed. "Let them all die!"

Norman poured out another collection of wrongs that result from abortion. He was particularly strident against organized groups that were doing the Devil's work.

"Make no mistake about it, the pro-choice movement in this country is elitist, racist, and genocidal. Those people must be eliminated by whatever means necessary."

He glanced at his watch. It was time to conclude his tirade, but before he finished, he wanted to single out one particular medical practice for condemnation.

"Do you know what some so-called doctors are doing to the unborn? Doctors who are sworn to protect the sanctity of life? They're sticking a needle into the protective sac around the little baby to see if the child isn't absolutely what the parents want. It's called amniocentesis, and its purpose is evil."

The faithful had heard enough. The swaying and moaning men and women were nearly overwhelmed by the litany of affronts to God.

"You don't want a boy? Kill him! You don't want a baby who might have an inconvenient medical problem? Kill him! It's legal."

This drew sharp screams from the thousands.

"Every baby should be given a chance to live, no matter how deformed or mentally defective it might be. To destroy these little ones, handicapped though they may be, is to set up an elitist society in which only the perfect may live. It is the first step toward the breeding of a master race, the Third Reich all over again."

The orchestra, on cue, began a muted rendition of "Glory, Glory, Hallelujah."

"When the righteous are in power," Norman spoke over the building melody, "the people are happy. We are the people who understand what God wants. We are the ones He's expecting to rule over His land."

The orchestra sound increased, and waves of the devoted and the newly committed began standing and singing. Norman put the microphone back into its holder and held out his arms. He stood with his palms open toward the throng of worshipers for nearly a minute. Few noticed that his orchid had wilted.

"And now, my children," Norman resumed, "there are many of you who wish to accept Jesus, to publicly acknowledge that you have been born again. Others of you once accepted Him, but you've been walking the world's way. If you wish to make a commitment, to get right with God, or to obtain counseling, just come right down to this beautiful altar."

As hundreds rushed forward, Norman spoke again.

"My brothers and sisters, I want you to go forth," he admonished the multitude, "and take action into your own hands. Do not be afraid. God is with us. God will protect us. God will save us. And if we mend our ways, God will bless America again!"

As 15,000 voices became one and sang the remainder of the sacred piece from the depths of their emotions, Norman reached to his left. Bunny was already beside him. He took her hand, and together they bowed and departed. The sobbing penitents at the altar were left with local volunteers who took their names and addresses and listened to the confessions and cries for mercy.

St. Francis Hospital, Tulsa
11:47 a.m.

Don Evans stood and retrieved his overcoat from the back of the chair.

"Meridian Tower, east of Yale off I-44. Suite 950. Four-thirty tomorrow afternoon." The FBI agent had been sitting across from Jack for an hour and a half. Their discussion had been almost nonstop. He pulled on his coat.

"I'll be there," Jack replied as he rose and walked with Evans to the door.

Evans opened the door and looked outside.

"Young lady," he smiled, "he's all yours."

Rachel moved around a policeman and approached her father tentatively. Then she ran to him and hugged him tightly. "I need you, Daddy," she pleaded.

Her body trembled in his arms. Jack stroked the back of her head. "I need you, too, Rach. Let's go home."

"One more thing, Jack." Evans stood in the corridor. "Ted Colyers, a deputy U.S. marshal, is waiting in his car outside the emergency entrance. That's the most secure place to depart the hospital. He'll drive you home."

Jack kept one arm around Rachel and signaled with the other. "Thanks again, Don."

"Ready, folks?" It was Sergeant Harjo of the Tulsa Police Department.

Jack looked down at Rachel. She turned toward the policeman and replied with a smile.

"Yes, sir. My Dad and I are ready for anything."

Kansas City Renaissance Hotel
12:30 p.m.

The buses of the Christian Cavalcade, engines purring, stood ready for their departure to Denver. More than a thousand well-wishers lined the hotel corridor. Norman and Bunny grasped the hands of their supporters and made their way to the parking lot.

"Bless you," Norman exclaimed as he stopped and kissed the cheek of a woman in her fifties. He reached toward a boy who stood next to her.

"Your son?"

"Oh, no," she giggled. "He's my ten-year-old *grand*son."

Norman held the boy's hand in both of his. He squeezed it affectionately. His tongue showed through his lips as he stared into the boy's eyes.

"My, but isn't he handsome."

The woman beamed.

Tulsa
12:37 p.m.

Flora peeked out the window and realized it would be any minute now. She had staked out her usual observation post in the dining room. From innumerable times waiting for Jeff and Rachel's school bus, she knew that if she moved the drapes aside just about a foot, she could see all the way to the intersection six houses away. It would give her the lead time necessary to get outside before they arrived.

When an unfamiliar automobile suddenly pulled into the driveway, Flora blinked in surprise. Who could that be? She brought her hand to her mouth as she remembered that Rachel had gone to St. Francis Hospital with the marshal in a government car. She started waving excitedly and kept waving as she rushed for the front door. Within seconds, she was across the frozen lawn and alongside the car.

"Mr. Stroud. Oh, Mr. Stroud."

"Flora!" Jack called through the glass. "You're going to catch cold without your coat." He winked at her and opened the door. She gave him a teary embrace after he stepped out.

"Mr. Stroud, I'm so glad you're home."

Jack held her. "It's great to be back, Flora." He put his hands on her shoulders and drew back a bit. He looked into her eyes. "I missed you."

"Oh, I missed you, too." She noticed his pullover cap. "You have a hat?"

"Only for a few weeks." He wrinkled his nose. "You know I don't like these things."

She hugged him again.

The marshal finished unloading the trunk and closed the lid. Rachel came around the side of the car with Jack's suitcase. He saw her from the corner of his eye.

"Here, let me take that, sweetie."

"No way, Dad." She lugged the suitcase past her father. "You're *my* patient now."

"Mr. Stroud?" It was Colyers. "It'd be best if you went on inside, please."

"Yes, Mr. Stroud." Flora patted her hands together. "I have a nice lunch all ready for you."

Jack laughed. "*No* one sets a table like you do, Flora."

She smiled proudly. "I knew they wouldn't take care of you the way you deserve, so I called Petty's yesterday, and they sent out all of your favorites . . . rib-eye steaks and freshly squeezed orange juice and their famous English muffins and . . . "

"I don't believe it," Jack interrupted. "For lunch?"

"Oh, no, sir." She didn't see the twinkle in his eye. "I want to have all the right things for every meal from now on. You and Miss Rachel deserve only the best."

The White House
Wednesday, January 6, 9:00 a.m.

With his back to his visitor, the president sat in the Oval Office and stared outside in silent contemplation as tiny snowflakes drifted and swirled past the bulletproof windows. The frozen precursors of a strengthening winter storm had arrived six hours earlier than predicted, and they touched and teased at the buildings and monuments of the city.

Thousands of others in the District looked out their windows at the white crystals and grumbled and began computing alternate times and routes home, for they knew that rush hour would be a tormenting hassle of heartburn and fender benders. Few residents of metropolitan Washington appreciated this kind of weather. Especially if they had to drive, which most did.

The president removed his reading glasses. He closed his eyes and gripped the bridge of his nose. Finally he turned in his leather chair and placed his spectacles on top of Brand's summary.

"I've read better fiction."

The FBI director took a deep breath and sighed. "But what if he's right?"

Neither man said anything for a few seconds. The president leaned forward and laid his hands, palms down, on the polished surface of the desk. "So you agree with him?"

The federal lawman shifted in his chair.

"We currently have active investigations at three other locations within the continental United States, but, quite frankly, they don't compare to what's happening in Tulsa—particularly in light of the discovery of a large cache of explosives coming in at the port there and the suspicious financial arrangements." He paused. "I've given Corley Brand carte blanche to pursue every lead, but he keeps coming up with that ministry."

The president stood.

"Well, that's just great."

He tucked his hands into his jacket pockets, walked to the front of the desk, and propped himself against its edge and faced the director.

"A prominent Christian ministry backing a bunch of terrorists, probably Middle Eastern. Who in the hell's going to believe that?" he snapped.

The FBI chief hesitated. "With all due respect, sir, if you'll recall, Brand thinks it's the other way around."

"Oh . . . yes." The president nodded and walked back to his chair. "Well, that's even *more* insane." He gripped the top of the leather seat with one hand and turned around. He glared at his guest. "All right, crazy or not, I'll give you the benefit of the doubt. Temporarily. What's his plan?"

"To find the missing link, the 'smoking gun.' Best bet is by search warrant."

"When?"

"Looks like the day after tomorrow."

"Not sooner?"

The director shrugged. "It's possible, but Brand doesn't want to make the mistake of digging in the wrong places. It's a big campus out there, and with the stakes being what they are, he can't afford to select empty buildings. He's got to be specific, and justify his choices, in order to get the search warrant. But I'll see what I can do."

The president pointed at the director. "You tell him I'm expecting results."

"Yes, sir. The Bureau's already forming a task force with the ATF and a couple of other law enforcement groups in Oklahoma, specifically targeting the ministry." The FBI man added, "I'll see that any other steps needed to be taken *are* taken, in order to expedite results."

The president checked his watch. "Time to tell it to the NSC. Let's see if they have the same faith you do."

The FBI chief rose. The president took him by the arm. "I hope to God Brand's right. We need a major break. One more disaster could tip the country into anarchy." He shook his head as they started for the door. "And everyone worried that the Korean situation would be our severest test after the Gulf War. Then we had New York and Oklahoma City. Preludes?"

The president stopped.

"I'm going to hold your feet to the fire for quick results. I'm scheduling a news conference for Friday evening . . . to announce a breakthrough."

Tulsa
10:51 a.m.

Jack's housekeeper advanced toward his desk with the morning mail.

"Heaven's sake, Mr. Stroud, I've never seen so many catalogs *after* Christmas in all my life." She held out a collection of some two dozen pieces of advertising. "Maybe only two or three important things among them." She grinned. "Like—¿cómo se dice?—bills."

Jack peered over the top of his reading glasses as he accepted the bundle. "Catalogs? Purely fishing expeditions, Flora. In case anyone has any money left after the holidays." He smiled. "Bills? They're always in season."

The woman put on a frown. "Now, don't forget, Mr. Stroud." She shook her index finger. "Lunch at noon, then your nap. To make sure you get better."

Jack waved his acquiescence as she started to leave. It had been more than ten years since the rotund little lady had proudly come to Tulsa Bible College to enroll her freshman son. And it was only shortly afterwards that she had smiled her way into the Strouds' hearts.

The woman turned around. Her black hair, accented with ribbons of silver, was pulled back into a tight bun to reveal her happy, moon-shaped face. She stroked the sides of her white apron.

"Mr. Stroud," she spoke awkwardly, "I'm . . . I'm so glad you're home."

Jack winked. "I am, too, Flora. Thanks for being here for Rachel and me, and thanks for being you."

As soon as she left, Jack began to examine the mail. He found the envelope almost immediately. He lifted it up and held it in both hands. Its appearance was unique, yet something about it seemed familiar. He ran his fingertips across the crisp onionskin paper, then considered the way his name and address appeared. The typing looked as if an old manual machine had been used. Some of the letters were not evenly aligned. Tulsa became "Tul a." He tilted the envelope for oblique lighting and noticed that the top of the missing "s" was barely evident at the base of the "l" and the "a."

Jack opened his desk and extracted a letter opener. As he slipped the sharp end into the fold at the back of the envelope, it dawned on him. This was the same kind of stationery used for the message the man pressed into his hand after Laura's and Jeff's memorial. Typing, too. Jack knifed the envelope open and took out a folded piece of paper. He laid the opener aside and unfolded the letter. Same typeface as on the envelope. He was now sure it was the same as that on the mysterious note of almost a week ago. He read.

J. Stroud—
After Thanksgiving vacation, forty foreign students at Tulsa
Bible College did not return to campus. All majored in political
science and are still listed on current school rolls. Sincerely worried
their disappearance connected to attacks against you and America.

Jack frowned. There was no signature, date, or return address. The envelope was postmarked the previous day, and it had been mailed locally. He folded the letter and returned it to the envelope.

"Flora?"

He was already out of his chair. Jack carried the envelope to the hall closet and laid it on a nearby table. He picked out a sports jacket, put it on, and tucked the envelope into an inside pocket.

His housekeeper came around the corner from the kitchen as he slipped into his overcoat. She was wiping her hands on a towel.

"You're going *out* for lunch, Mr. Stroud?"

"No, I'll be with the FBI. I should be back in an hour or so. I'll definitely be here before Rachel gets home from school."

She reached into the closet and handed him the wool cap. "Well, be sure to keep this on. You don't want to catch cold."

Jack fitted the cap over his bandage and smiled. "I don't want to show my bald spot, either." He fumbled for his keys before he remembered the deputy marshal outside.

"Oh, who's on duty this morning?"

"I think it'll be Mr. Colyers. He takes over at eleven."

Jack referred to his wrist. He made a face. "Flora, have you seen my watch?"

"No, sir."

Jack returned to his study with Flora in tow. Both gave the room a cursory once-over. When the timepiece wasn't found, Jack thrust his hands into his coat pockets.

"I don't remember wearing it home yesterday. I'll bet I left it in my room at the hospital. They moved me so many times, I wouldn't be surprised." He started to leave.

"Flora, would you call St. Francis? Maybe someone there found it."

He was out the front door before she could say anything.

City Hall, San Francisco
11:00 a.m.

Mayor Vincent Nomura saw the signal from his security man at the door and turned again toward the full-length mirror on the inside of his office closet.

"Coming, coming."

He held the knot of his four-in-hand with his right thumb and forefinger and gave one last tug to the shorter end of the tie. He twisted his medium frame and appraised himself. He was quite satisfied at the reflected results. The media close-ups would encourage some writer at the *Chronicle* to comment again on how fortunate the City by the Bay was to have such a distinguished-looking man representing their sophisticated metropolis. It never failed, and it always boosted his standing among the voters. Not to mention his ego.

Once more, Nomura checked the drape of the jacket of his expensive suit and made sure his French cuffs and gold cuff links extended slightly beyond the sleeves. Only then did he adjust his smile and walk toward the door. The security man opened the partition into the brightly lit conference room and motioned the mayor to the podium, which bore the city seal. On either side of the stage were the obligatory flags, Old Glory and California's proud banner from the days of the Republic. A row of television cameras lined the back and side walls of the room. Impatient reporters and proud city dignitaries crowded together and provided the mayor with the essential elixir of any politician: attention. He attempted to acknowledge their gift by singling out a lucky few for a personal greeting.

"Good morning, Ben. Appreciated the Christmas story on our friends in Sausalito. Nice touches. Carlyle, we need to have lunch next week. Oh, hi, Amy. Tell your dad we're thrilled you're on board."

Nomura adjusted the microphones and noted the presence of two representatives from Sacramento. The governor had maintained a close liaison with the city ever since the U.S. Commerce and State departments had given this conference their respective priority rankings. He felt for his water carafe and glass on the second shelf and winked at a pert female television reporter who smiled at him from the second row. He reached inside his jacket and extracted the stapled notes, which he laid face up on the podium. He cleared his throat.

"Ladies and gentlemen," the mayor thrust out his chest and began, "this is my third report to you in as many weeks concerning another proud moment for San Francisco."

He looked around the room and beamed.

"As you know, a week from today we will be honored to host the thirteen-nation Pacific Rim Summit. It's been in the planning stages for three and a half years, and now it's about to come to pass. We will have in town the presidents of the Philippines and Indonesia, the premier of China, and the prime ministers of Japan, Singapore, Australia, New Zealand, Malaysia, Thailand, Canada, South Korea, and Taiwan. Secretary of State Arthur Cromwell will represent the United States, and the president will be the keynote speaker on Thursday."

The mayor paused after reading the list of attendees. He checked his notes.

"Just to recap, the major functions will be held at the Westin St. Francis and the Hyatt on Union Square. These heads of state and their various delegations will be our guests at a number of functions around the city. There is a schedule of the many events, and if you don't yet have a copy, you can pick up one at the door."

Nomura reminded everyone of the goals of the conference, the prime one being the continuing unity and cooperation of the thirteen countries for their common good during the explosive economic expansion in the Pacific arena. Not far down his enumeration was a plan to assure San Francisco a key participatory role in the growth. And that step would start with a successful conference.

The mayor ended with an exhortation that the community extend a most gracious welcome to its special visitors.

"What an opportunity this will be for us," he gripped the podium and boomed. "When you count the number of business leaders and their families who will accompany each country's delegation, we'll have 1,300 VIPs here. Thirteen hundred," he repeated, then waited for a moment before continuing. "I ask you again . . . let's show the world the special graciousness and charm for which San Francisco is known." With this close, and a broad grin, Nomura tucked his notes away and bowed formally.

Beggs, Oklahoma
12:52 p.m.

Ever since they'd pushed Lester Graham into his basement cell on Sunday, the simple routine hadn't varied. Three meals a day were delivered with stopwatch regularity, and the plastic plates and utensils were always picked up half an hour later, not that it took him that long to eat the usually unappetizing fare. At least once every twenty-four hours, there would be a surprise intrusion by the guards. They'd bolt in and stand and stare at their prisoner. Then they'd leave. Always without explanation.

It was just after lunch on his third full day of captivity when Graham's curiosity finally paid off. He was lying on the bed, staring at the back wall. Something about the wood paneling hadn't sat well with him since the first night, but he couldn't figure out why. All of a sudden he realized what was wrong.

"Hot damn!"

He jackknifed to a sitting position. Of *course* there was nothing wrong with the back wall. *And that's what was wrong!*

He raised his head in thanksgiving and pounded his fist into his palm as the memory came together. When old man Cummings built this basement, it was only a rectangular pit lined with bare concrete. Then he'd covered the walls with dark wood paneling to make the place look more presentable. And it had been a really nice room, until the almost continuous seepage of water between the concrete of the back wall and the paneling caused the top part of the wood to mildew and warp. Varnish concealed the truth and postponed the inevitable for a year. However, Cummings had finally ripped out the entire back wall and made the appropriate repairs. Repairs that just might spell opportunity, Graham thought, as he got up and sauntered over to the wall.

He studied the dark brown surface. It was some fifteen feet wide by eight feet high, and it consisted of paneling set vertically, with matching molding where the wood met the ceiling. It showed its age, but it still looked solid.

Graham turned around and stared at the door. He had never before stood and examined a wall for so long. It would certainly look suspicious to anyone peering in through a peephole. He waited and watched for another minute. There was no sound from the outside. Finally he thought it best to check out the rest of the room while he was at it, to see if there were any obvious places where someone could see into the cubicle.

He stepped along a side wall and watched for suspicious cracks or punctures in the covering. Then the front, past the door, and back alongside the other wall. Everything seemed as intact as it had been when the old man had entertained years before. There were no new holes, no peekaboo slits. Graham blew out a breath and put his hands on his hips. If he were right, and if the new owners hadn't made any changes to the foundation, there might be a way out of this dungeon after all.

He moved to the back wall again and held out his open hands. His fingers contacted the hard surface at shoulder height, and he pushed against it. The surface yielded slightly. If memory served him well, there'd be a good fifteen inches between the replacement paneling and the original concrete wall. Graham stopped and remembered that he had come over once or twice to visit while the old man was making his repairs. It was afterwards that Cummings divided the room. So maybe there'd be an adequate crawl space behind both this room and the adjacent one. Where it might lead . . . well, he'd just have to find that out.

Graham looked in the direction of the door again. He hoped he hadn't overlooked a prying eye somewhere. Still, nothing looked suspicious. He turned and rapped the wall gently with his knuckle. The muted tap echoed back the hollowness behind. Graham smiled and moved along the wall and did the same thing every couple of feet. He heard the same sound. There *was* a space behind the thin board. Now, if he could just figure out the best way to get behind the outer covering without attracting attention and getting caught. He shook his head. The whole effort might be a waste, when all was said and done. He might simply find himself between wood paneling and a cement wall. He returned to the bed to consider his next move.

Ron Oliver, special agent in charge of the FBI in Oklahoma, motioned the others into the conference room. Special Agent Gary Duvall brought up the rear. The younger man came through the door with a pencil in his mouth, and he carried a sheaf of papers and a coffee cup. He nodded at Oliver as he passed. Already around the elongated table were Tom Bentley, the Tulsa office's supervisory senior resident agent, and agents Don Evans and Harriet Blake.

When Duvall took his place, Oliver started.

"If the reason we're here turns out to be valid, today will mark the beginning of a major national role for this office. We could be in the eye of the most devastating political hurricane the country has ever encountered. This morning the president gave his personal approval to our effort. A great deal has come into focus over the past couple of days." The SAC looked to his right.

"Tom, you begin."

Bentley remained in his chair. "Corley Brand's summary of the various terrorist incidents with a possible Tulsa nexus was faxed to us this morning. You've all read it, so let's proceed." The SSRA pulled himself to the table. "We've been directed by the deputy director to form a special task force to determine the extent of criminal activity, if any, taking place at the Gentry Ministries, with particular emphasis, of course, on any relationship to terrorist actions."

Bentley clasped his hands together and nodded toward his colleague. "Since Evans has been spearheading this up to now, I want him to continue being case agent for the investigation." He glanced around the table. "We have enough probable cause to go for a search warrant, but I don't want any slippage. Understand? No wasted motions out there. No wildgoose chases. We can't afford a screw-up." He rubbed one hand with the other. "I'm allowing thirty-six hours to put all the pieces together to make our case to the U.S. attorney. No more."

Bentley clasped his hands together again and rolled his thumbs back and forth.

"We have twenty-four agents operating out of the Tulsa office. We might have to double that . . . if this is the real thing." He referred to his watch. "A former military guy, Jack Stroud, is coming in at four-thirty. Don, why don't you fill us in concerning his involvement in this case."

Evans started with a review of Jack's background, from his Navy days to the present. The FBI agent mentioned the SST crash on December 28 and continued through the kidnapping of their fellow agent Carmichael from the Stroud home. He concluded with the meeting he had had earlier in the day with Jack concerning the latest anonymous letter.

"He's certainly in the eye of the storm already," Harriet Blake observed. "We're protecting him, aren't we?"

"Since last Saturday," Evans replied. "Deputy marshals. His daughter, too. We're treating them like witnesses."

"Twenty-four hours, for both?" Oliver asked.

"While Stroud was in the hospital, Tulsa police sat outside his door. The marshals checked on his daughter after school only. But we went to around-the-clock coverage yesterday for both, as soon as he was released."

"Well, if this is what Brand thinks it is," Oliver observed, "the guy could be in a hell of a lot of danger, especially at night. He may be our only key." The SAC went on. "Depending on what we uncover, we might want to move him to a safe house."

Evans shook his head. "Already proposed that. It's a no-go. Stroud made it abundantly clear to me that he was going to stay out in the open. He said his effectiveness to us would be compromised otherwise. I really couldn't disagree."

"Damn it," Oliver exclaimed, "we can let a private citizen ferret out facts for us and maybe get himself killed in the process!" Then he paused. "Or we can lock him up and get nothing." The SAC waited a second before continuing. He nodded at Evans.

"All right, tighten in the marshals and let him roam."

Oliver went on. "I'm calling the ATF, the Tulsa police, and the Oklahoma Highway Patrol for a meeting in the morning at eight." He tapped the table. "In this office. But before then I want to talk with Washington, probably tonight, so we'll have the latest they've come up with. I'll also want a current map of the entire Tulsa Bible College campus and aerial videos for the meeting." He looked at Evans. "Can you handle that?"

Evans nodded. "Map's a done deal. The most detailed one is sold at the bookstore out there. I already have a copy. As far as the aerial pictures are concerned, I'll probably want to use a helicopter."

"From one of the local radio or TV stations?"

Evans shook his head. "Too small. There're not stable platforms. They'll also attract attention. I was thinking of one of the hospital Life-Flight units. It'll be easier to keep what we're doing under wraps, as far as leaks are concerned." The agent thought for a minute. "Because of the early meeting time here tomorrow, we won't be back with the videos until eight-thirty or nine. But we'll have night and sunrise shots, for contrast. That OK?"

"It'll have to be." Oliver pushed his shirt cuff back to expose his watch. "Let's get Stroud in here."

4:30 p.m.

Jack picked up a copy of *Newsweek* from the end table. He had arrived early at the FBI office, and the receptionist, behind a bulletproof glass partition, told him it would be another five minutes or so. He contemplated the cover of the magazine, which was a montage of disaster scenes, in color, beginning clockwise from the top with the SST crash. He tossed the copy aside and shook his head, fighting against tears for the hundredth time.

He surveyed the twenty-by-fifteen room. The walls were covered with a muted gray fabric, the carpet a royal blue. The furniture was steel and leather. He thought the look attractive, even stylish, especially for a government office. A large color representation of the FBI's shield hung alone on one of the walls. Jack read the Bureau's three professed strengths, "Fidelity, Bravery, and Integrity."

Out of habit, he looked down at his wrist for the time. He winced when he recalled that his watch was missing. It was a moderately expensive Cartier with an elongated, curved case of eighteen-karat gold and a crocodile-leather strap. But, more than anything else, its real value was sentimental. The watch had been presented to him by Reuben Gentry himself on Jack's fifth anniversary on the board of Tulsa Bible College. He distinctly remembered looking at it sometime yesterday morning, before Dr. Cunningham came in to change the bandages for the last time. Flora was to call housekeeping at the hospital this morning. He hoped someone had found it.

A door opened at the end of the room.

"Jack?" It was Don Evans. The agent held open the buzzer-locked door with one hand and pointed over his shoulder with the other.

"You're on."

At the same moment, as if on cue, the main door to the reception area opened, and in walked Corley Brand. The counterterrorism chief lowered his suitcase to the floor and pulled off his gloves. He smiled at Jack. "That's a mean bunch in there, ol' buddy. I thought you might appreciate some help."

San Francisco
5:14 p.m.

The aroma of freshly baked bread wafted around the three muscular young men and the two attractive women in jeans and T-shirts who sat on bleached-wood stools against a brick wall and gave their full attention to a fourth man squatting on the tiled floor in front of them. He made a thumbs-up gesture and pointed over their heads.

"Sourdough from SFO." He laughed as he pronounced the company's rhyming name. Then he mimicked the lilting voice of the Asian woman who represented program planning for the Pacific Rim Summit.

"Everyone in America's heard of them. Since they sell so much bread at the airport and in seven other cities in Northern California, the committee decided to include their bakery on the tour."

"Dumb fuckers," one of the women spat out. "And right across the street."

The squatting man smirked. "Yeah, and the only security check we'll get is that token walk-through by the Secret Service on the thirteenth." He rubbed his hands together. "A week from tomorrow, with the whole world watching on live television, hundreds of representatives from a dozen nations will come to see the ovens of Sourdough from SFO."

One of the women put on a sad face.

"Too bad they're going to have that little fire over there the night before. But maybe someone will be able to persuade *another* bakery to let all of those VIPs walk through a stainless steel oven. Wonder who'll get asked to help salvage the tour and the city's reputation for hospitality? Oh, won't you please let them in your seven-hundred-degree oven? Pretty please?"

Everyone laughed.

Tulsa
5:29 p.m.

Rachel stared at the blank screen of her Macintosh computer. She had planned to update her electronic diary this afternoon, but the clouds gathered again in her heart. Her face tightened, and her tongue played irregularly against her upper teeth. A tear coursed down her cheek. She reached out, extracted a Kleenex, and held it against her closed eyes. She bit her lip, but it didn't work. The emotions welled up uncontrollably, and she began to sob.

"Oh, Mom, Jeff . . . ," she moaned. *"Why?"*

Rachel shook and lowered her head to her crossed arms and cried from the depths of her soul. In rolling wails, interrupted only by breath-catching gasps, she resumed her agonizing journey through the raw emotions of grief. Her father, her doctor, and her minister each had held her and told her what she had already known intuitively—that ultimately, mercifully, she would make the irrevocable split with the past . . . by accepting it. But she couldn't believe them. Not yet. She'd never get over this sorrow. Her mother and brother were still hers. She would release them if she could, but she didn't know how to do it. New convulsions rose, and her sobbing continued.

"Miss Rachel?"

Rachel didn't hear the taps on her bedroom door. "Mom," she moaned, "come back. *Please,* Mom, I need you so much. I'm sorry for everything I ever did." The teenager again cried out in long, racking wails.

The door opened, and Flora peered around.

"Miss Rachel?" the woman called again.

Rachel sucked in her breath, sat up abruptly, and hurriedly wiped at her eyes. She blinked and tried to focus on the computer screen.

Flora came across the room, stopped behind Rachel's chair, and reached out. She held her open hands an inch or so from the young woman's shoulders, uncertain what to do next.

Slowly, Rachel stood and turned and stared through the tears.

"Oh . . . Flora."

She embraced the older woman tightly and started to cry again.

Flora didn't attempt to say anything. She stroked Rachel's hair.

The teenager sobbed, "What am I going to *do?*"

"Here, Miss Rachel," Flora directed. "Let's sit down and just be together."

Flora guided Rachel to the edge of the bed.

"You talk if you want to."

Rachel buried her face in Flora's ample bosom and continued to moan.

Flora looked around the teenager's room, with its purples and greens, pinks and blues, the posters of rock stars and a busy bulletin board starring football schedules, paper napkins from restaurants, and dozens of overlapping photographs of various school activities. On one of the walls were three prints of horses, which she had received on her sixteenth birthday from her grandfather Gentry. A combination stereo-CD unit sat mute on a table next to a well-filled bookcase, which contained on one of its shelves stair-step-size horse-show trophies, three stuffed animals, and color pictures of two erstwhile boyfriends. Rachel's wastebasket overflowed with wadded discards of notepaper and tissues damp with tears. Two outfits of clothes lay across the other end of her bed. In front, on her desk, were a Garfield telephone, the charm bracelet with the horse that she had also received from her grandfather, and a formal family photograph. The latter, a Christmas present from her mother, showed the four Strouds in a colorful garden setting. The picture had been taken last summer, and the happy expressions of the close family members would radiate from that portrait and remind her of their happiness long after today's agony had faded.

Flora also noticed that standing proudly on Rachel's desk was the Christmas present from her brother, a finely detailed, nine-inch-high pewter representation of an Arabian stallion, his mane billowing in the breeze. Jeff had worked part-time for most of the year in order to be able to buy it and offer it with love to his twin.

Flora extended her arm toward the desk and extracted a Kleenex for herself.

Los Angeles International Airport
7:12 p.m.

The two large hangars owned and operated by Western Air Freight Systems stood on the south side of Los Angeles International Airport. One was designed for shipping and receiving, the other for line maintenance for the airline's fleet of seven DC-10s. In between stood a squat, two-story administration building.

Western Air had become a formidable competitor to DHL, FedEx, and UPS in the frenetic business of transporting large cargoes between L.A. and Dallas, Chicago, New York, and, recently, Honolulu and Tokyo. Tonight three of the McDonnell-Douglas jumbos were being loaded for their regularly scheduled runs. Two were eastbound; the third was set for the transpacific route.

A Buick LeSabre turned off Imperial Highway and drove to the visitor area outside the busy main office building. A diminutive man in his early thirties braked and eased the car between the yellow parking stripes. He turned off the ignition and stepped out into the cool evening air. He put his hands on his hips and stretched backwards from his waist, taking in the scene. There was a constant flow of customers toward the entrance of the building. The man joined the procession and walked inside.

"Yes, sir?" A heavyset woman behind a long desk made a notation on a sheet of paper and laid it aside. She looked up. "May I help you?"

The man reached into his pocket, withdrew a business card, and handed it to her.

"I'm with Farmington Novelties."

"Oh, yes." The woman smiled. "You're one of our favorite customers."

The man nodded curtly. "I'd like to check on your rates for a special shipment of toys to Chicago. There's a new trade show up there, starting this weekend. Last-minute decision for us to attend." He fumbled for a notepad in his jacket. "Here it is." He checked his figures. "There'll be eleven crates, sixty-four cubic feet each. Twenty-two hundred pounds altogether."

The woman turned and faced a computer screen. She placed her fingers over the keyboard and tapped in the information.

"Do you want us to pick up and deliver?"

"No, we'll do that."

She touched several keys. "OK, it looks like $2,600 even."

The man looked at her. "We'd like to ship tomorrow night."

"Oh, no problem, sir. Thursday's fairly light for us this time of the year, especially to Chicago. That flight leaves at eight." She leaned toward him. "Now, you know you'll have to have the crates at our loading dock by five. For the paperwork and the inspections."

"Five o'clock?"

She nodded.

"OK, is there anything else I have to do?"

She shook her head. "No, sir." She referred to his business card. "I'll just make a note that Farmington Novelties will have a 2,200-pound shipment, in eleven crates, to Chicago on Thursday, the seventh. Right?"

"You've got it."

"But please," she added with emphasis, "call us by noon tomorrow if you want to change or cancel. With all of this terrorism stuff, we're having a horrible time figuring out who's going to ship and who's not. And who *shouldn't* ship. Know what I mean?"

The man smiled curtly.

"Don't worry, we won't cancel."

Tulsa
7:43 p.m.

The silver Monte Carlo slowed as it approached the house. It stopped at the curb in front, and the headlights went out. A slender woman emerged and started up the sidewalk for the lighted front porch.

"Hold it, miss!"

A man jumped out of his car across the street and ran toward her. She appeared startled by his sudden appearance.

"What?"

"Stay right there, please," the man pointed. He moved between the woman and the house and opened his credentials.

"Deputy United States Marshal, ma'am. Who are you?"

The woman stared at him before responding. "I'm . . . a nurse. At St. Francis."

"Name?"

"Andrea Singletary."

"Business, please?"

"Business?"

"Why are you here, ma'am?"

"Oh, Mr. Stroud left his watch at the hospital when he checked out yesterday." She opened her purse and extracted the gold timepiece. "Here it is."

The marshal kept his eyes on the woman while he reached for the watch.

"I'm returning it. His name's on the back," she mentioned helpfully.

In the dim light, the marshal could make out "STROUD" on the case.

"I'll still have to see some identification, ma'am, and examine your purse."

"Well, if you say so." The woman drew out her driver's license and hospital security badge. Both featured her photograph. She handed them over.

The marshal examined them and gave them back.

"Now your purse."

The man took the small leather bag and checked the contents with a practiced hand. He returned it. "I'll take the watch to him."

"No, please," she begged. "I'd really like to give it to him in person." She smiled coyly. "That is, if you don't mind."

The marshal hesitated. "OK, but I'll have to go with you."

"Thank you very much, sir."

The two walked toward the house, and the agent rang the bell. Flora opened the door.

"Ma'am, this lady would like to see Mr. Stroud. She's a nurse from the hospital, and she's returning his watch."

Flora appraised the woman for a few seconds.

"I'll get Mr. Stroud. I know he'll be grateful. We've looked everywhere for it."

The marshal and the woman entered and stood in the hallway. The woman brushed back the soft light-brown hair from her face and smiled at the agent. A moment later Jack appeared. He recognized Andrea immediately.

"Oh . . . hello again."

"Mr. Stroud," the marshal attempted to intervene, "this woman's from St. Francis. She has your wristwatch."

Andrea stepped forward and held out her hand. "Andrea Singletary. Remember me?"

"I certainly do."

Jack clasped her hand and noticed that her skin was warm and soft. He thought he detected a hint of Shalimar, but the pleasing scent dissipated before he could be sure. She withdrew her hand and, opening her purse, found the watch and handed it over.

"I knew you'd like to have it back as soon as possible, Mr. Stroud, so I brought it myself."

Jack accepted the watch. "Well, I'm so glad you did. How nice of you." He motioned toward his study. "Come in. And please call me Jack."

The marshal turned to return to his car.

"Where was it?" Jack asked as he escorted the woman inside.

"You left it in the drawer next to your bed."

He laughed. "Doesn't surprise me. I was in such a hurry to get out of there. Would you like something to drink?"

"Oh, no, thank you. I really have to go."

"Surely you can stay for a minute."

"I still have some grocery shopping to do. But thanks anyway."

"Who was it, Daddy?" Rachel entered the room. When she saw the woman, she hesitated. "Oh, I'm sorry."

"No, come in, sweetie. This is . . . " He winced. "How embarrassing. I don't remember your name."

"Andrea." The woman smiled. "Andrea Singletary."

"Yes, this is Miss . . . *Mrs.?*"

"Miss."

"Ah, yes. Rachel, this is Miss Singletary. She's a nurse at St. Francis, and she found my wristwatch."

Rachel advanced and extended her hand. "Glad to meet you, Miss Singletary."

"I'm Andrea," the woman insisted as she shook the teenager's hand. "And I'm very glad to meet you, too, Rachel."

25

"Gentlemen, they're here."

A pretty secretary stood in the doorway of SSRA Tom Bentley's office. Ron Oliver, Oklahoma's special agent in charge, sat in one of the two chairs facing Bentley. Corley Brand stood at the window and looked out over south Tulsa.

Oliver glanced over his shoulder and held up his hand.

"Two more minutes, please, Janet."

He turned back toward the supervisory senior resident agent.

"Let's tell them everything up front. I want smooth sailing every inch of the way."

Bentley nodded. "Agreed."

Oliver went on. "We've called in Alcohol, Tobacco, and Firearms— obviously because of the explosives. Also the Tulsa Police Department and the Oklahoma Highway Patrol, in case we have to ask for more local control. No, I don't want any turf problems on this one. It could be our most important case ever." He looked toward Brand. "Anything to add?"

The FBI's Counterterrorism Section chief kept his gaze fixed on a distant collection of buildings that reflected the newly risen sun. After a pause, he replied without moving. "We may be just seven miles from hell, gentlemen. I wonder what kind of beast—or beasts—we're going to encounter out there."

Bentley punched the intercom. "Our people ready, too?"

"Yes, sir. Everyone's in the conference room."

Tulsa Bible College
9:30 a.m.

Jack adjusted the knitted cap over his bandaged head and motioned his driver toward the special parking space. The unmarked acorn-brown Chevy pulled in and braked where a small iron sign read TRUSTEE. The Reuben Gentry Ministries, as a courtesy to its sister institution, always kept two spaces in front reserved for the VIPs of Tulsa Bible College. Because of Reuben's special request of him six weeks ago, Jack was the only TBC trustee who regularly parked here. Today was his first day back. He grabbed for his gloves and briefcase and opened the door as soon as the car stopped.

"This shouldn't take more than thirty minutes." He stepped out into the cold morning. "Surely they haven't left anything for me to find." He closed the door. "Be good to get back to my real job on Monday."

Corley Brand locked the car and caught up. "Take a look to the left."

Both men watched as a high-pitched whine rolled across the campus and an Aerospatiale Dauphin twin-jet helicopter lifted slowly from the landing pad on the east side of the TBC hospital. The large craft climbed to fifty feet and hovered for a few seconds. Then it began a gentle ascent in their direction. As the white helicopter came overhead, Jack saw "St. Francis Hospital—LifeFlight" stenciled on its belly. The helicopter swung northward and disappeared over the ministry's administration building.

"Hope he got a picture of my best side," Brand commented as the noise of the turbine engines faded.

They entered the building through the main door and crossed the foyer in silence. Jack nodded to a woman in the information booth. He pushed the "up" button at the bank of elevators.

Neither man spoke on their way to the third floor. Jack wondered what other interesting information might still be available on the computer. And who had tried to take the floppy disk from his house when they kidnapped Carmichael? And how did that little shit Norman fit into the picture? When the elevator doors opened, the two men started down what was a familiar corridor to Jack. He sniffed the air. It even smelled right, he concluded. He was thankful Reuben had given him an office. Otherwise there'd be no practical way to do this kind of snooping. Jack intended to ease back into his role with the ministry, using his medical condition as an excuse for limited visits and for different-than-usual hours.

"Good *morning*, Dolores," he greeted his sixty-one-year-old secretary as he held the door for Brand. He motioned toward the FBI man. "Dolores Hopkins, meet Marty Bryant, an old friend of mine from my Navy days. Marty, this is the lady Dr. Gentry was kind enough to assign to me last fall. She is not only the finest at the sophisticated craft of making things happen around here, she's also become a very good friend." He twisted out of his overcoat and reached for the closet door. "But to tell you the truth, Dolores, there were many days recently when I thought I'd never be back."

The woman had a puzzled look on her face. "Mr. Stroud, haven't you heard?"

Jack frowned and walked to her desk. He placed his briefcase on the floor and rubbed his cold hands together. Corley Brand stood by the door.

"Heard what?"

Jack's secretary squirmed in her chair.

"Sir, we were instructed yesterday . . . " She paused and glanced around for her purse. "You can't go into your office, Mr. Stroud," she whispered in a pained fashion.

"What?" He leaned forward.

She found her purse and extracted a handkerchief. There were tears in her eyes when she looked back at him. She dabbed at her eyes.

"Sir, you no longer have an office here."

Jack was genuinely caught off guard by this strange scenario. He didn't move.

"Why not, Dolores?"

"Sir, it came directly—" she struggled with the answer—"from Norman Gentry."

That little bastard, Jack thought. He realized he'd been coolly upstaged, but there was little he could do about it.

The woman started to cry. "Your things are to be delivered to your home this afternoon."

Jack attempted to suppress his outrage. "Look, surely there's been a mistake. Where's Norman's caravan?" He forced a smile. "I'll call him right now and straighten this out. We'll have things back to normal in short order."

Dolores held the handkerchief tightly in her fist. There was a sterile tone to her voice.

"Mr. Stroud, if you don't leave immediately, I've been told to call security."

Jack shifted awkwardly. Then he heard Brand open the office door. Jack made an open-handed gesture of helplessness and retrieved his coat. Without saying anything, the two men departed.

Twenty feet away, behind a closed door in what had once been Jack's comfortable ministry office, a man sat at the desk and picked up the telephone. He keyed in a number. Three seconds later he made his report.

"Stroud and a Navy friend of his named Marty Bryant are going for the elevator right now."

"Change the lock immediately," came the response. "And the other man wasn't any Navy buddy. That was our first big fish from the visiting team."

Jones Airport, southwest of Tulsa
9:57 a.m.

The FAA man picked up the telephone and looked out over the busy general aviation field that was the main reliever airport for Tulsa International.

"Tower. Carlin."

The woman's voice sounded agitated.

"Sir, my name is Nellie Davis, and I meant to call you earlier, but we had to go down to visit kinfolks at Ardmore for New Year's. . . . "

Carlin withdrew a ballpoint pen from his shirt pocket and clicked the point into position. His caller sounded to be in her sixties.

"Yes, ma'am. How can I help you?"

"Well, just before we left, I saw a little plane land nearby. It seemed to be in trouble. I thought you'd like to know about it."

Carlin was used to reports from area residents who complained about low-flying aircraft. The tower fielded an average of ten calls each week. He reached for the FAA's formal report pad.

"Ma'am, I'm sorry you were bothered. Did you get its registration number? That's what's painted on both sides of the fuselage."

"No, sir. I waited for it to take off, but it never did. Now, it could've left while we were gone, but our foreman says he didn't hear a thing."

Carlin raised his eyebrows. "Where do you live?"

"We have a farm north of Beggs. Our property is seven miles west of U.S. 75, and it runs basically north and south from the intersection of the two county roads. We have the big pond where the little boy drowned a couple of years back."

Carlin continued writing. He nodded. "I know where that is. Now, when did the plane land?"

"A week ago Tuesday." She calculated for a moment. "December twenty-ninth."

Carlin didn't say anything as he completed the report. "Well, thanks for the call. I will need your telephone, Mrs."— he looked at the top of the page—" Mrs. Davis. I'll report the incident and get back with you as soon as I have some answers." Carlin wrote down the woman's number. "Thanks again, ma'am."

He'd already guessed that the plane belonged to the Southwest School of Aviation, which had a large fleet of training aircraft based at the airport. He dialed the school's number and got Hap Powers, the chief flight instructor.

"Hap, Ron Carlin. Do you guys have a plane missing?"

"As a matter of fact, Ron, we do. One of our commercial students checked out a 152 last week for a personal flight to Louisiana. He was supposed to be back last night, but we haven't heard a word from him since he left."

Carlin recounted what the woman had reported, then thought of something.

"Let me see if Dutch is in his office. I'll ask him to take a look next time he's down that way."

"Good idea," Powers returned. "The guy's got eyes like a hawk. Keep me advised."

Carlin smiled after he hung up. "A hawk with bifocals." He rang the airport number of Dutch Dennison, the Oklahoma Highway Patrol's senior pilot for the area.

"Hell-o?"

Carlin recognized Dennison's rolling Oklahoma accent.

"Hey, Dutch, there isn't a cloud in the sky. Why aren't you out there clocking cows like you're supposed to?"

The OHP pilot knew who it was and laughed.

"OK, Mr. Smart Ass, next time I see that red Honda streaking down Elwood for the airport, you can count on a full roadblock. Breathalyzer, pat-down. With any luck, you'll only be a month late getting to work. Now, what's on that mini-mind of yours?"

Carlin grinned. He and Dennison had known each other from their Air Force days in California as fellow jet jockeys. Carlin had gone to the FAA's training facility for controllers in Oklahoma City immediately afterwards, while Dennison went to work flying for a Tulsa oil company. When the firm closed its aviation department in the mid-'80s, Dennison joined the highway patrol and was assigned to fly for Troop B, headquartered in Tulsa. A year later, when he was returning one afternoon in the patrol's Cessna 172, a voice on the radio ordered him to call the tower upon landing. Dennison knew that was the way controllers chose to chew out a pilot for a violation of the federal aviation regulations. It was usually the private beginning of a very public hearing process that could, and frequently did, lead to a license suspension or revocation. No pilot relished being told to make that particular telephone call. Dennison was no exception, and he reviewed his flying procedures minutely as he taxied to the hangar.

"You son of a bitch!" he'd yelled into the receiver when he recognized Carlin's voice. "I dumped twenty pounds worrying about what I'd done wrong."

"Hey, I never said you did anything wrong," Carlin pleaded. "But you have to admit it got your attention."

The renewal of their relationship on that note led to periodic practical jokes by both men. Today, however, they were all business.

"Dutch, a woman just called in. It wasn't the typical gripe."

Carlin explained the conversation.

"I know right where her place is, Ron. I'm supposed to be up in Osage County for the first part of the afternoon, but I'll be able to go down to Beggs afterwards. I'll let you know if I find anything."

Denver
10:00 a.m.

The Christian Cavalcade crossed the flatness of Kansas and eastern Colorado and entered Denver Tuesday evening, five days after the grieving city's popular mayor was murdered. The buses remained in procession and turned off at the Colfax exit. They had braked and negotiated their way to the hotel complex in the center of downtown, just a block from the spacious Municipal Auditorium. Norman's removal from his bus was easier than usual. It required a record seven minutes to ensconce him in his suite for the obligatory drying out.

Norman had started his heavy drinking two years earlier. Everyone in the ministry knew about it, but no one could pinpoint a precise reason for its sudden onset. Some felt it was his deteriorating relationship with his father, while others referred to intense arguments between Norman and Bunny. A few said it was due to the financial troubles at the ministry. Norman didn't get drunk on every trip. Sometimes he would just sit and stare out the windows of the bus. He had been known to remain aloof and unaware of his surroundings for hours along the way. There were rumors that he had an incurable disease and was finding it difficult to make his peace with the Lord. But this trip looked like another garden-variety, booze-anesthetized run from city to city where, a day or so into each leg, he would be at his usual and flashy best.

The Colorado crowd was as frenzied as Tuesday's gathering in Kansas City. Denver's Municipal Auditorium was standing room only when the couple made their grand appearance. Today's topic was the sanctity of marital sex, and those who rose in the tumultuous welcome for Norman and Bunny righteously waved their Bibles and knew in their hearts that God's one-man-for-one-woman stricture was the only way. And that Norman would confirm their beliefs.

The lights flashed off and on, cued by professionals who had developed their craft to a psychological art form. The audience screamed and swayed in the emotionally charged atmosphere. Norman's motions for quiet were cleverly designed to produce precisely the opposite reaction. He beseeched with his arms, then he rolled his eyes and acted overwhelmed at their display. They poured it on and delivered their heartfelt and thunderous acceptance.

"Oh, my dear brothers and sisters," Norman started as he paraded across the stage when the roar finally subsided. "You and I know a secret." He stopped and pointed toward heaven.

"Almighty God is *furious* with America."

His new standard opening was under way, and the crowd loved it. Men and women yelled and screamed, and many who had brought babies held up to the Lord the fruits of their monogamous loins. It was a satisfying sight to the already sweating minister. Almost as satisfying as the thought of the filled plastic baskets being emptied and the money counted in a room backstage.

Jones Airport
4:46 p.m.

Dutch Dennison reached Carlin at home.

"Didn't see a plane, Ron. I made a half-dozen circuits of the whole area at five hundred feet."

"Then what do you think she saw?"

"Well, let me finish. There's a level grass strip on a quarter-section northwest of the intersection of the county roads. The rest of the surrounding countryside is fairly rough or covered with trees. I did see what looked like a set of grooves in the frozen grass on the strip. Could have been caused by a plane making a touch-and-go."

Carlin felt there was something out of focus.

"Dutch, that lady said it landed. She said she watched for it to take off, but it didn't. And it's still missing."

"I'll tell you what," the OHP pilot offered, "I'll go out there in my cruiser, first thing in the morning. There's a house where that strip is, and I'll see if they know anything. I'll even do a little snooping around while I'm there."

"Thanks, Dutch. It's got my curiosity up."

"Mine, too, Ron."

Los Angeles International Airport
7:37 p.m.

Fifty-one-year-old Lewis Ashcraft sat in the left front seat of the fully loaded Western Air Freight Systems DC-10-30 and surveyed the glowing instrument panel. The phosphorescent greens and reds of the cockpit's electronic illumination played off his half-moon spectacles. He peered back at the gauges and verified their information to First Officer John Haversham's rapid-fire checklist before engine start. He repeated the last call.

"ATIS information 'Yankee.' Altimeter setting, two-niner-niner-four."

Second Officer Barry King resumed the checklist for the short, "just-priors" tally of the flight engineer's panel. As soon as that was completed, Ashcraft rotated his right index finger toward the overhead panel.

"Light number three, Jack." He smiled at his copilot. "We're 'go.' "

Haversham coordinated the engine start with King. The first officer then tightened his over-the-shoulder restraints and clipped the Seal Beach Departure plate to the control column. He dialed up ground control and waited for an opening to squeeze in his request to taxi. The controller's eventual reply was buried with other clearances on the heavily congested frequency.

"Delta One-Ten, hold short of Taxiway Eight-Juliett. Right where you are, sir, if you can. Got an American Boeing 'seven-six' comin' across the end of Two-Five Right to maintenance. United 268 Heavy and United 1377, hold your positions for the VIP limo ahead and to your right. Continental ... is that *Four*-Fifteen? Roger, *Five*-Fifteen ... what I thought. Want you to keep going on Kilo Inner, please. The Varig stretch is waiting, has you in sight. Western Air 201 Heavy, are you the first DC-10 on the apron over there? Air Canada 889, negative push this time, ma'am. Northwest 1212, you the MD-11 who wants to go to your hangar on the north side? OK, sir, be a ten-minute wait. We're starting to get busy."

Haversham tried again to get in his response. Finally he shook his head at the logjam, sat back against the cloth-and-vinyl seat, and sighed. He still wasn't accustomed to this.

Ashcraft looked to his right and grinned. As one of Western Air's senior pilots—with a total of 23,000 hours in the air, 3,100 in the DC-10—he knew that patience was the only virtue at LAX.

"Like trying to swim in cold molasses, isn't it?"

Haversham rolled his eyes.

Ashcraft wasn't the only experienced professional in the cockpit tonight. Haversham had flown a total of 8,200 hours, and King, 14,000. The two junior men had 1,900 and 1,700 hours respectively in the McDonnell Douglas widebody. All three men had forsaken airline careers for the uncertainties, and the sometime financial rewards, of being owners of the nation's fastest-growing air-cargo company.

Once more Haversham pressed the red communications button with his thumb.

"Western Air 201 Heavy. That's us over here."

This time it worked.

"Roger, Western Air 201 Heavy. Taxi to Runway Two-Five Left. Give way to the JAL 747 comin' out of their cargo area ahead of you."

"Wilco."

The controller was directing seven new planes around the bustling maze of the South Complex. He didn't hear Haversham's reply.

Ashcraft gripped the nosewheel tiller with his left hand. He curled the fingers of his other hand over the rounded tops of the levers on the center pedestal and gradually advanced the throttles. The three General Electric CF6-50-C2 turbofan engines spooled up smoothly. He nodded at the saluting lineman outside as the 286-ton aircraft swung slowly to the right and headed for the taxiway. At 182 feet in length, his DC-10 was more than sixty feet longer than Orville Wright's entire first flight at Kitty Hawk.

"There's Tokyo," he pointed as a white Japan Air Lines jumbo headed for the same taxiway 1,500 feet ahead.

"Got him," Haversham smiled. He always liked flying with Ashcraft. This captain flew by the book, but his cockpit attitude was friendly. Never overbearing like some of the don't-question-me skippers.

Second Officer King requested their attention for the final ground checklist. " 'Before takeoff,' gentlemen?" Ashcraft and Haversham concurred and began responding to King's itemized challenges.

A mile later, as they neared the turn for the runway, Haversham changed frequencies and reported their readiness.

"You'll be number two, sir," the Los Angeles tower responded. "Have to give you a couple of minutes for separation behind the 747."

Ashcraft looked aft out the side-panel window. He saw his company's LAX to Dallas–Ft. Worth and New York Kennedy flight taxiing out.

"Looks like we're all on time," he observed.

There was an unexpected break in the traffic, and the JAL freighter was cleared for an immediate takeoff. The departing 747 lumbered away in a roar and lifted off into the hazy darkness. The DC-10 was told to taxi onto the runway and hold for its release.

As Ashcraft turned his aircraft onto 25L, set the brakes, and looked out at the parallel white lights for 11,096 feet of pavement ahead, he reminded his first officer of the reported turbulence at the lower altitudes.

"Don't be surprised if we get a bit of a wiggle between one and three thousand. Light-to-moderate chop's been called in by everyone tonight."

"Thanks, Lew," Haversham replied with a smile. "I'll be ready."

Disneyland
7:49 p.m.

Seventeen thousand invited guests, with their spouses and children, crowded into the nation's second-most-popular theme park, queuing for the attractions and happily waiting for the evening's special fare at 9:30, a preview of the revised mini-spectacular known as the Festival of Lights. It was a new, abbreviated version of the summer's famous Main Street Electrical Parade.

January used to be a slow month for Disneyland. Now it provided almost as many visitors as when the schools were out for the summer. Disneyland was open seven days each week, but it closed at six p.m. weeknights during January. Tonight's private party, which had begun at seven, was being held for the Disney corporate family in California—those who put the "magic" into the Magic Kingdom, and their loved ones. Mickey and Minnie cavorted with forty other Disney characters and posed for the obligatory photographs throughout the theme park. Even though everyone this evening was in some way associated with the company, the aura of the dazzling establishment captured the hearts of all, executives to street sweepers, and yielded an atmosphere no less exciting than when outsiders attended.

The temperature was an even sixty degrees—cool but no damper on the festivities, which would last until ten, culminating with a spectacular music-and-fireworks show known as Fantasy in the Sky. Throngs of laughing guests poured into the inviting shops and restaurants in the seven areas of the park. They bought instant treasures and gobbled down hamburgers and chocolate-chip cookies and reveled in the party climate, which was famous the world over.

Belgian horses swinging their white tails clopped between the flickering gaslights atop the ornate lampposts of Main Street, U.S.A., and pulled streetcars filled with dozens of beaming youngsters and their adult escorts. Cameras flashed at a motorized turn-of-the-century fire engine as it rang its heavy bell and maneuvered down the 1,800-foot street, while melodies of barbershop quartets and the sound of a ragtime piano wafted over the happy crowds.

Groups of wide-eyed ghost-seekers stood and waited their turn at the portico of the Haunted Mansion and talked excitedly with their companions about the forthcoming experience. A few little ones looked around fearfully and tugged again for reassurance from their parents. Guests moved into the eerie attraction without ever catching sight of those exiting. It was all part of the illusion that people entering the spooky place might not emerge. In the distance, through berms effective at blocking the visual, came the repeating music from It's A Small World. The maddeningly simple lilt didn't dispel the anticipation of those waiting their turn to enter the forbidding house looming before them.

Across the way stood the spired Space Mountain, one of the best "dark rides" in the country. Tonight's lines ran past the hour-if-you're-standing-here mark, but few complained at the wait, which would eventually give way to a splendid experience to be repeated as often as they could come back.

The annual party was again an assemblage of joy. Employees found in the beaming faces of their families a validation of their earlier decision to become a part of this giant happiness-generating organization. There was no better place on earth to work.

Los Angeles International Airport
7:53 p.m.

The wind was a steady ten knots off the ocean, right on their nose. When the takeoff command came from the tower, Captain Ashcraft advanced the throttles to the "stand-'em-up" vertical position, while First Officer Haversham released the brakes.

"Your throttles," Ashcraft notified his copilot.

Haversham reached over with his left hand and smoothly pushed the thrust handles forward for maximum power. Each of the DC-10's three engines powered up to 51,000 pounds of thrust, and the giant plane began its roll down the centerline.

"Set max power," came the command to the second officer.

King leaned forward from his position behind Haversham and adjusted the throttle settings for optimum thrust. At this point Ashcraft reacquired temporary engine-power responsibility. It was a standard safety procedure for the senior member of the flight crew to handle the throttles from max setting by the second officer until the aircraft was committed to fly. In case an abort became necessary, power would be in the hands of the most experienced pilot.

First Officer Haversham maintained his firm grip on the control yoke as the two front-seat men choreographed the acceleration of their ship toward the dark and inviting sea aloft.

Western Air 201 Heavy was airborne in fifty-one seconds.

The procedure for the Seal Beach Departure, which most eastbound flights used, called for a climb on an initial westerly heading of 250 degrees magnetic. Departure Control routinely gave departing aircraft a left turn down the coast, then a vector at the Palos Verdes peninsula for the inland Seal Beach VORTAC, a radio navigation facility southeast of the Long Beach airport and 20 miles from LAX.

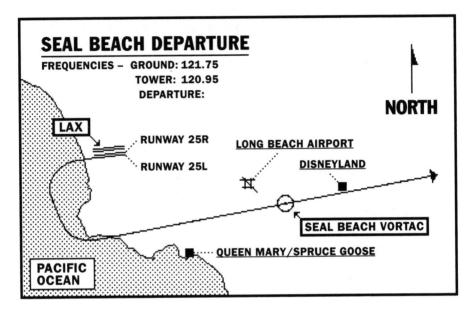

The DC-10's gear folded noisily into the wheel wells, and the order came from the tower.

"Western Air 201 Heavy, contact Departure. You guys have a good evening."

"Intend to. Western Air 201 Heavy. S'long."

Ashcraft selected 125.2 and listened for an opening. He keyed his microphone.

"Departure, Western Air 201 Heavy, out of seven hundred."

"Western Air 201 Heavy, Los Angeles Departure. Radar contact. Leaving three thousand, turn left, heading one five zero. Climb and maintain one zero thousand."

"Okiedoke, left to one-fifty out of three and up to ten grand. We're out of nine hundred now. Western Air 201 Heavy."

As expected, the aircraft entered an area of rough air. The plane shuddered and porpoised slightly before it began its climbing turn.

Ashcraft grinned. "Nothin' to write home about." He looked out briefly at the panorama of lights in the wide Los Angeles basin.

A minute later, Departure was back. "Direct Seal Beach, on course. You can expect Flight Level Three Three Zero from Center in about two minutes."

Ashcraft acknowledged. "Roger, left to Seal Beach now and on course. Higher shortly."

He unclipped the Jeppesen Standard Instrument Departure sheet from the control yoke and put it back into his binder. He replaced it with another chart. The air was now smoothing out.

The DC-10 passed back over the southern California coastline. Shortly afterwards, it crossed the Seal Beach VORTAC and climbed upward toward O'Hare at nearly 2,000 feet per minute.

Garden Grove, California
8:01 p.m.

A man sat in his parked car off the Garden Grove Freeway at Beach Boulevard. The latest clearance for Western Air 201 had just come over his portable aviation radio. He pushed open the door, stepped out into an alley, and squinted into the night sky. Even with all the brightness of the area, he saw the DC-10's navigation lights as it passed over the nearby VORTAC. The man leaned back inside the car and picked up a small metal box. He pulled out an antenna and waited for a few seconds. Then he pressed a rectangular button on top of the box and looked up again.

A dot of white flashed where the plane had been. A millisecond afterwards, an expanding ball of blinding fire appeared. The huge orb swelled outward and held for a moment before it contracted, and the man saw spiraling blood-red pillars spewing outward and falling toward the ground. He snickered and tossed the transmitter across the front seat of his car. He got back inside and twisted the ignition key.

The explosion burst through the left-aft fuselage of the DC-10 as if a knife had suddenly cut raggedly through the airplane near its tail. Streamers of metal and wiring held on in the 280-knot slipstream for a fraction of a second before they yielded to the separation. The massive tail structure, with its number-two engine, fell away and descended into the night. The forward part of the jumbo jet yawed awkwardly to the left and began its disintegrating tumble.

Disneyland
8:04 p.m.

Casually dressed men gripped their wives around the waist and patted excited little ones on the head as they boarded the Jungle Cruise ride in Adventureland. The skipper of their boat was already telling his tall tales and warning the smaller set of the dangers they might face from crocodiles and hippos ahead. The boom in the distance caused a few of the guests to wonder if the fireworks show had begun early.

The forward fuselage and one wing of the DC-10 careened out of the hazy sky and impacted explosively at the entrance to the Jungle Cruise. Massive parts of the truncated aircraft blasted a hole thirty feet deep and sixty-five feet long in the narrow walkway in front of the ride, smashing 181 humans into instant oblivion. Huge pieces of the jumbo jet bounced outward in geysers of burning fuel, cascaded over the men, women, and children ringing the walkways outside the tree-lined Central Plaza, and plowed into the side of the Sleeping Beauty Castle, severing and igniting its top. White-hot metal and flaming liquids spewed across and smashed into the throngs beyond, hacking and mangling and annihilating another 1,100.

The severed port wing of the DC-10, with its pylon-mounted engine, twisted crazily onward to the northeast and sliced into a popular coaster ride known as the Matterhorn. The wing's full complement of jet fuel disgorged upon impact, spraying thousands of gallons of liquid fire into the enclosed 147-foot steel-and-plaster structure. Eighty-seven bobsled riders writhed and were cremated in their seats. One connected assembly of cars barely emerged from the base of the mountain before burning fuel gushed out of the exit tunnel and consumed its screaming occupants. Three Disney gardeners watering Chinese tallow trees on the outside were shaken from their perches by the violence and fell to their deaths. The entire attraction exploded.

The tail section of Western Air's Flight 201 crashed into a fast-food outlet on Harbor Boulevard a mile and a half away. The blazing impact caked two dozen customers against the walls of the building. Severed turbine blades from the ruptured engine sliced into the night and dismembered another twenty-one in the parking lot.

Eleven minutes after the aerial detonation over the Seal Beach VORTAC, 2,400 people lay dead, most of them inside the perimeter of Disneyland. Seven hundred others would succumb from third-degree burns within a week. Another 3,000 suffered hideous wounds that would forever remind them of their evening out.

J. Edgar Hoover Building, Washington, D.C.
Friday, January 8, 6:09 a.m.

Jerry Reynolds, the FBI's deputy director, stood at the narrow entrance to the conference room inside the Strategic Information Operations Center and held open the soundproof door with his foot. He waited while Douglas Redding, the heavyset assistant director for the Criminal Division, trudged toward him. William Colquitt, assistant director, National Security Division; Loren Turner, assistant director of the Laboratory Division; and Lewis Bittker, SIOC's chief, were already seated around the table. All five men had made it through the snowy night and had been at headquarters since 3:00 a.m. Early editions of *The Washington Post, The New York Times*, and a half-dozen other morning newspapers were stacked irregularly at the far end of the table. Each of the periodicals prominently displayed a photographic accounting of the aftermath at Disneyland.

"Lab's gonna take another three, maybe four hours, Jerry," Redding exclaimed as he clumped past. "Stuff came in from California less than an hour ago." He nodded an acknowledgment to the others while he continued talking. "There's a lot to be separated out before they can start chemical and spectrographic."

Reynolds gritted his teeth and released the door. It swung shut and sealed itself behind him. "Well, it probably doesn't matter anyway." He followed Redding into the room. "I'd be surprised if we get any surprises."

Redding grabbed the back of a chair and pulled it away from the table. "Gellex or RDX again, for my money." The big man gripped both armrests and lowered himself into the seat.

Reynolds took his place at the table and motioned to the SIOC chief. "You start, Lew. How are you handling it?"

Bittker stood and walked to the thick glass separating the conference room from the second of SIOC's two main operations chambers. He pointed ed toward the rear of the adjacent room.

"We've improvised the DC-10 crash around the Phoenix gassing incident, for now."

The other men turned and looked through the transparent partition at a group of FBI specialists in the tiered facility next door who were segregated from a similar group of analysts by a stacked wall of binders, reports, and briefing materials.

"That's Phoenix in front. We're almost on top of each other." The SIOC chief faced his audience. "But we haven't missed a beat." He started for his seat. "At least not yet."

Reynolds picked up his ballpoint pen.

"You *are* going ahead with the consolidation, aren't you?"

"That's almost ready, Jerry," Bittker confirmed. "We should be running everything out of one room by seven o'clock."

The deputy director gave a thumbs up. "That's definitely a record for pulling everything together." Reynolds leaned forward and eyed everyone at the table.

"It was just a week ago that Corley Brand first advanced his proposition that the source of this outbreak of terrorism is within the United States. He went way out on a limb at the time, but he's developed a convincing argument, and data to go with it, that narrows his search to the Reuben Gentry Ministries in Tulsa, Oklahoma. Step by step, incrementally, Brand's convinced me, the director, and . . . almost . . . the president. After last night's disaster at Anaheim, he'd better be right. For alternatives, we have nothing else that even comes close, and we're out of maneuvering room."

Reynolds looked at his watch.

"Brand's in Tulsa. He's going for a search warrant before noon. Plans to be at the ministry right afterwards. The president wants to reveal the discovery of the 'smoking gun' tonight at eight. Keep your fingers crossed we'll find it in time."

The large television screen on the wall next to the door flashed on silently and displayed a blue background. Then orange letters popped into position, revealing the name of the location: Berlin. Underneath the city's name, a digital timer showed "12:15—Local." The men in the conference room adjusted their chairs, readied their legal pads, and waited for the transmission from Michael Kinney, the Bureau's legal attaché in Germany.

"Jerry?" Kinney's face appeared.

"Yes, Mike. Can you hear me?"

"Loud and clear."

Reynolds clicked his ballpoint.

"Then let's get rolling. With me are Doug Redding, Bill Colquitt, Loren Turner, and Lew Bittker."

Kinney started. "Gentlemen, the German foreign intelligence service made contact with their informants outside Damascus the day before yesterday, as planned. But before I get into that, let me recap a few things." Kinney looked into the camera. "At least two training camps in the Bekaa Valley have been under the control of that new extremist group called the Brotherhood of the Ultimate Ijima." He looked back at his notes. "One was completely abandoned on 29 or 30 December. There's no activity whatsoever at that place now. Not even a lone guard left behind."

Kinney read from the papers in front of him.

"But the second camp is still operational, although things there quieted down on the twenty-ninth, as I'll get to in a minute. That second camp is extremely well secured by double and sometimes triple perimeters of electric fences and armed gunmen. You'll remember that I reported on 3 January that an informant of the BND in the town of Baalbek said that a camp in the Bekaa Valley was preparing teams for service in North America. Well, it looks like the guy was talking about the second camp."

His SIOC audience kept writing.

"Concerning the two men the BND interviewed on the sixth, they're Syrian carpenters, and they've worked in the Bekaa Valley since the mid-to-late '80s. They've been employed inside the second camp on two different occasions. The first time was three years ago, when they helped build the place. They had free access to all seven buildings. After they finished the basic construction, they were laid off. They were called back last March to build a series of rooms within one of the empty buildings. When they returned to the camp, they were told they would be part of what was called the 'secondary allegiance' portion. That meant they were restricted to five of the seven buildings. They think the places they couldn't access were special living quarters, probably for trainers and recruits. At least that's what those buildings were originally designed to be. Could have been changed into something else, though, during the time the informants were away."

Doug Redding stopped writing. "What about those rooms they worked on?"

"Classrooms, they think. Plus some sort of television or radio or other kind of studios. Three of those. It's a big building."

"Television or radio studios?" It was Loren Turner. "How in the hell would common carpenters know anything about that?"

"Well, one's a college graduate, and both speak passable English. Anyway, they've done this kind of work before. There were all sorts of portals and other provisions for electrical lines. Panels, conduits for floor wiring, too. They said the camp had the most preconstruction set-up for electrical equipment they'd ever seen."

"Mike, Bittker here. Why use outsiders for any kind of work? Here we are, the FBI, reviewing floor plans of a secret terrorist base. Wouldn't they figure that something like this could happen?"

"Calculated risk, Lew. Outsiders bring in needed skills for one-time tasks, but, more importantly, they bring bits of intelligence from the surrounding area. That can be critical. The terrorists pay well, too, and this helps to maintain the goodwill they have with the locals. Good two-way street."

Reynolds raised his eyebrows. "Any North Koreans over there?"

"Yes, Jerry. That's one of my concluding points. The Mossad has kept a pretty good count of the number and location of North Koreans in Lebanon, ever since they started seeing them coming in again, back in 1989. But the Israelis have nothing at all on that camp. So when the BND informants started talking about cold-blooded Asians who dressed alike, spoke American English, and kept to themselves, everyone perked up. That's why the BND thinks we're going to have real problems from that camp. Their best guess is ten North Koreans."

"Trainers, all right," Colquitt concluded. "If they sound like us and they're kept under wraps, they're the best Pyongyang has to offer. Probably even alums of one of the old Crimean camps."

"Are you ready for the grand finale?" Kinney's expression was earnest.

Reynolds pulled himself to the table. "Go, Mike."

"The informants said there was some sort of a send-off on 28 December." Kinney referred to his notes. "About two hours after sunset, two helicopters arrived from the southeast. No running lights on either one. The informants saw two groups of three men each run out and get on board. The helicopters took off immediately and flew back to the southeast. It was all over within five minutes."

Reynolds posed, "Did the informants know who they were?"

"No. They couldn't see too well in the darkness. The only outside light came from a security bulb above one of the buildings."

"Then what makes them think the send-off was something special?"

Kinney tapped his notes. "That place was frantically active before the six men left. Afterwards everything became very quiet, and it's stayed that way. Camp's still open, but barely. They said it reminded them of a bee colony when the queen leaves."

After a moment, Reynolds broke the silence.

"And thirty-six hours later, six suspects with Syrian passports showed up in Frankfurt and flew to Tulsa, where they vanished." The deputy director doodled on his pad. "The informants said the helicopters flew from the camp to the southeast. How interesting." He looked around the table. "The Syrian border is only a few miles away, in that direction."

Tulsa
7:11 a.m.

As Jack Stroud stepped from Brand's government car, he saw Don Evans's raised-newspaper signal from a window of the restaurant. He acknowledged with a nod as he and Brand walked toward the entrance.

Evans had arrived fifteen minutes earlier in order to select a secluded booth. It was wedged into a back corner of the most remote area of the otherwise busy facility. There was a solid wall on one side and a window on the other. The closest tables for other customers were more than ten feet away. The FBI agent sat with his back to the main dining area. There would be little chance that a conversation in lowered voices could be overheard.

Jack and Brand squeezed past a line of waiting patrons and headed for the booth.

"Morning, Don." Jack greeted the agent with a handshake and sat next to the window.

Brand slipped into the leatherette seat next to Jack and looked around.

"Good location." He started to say more, but a waitress intruded.

"Welcome to Denny's!" The young woman smiled. "Coffee for you guys, too?"

The newcomers nodded.

"Cream?"

Brand held up a finger and looked in Jack's direction. "I guess I'm the only one," he concluded.

As soon as the woman left, Brand leaned toward Evans.

"We're late because Jerry Reynolds called me at the hotel as I was leaving. Because of the DC-10 crash, they had an emergency SIOC meeting this morning."

Brand reported Mike Kinney's findings, including the juxtaposition of the account of six men seen leaving Lebanon with that of six men who flew from Frankfurt and disappeared in Tulsa.

"There's not a doubt in my mind that those two events are connected. I'm absolutely certain that what's happened over the past two weeks has a Tulsa nexus, involving the ministry. And we damn well better succeed with our search warrant today."

Brand was interrupted by the waitress. She poured coffee into the two cups she balanced on her small tray and placed the carafe at the middle of the table. When the woman set the cups down, she plopped a dairy substitute next to Brand.

Evans reached for his coffee.

"Speaking of today, let me give you the latest on our strategy." He leaned across the table. "Yesterday morning, when you guys were on your way to being kicked off campus, you saw us just after we'd paid them a little visit in one of St. Francis Hospital's LifeFlight helicopters. Our run should have appeared purely routine, even to someone with a suspicious mind. We took a patient over to the TBC hospital, a trip which was already scheduled, and we got a current video of the entire campus on the way in and, as we left, some nice close-ups of the maintenance building and the garage, both places where we think they'd be likely to hide explosives and trucks that might haul such stuff. This precision should help us expedite the process of getting a search warrant. We can point to exactly where we want to go."

Jack sighed. It was still hard for him to accept that his adopted family business could be the center of evil that they suspected.

Brand stirred sugar into his coffee.

"Don, when you reviewed the pictures, did anything stand out? Suspicious trucks or equipment?"

"Nope. Just looked like a quiet place where nice young kids study hard and pray a lot."

Brand turned toward Jack. "Are you meeting today concerning the exhumation of Reuben's body?"

Jack shook his head. "Monday at ten. The D.A. will still have to go before a judge to ask for an exhumation order. The only potential hitch is that the judge will have to schedule a hearing and give at least five days' notice to Reuben's family. And that means telling Norman." Jack made a wry face. "Now that he's kicked me out of the ministry's affairs, I guarantee you he'll be fit to be tied when I go for the autopsy."

Jack looked down at his coffee. What a terrible thing to have to do, he thought, to yank Reuben's body unceremoniously from its repose, in order to prove the existence of a horror that has perverted the place the old man founded and loved so much.

Evans held his coffee cup at chin level and looked across at Jack. "Norman will be in Albuquerque through tomorrow?"

"Only until after the camp meeting. The caravan leaves for Phoenix in the afternoon."

Jack moved his head to one side and stared toward the waiting area near the cashier. He squinted and jerked forward.

Brand noticed his reaction. "What is it?"

"Well, I'll be *damned*." Jack continued to stare.

Brand turned and saw a man wearing an overcoat and hat who appeared to be in his late fifties. The man glanced in their direction. He seemed to hesitate before walking briskly out the door.

"You know him?"

"Let's go." Jack pushed against Brand's arm. "*That's* the guy who gave me the note after the service for Laura and Jeff."

Brand raced to the front of the restaurant where Jack, a few steps behind, added, "Wrote the message about the missing students, too. Same typewriter."

Evans caught up with them as they burst through the main door of the restaurant. The three men fanned out across the parking lot. There was no sign of the mystery man. They stopped when they saw that the only moving traffic was that passing by on adjacent Yale Avenue.

Jack jogged from car to car in the parking lot. He made a complete circuit and returned to the FBI men. "Gone," he huffed between breaths. "But that was our note-writer all right."

"Shit!" Evans exclaimed. "If he's got all sorts of information, why in the hell doesn't he just give it to us?"

Brand put his hands on his hips. "I hope we get to him before his time runs out. That guy's a walking bull's-eye."

"I'm sure he knows it," Jack observed. "That may be why he came to see me today, even in public." Jack looked at the FBI agents. "But I think he was spooked by you two. He doesn't know whose side you're on."

The White House
8:00 a.m.

The briefing room was jammed. Press Secretary Kevin Howard took his position at the podium precisely on the hour. Mounted against the curtained backdrop behind him was the oval White House logo. He waited for the reporters to sit down.

"We're *not* going to hear from the president himself?" a man from NBC-TV questioned with upstretched arms. "For Christ's sake, even at a time like this?"

Howard shook his head. "Tonight."

Frustrated reporters disciplined one another for excessive noisiness, and the atmosphere gradually quieted.

"Ladies and gentlemen ... " The press secretary nervously traced the edges of the sheet of paper he had brought with him. He looked down and began to read. "The president is shocked at the tragedy last night at Disneyland. At a time when our nation has already suffered grievously from many senseless acts of violence, it recoils again in horror. We do not yet know the cause of this terrible incident, but we do know that America is stronger than all adversity. The president extends his prayers and deepest sympathies for the victims and their families."

"That's it?" One reporter waved her copy of the announcement. "Three thousand more dead, and that's all he's got to say? Damn it, Kevin! When is he going to level with us?"

"Tonight, Helen. Please."

Another reporter jumped to his feet. "You've never kept the lid on this tight before. Oklahoma City was a friggin' open book by comparison. I don't need to tell you that every major paper around the country is following the *Post's* lead: a paralyzed administration. Stuck. Dead's a better word. The country's being attacked. All we're asking for is something of substance from the president—some explanation, some glimmer of hope. Even in your own words ... for the love of *God!*"

Howard hadn't relished this morning's session. Or any of the recent media briefings, for that matter. He sighed. "We don't know what caused the California crash, David. It could have been purely accidental. The president will address the nation tonight at eight, on everything."

A third reporter stood with his hand in the air. He had a look of frustration on his face.

"The Disney people now say they're going to level the place. No comment from him on that?"

The press secretary shook his head.

Beggs, Oklahoma
8:05 a.m.

"Thank God for dry rot."

Lester Graham knelt at the back wall of his basement cell and stabbed at the adhesive residue. His makeshift chisel was the metal clasp of his wristwatch. He cleaned away the powdery debris with his fingers. The vertical wood paneling was three-eighths of an inch thick, and he figured he'd just about penetrated the weakened glue at a point a foot above the floor. He probed again, and the last dried crust gave way. Graham leaned closer and blew into the small opening. He pushed his watch clasp into the crevice just to be sure. He grinned. He'd broken through.

8:16 a.m.

Oklahoma Highway Patrol trooper-pilot Dutch Dennison steered his black-and-white cruiser off U.S. 75. As he started westward on the narrow, two-lane county road, he reviewed what Ron Carlin had told him about the missing airplane. Dennison already knew this area of the state had more than its share of strange occurrences, from reports of satanic cults and secret burials of toxic wastes at night to frequent sightings of groups of men standing in fields with their arms outstretched, as if attempting to communicate with UFOs. He himself had seen the latter from the air on a half-dozen occasions. When investigators followed up on the ground, there was never anything damaged, moved, or left behind. No evidence whatsoever of their having been there. Now this curious matter.

Dennison checked the odometer. Six miles. One more to go before the intersection. He watched for the house of the woman who'd called the tower at Jones Airport. He spotted her place just before he slowed for the intersection. He figured it was a maximum of 150 yards from where she said the plane landed.

He braked at the stop sign and peered to the northwest. There was a rutted driveway near the intersection that extended westward across a flat field. It passed next to a house. Dennison checked for traffic and accelerated across and onto the driveway. As he approached the house, he noticed a mowed area on his right. Must be that grass strip. He continued toward the house and pulled his car alongside the structure. He reached for his hat and got out.

"Got a problem?" a loud voice called out immediately. Dennison hadn't noticed anyone at the front door when he stopped. A burly man advanced down the steps.

Dennison pressed on his hat and rested his right palm on the butt of his revolver. "Maybe."

The man stopped five feet away. He was taller than Dennison, and the trooper surmised that behind the insulated jacket and black jeans was a physique that would be the envy of the steroid set.

The man crossed his arms. "Like what?" The expression on his face was defiant.

"We've had a report that a plane landed on your property early last week. Do you know anything about it?"

"No."

The man held his confrontational pose. Dennison watched the man's eyes for any sign that he was hiding something. The trooper had learned that the eyes usually give away what the mouth conceals. Windows to the soul, someone once said. This man's eyes, however, displayed nothing but contempt, which matched his tone of voice.

"Could I have a look around?"

The man shook his head. "No."

Dennison tried again. "I'd just like to walk around that grass strip for a few minutes," he proposed with a jerk of his thumb. "Maybe the plane landed and no one here saw it. There might be something I'd notice. Won't take more than a couple of minutes."

"Get off the property!" the man demanded. "I told you no airplane landed here."

Dennison realized any further conversation would be futile. He turned. Once alongside the cruiser, he saw that the man hadn't moved. Dennison started the engine and backed into an angry turn. As he headed down the driveway, he glanced up into the mirror. The man was still frozen in his crossed-arms stance. Dennison shook his head. "I'll be back, buddy," he promised out loud. "You can bet on it."

Instead of going back to Tulsa immediately, Dennison drove the nine hundred yards to the entrance of a house just south of where he'd been. He steered his cruiser onto the adjacent property and pulled alongside a small frame dwelling. He stepped out and followed the sidewalk to the back door. He peered through the window and rapped against the glass of the storm door with his ring finger. The sound of metal on glass was sharp. Dennison stood back and adjusted his leather, bullet-laden belt. There was no response. He signaled again, although he was doubtful it would produce anyone. Dennison reached into the left pocket of his jacket and extracted a card. It displayed the Oklahoma Highway Patrol shield as a background, in yellow, and it bore Dennison's name and telephone number. He turned it over and pulled out a ballpoint. He wrote "Please call me ASAP" across the back of the card. Dennison fitted it between the glass and frame of the door and returned to his patrol car.

8:52 a.m.

The sounds surprised him. They'd never come in between breakfast and lunch. Graham only had time to slap away the powder along the floor and throw himself across the open toilet before the door burst open. It slammed against the wall.

"What the fuck are you doing?" a voice boomed.

Graham lifted his head from the ceramic bowl and saw a brawny man advancing from the doorway.

"I think . . . I'm sick."

"You're going to wish you were." The man grabbed Graham by the collar and jerked him to his feet. He yelled over his shoulder, "Get him downstairs."

Two other men entered the room. One seized Graham's arms and secured them behind his back with plastic cuffs. The other covered his eyes with a blindfold and tied it so hurriedly that some of the farmer's hair was caught in the material and yanked out as the man tightened the knot. Graham winced but decided to keep his mouth shut. Someone grabbed him by the upper arm and pulled him out of the room.

He half-stumbled along an unfamiliar passageway. The new owners had constructed a hallway where there hadn't been one before. It was damp and cold, and there was a nasty smell—part mold, part rotted food. Graham sensed that the walls were bare concrete, and his footfalls were muffled by what he figured was cement dust. Twenty feet or so down the hall, someone restrained him by pulling back on his collar.

"Step down!"

Graham felt tentatively with the front of his shoe and found the stairs. His feet ground against sand on the wooden steps. It was a circular staircase. He counted as he went. Twenty-four steps in all. At about six inches each, Graham figured he'd descended twelve feet. Twelve feet *below* the basement floor? This here place sure hadn't existed when it was old man Cummings's house, he told himself.

Late Morning

The two pilots looked out at the occasional bursts of snow and waited for their clearance. The boxy Cessna Caravan stood on the concrete ramp of the small terminal building at Gaithersburg, Maryland, its turbo-prop engine whining. They had loaded their cargo and boarded in anticipation of an 11:40 a.m. departure.

Montgomery County Airpark, eighteen nautical miles north-north-west of the White House, was an uncontrolled field, and pilots had to file their instrument flight plan with the FAA's Flight Service Station by telephone.

Just after they closed and secured the door in anticipation of receiving their requested departure time, the copilot called the airport's fixed base operator on a special frequency.

"Montgomery County Unicom, this is Caravan 6783 Charlie. We've filed for an IFR run down to National, with a departure time of 16:40 Zulu. Would you check on it for us, please?"

Both pilots continued their preflight work. Two minutes later, the man radioed news they didn't want to hear.

"Eight Three Charlie, they've got a little problem with the weather down at National. Couple of snow showers have cut visibility and slowed operations. There's a hold all around the TCA. I'm to call them in a couple of minutes. Sorry."

The copilot clenched his fist. "That'll put us there too late."

"Nothing we can do about it." The pilot watched the white flakes swirl around the nose of the airplane. "Besides," he smiled at his companion, "I don't think we're going to miss anything, ten or fifteen minutes either way."

Finally, at 11:49 a.m., the FBO was back with their clearance. The copilot crosschecked his wristwatch with the chronometer on the instrument panel. Both showed 11:50:30.

"Let's move," the pilot ordered. His right hand gripped the power lever on the center console and pushed it forward. The turbine engine spooled up and pulled the three-ton aircraft away from the terminal and toward the narrow taxiway leading to Runway 14 for their southeast departure.

The airplane made the turn onto the runway, centered, and roared down the 4,235-foot strip. As the nose rose upwards into the cold slipstream, the copilot called out, "Time off: 1656 Zulu." Within twenty-five seconds, their outside world was completely obscured by clouds so dense that the tips of the Caravan's wings were barely perceptible from the cockpit.

While the pilot made a sixty-degree course correction in a climbing turn to the right, his copilot tuned the Automatic Terminal Information Service at National Airport. The copilot listened to the recorded particulars of the latest ceiling, visibility, wind, barometric pressure, and other critical data for the airport. He dialed in the numbers on the VHF radio and received instructions from Washington Approach.

"Caravan 6783 Charlie, Washington Approach. Radar contact. Fly heading one-eight-five, descend and maintain 2,500. Expect vectors to the final approach course for the VOR DME Runway 15 approach."

The pilot nosed the aircraft over for the required five-hundred-foot descent. He took up the assigned heading of 185 degrees magnetic. The weather at the new altitude remained solid clouds. It was smooth, though. As the aircraft droned on toward the south in the grayness, the copilot selected the proper frequency for the Washington VORTAC, the navigation facility located at Washington National Airport. His calculations indicated that their turn on course toward the airport was less than five miles away. Slowly the needle centered on the VOR dial, and the autopilot intercepted the radial and turned the plane to the southeast. The aircraft's distance measuring equipment indicated they were now exactly 9.3 miles from the Washington VORTAC and National Airport. The pilot initiated another five-hundred-foot descent, in accordance with the approach procedure. Their airspeed was maintained at 125 knots, as requested by air traffic control.

The copilot switched frequencies again. "Washington Tower, Caravan 6783 Charlie. We're three DME out."

The tower at National gave them the green light to continue. "Caravan 6783 Charlie is cleared to land, Runway 15."

"Cleared to land. Eight-three Charlie."

At 690 feet the Caravan broke out underneath the clouds. The pilot kept his eyes on the instruments.

"Airport in sight," the copilot called out. The pilot glanced up.

The visibility had improved considerably, and both men looked out at the panorama that was the nation's capital. Their southeasterly route was over Virginia, south of and parallel to the ice floe–filled Potomac River. The main part of the city lay to the left. The airport was slightly to the right of their nose, and both men could see the strobe lights flashing at the end of Runway 15.

Suddenly, at precisely 2.1 miles from landing, the pilot twisted the control yoke to the left and jammed the power forward. The Caravan surged into a turn just north of the Lincoln Memorial. The new course was one hundred degrees magnetic.

"Eight Three Charlie!" the tower controller yelled. "Eight Three Charlie, make an immediate right turn to heading one-eight-zero. You have entered prohibited airspace. I repeat, you are in prohibited airspace!"

The copilot reached over and turned off the radio. The Caravan continued accelerating. In less than thirty seconds, at an altitude of 450 feet above the ground, it streaked past the Ellipse and the White House to the left, the Washington Monument on the right. It headed directly for the center columns of the U.S. Capitol. The structure grew rapidly in appearance as the plane closed in. Once a miniature representation, far away, the building now filled the entire field of view from the cockpit. At the last second, crowds standing on the steps of the massive edifice turned and stared at the airplane. Their mouths opened. Then there was nothing.

"Good job," a voice came over the pilots' headsets. Both men slumped against their control yokes.

"Be sure to make your left turn while the DME is changing from 2.2 to 2.1. Don't wait. Otherwise you've got the potential of zeroing in on the Washington Monument instead. And you might clip it a hundred feet below the top. OK?"

The pilot acknowledged with a muted "Roger." Slowly, both pilots sat up and pulled off their headsets. They unhooked their harnesses and extracted themselves from the confinement of the cockpit. Their faces were drenched. A man carrying two towels and a clipboard walked forward and extended his hand to the pilot. "As I said, good job." He then shook the copilot's hand. "A few more times, different weather conditions, and you'll be ready." He handed each a towel.

The man referred to his clipboard, which held current Jeppesen approach charts for Washington, D.C.–area airports. Two sheets were marked with color clips.

"We'll have you make the run from a couple of other places, just in case we change our plans. That way you'll be prepared, no matter what."

The pilot dried his face and smoothed his moustache with his index finger. He smirked.

"We don't want to take any chances, do we?"

The man with the clipboard gestured at the electronic equipment surrounding them. "You take your chances here. Not on the twentieth."

The pilots quietly followed the man out the rear door and down the metal steps of the large white box. Their footsteps on the concrete floor echoed back from the walls of the cavernous building.

FBI Office, Tulsa
Friday, January 8, 10:30 a.m.

Jack Stroud stood at the window. Nine FBI agents, seven men and two women, sat and tapped fingers or made marks on legal pads at the conference room table, where crumpled paper and empty cups competed for space. It had been a long time since Jack had been in a meeting where any of the participants smoked. He had forgotten how badly a half-consumed cigarette could foul a room. Next to him at the window was Ron Oliver, Oklahoma's special agent in charge, and Special Agent Gary Duvall. The occasion reminded Jack of innumerable excruciating waits in countless other places, when even the most urgent plans were put on hold pending the approval of someone far removed from the immediacy of the moment. In truth, it felt good to be included in the "hurry-up-and-wait" fraternity once again.

Duvall glanced down at his crossed arms. His watch extended beyond the cuff.

"They've been in his office for at least twenty minutes."

Oliver kept staring out the window. "Probably more." He scratched his nose. "Maybe they had trouble at the U.S. attorney's office."

"Trouble?" Duvall looked alarmed.

"Naw, nothin' serious. You know, getting the affidavit typed."

"I wish we could locate that note writer with a search warrant," Jack offered under his breath.

"Yeah, strange character," Oliver returned. "It's like he has to get up his courage or something. If he really believed what he wrote to you and us, you'd think he'd be breaking our doors down."

The agents at the table maintained their silence. Denny Usera, the only smoker, sat segregated with his habit at the far end.

The phone rang. The SAC grabbed it.

"Oliver."

"Ron, it's Tom. It's a go. The U.S. magistrate signed the two warrants less than a minute ago. One for the ministry and one for TBC."

Tom Bentley, the supervisory senior resident agent in charge of the Tulsa office, repeated over the telephone the questions that he, Special Agent Don Evans, and Counterterrorism Section chief Corley Brand had been asked by the magistrate in support of their sworn statement to obtain the authorization to search for evidence at the two facilities. "I was worried he'd think three separate places out there would make the warrants unconstitutionally broad, especially since two of them were large buildings. The old 'fishing expedition' concern, you know. But the nature of the problem, the national security consideration, was decisive. Don's videos of the place were the icing."

Oliver grinned. "Good job, Tom. See you shortly." He held on while Bentley added something. "OK, got it. I'll tell everyone." The SAC replaced the receiver and turned to the group.

"Bentley got the warrants, and they're on their way back. ATF will be here at eleven. I want to review everything once more. We'll leave right at one." He faced the man standing next to him.

"Hope you don't mind sitting this one out, Jack. Legally, we can't . . ."

"I understand." Jack felt his heart sink. "Just wish I had my old badge, but, well, I've got some work to do at home. Rumor has it I'm president of U.S. Simulation Systems. It'd be nice if I were up to speed when I go back to my office on Monday morning."

"We'll call you when the smoke clears," Oliver promised. "Oh, Tom said when he was leaving, the magistrate stopped him and told him he'd never heard so much 'cause' and so little 'probable.' The judge said the whole country was counting on the FBI for a breakthrough in this madness. The old man's an Indian, part Creek, and he said Tom had better return with some scalps."

Jack smiled. As the agents poured new coffee and gathered their files in preparation for the next chapter in the chase, he went for his overcoat. He wished he could be in the lead car.

Albuquerque
12:30 p.m.

Dozens of acres remained scarred ten days after the 274,500-pound chartered TWA jumbo jet slammed down, killing all 279 aboard. The National Transportation Safety Board, the FBI, and the other investigators had finished their site work on the sixth. Earth-moving equipment worked all day Thursday to fill in the main crater and to restructure most of the remaining terrain. Even so, signs of the devastation lingered. From the air, it looked as though the tines of a giant fork had raked back and forth across the hilly land.

Norman Gentry's Blue Team, which had come directly from the Kansas City camp meeting, spent two hours setting up bleachers along the north edge of the traumatized area. The metal-and-wood seating was now filling with the ministry's followers, some 250 this afternoon. The electronic media had staked out positions around the bleachers that allowed for quick panning of the disaster site during the address.

A few supplicants who had gathered on the periphery turned toward the Interstate to the north as sounds of approaching buses rose and fell like the moans of a coyote. Suddenly two gleaming coaches roared over a rise and began braking as they drew closer. Beige powder from the rutted roadway billowed and surged forward as the buses stopped alongside the bleachers. The security detail in the lead vehicle emerged before the dust settled. Men in dark glasses mouthed commands to others of their kind who were interspersed with the crowd and, after a minute, they judged the area secure for Norman's dramatic visit to another place where God had shown His soaring displeasure with America.

Tulsa Bible College
1:30 p.m.

Three unmarked cars roared west on the entrance drive and pulled into the parking lot of the Reuben Gentry Ministries' main building just as the chimes in the TBC chapel bell tower announced the half hour. In the lead vehicle were Tom Bentley, Don Evans, and Corley Brand. The second car brought Larry Harrington, Roy Meeker, and Carl Webb of the Bureau of Alcohol, Tobacco, and Firearms. Harrington was the ATF's Tulsa "RAC," the resident agent in charge. The FBI's Gary Duvall, Harriet Blake, and Clay Olsen rode in the third car. The three vehicles stopped next to one another in adjacent spaces stenciled for visitors. The five-story administration building loomed ahead.

The three ATF men waited in their car as the six FBI agents jumped out and made their way briskly through the main door to the reception area. They moved to a circular desk marked "Information" that housed a woman in her late sixties. Her white hair was drawn back severely and clumped in a bun.

"May I help you?" She wore the tight, ubiquitous smile of a self-assured ministry worker.

Don Evans stepped forward. "I'm Special Agent Evans, ma'am. FBI. And I have a search warrant." He held open his credentials, then one of the legal orders. "May I see the business manager, please?"

The woman's smile evaporated. She glared at Evans as she picked up a telephone and tapped in a number. "Jolene, it's Bertha at the front. Please ask Mr. Lacey to come out. There're some people here." She hesitated. "The FBI." She lowered her voice. "That's right, the FBI." The woman hung up. "Mr. Lacey will be with you in a moment," she advised in a prissy tone. "You may wait over there by the door." She directed them with a dismissive flip of her wrist.

Evans and the five others walked the ten yards or so. Just as they stopped and started to look around the foyer, a door hidden in the wall opened and out stepped a lean, fiftyish man. He walked toward the agents.

"You're FBI?" The man seemed slightly nervous as he eyed the five men and one woman.

Don Evans nodded. "Yes, sir." He presented his identification folder. The man leaned closer to see, then he straightened up.

"Well, I'm Bernard Lacey, business manager of the ministry." He offered a handshake.

Evans extended the legal documents instead.

"We have search warrants for the Reuben Gentry Ministries and for Tulsa Bible College, Mr. Lacey. Here are your copies. You *are* an officer of TBC also, aren't you?"

The man took the papers and examined them cursorily. "Yes, I am." He looked up with a somber expression. "May I ask what exactly you're looking for?" Then he smiled. "Perhaps I could direct you and make your job easier."

Evans figured the man either hadn't seen too many search warrants—everything the FBI wanted was clearly spelled out, line by line—or he was playing dumb, hoping to restrict their attention and expedite the visit.

"Mr. Lacey, there are three areas specifically covered by the warrants. First, we want to see all ministry organization charts, all files relating to the ministry's foreign bank accounts, a list of all related or subsidiary companies of the ministry, whether active or not, and a list of all foreign students at TBC, together with a report on their status. We also want a list of all teachers at TBC who were not born in the United States. Second, we want to inspect the ministry's maintenance area. Third, we want to inspect the ministry's main garage and the adjacent storage area. If you need precise addresses for the latter two facilities, they're on the ministry's search warrant."

The business manager folded the warrants and held them in front of his chest with the thumb and forefinger of each hand. "Heavens." He made a face. "You're asking a lot. Could take days."

Evans glared at the man. "Mr. Lacey, how about *minutes?*"

"Oh, no." The man scowled. "First I'm going to have to get permission, and ... "

"Sir," Evans shook the original documents in his hand and growled, "these search warrants give you all the permission you need. We'd appreciate your immediate compliance. Otherwise, I assure you, you *will* answer to a federal judge." He put his face inches from the business manager's nose. "For contempt, sir."

The little man made an "O" shape with his lips, but no sound came out. He motioned awkwardly toward the door in the wall behind him.

"Please. Let's not have any trouble. We can begin in my office."

The FBI agents followed Lacey through the door and entered a narrow corridor. Fifty feet beyond, they walked into a spartan waiting room. A middle-aged woman with a beehive hairdo sat at a dark metal desk. She looked up and smiled. Brand knew he hadn't seen a coiffure like that since the sixties. It was even tinted blue. He smiled back.

"Jolene, would you please call campus security," Lacey requested from the doorway to his office. "Have Leonard Bolt come over immediately." The woman nodded and reached for the telephone. Lacey turned and faced Evans. "I want the security director with you when you go to the garage and the other places. OK?"

"Fine with us." Evans stayed right behind the business manager as they walked into his office.

Lacey motioned as he took his own chair. "Please be seated. We can plan this out in a minute or so, I'm sure."

"Excuse me, sir." The woman smiled from the doorway. "Mr. Bolt will be here within five minutes."

"Thank you, Jolene. Oh, just a second." Lacey extended his open hand in the direction of the door. "Folks, this is my secretary." The agents nodded. "Jolene," he went on, "these people are with the FBI."

The woman maintained her pleasant expression. "Yes, I know."

Lacey wagged his finger. "Now, listen carefully, Jolene." He inclined his head toward Evans. "Would you read that list again, please. What you want from the files. We probably have a couple of the things you want right here in the office."

Evans repeated the roster that was contained in the two search warrants. When he finished, the business manager stood up.

"Organization charts? Here in the office. Right, Jolene?" He didn't wait for her reply. "Foreign bank accounts? Never heard of those. I'll have to take you to our comptroller. But he's right upstairs, unless he's out of town. And what were the other things you wanted?"

"All information on related companies," Evans responded. "Plus the data on the students and faculty at TBC."

"Oh, yes. Well, I think we have that here, too."

Evans pointed to Blake and Olsen. "You two get the items here." Both FBI agents were computer-literate CPAs, and neither had any patience with diversions or dilatory tactics. If the requested information was available, they'd get it. Evans concluded, "The rest of us will go with Mr. Lacey."

"No, I'm very busy today. It'll just be Mr. Bolt."

All of a sudden, a voice boomed from the doorway. "You want me?"

Evans turned and saw a massive human being whose tan suit looked as if it had been welded on at the gene factory. The man was a solid block of 6-feet-6, with at least 250 pounds of muscle and gristle at the ready. Good God Almighty, he mused, I'd sure hate to be late for chapel around here and have that thing looking for me.

"Yes, Leonard. These people are FBI agents. Mr. Evans, this is our security director, Leonard Bolt."

Evans stared at the man without offering to shake his hand.

"We want to see the ministry's maintenance area and the main garage, including the adjacent storage area. I understand you're going to take us there."

"You *want?*" The big man slowly crossed his arms. "You say you *want?*"

"Leonard," Lacey mumbled nervously, "they have a search warrant."

The three unmarked government vehicles bounded behind the security director's white Chevrolet Caprice. As the four cars rounded a turn at forty, Evans remembered that the campus speed limit was posted at twenty-five m.p.h. "What's he trying to do, get us arrested?" he exclaimed while he wrenched the wheel to the right and accelerated again.

"With those blackwalls," Bentley observed as Evans pulled within thirty feet of the security director's car, "his Chevy looks like one of ours. Except for the color, of course."

"Not to mention its King Kong driver," Brand added laconically from the back seat.

Bentley turned around. "That guy's something else, isn't he? He was actually prepared to resist us there in Lacey's office."

Brand made a face. "Probably an ex-professional wrestler who doesn't know when to quit." He looked out the window. "Too bad Stroud's been scratched as a consultant around here. We could use all the inside help we can get."

"At least we still have our note writer out there somewhere," Bentley grunted.

Brand exhaled. "Let's hope."

Bolt led the convoy to the southwest portion of the campus. As they made the last turn and slowed, Evans noted that the architecture across the four hundred or so acres had remained consistent.

"You could mistake this place up ahead for dormitory row."

Even here, in a corner of the campus where things were hidden away to be overhauled or greased and where storage facilities supplied the city that was Tulsa Bible College and its ministry offshoot, everything on the surface maintained the façade of similarity and cleanliness. The procession closed the gap behind the lead car and pulled to a stop outside a two-story building. In a stylized typeface, a sign above the entrance read simply, "Maintenance."

The three FBI agents piled out of their car and assembled with Special Agent Duvall and the three ATF men. Leonard Bolt started for the door.

"Just a minute, please." Brand pointed at the security director. "We'll all go in together." Bolt stopped and glared back.

Brand stood in front of the group, like a quarterback preparing his team.

"Open everything and dig everywhere. The ministry warrant's good for the entire place, so don't overlook anything. Attics, basements. Check all cabinets, too. Even private offices. Assume they're hiding explosives, or evidence of explosives, in the most unlikely places. Because they probably are."

The FBI's terrorism chief looked at Larry Harrington, the Tulsa head of Alcohol, Tobacco, and Firearms, and checked the faces of his men.

"ATF ready?"

Harrington put his hands on his hips and thrust out his jaw.

"You bet."

Brand rotated his raised index finger. "Then let's go."

3:30 p.m.

An occasional current of biting cold air rounded the corner of the administration building and cut across the downcast faces of the nine government agents who stood silently in front of their three parked cars. Finally FBI agent Gary Duvall made a fist and pounded the hood of the middle vehicle.

"Shit!"

The dark metal reverberated for a second. He backed away and kicked the bumper.

"A goddamned *nothing!*"

It had been less than two hours since the six FBI and three ATF agents arrived on the campus of the Tulsa Bible College and the Reuben Gentry Ministries with their search warrants.

Corley Brand, with his back to the administration building, motioned everyone together. Before he spoke, he shook his head.

"Well, we didn't hit a home run. No RDX truck, or any other truck, for that matter. I can't believe we didn't find anything relevant or suspicious in the garage or maintenance area."

He held out a file folder of documents.

"However, we *did* get organization charts and financial records. On the surface, they look like plain vanilla and incomplete stuff. For example, there's no mention of that 'Christ's Believers' subsidiary that owned the truck carrying the RDX. Then, according to the comptroller, there aren't any foreign bank accounts. But we know that to be untrue, since we're in the process of freezing four of them right now. Also, we have the roster of the foreign students and foreign-born faculty at Tulsa Bible College. The lists may look innocuous, but *someone* thinks they're pretty important, and we intend to find that someone."

He put on an optimistic expression.

"So call it first base, maybe, but we certainly didn't strike out."

Brand tucked the folder under his arm and looked into each of the faces before him.

"Frankly, I have to admit that this place checks out as if it were primed for our inspection. It's a classic Potemkin village, and there's a key somewhere around here that opens the door to the truth behind the cover. We just didn't find it today. But it's *some*where." He patted the folder of papers. "Maybe closer than we think."

He looked over the TBC campus.

"I don't relish calling Washington. The president's address to the nation is in three and a half hours, and I don't think we're going to locate that key before then. I just hope the gun is still smoking when we find it."

He walked for his car.

Tulsa
3:35 p.m.

The deputy U.S. marshal jogged to intercept a woman who was heading for the Stroud home. She was wearing a heavy, three-quarter-length parka with a fur-lined hood. As he drew closer, he recognized her from two evenings earlier, when she'd returned Jack's watch.

"Miss?"

She turned toward him and continued walking. "Oh, hello."

"I'll need to check your purse, please." The marshal came alongside and extended his hand in the direction of her handbag.

She stopped. "Again?"

"Yes, ma'am."

The attractive woman shrugged and held it out toward him.

The man didn't say anything as he opened the simple leather case and poked among the contents of lipstick, nail file, hair pick, and an address book.

"No atomic bomb or anything," she joked.

The marshal continued inspecting and touched a small billfold, handkerchief, large key ring, and a baby blue box of Johnson & Johnson dental floss. There was a clear plastic dispenser of round pink birth-control pills. A bottle of makeup and an errand list completed her belongings, except for a small gift-wrapped package and a card.

"Something for Rachel," the woman explained as the man lifted up the parcel. "You can open it if you have to."

After a moment's examination, the marshal put the package back and handed her the purse.

"Sorry for the inconvenience." He nodded and headed for his car. At the curb, he glanced over his shoulder as the woman stepped onto the front porch and rang the doorbell.

Flora looked through the window and recognized the nurse from St. Francis. She squinted and studied the woman for a few seconds before she pulled open the door. "You're from the hospital . . . ," she began as she pushed out the glass storm door.

The woman smiled. "How nice that you remembered me, Flora. Is Rachel here?"

Flora shut and secured the front door. "She just got home from school. I'll see if she's available."

"Please. I have something for her."

Flora forced a curt smile and stepped down the hall toward the teenager's room. She pushed against the door with a series of knocks. Rachel was at her desk, holding the telephone with one hand and gesturing with the other. Flora caught her attention and signaled toward the front of the house. It took nearly half a minute for Rachel to interrupt the conversation and put her hand over the mouthpiece.

Flora spoke in a lowered voice. "That nurse from the hospital is here again."

"Andrea?" Rachel raised her eyebrows. "Oh, awesome! Tell her I'll be right there."

Flora closed the door and returned to the front hall. The woman was looking at a display of family pictures on a table. "So sad," she said as Flora drew closer.

"Miss Rachel will be out shortly. I think Mr. Stroud's asleep." Flora returned to the back of the house.

"Hi, Andrea." Rachel popped around the corner. "What's up?"

The woman retrieved the package and card from her purse. She smiled. "I've been thinking a lot about you since the day before yesterday." She held out the offerings. "I brought you a little something."

Rachel put her hands to her chest and approached.

"For *me?*"

She took the card first. It was a glossy Hallmark showing a girl standing in riding clothes and stroking the nose of her horse. Inside, the message read, "You're special to me."

"Oh, Andrea, that's so sweet." Rachel then took the package, removed the ribbon, and opened the box. She lifted out a piece of jewelry. It was a silver pin in the form of a horse. She beamed. "How'd you know I like horses?"

"I noticed your charm bracelet the other night. You seemed to give the horse loving attention."

Rachel gripped the gift in one hand and hugged the nurse. "I don't know what to say."

The woman held the teenager tighter.

"Mr. Stroud will be here in a minute," Flora announced tartly from the doorway.

Andrea looked up and smiled. "Thank you, Flora."

"And Miss Rachel has to leave now," the housekeeper added.

"Oh, yeah!" The teenager popped away from the embrace. "Flora's taking me shopping, then to dinner." She winked at the woman. "But I'm driving."

Andrea reached out and seized Rachel's hand. "Have a wonderful time. I'll see you later."

Jack stood before the full-length mirror in his bedroom and appraised himself. He had just awakened from a short nap when his housekeeper knocked at the door and informed him that "that nurse" was waiting in his study. He'd covered his T-shirt and briefs with his robe and put on his slippers; he wished he could have slept longer, but his mind was preoccupied. He expected to go to the FBI office within the hour for a recap of the search at the TBC campus.

He tightened the belt of his robe and stared at his reflection. In spite of the circles under his eyes, he had to admit he was still a reasonably good-looking survivor of life's recent and terrible challenges. As he turned to check his profile, he suddenly felt a mixture of apprehension and anticipation. It seemed eons ago since he'd given himself the right to appreciate his appearance like this. That was when Laura used to compliment him regularly. "You know I'm just using you for your body, you sexy hunk," she'd often tease before they made love. Now a new woman waited for him.

A *new* woman? A blade of raw guilt cut into him. What kind of thinking was that? Laura hadn't been gone for two weeks yet. Was he already trading her in? He shuddered at the improper and unwelcome fantasy and condemned himself for entertaining a carryover from some erotic dream. Or better, nightmare.

But could he trust his feelings now? When would that be safe again? How *should* he dress for Andrea? Was a robe an unconscious invitation? Or conscious? He shook his head to dispel the thought. Why was he manipulating these emotions in the first place? The woman had simply found his watch and was kind enough to return it. That's all there was. Business. This internal debate was an embarrassment.

He considered his image in the glass again. Yes, he'd wear the robe. Surely she'd understand his informality, especially after what he'd gone through. Wasn't he entitled to be comfortable in his own home?

Jack patted on several drops of Obsession and checked his face and hair, then opened the door and padded down the hall.

"Hello," he said as he rounded the corner of his study. "Please excuse my attire," he continued matter-of-factly. "I've been lying down."

"Oh, I didn't mean to disturb you." Andrea stood and brushed a lock of hair from her face.

Jack contemplated an enchanting apparition. Her form-fitting black knit dress was accented by a pearl necklace and earrings and a silk scarf. Appropriately for the weather, she wore midcalf black boots. Her caramel hair fell to her shoulders in sculptured layers, and her tan emphasized her jade-green eyes. There was a heavy gold ring on her finger, and she clutched a black lizard purse. He had never seen her like this before—out of uniform, so to speak. She was magnificent.

Jack collected himself, stepped toward her, and clasped her hand in both of his. Hers was warm and soft. This time he *knew* he detected a hint of Shalimar, Laura's favorite.

"I came by to see Rachel," Andrea explained. "I brought her a piece of jewelry. A little silver horse, for her blouse."

Jack beamed. "How nice of you to do that, although I'd better warn you she has very expensive tastes. So watch out from now on."

Andrea inclined her head and pouted. "But she's such a sweetheart. Anyway, she and Flora just left. I'd better be on my way, too."

"You don't have to rush." Jack motioned to where the woman had been sitting. "Please."

He took his place in an adjacent chair. "Again, I hope you'll excuse my informality."

"I don't mind at all," she spoke softly. "As a matter of fact, I'm envious."

"Would you like something to drink? I know it's early. Perhaps some wine?"

Jack had a quick flashback to the first time he'd brought wine home. Laura had been shocked, but he'd been adamant.

"This is my house, too, and I want to have something to offer guests when they come by." He'd grinned. "I'm not going to drink it all."

She'd fought it briefly and then given in gracefully, as only she could. Oh, Laura. The pain knifed through him even as he gazed at his very pretty visitor.

"Perhaps some sherry?"

"Oh, no, but thank you." Andrea looked across at him. "Jack, I want to tell you how sorry I am about your wife and son."

Jack tightened his lips. "Thank you."

"And, then, about what happened to you." She leaned forward, as if to see his injury.

Jack rubbed at the stitched wound on his shaved scalp and laughed.

"First case of baldness in my family."

"May I see it?" she asked, then she smiled. "I *am* your nurse, you know."

"I'm yours to command." He inclined his head in her direction.

Andrea rose and walked behind him. She placed her fingertips in his hair alongside the wound. "Oh, it's healed much better that I'd expected. Does it still hurt?"

Jack took a deep breath at her gentle touch. "No."

She stroked his scalp around the wound.

"Do you feel this?"

"Mm, yes."

She maintained the rhythmic motions. "Sometimes the nerves are affected, you know."

In spite of himself, Jack wanted her to wrap her arms around him and hold him tightly. It'd been so long since anyone had comforted him. He felt a stirring in his groin.

Andrea gently smoothed at his hair several more times before returning to her chair.

"So I'll survive?" He watched as she sat down and crossed her legs.

"You'll be fine, just fine." Her eyes focused on his. "May I be personal with you for a moment?"

Jack sat up straight. "Why . . . yes."

Andrea twisted at her ring for a few seconds.

"Please understand, I don't want your sympathy," she began. "Certainly not at a time like this, with all that you've gone through, but I lost my husband last July . . . to cancer."

"Oh, I'm so sorry." Jack felt drawn to her. He understood her pain.

"It took two years for him to die, and it was horrible."

Jack's empathy grew. Andrea continued.

"I loved him so much, but I've had no one to talk to. My family doesn't live here. I guess I thought that, well, with your terrible loss, perhaps you . . ."

Jack reached over and took her hand and caressed it. "I understand. Really, I do."

Andrea fumbled for her purse and extracted a handkerchief. She pressed it against her eyes.

"How does one go on, Jack? When does it stop hurting?"

He took her hand again and held it tightly.

"Andrea, I've been wondering that myself. I've asked myself a thousand questions, but the ache won't go away. I know everyone says it will get better with time." He paused. "I'm glad you're allowing me to share in your loss. You're helping me put some of my own feelings in perspective." He took a deep breath. "I . . . I hope you won't think this inappropriate, but may I . . . hold you?"

The woman nodded. "I'd like that."

Andrea rose and faced him. He stood and opened his arms and embraced her tightly. Their bodies pressed together from shoulders to hips. She started to cry. Jack kissed at her tears then bent to place his lips on hers. His hand smoothed at her hair, and his tongue sought entrance to her mouth. He shook away a pang of guilt.

Jack sat down on the edge of the bed. He was acutely aware of his naked and aroused body. The light from the late-afternoon sun cast a glow on Andrea's face. She was absolutely breathtaking, he thought. As he leaned over to kiss her, a strange sense of freedom washed over him. If there's a God in heaven, surely He wants the living to go on living, and loving. It was as if he had finally been given permission to be a human being once again. Their lips met, and his tongue hungrily sought out hers again—at first tentatively, but, then he began to deepen his kisses as his pent-up cravings urged him onward.

Jack lifted the covers. Seeing her exquisite body further heightened his desire. He slid in beside her and held her tightly. His erection pressed against her lower belly. Her breath was short, and she moaned her readiness. His tongue searched her mouth, and he felt her hips begin to move. Almost automatically, he bent over and traced his lips down her chest. His mouth found a breast and eagerly closed over its brown nipple. He alternately sucked and ran his tongue around it. He did the same to the other breast.

Andrea encircled his erection with her fingers. He gasped and quickly rose to position himself over her. As her hand guided him between her legs, he felt the tip of his penis slip into her warm moistness. It was a glorious sensation, ordained by an understanding and benevolent God for His struggling creatures, especially—Jack was sure—in their moment of grief, and he thrust deeply into her. Male and female, separated from each other by the taking of the rib in the Garden of Eden, forever longed to reunite, and Jack cried out in pleasure in his union with Andrea.

They moved together as one and acknowledged their primal act with gasps. Finally Jack could hold back no longer. Simultaneously they brought their bodies to the heights of physical unity and touched paradise. In his spasms of ecstasy, Jack realized that a chapter of the past was being closed forever. He and Andrea were now the only present and future.

Moments later, with a kiss, Jack separated his body from hers. He rolled next to her. He knew they'd make love again.

The White House
7:41 p.m.

"Jesus Christ, the only thing I *could* do is cancel!"

The president stood at the side of his desk and held the telephone with his left hand. He shook his right fist.

"Sit here like an idiot and say I don't have anything to say? Tell the nation that our almighty FBI hasn't a goddamned clue? The country's being ripped apart, and I haven't the slightest idea where we go from here? No, Mister Director, I'm not fixing to do that. Doing nothing is preferable to doing something as incredibly stupid as that."

The president walked around to his chair.

"But I'm not going to *do* nothing." He stopped at the back of his desk. "You listen to me." His voice became a low growl. "This very minute I've

got a group, including the attorney general, working out the steps to insti-
tute martial law. I've already ordered the Pentagon to figure the logistics
for placing troops in cities of 50,000 and larger and at strategic sites around
the country. I'm going to use every power at my disposal to shut down this
national mayhem. Obviously without your help."

He slammed the telephone handset into its holder.

28

Albuquerque
Saturday, January 9, 12:09 a.m.

The slender man tapped impatiently at the coins he'd laid on the scratched metal tray beneath the public telephone unit and waited for the connection to be made.

"How much?"

He selected and deposited the requested amount. There was a click, followed by a delay, then a ringing sound. And a second.

"Hello?" The woman's voice was faint.

The man turned his back on the traffic outside.

"Is this the National Weather Service, for forecasts?"

There was a pause. "No, they changed their number last October. Do you want me to look it up?"

"There's been more trouble," the man barked into the receiver. "Take the girl to the facility."

"Yesterday went perfectly," came the reply. "He'd let me take the bitch to hell if I asked."

The man hung up. He gripped the handle of the hinged metal-and-glass door and pulled it open. He flipped up his coat collar and returned to his car.

Beltsville, Maryland
7:17 a.m.

The morning was crystal clear and bitterly cold. The last of seven inches of new snow was nearly twenty-four hours old. Within the paved inner perimeter of the Secret Service's Technical Development Division, Ray Shaffer, chief of the White House detail, stood next to agents Tim Vance and Rick Hayes, both of whom were assigned to the Presidential Protective Division. The three men watched the gray tractor-trailer combination back in. Even though the long truck displayed Department of Transportation numbers and bore a valid-looking set of Maryland license plates, all of its identification was fake.

Four other armed Secret Service agents were positioned in front of and behind the truck, two on either side. They walked forward as the driver maneuvered the big rig backwards. The rear portion of the trailer closed the gap and passed under an overhang, and the agent at the left rear of the truck signaled "stop" with crossed arms.

Shaffer looked around.

"Top secure," came an observation through his earpiece.

"Sides, too?" Shaffer questioned and motioned for Vance to confirm. The agent scurried to the overhang and saw that the rear portion of the truck had extended itself well into the loading area. There was now no way that the curious—with anything from binoculars to an orbiting spy satellite—could observe what the Secret Service was about to do.

"Sides secure!" one of the agents answered.

"Sides secure," Vance echoed. Shaffer nodded acknowledgment.

"OK, let's unwrap," the White House chief ordered.

The truck had made the 516-mile trip from Chrysler's Special Transportation Facility at Highland Park, Michigan, in just over eight hours, nonstop. Its cargo was so valuable that the rig had been shadowed on the way by three helicopter gunships and seven unmarked Secret Service cars. In addition, a half-dozen heavily armed agents rode inside the trailer the entire distance.

An agent wearing a headset inserted a communications plug into a receptacle on the side of the trailer. There would be no open radio transmissions until the offloading had been completed. He positioned the boom microphone next to his mouth.

"Black Magic, this is Merlin. Ready for release?"

The reply was almost instantaneous. "Merlin, we're 'go.'"

The agent pulled the connection, backed away, and nodded to two men at the rear doors.

The driver and his armed companion remained inside the bulletproof cab while the agents on the dock punched in sets of seven-digit codes to disarm the triple security systems. They then signaled the driver to lower the air pressure inside the trailer from slightly more than sixteen pounds per square inch to that of the ambient atmosphere. This had been one more step in the ironclad security procedures. Any attempt to breach containment during the trip, even by so much as a pinhole, would have set off alarms in more than a hundred sets of ears. There was a hiss as the pressure vented at the front of the trailer.

With a single pull on the handle, the locking mechanism whined and gave way, and the doors swung open. Holding onto the large doors, the two men walked around to the sides of the trailer, where they locked them into their full-open position.

Shaffer, Vance, and Hayes came underneath the overhang and looked inside the windowless trailer. This was the moment they'd awaited for more than half a decade. In the internal darkness of the truck, reflected glints of light hinted at the special cargo. The six agents who had ridden inside from the Chrysler plant moved into positions closer to their consignment. Another six men bounded aboard and disappeared in the blackness of the boxy enclosure. Suddenly the interior of the trailer was illuminated.

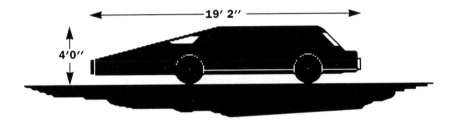

There, low-slung and proud, waited two gleaming black turbine cars.

"Oh . . . my . . . God," Hayes whispered in awe. "They're absolute beauties."

Shaffer nodded. "And they got here just in time."

Built at a total cost of $22 million and already designated internally as the "Black Mamba" and the "Black Widow," these classified, three-hundred-m.p.h. handmade vehicles had been the apple of the Secret Service's eye since the go-ahead to order them had been given in 1992. Interest in exotic getaway cars had waxed and waned over the years after the Kennedy assassination, but when President Reagan was shot in 1981, the Service pulled all stops in its effort to secure the vehicles. No one intimated that the cars would have prevented the attempt on the chief executive outside the Washington Hilton, but the Service argued persuasively that the one missing link in its protective coverage was an effective way to remove the president from the scene of an attack if helicopter or other aerial extraction methods weren't available or appropriate. The forty-one extraordinary and specific threats against the president following the war with Iraq, and the three dozen since, most of which had been denied or soft-pedaled in public, changed the minds of the few remaining opponents in Congress. After the most recent attacks on the White House, by three crazies with automatic weapons and one in an airplane, the cars became a necessity.

The armor-plated jetmobiles were expressly designed to provide high-speed "exit" transportation for the president. Both vehicles, with their smoked-black windows in front and back, looked identical from the outside, and that, of course, was on purpose. In truth, however, the Black Mamba was intended to transport the president, along with a driver and his relief—both of whom were called "pilots"—and an agent known as the "tail gunner" who manned, in a swivel chair, antiaircraft and antitank weapons in addition to Uzis and an array of other automatic weaponry. The Black Widow was the chase vehicle, and it was designed to carry five Secret Service agents whose job was to provide protective and diversionary cover for the president's car.

The agents carefully rolled the two cars out of the van for the initiation of the performance and acceptance trials, which were scheduled to last for three days. Afterwards the Signal Corps would coordinate the installation of the sophisticated communications equipment, which would be a close approximation of the multimillion-dollar array in the White House and Air Force One. The first officially planned deployment of the black marvels was for the inauguration, eleven days away.

"Poor old Bruce Wayne." Tim Vance stood with his hands deep in his overcoat pockets. He rocked back and forth and grinned at Shaffer.

"He only had *one* Batmobile."

J. Edgar Hoover Building, Washington
7:29 a.m.

Whenever "the DD and RC" were summoned to an emergency meeting with the director, everyone at headquarters knew that the Bureau had reached the apogee of a crisis. All three—Jerry Reynolds, the FBI's deputy director; Doug Redding, assistant director for the Criminal Division; and Bill Colquitt, the AD for the National Security Division—were veterans of many of the FBI's difficult periods. But with the failure at Tulsa, the Bureau hurtled into its blackest tunnel ever. Its one promising hope for a breakthrough in the national madness was now gone, and the three leaders looked as glum as they felt as they filed into the director's office.

The FBI chief sat on a leather couch in the corner of the paneled room. His suit jacket and tie were draped over an arm of his desk chair. With an impassive expression, he motioned the men to the seating arrangement in front of him. The cream-tint lighting from the table lamp gave a pasty coloration to his face. He didn't make any attempt to hide his exhaustion.

The director nodded toward a flashing button on the telephone console. "Brand's holding. We'll get to him in a minute."

He waited until the men were seated before he began.

"The president's going for a declaration of martial law. That hasn't been done since Lincoln, in 1861. The White House counsel and the AG are working on the executive order now . . . probably'll announce it tomorrow." He made a fist and hit the surface of the adjacent table with his knuckles. "He worked me over pretty well last night, gentlemen. It was as if the FBI hasn't done a goddamn thing since all this began. We're likely to catch more flak from him when he addresses the nation."

The three others negotiated with their own thoughts and wondered which approaches to the problem might have been overlooked among the debris of the past two weeks.

The director stared across. "Jerry, what's your best proposal?"

Reynolds knew his suggestion wouldn't be in vogue. "Stick with Brand," he answered in a tone that was almost a question. He hadn't meant it to come out that way. He cleared his throat and tried to retrieve a resolute posture. His voice was an octave lower.

"Probably pick up Norman Gentry for questioning, too."

The FBI director looked at Redding. "Doug?"

The heavyset Criminal Division leader rested his elbows on the chair arms and rubbed his hands back and forth.

"Hell, I don't know. Not counting the missile attack at Albuquerque, there've been three different types of explosives used—Gellex-4, RDX, and phosphorus. There was the gassing in Phoenix. Then we had the gimmicks, like the plastic mold that derailed the Metroliner, the dart pen used to kill the Interpol agent, and the puncturing of the Denver mayor's neck. You tell me where the common denominator is. Our lab certainly doesn't see one."

"Bill?" The director stared at the assistant director for national security, who shook his head.

"Negative input from everywhere. No actionable suggestions, other than what Brand is chasing. But I did check with NCIC just before this meeting."

"And?" The director looked interested. The National Crime Information Center, the FBI's private Internet, was his pride and joy.

Colquitt shook his head.

"Nothing. However, we instituted a program last night to flag about twenty different types of items, from suspicious vehicles and aircraft to stolen license plates and all reports of stolen explosives. Maybe it's a needle-in-the-haystack effort, but we're scouring every way we can think of."

The director looked each man in the eye, starting with Reynolds.

"No miracle answers, in other words?"

All three shook their heads.

"I didn't expect any. OK, let's see what Brand's got." He punched the flashing button and twisted the volume knob. "Corley, can you hear us?"

"Yes, sir," came Brand's voice.

The director rubbed his forehead. "We've struck out in the new-idea department. The president tore me a new one last night. He's now only hours away from announcing martial law. Our reputation's the pits, as far as he's concerned, and we're in for even more when he goes on television. We could use some good news. Got any?"

There was a moment's silence. Despite the impersonal hiss from the telephone console, everyone knew Brand was there, thinking.

"First of all," the counterterrorism chief began, "I have *no* regrets whatsoever about pursuing the ministry angle."

Reynolds started to smile. Brand's legendary self-confidence was still with him.

"No, there's nothing I would do differently. Everything pointed to that place. Maybe we didn't get the smoking gun, but, in addition to the financial data, we did get the names of the foreign students and the foreign-born teachers. We're culling them now. That's more than nothing. I'd do it all over again."

The director leaned toward the console.

"Since you were so sure you'd find the smoking gun, Corley, and you didn't, sum up what you think happened."

"As I told you last night, and I'll sing the same song tomorrow: They knew we were coming. It's as simple as that."

The director rubbed his face with both hands.

"You know something, Brand. You beat all."

"Sir, we were slicked. Listen to the list again: the foreign bank accounts, the six men from Syria, the truck with the RDX, the attempts on Jack Stroud's life, the notes from someone on the inside, the latest of which says the missing students at the college are linked to the terrorist acts. Finally, Carmichael. All of this is somehow connected to the ministry. Downplay it as much as you want, but it *still* overwhelms what we've got-ten anywhere else. Let's at least do two more things: check out the missing-students angle and find the guy who wrote the notes."

The director watched the three men in his office. Colquitt indicated that he'd like to say something. The director nodded.

"Corley, this is your devil's-advocate boss. You've heard most of this before, but the foreign bank accounts could be totally unrelated. The six men on the TWA plane were going to a flying school in Tulsa, not to the ministry. The truck—were those explosives or just bad labels? Missing foreign students? Happens all the time at every college in the country. As I see it, the only possible lead, if you can call it that, is your note writer. Beyond him, there's nothing else that points unequivocally to the ministry. Right?"

"Bill, I'll match my one lead against your none any day."

The men in Washington looked at each other. Colquitt shrugged.

"All right, then," he proposed, "*find* that guy. And let me suggest something else. Interview Norman Gentry. He's got to be wondering what we found yesterday, and we just might learn something from him."

"Agree. You want to set it up with Albuquerque? He's got a big show out there at ten this morning."

Colquitt referred to his watch. "Yeah, we'll handle it."

Beggs, Oklahoma
9:05 a.m.

"Let's go, asshole."

A man yanked Lester Graham up by the arms and pulled him backwards. The farmer tried to accommodate, but the blindfold didn't help his coordination. He stumbled to one side, but his fall was blocked by the man's knee against his ribs.

"God damn it, straighten up!"

The farmer blanched. The man's mouth was right in Graham's face, and his breath smelled like decayed meat.

"Hands behind your back." A plastic handcuff was slipped on and tightened.

Graham had been imprisoned in the new subterranean room for a full day. He'd been kept blindfolded, but they'd cut his wrist restraints when they pushed him inside the door the previous morning. He was ordered not to remove the cloth that was tightly secured around his head. He hadn't tried, even though it had given him a continuous headache.

A hand shoved him forward and through a door. Then came the steps upstairs. Again he counted twenty-four. He was pushed down the corridor, which he knew led to his original cell. A few feet later, a hand grabbed him by the shoulder and pulled him to a stop. He was turned to the right. There was a scraping noise—metal against concrete—and Graham could hear a door open. With an audible clip, the plastic restraints were cut.

"You're home," the same voice snarled. A hand pressed against the small of his back and pushed him forward.

"You're lucky you're not dead," the man added before the door slammed shut.

Graham pulled down the blindfold. As soon as he could focus his eyes, he went to the rear wall and placed his fingers on the paneling, testing it with gentle pushes. It apparently hadn't been disturbed while he was gone.

"Gotta get the hell out of here before them turkeys decide to move me again . . . or cook *my* goose."

He squatted and found the separation he'd made before he was dragged away. Without worrying if he was being observed, Graham took off his watch and started scraping again at the glue.

Albuquerque
10:11 a.m.

Norman hadn't been alone at center stage for thirty seconds before the screams and swoons of his thousands of followers began interrupting his sermon at the carefully programmed emotional triggers. Minutes earlier, as usual, Bunny had waved energetically before retiring to a back chair, out of the spotlight, while Norman pretended to be overwhelmed at the tumultuous greeting. He made embarrassed-by-it-all gestures with his hands and shoulders and waited for the expressions of adoration to subside. Silence finally fell, in anticipation of the tirade they had come to hear, to take home in their hearts. Norman found a handkerchief and dramatically unfolded it, pulling the monogrammed linen across the wetness of his brow.

Today's production would be similar to the successful camp meetings in Kansas City and Denver. Not only would it be an equally flashy, professional program, with the white-clad Gentry Singers and the attendant laser-light show, but gate reports had already established that this outing would be immensely rewarding where it really counted: at the bottom line. There was one difference, and it was spotted only by a few longtime supplicants who found ways to poke and invade behind the stage. Without question, there was a heightened level of nervousness among some of the production directors. It seemed almost as if those responsible to see that everything was carried out smoothly were themselves in a near-desperate hurry to finish and be on their way. Men of the ministry were overheard shouting at one another, even cursing, both of which were uncharacteristic among the members of the so-called "family of God's people" who traveled with Norman.

"Oh, brothers and sisters," the pudgy minister followed the script and warned, "God is punishing America for her many sins, and He will do more until we eventually get the message."

"Lord have mercy on us," came a scream from a woman in the audience. It was followed by other shouts and moans.

As Norman reached again for his handkerchief and a moment to savor the din, a skinny man in a brown suit appeared from the darkened side of the stage and approached briskly. The minister looked surprised by the intrusion. The man stopped and leaned into the microphone.

"Brother Norman, I am sorry to interrupt you, but I have some very good news, which I must share with you immediately."

He held up a fistful of slips of colored papers.

"These are major pledges—fifteen in all—which we have received from some of the good people who are with us today. *Major* pledges."

Norman's initial expression of bewilderment changed to one of joy.

"Oh, praise the Lord," he boomed as he accepted the papers. "Thank you, Clifford. Thank you for bringing these to me."

Norman glanced down and paged through several of the handwritten offerings while the mousy aide stood at his side.

"My, here's one for $5,000. Another for $5,000. And one, two, three, each for $2,500," he added excitedly.

That's when he saw the typewritten note. It read simply, "FBI here, wants to meet with you in the hotel at 11:30."

He held up the note and screamed, "Here's one for ten ... thousand ... dollars!" The crowd gave its all in return. Norman grinned and forced the papers into his jacket pocket.

The little man next to him bowed and scuttled toward the curtain.

Norman held his arms open in appreciation. "Thank you so very much, my brothers and sisters." He turned as the aide reached the back of the stage. "What a wonderful surprise, Clifford," he called after him.

The man waved and slipped out of sight.

Norman unscrewed the microphone from its pedestal and started to strut.

"I am going to reveal to you today the facts of a putrid stain: the stain of pornography!" He stopped at one side of the stage and reveled in their uncomfortable squirming. He swung around and stepped back to the center spotlight.

"First I want to tell you about an unfortunate child of God who was nearly *killed* at the hands of the evil pornographers. Her name was Amy. This sweet little thing, a beautiful child of only five years, with blond hair and blue eyes, was playing in her yard one afternoon, so innocently, when this ... this *beast,* who was known to subscribe to so-called 'men's magazines,' drove by and saw her. He stopped his car and asked if she would help him find his lost puppy dog. Now, as one who had been taught by her parents to be respectful of her elders, she agreed and got into his car and drove off with him."

Many members of the assembled looked on with open mouths, knowing that no good could possibly come from the little girl's innocent acquiescence.

"Two days later a Christian family on a picnic heard a child's voice coming from a public toilet next to a highway. They went to this foul-smelling wooden outhouse and looked down one of the openings into a pile of fly-covered excrement and found little Amy, knee deep, smiling up at them."

The audience gasped. It was at least as bad as they had anticipated.

"Yes, yes, that's where she was, and she was *naked.*"

Oh, no, many thought. It was worse than they had imagined.

"When the police later questioned her, little Amy said that once she had been taken away from her neighborhood, the man had brought out one of his filthy magazines and had pointed to the picture of a naked woman and asked little Amy if she could pose like that. Well, she was taught to obey, so she tried her best to comply. That's when the man started to fondle her. He later took pictures of her in those awful poses."

"Oh, God Almighty, God Almighty," they began to cry out in unison.

"And we wonder why God is furious with this country?"

There was now a cadence to the audience's growing response, a lilt to their multitudinous voices, and Norman rode it easily with his continuing recitation of the obvious to the committed.

"*That,* my dear brothers and sisters," he went on, "is just one of the certain consequences of the filth of pornography. God's promise to us, His guarantee, is that we will descend into utter degradation unless we eradicate all pornography from the earth. He has told us that it fosters premarital sex, it encourages the molestation of a million children each year in this country alone, it promotes homosexuality, AIDS, incest, and genital herpes. Oh, brothers and sisters, pornography may be the worst single negative influence in America today."

Many in the audience still wiped at tears and moaned at the thought of what little Amy had gone through.

"Now, I want you to know that so-called 'sophisticated' people laugh and ridicule those of us who fight this vicious and putrid infusion. They think all we care about is the banning of certain magazines and books. They have no concept of the larger picture. For, you see, it is not one magazine or one book. It is the larger matter of the commission of sin. One sin leads to another. So, when a man or boy views one of these sinful magazines, he will be led on to a greater sin. He cannot simply back away. He is hooked, ensnared by the Devil himself! And we all know that Satan must destroy."

"Why?" many asked themselves and their spouses as Norman continued, "Oh, why couldn't the rest of the country see what pornography was doing to the fabric of this great nation God had ordained?"

Norman swung his arm in an arc covering the room.

"Everyone who has studied the issue of pornography knows that it is addictive. Yes, this is a fact that the experts all agree on. Once it seizes you, you cannot get away. It draws you in, to the Devil himself. And the sad truth is that most pornography eventually falls into the hands of our children! We all know that an alcoholic needs one more drink. One after another. That's the same way it is with pornography! Once you've had a certain level of excitement, you want more. You want to see something beyond the first level. This means more and more perversion as you delve deeper into the maze of filth. You progress downward, for that is the nature of pornography."

The cumulative effect of his words nearly overwhelmed his audience of the righteous, who had determinedly led crusades in their own communities. If it wouldn't have appeared impolite, they would have marched out immediately and returned home to carry on the fight for decency. Most, however, wanted to absorb as much ammunition as possible. So, in spite of the emotional tugs toward places in need of their righteousness, they stayed.

"Experts say that an actual chemical reaction takes place in the brain when a man looks at a picture depicting a pornographic scene. A 'groove' is established that will forever remain and seek more stimulation, and the degradation of the individual will continue. The Devil wants to claim as many souls as possible, to damn for eternity as many of God's human beings as he can. The Devil wants to cause chaos, so he jealously guards his rich field of pornography. He lures men from their families and from God. Once the devil has started that groove, there is little chance that the unfortunate individual can be pulled back. The individual hooked on pornography must have more and more. And it must be stronger each time, too. It's truly a diabolical addiction, which has taken over control of that person. Step by step, he slides away from all that he has known. He becomes consumed by the awful horror that is pornography. Pictures of naked women no longer satisfy. He must see naked women being hurt. Possibly even being killed! He starts lusting after pictures of children being molested. Then his interests start to lean toward molesting children himself. And on and on. Soon, the man has lost all sense of reality. He's addicted to pornography! Just like Ted Bundy, the diabolical serial killer who was finally executed in Florida back in 1989."

Norman stopped his pacing and peered through the bright lights. He saw that the room was nearly evenly divided between those who copied down his words frantically and those who simply listened and drew his message to their hearts. For any who wished, copies of his entire speech this morning would be available by mail within two weeks, for the modest offering of $49.95, plus tax. Visa and MasterCard accepted. Today's message was good for at least 2,000 orders from the faithful present and another five or six thousand from those who were following at home.

"Once a man is addicted," Norman boomed on, "he is desensitized. He is in total bondage to the Devil. And things get *worse*. Sometimes the man gets his wife or girlfriend to serve his vile intentions. If she won't cooperate, he will go elsewhere in search of his bodily satisfaction. He will accost strange women. If he can't find them, he will definitely go after children. Maybe even *your* children. He can't be stopped now. He's on a virtual rampage. He'll rape ... he'll murder ... to gain his sexual release. And all because of the horror of pornography. Oh, my! What degradation!"

The sweating minister turned and faced the back of the stage. He raised his arms toward heaven and held the pose until the vast auditorium was nearly completely quiet. Then he brought the microphone to his mouth and began to speak in a low but clearly understandable voice.

"My dear friends, I am told that our little ones, our children, are frequently lured into traps by those addicted to pornography. Here the little ones are forced to serve men whose minds were initially warped by the sights of the naked bodies of women in those abominable skin magazines. Oh, how will God choose to resolve our terrible condition?"

He spun around and faced the audience.

" 'Order a child of your liking,' the ads read. That's right, a sick man can actually place his order for a little boy or a tiny girl. He can choose their age, height, and weight. Does he like chubby, rosy-cheeked little ones? How about two at a time, maybe sweet little ones from the same family?" He paused before asking, "Do you know that many of these moppets are later *killed* by these evil pornographers?"

The audience moaned.

"There are hundreds of color magazines out there on newsstands today that are directed to these child abusers. Magazines featuring the innocent faces, and explicit features, of little girls and boys, from age three to eleven. There's something for everyone! If a man—God forbid—likes little boys, with their taut, sweet-smelling bodies, why, he can pick up a copy of specialty magazines designed for the committed ... er, chicken hawk. Yes, yes! That's what they call those men who prey upon little boys. Chicken hawks!"

He had to stop to wipe his face. It appeared he needed time to catch his breath. Thousands of pairs of arms reached up and moved from side to side in silent prayer to a God who had every right to be punishing America.

Luis Hernandez and Kenny Powell picked among the shrink-wrapped audio cassettes. Most of the tapes were hour-long addresses by Norman and song selections from the Gentry Singers. Other speakers and vocal groups were represented, but their offerings didn't receive the optimal "facings" that the Gentry labels did. In the background, from inside the auditorium, Norman's amplified voice boomed forth from the mammoth speakers. Only a few were out of their seats during the minister's hypnotic delivery, and most of those were making painful dashes to the restrooms.

The two men finished their perusal of the tapes and sauntered from the well-stocked table.

Hernandez inclined his head toward a concession stand. "Coke?" All of a sudden a hefty man bumped into Powell, who courteously turned to apologize.

The larger man grunted, "What are *you* two doing here?"

Powell's smile disappeared. "I beg your pardon?"

"You got a complaint, buddy?"

Powell put his hands on his hips. "Mister, I don't know who you are or what you're talking about."

"Or didn't you FBI pricks get enough religious inspiration during your little excursion in Tulsa yesterday?"

Inside the auditorium, Norman was wrapping up. He could see that the content of his message would weigh upon these committed people for months.

"What can we do about the scourge of pornography? There's one basic course of action: We can stand up. Stand up *now.*" Norman motioned for them to comply. "Stand up and say 'no!' "

Ten thousand followers rose and screamed forth, "No!"

"Say it again!"

They bellowed even louder.

"No!"

"Stand up whenever we see the viciousness of pornography in our communities. Stand up and demand that drugstores and newsstands cast out the magazines of filth. Stand up and fight the secular humanists who have ensnared our public schools. Otherwise, God will do it for you. He will expand His rule of punishment, which He is employing across the land today. Glory *be!*"

With a throwing motion, Norman extended his arms to heaven and stood immobilized as the main curtain quickly and dramatically closed and shielded him from view. It was as if he had been taken from them by a God who was ready to end it all.

11:30 a.m.

The three FBI men stood inside the alcove at the double doors to the Presidential Suite. Special Agent Colin Andrews had already knocked twice, without response. Waiting with them was one of the hotel's assistant managers, who'd insisted on being present. During the unexpected silence, he awkwardly jingled the change in his pocket.

"We certainly don't want anything to embarrass our distinguished guest, now, do we?" he'd fussed as they rode up in the elevator.

Andrews knocked again, this time as hard as his knuckles could bear. There was still no reply. The assistant manager leaned closer and placed his mouth at the crack between the two heavy doors.

"Mr. Gentry? Sir?"

"Lookin' for Brother Gentry?" A black maid pushed her housekeeping cart toward the waiting men. She shook her head. " 'Fraid he ain't returned." She anchored the cart a few feet away and started counting miniature bars of Neutrogena soap. " 'Course, his friends has."

Andrews moved toward her. "Friends, ma'am?"

" 'Bout an hour ago. Four of them big men. Guards, like. Ya know, with the dark glasses? They come up here and moved all his stuff out of the room. Didn't take 'em no more than one trip, neither."

Andrews frowned. "Then this room's empty?"

"Sure is. They left the doors wide open when they left. I closed 'em. I can't clean the place just any ol' time. I have my schedule, ya know."

"Hernandez," Andrews barked, "find out if Gentry's checked out. Powell, see if their buses are still here."

The agents dashed for the elevator.

Tulsa
Noon

The doorbell rang twice before Flora could make it from the kitchen. She wiped her hands on a towel, then twisted the knob and pulled the heavy door open. She sighed, then motioned for the woman to enter.

Rachel flew around the corner.

"Andrea, let's go! We have some serious shopping to do!"

The nurse held out her arms and caught her speeding charge. She laughed and spun around with the teenager.

"Hey, slow down, kiddo. Save some of that energy for the mall."

Rachel wiggled free and waved at Flora. "We'll be back when we get back," she promised the older woman.

Flora tried to say something, but the girl was already out the door.

"I'm driving, you know," Rachel called over her shoulder to Andrea.

2:33 p.m.

Jack touched his scalp. It felt completely different now that Leland Marks had removed the stitches and the area was naked and obvious.

"Don't forget to wear a soft hat when you go outside," his physician had counseled at the door of his medical office.

"I'll wear one."

Jack had tried a bareheaded excursion outdoors, before the remaining bandages had been removed. When the cold air hit the wound, it had the impact of a piercing toothache.

As he walked to his study, the telephone rang. Jack felt an immediate pain in his head. A reminder, he knew, of another call just eight days before. He turned and looked out the window. There were no ominous signs this time. Jack reached for the handset.

"Hello?"

"We have your daughter, Mr. Stroud." The man's voice was coldly clinical. "If you want to see her alive again, listen carefully."

The horror of the message slammed into his chest. Jack slumped into his chair.

"*What* did you say?"

The voice went on.

"You are not to pursue the exhumation order with the district attorney. You will meet with him at eight o'clock on Monday morning and instruct him to disregard your previous request. Do you understand?"

Jack shook his head slowly.

"Look, I don't know. . . . "

"Do you understand?" the man shouted.

Jack struggled to regain control.

"I . . . uh. What if I can't . . . ?"

"Maybe you *can* understand this, Mr. Stroud." The voice was lower and measured. "If the district attorney does not terminate the exhumation matter on Monday, or if you report this call to the authorities before then, you will receive by noon Tuesday a color videotape showing the surgical removal, without anesthesia, of your daughter's breasts and uterus."

Tulsa
Sunday, January 10, 12:27 a.m.

In the leaden silence of the hour, Jack stood at a parting of the heavy damask draperies along the back wall of his bedroom and peered through the window. Not that he expected to see anything outside, as the reflection from the lamp next to his bed obscured all but the lone orb of a streetlight half a block away. He moved closer to the glass, and his breath frosted outwards in irregular circles against the frigid pane. Jack inhaled deeply and held his breath for a few additional seconds of thought. When he exhaled, he noticed that the humid column from his lungs added its full contribution to the collection of ice and spread the distant streetlight's brilliance into concentric rings.

He stepped away from the window and saw himself in the mirror. His haggard appearance was no surprise. He was still in yesterday's clothes, but that somehow seemed appropriate. He pushed his hands into the pockets of his trousers, clenched his jaw, and knew he'd never forget the sound of the man's voice on the telephone. As he replayed the inflections to himself, he shuddered again.

Emotional wounds are cumulative, someone had once told him. They keep worsening until you finally confront and deal with them, one way or the other. Some people retreat into themselves and build psychic barriers for protection. A few tortured souls eventually go insane . . . even commit suicide. He thought about the afternoon with Andrea, but he knew that the horrifying announcement about Rachel had focused his wounds and summoned him at last to be counted. To choose. And which way would he go? He'd asked himself that question a hundred times in the hours since the call.

Jack approached the bed and sat down. He pulled two fresh pillows from under the down cover and propped them against the headboard. He slipped out of his loafers, leaned back against the cool cotton, and swung his legs onto the bed. With a sigh, he gripped his hands together across his stomach. Yes, he thought as he bit his lower lip, the horrors of the past two weeks had found their catalyst in that one telephone call.

"I've lost Laura . . . and Jeff," he whispered. "And Reuben." His eyes watered, and he was now breathing through his mouth. He shook his head. "Now, God forbid, maybe I've lost Rachel, too. And I have no one to blame but myself!"

Yesterday, in the first few minutes following the receipt of the message, Jack had sat nearly paralyzed, staring at the telephone. Emotions boiled within, from hopelessness to anger and back again, and his limbs felt heavy and unresponsive. There was a putrid, metallic taste in his mouth. He had to force himself to breathe, and for a moment he worried his heart might stop pumping blood to a body that truly seemed close to giving up. At one point, floating before him in the ethers of his memory, he saw the apparitions of his wife and son. He saw them clearly and could almost touch them as they moved past, but they didn't look at him—or even seem to notice. Jack wanted to seize them, to bring them back into his arms, but he was powerless. He attempted to call out to them. It was worse than any nightmare.

Jack remembered how it was before the horrors began on December 28, when he'd felt confident he had irrevocably stepped over the last hurdle that most men regarded as the dividing line between becoming successful and being successful. Getting there was still called the "rat race," and if you hadn't won by your mid-forties—and were honest with yourself that you hadn't—you took time out to have a midlife crisis, to reorient yourself for the remaining years. He hadn't had to go through those pangs, because his path always seemed straight and true. There were wrenching experiences, all right, the drowning of his first wife and Laura's miscarriage, but his vision remained clear. He had stayed the course through the Navy and then to Tulsa to propel United States Simulation Systems to its current preeminence as the nation's largest builder of flight simulators. By most people's definitions, Jack was indeed a success.

He'd been looking forward to another ten years at the helm of his company before retiring to his dream home on the west coast of the Big Island of Hawaii overlooking the warm and vast Pacific, with the majestic and snow-brushed Mauna Kea standing guard in the background. For years, Jack and Laura had talked about their hideaway promise to each other. It had been but a bamboo hut in their minds when they first started planning—just a cover over two lovers who really needed only each other. As time passed, however, the home became wrapped in more solid finery, and it had just recently evolved into a 6,000-square-foot marvel of glass and open spaces, indoor waterfalls and Chinese artifacts. It would assuredly make the cover of *Architectural Digest*, and they would grow young again as they witnessed ten thousand sunsets together.

It was nearly thirty minutes after the terrible message arrived before Jack emerged from his trance. He'd lifted his head and immediately encountered Laura's and Jeff's smiles, which radiated from their last-ever photograph on his desk. He'd swallowed and stared. Maybe that's what brought him back to the present, he thought. Those innocent, trusting faces. He reached for the picture and slowly traced Laura's features with his finger. Then he touched Jeff, next to her. Reluctantly, finally, he looked at Rachel. Was there a clue for him in their expressions? Did Laura and Jeff look different than Rachel? Was there some common aura that he could identify? Did Rachel have it, too? He picked up the picture and brought it closer. He shook his head. No, all of them projected the wholesomeness of a happy family. And all looked vulnerable.

Jack focused on Rachel.

For some reason, he remembered the analogy of the half-empty versus the half-filled glass. How you saw it depended upon your perspective. He bit his lip. Was *all* his family gone? As he followed the lines and shadows that delineated and represented his daughter in the color photograph, the doubts fell away, and he made his choice: Damn it, he wasn't going to lose her. He was going to do *something*. He looked intently at his little girl. His voice was clear.

"Don't give up, Rach. I'm coming for you."

Jack felt a rush of anger as he repositioned the framed picture at the corner of his desk. With an invigorating flow of adrenalin, he rose and started pacing. He stopped with his back to the bookcase and crossed his arms. His heart was pounding. From his Navy days, he knew that kidnappers were unlikely to keep their promises. Regardless of their assurances that a victim wouldn't be harmed, the poor unfortunate was often dead long before the most accommodating response could be made. He remembered one case in which a sailor on leave at San Diego kidnapped the infant son of his former wife. The little boy was strangled on the way to the getaway car, yet the sailor didn't make his first ransom demand until nearly a day later. The pleading parents had complied immediately, but of course it hadn't mattered.

Then there was the caller's warning: "Don't contact the authorities."

Why in the hell did he say *that*? Just the standard line, like what was expected from a television script?

Jack started pacing again. Couldn't be. Rachel's disappearance was obviously related to this whole matter, which now involved the FBI. Whoever took her *had* to know about the U.S. marshal shadowing her. Why, they'd even given him the slip. Surely the caller knew the man would report it right away. Jack stopped and looked out the front window. Unless they planned to kill the deputy. He shook his head. Either way, the authorities would know about the kidnapping—without Jack's help. The caller's demand just didn't make any sense. And what had happened to Andrea?

Andrea. A warmth instantly washed through his exhausted body, and he felt embarrassed under the new circumstances. Still . . .

He remembered calling toward the door of his study.

"Flora!"

Seconds later, his housekeeper slipped into his office. She wiped her hands on her apron.

"Do you know where Rachel and Andrea were going?"

The woman smoothed the material of the apron. She peered at him.

"Mr. Stroud, you look terrible."

"Please, Flora. Where were they going?"

Flora drew back at his tone of voice. "One of the malls, sir." She looked at him again. "Mr. Stroud, what . . . ?"

"When did they leave?" Jack interrupted.

The woman brought her hands to her chest and glanced off to one side. "Let me see." She frowned. "The mantel clock in the dining room was chiming. Oh, it was exactly noon."

Jack stared into space, and Flora watched him for a clue.

"Thanks, Flora," he replied abruptly. Then he saw her anguished expression, and his features softened. He shook his head.

"Nothing you can do. But thanks."

Jack moved toward his desk. Flora waited until he sat down before turning to leave.

" 'Don't contact the authorities,' " he repeated out loud after she pulled the door closed. "Or, more precisely, it was 'don't call them until the exhumation matter is terminated.' "

Jack rubbed his cheek. "Can't wait," he concluded with a shake of his head. Then he saw Rachel's face on the photograph.

"Better yet, *won't* wait."

He pulled out the center drawer of his desk and rummaged through a partitioned section containing business cards. He spotted one particular white rectangle and picked it up. "Jones Brothers Chimney Sweeps. A. Jones, Proprietor." It was the card FBI agent Don Evans had given him in the parking lot on New Year's Eve. Jack referred to the number while he lifted the handset of the telephone. He punched in the seven digits. The number rang almost immediately. A woman answered.

"Afternoon. Jones Brothers." Her voice bore a heavy Oklahoma twang. "We're the 'clean sweep,' " she said cheerfully. "May I hep ya?"

"Uh, my name's Stroud." Jack started picking his way into a conversation. He knew he had to play it straight. "I've used our home fireplace for a month or so, but when I tried to start it a few minutes ago, flames came out of the bricks at the back. You know, on the wall, behind the logs. I couldn't tell, but the fire might have extended up the chimney."

He hadn't rehearsed it. He hoped it sounded natural.

"Good golly, sir. You probably got yourself a real healthy coating of creosote. How long's it been since you had your chimney cleaned?"

The woman's question sounded genuine, and it made him think for a second.

"Oh, probably five or six years."

"My-o-my!" the woman exclaimed in her nasal fashion. "Sir, you'd better not burn *anything* in that fireplace 'til your chimney's been scrubbed out real good by our people."

Jack could almost see her shaking her finger at him. Then he heard her turning pages.

"Now, we're kinda booked up," she went on. "You know, the cold weather and all. But I can probably get someone out to your place next Tuesday morning. How'd that be?"

"Tuesday? Not sooner?"

"No, sir. Like I said, we're real busy. So, a couple of our men will be there at . . . let's say . . . eight, Tuesday morning. Just use your furnace until then, OK?" The woman moved right along. "Address and telephone, please."

Jack complied, although he now questioned the whole conversation. Impatience and frustration boiled within his soul.

"All righty, Mr. Stroud," the woman concluded. "We'll see you next Tuesday. And thanks for calling. You have a nice day, y'hear?"

As she clicked off, he laid the business card on top of the others in his desk collection.

"Did Evans give me the wrong card?" He pushed the drawer closed. *Tuesday morning?* That woman was absolutely believable! He frowned and tapped at the desktop. Would the Bureau make contact? Did they even *know* about his call?

He didn't have to wait long to find out. When the doorbell rang thirty minutes later at the four o'clock shift change for the deputy marshals, Jack heard a man greet Flora loudly.

"Good afternoon, ma'am."

He didn't recognize the voice.

"Barnes. With the U.S. Marshal Service. Is Mr. Stroud in?"

Flora hesitated. Up to now, the marshals had remained aloof in their vigil. Rarely had they been inside the house, and those few times were at her direct invitation for a cup of hot coffee.

"Well, I . . . " She drew back at FBI credentials as the man eased the door shut and stepped closer. "But you're not . . . "

"That's right, ma'am." His voice was lower. "Mr. Stroud, please. It's extremely important."

The woman turned. "Mr. Stroud?"

"It's all right, Flora." Jack moved past his housekeeper toward a short, dark-complexioned man in his early thirties. He had intense brown eyes but an otherwise friendly face. The man pointed down the hallway.

"Back of the house, please."

Jack frowned at the order but complied. As soon as they turned the corner into the library, the man pulled off his glove and extended his hand.

"FBI, Mr. Stroud. Tony Alvarez. Everyone calls me 'Chico.' I don't think anyone can overhear us here."

"I'm certainly glad you came," Jack replied as they shook hands. "I didn't know if I'd reached the right number or not."

Alvarez was all business.

"We already know about your daughter, sir."

Beggs, Oklahoma
Before sunrise

In the predawn blackness, Dutch Dennison pushed up the turn indicator with his left palm and slowed for the exit.

"I'm back, you son of a bitch," he growled as the signal clicked through its repetitions and he left the main highway. He remembered all too clearly the surly, muscle-bound tough who'd refused his inspection of the property on Friday morning.

Dennison's Oklahoma Highway Patrol uniform and black-and-white cruiser were twenty-five miles out of sight to the north. This time he was in his decade-old yellow Chevy pickup. It was battered from uncounted hunting forays in unforgiving terrain, and three errant springs in its plastic seat had been taped into submission, but the old half-ton, at just under 100,000 miles, still provided reliable transportation. He braked and turned at the metal stop sign of the frontage road and accelerated westward on the two-lane county asphalt. There was no traffic. He noted the odometer. Seven miles to go.

"You're hidin' something, jerkoff, and I'm gonna find it."

Minutes later, Dennison halted at the "T" intersection and turned right onto the road that formed part of the section line. He accelerated and squinted to his left as he passed what he knew to be the location of the house. He couldn't see anything at all in the darkness. He then looked for the intersection with the road that ran along the north side of the property. He nodded when the perimeter fence ended and a flat area flashed past his peripheral vision. He drove onward, over a rise and fifty yards beyond so his brake lights wouldn't be noticed.

"This ought to do 'er," he commented out loud. He stopped the pick-up and peered over his left shoulder. He knew where the northeast part of that property was, with its grass landing strip, but he couldn't recognize anything yet. Which meant they couldn't see him either, he reminded himself. He stepped on the accelerator again, directed the vehicle into a shallow bar ditch a dozen more yards ahead, and braked to a stop. He was now well out of sight of the house.

Dennison held his wrist close to the lighted speedometer and checked the time. Sunrise was still nearly an hour away, but he knew he'd be able to make out basic outlines of objects from the initial eastern glow within fifteen or twenty minutes. He pushed off the headlights and settled back against the seat to wait. He'd decided not to use his flashlight in the search. The random stabs of light stood a good chance of attracting attention. "Dogs, for sure," he concluded. He then made a face. "And other undesirables." No, he'd wait until the first natural light yielded sufficient contrast to make his way onto the property. He probably faced little chance of being seen unless someone was alerted and actually started looking for him. He felt pretty good. On this cold and quiet Sunday morning, he figured the odds would be well in his favor.

As dawn approached, Dennison became aware of a fence line across the road. Then a lone tree took skeletal shape a quarter-section to the east. He pulled on his knitted hat and thick leather gloves, opened the door of the pickup, and stepped out into the ice-cold silence. There was no wind to make things feel colder . . . or to carry a scent. With both hands, he pressed the door shut with a barely audible click and started for the property.

It took him a couple of minutes to huff to the perimeter road, where he stopped and looked in the direction of the house and barn. His breathing forced out oblong puffs of condensation, which disappeared almost instantly into the frigid stillness. He squinted. Two thousand yards or so to the southwest, looking almost artificial in the first deep violet of the approaching dawn, stood the house and the large metal barn. There were no visible lights in or around either facility. The scene resembled a ghostly apparition that had risen out of the ground, and it reminded him of the first time he watched Alfred Hitchcock's *Psycho*. It was all he could do to keep himself from feeling the same way he did when he saw that eerie house in the movie years ago.

Dennison looked to both sides and proceeded in a measured walk to the fence that marked the northern edge of the property. He stared at the house as he continued. He concluded he hadn't been noticed. "At least I hope no one's watching," he told himself as he swung over the barbed-wire fence and squatted down just inside the property. He would have crossed his fingers if the gloves hadn't been so bulky. He lifted his head. Still no reaction from the house. He rose and started at a fast clip for the grass strip where he'd seen the evidence of a plane's landing.

Dennison stopped in the middle of the field. This was it, the sought-after mowed portion. He lowered himself to his haunches and rubbed a gloved hand over the flat surface. Even though it was the dead of winter, the thinner texture of the cellulose here was an easy giveaway. He was at the north end of the landing strip, which extended about a half mile to the south.

He stood up halfway, turned, and began reconnoitering. In a modified squat, he stepped gingerly down the middle of the landing strip. Nothing but straw-colored stubble within ten feet in any direction. He looked toward the house. It remained unlit. He moved on. He'd proceeded about a hundred feet when he spotted parallel narrow depressions characteristic of the marks made by a small plane's landing gear. They were probably the same grooves he'd seen from the air. Both seemed to stop in the middle of the strip. He looked around. There were no apparent taxi tracks. Maybe the pilot had made a "touch and go" after all, he considered. Then he saw something on the ground a couple of yards further. He approached and picked it up. It was a bent metal placard, approximately one and a half inches by three inches, black with silver lettering, most of which had been scratched off with deep cuts. Probably recently, he concluded, because the underlying metal was clean and still shiny. Dennison knew immediately it was from the instrument panel of an airplane cockpit. The registration number was even stamped on the lower right-hand corner: N36SSA.

"One of the trainers of the Southwest School of Aviation," he mouthed in recognition. All of their planes were registered with the FAA with the special three-letter appendage, "SSA." And it definitely wouldn't have fallen out from a touch and go. More like a crash.

As Dennison tucked the placard into his coat pocket, what sounded like a bumblebee streaked past his right ear. He raised his head. Then he heard the sharp report from the direction of the house.

"Shit, someone's shooting at me!"

Dennison ducked and ran for the fence. Another bullet whistled overhead, missing him by barely two feet. He vaulted over the fence and tumbled into a ditch on the other side as the sound of the second firing reverberated in the morning silence. In an adrenalin-fueled crawl, he propelled himself to the intersection and across the county road into the relative safety of the deeper ditch beyond. There was no third shot. He checked his pocket. He still had the placard.

Sunrise

The sharp sounds sent Lester Graham scurrying back to his cheap mattress. In the dark, he had been quietly moving debris out of the way in the crawl space he'd discovered behind the wood paneling at the back of his basement cell. He'd broken through on Friday morning, just before they yanked him downstairs, blindfolded, to that other room. He'd started in again when they returned him here yesterday.

The first noise was so uncharacteristic for the early hour that Graham cocked his head in disbelief. Had he actually heard something? Then came the second one. Yep, heard it, all right, he told himself as he backed out of the tight space and began a quick dust-off. Rifle shots, for sure. His hands located the smelly army blanket, and he dragged the woolen covering up to his chin.

"What the hell's going on *now?*" he questioned under his breath. While he waited, wondering if they'd come for him again, he reviewed his progress.

Each vertical wood panel was hinged at the edge of the suspended ceiling, and he was correct about the size of the space between the paneling and the original concrete wall; fifteen, maybe even sixteen inches in places where the wall was uneven. Certainly not a lot of maneuvering room for someone of his girth. He wouldn't be able to make it at all if he wore heavy clothing, although being poorly dressed would pose a separate risk for him if he got outside into the dry-ice-like conditions. He thought about that for a minute, then suppressed a laugh. Where was he going to get a lot of heavy clothing anyway? His stuff was in a closet at home, and these jerks weren't about to let him go get it . . . or lend him theirs.

When he first pulled open the section of wood paneling, he'd seen only a filthy, dust- and debris-filled space. Graham pushed aside the trash and peered upwards. His caught his breath and could hardly believe his good fortune. For there, incredibly, was quite possibly his salvation. Ten feet above, not far beyond the lowered ceiling of his cell, was a basement window. It looked to be large enough for him to squeeze through, *if* he could get to it.

Graham was determined to give it a try, in spite of another intervening obstacle he'd noticed ... the spiders. Or, rather, what was left of them after a bountiful summer of eating and breeding. He'd found out about the once-teeming colonies of arachnids the first time he'd thrust his hand into the dark recesses of the crawl space, where he couldn't see. It came as a distinct surprise when his fingers encountered what felt like collections of gritty cotton candy. He jerked his hand back, unintentionally bringing with it generous samples of his discovery.

"Holy shit!" he exclaimed as he frantically slapped away a dozen stringy web remnants with their attached egg sacs. "Darn black widows." He blew at one sinuous strand, with its wrinkled cocoon of suspended life, which impudently swirled closer and threatened to fasten itself to his bare arm.

"Be a thousand of them crawlers hatchin' under every house around here in a couple of months," he exclaimed as the errant floater gave up and drifted toward the floor. "But you devils won't find me." He checked himself for other vestiges of the tiny creatures, then smiled in relief.

"No siree. I'll be long gone from this here place."

The White House
Early morning

The president was alone in the West Sitting Hall on the second floor. He stood against a cheerfully upholstered sectional and stared out the large Palladian window that overlooked the West Wing. Frost coated the panes, but the massive Executive Office Building was clearly recognizable in the background. The chief executive wore a new, cherry-red cashmere robe, a Christmas gift from his children, and he'd put on the comfortable fur-lined slippers he'd bought in Iowa during the campaign. He gripped a copy of *The Washington Post*. After a second, he tossed the newspaper onto the end table. He heard a tap at the door.

"Mornin', Mr. President."

It was Jacob Briley, his favorite steward, right on time with a silver tray bearing coffee and orange juice. The older man lifted off two stainless-steel carafes of the hot beverage and a large crystal pitcher of cold, freshly squeezed juice. Already on the polished table were three china cups and saucers and three glasses. Linen napkins with an embroidered "The White House" lay to the side.

"Jacob, the other gentlemen will be here in five minutes."

"Yes, sir, I know." The steward smiled. "I'll bring the croissants and rolls then. That way they'll be hot and fresh." Briley took his leave.

The *Post* this morning was no more charitable than the rest of the media, the president reflected as he walked to the table and poured himself a cup of coffee. Editorial writers weren't taking any prisoners today. The *Los Angeles Times* started with, "The fallout from the president's canceled address to the nation on Friday was devastating to an administration already gravely wounded and seemingly adrift at this time of national peril. Such last-minute action, under the circumstances and without a serious attempt at an explanation, is inexcusable." The president could have memorized the entire editorial if he'd read it twice. He didn't intend to make the effort.

"Sir?"

It was the gravelly voice of a Secret Service agent. The attorney general and Clark Thornton, counsel to the president, entered and started for the arrangement of chairs where the chief executive stood. The agent pulled the door shut.

The president offered coffee and juice as he sat down. "We'll have rolls in a moment."

The two visitors took coffee. The president held his cup at chin level and stared at them.

"Well?"

Thornton spoke first.

"You can do it, Mr. President. Civil authority has become ineffective in many parts of the country. Martial law is your Constitutional prerogative. Article I, Section 9."

"No, damn it!" The attorney general shook his head. "That article empowers the legislative branch, not the executive. It was settled once and for all in 1861 by Chief Justice Roger Taney in the Merryman matter."

"But Lincoln went ahead and suspended habeas corpus anyway," Thornton boomed.

"Against the clear decision of the Supreme Court!" the AG sputtered in return. His face reddened. "A blatant violation of the Constitution, and you know it!"

"But Lincoln did it," Thornton continued confidently, "because he knew what had to be done to save the Union. And he was never second-guessed afterwards. You know why? Because he was *right*." The White House counsel sat back and crossed his arms.

"I don't give a healthy crap if he rescued the entire goddamn universe!" the AG nearly screamed. He was now half out of his chair, waving his finger in front of Thornton's face. "It was unconstitutional, it was impeachable, and I'm not going to lend one ounce of my prestige or that of the United States Justice Department to a repeat of the whole sordid thing."

"Gentlemen, *please.*"

The president put his cup and saucer on the table. His guests glared at each other.

"I happen to think you're both right." The chief executive placed his hands on his knees and rubbed them back and forth.

"I know what Lincoln did, and I know what Taney did. *They* were both right, too. For different reasons, of course."

He stood and went to the window again. He spoke with his back to his two advisors.

"But Lincoln was the president, and now I'm the president. I swore to preserve, protect, and defend the Constitution. Yes, I could get into a technical debate with the Congress over who has primary authority to act, but I'm not going to do it."

He toyed with the belt of his robe.

"That could take weeks. We don't have weeks. We've had panic and general turmoil across the country since all of this began. Thousands are dead, and we're at the breaking point. This is the worst domestic state of emergency since the Civil War . . . when Lincoln did what he had to do."

The president turned around.

"I'm going to act." He returned to where the two men were sitting. "Then I'll go for permission, or ratification, or whatever. But at least during the interim, as commander in chief, I'll put the lid on this mayhem."

He addressed Thornton. "Give me a thorough brief on the law and some appropriate language for a declaration of an Executive Order. I've got to get with Sandy McConnell and the Pentagon. I'll announce this to the nation tomorrow night."

"Mr. President, if you *please* . . . " The AG rose and attempted to fashion another perspective.

The chief executive shook his head.

"Goodbye, gentlemen."

As the two men departed, the steward appeared in the doorway holding a covered tray. He looked surprised that the meeting was over so soon. Thornton lifted the cloth as he passed and plucked out a sweet roll. The AG glowered after him.

Jones Airport
Sunday, January 10, 10:30 a.m.

The yellow Chevy pickup careened off U.S. 75, swerved in behind a station wagon on the frontage road, and skidded to a stop at the intersection. It turned right and headed for nearby Jones Airport.

Dutch Dennison jammed on the brakes alongside the FAA control tower. The out-of-uniform highway patrolman bounded out of the pickup and pushed the button on the freestanding intercom next to the door. The speaker unit crackled with static.

"Tower."

"Dennison here," he panted. "Carlin up there?"

"Naw, he's off today."

"Well, buzz me in anyway. I gotta call him."

A low-pitched sound signaled that the door lock had been tripped. Dennison pulled on the handle and dashed up the stairs to the tower cab. He bolted into the bright enclosure and nodded to familiar faces as he reached into his pocket and withdrew a slip of paper.

"Ever find that Cessna?" one of the controllers inquired without taking his eyes off the airplanes taxiing outside.

"Sure did. Piece of it, at least." He picked up the phone and, referring to the paper, dialed Carlin's house. After five rings, a sleepy voice answered.

"Hullo?"

"Ron, it's Dutch. Sorry to call you on Sunday morning, but I just got back from that place down near Beggs. You know, where the plane was reported missing? Guess what I found?"

"Dutch?"

"Damn it, Carlin, wake up. I found a placard from the instrument panel of that missing plane. I've got it with me." He heard a loud yawn.

"You talked with Southwest yet?" The FAA man sounded more in charge of himself.

"Next call," Dennison replied. "Then probably the FBI, just to make it official. Hey, you'll be happy to know they don't cotton to trespassers down there."

"About got your ass shot off again, didn't ya?"

The highway patrolman nodded. "Yeah, but I'm not through with that place."

Carlin went on. "You know, that pickup of yours ought to look like a piece of Swiss cheese by now, from all the bullets fired at it."

"It *is* the right color," Dennison laughed. "Gotta go." He broke the connection and punched in the number for the Southwest School of Aviation. As soon as the receptionist answered, he was under way.

"Who's on duty over there this morning? This is Dutch Dennison, OHP."

"Uh, well, no one really," the woman replied. "We're officially closed until noon. Let me see who's in the main hangar." She put him on hold. Someone clicked on.

"Hey, flyboy, it's Taylor. Doesn't the law ever rest?"

Dennison rolled his eyes and sighed. "No, and we never get any respect from certain people, either. Seriously, Jimbo, I need to know the 'N' number of your 152 that's missing. Got it handy?"

"Sure do," came the immediate reply. "It's on the scheduling board right in front of me. The registration's ... uh ... 'thirty-six,' with our company 'SSA' at the end."

Dennison retrieved the bent placard from his pocket and stared at "N36SSA."

"You know where our plane is?" Taylor asked.

"I know where it *was*. Let me get back with you, OK?" He was already juggling the Tulsa telephone directory into position as he hung up.

"FBI ... FBI. There it is ... 664-3300."

J. Edgar Hoover Building, Washington, D.C.
1:00 p.m.

Through the window of the conference room of the Strategic Operations Information Center, Deputy Director Jerry Reynolds saw the three-fingers signal from a technician outside. He nodded and punched the third lighted button on the telephone console. It was one of SIOC's seventeen scrambled lines.

"Corley, you there?" He twisted the plastic volume knob.

"Here, sir."

Reynolds looked at his watch.

"OK, another thirty seconds. They're hooking the satellite signal directly to the telephone line."

Reynolds pulled back a chair from the long table and sat down. The television screen at the end of the room flashed on. It was precisely 7 p.m. in Berlin when Michael Kinney's face appeared from the FBI's office in Germany.

"Jerry Reynolds, Mike. Can you hear me?"

Kinney nodded. "Yes, sir, like you're in the next room."

"Corley Brand's in Tulsa. We're all patched in together."

"I can hear you both," Brand acknowledged.

"OK, Mike." Reynolds leaned back in his chair. "Give it to us."

Kinney picked up a sheet and began.

"As you know, Germany's Kommissar system is still the world's best cross-reference of individual terrorists and their various organizations. Even so, sometimes there are time-consuming wild-goose chases in getting a positive identification, regardless of the number of input identifiers used."

Kinney read the bulleted highlights of his report. "After we gave the Germans the information on the 30 December TWA murder, together with the visa data from Immigration, I thought we'd get a good ID, photos and all, within twelve hours at the most. But they had absolutely nothing for us forty-eight hours later. I went over there and checked myself and found that they'd gone to backgrounds to get more cross-references. They even made twenty direct calls to *Bundesnachrichtendienst* operatives in the field, risking a bunch of people's covers in the process. Anyway, to make a long story short, it turns out they got snookered by the guy himself. He'd had facial plastic surgery, something they'd factored in, but what kept throwing them was the four-inch scar on his right hand, which the flight attendant reported. It was a one-hundred-percent phony, a peel-off. Once that was disregarded, the other pieces snapped together. TWA passenger Salim El-Asail, gentlemen, was none other than Abu Kuttab."

"Jesus H. Christ!" It was Brand's agitated voice. "He's the number-one henchman of Jamil Nasir. They call him 'the Scorpion' because he stays out of sight and strikes from hidden bases, usually when least expected. Kuttab's directly responsible for more than a *thousand* murders during the past decade. And one of his groups masterminded the Sadat assassination in '81. He was reported all over Europe during the war with Iraq, and he definitely arranged the American Express and Citibank bombings in Greece. His fingerprints are all over the IBM attack, too. Really, really bad news." Brand paused. "I'd bet my retirement he's directing that 'Brother-hood of the Ultimate Ijima' the BND warned us about last month."

Reynolds pulled himself to the table. "OK, Corley, why?"

"Hell, Jerry, he's the second-best of the worst in the grisly business of terrorism, and he comes out of Lebanon, where that group is located. I'll tell you exactly what's going on. Someone called someone at the Frankfurt airport the day before Kuttab and his henchmen boarded the TWA flight. I say that someone called Kuttab. And what did the caller tell him? Hold on, I wrote it down. 'The final jihad has begun. The first wounds have been inflicted. Go sever the head of the pharaoh and complete the cleansing. The Brotherhood is with you. Allah akbar.' Gentlemen, Kuttab and his group are now over here to do something very specific, namely to 'sever the head of the pharaoh,' whatever that means. I know what I *think* it means. In any event, it spells big trouble for us. And it's going to happen soon."

"How so?" This time it was Kinney.

"If he had all the time in the world, and assuming the base is here in the middle of the U.S., Kuttab would have entered at one of the major airports, such as New York or Chicago, and dropped out of sight en route. He'd have driven to Tulsa over a week, or longer. He absolutely doesn't like anyone to get ahead of him, to anticipate his moves. But he didn't cover this time. He came directly here, to Tulsa."

"But what if that was to throw us," Reynolds suggested, "because his real target is elsewhere, like on one of the coasts?"

"No way. His people are here, and he's coming to them. Airport security at Frankfurt and Customs in St. Louis said he had nothing out of the ordinary with him. Nothing shipped separately, either. No, he's going to pick up whatever he needs here."

"At your so-called American base," Reynolds added.

"At *his* American base," Brand corrected.

"He probably didn't think he'd be recognized," Kinney offered. "Ahmed Pasha paid with his life, but if it hadn't been for him, Kuttab might never have been noticed. It was all so neat and tidy—foreign students simply coming over for school. It would have remained that way, but for Pasha."

"All right, Corley." Reynolds closed his eyes and rubbed his hands over his face. "What's our next step?"

"Jerry, believe me, Kuttab's within twenty-five miles of me this very minute, and he's tied in with that ministry somehow."

Brand anticipated Reynolds's next question.

"I know we didn't get anything out of the search last Friday, but within twenty-four hours of it Norman Gentry disappeared and Jack Stroud's daughter was kidnapped. Hardly coincidences. No, we're awfully close now. I'm going to interview Stroud, then I'm going out to the Southwest School of Aviation. Kuttab's here, and I intend to get him."

Kinney patted a document. "Gentlemen, I've got his historical bio."

Reynolds faced the television screen.

"Mike, let's hear it."

Kinney opened a file.

"Born 10 August 1962 at the northern Egyptian town of Al Mazar. One sister, Rima Ameen, reportedly born in 1963. No further information on her. Supposedly, Kuttab has few memories of his mother or father other than that of their deaths during an Israeli strafing of their town on the last full day of the 1967 War, two months before his fifth birthday. An aunt, born in 1948, raised him to the age of eleven. She was killed in a 1973 attack when the Israelis crossed the Suez Canal."

He turned the page.

"In March 1980, Kuttab was interviewed by *Paris Match*. That was before the Sadat murder, and it's the only substantive look we have into his motivations. He said the way his parents died was the number-one reason he joined the Palestinian movement at age eleven. According to the magazine article, Israeli pilots frequently unloaded their unused bomb loads on Egyptian villages as they crossed back into Israel after a raid on military targets. On 9 June 1967, a 2,000-pound bomb obliterated the building next to his family's apartment. The concussion collapsed their three-story dwelling, crushing most members of four families, including his parents. Kuttab said he remembered running toward the boiling smoke and dust and finding his mother's mutilated torso. The only thing recognizable about her shredded body was a colorful smock. Not much more stayed in his memory, other than the beginnings of the hatred that grew to a fury, which has motivated him ever since. It's a fury, he told the writer, that united him with thousands of his fellow Muslims and that will be with him until its eventual release at his death."

Reynolds sat at his post and shook his head. Kinney went on.

"Kuttab entered manhood in the service of his religion, and he quickly fell under the influence of the 'Ikhwan,' the Muslim Brotherhood. During the late 1970s and throughout the 1980s, Kuttab took part in numerous attacks against Israeli and Western interests. His intention was to see, in his lifetime, the destruction of Israel and the removal of all Western influences in the Middle East. The path to both was an unyielding adherence to fundamentalist Islam. He developed into one of the best of the worst and attracted the attention of Jamil Nasir after the Sadat killing. Nasir had also started as a religious zealot, but he quickly evolved into one of the five or six most effective terrorists for hire, like Ahmed Jabril. In Nasir's opinion, Kuttab had an effectiveness that transcended the religious. Kuttab and Nasir met on the sandy wastes of the Bekaa Valley in 1983, and they formed a tight bond almost immediately. Together they represented the fists of millions of the disaffected, the deluded, and the disinherited whose ice-cold fury wanted to destroy everything Western."

Kinney paused to turn the page. "He was a prime suspect in the first few hours after the Oklahoma City bombing."

"Mike?" It was Brand. "What's the latest on Nasir?"

Kinney squinted at a separate sheet.

"We don't know where he is, Corley. We've had no positive contact with him for years. He remained totally underground during the Iraqi situation. However, the Mossad credited him with setting up one of those major training operations in the Bekaa Valley. Now, with the movement of Kuttab and five of his men to Tulsa, all probably originating from the Bekaa Valley, the Israelis were likely on target with their assessment."

"Is that the base that was recently closed down? Or seemed to be, after the departure of the trainees?"

"Possibly, but the BND's informants couldn't positively identify Nasir as one of the regulars at that particular place. Matter of fact, they don't think they ever saw him there."

Brand picked up the story.

"Well, we know Kuttab came to the United States on a Syrian passport and F-1 student visa. His ostensible reason was to be an aeronautical student at Southwest School of Aviation in Tulsa. According to the paperwork I've seen, he was to become a licensed aircraft mechanic. Then he was to obtain the necessary training from private pilot all the way up to and including the airline transport license. The entire curriculum would require nearly four years. But he disappeared in Tulsa and never showed up at the school. Of course, he never intended to enroll in the first place. And no one at INS has a clue."

Brand laughed. "Inscribed on the bottom of the plaque at the Statue of Liberty should be Immigration's proud footnote: 'Student visas available for all, no waiting, and no questions asked . . . now or ever.' "

Kinney continued. "I've got more on the Brotherhood, if you want it."

"Floor's yours," Reynolds barked.

"The BND's contacts filled out more of the picture we have. It isn't just a pan-Islam movement of some sort, with the Shi'ites, Sunnis, and the other Muslims. It's thoroughly anti-American, like some of the mujahadin offshoots. A tightly organized cadre of well-trained, high-tech commandos. Two of their slogans are instructive. The first one sounds like old Marxist-Leninist lingo: 'We will bring ultimate victory for the oppressed over the oppressors.' The other one is more disturbing: 'We are the avenging angels. We are bringing the future to you.' "

Kinney picked up his notes. "Everything else the BND has obtained confirms a vitriolic hatred of the United States. There's very little of the usual language of religious fervor, like what we heard from Hamas. But . . . who knows?" Kinney tapped the pages into order. "That's it."

"Good report, Mike," Brand called out, "but you left out the most important part."

"Which is?"

"The 'who.' Who's behind all of this? Not just the name of an organization, like 'the Brotherhood,' but the real people putting up the money. Who are they, and what's their ultimate goal? During the 1980s, the threat to the United States by international terrorists, principally Islamic fundamentalists, was focused in the Middle East. I remember the report of a Reuters journalist, when he looked over the smoking remains of the Marine barracks in Beirut. He lamented that he was witnessing the beginning of a movement that would one day wash ashore in America. 'When that day comes, America will grow up,' I think he said. In other words, the rich and corrupt Americans, who did not understand the roots and sustenance of the movement, would have their mouths full of shattered teeth. Then this threat was reinforced after our war with Saddam Hussein. Over the years, presidents have reacted to the growing violence against U.S. interests by threats and attempts to interdict and infiltrate. Such actions only fed the wrath of the hordes. Look at France. Now someone has apparently decided that the ultimate answer is the elimination of a leader, as in, 'go sever the head.' "

Reynolds frowned. "Your conclusion, Corley?"

"Jerry, remember I said earlier that Kuttab was over here to do something very specific and very soon? Well, I think it's time to get the Secret Service involved."

Tulsa
3:28 p.m.

"Mr. Jack Stroud, please." The woman's twang sounded familiar.

"Speaking."

"Oh, hi, Mr. Stroud. It's Becky down here at Jones Brothers Chimney Sweeps. Remember me? I was the one who scheduled you for next Tuesday."

"Yes, Becky." Jack felt a clutch in his chest. Had they found Rachel?

"Well, you know the Taubs? They're your neighbors a couple of blocks to the east. Anyway, one of our crews was supposed to do their chimneys this afternoon, but they're still away on vacation. The Taubs, that is. Not our crew." She laughed at the possible misunderstanding. "Anyway . . . "

"You people work on Sundays?"

"Oh, you betcha, this time a year. Now, if you want, I'll tell that crew to start your place today instead of Tuesday. OK?"

Jack didn't hesitate. "Certainly. When?"

" 'Bout a half hour. I just need to call 'em on the radio."

The second workman through the door lugged a protective roll of floor and furniture covering over his shoulder. Even with the Jones Brothers hat, uniform, and dark glasses, his identity was unmistakable. Jack recognized Corley Brand.

"Nothing yet on Rachel," his FBI friend whispered out of the corner of his mouth as he laid the roll next to the fireplace.

The other Jones Brothers "workman" spoke into an FM transmitter as Jack and Brand headed for the back of the house. As they entered the sunroom, Brand continued in his normal tone of voice. "We interviewed the deputy marshal again to see if he'd overlooked anything. No luck, same story. The nurse and Rachel went into a ladies' room on the first level of Woodland Hills Mall and didn't come out. Someone was waiting for them inside, or the nurse was involved."

Jack's heart pounded at Brand's last statement. "What about the nurse?"

"Just the usual 'everyone's a suspect at first.' We're still checking her out. So far, what they've got on her at St. Francis looks legit. Apparently the two of them went out or were taken out a window into a service alley. No one saw them. No prints, either."

"Corley, I haven't told you everything."

Brand raised his eyebrows.

"Not only was I not to contact the authorities," Jack explained as the two men sat down, "I'm not supposed to pursue the exhumation order with the D.A. tomorrow. I've been wrestling with that. I figured there'd be no harm done if I didn't tell you about it until later, since nothing's set to happen before tomorrow."

"They took Rachel to keep you from having Reuben's body exhumed?" Brand shook his head. "Who'd believe that?"

"No one. Especially since Norman could probably prevent an exhumation all by himself, as the son."

Brand shrugged his shoulders. "Except that he's disappeared."

"No, they took Rachel for a lot better reason than that, Corley. They took her to neutralize *me*. We're getting too close to something, and they wanted me out of the picture. They haven't been able to kill me, so the next best thing is to control me."

Brand crossed his arms and nodded. "I think you're right. That something we're getting close to may be more than we ever imagined." He summarized Kinney's report, then added his own deduction.

Jack squinted. "You think they've come *here* to kill the president?"

"I think this is where they've based their actions so far, and it's where they're probably organizing everything to 'sever the head.' That could take place anywhere. We've notified the Secret Service."

"Why are you so sure it's the president, Corley? The word 'head' could mean a number of things."

"Not to Abu Kuttab."

The two men sat quietly for a moment. Jack wondered if he should tell his friend about Friday afternoon with Andrea. He decided against it. Finally he spoke. "OK, how do we play the exhumation matter?"

Brand rubbed his hands together.

"First thing tomorrow morning I'll see the district attorney and ask him to put out the word to his staff that the exhumation order will not be pursued, at your request. If someone's sniffing around, that should work. In the meantime, since a crime's been committed—Rachel's kidnapping—and the exhumation, according to the caller, appears to play a role in it, we'll go for an emergency, but sealed, court order to exhume immediately. I'll take care of that, too."

Beggs, Oklahoma
11:40 p.m.

Lester Graham stood wedged between the cold, bare concrete wall of the basement and the wooden furring strips on the back of the paneling. His breathing was rapid in the tight crawl space. He had just completed an arduous thirty-minute vertical climb of ten feet from the floor level of his cell. The wood strips on the paneling were thin, and he'd lost his footing a dozen times when narrow pieces snapped under his weight. Thank heavens, he thought, for the occasional metal rod that stuck out of the concrete. Otherwise he wouldn't have had a prayer of reaching the top.

Graham braced himself and pressed his cobweb-streaked face close to what used to be a window. Now that he was here, he wondered how he ever thought this small opening might be his salvation. Or even assumed he'd be able to get it open. First he traced a finger along the edge of an aperture no bigger than fourteen by twenty-four inches. He smiled. They'd only shut the window, broken off the handle, and painted the glass. There didn't seem to be any putty or other sealant between the window and the frame. With a little luck, he might indeed be able to pry it open.

Graham looked down. The only light came from the basement below, and by the time it had filtered up through the supports, there wasn't much left. He hoped again that no one would decide to check on him. They hadn't come in before at this hour of the night, but there was always a first time.

Suddenly Graham froze at the sounds of voices. He couldn't tell how many people there were or what they were saying. He craned his neck. Inside or out? The voices faded. He waited a few minutes, then decided to continue working.

He slipped his hand into his shirt pocket and took out the two large nails he'd found among the debris on the floor inside the crawl space. He pushed both into cracks at the top edges of the hinged window, one on either side, and forced them tightly into place with his palm. He tapped against them. They held. He took a deep breath, then grabbed the nails and began a slow rocking effort, up and down, followed by circular motions.

"Hope this isn't sealed from the outside."

Then it dawned on him that the whole area around the house's perimeter might be wired to an alarm system. He surveyed the window frame as carefully as he could in the bad light. No telltale signs of wiring that he could see. Not that that gave him a lot of comfort in an age of sophisticated electronic systems.

Graham went back to working the nails. After another minute, he thought he saw movement. Yes, there it was again. The right side was definitely yielding to his rhythmic cadence. He intensified the pressure on the left side of the window. Finally it, too, showed signs of separating. Then he heard voices again. They seemed to be coming from outside. He waited. Yes, he was sure of it. And whoever the people were, they sounded a lot closer. Maybe they were only a couple of feet away, just waiting for him to open the window.

Graham stopped his work and listened.

The voices continued. Whoever was talking didn't seem to be next to the house. And if they were really watching for his attempted escape, wouldn't they want to be quiet, to surprise him? The more he thought about it, the more he felt confident that no one was lying in wait. But he didn't continue his work.

Another minute passed. Then there was complete silence outside. At first Graham didn't know what to think. He didn't like the situation. Maybe they were right there, keeping quiet and waiting to catch him. Or, worse, maybe they were on their way to his basement cell. With that thought, he maneuvered across the wooden infrastructure and down, an awkward step at a time, toward the hinged panel. Couldn't be too careful now that I'm this close, he decided.

As his feet contacted the floor, he thought he heard sounds from the direction of the door. The possibility of being discovered between the walls nearly panicked him into a clumsy reentry into his basement cell. The blind way he descended, he could have fallen against the paneling, causing one or more sections—or the whole wall—to fall into the room. He stopped and told himself to cool it. The sounds didn't seem to be any closer.

He carefully pushed open the loosened panel section. As soon as he saw that there was no one else in the room, he stepped inside and secured the panel at the floor. He loped across his cell and put his ear to the door. There was a hum of mixed noises but no indication of anyone's being immediately outside. He decided to wait for as long as a half hour to see if someone was going to check on him. He moved toward his bed and sat down in slow motion.

Probably a good time, too, to think about his escape plans again.

Graham figured he knew his property better than anyone else. Unless they'd walked it thoroughly while he was in here, there was no way they could know all the nooks and crannies, especially at night. He reminded himself he was not planning to return home. At least not until things were under control. One of the jerks would probably seize him there in a minute, before he could call and report what he'd seen and heard. They'd probably cut his telephone lines anyway. If he could, he'd head southwest for the grove, then south, using the trees as a cover. Once he got across the property line and in view of his own house, he could decide whether or not he should bolt across his property toward the east or if he'd be better off running further south. There were neighbors in both directions, and he'd have to decide who was home and who would be most likely to give him a ride to the sheriff's office.

Graham checked his watch—11:56 p.m. He figured he'd might as well get back to work. There was no time to waste. He went to the door one more time and held his ear against the solid wood for nearly a minute before giving himself permission to feel secure. Or, he thought, as secure as any rat in a cage could feel.

He returned to the back wall and carefully pulled at the loose paneling. As before, he propped it open with the spare roll of toilet paper they'd issued him. The light that filtered up into the cavity seemed even weaker than last time, but he knew that once his eyes got used to the darkness again he'd be back in business.

Graham squeezed into the tight crawl space between the original concrete wall and the newer partition. He stepped carefully onto the edges of the furring strips and elevated himself a foot at a time toward his perch near the ceiling. This time the ascent went smoothly and quickly. Once back in position at the top, he looked around and wondered just how he was going to raise himself up and through the window, assuming he could get it open in the first place. There was about six inches of space between the top of the window and the ceiling, and the window hinges were on the bottom. He realized there was no way he'd be able to get out unless he could break off the window unit itself. Even so, how he was going to gain the leverage to maneuver himself up and out remained an open question.

The two nails were still in place. Graham grabbed them and rocked once more at the sealed window. With a single snap, it popped open. He tucked the nails into his pocket and pinched the fingertips of both hands into the separation between the lip of the window and the frame and squeezed. The window opened further. With one final motion, he pulled it wide open.

A solid piece of plywood on the outside blocked the way. "Well, if it ain't one thing . . . "

He took a deep breath and placed both hands against the wood. He anchored his legs to give himself leverage and pushed. The rectangle cracked away into the cold night and thudded against the hard ground. Graham grinned in satisfaction. That's when the blinding lights flashed on.

"What the hell?"

His field of vision became virtual daylight from banks of intense spotlights mounted under the eaves of the house. He jerked back and hit his head against the interior wall.

"Damn!"

He thought about retrieving the board until he heard the pounding of feet in the house upstairs and saw people running outdoors toward the helipad. There were five or six figures clad in black, and each one carried something under his arm. Graham leaned closer to the opening. The noise of a helicopter thumped in the distance. All of a sudden the craft roared over the house and started its descent to the lighted helipad. He pulled back and shut the window. His heart pounded. The piece of plywood was out there on the ground, in the open, but there was nothing he could do about it.

Curiosity impelled him to have another look at what was going on outside. This was better than a couple of county fairs and a goat roping, he deduced. He reached up and squeezed his fingers between the painted window and the frame once more and moved the window just enough so that a sliver of light came into the closed space. He adjusted his position so he could see out one of the corners of the window. As he stared, he saw that the helicopter was on the ground and that figures were hurrying to get aboard. He definitely counted six who got on. A minute or so later, two more people ran out and boarded. They both looked like women, a taller one pulling a shorter one by the arm. Then the slap-slap-slap sound of the helicopter increased, and its downdraft grew more powerful. Pieces of snow and dirt flew into Graham's face and stung his eyes. As he spit and blinked away the debris, the rotor blades sliced and pulled the helicopter upward from the landing pad and into the black sky.

After a moment the sounds faded, and the exterior lights were extinguished. Graham listened and waited. There was only the moan of the wind as it threaded its way around the house and its exposed downspouts. He took a deep breath.

Time to go.

Lester Graham had fully intended to be long gone by now. He was sure the helicopter's departure just after midnight would have meant that everyone's attention would be back inside the house again.

"Bunch of jerks," he grumbled at the bad timing of his so-called neighbors.

He'd been forced to change his plans again when he heard the unexpected rumble of trucks. Graham had already broken the hinges, freed the window, and been half out the window when the lights of approaching vehicles appeared on the road that went around to the back of the large metal building. He'd wiggled back down into his perch and pulled his head inside. He reinserted the painted window.

"Shoot, glad I didn't toss that away," he muttered when the seal was complete.

As he waited, the engine sounds increased as the trucks drew closer to the house. Seconds passed, yet the noises remained loud and steady, as if the vehicles had braked right outside. Then he heard doors opening and closing, and voices. Must be some sort of convoy that had paused, and its drivers were talking. More time passed, yet the trucks remained. Were they loading something? What in tarnation could those turkeys want anyway? Then he heard noises from upstairs.

"Hell's bells, they might be fixin' to load *me!*"

Graham looked around and wondered if he should remain in place or return to his bed. He concluded that if his captors were coming for him, they'd get him either way. On the other hand, maybe he'd be better off in bed. If they did pull a room check, they wouldn't have anything to be suspicious about. He could climb back up here again once the trucks were gone. He rubbed his hands together and gave himself a nod of approval. Momma Graham didn't raise no dummy.

It required five minutes for him to lower himself from the precarious scaffolding and get under the scratchy blanket on his bed.

3:36 a.m.

Graham had had to wait in the darkness of his basement cell for two and a half hours before all the sounds subsided.

"The whole friggin' night's about gone!" he growled when silence fell at last. And the trucks weren't the only strange noises he'd heard. There'd been more muffled voices, which seemed to filter in from all directions. Then there were ratcheting sounds—like machines—grinding and whining. Occasionally there were dull thuds that reverberated throughout his underground post. Graham couldn't identify any of them. Fortunately no one had come to check on him since supper last night. Did that mean he wasn't under as much observation as before? No siree, he decided, that would be flat-out wishful thinking. Indeed, he had a queer notion that he was quite high on someone's list of concerns, and that feeling told him he'd better get out of here pronto. And who could say? They might move him again, and all opportunity to escape would be lost.

Graham sat up in bed and thought about the challenge ahead. It was a crazy scheme, all right. But it just might work. He peeled back the blanket. There were probably a dozen marksmen waiting in the darkness outside, armed and ordered to shoot to kill. He shrugged. He didn't care anymore. It was still quiet both outside and upstairs. Downstairs, too. He placed his feet on the floor. He stood up in the blackness and considered the fact that ever since he'd been captured a week and a day ago, he'd been imprisoned in a world that wasn't at all what it'd seemed. This was the old Cummings place in structure, but it was definitely a different world in every other way. Haunted wasn't too strong a word. Graham moved toward the door of the basement room and kept his train of thought.

He'd never forget the creepy feelings he'd experienced during the forced walk down to that other place on Friday, to the subbasement where they'd kept him for a day. It was like a damn cave of ghosts, a netherworld beyond. He'd been kept blindfolded all the time he was there. But they hadn't plugged his ears, which had gotten him an education, a lot of which he still didn't comprehend. He did know from the echoes of his footfalls that the corridor downstairs was a lot wider than the one at this level. As a matter of fact, there hadn't been any reflected sounds at all in places, so, at times, there was no way to tell if he was still being led down a passageway or if he'd entered a large room.

Then there was that little cubicle where he'd been kept. They'd guided him to a corner and pushed him onto a narrow wooden bench. There was no padding, and the wood smelled of kerosene. Not strong, he remembered, but someone had probably stored a leaky can of the stuff on the bench not too long ago. From the echoes, he figured his new cell was small—maybe, at most, ten by ten. And it had seemed empty. One voice did talk about a pile of cardboard boxes inside the door. Another man removed it. And the door itself must have had an opening in it, because once the men left, Graham could hear people talking about him outside, yet they sounded very close, like they could watch him through a window. One time the voices were in English, and they said he was to be kept blindfolded. The other times they jabbered in a language he couldn't understand.

Down there, he'd gotten something to eat—sandwiches—twice a day. And both times, dried ham. No, he thought again, more like dried *bread* and ham. The ham at least had a little moisture in it. Plus they provided a paper cup of water with each meal. Whenever he banged on the door for a trip to the crapper, they led him to a smelly area with an exposed toilet. While he was doing his business, he heard more of that foreign talking, and there were definite sounds of vehicular movement. Whines of electric motors rose and fell and accompanied the voices. It was as if people were riding around on some sort of underground transportation.

There was also the push of air. It seemed like a long column of it was moving from far beneath the surface, first in one direction, then the flow went the other way. Graham compared the sensation to the one he'd had in the caves in Missouri he visited as a boy. Marvel and Onondaga and Mera-mec Caverns, off old Route 66. He remembered that even when it was a hundred degrees outside, there were places in those subterranean worlds where you'd stand and shiver in the refreshing rush of cool air that had been chilled and purified somewhere deep within the bowels of the earth. He was thoroughly confused. There were no caves like that within two hundred miles of here. At least not natural ones.

Graham stood next to the door and reached for the light switch. He planned to flip it up and down quickly, giving him just enough illumination to read the time from his wristwatch. Then he thought better of the idea. The switch could also activate a signal somewhere else. He made his way to the loose panel at the back.

"This zoo's about to lose its caged monkey," he muttered as he slipped inside the crawl space.

The climb to the window wasn't as slow as Graham worried it might be. Because of the hour, he knew any sounds would carry far, and he'd planned on a careful ascent just to be safe. Even so, it only took ten minutes. The fact that he didn't slip on the way up seemed to be a good omen. Once in position at ceiling level, he anchored himself with his feet and knees and reached again for the window. He gripped the edges. The rectangular covering cracked opened an inch, then two, permitting the wind to swirl inside the crawl space. It was a biting cold, with the power to stick to his face and rip off his skin. He remembered he'd be braving the frigid night without his hat, coat, or gloves. The men had taken them away when they'd locked him up that first night. Damn! Why hadn't he brought the blanket from his bed? Nah, not worth going back down this friggin' wall. He grabbed the edges of the window and pulled it open just enough to get a look outside. He peered over the top of the covering. There was nothing immediately next to the house. He looked beyond and saw that the trucks were gone. He waited a few seconds to see if anyone would come along. No one did. The bitterness of the outside temperature burned his eyes and made them water. He'd really have to keep moving if he didn't want to freeze. He blinked away the wetness and removed the window altogether.

Graham contemplated the situation and shook his head. The fourteen-by-twenty-four-inch opening at eye level didn't look big enough to accommodate his post-middle-age girth, even after the nonmeals he'd had, and he wondered if he could really squeeze through. All he needed now was to get stuck trying to escape. They'd probably just shoot him at their leisure. Or maybe let him freeze to death, wedged half in and half out. Well, only one way to find out.

He held the window in both hands and lowered it to the ground outside. Then he thrust his head through the narrow opening. Even though his eyes were not yet acclimated to the darkness—or the cold—he could see that the frozen earth was only six inches below, and the discarded plywood seal lay a foot to one side, its white-painted face up. Thank God, he thought, the wood was camouflaged in the snow. Straight ahead, two hundred feet or so, was the helicopter pad. Across his field of vision from left to right was the paved road that came in from the highway and wound around the back of the house on its way to the metal building. He looked to the right. The big building was dark and silent. He cocked his head and listened. The night was still, except for a razor-sharp wind that came and went irregularly. He rubbed his bare hands together and blew warm air between them.

"Let's go, old man."

Graham reached up and grabbed the two sides of the window frame, considering again where the rest of his body should be positioned for the maneuver. He shifted and fashioned himself into a ready position by pressing his left foot against one of the metal studs on the concrete wall. The sole of his right foot rested on a horizontal furring strip on the back of the paneling. He'd tested it before, and it seemed strong enough. With any luck, he figured, he'd be able to hoist his bulk upward and through the opening in one motion. He started. At first he rose smoothly. All of a sudden, the thin furring strip gave way, and his right foot shot down out of control and banged loudly against the paneling. The wood wall covering creaked, but it didn't separate from the floor . . . or the ceiling. Fortunately he hadn't transferred all the weight from his other foot. Hanging onto the sill, he carefully felt with his right foot for another strip and started again. This time he decided he'd better lock his elbows against the sides of the window, just in case. Slowly, in one continuous motion, he lifted himself up and maneuvered the top half of his body through the window. Once he'd proceeded as far as his waist, he hesitated. Footsteps? More seconds passed, and he concluded that no one was coming. Like a snake shedding its skin, Graham wriggled free of the window and lay quietly on the hard ground.

God, was it cold! The bitterness of the black vault of the night penetrated his flannel shirt and work trousers like a billion steel needles and nearly paralyzed him before he could get started. His ears rang in the oppressive silence, and he reached up to touch them. They were beginning to hurt. He knew it wouldn't be long before they had no more feeling than plastic appendages. He'd been frostbitten before, on his hands and the tip of his nose. He'd never forget that episode. After everything hurt and began to swell, the skin hardened, and he couldn't feel anything anymore. Nope, didn't want to repeat that. Time was now his enemy.

There were no suspicious noises. Graham thought about suppressing his breathing sounds by keeping his face lowered toward his chest. He even considered exhaling into the front of his shirt, but he decided he'd better keep the shirt buttoned to maintain as much body heat as possible. No alarm had sounded. He raised himself on his elbows. The cold now penetrated his heavy boots. He knew from experience he'd have to be quick in finding shelter, for this temperature would eventually kill him. He rose to his feet and scrambled for the scrub oak grove seven hundred feet to the southwest, just inside the property line. He padded past the heliport and across the paved road and stumbled into the welcoming reach of the branches of the small woods. He ducked and weaved and broke off a few finger-size pieces of wood as he went. Another dozen yards and he encountered and scaled the fence bordering his land at its northern edge. He tumbled to the ground on his own property.

"By golly, I did it," he congratulated himself between breaths. "Now if I can only make it south a half mile or so, I'll be far enough away to consider my options. In spite of the cold, I won't go home right now. That's the first place they'll look. Nope, better keep on movin'. Maybe stop at one of my neighbors when the cold gets to be too much."

Graham pressed his bare hands over his ears and rose to continue his trek. As he did so, he looked over his shoulder. All of a sudden, a fifty-foot perimeter around the house and the adjacent metal building was illuminated as brightly as if it were the middle of a summer day. He couldn't imagine where all the high-intensity light was coming from. He'd never seen any bulbs on trees or poles, let alone suspected their presence. He squinted. The brilliance was blinding. Almost as soon as the lights blazed on, dogs started barking. Graham's jaw dropped. He'd never heard a peep from a dog while he was cooped up in the basement, but now he witnessed the ruckus of a pen full of the animals. Then came shouts. For a split second he wondered why all the commotion. He rolled his eyes when the absurdity of his question registered. "Oh, for cryin' out loud, what other reason could there be?" But why'd they turn everything on now? Maybe he'd tripped some sort of trigger, or maybe a motion detector had picked up his presence when he came over the fence. He dashed ahead through the wooded area and looked over his shoulder again as he entered a clearing. He tried to focus as he bobbed up and down. Where were the dogs now? How about men? Even with the help of the bright lights behind, he couldn't see anyone pursuing him. But he still heard the barking. He continued running through the grove of scraggly trees. The barking sounds seemed to fade, as if the dogs might be headed west or north. In any event they were going away from him. That's when he heard the muffled roar of engines. He looked back toward the large metal building and did a double take.

"I don't much like the looks of this. . . . " he huffed as he kept up his pace. There were two, then three Jeep-like vehicles tearing around the bend in the driveway. He had an urge to stop and watch as the vehicles drove for the highway. Their movement didn't make any sense to him at the moment, and he was curious about their plans.

"Oooh, shit!" All of a sudden it made a lot of sense, and he veered off toward the southwest and increased his speed. The Jeeps roared out of their driveway, then skidded noisily on the pavement of the county road and headed south. Graham was sure he knew exactly where they were going.

"Damn jerks'll come right in through my open gate."

He was right. The three vehicles bounded onto his property. The first Jeep roared to the north of his barn and headed toward the northwest. The second vehicle sped past the barn to the west and aimed directly toward him. The third followed the second but turned toward the southwest and porpoised across the rutted field. Graham figured he had nearly a hundred yards of trees between himself and the second vehicle, which was pointed in his direction. He retreated further into the wooded grove to the west of his house and hoped his exact location hadn't been spotted. He figured a minute and a half to the fence line of his western boundary. As he dashed through the trees, a limb ahead popped and sprayed into powdery debris. A second branch, another fifty feet further, exploded in its entirety. He dove for the ground as other limbs banged to the ground nearby.

"I don't believe this! It's like they're lookin' right at me!"

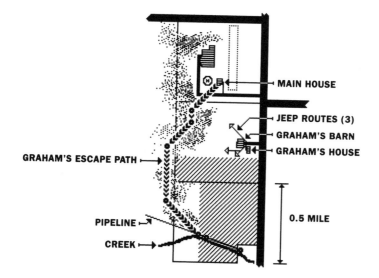

Another fusillade of bullets zinged overhead. Graham rose to his hands and knees. His heart raced as he made his frantic way to a denser gathering of trees. It was almost by feel that he encountered the barbed wire at the property line on the west side. He seized the metal fencing and propelled himself over the barrier. Onto safer land, he hoped. Without looking back, he ran another two hundred feet toward the southwest.

The third Jeep caught his attention. It was about a hundred yards farther south of his position, and it had stopped short of the property line. He could make out two figures who pointed at a grove of trees to their west. The next instant Graham heard a buzzing sound and saw through a clearing that some sort of weapon was mowing down the trees, literally clearing the area to ground level. He stared in awe. Whatever the weapon was, it was mounted at the middle of the open vehicle, and it made a whooshing sound. Like a silent Gatling gun. The firing was so intense and precise that an entire grove of scrub oak was reduced to sawdust and slivers in less than a minute. A man then directed the weapon at another gathering of trees. In spite of the obvious danger of remaining in place, Graham couldn't bring himself to move. This time the gunner trimmed the tops of the trees with a fluid back-and-forth motion. The grove looked as if it had received a '50s-style buzz haircut.

"Once more, folks," he exclaimed to himself as he took off again, "oooh, shit!"

This time a whole new navigational sense took over. If I'm ever gonna make it away from those SOBs tonight, he lectured himself, I'm going to have to get all the breaks. Maybe a prayer'll keep 'em one step behind me. The hand of Lady Luck herself wouldn't hurt, neither.

Graham bent and zigzagged around the trees and loped down a slope that carried him below the line of sight of the men in the Jeeps. He ran toward a nearby tree and, grabbing onto the heavy trunk with one arm, swung himself around behind it. He could hear the bullets tearing into trees again. But the men seemed to be aiming farther south. Not that it was any great news, he reflected, since that was the direction he was headed. He waited and listened. He could still hear the whooshing sounds coming from the gun mounted on the third Jeep. What worried him now was the fact that he had no idea where the other two Jeeps were. He knew where *he* was, though . . . a good half-mile west of his house. He couldn't see it, but he knew its exact direction and could walk to it blindfolded. He shook his head at the thought of the obstacles in the way tonight.

He rose and moved ahead in a modified crouch. A bit more to the west, three or four minutes maybe. Then due south to the creek bed. That'd probably be five hundred yards. As he slipped among the trees, he heard shouts from the third vehicle; then he noticed the crackling of a radio. Apparently the Jeep had reached the edge of the woods, and the men were in contact with the others. Did they know where he was? He got his answer when the pop-pop-pop of a weapon was echoed by the sounds of nearby trees being sliced into. Graham zigzagged south, then southwest, and ran up to his western fence line. He looked toward the north. There, at least a hundred yards away, was the stopped vehicle. Its lights were directed into the woods. He vaulted over onto his own property and fell to the ground. He raised his head at a new noise.

"The dogs!"

He hopped up and made his way as fast as he could through the trees. He knew his property intuitively.

"Gotta get to the creek."

Graham ran onward. Behind him, barking sounds rose and fell in the clear night air. He was sure the animals were closing in. They knew what they were looking for . . . the smell on the clothing taken from him. Fifty more yards to go, he calculated. He looked down and noticed that when he moved his fingers he didn't feel anything. He knew he was literally freezing. "God help me, I'll never bellyache about a hot summer day ever again," he promised between breaths. In the summer, there'd at least be some water in the creek, and he might be able to wade in it a while and throw off the dogs. But, he thought, if his luck held, he just might be able to do as well tonight.

Where exactly did the pipeline come in? He knew its location on his land, where it paralleled the small creek in a northwest-to-southeast direction. But it intercepted the creek near the edge of his plowed land. That pathway of tubular steel just might save his life, he considered as he stumbled ahead. Most of it had been completed before being abandoned by the oil company years ago. They'd given up their easement and had deeded it over to him. He'd thought about having the pipeline removed and sold for scrap, but there wasn't much of a market for it at the time. And it really didn't interfere with his farming, so he'd just left it. It'd never been used, so he wouldn't have any poisonous gases to worry about. Just darkness. And the cold. Graham peered ahead. Can't be much farther, he puffed. The sound of the dogs hadn't changed. They were still behind him, probably a thousand yards. At most, two.

Ah, there it was. The gentle slope of the ground pointed the way. He was now less than a hundred feet from the narrow cut in the land. The creek was only three or four yards wide and up to ten feet deep at spots. He reached the edge and stopped. The sound of the dogs grew louder. All right, he concluded, there was no time like the present. He hopped down into the dry creek bed and rubbed his body around generously. He scuffed at the hard soil and tried to spit, but his mouth wouldn't cooperate. Then he climbed the opposite side, throwing his arms up and down and spreading his scent. Once he was out of the creek, he resumed his running.

"Hope that was the right place," he huffed as he stumbled ahead.

He ran headlong for another half minute. Then he stopped and retraced his steps as fast as he could. At the southern edge of the creek where he had climbed out, he moved aside in one wide step and jumped forward into the darkness. In a jarring tumble, he bounced against the opposite side and slipped to the sandy floor. In the distance, the sounds of the dogs grew louder. He struggled to his feet and began to feel along the dark creek wall.

Where was it? It *had* to be here. Graham patted frantically.

Clang. Great! He'd located the pipeline. Now, where in the hell was that pig valve? He continued foot by foot, patting his hands against the pipeline. Then he found it. Without wasting a second, he felt around the cap of the flange and found the release handle. He gripped it and pulled the cap open. There was a sound of hollowness from within the three-foot-diameter tunnel. He held the metal cap open with one hand and hoisted himself up and into the empty pipeline. His heavy boots banged as he pulled his feet inside, and the sound echoed up and down the length of the metal casing in a series of booming waves. The reverberations made him wonder if anyone outside could have missed hearing. But he couldn't worry about that. He pulled the cap closed from the inside.

It was the ultimate blackness, oppressive and complete. He could never have imagined the claustrophobic sensations that nearly overwhelmed him. "Stop it," he demanded of his mind. He knew he had to master his emotions immediately if he was to stand any chance at surviving. This was his only passage to safety, a quarter of a mile away where another outlet was located. One thousand three hundred and twenty feet of steel hardness against his palms and knees as he crawled for his life. He was thankful that the air seemed free of contaminants.

Level head, level head, he told himself. How about a count? A quarter of a mile . . . that's 1,320 feet. Level head . . . *think!* Instead of crawling a foot at a time, how about paces of eighteen inches? Yes, good idea. That means it won't require as many paces, right? Two-thirds as many, if his farm math was on target. So two-thirds of 1,320 would be, uh, eight hundred . . . and eighty? Wouldn't it be? At a pace a second, that'd mean he'd cover the distance in fifteen minutes. No, no, he couldn't maintain that rate. A pace every two seconds was more likely. Even at that, the trip would be an exhausting thirty minutes. No choice. All of a sudden he realized that he had already started crawling, propelled by fear. Must have already made ten paces, he guessed. Can't forget to keep count. Think! Eleven, twelve. Graham was aware of what he'd survived to make it this far. No way I'm going to give up now. Thirteen. Thirteen? No, he'd gone fourteen, maybe fifteen paces.

"All right, quit thinkin', old man," he changed the orders. "Just count."

He stopped to take stock. No more idle thinking or talking, he ordered himself. As he was about to begin crawling again, he became aware of something that he thought was stuck to the bottom of his right palm. It made a smacking sound as he lifted his hand from the steel to exercise his fingers. He sat back on his haunches and felt for the object with his left hand. Both hands were so cold that nothing registered—something was there, but he couldn't feel a thing. One possibility suggested itself. When the pipeline was welded together, length by length, a residue of metal slivers stuck inward at all the seams. Maybe he'd picked up a collection of them. "Yeah, must be it." He crawled onward as fast as he could.

"Damn, *now* what's the number?" He'd gone for unknown minutes, and paces, because of being distracted by the problem with his right palm. "A hundred? At least," he figured. He hoped. He continued counting.

"Now what?" He stopped at 305 and sat back. There had been a slapping sound from his knees as he proceeded. With his numb hands he felt both. He patted, then hit at the joints, but there was no feeling. Probably more metal, being picked up by his pants. He decided to go on, one unbalanced crawling movement after another.

"Four hundred?"

He stopped again. He had no idea what the count was anymore. He even began to doubt that he had been moving at all. He reached for the entry flange. Maybe it was still there, and all of this was a hallucination. He banged at the wall of the pipeline. No flange. He started crying. Better resume the count at 410. He'd probably gone further, but that number would be safe. He'd rather reach 880 early and have to feel for the outlet at the other end than go past it. He smiled at his sense of control.

His heart almost stopped at the next thought. When the oil company built the pipeline, they'd planned for it to be a main gathering line for crude oil that would be pumped to a refinery they were planning to build near Okmulgee, just to the south. On his property, they'd fitted the pipeline with two outlets for hookups by smaller conduits, the first where he'd gotten in and the second one ahead of him, where he intended to get out. However, when they abandoned the pipeline, the company left intact a ninety-degree bend to a steel plug fifty feet straight down. That was only twelve or so feet beyond the outlet he was heading for. Graham shuddered. If he somehow missed the exit flange and crawled beyond, he would fall headfirst to a certain death five stories below the surface. And the only way he'd know he was in danger would be when he actually fell into the abyss. There'd be no warning whatsoever.

He blew out a chestful of air. He was getting nauseated now, a product, he was sure, of the disorientation of his situation. Not to mention the horror of its possibilities.

"Five hundred? A thousand?" How the hell many feet was he now? No, he corrected himself, it was inches he was supposed to count. Inches? No, paces. He started to laugh, and he fell over and hit his head on the hard metal. For a moment, everything started spinning, and he wanted to vomit. Oh, dear God, he confessed, what difference does anything make anymore?

Suddenly he popped back to his hands and knees and started moving again. He felt totally in control. He kept going for another ten minutes before he slowed. The fears he had banished swept over him again. The pipeline extended a half mile across his property. He could be anywhere from a thousand feet from the exit flange to right next to it. He raised his hand to the side wall to feel for the cap as he went ahead. He'd hit at the wall a half dozen times before he realized he felt nothing. Of course he couldn't feel anything, he announced to himself imperiously, because, damn it, he'd become a snowman. And snowmen didn't have nerves. He frowned at the statement. Was that a logical thing to say? He continued forward, hitting to his side as he went. The only way he knew he was contacting the metal was the reedy sound, like bamboo, that reverberated inside the pipeline.

"Am I hitting it that hard? What kind of a noise is that? That's my palm, isn't it? It shouldn't sound hard against metal."

Left knee, right knee . . . left, right, left. The curved bottom of the pipeline kept him centered, even though he was moving in a slight zigzag. On he went, for what seemed like ten minutes more. Or was it fifteen? Still he found nothing. The air was dead. Soon, his brain calculated, he would be, too. Now, *that* was logical. He wanted to stop and think about it. But he didn't.

Squish, scrape, squish, scrape. What kind of sounds were those? Is that what I'm supposed to be hearing? he wondered. I know, there's water in here now. He started singing, and he wanted to stop crawling. But he forced himself ahead. Agonizing foot after foot. Was there an end to this? Why did he have to stay? Hadn't he seen this movie before?

That's when he heard the barking sounds.

"Oh . . . dogs. I love dogs. Here, doggy doggy."

He proceeded a few more feet before reality shook him out of his delirium. He began a frantic pace. "Oh, my God, they've found the upstream flange, and they've put them dogs into the pipeline!" He bent forward and increased his speed. His right hand slapped at the solid steel wall. "I know I'm almost there. I know I am. Please, God, where is it?" The dogs were now running at full tilt, enticed by the flesh-and-blood trail. They were seconds behind him.

Graham found the indentation almost immediately. Without pausing, he lunged against the seal, and it broke away, spilling him outwards and down four feet of night to the hard creek bed. He impacted on his left shoulder. The pain surprised him. It was so novel, he was glad to experience it. As he lay on the ground, gasping for breath, the sounds of the dogs grew to a level that he knew they'd fly out the opening and be on him in an instant. He dragged himself to his feet and staggered back to the pipeline. He patted his clothes and found his soiled handkerchief. He reached inside the pipeline and tossed the wrinkled cloth in the direction he'd been headed. Then he slammed the cap over the opening and fell backwards to the ground. The barking sounds roared past the flange. All of a sudden, yelps and fading moans confirmed that the dogs hadn't been able to stop before they encountered the deep drop-off. Graham wanted to stay where he was, to sleep.

4:58 a.m.

The blackness of the early hour was like a warm dawn to Graham. Had he slept? Was he sleeping now? All of a sudden, someone's hands scooped under his arms and lifted him.

"What the . . . ?" Graham bobbed drunkenly as he was brought to his feet. He twisted back to try to take a swing.

"Whoa, buddy!" a voice interposed. "Dutch Dennison, Highway Patrol."

Graham stared in disbelief. "Well, thank God and the governor of the great state of Oklahoma." He weaved to one side. "Let's get the hell out of here. Them guys is right behind me."

The trooper reached around and supported him.

"I've got my pickup nearby."

The two men shuffled forward. They rounded a small bend in the rutted, irregular creek bed and reached a staggered edge of rocks along the south side. Dennison helped Graham up the stairstep incline and out of the creek. Suddenly bullets zinged past their hips and impacted in the hard dirt beyond. Dennison pushed Graham to the ground. "Stay down!" he ordered and withdrew his revolver. An additional burst whistled overhead.

A massive explosion erupted to the north. Both men turned to see a huge fireball boil reds and yellows, cauliflower-like, into the night sky.

"That's *my* place," Graham shouted.

Dennison saw five or six figures a hundred yards away, running toward them. The trooper jerked the farmer in the direction of his pickup.

"We've got to get out of here!"

The farmer stumbled on, but he kept looking around at the fire to the north. A second explosion erupted, sending upward another ball of red and yellow. By this time Dennison had established a brisk run, and the lawman's grip on Graham's shoulder ensured that the two stayed in tandem.

The men reached the pickup. Dennison eased his charge inside. All the pain Graham had been spared now shot up his legs and arms and knifed into his skull. He started to moan. Dennison turned the key. The old

Chevy roared to life. The trooper was glad he'd parked it headed south. In his rearview mirror he saw the fading light of the fires. He jammed his foot against the accelerator and fumbled for the handset of his cellular telephone.

J. Edgar Hoover Building, Washington, D. C.
Monday, January 11, 8:50 a.m.

The dispatch on his desk was the confirmation of the telephone call Jerry Reynolds had taken an hour earlier in the Strategic Information Operations Center.

"Damn!"

Reynolds stood over his desk.

"Twenty-one and a half million flushed out of nine foreign banks the moment they opened this morning." He looked through the doorway and motioned at his secretary. "Carol, get Brand on the line, please. And quickly." The FBI's second in command pulled out the chair and eased himself into it. He picked up the document. "That minister disappears on Saturday, and his money's pulled first thing Monday. Something's definitely coming to a head."

Tulsa
10:00 a.m.

"District Attorney Clayton's office."

The receptionist held her finger over an array of buttons on the console and prepared to direct the call.

"Good morning, this is Special Agent Terry Neville, FBI Tulsa office. Has Mr. Jack Stroud arrived yet for his appointment with the D.A.? He said Friday he planned to see us afterwards. I need to relay a message to him, if that's all right."

The woman hesitated as she looked for the prepared note. She read the typewritten lines.

"I believe that meeting's been canceled, sir. At Mr. Stroud's request." She raised her eyebrows. "Would you like to speak with Mr. Clayton?"

"Nah," the caller responded. "But thanks." He hung up.

The receptionist turned to her right. "It was one of your local people, Mr. Brand. A 'Terry Neville.' "

Corley Brand shook his head. "We don't have anyone in Tulsa by that name. If he calls back, let me know."

Phoenix
10:00 a.m.

The crowds had filtered through the twenty entrances of the Convention Center ever since the doors were swung open at eight. The rumors of the problem at Albuquerque had reached the upper echelon of the local followers of the Gentry Ministries, but even they couldn't believe that Norman wouldn't appear, to exhort and inspire. So they, too, pulled on their best clothes, made their way to the auditorium, and took their places alongside those who had held tickets for months and wouldn't have missed the event for anything.

Thirty-one thousand excited devotees had already taken their places when the magic hour struck. Another 3,000 moved toward their seats as the orchestra began its introductory number. Maybe he'd show and everything would be all right, a few of the local ministers concluded as the performance got under way. Most of those in the audience gripped their Bibles and tapped their feet to the inspirational medley. A few bobbed their heads and read Norman's message at the front of the program.

"Oh, let me tell you, my dear friends," the open letter began, as an introduction to the subject matter of his scheduled address, "this is a story of one of the most sickening sins against God. It's the story of a precious little child who was sexually ravaged by her demented stepfather. It happens all the time in this sinful land of ours, a nation of degradation and perdition. Without question, this terrible sin always appears and spreads just before great empires fall. As we look around our country today and witness the wrath of God against our sinfulness, we know that the end of America could well be very close. And it will come through more of these horrible actions that we have witnessed over the recent past. I specifically refer to the awful gassing of the little schoolchildren right here in Phoenix just a week ago. I will show you, in pictures, why the hideous sins of incest and pedophilia are reasons this great land of ours is being punished by Almighty God."

As the orchestra concluded its selection, security men throughout the hall seemed particularly animated. Those who stood in the back of the auditorium with their FM transmitters answered others hidden along the parapets above. The perimeter lights flashed on and off as a signal that the performance was about to begin, and tardy attendees nodded at new neighbors, settled into the tiered seating, and watched as a large man walked to the center of the stage. It wasn't Norman, they whispered. Unease affected many as the strange man took the microphone and began to speak.

J. Edgar Hoover Building, Washington
11:41 a.m.

The FBI courier waited in the corridor and handed the envelope directly to Jerry Reynolds as he entered his reception area. The deputy director crossed the carpeted expanse and drew out the communication. He started reading as he closed the door to his office and stepped to his desk.

"God *damn.*"

He sat down and stared at the data. "A minimum of forty F-1's missing. And no idea where they are." He took a deep breath and shook his head. "God *damn.*"

"Carol," he called into his intercom, "would you get Brand on the phone again?"

Corley Brand was at the FBI office in Tulsa. As soon as the connection was made, Brand began the conversation. "Jerry, get this. . . . After you called earlier, I checked . . . "

Reynolds cut him off. "INS has lost those forty students who disappeared after Thanksgiving. Count 'em, Corley, four zero! Their names check out against the list you got during the search, and every one of them came in under F-1 student visas and disappeared just like the six from Frankfurt on the thirtieth. Not a clue."

"And Immigration said they'd cleared up all the search lapses during and after the Iraqi war when they had to go looking for more than 3,000 they'd lost touch with," Brand reminded him.

"Same crap," Reynolds barked. "Anyway, like the letter said, the TBC students were enrolled in political science courses. I think you'd better have a talk with the poli-sci folks out there. Fast."

"Wilco, Jerry. Now, are you sitting down?"

"Shoot."

"OK, I spoke with the banks in Paris and Frankfurt. I've dealt with their VPs before, and they gave me the name of their counterpart at Barclays in London, whom I called. All three were willing to talk to me without attribution. For anything official, however, we'll have to get court orders. Anyway, these particular banks were notified of the withdrawals last Saturday morning between six and seven, local time. They all have weekend procedures for their bigger customers, and the Gentry ministry certainly qualified."

Reynolds couldn't hold his curiosity. "Who notified them?"

"Don't know," Brand answered, "but whoever it was has some mighty interesting friends."

"Make your point."

"The banks were instructed to wire transfer the funds to the same numbered account at Credit Suisse in Zurich. From all three banks to that one Swiss account. Immediately."

"Well, let's start putting together the petition for disclosure under their secrecy laws. We ought to know whose account it is by noon tomorrow."

"No need to bother, Jerry. I've already found out. According to my Swiss bank cohort, the account's in the name of an outfit called . . . my German's rusty, so I'm probably going to mispronounce this . . . 'der entscheidende Religionskrieg.' "

"What's that, another religious group?"

"I *wish*. No, it translates to 'the final jihad.' "

Reynolds winced. He didn't need to be reminded of the message intercepted at Wiesbaden two weeks earlier by the German foreign intelligence service.

"That's bad enough, Jerry," Brand went on, "but there's more, and I suggest you hold onto your chair. Before the Berlin Wall came down, that particular name was used by a branch of the East German Stasi when they set up a conduit for financial support to terrorists in Iran, Iraq, and Syria, but the BND isn't sure it was ever used for that purpose. After German reunification, everyone considered the name to be nothing more than a historical curiosity, another odd tidbit from the files of the East German secret police for some scholar. Now, however, 'der entscheidende Religionskrieg' appears to be the financial conduit for a very active and well-funded something, and the BND says that something could be a terrorist training base in Lebanon, run by Jamil Nasir."

"Nasir? Oh, fucking great! And who's got the deep pockets?"

"None other than our old hard-line friends who used to office near the Moscow Ring Road, the Komitet Gosudarstvennoy Bezopasnosti."

"Shit!" Reynolds exclaimed. "Well, we know that those bastards are heavily involved in terrorist activities, but it would be really bad news if the new KGB, or one of its offshoots, is financing a Jamil Nasir operation in Lebanon. Now, with known terrorists emerging from Lebanon, possibly from Nasir's base, and going to Tulsa, we could have a completed circuit— one made in hell."

"Couldn't have said it better myself," Brand replied. "We'd better get a handle on this money trail ASAP. The reconstituted KGB probably has most, if not all, of the billions that disappeared from Soviet bank accounts in Switzerland during 1990. With that kind of money, they could buy more trouble than we could ever imagine."

Tulsa Bible College
2:00 p.m.

Perhaps the political science people could offer some insight about the missing students. Corley Brand certainly hoped so.

When Jack received the message from the so-called note writer about the forty foreign students in the United States who hadn't returned to TBC after Thanksgiving, there'd been no cooperation whatsoever from the school in cross-checking names. The registrar told the FBI curtly that all forty were still attending school. A subsequent request for an interview with the head of the department was turned down without explanation. But that was last Wednesday. They'd gotten the list on Friday when they searched the school records under a court order. A chance call today resulted in an invitation to come over right away.

Before he left the FBI office, Brand received another telephone call from Jerry Reynolds with some special news involving Jack, then a curious message from Don Evans, who was at St. Francis Hospital waiting to interview an injured man, and, finally, a call from Jack himself.

Brand reached inside his coat and took out his notes. What was this man's title again? He turned a page. "Professor of Political Philosophy." Interesting name, too.

"Mr. Brand, I thought you'd never come."

A short man in his late fifties emerged from an office and extended his hand toward the agent. The man's English was strongly accented, his expression grim. Brand immediately recognized him from his brief appearance at the Denny's restaurant on Friday. This was the man they were looking for.

"I'm Aleksandr Voronov," the Russian introduced himself. "Please come in."

"You're Jack Stroud's note writer."

"Yes, and there's so little time."

3:07 p.m.

The Jones Brothers Chimney Sweeps truck pulled into Jack's driveway and jerked to a stop. Brand set the emergency brake and got out. As he walked for the door, he cupped his exposed hands to his mouth and tried to warm them with his breath. Because of the national maelstrom, he'd almost forgotten which month it was.

"Hello, Flora," he greeted Jack's housekeeper. He rubbed his hands together. "Would you tell Mr. Stroud I'm here?"

"He's on the phone, sir," she announced and indicated the way. "But please," she motioned, "he's expecting you. May I take your coat?"

"No, thanks." Brand moved past her. "I have a present for him in my pocket."

So he's using his home phone openly now, Brand observed as he turned the corner into Jack's study. Two calls to us that I know of. What the heck is he doing? Who knows who else he's telephoned, and what he's said. So much for our special procedures for lines suspected of being compromised.

Jack hung up and saw his visitor. "That was my office. I'm going to take some more time off, officially as a vacation, so I can do whatever is necessary to find Rachel." He pointed toward a chair. "Have a seat. I've got to tell you my decision."

Brand laid his coat over the back of the chair. "Why don't you start with your disregard for our telephone procedures?"

Jack sat opposite his old friend. He waved an open hand. "Just hear me out."

Brand shrugged conditional acquiescence. Jack moved forward in his chair.

"Corley, no more pay phones, no more marshals, no more hiding. Whoever has Rachel knows all about the FBI's involvement, and they're not about to kill *me* while they have her. As I've said before, they took her so they could exercise control over me. They'd lose that if they harm her. They got me to call off the exhumation request, and they may have more demands, which they can pass along to me—with or without your armed guards. By taking Rachel they've already shown they can still do a lot, regardless of the protection you might set up."

Brand tried to interrupt. Jack waved him off.

"No, let me finish. Rachel's been pulled into the middle of everything that's going on around here. If I'm to get her back, I'm going to have to help you. And vice versa. So you might as well get used to having me around. Not just professionally . . . I'm personally involved." He paused. "This is my daughter we're talking about. My decision is final."

Jack sat back and crossed his arms. Brand waited a few seconds.

"Is that the end of your speech?"

Jack shrugged. "I guess so."

"OK," Brand took over, "now it's my turn. First of all, I accept your decision. No argument."

"That was easy." Jack smiled.

"Second, I met with your note writer this afternoon."

"You found him?" Jack sat up in his chair. "Where, Corley? Who is he?"

"At TBC. He's a professor of political philosophy. You've met the guy, even had dinner with him."

"I did?" Jack looked blank.

"Aleksandr Voronov."

Jack snapped his fingers. "The Russian! He's the guy Reuben got out of prison over there. We *did* have dinner, a formal one with all the TBC trustees, just after he arrived. But no wonder I didn't recognize him ... he's shaved off his beard." Jack leaned closer to Brand. "What's his story? Why the notes? Why to me?"

"Voronov and your father-in-law spent a lot of time together from the moment he moved to Tulsa. Within a year, Gentry apparently trusted Voronov completely, and your father-in-law confided in him about the suspicious, behind-the-scenes activities at the ministry. We'll have to interview him at length to get all the details, but there were three main points he wanted to pass on to us. First, Gentry told him he'd discovered mysterious foreign bank accounts in the ministry's name. Second, he found out about a group of outsiders who were carrying out certain operational duties on behalf of the ministry, under orders from someone within the ministry. Your father-in-law was to meet with Voronov the night before he died, to pass along details, but he never showed. And third, Gentry had learned there was some sort of training or staging facility south of town. A big-time something, supposedly in the vicinity of Okmulgee, but he never got a handle on it. That last item, according to Voronov, worried the hell out of your father-in-law, if you'll excuse the expression."

Jack shuddered. "Makes the autopsy even more important, doesn't it?" He shook his head. "Well, we know something about the first item, the bank accounts. But the second? Under orders from someone within the ministry, and Norman's missing?" He looked up.

"Anything on that last item?"

Brand told Jack about the possibility that a resuscitated KGB was funding a Jamil Nasir base in Lebanon that could be sending operatives to Tulsa. He also repeated the information about the ministry's funds being transferred to a KGB account. Jack shook his head slowly.

"Then there's the call from Evans," Brand added. "He's waiting for me at St. Francis with a man who just might have escaped from that place your father-in-law worried about."

Jack sat silently and considered the converging facts. He glanced at Rachel's picture before he spoke.

"What else do you have on the possible KGB-Nasir tie, and to something here?"

"You know all that I know, but I wouldn't be surprised at anything. Do you want to go with me to the hospital?"

"Damned right I do." Jack stood up. "I'm going to be your Siamese twin from now on."

"Then," Brand said as he went for his coat, "you're going to need this." He handed over a wrapped package. "Maybe you should call it a late Christmas present. Matter of fact," he added with a nod, "hope you'll let it make up for a lot of missed Christmases."

Jack opened the parcel and lifted the hinged lid of a polished wooden box. Inside, on a bed of red velvet, lay a brand new, blue-steel .45-caliber automatic. Two full eight-round magazines were fitted in the display case on either side of the gun.

"Corley, I . . . I don't . . . "

Brand grinned. "Then don't. They call it a GSP .45. It's built on the Springfield armory pistol, and it's the best of its kind. Wish the Bureau would issue that baby to us, instead of the 10-millimeter 'spray and pray' special we have to carry."

Jack picked up the gun and turned it over slowly. "Thank you. It's magnificent." He frowned. "But there's just one problem."

"Which is?"

"I can't haul this around, not if I expect to be in the trenches with you."

"Oh? Why not?"

Jack laughed. "Hell, Corley, I don't have a permit. And I certainly couldn't carry it concealed, especially across state lines, without having you arrest me."

Brand shook his head. "You don't need a permit. You've just been recalled to the Navy for the duration of the crisis. On the president's orders. Reynolds heard it directly from the CNO a couple hours ago." He saluted. "Captain Stroud, proud to serve with you again, sir."

Jack could only smile at his friend.

St. Francis Hospital, Tulsa
3:10 p.m.

"That guy's almost a textbook study in cryogenics, and he has every reason to be dead."

The lanky physician stood at the window and nodded toward an inert figure in the intensive care room beyond.

"Yet there he is, still breathing."

OHP Trooper Dutch Dennison and FBI Special Agent Don Evans watched while an ICU nurse checked an intravenous flow at Lester Graham's bedside.

"Severe to extreme hypothermia. He's had a very dangerous experience." The physician looked at Dennison. "Lucky you picked him up when you did. I figure another ten minutes—max—and he'd have lapsed into a coma. A few minutes more, and his body temperature would have been down to ninety or so, and he'd have died."

The physician crossed his arms and nodded toward his patient.

"The guy was frostbitten all over. We had to amputate two toes. He'll probably lose another one before he gets out of here. Gangrene in his ears and fingers, too, but we think we can save those. He must have kept his fingers moving, and he probably warmed them occasionally with his breath. His face was like cardboard from the effects of the cold. His palms, knees, and shins were scraped clean of flesh. He wore off lots of bone at the knees, and he must have left a long, bloody trail getting that much damage. Three hours in surgery for his knees alone."

The doctor looked at his watch.

"We're going to take him to his room in an hour or so. I'd say you'll be able to ask him a few questions by five o'clock. But no more than ten minutes with him today, OK?"

5:11 p.m.

Jack Stroud greeted Don Evans at the door. "Sounds like we have a good ol' boy VIP on our hands."

"Sure do, and he told the OHP trooper quite a story," Evans returned.

Corley Brand came around the corner, and the three men entered the room. They walked toward a nurse who was checking an oxygen cannula attached to the nose of the bandaged figure.

"How's your patient?" Brand inquired as he grasped the protective metal bars attached to the bed.

The woman turned. "He's been through a lot, but he's one tough customer."

The man in bed opened an eye and regarded his audience warily. Evans winked at him. The man's other eye popped open, and he scowled at the strangers.

"Well, folks," Brand announced with a sweep of his arm, "we finally found him. Meet 'Mister Gun.'"

The groggy farmer tried to sit up. "What in tarnation's going on here?" He sank back, and his voice dropped to a growl. "My name's Graham, sonny boy."

"Mr. *Smoking* Gun," Brand completed with a wide grin.

JUDGMENT DAY

And the beast was taken, and with him
the false prophet that wrought miracles
before him, with which he deceived them
that had received the mark of the beast,
and them that worshipped his image.
These both were cast alive into a lake of
fire burning with brimstone.

Revelation 19:20

Damascus, Syria
Tuesday, January 12, 12:01 a.m.

Hassan Kadry reclined in an overstuffed leather chair in a corner of his office, surrounded and comforted on two sides by ceiling-high shelves of his treasured books. This was the first time he'd been alone all day. Being the new prime minister added many new burdens to his load while the regional adjustments continued in the aftermath of the fall of the Soviet Union. Vast new opportunities for Syria, he thought, yet how numerous the disparate voices of advice from the secular and religious forces. Irreconcilable demands? He closed his eyes and tapped the soft padding of the armrests to the metronome-like cadence of the antique timepiece on the mantel. The boxy clock his parents had carried with them nearly fifty years earlier faithfully kept track and informed him of the passage of his life. He drew a deep breath, opened his eyes, and looked across the room. In the yellow aura from the table lamp next to him, he saw that the large brass hand had cleared its smaller brother on the ornate dial, indicating that a new day had indeed begun.

A new day. Yes, he reflected, and they just might be able to go back home, once all the political sessions had ended and the necessary accords and protocols had been signed and enforced. Perhaps soon, too, and for good.

Kadry shifted his center of gravity and reached for his pipe on the table. With generous pinches from the humidor, he filled the hand-carved bowl with a renewal of the dark, aromatic tobacco he favored at times like this. My "thinking" tobacco, he used to tell associates in Ottawa when he was ambassador to Canada. He tamped at the humid shavings and extracted a wooden match that jutted from a box in the middle of an ashtray.

Home and soon. It sounded so comforting . . . and so easy. He struck the match. If the miracle took place. No, he'd have to stop saying "if." It was "when." He puffed the pipe to life and waved out the match. But first, of course, he had to relay the second file.

Kadry leaned back. He wasn't an old man by any means, but he didn't want to wait any longer. As he watched the bluish-gray risers swirl upwards in the thermals from his pipe, he remembered. He couldn't forget, really, for his history had been his destiny. Such it was for millions of his fellow Palestinians also.

He'd been born at the Syrian port city of Latakia in 1949, just after his parents fled north along the Mediterranean coast following the establishment of the State of Israel. They had remained in their homeland for six months after the new country was declared independent in May 1948, but increasing tensions of their peoples against the new inhabitants made it imperative for them to join the other Palestinians who migrated from their native soil and took up posts around the world to wait for the inevitable call to return. His father and mother had stayed within sight of the coastline as they crossed Lebanon, entered Syria, and pushed farther north, following the line of the gentle Jabal an Nusayriyah mountain range, through the port city of Tartus and onward the seventy-five kilometers to their new home. The fertile land underfoot was a consolation of sorts for what they had left behind, and it was good to them for decades, but they knew they'd go back someday. His father had promised.

Kadry checked the enclosures in the brown envelope. All seven pages were there, plus the map. He rose, walked to his desk, and pressed a gumball-size red button on an ornamental silver box. His secretary appeared almost instantly. In silence, she reached for the envelope. There was no need for conversation between them, for it had been decided. As she left and closed the door, he remained standing at his desk. He turned and noted the time. Nearly half past twelve. He knew that within five minutes facsimiles of the documents would be on the Syrian ambassador's desk in Washington, where it was only rush hour yesterday. The meeting at the White House would probably occur by nine this morning, Washington time.

I've done all I can, he told himself. It's now up to the Americans. With this data on the special operation in the Bekaa Valley, the president will have to accept our sincerity.

FBI Office, Tulsa
1:22 a.m.

Jack Stroud sat with Corley Brand. They watched CNN's news recap on the television console in the corner of the conference room. Other agents padded in and out and peered at the screen, but most wouldn't be seated at the table until the meeting at two o'clock.

The litany of news stories had begun with a replay of the president's declaration of martial law the previous evening and had continued through the furious congressional reactions and near national hysteria, on to a summary of the events that had led to, as the chief executive had characterized it, "one of the gravest moments in our history." One after another, in assembly-line fashion, the political personages appeared and delivered their opinions. The president said he was acting to prevent anarchy in the face of a series of unprecedented attacks against America. Homer Jenkins, his bow tie askew, shook his fist and railed against an administration that, he said, hadn't done anything for two weeks, "then yanked the props from beneath every American with this blatant violation of the Constitution." Jenkins hinted twice, in answer to questions from reporters, that impeachment proceedings could well be the first order of business of the new Congress.

Brand punched off the sound. "Too bad we didn't find Lester Graham two weeks ago."

"Or a year ago," Jack offered. He watched his friend.

Brand pointed at the brewer in the corner. "More coffee?"

"No, thanks."

Dozens of times, years ago, Jack and Brand had discussed their cases, just the way they were doing now. Professionals first, friends second. Regardless of the complexity of the pursuit at hand, they always assured each other that they knew exactly where they were in relation to where they wanted to go. Jack remembered that he'd never had any doubts about finding the missing evidence, or interviewing that one critical witness, or discovering the final pieces of the puzzle in their past cases. But the resolution of each chase always presented surprises, and Jack felt certain that this one would be a world-class eye-opener.

The FBI man leaned forward and pulled his briefcase across the table. He lifted the top and removed a manila file folder.

"OK, why don't we go over the report together before everyone else gets here?"

Jack nodded. Brand closed the briefcase, stowed it under the table, and started reading.

"Early yesterday morning, Trooper Dutch Dennison of the Oklahoma Highway Patrol went back to the area he was investigating northwest of the town of Beggs, after he'd found the metal placard from a missing airplane. Sometime around four o'clock, Dennison, nearby in his personal pickup truck, saw three Jeeps emerge from the subject property. They exited their driveway, traveled south, and entered the adjacent property in apparent pursuit of something or someone."

The FBI's chief of counterterrorism hesitated. Jack knew it was time for Brand's editorial comment.

"Isn't it always like this? I mean, we have the most technically sophisticated investigative tools and techniques in the history of the world, yet we're still dependent as hell on lucky breaks. Oklahoma City? Another OHP trooper." He looked back at the paper. "Old man Graham would have been a dead duck if Dennison hadn't been tenacious, and we probably wouldn't have located the smoking gun, or what's left of it."

"Keep going," Jack interjected, pushing his chair away from the table. He shook his head. "Old Graham's a tough bird. I think he'll be okay. He's not the problem, but something about that Beggs story is not computing."

Brand continued. "Dennison told Don Evans what he'd learned from the farmer on the way to the hospital. Some of it sounded to the trooper like disconnected ramblings from a seriously injured man, but Graham told the exact same story later. It included an account of strange neighbors in a house with a subbasement, perhaps occupied by numerous people. There were inappropriate sounds for the area, such as the operation of heavy machinery or electrical equipment, and Graham noticed large cylinders being hauled by tractorlike trucks to a helicopter. Those tanks were apparently the same size as the ones spotted near the port a week ago Sunday."

Brand shook his head at the long list.

"These items aren't in chronological order, but I guess everything is written down the way Graham related the situation to Evans. Anyway, the farmer watched a small plane land and get cut up, and saw the pilot taken away. It's not known where the pilot is now. Graham heard a foreign language being spoken. No idea what it was. Then, just before he escaped, he saw six people dressed in black leave by helicopter. He was sure there were two females who boarded with them. One taller, one shorter."

Jack's heart stopped for a second. He could feel Brand's gaze. He knew both of them were thinking the same thing.

"Then," Brand went on, "Graham passed out in the trooper's pickup."

"Nothing from the FAA on that helicopter?"

Jack couldn't take his thoughts off the statement about the shorter woman who had apparently gotten on the helicopter. He hoped his voice had sounded dispassionate.

Brand shook his head. "Not as of midnight. We've taken a look at the tapes the local radar controllers at the Tulsa airport saved for us. Nothing. Their range is thirty nautical miles, and the Beggs property is right at twenty-nine. However, air-traffic control radar isn't effective at spotting objects close to the ground, at that distance. Also, the helicopter didn't need any kind of a flight plan for its operations. It just, well, vanished."

Jack looked at his associate. "Where would eight people go in a heli-copter at that time of night?"

"A local airport?"

Jack considered the possibility. "Maybe. But why not take a car?"

"Because the airport's too far away?"

Jack rubbed his hands over his face. Then he slammed his fist on the table. "Damn it, Corley!"

"Hey," Brand assured him, "we'll get another break." He put his hand on Jack's shoulder. "And we *will* find her. *That* I have no doubt about."

"Yeah...."

Brand returned to his report.

"OK, once Dennison got to the hospital and handed Graham over, the trooper called us. Last Sunday morning, he'd informed our office here of his discovery of the placard from the small plane. Unfortunately his report seemed more routine than revolutionary at the time, so one of our agents treated it as simply a stolen-aircraft matter and planned to look into it this week. With all of Dennison's new information, however, it became front-burner material." Brand ran his finger down the page. "Let's see.... Evans went out to St. Francis immediately and met with the trooper. He was able to interview Graham twice yesterday."

Jack held up his hand. "When did we receive the report concerning the explosions down there?"

Brand wrinkled his nose and looked over the sheet. "Hmm, I'm not sure we ... " He referred to the first page again.

"About the time we were at the hospital, wasn't it?" Jack suggested.

"Mmm, right."

"Twelve hours, then." Jack sat back. "That's a good ballpark figure."

"What do you mean?"

Jack shifted. "We're twelve hours behind the people who blew up that property. Not great news, but at least we have a fix."

"Hey, remember when you were in the hospital and I asked you to let me in on whatever you're thinking? Would you cut me in again?"

"I think it makes a lot of sense, Corley. Here's how I figure it." Jack faced his compatriot. "We're still getting historical information. In other words, it's old, and we're behind. Late ... out of touch ... whatever you want to call it. Our most recent encounter, yesterday, shows we're about twelve hours behind." He tapped his wristwatch. "So whatever they're planning to do, if they pull it off, we'd walk in half a day late, under most cir-cumstances. That'd be an absolute disaster." He stopped and thought about his daughter. Then he raised his head and continued.

"No, we've got to close the gap. Once we merge into real-time monitoring, or get close to it, we can finally start being effective."

Brand looked quizzical. "You never told me about *that* system of yours before."

"I use this method solely to measure my pace. If I start crossing someone's path progressively at ten, eight, six hours after that person's been somewhere, I know I'm doing the right things. On target, if you will. I know it's not an investigative technique, but it's a mental checklist." He cupped a fist in his other hand. "Maybe it serves mostly as a motivator when I think I'm at a dead end. When we used to work together in Washington, I felt I needed all the help I could get to keep up with you."

"Thanks for the compliment." Brand laughed. "But who do you think was grateful he had twenty-four-hour access to a high-tech lab so he could stay even with a certain counterterrorism genius from the NIS?"

Jack smiled.

"And just how do you see us closing that twelve-hour gap?" Brand seemed intrigued with Jack's mental checklist.

Jack placed his elbows on the table and rubbed his palms together. "Why don't you finish your report first. Maybe there's a clue salted in it somewhere."

Brand found his place. "Our people went out to the Beggs site late yesterday afternoon, with ATF agents, but everything was gone, blown up. The volunteer fire department down there reported that Graham's house apparently went first, then the house to the north, followed by the metal building. That's based on a couple of neighbors' comments."

As Brand read, Jack thought again about the farmer's statement that he'd seen two women running for the helicopter. "One shorter." He didn't realize he'd said the words out loud.

"What?" Brand looked up.

"Sorry." Jack shook his head. "Go ahead."

"OK, there was lots of ice all over everything when our people got there, from water used on the debris, but no sign of anything significant or out of place. Our agents and the ATF boys poked around and took samples until about nine last night. And, of course, you and I are going to be with them on-site this morning. Maybe we'll spot something in the daylight. That's my report. See anything?"

Jack stared at the opposite wall. Then he turned toward Brand. "Nope."

The FBI man reached over and placed his hand on Jack's shoulder again. He looked into his friend's eyes. "You and I will find her."

Don Evans pushed open the door. "Ready for us?"

Brand sat back and checked his watch. "Two o'clock already? Oh, it *is*. Yeah, let's get started." Evans nodded and went to get the other agents. Brand turned back to Jack. "We'll *find* her, my friend."

Jack sighed. "I know we will, Corley." He tried to quell the anxiety that rose in his chest. "We *have* to."

Beggs, Oklahoma
6:15 a.m.

Jack had been up all night. They all had. Their meeting at two had run until five-fifteen, primarily because Brand wanted everyone who was currently involved in the investigation, both FBI and ATF, to have the big picture. Jack was glad the others got to hear Brand's unique observations, because when the FBI visitor from Washington finished, everyone looked wide awake.

Jack read the *Tulsa World* on the way to the site. The newspaper reported simply that no one had been injured early Monday morning when two residences and a metal barn northwest of Beggs were destroyed by a series of large explosions. Volunteer firemen, who reached the scene after the devastation was called in by a neighbor, reported that all three structures were completely leveled and it appeared that none was occupied at the time of the blasts. The firemen extinguished a few small blazes along the periphery of the foundations. Speculation by local law enforcement authorities was that an underground natural gas transmission line had suffered a break due to the extremely cold weather. A spokesman for the Okmulgee County sheriff's department said that leaking gas from such a rupture could have migrated into the three facilities and been ignited by an open flame, such as that found in water heaters. The article gave only a two-line reference to the presence of agents from the Bureau of Alcohol, Tobacco, and Firearms.

Jack and Brand stepped out of the FBI car and encountered Carl Webb of the Tulsa ATF office. Brand looked at Webb and inclined his head toward Jack. "You know Jack Stroud, don't you?"

"Sure, I know who he is." Webb grinned as he shook Jack's hand. "We talked about you a lot when we searched the TBC campus." The big man frowned. "Too bad we didn't find much. I guess we're not doing any better out here, either. We're just a step behind, it seems."

Webb indicated the debris with a swing of his arm. "This wasn't any gas leak, gentlemen. We've got suspicious residue on everything from plasterboard to concrete." He faced the new arrivals. "We should know in a couple of hours from the samples we took last night, but if you want my two cents' worth, it's a good plastic, like Gellex-4. Same stuff, all three places. And as for being accidental? Virtually simultaneous explosions . . . doing that much damage?" He shook his head. "No way. These were definitely planned detonations."

Jack pulled on his gloves as they started walking toward the rubble that had once been the old Cummings house.

"Other than the use of explosives, anything else look suspicious?"

"No, sir."

Webb pointed to where the metal building had stood. "We poked into a lot of debris over there. All typical construction materials. We're going over this house now. There's a basement, which appears to have been partitioned off. Hard to tell much of anything, though, after the blast. Some of the debris was as far away as a quarter of a mile. However, nothing strange in what we've found, except for the probability of Gellex. Just the same sort of stuff you'd expect from a house explosion."

The three men walked toward what was left of the dwelling. Jack walked to the edge of a crater. The remains of the house itself were pieces of wood, shredded and strewn away from a ground zero that was now only a hole in the earth. He noticed that even the cement walls of the rectangular basement had buckled. In one corner was the shattered porcelain of a toilet.

"Did you go down and inspect the basement?" he asked the ATF agent.

"Yes, sir. We checked the walls, what's left of the floor, pipes, everything. What you see is what you get . . . a destroyed house. Nothing more."

Jack pointed. "How about the other two places?"

"Same, except that they didn't have basements."

"What about further out?" Jack looked at the man. "Say, a radius of fifty yards?"

The ATF agent shook his head. "We've crisscrossed all three sites about that far away, looking for more samples of explosives. Found those, but nothing else."

Jack indicated the debris-littered cellar. "I'm going down to check it out for myself."

8:50 a.m.

"Corley, it's just not possible."

Jack removed his gloves and tossed them onto the trunk of the car. He accepted a cup of coffee from Brand.

"That there was a big operation here, like Graham said?" Brand questioned.

"No, that they removed a full-scale flight simulator."

Brand frowned. "You believe the guy really saw one?"

"Look," Jack stressed, "what he described was a simulator of some kind, most probably aircraft. A large, boxlike object, standing on stilts, with wires and hoses coming out of it and going into a wall. I ought to know what one looks like. It *is* my business, you know. That is, it *used* to be my business." He took a sip of coffee. "No, Graham was too specific about things he had no experience with. I think he saw it, all right. Now it's up to us to track it down."

"Well, there's no debris from it, just wood and the other construction ingredients of a house. If it existed, which I doubt, they could have hauled it out of here in one of those trucks he saw. Cut it up first, like the airplane."

"Could have, Corley, but probably didn't."

"OK. If they didn't, what happened to it?"

Jack shrugged.

Brand crossed his arms. "Speaking of a subbasement, where is it? How do we get into it? You even poked around the basement of the house and looked for the steps to it, where Graham said. No sign, right?"

"Right."

Brand pointed. "And no sign of it over where the metal building stood."

Jack nodded again. "Right."

"See?" Brand placed his hand on Jack's shoulder. "We've probed around all three structures and found nothing. Even had the acoustics man out yesterday listening for gas leaks. He found nothing. No trapdoors, no hollow chambers beneath the ground level. No soundings of anything but dirt underneath. Nothing's been discovered among the ruins that might have been part of a complex machine like a simulator. So I say if Graham really saw one, it must have been taken off the property prior to the explosion. Too valuable a piece of equipment to blow up, or even cut up. Logical conclusion, right?"

Jack didn't say anything. He finished his coffee and dropped the paper cup into a trash box next to the car. Finally he replied. "Corley, something that bulky could have been removed intact only by a very large truck, unless they disassembled it first, which is unlikely. It would have been a prohibitive, time-consuming job to separate the thousands of parts, electronic panels, and boxes from the metal frame. The Oklahoma Highway Patrol said that no vehicle capable of carrying such a load was reported by curious neighbors. In addition, Graham reported he heard many voices in and around the house."

"So?"

"What a busy place this was. Full of people and equipment." Jack's voice lowered. "Graham escapes, and they immediately disappear, without a trace. Except a handful on a helicopter."

"OK, consider this, Jack. It *was* a staging area of some sort, we tipped our hand when we searched the ministry and the school on Friday, and they had four days to pack up and move out. That would be plenty of time to leave nothing behind."

Jack stared at the silent remains strewn across two quarter sections of frozen land. An erratic wind vibrated pieces of debris.

Brand watched him. "Damn it, what *else* could have happened?"

Jack motioned to his friend. "Let's get in the car."

As soon as they shut the doors, he spoke. "They didn't go anywhere, Corley."

"What?"

"They're still here."

"Underground?"

"We've combed the property and found nothing," Jack continued. "Yet Reuben told Voronov there was a big staging or training area out here somewhere. Graham said he was imprisoned by strange people in a strange place. The surface structures here were intentionally blown up, probably by Gellex, one of the explosives the terrorists have used around the country, yet we can't put two and two together. Maybe they did move some things out, but I'll bet my reputation there's a lot left behind. Like the simulator."

Brand rubbed his forehead. "All right, Jackson, assuming you're correct, what the fuck can we do? Dig holes everywhere? We've had technicians all over the area, and they haven't detected anything out of the ordinary. Certainly no indication of anything underground."

"Corley, we can't afford the luxury of chance anymore. I think Graham saw everything he said he saw. We have to make some direct hits. Starting right now."

"OK, I'm all ears. What do you suggest?"

"If the simulator's here, there's probably only one way to find it quickly. A magnetic analysis of the area. From the air."

Brand rolled his eyes. "Oh, yeah, call the Air Force and ask them to take pictures. You're going off the deep end, old buddy."

"I'm not talking about mapping the surface, God damn it. There's more than one way to skin a cat." Jack jerked his thumb toward the north. "I've got a friend in Tulsa who does aerial magnetic work for oil companies. Deep stuff. If he's available, he can probably be down here today. All we need is an indication of *something* where there shouldn't be anything. Then we can take the next step."

"Which is?"

"Precise infrared measurements for thermal anomalies. They'd tell us the extent of habitation. In other words ... "

"I know, I know," Brand muttered, "whether or not someone's been left behind to guard the fort." He pulled out a notepad. "What's your friend's name?"

"Albert McCollough. Company's called McCollough International."

"Is he clean?"

Jack was silent for a moment. "As far as I know. I've known him for at least ten years."

"OK, Jack, your idea beats anything I could offer. Let's get back to the office. You call your friend and get with him as soon as you can. See what he can do for us, but don't tell him the FBI's involved or what we're up to or where we're looking until I check him out. If you're right about this place, there's nothing to be gained in letting anyone else know what we know. Also, I'll see what kind of a deal we can get later tonight for a picture from someone with a reconnaissance satellite, like Landsat 5. Maybe even one of the CIA birds. Let's make the assumption your man will find something worth photographing." Brand extracted himself from the back seat. He turned and looked at his friend.

"I don't think I've ever seen you this intense before."

Jack stared back. "I haven't been, Corley. I'm putting together the most important jigsaw puzzle of my life. The completed picture will be the smiling face of my daughter." Jack felt a shiver. But what if he was wrong? What if this turned out to be another wild-goose chase?

J. Edgar Hoover Building, Washington, D.C.
10:00 a.m.

"They bypassed State, if you can believe that."

The FBI director pointed to the report Jerry Reynolds was reading.

"The Syrian ambassador himself showed up at the White House this morning to deliver it. He called the information 'a gravest matter concerning your national security.' He made his presentation and left. He was only there for fifteen minutes."

"Incredible," the deputy director observed as he looked over the seven sheets of data with their accompanying map. "Their first information basically repeated what the German BND had already passed along, namely that there were bases in the Bekaa Valley that were training people to carry out terrorist acts against American interests, possibly even here at home." Reynolds tapped the report and shook his head. "The Syrians have never before given us anything this sensitive, nor have they ever gone directly to the president."

"The Secret Service is all ginned up about it," the director added.

"Well, I can imagine." Reynolds waved the papers. "Less than a week to the inauguration, and this arrives."

"In a nutshell," the director reviewed, "Abu Kuttab, who was on that TWA flight on the thirtieth of last month, came from a training camp in the Bekaa Valley that is or was under the control of Jamil Nasir, and he's here to 'sever the head of the pharaoh.' "

Reynolds could only grunt. "But Nasir himself hasn't been seen around his own camp in months. Guy's in charge of a place, yet he's nowhere to be seen."

"I'd say that if whatever they're training for is a major effort somewhere, he's gone ahead."

"That's what Brand thinks, too," Reynolds commented. "Just talked with him. He's got a request, but consider this last part from the Syrians: Kuttab has a sister. Name's Rima Ameen. We've had no substantive knowledge about her before, but it's apparent she's an active little soul. The Syrians say she's always in the shadow of her brother, and she's every bit the killer that he is. Wherever he is, she'll be there, also. Undercover, background. According to the Syrians, she fits in—works as flight attendant, secretary. You know, service-oriented jobs where she has ready access to public situations." Reynolds looked at the summary again. "Born in 1963, she's five feet six with black hair and jade-green eyes. Her hair color changes with the needs of the moment. She's sometimes a blonde but usually a brunette. She's got a lighter complexion than the Mediterranean tan of her brother, so the Syrians think she might have had a different father. Oh." He paused. "Here's a nice touch. I see they even sent us the little darling's fingerprints."

FBI Office, Tulsa
10:00 a.m.

"If Kuttab's here, she probably is, too? Holy shit!"

Brand came around Don Evans's desk and sat down.

"Give me her description again, Jerry, then send the rest of the information on the secure fax."

He copied the woman's attributes. Suddenly he sat bolt upright.

"I don't believe this. . . . That description precisely fits the nurse from

St. Francis Hospital. The one who disappeared with Jack Stroud's daughter! And you have her prints?"

"Sure do. This gal's had nurse's training all right, but she got it at Amman, Jordan. Since then she's worked Palestinian causes, until she went completely underground a few years ago. Even the Syrians had trouble hearing about her after that."

"Jerry, I think we might be able to obtain a match of her prints from here. People applying for most jobs at hospitals get printed, and I'll bet that happened to Miss Ameen at St. Francis. She probably didn't even mind because she knew she was clean with us, Interpol, and the others. I'll check right now."

"Where's Stroud?"

"With his oil-field friend, arranging a magnetic sweep. We may be able to have it by six tonight. As for his personal condition, I've never seen him more focused. Understandably, of course."

"Did you find out who owns that property?"

"Yeah, some outfit called the Beggs Health Ranch."

"Health ranch? I'll bet. Corporation?"

"A d.b.a., signed for by a guy named Victor Souter."

"Ring any bells?"

"Nope. Hey, wait a minute! Jerry, I just had an idea. Might save us hours. Keep your fingers crossed. Talk with you later."

Brand hung up and waved at the receptionist as he bolted out the office door.

"One hour. I'll be at Stroud's house."

He crossed fingers on both his hands as he waited for the elevator.

34

"Sorry, Jack. Won't work."

Al McCollough sat at his desk and shook his head.

"An aerial magnetometer survey of that area wouldn't locate anything smaller than the White House."

Jack had laid out his idea to the man most in the oil patch considered the best at finding things. Usually what McCollough looked for—and found—was oil and gas and hard minerals.

"Trucks? Habitable installations and equipment?" McCollough made a thumbs-down gesture. "Not a chance. Way too small."

"Well, I was hoping for some better news."

Jack stood to leave.

"Hold it." McCollough raised his hand. "Who says there isn't another way?"

Jack lowered himself into the chair again. "I should have remembered you didn't get your reputation by giving up on the first try. What do you propose?"

"We do a lot of our initial work on the surface, especially in areas hostile to airplanes. Mountainous terrain, along riverbeds crisscrossed by power lines. Those kinds of places."

"But don't you have to set off charges of some sort?"

"For seismic work, yes, but not to find magnetic anomalies."

"So?"

"We can use a portable sensor, which weighs less than twenty pounds. A man walks off an area, then returns to the office. We plug the sensor into a computer analysis unit here, and in seconds we've got a nice picture of the place, anomalies and all."

"When can you do it?"

"Hey, if the area's close, I can have it done, analysis and all, within a couple of hours."

Jack felt a jolt of adrenalin. "Al, you just made my day."

10:23 a.m.

"Yes, sir. I remember she got one," Flora said as she led Corley Brand to Rachel's room. "It should be in her desk, where she keeps that kind of stuff."

"Have you or anyone else touched it?"

"No, sir."

"Let's hope she was so excited getting the silver pin that she didn't touch it much herself."

Flora opened the center drawer of the desk and pointed.

"That's the one. I could never forget it."

Brand scooped up the Hallmark message with his business card and tunneled it into a plastic envelope.

"Thanks, Flora. This may help us find her."

FBI Office, Tulsa
10:49 a.m.

Jack paced from one end of the conference room to the other. He'd segregated himself here, to think. McCollough had agreed to do the magnetic mapping job himself.

The door burst open. Corley Brand dashed in, waving an envelope.

"I got it . . . the card that nurse gave to Rachel. We're having a courier take it to Washington immediately. If there's a good impression and the prints match . . ."

"What the devil are you talking about?"

"Oh, that's right, you don't know. Sit down for this one."

Brand told Jack what the Bureau now knew about Abu Kuttab's sister and what the FBI suspected. As he spoke, Jack's face grew ashen. Oh, God, no. The horrifying and humiliating juxtaposition of making love to his daughter's kidnapper nearly overwhelmed him. He placed his palms on the table to steady himself. He'd been a fool.

Brand squinted across. "Are you all right?"

"No!" Jack took a deep breath and slowly raised his fist. He slammed it down. "God *damn* it, Corley!" After a moment he closed his eyes, then hit the table again. "I fell for it."

"Don't be so hard on yourself. There was no reason for you to be suspicious."

"No reason?" Jack jerked upright. "Just after my wife is killed, a good-looking woman starts paying attention to me?" He shook his head and stared at the wall. "First it's the watch, then a little gift for my daughter. Oh, real smooth and believable. She's all empathy. Lost her spouse, too, she says. She reaches out to me . . . Mr. Completely Vulnerable, and she god-damn *uses* me to get to Rachel. A classic effort by a 'swallow,' Corley. Why, I couldn't write a better scenario for Intelligence 101. Me! I've taught this kind of stuff to rookies. Yet I fucking fell for it!"

Brand cupped his mouth with his hands and exhaled.

"You didn't screw her, did you?"

"Shit yes, I did!"

Jack got up and ran his hand through his hair. "And to think I was feel-ing guilty for seducing some sweet and lonely nurse who cared about my daughter and got herself kidnapped for her trouble." He glared at Brand. "I even had nightmares that Laura and Jeff paid the ultimate price, in advance, because I took advantage of that poor woman. Now I'll have to face myself and the world for being solely responsible for the taking of my only surviving child."

Brand pointed to the chair. "Sit down."

"The wonders of a goddamned hard-on! My leftover Catholic upbringing has come full circle, Corley. Sins of the father and all. Time to pay the piper."

"I said, *sit down!*"

Jack turned and saw the determination in Brand's eyes. He scratched at his cheek and took his place at the table again.

"You don't have any idea what I'm going through, Corley. You can't."

"Now you listen to me," Brand commanded in an even tone. "Maybe I can't, but maybe she didn't do it. The prints might not match. Have you thought about that?"

"Oh, they'll match all right. She did it. I'm not thinking with my prick this morning. She's the one."

Brand sighed.

There was a knock at the door. Brand turned. "Come in."

"Mickey Boucher, Corley. I can go. There's an American flight to National in, ah," he checked his watch, "a little less than an hour. I'm already booked on it."

"Great." Brand handed over the manila envelope. "Who's going to meet you?"

"Just talked to Loren Turner. He'll have a lab man waiting."

"Good luck, Mickey. It's extremely important. And thanks."

The FBI agent nodded and left.

The intercom buzzed. Brand picked up the handset.

"Mr. Brand?" It was the receptionist. "The Oklahoma State Bureau of Investigation on three."

"Thanks." He pushed the button. "This is Brand, who's this?"

"Brad Terrill. I have the employment application information on one Andrea Singletary. We've got her prints, too. Did you want those sent over?"

"Not yet, just the relevant data she gave the hospital." Brand positioned his pen over a legal pad.

"Well, as you know," the OSBI agent began, "we always check employment prints against known warrants."

"I know, Brad."

"We didn't find a thing on her."

"What about her bio, please?"

"Oh, yeah. When she applied for work at the Tulsa Bible College Hospital a year ago last month . . . "

"Whoa!" Brand nearly came out of his chair. "*Bible* College? Is that what you said?"

"Yes, sir. The Tulsa . . . "

"But she was a nurse at St. Francis."

"Yes, sir . . . later. Last September."

"Jesus Christ!" Brand exploded. "Of course! She established her cover at TBC. It was a piece of cake to transfer."

Terrill picked up his recitation. "She was born in Rantoul, Illinois. Grew up in Chicago. Attended nurse's school there."

"Hold it, Brad," Brand interrupted. "Is that the only kind of stuff you've got on her? U.S. locations and jobs?"

"Yes, sir."

"Thought so. It's worthless. But thanks." He hung up.

"Well, Jack, don't feel like the Lone Ranger. Looks like we both got slicked by that woman. I should have known. I mean, we're targeting TBC, and I never connected her with the hospital out there. A nurse! A hospital!" He raised both arms and looked toward the ceiling. "Damn!"

The telephone rang again. Brand leaned over and picked up the receiver. "He's here." He handed the telephone to Jack. "It's Flora."

"Mr. Stroud?" His housekeeper sounded worried. "You'd better come home."

"Why?"

"Sir, someone left a package at the front door. Rang the doorbell and left."

"Flora, did you touch it? You didn't open it, did you?"

There was a long pause before the woman answered.

"I did."

"And?" His first thought was, thank God it didn't blow up.

"It's a videotape, sir."

Tulsa
12:00 noon

Jack turned into his driveway. Brand had the door open before the car came to a stop.

"Where'd you find it?" the FBI man asked Flora the second she opened the door.

"Right where your foot is," she pointed. "At first I didn't see it. I was looking to see who had rung the bell."

"Did you see anyone?"

"No, sir."

Jack seized her by the shoulders. "Flora, you shouldn't pick up something like that, especially not with all that's been going on. I don't want anything to happen to you."

"It wasn't heavy, Mr. Stroud. So, I didn't think it could be a bomb."

"Where is it now?" Brand was already inside the house.

The housekeeper started twisting the belt to her apron. "I really didn't mean to cause ... "

"Don't worry about it," Jack assured her with a hug.

"Where, ma'am?" Brand was impatient.

She pointed. "On Mr. Stroud's desk."

Jack followed Brand into the study and saw the plastic cassette. To Jack, it looked threatening. He couldn't forget the warning the caller had made after Rachel was taken.

Brand circled the desk and considered the black object for a moment. "There probably weren't any prints on it in the first place. Those people aren't amateurs." He took out his pen and pushed the cassette toward the edge of the desk. He reached toward the bookshelf behind and picked up a magazine, which he held at desktop level. He then guided the cassette onto it.

"VCR?"

Jack pointed. "Over here." He walked to a cabinet, opened it, and pushed the "on" button of the recording unit. He then turned on the TV. "Uh, Flora ... " Jack began as Brand loaded the VCR. His voice caught in his throat.

"I understand, Mr. Stroud. I'll be in the kitchen." She nodded and left the room.

"Jack, are you ready?" Brand held his finger next to the start button. "You know how bad it could be, don't you?"

Jack sat down. All of the emotions of the past fifteen days seemed to return in a cascade. Fury and anxiety warred within him. He gripped the armrests.

"I'm ready."

Brand pushed the "play" button. Color bars appeared and held for a quarter-minute. Then an obvious surgical procedure filled the screen. The two men leaned forward. Jack's heart raced. He began to feel nauseous as the gruesome chronicle continued in silence. Glove-wrapped fingers held something fleshy while a scalpel sliced away at restraining muscles. The fingers grabbed and pulled as the cutting motion continued. Blood and clear liquids flowed copiously and reflected in the bright lights. Jack began to feel faint as the obscenity continued. Suddenly he propelled himself out of the chair.

"No, Corley, *no!*"

Brand threw his arm around his friend and held him.

Suddenly a scream from the speaker pierced the silence. Jack's legs nearly buckled. The hideous sound continued for a minute while the excision scene was completed.

"Did you like that, Stroud?" a man's voice boomed from the tape. Then he laughed. "I didn't want to tell you this, but, unfortunately, that wasn't your daughter." He laughed again. Then the voice became very serious. "You listen to me, you son of a bitch. That would be too good for her. No, your daughter's going to experience terror beyond imagination, just before she dies. And her pain," the man concluded, "will be a hundred times what it would have been from bad surgery. You fucked up, Stroud, and now *she's* going to pay." The television screen went to snow.

San Francisco
1:01 p.m.

"Door, please!"

Stanley Davidson, the legendary director of the U.S. Secret Service, motioned impatiently at one of his local agents. The woman, in turn, signaled to associates outside and quickly sealed the room.

Representatives of the FBI, the San Francisco police, the California Highway Patrol, and the Secret Service sat in groups at the front of the room as the big lawman orchestrated the beginning of the task-force meeting. Six and a half feet tall, Davidson had lumbered to the podium five minutes early. *The Washington Post* once called him "a plodding, elephantine figure who relishes being in the eye of the storm," adding that he never forgot anything important and could retrieve, years later, a nuance from some investigation. When Davidson headed the Presidential Protective Division, his tenure was highlighted by almost-daily complaints from the media that the Secret Service took its job too aggressively, nearly hiding the chief executive from view. Wags suggested that God Himself would have trouble getting through to see the president. "With Stan in the way, He probably wouldn't even bother."

Latecomers to the meeting avoided Davidson's glare as they entered the room and aimed for seats. Loudspeakers cracked as he flipped at the microphone, his version of dimming the lights. Aides made their final adjustments to covered display boards, activated an overhead projector, and retreated to the relative calm of the back of the room.

"The last two cities on their agenda were here and Seattle," Davidson boomed. The session was under way. "And we can bet they planned something for both stops."

He had jumped to the second item on the agenda. One of Davidson's characteristics was to eschew the preliminaries, which sometimes meant even dropping official parts of the organized program. "Give it to me shorthand," he demanded from his people. And they did. "Minute Man Stan" was an appellation of which he was proud. Agents knew that if they had a scheduled meeting with him, they had sixty seconds to make their point. Otherwise they'd be back in the hallway, and they'd have to call for a new appointment.

"You heard the latest on the Tulsa situation from Crabtree," he barked. "We still haven't found that Norman guy, FBI's microscoping everything around the ministry out there, we're ratcheting up the temp in D.C. for the inauguration. . . . "

There were few transitional phrases in Davidson's speaking style, and even fewer pauses of more than three seconds. Certainly no "uh"s, "er"s, or "you know"s. The Secret Service chief usually spoke so rapidly that his material hovered at the outer edge of comprehension unless the listener remained totally alert. Virtually everyone present in the audience today wished that tape recorders were not banned. Tomorrow's complaints would include writer's cramp.

"Don't need to tell you that because of the foreign heads of state, Secret Service's in complete charge of security of this conference. You will be following our order of priorities. You're certainly free to disagree, privately, but it won't do any good. This is *our* ball game."

Old-timers in the audience enjoyed the performance. It was classical Davidson: Stiff-arm up and down the field, intimidate potential opposition, and eventually score at will. Regardless of the setting, he always went through a similar protocol to maintain his reputation as the preeminent in-the-trenches lawman. However, those who had been around a bit knew that behind the façade of bluff and bluster, there wasn't one mean bone in Davidson's body.

D. J. Crabtree, the FBI's San Francisco special agent in charge, made occasional notes. It was his office that had first notified the Service of the potential threat to the attendees of the international conference. After he learned of Norman Gentry's disappearance the previous Saturday, together with the missing funds from the foreign bank accounts and the appearance of some sort of incursion into the United States involving known terrorists and the ministry, Crabtree called Davidson directly and offered full cooperation.

"Hell, D.J.," Davidson had commented over the telephone, "we've already been getting stuff from Corley Brand on a possible attempt on the president—what he heard from the Germans. Then there's the action out of a potential base in Oklahoma. Now this. It's spreading us pretty thin, with alerts on both coasts and the center of the country at the same time."

Crabtree had eleven FBI agents with him for this meeting. Davidson began his wrap-up.

"Very probably they'll be attempting something here. Again, what occurred elsewhere on the ministry's itinerary was designed for maximum public—and demoralizing—effect. We'll continue to look at all appropriate gatherings, sports events. Anywhere television could augment the destruction. But, of course, the obvious place for us to concentrate is the Pacific Rim conference. Now it's time for our last circuit."

Davidson put his hands in his pockets.

"Ladies and gentlemen, if we're not satisfied with the intelligence generated during the next six hours, we'll take whatever steps are necessary to ensure the safety of the president and the foreign participants. This includes the possibility of canceling the whole event. I've personally explained our policy to the mayor. Needless to say, he isn't pleased at the prospect, but that's the way it's going to be. The mood in the country is dark, and no one in our position can tolerate another attack on America. Period." He motioned for the lights.

"Time to move out for your intensive on-site inspections of the places the VIPs are scheduled to visit on Thursday. We'll meet again tonight at seven. Be ready for a workshop and a late night. Bring your notes, audio- and videotapes that you make, and be prepared to defend each location. If I find one open circuit, one lapse in security, the place's off-limits."

FBI Office, Tulsa
7:21 p.m.

"You asleep?"

It was Reynolds's voice on the telephone.

"Guess I was." Brand sat up on the couch and looked at his watch.

"We're getting some cots in here, Jerry." He yawned. "I think we're going to need them."

"Damned right you're going to need them, Corley. Because they matched."

Brand woke up completely. "The nurse's prints?"

"Got a perfect thumb, plus parts of two other fingers. Andrea Singletary, nurse, is definitely Rima Ameen, world-class terrorist."

"Holy shit!" Brand moved the handset to his other ear and contemplated the significance of the confirmation. "Jerry, she's been here for more than a year. And she's never been known to be more than five minutes from her brother."

"I know. Either he came into the country earlier, before his F-1 visit, or she's been here without him. As far as anyone knows, she's never done that before."

"How did they get her prints?"

"From a goddamn Diet Coke can in Baalbek, Lebanon, back in '89. The Syrians started keeping tabs on outside terrorists about then. Not that she was unknown to them, but they didn't have her prints, and they didn't know who her current employers were. So they marked cans and got prints from Rima and two others. They figured it might be worth something later on if her prints were available. For identification . . . or there's always the possibility of compromise."

"Yeah," Brand took over, "my guess is she went through the ID process in Tulsa at the hospital, probably at a number of other places earlier, not worrying about being unmasked. She figured any copies of her prints wouldn't get together for comparison. Of course, if they had, someone would have noticed that she was using different names for different jobs. Anyway, the types of jobs she held were different from one another, so there was never any central point or clearing place. She wouldn't get our attention because she didn't apply for a position requiring clearance with us. Plus, we didn't have her prints to start with."

"Corley?" It was Don Evans at the door. He pointed. "They're in my office."

Brand stood up. "Jerry, Jack Stroud's here. Hope he's got something. I'll call you back." He hung up and followed Evans out the door and down the hall.

Jack stood at Evans's desk. Al McCollough spread out a large sheet of white paper and secured it at the corners with an ashtray and three magazines.

Jack pointed to a series of interrupted lines along the edge of the paper. "Looks like a Picasso, doesn't it?"

McCollough placed his finger on the exact spot. "Right there. No mistake about it," the geophysicist confirmed. "I've gone over the data a half dozen times. There are more solid indications of metal, concentrated in one area, than I've ever seen, even in heavy iron ore country. Most of it's localized, too." He punched at the paper again. "Right to the southwest of the remains of the metal building. But then there are ripples from some other things, as many as five in all, to the west of the main concentration. I wasn't able to go over that far in the time I had, so I have no idea what they might be."

Brand stared at the oilman. "What do you think the heavy concentration is?"

McCollough shook his head. "Don't know, but it's nothing natural. I've got some old charts of the area, from the '50s and '60s. They were devoid of any such anomalies." He took a step backwards and looked at the men. "Now, that part of the state is famous for its late-night burials of toxic waste and other contraband, but you'd almost have to have 10,000 pounds of mercury waste there to make those bumps. And you'd expect surface signs, like scraping or filling. There weren't any." McCollough crossed his arms. "Beats me."

"Well, we'll soon know if you're right." Brand checked his watch. "We've got an emergency request in at the CIA for a thermal look at the area from a recon satellite." He looked at Jack. "We don't know what they'll be able to do for us on such short notice. Maybe they won't be able to reposition one of their most appropriate infrared birds, but with what we may have found, we've definitely got priority. We're supposed to have something by early morning."

Jack started for the door.

"I hope you gentlemen don't mind, but I've got an appointment. Then I'm planning to get some sleep. I don't need any more of today, and I have a feeling that rest will be a luxury by tomorrow."

En route to St. Francis Hospital
7:52 p.m.

"I'm glad you're going with me, Flora." Jack glanced over at his diminutive housekeeper. "You're very special to me." She smiled back and fidgeted with her hands.

He'd decided to ask her to accompany him to see Lester Graham. He knew it was the right thing to do. The FBI had completed its interrogation, but Jack felt he should visit with the man who had unwittingly played a crucial role in tying together events and conclusions that might indeed lead him to his daughter. Jack especially wanted to hear about the departure of the helicopter.

Flora seemed lost without Laura and Jeff, and she'd had to be alone while he was in the hospital after being shot. Now Rachel was gone. The woman had personally suffered as if it were her own family. Well, he thought, it *was* her family. Her husband had died years earlier, and her only child, a grown son, now lived a ten-hour drive away in San Antonio. So, in effect, this was her home, her family. Or, Jack reflected, what was left of it.

"I've taken you for granted, Flora. Ever since Laura and Jeff . . . well, I've leaned on you but I haven't talked with you enough. And I'm sorry. I really am."

"But, Mr. Stroud, I'm glad you have taken me for granted," she responded. His surprised expression brought forth her explanation. "I know you've had your mind on many things, so it makes me happy to know you feel you don't have to talk to me all the time. I am glad I can get things done the way you like, so you can do what you have to do."

Jack smiled. "Flora, you're one in a million." He looked over at her. "I can't thank you enough."

"I must thank *you* for what I have," she replied. "You have given me such an opportunity here in America, Mr. Stroud. I remember when I used to take little Jeff and Rachel to the park to watch the swans. There were other children playing, and I thought how beautiful this country was to allow everyone to share in its openness and wonder. Oh, no, Mr. Stroud, I owe *you*."

Jack kept his eyes on the road.

"Flora, you're the only link I have with all that's important to me. You've been a wonderful part of our family."

"There is something I must tell you. I . . . I have found it hard to say before now."

Jack turned. "Oh?"

"Yes, well, Rachel came into the kitchen last week. We've talked about things often, and I could see that she wanted to tell me something." Flora took a deep breath before she continued. "She said she was the luckiest daughter in the world, to have you as her father."

Jack's heart turned over. He could only nod as they drove on in silence.

St. Francis Hospital, Tulsa
8:03 p.m.

"Ready?"

Jack motioned her to go into the room ahead of him, but Flora hesitated. She gripped a package with both hands and looked to one side, then the other. He realized she was concerned about her appearance.

"You look fine." He remembered her comment before they left home: "Mr. Stroud, what a terrible thing to happen to someone. I want to look my very best. And from what you say he seems such a—*¿cómo se dice?*—decent man."

Jack pushed open the door and thought yes, a decent man, indeed—maybe even like Señor Hernandez, her late husband. The room was dimly lit.

"Oh, Mr. Stroud," Flora tugged at his coat sleeve and whispered, "we have come at a bad time. He needs the darkness to sleep. Maybe we should come back later."

A man's low voice broke the silence. "Who's there?"

With Flora in tow, Jack stepped into the room.

"Mr. Graham? It's Jack Stroud. I was here yesterday with the FBI. Oh, and this is Flora. She's part of my family."

His housekeeper looked at Jack. "Oh, my, I didn't mean to wake him up."

"Who can sleep around here anyway?" Graham's voice sounded solid. He adjusted himself in the bed.

"Flora's brought you some oatmeal cookies. She baked them herself."

"But you don't have to eat them if you don't want to," the woman assured quickly. "They're full of raisins, too, and I thought you might also want some . . . "

"Hey, slow down." Lester Graham frowned. "You're talkin' a blue streak."

"I was going to say I thought you might want some conversation, too." She finished her sentence and immediately blushed.

Graham's eyes were fixed on her.

"Yes, ma'am, I sure would like that."

"Well, I just . . . I mean, you know. . . . "

Flora lowered her gaze, and Jack helped her out of her coat. He noticed she appeared to be as nervous as a schoolgirl on her first date.

Twenty-two miles north of downtown Washington, in the undulating Maryland hills east of the Baltimore-Washington Parkway, on a thousand acres within the perimeter of Fort George G. Meade, lay the massive, interconnected, campuslike facility of the highly secretive National Security Agency. The nearly 200,000 civilian and military people around the world who were directed from this one location manned computers and monitored satellites and secured listening posts that provided information vital for the operation of the United States armed forces.

Even at this early hour, 3,000 intercept specialists of the Special Operations Office were actively at work eavesdropping on clandestine transmissions from selected installations in Syria, Lebanon, and Mexico. Their ranks had grown a hundredfold since the second of January, when the Pentagon ordered intensified monitoring of specific telephone and radio communications following the loss of the KH-12 reconnaissance satellite in the *Encounter* space shuttle disaster. Now a separate section staffed by eleven NSA operatives had been hurriedly partitioned for a related domestic assignment for the FBI.

In an underground bunker that resembled the control room of a television studio, two image data-processing analysts sat and watched as an interpretation unit yielded on their computer screens a black-and-white representation for the coordinates requested. The single picture had been transmitted after an earlier practice series of a dozen shots while the satellite was over the western Atlantic and the eastern United States. In a burst of data from 1,000 nautical miles away, the photograph was downlinked directly from an advanced, digital-imaging KH-11 Strategic Response reconnaissance satellite in polar orbit to the nearby array of NSA antennas. During its brief mission over eastern Oklahoma, the secret Air Force spacecraft was at 340.2 kilometers. The resolution of objects photographed in the infrared wavelength at that altitude was the width of a human hand.

One of the analysts noted the coordinates in the box at the top right of his screen. He spoke into the boom microphone of his headset.

"Target was north 35 degrees, 45.5 minutes and west 96 degrees, 05.7 minutes. We framed it at five nautical miles."

The other man followed the abbreviated logistics text as it spilled across the screen. "OK, single pass ... four minutes ago at 0928 UTC, which was 3:28 a.m. local time out there ... ground track right across the target, probably no more than a thousand meters off the aiming point ... looks like no measurable slant whatsoever." He turned to his companion. "I'd call that a bull's-eye."

"Level Five and print it," the analyst signaled.

For the large scale preferred by the FBI, forty by sixty centimeters, and the details desired, the cycle required fifty seconds to produce the filtered infrared representation. When the printer's status light changed from yellow—processing to flashing green—ready, the man lifted the door, removed the sheet from the output tray, and laid it on the slanted view board. He selected a lens from the velvet-lined rack and bent over the copy. He moved his head up and down.

His associate stepped off his stool and walked closer.

"Anything different from what the computer gave us?"

"Nope," the man answered without looking up. "Still looks like a giant fork." He held his position. "Damnedest thing I've ever seen."

The analyst moved alongside.

The other man sat up. "Here, see for yourself." He handed over the viewer and yielded the stool. "Check the evenness of the thermal striae extending west from the target. Something's maintaining a stable temperature in the five, uh, corridors. What and why ... your guess is as good as mine."

The analyst leaned over the picture. After a moment of silent contemplation, he looked to one side.

"Giant fork ... or maybe a hand." He gave back the lens. "What do you make of the western ends of the striae? They're like cooler fingertips to the hand."

The man reclaimed his seat. He shook his head. "Don't know. Obviously, from the temperature differentials, there's some sort of barrier separating the tips from the corridors. Seals, maybe." He checked to make sure that the tape recorder was rolling, then he held the viewer over the picture and started his conclusion.

"Uniform temperatures are indicated, which radiate in a westerly fan shape from a larger, central heat source, which was the target of our shoot. The smaller heat sources enlarge into five straight lines, resembling corri-

dors, which proceed further west. The bottom four of the five paths terminate at the same point of longitude 800 meters, or approximately one-half
mile, from the central heat source. The top one, the most northerly, termi-
nates somewhat sooner."

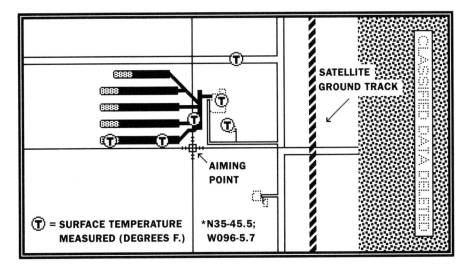

The man checked a computer screen, then leaned over the view board.

"Temperature analysis: The surrounding surface is uniform at sixteen
degrees Fahrenheit throughout the area photographed. Above the central
heat source, it rises to slightly under seventeen degrees. We've programmed a ten-degree increase per meter in depth, so if the heat source is
six meters below the surface, an increase of sixty degrees is probable, yielding a temperature of seventy-seven degrees at approximately twenty feet
down."

He took a deep breath and checked the position of the microphone.

"Of course, the heat source could be much deeper, but an origin more
than fifty feet is not likely because it would produce a strong diffusion outwards due to normal subterranean absorption and scattering, and it would
not maintain the integrity of defined edges and angles, such as we have
here. There is the appearance of an organized pattern, such as is seen with
underground geothermal pools plus their gathering lines. The temperature
of the five corridors is slightly less than the central heat source. The termi-
nus of each of the corridors is substantially cooler. Best estimate for them
at a twenty-foot depth is thirty-seven degrees."

The man placed the viewing lens on the rack.

"There's no evidence of surface venting of the heat." He crossed his
arms and looked at his partner. "Some sort of a sealed world down there.

The computer says it looks like geothermal. What do you think it is?"

The analyst glanced at the glowing monitor, then at the hard copy. He shook his head. "That's not geothermal activity. And nothing is pumped underground in pipelines at those temperatures . . . usually only cold liquid or very hot gas." He shook his head. "No, anything close to seventy-seven degrees is what you'd expect for something that's temperature sensitive."

"Like what?" his associate asked.

"Like something alive," the analyst concluded. "Expedite that photo to the FBI."

J. Edgar Hoover Building, Washington, D.C.
5:16 a.m.

The armed courier stood at the door with his sealed briefcase. At his side was an Air Force guard who had accompanied him on the drive from the National Security Agency. Both men were in civilian clothes. Behind them, in the shadows of the corridor, was their FBI building escort.

Jerry Reynolds had been in the Strategic Information Operations Center when he was notified of the unmarked car's arrival at the electric gates of the underground garage. He stepped off the elevator and walked briskly toward the men waiting outside his office. He nodded at the courier.

"We've been expecting you."

Reynolds punched in his personal code and opened the door to the reception area. He noticed that the courier smiled at his greeting and realized it was probably because no long-term NSA employee ever knew a time when the FBI didn't want a sought-after message delivered yesterday.

Reynolds motioned the three men to enter. He followed them past the four vacant secretaries' desks and through the door of his private office.

"You can use that table, if you'd like," the deputy director pointed as he walked across and adjusted the security curtains behind his desk.

The courier and the guard moved to a narrow buffet along the wall. The man pushed aside a stack of magazines while the guard keyed a seven-digit code into his FM transmitter, which advised security agents at Fort Meade that the classified item was in the physical presence of the authorized recipient and was about to be delivered. The courier had his own code to enter on a belt-clip radio. Then he flipped up a spring-hinged covering under the handle of the briefcase and punched in the same numbers on a dial. He moved his hands to the edges of the case and popped the locks.

"Signature you know where."

The courier picked up a single manila envelope and handed it to Reynolds. The man closed the briefcase and reversed the order of the cod-ing process. The Air Force guard tapped in the delivery-has-been-effected numbers. Reynolds scribbled his name on the "eyes-only" receipt attached to the envelope and gave it to the man.

The courier tucked the paper into an inside pocket. "Good day, sir."

Reynolds acknowledged with a nod and sat down at his desk. The men, with their FBI escort in tow, left his office and pulled the door shut. Out of the corner of his eye, Reynolds saw the flashing light on his desk go steady after a few seconds, indicating that the sound sensors in his reception area no longer detected the presence of the visitors. He found a letter opener, slit the top of the envelope, removed the folded single-page infrared photograph, and placed it on the desk. He opened the picture and reached for his private telephone just as it buzzed. He picked up the handset.

"Well?" It was Brand's voice.

"Just got it," Reynolds replied. "Hold on for a second." He scanned the black-and-white picture. "This is absolutely incredible, Corley. It's just as Stroud figured. There's an underground facility at Beggs, all right, with five corridors extending—Jesus Christ!—about a half mile from the main place." He removed a paper clip and held up a typewritten sheet. "NSA's attached a summary analysis." He read for a second. "Listen to this—the place's sealed, apparently no venting, and they've even gone so far as to say it could be habitable."

"So not only might a simulator be down there," Brand offered, "but the people who operate it, too."

"Yeah," Reynolds agreed as he looked over the summary again. "Absolutely incredible," he repeated.

"Well, that's our base, Jerry, and my hunch is there are probably a lot of really bad eggs down there right now, just waiting for us to go away. They never figured on a Jack Stroud and a confluence of coincidences zeroing in on them."

Reynolds cradled the handset against his shoulder and picked up the photograph.

"OK, Corley, I'm sending this to you right now on the secure fax. I'll get everyone here for a meeting at eight. Can you be at our Tulsa office then for a hookup?"

"Hey, señor, just where do you think I am right now?"

FBI Office, Tulsa
7:32 a.m.

Jack Stroud held a coffee cup in one hand, the telephone to his ear with the other, and spoke with Ron Oliver, the FBI's special agent in charge for Oklahoma.

"Corley's still talking with Jerry Reynolds in Washington, Ron." Jack spoke loudly in order to be heard over the other conversations in the conference room. In a corner, Tom Bentley made notes while he sat with Larry Harrington, Tulsa head of the Bureau of Alcohol, Tobacco, and Firearms, who had come directly from his home to the FBI office.

"Yes, it's confirmed." Jack laid the cup on the table and pressed a finger to his free ear. "That's right, a massive underground bunker of some sort. We've got the infrared picture, which the National Security Agency took less than four hours ago. Reynolds faxed it to us."

"What's that, Ron?" Jack squinted. "Yes, a task force. Exactly what Corley had in mind, and he'd like to set up a meeting for noon here. We're going to have to get everyone together who is capable of breaching that place, and we're going to have to plan the assault. Oh, hold on. Brand just got off the other line."

"Oliver?"

Jack nodded. Brand reached for the telephone.

"Ron, can you be here at noon?" He maneuvered a pad of paper in front of him. "Great. Jack told you about the NSA photo? OK. I'd suggest you notify the governor and the chief of the Oklahoma Highway Patrol. They still have their tactical teams, don't they?"

Brand drew three boxes on the top sheet. He labled them "FBI," "ATF," and "OHP." The FBI box was on top.

"All right. Well, they were always great when they practiced with us at Quantico. Anyway, I think we ought to use our Hostage Rescue Team, the similar group from the ATF, and the tac team from the OHP. See if you can bring one of the OHP team commanders to the meeting."

"Righto. See you at noon." He hung up and looked at Jack. "I've been thinking about your system of measuring the progress of a chase ... the mental checklist you told me about yesterday. You know, ten hours, eight, six?"

"And?"

"Well, I think we're about to reduce that time frame of yours to zero."

Bentley and Harrington came over and pulled out chairs at the table.

"Larry agrees with you, Jack," the local FBI chief started. "In spite of the depth. We'll see if the Tulsa police can spare a few of their German shepherds this afternoon."

Inglewood, California
10:00 a.m.

The Southern California camp meeting was to have been the biggest gathering of the faithful along the Tulsa-to-Seattle pilgrimage of Norman

Gentry's Christian Cavalcade. Instead, the entire event was in disarray. Even so, by sunrise, as would have been expected before the curious events of the past four days, the parking lots at the Forum were already half filled. Virtually everyone this morning had heard about Norman's disappearance in Albuquerque on Saturday and of the strange substitute program at Phoenix on Monday, but only those few whose faith wavered could not imagine that the young evangelist would return in triumph to lead his followers today and then onward toward San Francisco and Seattle. Thousands who had forsworn the influence of newspapers and television and professed to be unaware of the rumors and suspicions surrounding the ministry now came and whispered together outside the auditorium and passed along the latest word that Norman had been kidnapped or possibly even killed. As their concerns grew, it became necessary for those assembled in the parking lots to move forward, to try the locked doors and to see for themselves the signs that read, "Event Canceled." They stood quietly at the glass, shook their heads, and wondered what indeed the world was coming to.

Westin St. Francis Hotel, San Francisco
10:30 a.m.

"Ladies and gentlemen," the mayor's voice boomed over the loudspeakers of the Golden Gate Room. He beamed and extended his arms. "Welcome to San Francisco and the opening of the thirteen-nation Pacific Rim Summit."

Applause spread across the packed ballroom, and 5-foot-11 Vincent Nomura gloried in the corridor of light that shone from the ceiling. After a moment, he brought his arms together and tugged at his French cuffs to make sure the eighteen-karat-gold links flashed in the brightness of the podium. He'd looked forward to this moment for three and a half years, and he reveled in being at the center of international attention.

Thirteen hundred dignitaries and representatives, including presidents and prime ministers, from Japan, China, the Philippines, Singapore, Australia, New Zealand, Malaysia, Indonesia, Thailand, Canada, South Korea, and Taiwan sat with those from the United States and readied themselves for today's general session. Secretary of State Arthur Cromwell was in attendance with the U.S. delegation, and the chief executive himself was scheduled to address the assemblage tomorrow night. The attendees also looked forward to outside events and tours, which were interspersed with the formal learning sessions here and at the Hyatt on Union Square.

"It gives me great pleasure ... " the mayor maintained his consummate political speaking style as he moved the program along, " ... to introduce our first speaker, the United States deputy assistant secretary of commerce."

Tulsa
10:33 a.m.

"Methacholine, for sure."

The assistant medical examiner pulled off his surgical gloves and plopped them into a stainless steel disposal unit at his feet. He flexed his fingers and looked at his associate.

"I've seen it done with ephedrine. You can get that over the counter, but it takes a lot more to pop off the top of the head. I have no doubt, though, that this death resulted from a nice dose of methacholine."

His associate nodded. "Fools the emergency-room docs every time."

"Look here." The ME pointed to the adrenal medulla. "Squeezed it dry. Yep, methacholine, all right. What a beautiful and almost undetectable way to cause a massive hypertensive crisis. Probably had it sprinkled in his food. Like in a sauce."

The associate stared at the exposed brain. "Yeah, a couple hundred milligrams would never have been tasted by the poor guy."

"OK, let's get the samples to the lab and make it official."

FBI Office, Tulsa
12:00 noon

The seven men sat down in the conference room precisely at twelve o'clock. At the end of the table, with his back to the door, was Corley Brand. Jack sat to Brand's right with Ron Oliver and Don Evans. On Brand's other side were Tom Bentley, ATF's Larry Harrington, and Oklahoma Highway Patrol chief Orrin Birdsong. Somehow all of this talent gathered in one place gave Jack the reassurance he needed. Rachel was still alive, and they'd find her. He closed his eyes for a second. He couldn't let hatred and frustration rule him. A cool head was what he needed now.

"You there, Jerry?" Brand adjusted the knob on the telephone console.

"Yes, and I have Tex Follett with me, Corley." Reynolds's voice was crisp from his office in Washington.

Jack remembered the days before Follett was asked to reform and refine the FBI's Hostage Rescue Team. Tex, he'd never forget, was the greatest advocate of a full-time HRT, rather than the on-again, off-again approach that characterized the Bureau until Pan Am 103. The World Trade Center bombing and the terrible events at Waco had sealed the decision to make the sweeping changes. One of Tex's stellar performances came when the FBI thwarted a plan to take over the nuclear submarine *USS Trepang*. The terrorists were stopped literally seconds before they were to cast off. Their plan was to put out to sea, fire a nuclear missile at an American city, and sell the submarine to Libya. Tex was now the unit's full-time commander.

Jack listened to Brand's recap for the benefit of Washington.

"We've got seven German shepherds, with their handlers, on their way to the property right now. We should know the results by five or six today."

"Jack, can you hear me?" It was Follett.

"Loud and clear, Tex."

"That underground layout looks like a giant book of matches to me, and I'd say you're right on target about the ends of the damn things. Makes all the sense in the world that they'd store explosives far away from anything else."

Jack nodded. "And if the NSA is correct about the depth of the stuff, Larry Harrington here with the ATF says we should still get a reaction from the dogs."

"Well, good luck. Expect eight of us there tonight. We'll leave as soon as they get the shaped charges to us. I'll tell you all about my strategy when we arrive."

Brand took over again. "Let me summarize what we're up against. Then I'd like to have everyone's strategic thinking."

As Brand reviewed the facts, Jack's concentration moved to the who and the why. To finance their operations, most terrorist organizations used bank robbery or kidnapping, but it looked like this group had plenty of money . . . in those accounts. At least it did before the funds were transferred, apparently to a KGB-controlled account. The old KGB certainly had a long history of being the financial benefactor of numerous terrorist groups. And the typical terrorist target list included oil facilities, offshore rigs, refineries, supertankers, oil fields, power facilities (especially nuclear ones), water supplies, and computer systems. But not with this outbreak. He wondered—were the old Soviet bastards trying to profit from these terrorist activities? The Russians, even under their new leadership, were trying to export everything else for a buck.

"Mr. Stroud?"

Jack snapped out of his reverie. It was a secretary. He raised his eyebrows and leaned toward her.

"Urgent telephone call, sir," she whispered. "The district attorney. He wants to see you right away."

Tulsa County Courthouse
1:06 p.m.

"Jack, I wanted to show you this in person." District Attorney Barry Clayton held up a file folder as Jack crossed the room. Clayton indicated a chair.

"Reuben Gentry was murdered, just as you suspected."

Jack sat down in silence. He was more saddened than shocked. The DA went on.

"By court order, the exhumation of your father-in-law's body took place early this morning, secretly, and the autopsy was conducted at ten. Based on the physical appearance of certain organs and the subsequent chemical analysis, they tell me Reuben Gentry had enough methacholine in him to burst an elephant's brain. His heart probably had its load tripled, and his blood pressure must have gone off the chart."

The DA sat against the edge of his desk and opened a folder. He adjusted his reading glasses.

"Dr. Gentry died in Tulsa Bible College Hospital at nine on the morning of December 28. According to their records, he was brought in by ambulance minutes before he expired. He was unconscious from the time the paramedics picked him up until his death."

"I knew he had high blood pressure," Jack offered. "He'd been cautioned by his doctor to stick to his diet and medication regimen."

Clayton nodded, then returned to the file.

"According to the autopsy, the body showed evidence of methacholine ingestion over at least twelve hours, so he probably started getting the drug around mealtime the evening before. Methacholine comes in powder form, so it could have been sprinkled on his food. In a sauce, maybe. He wouldn't have tasted or smelled it, and as little as two hundred milligrams would probably have done the job."

Jack looked at the district attorney. "Methacholine?"

"It's a prescription product used mostly for diagnostic testing and inhalation therapy. Get it at any pharmacy. It's not controlled, so they don't keep very good records on it. There's 'shrinkage' all the time, just in the way it's regularly handled. Methacholine causes the smooth muscles to contract, which means in the case of the vascular system there's less space for the same volume of blood, so the pressure goes up. In Gentry's condition, with his history, it produced an aneurysm and a massive cerebral hemorrhage. He probably died without feeling anything. Happened too quickly. This was definitely no accident, though. Your thoughts?"

"Well, it was completely in Reuben's style to have dinner at nine or so in the evening. He called me around eight the night before he died, when I was at the Las Colinas hotel in Texas. He didn't say anything about feeling ill. How quickly does that stuff work?"

"Pretty fast." Clayton closed the folder and walked around to his desk chair. "If he'd talked with you more than a minute after taking it, you would have noticed." The DA stood behind his chair. "In any event, from what the lab says, he probably got his first dose at dinner. That didn't kill him, so someone finished him off the next morning. There's evidence he may even have been given some of the drug on the way to the hospital, just to make sure. Since he had a history of hypertension and he died under a doctor's care, there was no reason for an autopsy under Oklahoma law. Nice and neat. That is, until you came along with your suspicions."

Jack squinted. "What astounds me is the fact that when I called, Norman told me in a nonchalant voice that his father had simply suffered a stroke and was unconscious. Yet that was exactly the time Reuben was dying at the hospital, or was already dead, and the little son of a bitch knew it! But he was more concerned about my catching the flight . . . the flight that killed Laura and Jeff." He paused and looked to one side. "It's exactly as Brand said. *I* was the target."

"Jack, you still are." Clayton spoke slowly. "They're going to use Rachel to get to you, to use you if they don't—or can't—kill you."

Jack shook his head. He stood up and reached for his coat. "No, you're wrong on three counts, Barry. First, I'm not their target anymore. Second, no one's going to use Rachel for anything. And, third . . . " He walked to the door and stopped. "I don't care what I have to do, I'm personally going to get her . . . those . . . " He left without completing the sentence.

San Francisco
4:00 p.m.

"That's right, miss. Secret Service," one of the two men in business suits spoke into a metal speaker unit at eye level to the right of the front door. "We have an appointment."

The young woman inside the brick building waved two fingers toward a man in an office before she reached underneath her table and pressed a black button that buzzed open the door lock. A moment later, the government men stood in front of her.

"My name is Simms; this is agent DeBona."

The woman, a brunette, was in her mid-twenties. "Yes, of course. We've been expecting you." She smiled and indicated the man who walked toward them. "This is Karl. He's the manager."

The agents turned and saw a muscular man, about thirty years old, dressed in jeans and a golf shirt. He covered the remaining twenty feet in long strides and held out his hand.

"Karl Boerner. You're here for the Secret Service tour, right?"

"In a manner of speaking, yes," Simms replied. "We'd like to see every room, storage areas included. As we requested when we called last week, we want a list showing the names and addresses of the owner and all employees, with their Social Security numbers."

The man hooked his thumbs into his belt.

"Hey, no problem. Let's do the walk-around, then we can pick up the list when we finish."

The agents nodded and followed him down the tiled corridor. The aroma of fresh bread almost made the tour of the bakery a pleasant diversion for them.

"First we have our offices." The man pointed. "That's mine. Do you want to go in?"

The lead agent nodded. "If you don't mind."

"OK by me," their host replied and led the way into a twenty-by-fifteen cubicle. "Just the usual stuff. You know, a desk, a chair . . . " He laughed. "Nothing threatening."

The men scanned the room from ceiling to floor. There was a small window that faced the street.

"I see there's no attic." DeBona checked the view from the window. "Is there a basement to this building?"

"No."

The man gestured toward the door. "The next two offices are just like this one. Then there's the main pantry, followed by the oven."

The Secret Service agents walked into and checked the other two offices. They were as the man had said, similar to his.

"Where's that door lead to?"

The man looked where Simms pointed. He frowned. "Uh, pipes, I think. Yeah, pipes."

"What kind of pipes?"

"Plumbing. That's all."

The agent walked over and turned the knob. The door was locked.

"Do you have a key? I'd like to see for myself."

"Oh . . . yeah."

The man returned to his office and came back with a large ring of keys. "This ought to be it." He selected one and inserted it into the lock. With a twist, the lock clicked. He opened the door and found the light.

In the weak illumination, the two agents saw a narrow wooden staircase that descended beneath the main part of the building. They stepped down and entered a musty room that measured approximately thirty by twenty feet. It smelled of dead air. Plumbing and other pipes coursed in different directions beneath the ceiling.

Simms confronted the man. "I thought you said there wasn't a basement."

"We don't use this place." He shrugged. "I just kinda forgot about it."

Simms looked at his partner, who shook his head slightly.

"Any other places around here you don't use?"

"No, no." The man's reply was rapid. He held up his hand and smiled. "No, we're just humble bakers of the best sourdough in town."

"What about your competition across the street?"

"Sourdough from SFO? They're no competition, only bigger. A bread factory. No, we make the finest."

"OK, let's see the rest of the building."

When the man reached the top of the stairs, he turned around.

"How many people will be on that tour tomorrow?"

"I don't know," the agent answered as he followed up the stairs.

"Must be a good-size group to attract the kind of attention they're getting."

The agent didn't respond.

"Here's where we store all our supplies."

The man opened the door to a large room lined with shelves of cans, sacks, and boxes. There was a massive white refrigerator at the back. The agents walked in. DeBona pulled the latch and opened the refrigerator.

"Next we have our kitchen area, with the preparation tables and all. Then the oven."

The three moved along the side of a spacious kitchen. Two other men and a woman worked with pans and utensils and watched. When the agents made eye contact, the men looked away. The woman glared back.

"Here's our pride and joy, our stainless-steel oven." The manager unlatched a heavy door and pulled on the handle. He gestured. "Go ahead, gentlemen."

The agents entered a thirty-by-thirty room. To the left were rows of heavy shelving. To the right, along the metal wall, were three multiple-glass windows that looked like little portholes.

"It gets up to six hundred degrees in here," the man said with a grin as he pulled the door shut with a thud. "Walls are a foot of heavy-gauge steel." He touched the discolored steel next to one of the small windows. "This place really heats up when we turn on the gas."

"I'll bet it does," Simms observed.

"Well, that's it, gentlemen. Any more questions?"

Simms looked at DeBona, who shook his head. "I think not," the lead agent replied. "But we want that list from you. Ownership and the rest."

"Oh, yes." He pushed open the thick door and directed the Secret Service men toward his office.

4:41 p.m.

"There are six names on this list," DeBona recapped as they drove back to their office, "and I counted six people in the building. Four men and two women."

"We'd better have someone watching every one of them tomorrow," Simms suggested. "I don't like being lied to."

Jack clicked off the light and allowed himself to focus on the previous day. After meeting with the district attorney, he'd concluded that the session had both settled an issue and opened yet another door. Certainly it marked the end to the speculation over Reuben Gentry's death. However, that in itself didn't help answer the recurring question of why. And where had that bitch gone? Did she have Rachel? Was Rachel still alive?

He remembered he'd driven to the interstate that looped around the downtown area. It was necessary to think a little more, away from others. He needed the solitude his car offered.

Had it been only two weeks and two days? It seemed like a lifetime had passed since he'd waved goodbye to Laura and Jeff at the airport and let them go into eternity. He wanted to treat the memory like a tangible truth . . . something he would always have and could rely on to keep the bond intact. But it was already fading, like the colors in a favorite photograph. And he knew he couldn't do anything about it.

His personal tragedy had coincided with the beginning of the national madness. Martial law had indeed had its intended effect. The shock of the severity of the president's action seemed to make time stand still long enough to allow the hysteria around the country to begin to subside. Of course, the sight on television of armed troops stalking city streets had its effect, too. With few exceptions, the soldiers were serving the national interest just by being visible. Many commentators were already saying the military intervention would be short. As far as Jack was concerned, the president had done the right thing, and the relative calm during the forty-eight hours since martial law had been declared seemed to validate the action. The president would have to face his critics later. Probably in court, if the ubiquitous Homer Jenkins had anything to do about it.

Jack stared out the windshield.

The country had muddled through an extremely inflammatory experience. Most people had maintained their smiles and optimistic expressions, although genuine concern lay close to the surface. Attendance at public events was not prohibited, but most functions were canceled on the first day of the president's edict. The second day was better. Everyone sensed life would go on—and probably more safely—following the chief executive's dramatic action.

What was that exit?

Jack tensed and looked in his rearview mirror. Settle down, he told himself. Hadn't he intended to get away for a while? He decided to continue for two or three more exits before turning back.

"Two weeks and two days," he spoke aloud. Every additional second was another inexorable barrier between himself and all that had really mattered to him.

"Except Rachel." The thought of his daughter broke the spell. Then he pictured the woman who had taken his child. He pushed away the image of her nude body above his, her eyes staring down at him as she rode him. His anger boiled again, both at her and at himself, and he knew it was time to return to the FBI office. He engaged the turn indicator and slowed for the approaching exit.

There was one more thing to do before he yielded his afternoon privacy. It wouldn't take long. It might even help put things into perspective.

Jack drove to a parking area along the Arkansas River. He pulled into the lot and stopped next to a van with Missouri plates and a "Two Show-me's from St. Louis" sticker on the bumper. He opened the car door. His legs felt heavy, as if they resisted his attempt to duplicate the moment.

He and Laura had come here together uncounted times, mostly during the late spring when a half-hour walk would renew their feelings of belonging to nature and to each other. He felt he had to try again. There was an elderly couple ahead. Probably the people from Missouri, he thought. He started toward a path that paralleled the river. After a few seconds, he stopped and stared.

Laura preferred the early evenings so they could watch the retreat of the sun. Walking hand in hand, they would listen to the birds in the dusk and be awed while, as Laura had once characterized it, "the Master's brush strokes created a living painting" on the deepening western sky. The river usually reflected the colors in the heavens and in their hearts. Today it was an impersonal slate gray, and the cold, raw afternoon simply yielded to the night. And there was no one beside him to clasp his hand.

Jack returned to his car. The journey in memory had accomplished at least one thing: He'd thought of someone he needed to see.

Jack had arrived at the FBI office shortly before six the previous evening. The atmosphere was frenetic. As he slipped past agents, he figured the level of activity had probably tripled in the short time he'd been gone. There must have been forty men and women moving purposefully between telephones, fax machines, and conferences with each other. From snippets of overheard conversations, he knew the ties with Washington were now on a dozen levels. This office had suddenly become the focus of national attention.

"Thank God for martial law," came a familiar voice. It belonged to Don Evans. "Jack, our request to the White House at noon produced a direct call to Southwestern Bell for the immediate installation of forty new telephone lines. The crews were here by one, and ... " The agent pointed at an array of new consoles. "Voilà."

Jack followed Evans into his office.

Evans pointed to a document on his desk. "Take a look at that." He dropped into his chair. "Were you ever on target about the possibility of explosives."

Jack sat down and picked up the copy of the infrared photograph. Red plastic dots had been applied to the picture at the ends of the five corridors.

"All of them positive," Evans added. "Our original plan, of course, was for seven German shepherds to snoop around, but with your concern after talking with Follett, we radioed and held back six."

Evans scooted closer to the desk.

"Here's how it went. The dog and his Tulsa police handler arrived at the site around one this afternoon. In accordance with our revised plan, two vans we borrowed from Oklahoma Natural Gas exited a mile north of the usual access to that property. The first one was driven by the dog's handler, the second by another officer. They drove eight miles west, then nearly the mile south to be close to the northwest corner of the property."

He sat back in his chair.

"That's where the handler stopped and got out. He was dressed in an ONG uniform, just in case someone noticed his arrival, and he jogged into position about fifty yards to the north of the property. We decided he couldn't be seen by anyone from the south, at least not from ground level, because of a slight rise in the land adjacent to the road. The other van continued south."

Jack had originally supported having seven dogs released on the property. The initial thinking was, let them roam around ... they'd find the locations quickly if something was there. However, upon reflection, he realized that seven would be conspicuous. A pack of wandering German shepherds was definitely out of the ordinary in Beggs, Oklahoma. But a lone ONG man checking the area for gas leaks and encountering a friendly dog? Jack saw no major problem with that.

"OK," Evans went on, "the dog was taken to the south side of the property, where he could pick up the scent of his handler from the north wind. Our man entered from the north, about fifty yards to the east of where the explosives eventually registered. He continued walking south until he was about a hundred yards north of where his dog was being held in the van."

Jack laid the photograph on the desk.

"The dog was released . . . " Evans poked at a spot, "about there, and he ran for the handler, looking like a playful country animal." Evans traced his finger across the paper. "The man turned around and moved north, in the direction of the southernmost deposit, acting like he was writing something on one of his reports. The dog ran ahead, then stopped suddenly. He sniffed and sat down and looked at his handler. The man pretended to ignore the animal. The dog bounded forward again, only to repeat the scene a few hundred feet further north."

Evans grinned.

"What the guy was doing was marking and collecting a string he had fed out from the north edge of the property. The pooch stopped, the man marked, then it'd be repeated. Once they reached the northernmost corridor, the man retrieved the remaining string. Low-tech stuff, but it worked. The tunnels, according to the NSA photograph, appear to be about 440 feet apart. Sure enough, once we checked the marks on the string, we found that the dog had found something big almost exactly every 440 feet."

"Big?" Jack leaned forward and fixed his gaze on the marked areas of the picture.

"Yep. Those dogs can pick up the scent of explosives as insignificant as one part per *trillion*. The officer said his dog was nearly overwhelmed twice. He sniffed so much of something that he acted, uh, woozy. You know . . . . "

Corley Brand walked in. "Drunk as a skunk."

Jack kept looking at the picture. "So we hit the jackpot, then."

The FBI's counterterrorism chief seized the arm of a chair along the wall and brought the seat alongside.

"Looks that way," he observed. "Twenty feet down, through frozen soil, and the stuff still gave off a scent. Must be a hell of a storage area. Or five of them, to be exact."

Jack turned to his friend. "Is anyone watching Voronov?"

Brand frowned. "No.

"Well, he's gone. I stopped by his place this afternoon, and the outside looks like he took off after you talked with him. He hasn't picked up his newspapers since Monday."

"He said he told us everything Reuben told him. The foreign deposits, the strange men working for someone within the ministry, and the place south of town. You think we missed something? Maybe we didn't ask a key question?"

Jack shook his head. "I'd just like to know if he'd scheduled a trip and forgot to mention it. Maybe he told someone at the school."

Brand nodded. "OK, I'll have it checked out. It does seem strange he'd leave without telling us."

"How about Lester Graham?"

"Protection?" Brand gave a thumbs-up. "Tulsa police. Starting this morning."

Jack picked up the photograph and studied it.

"You have a name for the assault yet?"

"Operation something-or-other. We're open to suggestions."

"Well, I've got one." Jack pointed at the picture. "There's a little river that runs through that area. More like a creek, really. Called Deep Fork."

"That's what the place looks like, all right, a deep fork." Brand grinned. "Consider it done . . . Operation Deep Fork."

Jack knew he needed to sleep, but he'd not felt tired all evening, especially after the energetic discussion with Tex Follett and his seven team members who'd arrived at eight.

The thoughts kept returning. Jack remembered that when he came back to Tulsa on the twenty-eighth Norman had said that Reuben's death was a real blow to the ministry. He sat up in bed.

His own *father!* A real blow to the *ministry?* That little son of a bitch. The memory made him furious again.

And why the helicopter? Who the hell was getting away? He lay back against the pillow and stared into the darkness. Two women? One shorter than the other? Was the farmer sure of that? Jack was more troubled than ever.

The White House
3:55 a.m.

Ray Shaffer reached for the last of his coffee.

"I don't like any of the signs."

The chief of the Secret Service's White House detail sat back in his leather chair and drew in a mouthful of the tepid liquid. He looked around the small command post of the Presidential Protective Division, which was hidden beneath the Oval Office in the West Wing.

"If the FBI can't get a better handle on Kuttab and his wandering band of assassins before the inauguration, I won't take the chance. Reminds me of their incompetence in Dallas in 1963."

"Cancel the public ceremony?" Tim Vance raised his eyebrows. "You know the president wouldn't go for that. Especially not after declaring martial law." The agent shook his head. "He can't be perceived as cowering from terrorists now. It'd be a political disaster."

"That's not my concern."

Rick Hayes rubbed his hands together and looked at his boss.

"What's Davidson's temperature on this?"

Shaffer laid down his mug. "The director doesn't like it either, but he's got more faith in our FBI brothers than I do." He found a Lifesaver and tossed it into his mouth. "I can't figure why they chose to wait a day before telling us about the helicopter." He stared into space for a second. "Unless that retread civilian of theirs, Jack Stroud, has them so fixated on the bunker down there that they don't care. Something tells me our boy was on that chopper, and he's heading this way."

Shaffer stood up.

"Davidson notified all of our offices to be looking for Kuttab, but if I'm right, we're going to be the ones to find him."

FBI Office, Tulsa
4:00 a.m.

Brand was back less than five hours after he'd left for his hotel. The government facility looked as busy as it had before midnight. "Gotta start using one of our cots up here," he spoke to no one in particular as he popped open his briefcase in the spare office he had commandeered. "Waste of taxpayers' money to keep an empty hotel room in my name." Brand checked his watch. The main meeting was scheduled for eight. He'd let Tex Follett run the show.

Follett and his seven Hostage Rescue Team members had brought with them specially shaped explosive charges that would be employed to breach the underground facility at Beggs on Friday morning. The main challenge, as Brand saw it, was to coordinate the entire effort with the special Tactical Team of the Oklahoma Highway Patrol. "So little time." He sniffed the air. Someone had started a new pot of coffee. He sat down to wait. It was good to see Follett merge into this operation. That man had fought to establish a premier attack unit, and he deserved an opportunity to strut his stuff.

Since 1970 there had been over 13,000 acts of terrorism committed around the world—more than ninety-nine percent of them outside the United States. The 1972 massacre of the Olympic athletes in Munich was a seminal event in the development of quick response teams. Israel and West Germany had taken the lead. At the time, America didn't see terrorism as a major threat, so initially there was little interest in putting together a highly trained unit. Follett was a member of the FBI's early entry into the field, and he was frustrated when the Bureau disbanded the group shortly after it was formed. He knew that to be effective, the unit could not be a part-time, Minuteman-type organization. His lobbying started paying off in early 1989, when he was given the green light to study the utility of a full-time professional unit. The official reason noted was the general need to prepare for any terrorist acts in America that might result from the growing restlessness in the Middle East. Without question, however, the downing of Pan Am 103 in December 1988 was the catalyst for the FBI's newly found interest. The Bureau finally "got religion" when terrorists detonated explosives inside the World Trade Center garage. After Waco, Follett's team was finally accorded full-time status.

"Coffee ready yet?" Jack walked in and yawned.

Beggs, Oklahoma
4:53 a.m.

Because of the intense cold, the FBI sentries rotated their shifts every four hours. Even though they were protected by arctic hats, gloves, and layers of clothing, the climb back down at the end of their watch was a slow process because of ice and dangerously numbed limbs. But their work was too important to tamper with now.

The lookouts had been established at the large city water tower on Tuesday. Their primary duty was to observe the property day and night through binoculars or night-vision goggles from a height of two hundred feet and a distance of a thousand yards.

When the four-to-eight-a.m. sentry moved along the catwalk on his hands and knees in the cutting wind and took over, his predecessor reported no suspicious activity of any kind.

FBI Office, Tulsa
8:00 a.m.

At precisely eight o'clock, the door to the conference room was pushed shut at Corley Brand's nod, and the meeting began. It was standing room only. At the closed end of the tight cubicle waited Ron Oliver, the

FBI's special agent in charge for Oklahoma; Tex Follett, chief of the Bureau's Washington-based Hostage Rescue Team; and Brand. Tom Bentley, the supervisory senior resident agent of the Tulsa office, sat to the side. The seven other members of the FBI's national "super-SWAT" unit and ten men from the Oklahoma Highway Patrol's elite Tactical Team were positioned around the table. Along the walls stood five members of the Bureau of Alcohol, Tobacco, and Firearms and five local FBI agents. Jack Stroud stationed himself next to the door.

"I know we're crowded in here," Oliver began with a wave of his pencil, "but we don't have any choice. I can't vouch for the security of an alternate facility at this late date, and our effort must *not* be compromised."

The SAC continued. "As is usual for this type of operation, we'll set out both the strategy and the tactics. But initially, we're going to cover the background of the terrorist incursion and what we've found to date." He nodded toward his fellow speakers. "The meeting will be conducted jointly by Corley Brand and Tex Follett. We're calling the assault 'Operation Deep Fork.' " He then faced the man next to him.

"Corley?"

The chief of the FBI's Counterterrorism Section stepped forward.

"I'm going to do a short recap first. It's important for all of us to be up to speed, because what we're about to carry out is potentially the most significant security action ever undertaken in the history of the United States."

Brand waited a second for emphasis.

"If that place is what we think it is, we'll be breaching the well-defended command, training, and staging center—the very heart and soul—of the operation responsible for the string of criminal acts that have been unleashed across America during the past two weeks."

He moved to a large whiteboard and positioned it at an angle.

"Whoever masterminded the installation has probably given a lot of thought to the possibility of what we're planning to do to them."

He glanced around the room. "Mark my word, there'll be a lot of surprises waiting for us."

Brand wrenched the top from a blue marker and listed twelve terrorist incidents. "I've combined the killing of the two caterers at the Dallas–Fort Worth airport with the bombing of the SST." He didn't look at Jack. He then reviewed the probable chronology for the preparation and installation of the base and the terrorists' apparent ties with the Middle East and the KGB. He touched on the involvement of the ministry and Jack's personal interest in the resolution. He didn't mention the sexual encounter Jack had told him about.

"Everyone here knows it's the responsibility of the FBI to attempt to prevent acts of terrorism in the U.S., to investigate such acts if and when they do occur, and to indict, arrest, and convict those responsible." He faced his audience and tapped the marker in his hand. "These past two weeks have been a demonic whirlwind a hundred times what we've ever experienced before. We'd been fortunate in having a range of from ten to a maximum of forty secondary incidents per year, the worst being the bombings in New York and Oklahoma City." Everyone in the room watched him. He replaced the cap on the marker and secured it with a slam of his palm. "Let's make sure that tomorrow's action will put an end to this outrage."

Brand pointed at Follett.

"This man, as I think you all realize, is the best in the business. If you hadn't met him before, you did so this morning. If I know Tex, if you didn't introduce yourself to him, he sought you out. I'm pleased to present Tex Follett."

Five-feet-10, 160 pounds with salt-and-pepper hair, and a decade younger-looking than his forty-nine years, the HRT leader nodded toward Brand and grinned at the group. His own men and most of the others had heard him speak before and knew he was a no-nonsense taskmaster. Still, his facial expression looked disarming to the unsuspecting.

"I'm starting this operation with a smile," he spoke calmly, "and I'll maintain my smile throughout, because by the time we're finished down at Beggs you're probably going to be pissed off at me for something I've said or made you do, and the smile makes you realize that I really don't give a shit."

Two of the OHP men squirmed. One of the ATF agents cleared his throat.

"I'm a professional," Follett continued in his measured canter, "and all I care about is accomplishing the mission without having someone on my team get his ass shot off." He looked around the room in a smooth left-to-right motion and made eye contact with each man.

"Later, I may chew his ass off *myself,* but that's my privilege."

There were no more sounds from his audience.

Jack remembered the pecking order problems this FBI team used to have in terrorist and hostage matters before Follett assumed control. There were constant turf battles when various governmental groups fought for the responsibility, not to mention the credit, of handling headline-producing incidents. Such squabbles simply came with the territory, someone once said. After Waco, however, it only took one minor incident in Montana for the word to spread far and wide. Follett had personally tossed a local policeman into a trash bin when the officer blocked the way and insisted that a violent tax protester be transported to jail in his patrol car. The fact that the policeman had blatantly notified the media of his estimated time of arrival hadn't helped matters. Follett made it known afterward that as long as he was involved and could draw a breath, jurisdictional disputes would not be tolerated.

In less than a year from the time he was given the final green light by the director, Follett had implemented a streamlined command structure, an intensive training program, and the tightest personnel-selection process in the government. Additionally, he had acquired the finest weapons and equipment, and he had established ties and coordination with the appropriate intelligence and research organizations. Today his unit had the reputation of being one of the best in the world, ranking equally with, or even above, the British Special Air Service and the German Grenzschutzgruppe 9.

"We're a 120-man commando unit that has had intensive training in close-quarters battle, rappelling, assault tactics, entry techniques, hand-to-hand combat, negotiations and terrorist psychology, communications, the use of high-tech surveillance equipment, sniping and countersniping. We have skilled operatives, from pilots to scuba divers, and our people know high-speed and specialized driving, parachuting, mountaineering, field medicine, airborne and small-boat insertions, combat marksmanship, and demolitions."

He started to pace, and he pulled an imaginary trigger with his left index finger.

"We stress weak-handed shooting, malfunction clearance drills, tactical reloads, use of cover, firing under assault conditions, precise shot placement in hostage scenarios, and firing from vehicles and helicopters and while rappelling. In our so-called 'Killing House' at Quantico, we even employ FBI instructors as 'hostages' in live-fire scenarios."

He faced his audience.

"We're the best at what we do. And those of you with the OHP and the ATF know why I'm recounting all this." He paused. "You've had the exact same basic training at Quantico that we've had. That's why you're here. Together, we constitute the finest team ever assembled to do a job." He smiled broadly. "Now, gentlemen, let's get on with the planning."

Jack shook his head in admiration. He could almost touch the emotional bonding that had just taken place.

Follett moved ahead.

"In essence, Operation Deep Fork will be a three-part strike. We'll breach the bunker and corridors—first, to neutralize the terrorists; second, to prevent the detonation of explosives; and, third, to rescue any hostages.

The FBI will enter the bunker area, the OHP will access the corridors, and the ATF will secure the explosives once the rest of us have done our jobs."

He stopped and rubbed his hands together.

"As you know, in any such assault, the operator wants to gain intelligence about his objective, gain access to the objective, carry out the assault, attack the terrorists, and protect himself during the assault."

Follett reached for a poster that had been turned to the wall. He swung it around and positioned it against the whiteboard.

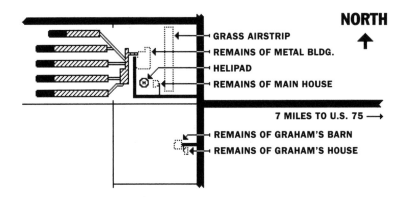

"We prepared this sketch from the infrared photograph taken by the Air Force satellite yesterday and recent aerials acquired by lower-flying aircraft. Generally speaking, in planning an assault like this, we want to carry out a personal, on-site reconnaissance of the area, checking the terrain for natural and man-made obstacles. Yet we don't want to risk exposure by alerting anyone who might be observing us from the bunker. We've already plotted the underground location of the explosives with the dog. The main question now is: Can we carry out a clandestine approach? We think so, but we must assume that whoever's there has fiber-optic equipment and is probably capable of excellent line-of-sight acquisition of any trespassers. Maybe even from a foot or more above the surface."

"Tex, I've got a problem."

Everyone turned toward Jack's voice.

"Or do you want me to wait until you conclude?"

"No, I want you or anybody else to stop me immediately if you see or hear something that doesn't seem right."

"OK. I met on Tuesday with Lester Graham, the farmer who escaped from that place. He said that from two summers ago to the present, numerous vehicles have entered and left the property. Starting after Thanksgiving, last year, there were buses. Forty-five-foot 'road cruisers.' Army-drab brown with smoked windows. Five at a time, and they stayed for a few days each visit. Then they left after midnight. But they were back in a week. The cycle was repeated at least a dozen times over seven weeks. That's at least sixty bus trips. It's obvious they were bringing something in or taking something out. Or both. Maybe they were bringing in people and equipment, and maybe they were hauling out dirt from an excavation. But look at the IR picture and your sketch. Those so-called corridors look relatively wide. Maybe thirty feet. By my count, there weren't enough buses to haul off that much dirt. So those couldn't be large-diameter holes or passageways."

Follett squinted at the sketch.

"But what sense does a flat excavation make? What about the rest of the place, the bunker to the east?"

"My best guess," Jack pursued, "is that the real stand-up depth is to the east. The fingerlike corridors are wide, all right, but they're not as deep. Those storage rooms at the ends are probably being kept cooler for safety's sake. But why keep the tunnels at virtually the same temperature as the bunker space? Doesn't make much sense unless you conclude that people are moving back and forth." He crossed his arms. "There's no way to tell from the IR photo, but I'd figure those might be crawl spaces between the main facility to the east and the tips where the explosives are. If they are, that'll make a big difference when you guys breach the corridors."

"Good analysis," Follett nodded. "I agree." He pointed at the FBI sketch. "OK, let's be sure of the places we're talking about. The 'bunker' is this main area we're targeting for terrorists and probably hostages, then these are the five 'corridors' that extend toward the west, and, finally, at the end are the 'tips,' which are the storage rooms for the explosives."

Oliver spoke. "We don't have any proof that there *are* hostages down there, but we're going on the assumption that there are. Maybe agent Charlie Carmichael, maybe the missing pilot from the aviation school, maybe others. If they're there, we don't know where they're being held, although we can suppose they're in the bunker."

"How much ground cover is down there, Tex?" one of the highway-patrol troopers asked with a raised hand. "From my own experience, I don't know of any berms or large trees in that particular area."

"Right. It'll mostly be the darkness we'll have to contend with on the surface," Follett responded. "But let me give you my own list of questions, to give you an idea of the points we have to consider. It's not complete, by any means. I want to paint with a broad brush right now. Then we can go over everything in detail and put together the most effective way of assaulting that place."

He started reading, and most of the men made notations on pads of paper.

"How many terrorists are there? Where is their 'command and control'? How is the bunker defended?" Follett looked around the room. "Is it wired with explosives or otherwise booby-trapped? Are there any pipelines under the property or other potential impediments to a breach with explosives?"

As Follett continued, Jack again remembered the naked woman sitting astride his pelvis. He shook away the thought and wondered for the thousandth time if Rachel had been that "shorter woman" who had been taken away by helicopter. He wouldn't allow himself to imagine the horrors his daughter might have endured.

The Westin St. Francis, San Francisco
Noon

The morning sessions in the elegant ballrooms of the Westin St. Francis and the Hyatt on Union Square ended at the same time, as if by a master cue. So smoothly had the Pacific Rim Summit coursed from its formal opening that Mayor Vincent Nomura had turned feisty and had begun to chide members of the Secret Service. His Honor had been incensed about the threat by director Stan Davidson to close down the entire affair if certain negatives cropped up.

"Where are those big, bad terrorists?" the mayor taunted one agent as dignitaries filed out of the Golden Gate Room for their three-course luncheon and a leisurely afternoon tour of the city before their return for a formal dinner and the address by the president.

"Shouldn't we watch out for UFOs, too?" Nomura called out as the agent moved ahead with the entourage. "Whoo, 'X-Files'!" When the Secret Service man didn't respond, Nomura grinned and turned toward his guests.

"Have a wonderful luncheon, madame," he urged a stately Asian woman. He rocked back and forth on his polished Ballys and beamed. "I know you'll be as enraptured by our city as we are." Nomura wiped his brow and wondered if San Francisco would really be spared the national madness.

Tulsa
2:37 p.m.

Brand kept the earpiece pressed in place while he swung the telephone handset up.

"They're still checking."

Jack glanced at his watch. The question had hit him like a bombshell. He'd signaled Brand, and they'd left the meeting.

"The buses, Corley!" he'd exclaimed the instant the door was closed. "The ones Lester Graham reported."

"So?"

"Remember the old joke about the guard at the factory who's supposed to be on the lookout for employees stealing things when they leave at night? Well, one suspicious-looking guy lines up at quitting time pushing a wheelbarrow with a load of straw in it. The guard pokes around the straw, finds nothing, and lets the guy go. This happens week after week. Years later, the guard, long since retired, sees the guy and stops him. 'Hey, remember me? I used to check you every day when you left the plant. I knew you were stealing something, but I was never able to catch you. You can tell me now. What was it?' The guy replies, 'Wheelbarrows.' "

Brand jerked his head back. "Of course! Where in the shit *are* those buses?"

"Graham said he saw a few leave the night he got away. They could be anywhere."

Brand ran to Bentley's desk, picked up the telephone, and punched the button for the new direct line to deputy director Jerry Reynolds in Washington. There was a pause.

"Jerry, we need to find anywhere from five to sixty buses—big ones, forty-five feet, smoked windows—the ones that came in and out of the Beggs property." Brand made a face, then shook his head. "Don't know the make, but they're probably all brown. I think you should alert Seattle, where the ministry was going to hold its big shindig on Sunday. I don't know what they were planning up there, but I'll wager it was trouble." He nodded. "Yeah, the D.C. area, too. And see if anything's turned up on NCIC. Someone might have noticed something out of the ordinary and reported it. Oh, and Jerry . . . better tell our friends with the Secret Service about this. Thanks. Yeah, I'll hold."

Jack walked to the window and stared into space.

"I wonder if those people on the helicopter rendezvoused with one of the buses."

"What?"

Jack started to repeat his observation, but Brand was back with Reynolds.

"Are you shitting me?" Brand rolled his eyes and took a deep breath. "Unbelievable! Well, this could be it, Jerry. And they got away?" He made a thumbs-up gesture to Jack, then flipped it over to a thumbs-down. "Alert the Secret Service right away. If those buses are en route to San Francisco, that could have been the plan all along. I understand the president's supposed to speak there tonight. 'Sever the head'? By something dramatic like buses full of explosives? Kuttab's style, all right." Brand held on for another fifteen seconds. His head bobbed twice. "OK, will do. Keep us advised." He hung up and whistled.

"Get this. Less than an hour ago, the California Highway Patrol stopped a bus for speeding. It was traveling behind two others, and all three fit the description of the ones that left here. Anyway, the patrolman pulled it over forty-five miles northeast of San Francisco. All three were heading south. When the patrolman got out of his car, someone fired a shot from the driver's side of the bus. The bullet grazed him in the neck, but he was able to get back to his car and report the incident. Plus the license number *. . . an Oklahoma tag, no less!*"

He whistled again.

"We would never have heard about it except for martial law. Seems the patrolman is a pilot in the reserve, stationed at Travis Air Force Base. They've set up a network to monitor suspicious activities near the field. They thought this shooting qualified, so they called us." Brand moved over and slapped Jack on the shoulder. "You just may have had the best hunch of your life."

Jack shook his head. "I don't know, Corley. If this was to be the big one, using buses, what the hell were they doing with a flight simulator?"

San Francisco
3:55 p.m.

The Secret Service command center at the Westin St. Francis broadcast the UHF message at 3:50 p.m., and all teams acknowledged in less than fifteen seconds. Within two minutes, 653 touring dignitaries were instructed to assemble next to their waiting vans and buses. Most of the visitors were aboard the vehicles and ready to return to the hotels nine minutes after being notified of the change in plans. However, one group, 194 VIP guests in all, still waited in the reception area of a small bakery. A muscular man dressed in jeans and a golf shirt blocked the exit and argued with a Secret Service agent.

"Look," he yelled, "we changed all of our schedules to accommodate you people after some asshole pressured us this morning after the fire across the street." Then he pointed toward the back of the building. "Do you know how long it takes to cool down that stainless steel oven from six hundred degrees to make it available?"

The agent remained expressionless. The man went on.

"And how much money do you think we're going to lose because of your goddamn decision? We won't even get the advertising effect of the publicity."

"I'm sorry, sir, but I have my orders. These people are to be returned to their hotels immediately."

The man ran his palm across his forehead and flicked the sweat toward the floor.

"You try to do something nice for the city, and this is what you get. You know something, you really piss me off."

The Secret Service man leaned forward. "Sir, please don't misunderstand me. If you don't step aside, I will arrest you."

The red-faced man breathed heavily and glared at the agent. Finally he backed away.

FBI Office, Tulsa
7:00 p.m.

Jack stood at the office window and talked to Jerry Reynolds on Tom Bentley's desk telephone. Brand was on the same line at the table unit against the wall.

Jack winced.

"How could it just *disappear?* I thought you told Corley the patrolman reported the shooting almost immediately. Surely someone picked up the chase."

"He reported it almost immediately, from his car," Reynolds confirmed, "and other units entered the highway at the next two interchanges, but they came up empty-handed. Damn bus just vanished. Oh, and get this, the tag number was a phony."

"The Oklahoma plate?" Brand asked.

"Yeah."

"Well, what sense does *that* make?" Brand looked to the ceiling. "If you want to be as inconspicuous as possible, you try to fit in by displaying the appropriate plates. If they were going to use phony plates, Jerry, why not phony California plates?"

"You figure it out, but because of it all, the Secret Service nixed the president's address tonight at that big conference out there."

Brand frowned. "Is the president already in San Francisco?"

"No, I think he's supposed to arrive from Washington in about an hour."

"So he's still going to be staying somewhere in the city this evening?"

"Think so, Corley. Probably where he was originally scheduled, the Westin St. Francis."

"Well, he's in danger as long as those three buses are on the loose." Brand's voice was on edge.

"Jerry, look at it this way: The only way phony Oklahoma license plates on those buses make any sense is if there was a change of plans where those plates would have fitted in, and there wasn't enough time to make new ones. Those buses would have been perfect at the ministry's grand finale in Seattle on Sunday, but now that's been canceled, and three of them are spotted heading south toward San Francisco, where the president just happens to be scheduled to speak. It's his first public appearance after his declaration of martial law, and what a hell of a greeting someone might be arranging."

"Corley, I'll pass this along to the Service. In the meantime, good luck. I'll talk with you before you leave for the staging area."

"Right," Brand replied as he hung up. He flinched when he saw Jack's expression.

"OK, now what?"

"Corley, they've had more than enough time to make new license plates, if they'd wanted to. They probably even had a complete set for all fifty states before they left here. A speeding bus? A gunshot?" Jack shook his head. "No, I think the phony Oklahoma plates were *intended* to be noticed." He looked directly at his friend. "This whole thing is like a hideous game someone's playing with us. Mocking clues and all."

37

Okmulgee Airport, Oklahoma
Friday, January 15, 12:41 a.m.

"That's the place!" Corley Brand pointed.

The white Phillips Petroleum pickup slowed in the cold stillness of the early morning, swung left across the empty northbound lanes of U.S. 75, and bounded onto the deserted expanse of the Okmulgee municipal airport, thirty-one miles due south of Tulsa. The small Chevy truck followed the bumpy, sparsely lighted two-lane access road to a green sign that spelled out its message in reflective white letters: "Welcome to OKM. Elevation—714."

Directly ahead stood a two-room terminal building where, during many of the endlessly humid summer days, curious locals waited and watched and waved greetings to the occasional private planes that taxied in to drop off a passenger or to take on fuel. Tonight the terminal was dark. Inside the wood-on-stone structure, six deputies from the Okmulgee County sheriff's department sat and peered into the blackness. The white pickup was the final vehicle they expected from Tulsa.

To the left of the metal sign lay a thin asphalt ribbon leading to four hulking hangars, which housed the dozen or so planes flown by prominent residents of the county. The pickup swerved in that direction and accelerated. Every few seconds, like a forlorn wanderer, light from the airport's rotating beacon crossed the road ahead in alternating swaths of green and white.

"Past the line of trees," Brand directed in a low voice from the passenger side of the cab. He pointed as the curved-roof buildings loomed into view. "Third one."

"I've got it," Jack Stroud returned.

Seconds later, the truck bounced onto an unlighted gravel parking area and slowed for a wooden sawhorse placed near the front door of a large metal building.

"Whoa!" Jack stepped hard on the brake to avoid knocking over the obstacle. They skidded to a stop. He pushed off the lights and looked around.

"Great place for a mobile command post. Certainly looks abandoned, and if I didn't know better ... " He wasn't able to complete the sentence.

"You're to park inside," came a gruff voice close by.

Jack turned and saw eyes staring at him through the glass of the driver's-side window. He nodded.

"OK. Where to?"

"To your left, a hundred feet or so. Then a right turn. They're waiting for you at a sliding door on the side of the hangar."

"We're on our way."

Jack seized the gearshift handle. The man outside was already gone. The sawhorse, too.

The pickup jerked forward, then slowed for the turn into a narrow passageway between two hangars. Fifty yards ahead, at hood level, a tiny red light flashed on and off erratically. Jack squinted and brought the vehicle to a stop when he made out a man's hand, palm open and facing him, forming a halt sign. A crack of light appeared from the side of the building as a floor-to-ceiling door was rolled back. When the opening had grown to ten feet, the man with the small red light waved Jack inside. Another man with a penlight approached from within the building and motioned toward a line of cars fifty feet ahead. As Jack aimed for a slot, he noticed that none of the automobiles carried government or law enforcement markings or license plates. A twenty-foot-high gray backdrop curtain ringed the perimeter of the parking area, preventing unauthorized eyes from seeing beyond. Jack braked and cut the engine. He and Brand stepped out.

The temperature of the cavernous hangar remained chilly in spite of the bright glow of a dozen radiant heaters mounted in the overhead rafters. Woven into the musty smell of the old building Jack detected the additional and unlikely combination of fresh coffee and cordite. He wrinkled his nose at the odd mixture. Almost immediately, he became aware of the sounds of movement. There were soft shuffles and scrapes and dragging noises, in all quadrants.

"I want you to see these sumbitches before we load them."

Tex Follett stepped through an opening in the curtain and pointed over his shoulder.

"They got here an hour ago and impressed the shit out of everyone."

The leader of the FBI's HRT team wore a one-piece black Nomex suit, and he held an anti-flash balaclava hood and a ballistic vest under his arm.

"Is everyone here?" Jack asked. He and Brand walked toward Follett, who nodded and pulled the curtain back.

"Yeah, and the place is secure out to the airport's perimeter fence.

Thanks to our friends at the local sheriff's department."

As Jack stepped beyond the curtain, he saw that the entire concrete floor of the large hangar was covered with pieces of equipment, which some fifty men were moving about or putting together. Most wore black assault outfits. Follett moved past his new arrivals and led the way.

"Over here."

The FBI man circled his arm in the direction of a sectioned-off area. "These augers are specially designed breaching units from the U.S. Army's ammunition depot down at McAlester. They'd been built for Persian Gulf action but were never needed." He looked over his shoulder at Jack and Brand. "But they're absolutely perfect for our operation. We were lucky to get eighteen of them."

The three men stopped at a row of wooden boxes that had been unloaded from a nearby truck. The thick tops had been pried open. Follett put his combat boot on the edge of a container and reached down.

"In essence, this is just a simple drilling device." He lifted up a ten-foot-long solid steel pole with a sharp, spiral-shaped bit at the end and steadied it with both hands. "But there's real beauty in the way it works."

Follett turned the pole upright, positioning the bit on the floor.

"Officially, they call this mother a 'boring lance,' and it's mounted in that tripod power unit over there. It's a one-time-use, solid-fuel system. The whole thing is placed over the target on its three legs and fired. Pow! . . . you've got yourself a ten-foot hole, twelve inches in diameter, in less than ten seconds." He grinned. "The ordnance boys at McAlester nicknamed this baby a 'screamin' reamer.' "

Follett righted the metal object and held it out to Jack. As he did so, he added with a wink, "What else would *you* call zero to 5,000 r.p.m. in about a second?"

Jack rested the pole across his open palms and figured the single-piece unit weighed at least forty pounds. As Follett kept talking, Jack squatted and placed the drilling pole back in its shipping box. He considered the possibility that Rachel might be imprisoned directly beneath one of the holes. He slammed the door on the thought. No, he had to get to her, and these boring lances were the quickest way. He had to focus on getting in first, then on finding her. He couldn't let worry blunt his goal.

"Yep, eighteen of them," the FBI man went on. "Of course, we'll only need nine for our entries, but I've always believed in hundred-percent redundancy."

Follett motioned in the direction of another segregated area on the hangar floor.

"Now, gentlemen, I want to show you the shaped charges we brought with us from Washington. The augers are impressive, all right, but these other babies gave the highway-patrol boys a hard-on."

J. Edgar Hoover Building, Washington, D.C.
1:52 a.m.

Jerry Reynolds stood behind Lewis Bittker and looked over the shorter man's shoulder. The chief of the Strategic Information Operations Center held down two lighted plastic buttons on the main control console and raised his head. He pointed with his free hand.

"I'm putting San Francisco on the first monitor."

Thirty-five feet away and slightly above eye level in the front of the large room, an oversize video screen flashed on. It displayed the FBI shield in color, then a black-and-white panel with the identifier, "SF— 01/14–01/15."

"Good," Bittker exclaimed and released the transfer buttons. "This is it." He checked the monitor selector switch and pressed his thumb against the "start" bar. "There's about a half a minute of leader tape first." He motioned toward a rack of headsets mounted on the side of the console.

"Would you get a couple of those, Jerry? We can listen in right here."

Reynolds lifted two of the lightweight sets and handed one over. Both men put on the devices and plugged the jacks into outlets on the console.

The SIOC chief looked at Reynolds. "Still hear me?"

The deputy director nodded.

"OK, sometimes the background static from the tape machine gets to be too much." He crossed his arms and watched as the screen went blank. "It's in two parts. The first is a shot of the buses where they found them yesterday afternoon."

When the picture flashed on, the scene, in color, was of the side of one of the buses, from about fifteen feet away. The brown vehicle had smoked windows. A hand-held camera started a circuit of the bus, toward the front. The audio snapped on, and a man's voice announced, "The three abandoned buses were discovered by a Travis Air Force Base helicopter that participated in the search after the highway patrolman's report. They had been driven to the back of an RV park north of Vallejo. Initial inspection revealed . . . "

Bittker turned down the volume. "That's all the hard news about the buses." He pointed to the screen. "Except this." The tape jumped to a shot of a rear license plate, an Oklahoma tag. "Same phony one on all three, Jerry. That farmer in Tulsa told Brand last night this bus looked just like the ones he saw leaving."

Reynolds frowned. "All three buses had the same license tag number? A *fake* number?"

"Right. Not something we see every day, is it?"

Reynolds kept staring. "What about the drivers?"

"That's another interesting part," Bittker replied and stopped the tape. "An attendant at a nearby Chevron station saw a beige van pull in behind the buses. It picked up the drivers and took off. The guy said it didn't stop for longer than ten seconds. Went south, back on the interstate. Then ... "

Reynolds interrupted. "I know Brand figured we should look around Seattle, but today's the day the ministry's San Francisco meeting was to have been held. Were those buses a part of that?"

"No telling," Bittker answered, "but they're obviously not now. And why were they coming down from the north when the main entourage of the ministry was supposed to be arriving from Los Angeles? Seattle, maybe? Who knows?"

Bittker started the tape again. "We may have a piece of the puzzle after all." He twisted the volume level. "Check this out."

The new picture was of a red brick building trimmed in black wrought iron. The camera panned to the right, revealing a burned-out structure across the street, and the sound came on.

"The Sourdough from SFO bakery, a San Francisco landmark for fifty years, was completely destroyed early Thursday morning by a fire of suspicious origin. The site was to have been a tour stop yesterday for a group of visitors to the Pacific Rim Summit. An adjacent bakery was asked to serve as its replacement. However, because of the peculiar facts surrounding the shooting of the highway patrolman near San Francisco, the Secret Service canceled all afternoon tours for the foreign dignitaries, but not before nearly two hundred of them had filed inside the second bakery. An argument ensued between the manager of the facility and a Secret Service agent when the agent attempted to escort the visitors back to their buses. The manager appeared extremely upset that the tour had been canceled, and he tried to block the exit. As a result of his action, the Service decided to put the place under temporary observation. At 4:40 yesterday afternoon, a beige 1994 Toyota van stopped alongside the second bakery on the Mason Street side. There were four men in the vehicle, including the driver. Not more than ten seconds later, a man emerged from the building and boarded the van, and it departed. The agent did not follow, but he did get the license number. According to the California Department of Motor Vehicles, the sequence of letters and numerals he reported has not yet been issued. The man who got into the van at the bakery fitted the description of the manager who had argued with the agent earlier."

Reynolds shook his head as the tape ended and the screen went blank. He removed his headset and waited until Bittker engaged the rewind function.

"So what do you make of all this?"

Bittker flipped off the monitor and pulled his headset down. He looked at his watch and shrugged. "Well, a little more time will tell for sure, but I think we've pretty well screwed up some major plans, maybe even broken the demon's back."

He looked directly at Reynolds.

"Everything started unraveling when we raided the Tulsa ministry, and there haven't been any more terrorist attacks since then. We've seen those buses out of place in California, the scene at the bakery, and the other signs of disarray. Chaos, almost. Nah, I'd say we've definitely got them on the run now, Jerry." He smiled. "And if that bunker in Oklahoma is their command center, the next couple of hours should produce the coup de grace."

Okmulgee Airport
2:33 a.m.

Jack peered inside the empty cab of a Dodge Caravan that was nosed into a corner of the hangar. He checked the clock on the dashboard. Operation Deep Fork was scheduled to get under way with a phased departure for the Beggs site in exactly twenty-two minutes. Jack stepped back several feet and looked at the unmarked vehicle, which glinted in the overhead lighting. A similar van stood twenty feet away, and two more just like them waited together, facing another corner of the building. The rear doors of all four were open, and groups of men dressed in black continued to load equipment in virtual silence.

Old feelings surged back. This was how it always was at the Naval Investigative Service before every major action, he reflected. Especially when he worked jointly with the FBI. Everything moved quietly and efficiently ... just before all hell broke loose. He sensed the flood of adrenalin that flowed through him. He was keyed and ready.

Jack nodded at one of the agents who sat on a crate and fine-tuned the sight on his submachine gun. Jack recognized the 9x19mm Heckler & Koch MP5 assault weapon. The FBI carried the model SG now, a slightly improved version of the H&K SD3 he himself had wielded on a dozen occasions a decade or so ago. It still had a telescoping skeleton stock, a six-inch barrel, and, if he remembered correctly, a cyclic rate of 650 rounds per minute. The highly accurate weapon was less than twenty inches long, and it weighed just seven and a half pounds. Since it was sound-suppressed, with a laser aiming device that placed a red dot at the point where the bullets would strike without otherwise illuminating the target, one could actually take out a terrorist at a hundred yards without alerting a compatriot standing right next to him. Jack wondered how many opportunities this particular FBI man would have to do just that in the hours ahead.

Behind the agent, Jack noticed that other HRT team members were preparing assault weapons with compact second-generation image intensifiers and self-contained power sources. It still impressed him to know that every man on the mission today had achieved a consistent target accuracy with these high-tech aids of one inch at two hundred yards.

Jack walked over to take a final look at the tactical maps before they were rolled and stowed. He thought again about Brand's comprehensive review during the trip from Tulsa.

The eighteen assault-team members would be carrying an array of equipment this morning. There would be handguns for backup use in case their submachine guns malfunctioned. A handgun could even become a primary weapon if someone got into an intense, close-quarters shootout. The Oklahoma Highway Patrol packed the Browning Hi-Power, a 9mm single-action autoloader with a thirteen-round magazine. The FBI's secondary firearm for the past few years had been the Smith & Wesson Model 1076 10mm in a drop holster.

Jack knew the men brought two special types of ammunition. The first was the Glaser Safety Slug, a particularly deadly bullet filled with small #2 shot. It was designed to fragment immediately after penetration, making it extremely effective against the human body. One properly placed round would cause a man's head to explode into pieces no thicker than beef jerky. Follett had said he particularly liked the Glaser for today's assault because there was little danger from ricochet in the tight quarters anticipated. The second type of ammunition was the KTW armor-piercing round, a high-velocity bullet covered with Teflon. It made short shrift of most body armor. As Brand had pointed out, whether the men chose head shots or chest shots, they had the appropriate ammo for either.

Each man also brought with him, in sling-carry position, a Remington 870 short-barrel, 12-gauge slide-action shotgun with two special rounds: the Ferret, a barricade-penetrating charge, and the Shok-Lok, for blasting hinges and locks off doors. If those didn't work, the men also carried air-powered projectile launchers and battery-powered thermal cutting torches.

Then there were the stun grenades, special diversionary devices that produced a blinding flash and a loud explosion. Everyone called them "flash-bangs." The latest ones generated 3 million candlepower and three hundred decibels. They were designed to surprise and disorient, to allow the assault team quick access with the least resistance. The FBI and OHP teams had both single- and multiple-bang versions.

Tex Follett was the only one who carried a sensitive listening device and a sophisticated thermal unit to detect the sounds and heat differentials of anyone, terrorist or hostage, who might be hidden in a special protective facility.

Lastly, nine men, one at each entry point, carried bullhorns.

Jack stopped at the table and leaned over a map, considering once more the steps that would be taken to accomplish the lightning raid. The underground bunker was almost exactly fifteen miles to the northwest by the route the convoy would drive. There would be no advance team. He knew Follett had considered air-dropping listening devices onto the surface an hour before the assault, but continuing concern about possible fiber-optic monitoring at ground level changed his mind. The attack units would roll onto the property nonstop from this staging area. The value of surprise was paramount.

Jack looked around the hangar. The equipment had been marshaled, the vehicles readied. So as not to attract attention on the way, there would be three separate sections to the convoy: two vans, one behind the other, followed by two more vans a quarter-mile farther back, with a follow-up command and control car at the rear. Jack and Brand would ride in the car.

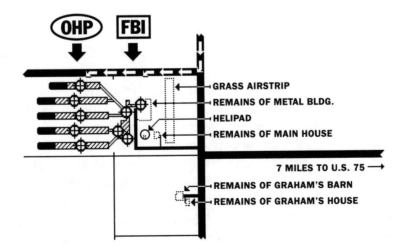

The first two vans would carry the men with the augers, five OHP troopers in one and four FBI agents in the other. They would enter the property at two predetermined points and would proceed south, slowing to drop a man with an auger at each of the prearranged penetration sites. Two more vans would follow, discharging another man at each site, five OHP men on the west side of the property and four FBI men on the east side. These men would carry the shaped charges. In all, there would be ten OHP and eight FBI men on the property for the attack. The follow-up car would not enter the property but would remain out of sight a quarter mile to the north.

The first teams would position and simultaneously fire the augers to open a ten-foot-deep vertical tunnel, and the second teams would drop and detonate the prefabricated charges, penetrating all five corridors and the central and eastern parts of the bunker. The OHP teams had been assigned the task of cutting off the terrorists' access to the store of explosives at the western ends of the corridors. The FBI men were to neutralize terrorists in the main bunker and rescue any hostages.

Jack remembered hearing that all outside surveillance would be conducted by FBI snipers and monitors in the car and on the nearby water tower. One of the communications men would align a man-portable satellite link for direct hookup with SIOC in Washington. A backup satellite link would be readied at the base of the water tower at 3:05 a.m. He wondered whether they'd find the pilot of the small plane and the kidnapped FBI agent. And Rachel.

"Not exactly a long-distance foray into hostile territory like Djibouti or Entebbe," Follett said as he came up from behind and put his hand on Jack's shoulder, "but I'll bet it won't be any easier. You ready?"

Jack turned and nodded. Both men walked to their vehicles.

"Don't worry, Professor Voronov. It won't be long now."

A woman's hand seized the blindfolded man by the hair and yanked his head backwards.

"You'll get to make your call. Assuming, of course, that he survives our little party out there."

U.S. Highway 50, Salem, Illinois
2:40 a.m.

One after the other, the two newly painted Road Cruisers pulled out of a darkened metal building and turned north on the old Centralia lake road. The forty-five-foot buses were seven miles from their right turn onto U.S. 50, near Salem, and an even fifteen hours from the steps of the U.S.

Capitol. In spite of their new air filters and special insulation, the acrid freshness of their paint jobs permeated the interior of both vehicles.

"Those fucking fumes better not last long," a woman yelled from a makeshift couch in the middle of the second bus. "It would be a cheap way for her to go."

She peered down at the gagged teenager strapped to a board. "With all the crap we've pumped into her veins, the little bitch is probably half dead already." She laughed. "But we can't let her miss the ride of her life." An elongated plastic bag containing liquid hung on a metal stand, and a clear tube extended down and underneath a bloody bandage covering the young woman's right hand.

"Shouldn't take more than an hour at highway speeds to dry everything," the driver called over his shoulder. "Until then, open the vents more. I'll crank up the heat."

At the intersection with U.S. 50, a clerk at the all-night Texaco held his hands over a yawn. He frowned as two buses pulled onto the main highway and accelerated toward the east. " 'D.C. or Bust: We're Disadvantaged Kids from Southern Illinois,' " the man read the side of the first bus as it passed.

"Never heard of *that* group," he mumbled and turned back to a small television set. "Probably from Centralia, going to the inauguration." He heard the diesel whine of the second bus. "What's the big deal about being there in person?" He chewed on a fingernail. "You can see so much more on TV anyway."

Beggs, Oklahoma
3:15 a.m.

Tex Follett's van maintained its separation of fifty feet from the lead vehicle, which carried five members of the Oklahoma Highway Patrol's tactical team. The OHP group had its own commander, a colonel, but, today Follett was the C.O. of the eighteen men on both units. He tapped at the illuminated clock on the dashboard.

"Twelve miles in sixteen minutes? Perfect."

The van kept the OHP vehicle within its headlights. Follett stepped over the hump in the floorboard and shifted to a squat facing his two associates in back.

"Remember, now, the targets have to be recognized and neutralized instantly. Exact shot placement, but keep your pop-up, friend-or-foe mentality. It's possible they'll dress any hostages in their own outfits. Might even give 'em a gun, for effect. Anyway, we'll have fifteen seconds from the activation of the augers until we're inside. They shouldn't have any more time than that to react."

"Three minutes," the driver noted.

The men in back said nothing, but Follett knew they were reviewing the planned tactics and their own particular assignments. For communications, the OHP men were to be called "Sooners," and the FBI team members were the "Cowboys," after the state's big college football teams. Even though all had laryngophones that connected everyone, Follett's voice was to be the only one transmitted as the mission unfolded.

Follett's and the OHP van ahead had separately programmed and GPS satellite-linked digital counters mounted on their dashboards, which the drivers would activate upon entry to the property. The OHP van's signal would beep every 440 feet as that van headed south across the expanse, and a man with a solid-fuel auger would immediately jump out and position it. The center locations of the underground corridors had been determined to be exactly 440 feet apart, the first one 440 feet from the northern property line and the last one 440 feet from the southern property line. The FBI's auger-positioning van would follow a different release pattern because of the particular arrangement of the bunker. Each auger would require a ten-second set-up time. Shortly before the first OHP and FBI vans made it to the south border of the property, the second OHP and FBI vans would enter the land and follow the same paths as their predecessors. Those vehicles, however, would deposit a man with a shaped charge at each site. Once all nine augers were in position with the shaped charges at the ready, Follett would give the command to activate the drilling, and the attack would be under way.

"Two minutes!"

The four FBI men donned fitted polycarbonate helmets with mounted night-vision infrared goggles and checked the UHF transmitters for their laryngophones. The press-to-test buttons produced green lights. They tapped their ballistic vests and recognized by rote a handgun, knife, flashlight, gas mask, and two stun grenades.

"Property line coming up," the driver called out.

Follett gave a thumbs-up to his men. "See you downstairs."

Their van turned right onto the east-west county road and slowed. Ahead, the OHP van pulled away and headed for its own entry point.

The FBI driver took a deep breath.

"Ten seconds."

One of the men in back depressed the handle and pushed open the rear doors. The night's frigid air and the sounds of the tires against the rutted pavement swirled inside with a roar. The man fitted staybars into place over both hinges to keep the doors from swinging shut.

The FBI van swerved to the left and slammed across a wide depression in the frozen soil. It wrenched and shook before bounding onward. The driver reached over and steadied the distance counter on the dashboard.

"Stand by, Cowboys One and Two."

An agent seized one of the bulky augers and placed the heel of his boot on the rear bumper. A second man held on to the overhead safety straps in readiness for his own release.

"Cowboy One, at my mark."

The van rocked from side to side and abruptly slowed to five miles per hour.

"Mark!"

The first man's foot hit the ground less than a second afterward. He pulled the auger out of its sleeve as the van accelerated away into the night, and he dashed toward the east.

Almost immediately the driver yelled again.

"Cowboy Two . . . mark!"

The second man was gone into the cold darkness. He carried his burden toward the west. Follett grabbed the release bar on an auger and stood by at the open doors.

"Five seconds for Cowboy Three. Ready . . . mark!"

The HRT chief retrieved the portable drilling unit as he landed on the hard field and jogged a tenth of a mile to the west, perpendicular to the path of the southbound van. He counted as he went. It was 211 thirty-inch paces to his predetermined position 528 feet from the centerline of the van route. Once there, he immediately extended and secured the wide support legs of the auger and set the unit upright. By feel, with a sliding motion of his thumb across two switches, he activated the firing unit. As he did so, he saw that Cowboy Four, the driver of his van, had stopped not far away and took up his own position. Follett couldn't see them, but he knew that nearly a half mile farther west, the five OHP teams, the "Sooners," were doing the same thing. He looked toward the north and saw the parking lights of the second FBI van as it headed in his direction. Within seconds, another agent stepped out of the back of the passing vehicle with his own bulky object. The man ran for Follett's position. He stopped ten feet away and laid the bullet-shaped charge on the ground.

Follett activated the transmitter for his laryngophone, then pushed in the button on the side of his watch. He watched the countdown flash across the lighted face of his timepiece. At exactly twenty-one minutes past three in the morning, Follett spoke softly into the darkness.

"Kick ass!"

Within five seconds, at nine separate locations across the stubble-covered field, orange-white fire flashed upward and held at forty-five-degree angles, and a deafening roar, like an array of rockets igniting all at once, seized command of the night. For a full half minute, the land reverberated under the onslaught. The effect in the sky above each drilling site resembled a Fourth of July celebration, with tracerlike objects spiraling aloft and popping high atop plumes of colorful incandescence.

As the steel bit screamed into the earth at Follett's position, icy dirt blasted up. Jagged flint rocks shot out, sparking against each another and pelting both FBI men. Seconds later, as the furious drilling ended, a gritty powder began to fall back to earth. Follett spat away the dirt from his mouth and retrieved the searing-hot auger and its spent power unit, while his partner moved into position over the roughly symmetrical wound in the ground and held the twenty-five-pound shaped charge by its detonator wires. With a swift hand-over-hand action, the FBI man lowered the explosive into the narrow ten-foot hole and fed out the lines while he retreated thirty feet to relative safety. He stopped alongside Follett, who nodded his readiness. Both men turned and crouched with their backs toward the point of detonation, and the man completed the electrical circuit. Another fiery explosion shook the ground, and a massive column of dirt rose nearly three stories into the night before breaking apart and falling outward in large clumps of rock and soil. The sounds of other percussions elsewhere indicated to Follett that the assault was going according to plan.

Both FBI men ran for the irregularly carved opening, now four feet wide, and Follett peered into the depths. There was no way to tell precisely how deep it was until he went into the cavity himself, but Follett knew the hole had to be at least twenty feet straight down. There was no sound or light coming from the bottom. He extracted a single-flash stun grenade, dropped it into the opening, and stepped away. The blast illuminated the vertical corridor for an instant and sent a shaft of noonday brilliance into the heavens. Both men waited until the ear-shattering percussion hit with a palpable force before beginning their descent.

Follett was first to hit bottom. He fell to his stomach and rolled to one side to make room for his backup, who was five seconds behind. The floor seemed to be man-made, but he couldn't be sure because of all the dirt and rocks. As his partner slammed down the shaft, Follett realized they were inside a fair-sized room. They had apparently accessed the bunker and not the small passageway toward the fourth corridor as anticipated. The other thing that wasn't quite right, he thought, was the lighting. This place was still brightly lit. In previous hostile breachings, someone always pulled the power the instant an attack was started.

Suddenly there were shouts in Arabic. Someone else was nearby, but for a second, Follett couldn't see who it was because of the remaining haze from the flash-bang grenade. Then he saw a man, dressed in black, standing in a doorway waving an Uzi. As the man swung the submachine gun around and started shooting at him, Follett popped the man's head off just above the eyebrows with a five-second burst from his own weapon. The man's body jerked and collapsed like an imitation of a mime act, and bits of brain matter oozed out of the bullet holes in the wall. Follett made a rapid perusal of the room for other terrorists.

"Door ... *again!*" his partner shouted.

Another man began shooting in their general direction. Follett felt bullets fan past his face as the man ran closer. In a sustained burst of fire, Follett's backup pureed the terrorist at point-blank range. The man danced a few steps sidewards across the floor before he hit a wall and crumpled. As his body twitched, the man's arm dropped and his fingers released their grip on a submachine gun.

Both FBI men turned. They heard other sounds of shooting—multiple bursts. The noises seemed to be coming from the south, the direction where Cowboy Four was to have entered the bunker. After fifteen seconds, however, everything was quiet.

Follett pointed to the west wall.

Most of the haze in the room had dissipated. He rose to a crouch and moved toward the door to the passageway that they had intended to breach. The thick metal seal was open, and a short tunnel beyond appeared unoccupied. Follett listened. There were no sounds coming from that direction—or any direction now, for that matter. He turned and considered the room again. It was approximately fifty feet by fifty feet, with a high ceiling of wood planks, and it was empty except for the two bodies. He wondered what the place had been used for.

Follett signaled with a touch to his nose and finger. His partner nodded and moved to the dead terrorists. Both were slumped with their heads bowed. The FBI backup pulled at their clothing and adjusted the bodies so he could see their faces clearly. He winced at the grisly appearance of the first man's scalpless countenance. The terrorist's bloody skullcap lay to the side. The FBI man extracted a Polaroid PistolCam from his vest, pointed it, and took pictures of both terrorists. Then he pulled out two fingerprint cards. He peeled back the plastic cover of one and pressed the fingertips of the dead man's hand against the sensitive pad. He did the same with the other terrorist. The entire effort for the two corpses took less than ninety seconds.

Follett watched his partner tuck away the camera and print cards. He considered their situation with a brief shake of his head. Even with all their sophisticated intelligence-gathering capability, he still had no idea how many other terrorists were close by, no knowledge of the armament they might have, and no clue how many hazardous rooms lay ahead.

He motioned for the advance to continue.

Both men moved toward a closed double door on the north wall. Remaining to one side, Follett extended the rubber-cushioned cup of an electronic stethoscope and held it against the portal. He squinted and listened, remembering pieces of his own training syllabus: Your eyes, ears, and nose are everything. Be alive to the possibility of danger everywhere. Find a target; don't become one. He shook his head. He could have heard a heartbeat next door. There was nothing immediately beyond but emptiness.

Behind the two men came another hissing rat-tat-tat. Once again, Follett felt sure it originated from the direction of Cowboy Four, his two men moving north. But where were they? Cowboys One and Two were coming south. It was a classical squeeze play that was supposed to produce terrorists in its pincer effect. Hostages, too, if they were here. So far, however, the effort resembled a low-key mopping-up operation the day after a battle.

His eyes returned to the closed doors. Maybe everything—everyone?—lay through there. He pointed at the knobs. His partner nodded and swung his shotgun into position. Follett backed off and pointed his submachine gun in support. The shotgun blast splintered the doors, blowing their remains into the next room. Both FBI men maintained trigger pressure on their weapons, but there was no hostile response. Follett motioned them to move ahead.

As they crept through the torn opening, the men saw what appeared to be another abandoned room, with a long hallway leading toward the north. Off the hallway were doorways to even more rooms. In case there was someone waiting, Follett made sure he didn't telegraph his presence with a gun muzzle or a foot as he approached the new doorways. A matter of training, he told himself. His weapon was in the low-ready position so as not to allow any adversary to make contact with him or the muzzle. Stop, look, and listen, the railroad crossing adage, applied exquisitely to this business. He remembered the endless exercises. Take an area by sections. Scan and think. Where's the target? Never turn your back on anything or anyone you haven't checked. Never assume. Move on. Secure as you go. This same procedure would be employed for the entire bunker. But if the rest of the place was as empty as this, he shook his head at the possibility, the whole effort might be wrapped up in short order. And he'd felt this assault had so much promise.

"They're *dead.*" A shrill voice inside Follett's helmet stabbed into his skull. "Jesus Christ, Tex, they never had a chance."

Follett froze. He thought he recognized the group leader of Cowboy One. He activated his transmitter.

"Say again?"

This time, the man's tone was more composed.

"It's Cowboy One. Two's been eliminated, wiped out. They apparently came down into bales of razor wire. Or . . . I don't know." There was a pause. "Maybe it came down on them. Anyway, the biggest body parts are . . ." The man hesitated again.

"Are *what?*" Follett snapped. A few seconds passed.

"Their heads, Tex. Their heads. Both severed. The wire sliced through everything. Dave still has his neck, though. Blood's everywhere. Never seen anything like it. Never."

"All right, Cowboy One," Follett ordered, "continue your advance. Copy?"

Twenty seconds passed before his command was acknowledged. It came as a simple "Roger."

All of a sudden, fifty feet ahead, a man dressed in black ran across the hallway and into a room. Then, as Follett watched, the man came back into the hallway and slowly retraced his steps. He wore a thick protective vest and wielded a pistol in the high-ready position. For a few seconds, the man seemed completely unaware of the FBI men's presence. Then he pointed his weapon toward them.

"Ooh, bad move," Follett mouthed as he pulled the trigger. The bullets from his submachine gun stitched a path from the center of the man's chest to underneath his right arm and penetrated his body at the armpit. His bulky vest served as a containment vessel that prevented the exit of the projectiles. The slugs dissipated their energy by making circuits inside the man's body at nearly the speed of sound. The effect was like a Cuisinart. The terrorist staggered to a stop and opened his mouth. Slowly a ragged column of strawberry-red froth, littered with rib chips and lung peelings, foamed out and started down the man's front. His own eyes watched as the bloody effluent involuntarily expelled itself. Finally the man pirouetted and collapsed.

"It's a trap!" someone screamed in Follett's ears. "It's all a fucking trap!"

He didn't recognize the voice as belonging to one of his men.

"Sooner Three," yelled the voice before Follett could ask. "This is OHP Sooner Three. They're coming out of the wall over here, and they've got Stingers. Shit, *no!* They're going to fire them down the corridor!"

Almost immediately, a massive explosion shook the room where the assault team leader and his backup stood. Separate pieces of the wooden ceiling wrenched loose and fell, and Follett had to place both hands on a wall to steady himself. Another explosion followed. He was thrown to the floor, and the room was partially upended. The lighting blinked out.

"Evacuate!" he yelled as he pulled himself to his feet in the darkness. He now noticed the strong smell of detonated explosives.

"Evacuate . . . *everyone!*"

He grabbed for his flashlight and, stepping over rubble, headed for the room they had originally entered. His partner was right behind.

A third boom rocked the floor as the two FBI men reached the chamber where they'd entered the bunker. Follett feared the explosions had been more than enough to collapse their tunnel to the surface, but as he came underneath and shone his light up into the vertical opening, it looked intact. Pieces of collapsed ceiling and wall covered the floor. Thank God, he thought. They'd serve to assist them in getting back into the tunnel. He grabbed a wooden plank and wedged it into position. Then another. There was more than enough debris to prepare a makeshift ladder.

Suddenly two men dressed in black pounded toward Follett and his partner from the passageway to the west.

"Sooner Four, Tex," the first man waved his arms and radioed, even though he was now close enough to speak without the transmitter. The two members of the OHP team stopped to catch their breath. Follett thought they looked as if they'd endured everything short of death. Both men's clothing was ripped, and both displayed open wounds and sprays of fresh blood over half their bodies. A fourth boom shook the room, spilling debris from the hole leading to the outside.

"Let's get the hell out of here!" Follett motioned to the OHP men. "Go!"

The two exhausted men maneuvered up the latticework into the opening and climbed by wedging themselves against the dirt walls a foot at a time. Follett's partner was next. Twenty seconds later, the FBI leader took a last look around with his flashlight and followed.

As the four men worked their way up the narrow, twenty-foot conduit, another explosion erupted. The violence from the blast was so strong that Follett's partner lost his footing and tumbled backwards, slamming both men to the floor.

The men in the follow-up car had had a warning, such as it was, of thirty seconds. An FBI communications specialist at the Okmulgee Airport reported to Brand through a secure cellular telephone the text of the two signals he'd picked up on his VHF scanner. The first had been a simple, unacknowledged voice transmission a minute before the convoy rolled onto the property. It was broadcast on 121.075 megahertz, and it sounded very clear and very close.

"Tell grandma five little piggies are on their way."

Because it was ambiguous in relation to the assault, the FBI man hadn't reported it at the time. Any aircraft radio could have been used for the messages, the specialist pointed out in a calm manner, and there were at least ten available planes tied down for the night at the Okmulgee airport. On the other hand, he admitted, it could have come from a hand-held portable transceiver. And if it had, there was no telling where the caller was.

When the man relayed the second message, Brand yelled it back as a question, " 'It's time to turn the piggies into bacon? Allah Akbar?' " He grabbed the UHF microphone. "Follett, God damn it, get the fuck out of there!"

Jack, Brand, and another communications man had waited in the car since the beginning of the assault, ready to monitor the events as they occurred and were broadcast by Follett and his team. Jack had toyed with a composite representation of the underground structure. While he waited for updates, he'd stabbed color-coded pushpins at the locations where the OHP and FBI men had entered the corridors and the bunker. At one point they'd even discussed how the media would be informed about the assault once the cleanup was under way. Would there be a formal news conference in Tulsa? In Washington? Here, at the site itself? By the FBI or by the president? Would there be a discussion of the actual tactics used in the operation? How about the sophisticated equipment that had made today's success possible?

Jack saw a flash to the southwest; then the first explosion shook the car. He squinted, but before he could say anything, three more flashes erupted from the property, in a sequence separated by seconds. Huge chunks of rocky dirt thudded into the car. The blackness outside turned fiery white, and the car was lifted backwards by the concussion. The windows imploded, and the vehicle rolled over twice before it came to rest on its side in a field.

"Laura," Jack whispered his dead wife's name just before he lost consciousness.

In the distance, a dog barked briefly. There was no response to its inquiry. Then the Oklahoma night once again became very still.

38

The cataclysm in Oklahoma early Friday morning had been detected by seismologists around the world, as the five explosions produced readings comparable to those for underground atomic tests. Residents within a hundred miles of Beggs were jarred out of their dreams by the series of thunderclaps, and cities as far away as Dallas had windows rattled by the artillerylike concussions. With one exception, however, a full appreciation of the violence wasn't realized by others across America until hours after the monstrous final explosion. That exception, of course, was the collection of specialists who had monitored the entire incident from half a continent away in the FBI's Strategic Information Operations Center.

Lew Bittker paced and watched and listened to the live satellite transmissions from the site as the strange clues from Tex Follett's team built toward the incomprehensible moment when the video camera rolled away from the massive blasts and the follow-up car was blown from its observation post. In the silent minutes that followed the interruption of the signal, the SIOC chief shook his head and considered it a near certainty that everyone was dead.

He stared at the blank screen. For the first time in years, he said a short prayer. How quickly the momentum of life can change, he reflected. The atmosphere of tense but optimistic anticipation at SIOC had collapsed so suddenly, so unexpectedly. Bittker decided not to sit down. He was afraid he wouldn't be able to get up. He grabbed the edge of the console and took a deep breath. The reality of what had happened was nearly overwhelming.

Ninety seconds after the satellite signal was lost, a nonsecure line into SIOC flashed. It was a call from a deputy sheriff at the Okmulgee airport command center. He had bypassed the FBI's main switchboard to report over an open telephone line that he'd lost contact with the monitoring car near the site of the assault. Bittker closed his eyes and sighed at the breach of security. Then he realized it was ridiculous to worry that the wrong person might find out about Operation Deep Fork. It was obvious that someone had known the FBI's plans and intentions all along.

The direct flow of information from the site itself began again seven minutes after the last explosion rocked the night, when an FBI communications specialist activated a second satellite dish at the base of a city water tower 1,000 yards to the south of the bunker. Although the man's audio-only message was frequently interrupted by static, his report was SIOC's first on-the-scene confirmation of the debacle. In the electronic green surrealism of his night-vision goggles, it looked like a moonscape, he whispered. Silent, desolate, pocked with craters. The specialist reported that he'd been protected by a gully, but the nearby two-hundred-foot water tower had been toppled, killing the FBI sentry on the catwalk.

The negative effects of the disaster followed its revelation as predictably as night followed day. While the first people to know, in addition to the FBI and the president, were the governor of Oklahoma and the head of the Oklahoma Highway Patrol, certain facts of the story were quickly pieced together by enterprising area reporters who'd been roused from their sleep. By 10 a.m. local time, the message was that some sort of joint assault, possibly involving the FBI, had been carried out against a fugitive underground hideaway, perhaps even a terrorist haven, and that there'd been heavy casualties. Almost immediately, the curious came by car and helicopter, and the Okmulgee County sheriff's department had to be pressed into service to maintain a protective cordon around the devastated area.

The shock felt in SIOC was duplicated and augmented by a sense of disbelief throughout the entire FBI organization. Because of the unprecedented loss of so many specialty personnel, no one at the Bureau believed that the real story behind the tragedy could go unexplained for much longer. Twice, in front of Bittker, the director wondered aloud if the FBI could snap back from the catastrophe and become fully effective in time to prevent whatever else the terrorists had planned. He also expressed concern over the forthcoming news conference and how the president would handle the explanation. The FBI would brief him beforehand, putting its most positive spin on the facts, but there was no telling how the Bureau would fare in the chief executive's actual presentation to the American people. Could he keep parts of the story under wraps and soften the effects? Would he even have any interest in doing so? Certainly all bets were off if there was an extended question-and-answer session after his prepared remarks.

Friday's Dow opened down a hundred points, and it continued to slip as the bare basics of the mission and the attendant rumors churned onward without an early statement from the White House. Bizarre amplifications of the story threatened to panic a nation already brittle and weary from the physical and mental tortures of three weeks of terrorist mayhem and the erratic strictures of martial law. One report that quickly made the environmentalist rounds was that residents near the site had inadvertently discovered a secret atomic waste dump and had somehow triggered violent government retaliation. Finally, at noon, press secretary Kevin Howard responded with a prepared statement that assured the country that all was indeed under control. Howard promised that the president would hold a news conference at four, at which time he would have definitive answers and would take questions. According to a *Wall Street Journal* columnist, writing for Monday's edition, this brief but to-the-point response, though delayed, kept financial markets from tumbling into the abyss.

Headlines in the afternoon newspapers showed that there were many more questions than answers, and editorial writers expressed hope that the president would lay out the full story. By two o'clock, CNN reported that something had gone terribly wrong during a significant paramilitary assault that involved the finest law-enforcement SWAT teams. Why they were there, what they were attacking, and what had happened were the three major unanswered questions. Adding further mystery was the fact that no interviews had been allowed with any of the surviving participants who were hospitalized in Tulsa.

Jerry Reynolds stayed at Bittker's side throughout the ordeal. This was to have been their finest hour, he observed with chagrin as more facts came into SIOC, yet eight of their best, the crème de la crème, had apparently walked into a trap, and six of them had been killed. The Oklahoma Highway Patrol's tactical team lost eight men in the devastation.

Since 5:10 a.m. Friday, SIOC had received two dozen specially requested satellite photographs of the area. Following daybreak, aerial and surface pictures were taken and reviewed. When the director himself came in for a final briefing at two-thirty in the afternoon, prior to going to the White House, Bittker scrolled down the list of more than a hundred available still photos and selected one of them. It was the least complex representation, and he felt it told it all. He placed it on the middle screen.

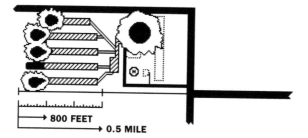

The image was a composite of the FBI's earlier drawing of the underground facility together with an artist's rendition, which showed, to scale, the size of the craters and the surrounding perimeter where most of the debris fell. According to the Bureau of Alcohol, Tobacco, and Firearms, the four craters to the west would have been nearly twenty percent larger and more circular in shape if a portion of their explosive force hadn't been directed horizontally through the underground corridors. It was those focused blasts that killed the men on the four OHP teams. The terrorists' explosives responsible for the large crater to the east had been stored less than five feet beneath the surface, near where the large metal building once stood.

"They had the whole arsenal ready for us down there, Jerry," Bittker said while the men waited for a replay of a Friday morning television interview. "Everything from RDX at the end of the corridors to Gellex-4 for the last detonation. And, of course, the Stingers. Someone had planned and coordinated it to the second."

The television excerpt came on the screen. It was a segment produced by the NBC affiliate in Tulsa and shown on the network's "Today" show. The interview was with Nellie Davis, a woman who lived near the destruction. Broken boards and puffs of bright orange insulation reflected the sunrise and formed the backdrop.

"Our place was completely leveled," she mumbled through tears, "just like a tornado had come through. Both our home and the barn out back." She opened her arms in a helpless gesture. "Nothing's left. Nothing."

Bittker ignored the concluding remarks of the TV reporter.

"Until we dig up the whole area, the best count so far is that we killed eleven terrorists. But there were no hostages. Not even a sign of any. No Carmichael, no missing pilot."

"What's the latest on Follett and our other man?"

"Terry Willits? Both still hospitalized, but they're going to be all right. Follett suffered three or four broken ribs from the fall with Willits."

"The OHP boys?"

"They nearly got buried alive, but they were close enough to the surface to get out on their own. One's got a knife wound. They'll make it."

"Brand? Stroud?"

"They should be patched up and released any time. I talked with Brand about an hour ago. All of them, which includes our communications man, got sliced from the waist up by broken glass when their windows blew in and the blast whipped the shards around the car. Equal cuts . . . kind of a democratic accident. Thank God they had their seat belts on."

Reynolds nodded toward a computer monitor. "What do we have on the deaths of the fourteen?"

Bittker punched at a keyboard. "OK, reconstructed order of death: Our men, Cowboy Two, were the first, when they fell into the electrified razor wire. Then Cowboy Four when they were electrocuted—fried, really—at that power unit. Sooner Three, just after they called the warning to Follett, then Sooner One, Two, and Five, in that order, when the missiles were fired at the explosives in their corridors. Cowboy One was annihilated in the final blast. Only our Cowboy Three, Follett and Willits, and the OHP's Sooner Four survived."

St. Francis Hospital, Tulsa
8:58 a.m.

Don Evans stared at the men in side-by-side hospital beds.

"You guys are damn lucky to be alive, let alone in one piece."

Oklahoma Highway Patrol tactical team members Tommy Coleman and Rich Fleming acknowledged with nods. Together, the muscular troopers had constituted the strike unit "Sooner Four" during Operation Deep Fork.

"Felt like I was sealed in cement," the redheaded Coleman responded slowly in his Oklahoma drawl. "Couldn't move at all for a spell." He shifted his position on the mattress and winced. "Oof, sorry." He indicated with his hand. "Ribs still hurt." The burly lawman opened his eyes wide and blew out some air. After a moment he continued. "The ground shook a little, like an aftershock, and I prayed the hole hadn't been rammed shut, only filled by cavin' in above me." He raised his eyebrows. "Somehow I found the starch to push against the sides of my feet, which I'd hooked against the walls earlier, and I popped my head up and out of the hole. A little more scramblin', and I was all the way out."

Coleman inclined his head in the direction of his partner.

"I chucked my gloves and dug down into that loose dirt like a goddamned runaway backhoe and found Rich's hand. It was wigglin' a little. I just grabbed it and pulled. And," he smiled at Fleming, "the rest is rock 'n' roll."

Evans took out a notebook and turned to Coleman's partner.

"Rich, you the team leader?"

Fleming nodded.

The FBI agent tapped at the paper with his ballpoint. "OK, give me the chronology, the scenario, from the time you both were inserted into the corridor."

Fleming shoved his fingers through his thick brown hair. "Well, after the big boom from our stun grenade, we went in like mountain climbers down a sheer cliff." He winked at Coleman. "Got used to that stuff as a kid, growing up in British Columbia. Anyway, we figured anyone inside the place should be pretty well disoriented by the 'flash-bang.' We hit the bottom and went immediately for target identification, then target isolation, in case the terrorists were near any hostages. We wanted to know how close they were to the storage area at the end and if they had detonators. We knew it would take split-second timing for the close-quarters battle down there. We just didn't figure it'd be *that* close."

"Meaning?"

"We felt it would be hard for the terrorists to guard all five corridors at the same time, so we thought we might not encounter anyone the instant we got there. Fat chance! There was not only a tight clearance in the corridor, but they were right there, waiting for us."

Coleman picked up the conversation. "Don, if you was to cut through the tunnel—you know, like a cross section—you'd see a 'T.' It was just like that guy Stroud figured at the meeting last Thursday. Ceiling to floor was some seven foot." The trooper motioned with his right hand. "It was about four feet wide, not hardly enough to let two people pass. Now, the crossbar of that T was maybe thirty feet wide, but only a couple feet deep."

Evans frowned as he wrote down the comment. "What was up there?"

"Never did find out." Coleman shook his head. "No sir, no time."

"No time, indeed," Fleming confirmed, aiming his hand as if he had a gun in it. "I had to drop a man almost immediately. He was running west, toward the explosives at the end of the corridor. Well, he turned and fired at me. Twice, from maybe twenty feet. But he was a bit off balance, trying to shoot on the run." Fleming grinned. "I had no trouble acquiring him, though. Pop, pop . . . two in the center of mass, as we say. Opened him up really nice. He went down spread-eagle-like." The lawman stroked at the stubble on his chin. "Sure glad I stopped him where I did. Just as we thought, it turned out there was a ruby-laser trigger beam protecting the end of the tunnel. If anyone broke it, the stuff blew. Seems our entry explosions sent terrorists running from the main part of the bunker toward the stored explosives. But none of them made it." Fleming looked at the ceiling. "It all should've worked out. We stopped every one of those bastards in all five corridors. The only reason the other troopers were done in was because of the damn pop-ups with the Stingers. Totally a surprise. Tommy and I were lucky to see our launcher coming out of the wall. Otherwise we'd be statistics, too."

Coleman gestured toward Fleming. "I gotta tell ya that pullin' him out of the cave-in was my payback for what he done for me. I let my guard down just once, and I would've bought the farm if Rich hadn't been there. Some SOB jumped out of a door on the side of the tunnel, and I pushed my 9mm into his face. But before I could pull the trigger, the asshole grabbed the barrel with his left hand and forced it away and held on to it, tight as shit. Well, I thought it'd be smart to yank the gun backwards . . . you know, to pull the guy off balance. It worked, all right, and I seized him by the throat. What I didn't know was that he had a big black knife in his right hand. I never saw it coming. They always tell us the most dangerous weapon is the one you don't see. Anyway, the guy grinned, like he knowed my life was in his hands, and he jabbed that knife right under my rib cage." Coleman touched his left side. "But the sumbitch saw something at the last second, and that must have kept him from pushin' the blade all the way in to the handle. What got the guy's attention was the laser dot from Rich's Browning, which showed up on his chest, right where his aorta was. He saw it about the time I did, and, before he could cut my guts out, his whole back exploded against the wall behind him. His head jerked up as he fell backwards into his own mush. He didn't say nothin', but I remember those eyes. They was mighty full of questions."

Coleman pursed his lips for a moment.

"I sure do hope he got some answers on the other side."

Evans kept writing. "I understand you took pictures."

"Got their prints, too," Coleman assured him.

It had been nearly 8 a.m. Friday before rescuers reached Follett and Willits. When the last, most violent explosion occurred, and the two men had plunged fifteen feet to the hard floor, Follett broke Willits's fall and four of his own ribs in the process. Soil poured down from the hole for a full minute before the earth sealed itself, leaving the FBI agents in the pitch-black bunker thick with hot, noxious fumes. By remaining prostrate against the floor and breathing with their mouths in the dirt, they'd been able to survive their four-hour entombment. Both were admitted to the hospital by midmorning, but only Follett was required to stay overnight.

Throughout early Friday afternoon, Follett talked with most of the FBI hierarchy, and he told himself after the conversations that it didn't take a rocket scientist to discern the embarrassment and frustration throughout the J. Edgar Hoover Building over the appalling outcome in Oklahoma. Not that they blamed it all on him, but he had been, after all, the leader of the assault. The captain of the ship, as it were. And duty, honor, and tradition dictated that he accept full responsibility and go down with his ship if necessary. He knew the official imposition of blame would come in the president's address at three o'clock, Tulsa time. Scapegoat? The word had crossed his mind.

He was glad there was no one else in his hospital room as the afternoon television programs were interrupted for the special report from the White House. He knew, however, that everyone in the Bureau was at rapt attention in front of TV sets, and the name Follett had probably been used a thousand times in vain.

"Ladies and gentlemen, the President of the United States." The picture switched from the presidential seal on a field of blue to the Oval Office. The president sat behind his large desk and stared at a single sheet of paper in his hands. As the camera tightened to a close-up of the chief executive, he kept his focus on the paper. The filtered yellow sun of the late afternoon gave the scene an aura of peace, of resolution.

Follett jerked upright in bed.

Oval Office? Shit! Then there wouldn't be any questions by reporters ... because there wouldn't *be* any reporters. For Christ's sake, this meant we were going to be picked clean. *Nuked* might be a better word for it. At least with skeptical reporters around, the president would feel somewhat constrained not to blame us for everything. Reporters always seemed able to get the man to soften a harsh statement, usually through a question that would force him to admit there might be a second side to the story. God knows we could use a little moderation today.

The president raised his head and faced the camera. His expression was somber.

"Good afternoon. For nearly three weeks, you and I have suffered the horrors of terrorism across this great country of ours. Thousands of innocent people have been murdered, and the toll in property damage is well into the billions of dollars. This obscenity has torn at our national fabric, subjecting us to ravages unknown since the founding of the republic. It has threatened all that America stands for."

The chief executive hesitated and looked down at the paper for a few seconds before continuing in his flat cadence.

"Ever since this plague began on December 28, we have aggressively—and prayerfully—sought to end it. This afternoon I am humbly grateful to inform you that our prayers have been answered."

Follett leaned toward the screen. His mouth was open.

"Within the past few days," the president went on, "following the most intensive search effort in its history, the Federal Bureau of Investigation located an underground terrorist base northwest of the town of Beggs, Oklahoma. Further inquiry has confirmed that this hidden facility has been the source of the major criminal acts that have been carried out across the country."

The president paused again.

"Early today, a combined force of eighteen highly trained and equipped members of the FBI and their tactical team counterparts from the Oklahoma Highway Patrol conducted a raid on the installation. The attack was a success. The facility was destroyed, and all terrorists there were killed. Tragically, however, the conflict was so intense that fourteen of our lawmen perished inside the bunker, and one FBI agent died outside. Further details will be revealed after we examine the entire underground structure, and these facts will be presented to you as soon as we have them. In the meantime, I want to say that if it hadn't been for the persistent efforts by the FBI and the heroic service and sacrifice on the part of both the FBI and the state troopers of Oklahoma, we would not have put an end to this diabolical infestation."

Follett could only shake his head. His mouth was still open.

"I have chosen not to answer reporters' questions just yet, for there are many facts still to be gathered. I hope to have additional information to present to you by tomorrow evening, and I will hold a full news conference at that time. Until then, as we conclude what has been an unprecedented national nightmare, I ask for your patience."

The television camera widened slowly to a ten-foot frame of the president and his desk.

"Finally, because of the successful elimination of the source of terrorism, I am at this time ordering a lifting of martial law. I will shortly ask for a confirmation by the Congress of my original action last Monday."

He moved the paper aside and clasped his hands.

"I believe that everyone can now see that the combination of martial law and the professional actions of our law enforcement community have rid the nation of a terrible scourge. It is truly a day to be thankful."

The president's sober expression gave way to a thin smile.

"May God continue to bless this great country of ours."

Tulsa
9:07 a.m.

Neither man had slept well Friday night. Even though they hadn't averaged more than four hours a night for the past week and were further debilitated from their harrowing ordeal in the car, both Jack Stroud and Corley Brand had spent most of the last evening wide awake, looking at the ceiling. Brand thought about the president's speech the previous afternoon. Jack couldn't keep his mind off Rachel.

They had been at St. Francis Hospital for two and a half hours, being examined and treated for numerous cuts. Afterward they went to the FBI's Tulsa office and called Washington. Until then, they hadn't known the extent of the fiasco at Beggs. They watched the president's address from the office.

"What in the hell was *that* all about?"

Brand had punched off the set when the president signed off.

"Declare victory and go home?"

Jack shook his head. "We get wiped out by a suicide squad, and the president blows the all-clear. What does he know that we don't?"

"Or what does he want us to *think* he knows?"

Now, twenty-four hours after the fiasco, even with the perspective of time, everything still looked as confusing. Both men met in Jack's study after breakfast. Brand's call to Jerry Reynolds in Washington brought the same response about the president's speech: We don't have any more idea what's going on than we did yesterday.

"But we intend to find out this afternoon," the deputy director replied over the speaker on Jack's desk. "The president's scheduled a meeting with the chiefs of the FBI and the Secret Service, probably to chew some ass privately. However, I've given the director a list of questions and our concerns. In the meantime, be grateful for small favors. The Big Man hasn't pummeled us yet, and the morning papers are actually talking about hope in America once again. We needed a breathing spell. Call it mass psychology, but it seems to be working."

"You can bet it hasn't fooled one particular individual who's right this minute putting the finishing touches on his plan." It was Jack. "He knows his strengths, what he's got with him, and why he sacrificed that bunker."

"Kuttab?" Reynolds asked.

"Damned right. I say the loss of that place had absolutely no negative effect on him. If we'd wiped him out, or a bunch of his equipment, it might have been a different story. No, the bottom line on the bunker was that *we* got kicked in the nuts, not Kuttab."

"Give me a one-sentence summary of your analysis."

Without hesitating, Jack looked at the speaker unit and replied, "The bunker was a trap to wipe out those who might be able to stop what he's about to do."

"We're back to the inauguration?"

"You got it."

Reynolds was silent for a moment.

"OK, I can't argue with you. Before we go any further, though, let's review what we found at Beggs. First, there was indeed a flight simulator in the bunker. The fifth explosion destroyed it, but there were enough recognizable pieces left over for us to make a general determination. We haven't yet been able to identify the specific type, though. Second, there were a lot of other metal scraps in places, but it's going to take a couple of weeks to learn if any were part of that missing airplane."

Reynolds cleared his throat.

"Then, remember the ratcheting sounds the farmer heard, grinding and whining? They came from two hydraulic elevator systems. One was inside that big metal building. It was used to lower the simulator, which was then moved north and placed under the Gellex supply. The other system was over near the underground power station."

Brand looked out the window. "Where Cowboy Four was killed?"

"Right. Both men landed on top of 33,000-volt leads and were electrocuted instantly. The first shooting Follett heard from their direction was probably the involuntary contractions of their fingers against the triggers of their weapons. From the condition of the bodies, full of puncture wounds, it appears that someone then shot them after they were dead. The men shorted out the power generator in their fall, but the lights were on and stayed on because of a battery unit. We learned that the only power ever sold to the property by the local co-op was small stuff, like what a farmhouse might use. That way no one got any ideas. No suspicions where there shouldn't be any." Reynolds continued. "We also found dozens of fiber-optic strands extending from the bunker to a point twelve to fifteen inches above the surface. To the uninitiated eye, they looked like weeds, waving in the wind. They were used to monitor activities outside the bunker. We believe they could spot people as far away as our men on the water tower." Reynolds rustled a piece of paper. "Got a little more. It's from the ATF. They confirm that the two explosives . . . "

"Excuse me, Jerry," Jack interrupted. "Still no sign of my daughter or that woman?"

"No, Jack," Reynolds answered. "But try to look at the positive. If they had been there during the raid, they'd both surely be dead now. I know this isn't much consolation, but there's still a chance, a good chance, we'll rescue Rachel."

"Yeah, Jerry," Jack replied, "I know. Still a chance. Thanks." Jack clenched his fists so tightly that he could feel his muscles strain against the cloth of his shirtsleeves.

The White House
2:05 p.m.

Tim Vance sat at the back of the command post under the Oval Office in the West Wing basement and checked his watch. Around him, agents stared at high-resolution video monitors attached to cameras with zoom lenses and night-vision amplifiers. Along a wall, Uzis and Remington 870 pump shotguns, modified for the Service, stood upright and ready. Nearby, one man, arms crossed, watched a screen showing the president on the telephone upstairs.

Vance absentmindedly flipped at the edge of a business card. In the center it read, "Timothy S. Vance, Special Agent, U.S. Secret Service." At the top left, embossed in raised gold, was the Service's star logo. At the bottom left corner, "Presidential Protective Division, The White House, Washington, D.C. 20500." He wondered if he still had those qualifications they'd said he had when he was hired: instant reflexes, judgment, nerve. He'd looked forward to being known as a man of granite, a soldier in a suit and tie, working in what many considered to be the most elite law-enforcement organization in the world.

There was a lot of mystique in the so-called *Sacred* Service, but the hours were shitty if you liked a regular home life. But then, Vance hadn't been married when he'd started his career at the Denver field office. Now, on the White House detail and married, he never counted hours. He told his wife he couldn't, because at least unofficially all his time belonged to the job. There were the nominal eight-hour duty times, but no one punched a clock. That's why they rotated you out of here after three years, he reminded himself. Mental pressure, sheer exhaustion, burnout. He winced. Not to mention divorce. His own had been in the works for a little over two weeks.

"This beats bustin' counterfeiters," he'd told his superiors when they asked if he'd prefer to be out in one of the field offices again. "Nah, there's nowhere else for me."

Without a doubt, Vance liked all the trappings of covering the president. He'd taken an oath to step between the chief executive and any danger, to shield "the Man" from an assailant. He'd driven both the limousine and the "war wagon," the follow-up black GMC Suburban that was loaded with firepower, "J-turns" and all. He'd played "tail gunner" in the swivel seat in back of the four-wheeler, wielding his Uzi and ready to take on even dive-bombing aircraft. He remembered one time when his driver had jumped the curb between the White House and the Treasury Building and had swerved back and forth before regaining control. The ammunition clips Vance had taped to the ceiling broke loose, bounced against his chest, and tumbled out the open rear window. If there had been any tourists in the East Executive Park, they'd have made off with prized souvenirs.

Yes, this was the career for him, wife or no wife. Vance even had personalized Maryland license plates reading LV MY JB. There was something electric about "working the Man"—shades on, security clearance tag ostentatiously around one's neck, fitted earpiece in place, special daily lapel pin properly displayed—moving alongside when the president walked the rope line, keeping one's gaze low and watching people's hands and purses. Or peering into their eyes. At any moment the warning could come over the earpiece, "Gun left!" or wherever the threat might be. Ever vigilant, coat always open, ready to draw. An incredible high.

They always looked for "the face," that expression that didn't belong. The grinning guy at a solemn ceremony, the sweating man on a cold day. With his sunglasses, Vance could keep ten or fifteen people thinking he was staring directly at each one individually. Sometimes, though, when he wanted to communicate with a specific person, the sunglasses came off, and he'd stare into the soul of someone who gave off the wrong vibes. Keep back, the look communicated. This is my turf, and I'll kill you *dead* if you make a wrong move.

"Davidson wants us to meet in the conference room," came a voice at the door. Vance looked up and saw Ray Shaffer, chief of the White House detail. Shaffer lowered his voice. "And he's really pissed."

Vance stood and rolled his eyes and followed Shaffer down the hall. "No shit. Wonder why."

2:15 p.m.

When Shaffer and Vance walked into the paneled meeting room, everyone else was in place around the table. Everyone, that is, except the director. Special Agent Rick Hayes sat and talked with two representatives of the Technical Security Division, the Secret Service's designers of the state-of-the-art ways and means to protect the president, from bulletproof clipboards and briefcases to electronic intruder detectors and seismic sensors buried in the White House grounds. Officially, Technical Security had oversight responsibility for the design and construction of the two new Chrysler turbine cars, although, in the interests of secrecy, all information on the vehicles had been maintained and monitored by the separate and little-known branch called the Technical Development Division.

Also waiting were three members of the Intelligence Division, specialists who dealt in plots and counterplots, read between the lines of letters to the president, and otherwise looked for those who might pose a threat to the chief executive. In addition, there were two members from Protective Research—agents who conducted advanced screenings and interviews—and two members from the Visual Intelligence Branch, photographic specialists who captured and maintained pictures of individuals and groups who might step over the line someday.

"Goddamned FBI," the 6-foot-6 Davidson grumbled as he pushed into the room. The leader of the Secret Service wore a dark pinstriped suit, his trademark.

"Oswald, then Hinckley."

Davidson walked to his chair.

"Thought I'd heard everything."

The talking stopped when "Minute Man Stan" dropped two leather briefing manuals on the table with an authoritative thud. As usual, he started right in.

"It's all going to be up to us." He fingered the chest pocket of his suit coat for his reading glasses. "The FBI has absolutely no idea where the devil that guy is, how many are with him, what his capabilities are." Davidson shook open the frames and fitted on the spectacles. He opened the top briefing book and started paging.

"This isn't any band of wackos or loner 'quarterlies,' either."

Vance looked across at Shaffer, who shook his head almost imperceptibly. Too bad, Vance thought, that one of the Service's real strengths, keeping tabs on potential threats to the president, often depended on their getting good leads and other timely information from other government agencies. Unfortunately, that data, even though available, sometimes didn't come over, and, when it did, it was often flawed or incomplete. The FBI had indeed failed to notify the Secret Service of its files on Lee Harvey Oswald and John W. Hinckley, Jr. The present situation, Vance observed, looked like another valid complaint against the Bureau.

The Service maintained two lists. The first contained the names of those who had made general threats or abusive comments about high federal officials or who had participated in demonstrations against the American government. Thirty years ago, this list contained the names of more than a million people. Today it had shrunk to around 25,000. The second, the "short list," was a catalog of people the Service never let out of its sight—those who had actually made an attempt on the president or anyone else the Service was responsible for protecting and those who had clearly stated they would like to make such an attempt. These were listed on quarterly reports and were thus referred to within the agency as "quarterlies." Their names were constantly cross-checked by computer against guests registered in hotels where the president might stay, those listed as attending a convention where the president might speak, prisoners scheduled for release, and patients about to be dismissed from mental hospitals.

"When I headed the Presidential Protective Division," Davidson boomed and looked around the table, "we maintained a shield around the Man that many in the media complained was virtually impenetrable. Well, if I'm right, Kuttab's arrival will be as bad as an attack by Satan himself. We'll have to make the seal so tight even air will have trouble getting through. Mark my words, it'll be ten times worse than anything we ever worried about during and after the Iraqi war or following the domestic Hamas threats."

The room was so quiet that two agents flinched when the heating system kicked on with an audible click.

Davidson squinted at his wristwatch.

"I'm to meet with the president in seven minutes, and I'm going to do my damnedest to get him to call off the outdoor part of the inauguration. Oh, and I want us prepared to take him to Raven Rock or Mount Weather. Camp David, as usual, will be a backup."

Everyone in attendance knew that the superior underground nerve center was at Camp David, the presidential retreat in Maryland's Catoctin Mountains. It was 134 acres of forest, surrounded by a high-voltage electrical fence trimmed with barbed wire and patrolled by U.S. Marines. But it was also the first place outside of Washington a terrorist group would go in search of the president. Therefore, in the event of an attack, the Secret Service planned to move the chief executive first to one of the other high-security hiding places. He could be taken to Camp David once they were convinced it was safe.

There were dozens of underground shelters in the mountainous region around the capital. Raven Rock Mountain in Maryland was a favorite of the Service. Mount Weather in Virginia was where the Cabinet, all the Supreme Court justices, and some 2,000 government employees would be housed in the event of an attack. Both facilities had massive bank-vault doors with elevators descending hundreds of feet to self-contained, fully staffed subterranean worlds. There were war rooms with banks of communications equipment, multiple dining areas, large storage pantries, underground reservoirs with water-purifying equipment, and beds for everyone selected for protection.

Vance had read the file on the scare the Service suffered in 1974, during one of its practice removals of the president. Never again, the agency vowed, would so many things be allowed to go wrong at once. At eleven o'clock in the morning of December 1, an overcast and blustery day across the mid-Atlantic states, a TWA Boeing 727-200 fought the turbulence above the Blue Ridge Mountains and descended toward the Washington, D.C., area. Flight 514 had left Columbus, Ohio, thirty-six minutes earlier, and it was scheduled to be at the gate at National within the quarter hour. On that day, however, brisk forty-five-knot crosswinds forced the FAA's Washington Center controllers to divert the airliner to nearby Dulles International. Tragically, the plane's pilots misunderstood the approach procedure and descended prematurely into the last ridge of mountains to the west-northwest of Dulles. At nine minutes and twenty-two seconds past eleven, local time, less than twenty miles short of the airport, TWA's Flight 514 slammed into the heavily wooded terrain a bare hundred feet below the top of Mount Weather and disintegrated. Ninety-two human beings were obliterated.

That's all the media reported. What the general public never learned was that President Gerald Ford was in the shelter underneath. The jarring impact of the 143,167-pound jetliner severed the primary national security communication links and set off every appropriate alarm at U.S. bases around the world. For an eternity of seventy-three seconds, the president and his advisors thought the nation was under attack. And they prepared to retaliate. Today, because of the potentially disastrous outcome of such an interruption in communications, all shelters where the president might be taken were equipped with multiple low-frequency radio transmitters and a gridwork of bombproof fiber-optic lines.

Davidson glanced at the clock on the wall.

"Hell, time for me to go."

He closed the cover of his briefing book. "We'll get to the rest tomorrow." He picked up the manuals and started toward the door. He turned. "I'm going to lay it right on the line: No public ceremony for the inauguration. No need for all the falderal anyway. He's automatically president for another four years as of high noon Wednesday—ceremony or no ceremony."

2:30 p.m.

"This won't take long," the president announced as he stood next to his desk with his arms crossed. "No need to be seated."

The directors of the FBI and the Secret Service glanced at one another as they entered the Oval Office. They took up positions behind the chairs they had intended to sit in.

"Three points," the president started. He looked first at the FBI chief.

"One. Kuttab's still out there somewhere . . . although I suspect he's already here in town for his ultimate mission during the inauguration. That bunker in Oklahoma served him and his fellow terrorists very well. It hid them while they honed their skills, and it sponsored their deadly distractions over the past three weeks, which kept the Bureau running every which way. When those people didn't need the bunker any longer, they let you find out about it and suckered your finest HRT boys in and blew them to hell." The president shook his head.

"Masterful."

The FBI director gripped the back of the chair and inhaled deeply.

"Two." The president looked back and forth between both men. "Thirty hours ago I received a new communiqué from the Syrians, who say they've uncovered evidence that there may now be another team of terrorists in the United States with the same objective as Kuttab's." He paused for a second. "Possibly independent, but more likely coordinated. Not a pleasant thought, so I decided on a little defensive maneuver of my own. Lemons to lemonade, in other words. My national address yesterday was specifically designed to make the two groups think—if they care to believe anything I say—that we're confident we've ruined their clandestine facility *and* their plans. The worst is behind us, and we can now lower our guard. That's exactly why I lifted martial law."

He looked straight at the Secret Service director.

"Finally, and this is precisely what you don't want to hear, but don't even begin to object: I'm *not* going to cancel the public ceremonies for the inauguration. They're going to be held on the West Front of the Capitol, as usual, because that just may be the only way to flush out and get rid of both groups."

The president paced in front of the men.

"No assurance of this, but if the Syrians are right, that second team won't show itself unless it has to . . . and that would be because the first team failed. The best way for that to happen is to keep a high profile on Wednesday, bring the first one to the surface and destroy it."

The Secret Service director started to shake his head.

The president held up his hand and continued to speak. "Between now and the twentieth, the Syrians are going to collect as much as possible on this second group. All they've learned so far is that it's supposed to be hand-and-glove with some of the old KGB masters and that it may be ten times more dangerous than Kuttab's team."

The president walked back behind his desk. He smiled.

"So step one, gentlemen, is for you to get Kuttab. Good day."

Tulsa
4:13 p.m.

Jack slept fitfully for most of three hours. He was absolutely exhausted. Continuing questions about Rachel pulled him out of unconsciousness each time he sank down the welcoming slope of a dream. He hurt all over. Psychologically he was numb, yet somehow he felt he was close to something.

But hadn't he examined everything and found nothing? Maybe it was just hope, that enduring emotion. Or maybe it was a real hunch, like those he used to rely on.

"All right, think!"

What was the one question about Rachel that incorporated all others? He nodded. It was "Why?"

Why did they kidnap her?

A logical sequence began to fall into place. They tried to kill me, then they took Rachel. She's still missing. Have they killed her? Are they about to? What has her kidnapping done for them? If they did it to control or manipulate me, how was that to happen? What am I doing—or not doing—as a result?

"Good God, that could be it!" Jack sat up as a thought took shape.

Taking Rachel has definitely done one thing: It's kept me from my office at U.S. Simulation Systems! Someone knew my background would have virtually guaranteed that I would join in with the FBI when she was taken. And I'd have stayed away from my office!

He searched for his loafers with his stocking feet. He grabbed his sports jacket and slapped the pocket for the keys.

"Flora, I'll be at Simulation!"

"What's that, Mr. Stroud?"

Jack closed the door on her question.

Washington, D.C.
Sunday, January 17, 12:04 a.m.

Tim Vance caught a ride to the site at the last second. He wasn't scheduled to go back before the turbine cars would be installed later tonight, but with all the heightened attention to security he felt it appropriate to familiarize himself with the revised housing and escape arrangements one more time. The implications of the disaster in Oklahoma produced an almost obsessive-compulsive reaction to double-check everything.

Their unmarked Mercury Topaz slowed, then accelerated, then braked and turned in typical Secret Service driving fashion, and finally nosed onto congested Pennsylvania Avenue at the southeast corner of Freedom Plaza.

Vance gripped the back of the front seat with both hands as they edged between two taxis crossing Twelfth Street and bolted onward. This traffic was like rush hour, he observed. If it were an ordinary winter's night—especially, as it was, a Sunday—the city would be virtually deserted. But this was the historic, once-every-four-years Inauguration Week, the culmination of another national presidential campaign, and many relieved Americans had decided to venture out again after their recent bout with terrorism. Galas associated with the major political event had started even before the lifting of martial law, and tonight, Vance noticed, out-of-town attendees returned to fashionable hotels and ignored unfortunates who hurried along the sidewalks with faces pinched from the cold. Limousines burst across intersections against yellow lights and transported their well-coiffed cargoes to the high rises of the District and the obscurity of the numberless mailboxes and winding driveways of Fairfax County. Saturday night's social offerings ranged from tony receptions in Georgetown to glittering how-do-you-do's in marble-lined ballrooms. In all, within a twenty-five-mile radius of the White House, there had been four "official" functions and a hundred times that many unsanctioned events. Washington was rising to the occasion. As it always did.

During the remainder of the six-minute drive from the Executive Mansion, Vance stared at the illuminated but largely vacant edifices along

Pennsylvania Avenue and shook his head at the cross-purposes of the people in their evening finery and those others out there, somewhere, for whom he was preparing. His job, his commitment, was to see that the two never met.

A Type One, he whispered as the car doglegged left onto Constitution Avenue and crossed Third Street. It's *got* to be a Type One. Vance watched over the front seat as the Capitol loomed to the right. Type One and Type Two . . . that's how some of the old-timers at the Service classified all inaugurals. Fortunately, most of the functions during the past century had been Type Ones—celebratory, filled with positive memories. Type Twos were the others, the flawed versions. Somber, solemn, quiet . . . a hurting blot on the nation's memory.

Vance remembered his history. September 14, 1901, when Teddy Roosevelt took the oath of office after President McKinley died of gangrene from an assassin's bullet in his belly . . . that was a Type Two, and it motivated Congress to place the Secret Service in charge of presidential protection. T.R.'s second inauguration was a Type One. Harry Truman became president in a crowded Cabinet Room on a Type Two day, following FDR's fatal cerebral hemorrhage in Georgia. His second inaugural was a euphoric Type One. Then there was Lyndon Johnson's terrible Type Two, inside Air Force One on that numbing November afternoon in 1963. His win over Goldwater twelve months later gave him his Type One.

Their car maneuvered over the curb and headed down a temporary path across the lighted northern grounds of the Capitol. Every twenty feet or so, red and black signs on either side warned, AUTHORIZED SECRET SERVICE VEHICLES ONLY. The narrow road was policed by three sets of grim-faced, pistol-wielding Uniformed Division guards who nodded at the driver's credentials. Seven hundred feet south of Constitution Avenue, two special agents in open trench coats, which revealed forty-round Uzis a grab away, waved the Topaz into the covered emplacement on the West Front of the massive building. The car stopped alongside a metal sign with the letters TDD. This was where the Technical Development Division would unload the jet cars in less than twenty-four hours.

Vance stepped into the cold room. His breath condensed and swirled as he rubbed his hands together. It was like a large tomb, complete with the earthy smells of moist dirt and cement. He squinted at wide rows of bright lights that ringed the room near the ceiling. They pretended to warm a cubicle that had been built between the two sets of outside steps leading down from the main terrace of the Capitol on the West Front. It was three times the size of the facility constructed for the last inauguration. That was only a complex of rooms covered with red, white, and blue bunting and filled with heavily armed Secret Service agents. Vance thought this place looked more like a garage—which, of course, was exactly what it was.

Construction work for the special inaugural platform had begun over five months earlier. The two-hundred-foot-wide structure of steel, reinforced concrete, and wood was now complete but for a few final touches of white enamel, and it extended westward ninety-five feet from the second-level portico, then down to ground level. To the casual television viewer, the ceremony on Wednesday would look like the three previous ones. However, this year's arrangements were unique, to say the least. There were two parts to the $3.4 million platform: a prosaic-looking outer shell with its TV-friendly tiered rows of seating for the leadership of Congress, justices of the Supreme Court, the Cabinet, and other important members of the executive branch and their families and guests, and the inner cocoon underneath, where Vance stood, which would remain unnoticed by the world, if all went well. The basic façade work was completed in mid-December, and the highly classified presidential escape facilities below would be ready in a day. Both parts of the construction effort were completely supervised by the Secret Service. By the time the jet cars arrived, the only personnel allowed inside the hidden facility would be agents assigned to the Presidential Protective Division.

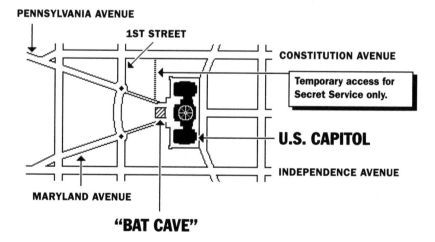

Vance smiled when he remembered that someone had nicknamed this place the "Bat Cave." Resembled the one in the movie, too, he concluded as he walked across the room. Banks of lighted communications equipment and television monitors were fully operational. Vance looked up at the padded chute that extended snakelike from the ceiling. He'd tried it himself, and it was head and shoulders above the inflatable slide they'd originally considered. He crossed his arms and studied the device. An airline-style escape mechanism absolutely paled against what the Technical Security crowd had arranged.

Most people were unaware that the president always stood inches from a rapid method of getting away from danger. At past inaugurations, safety lay in moving the chief executive into the Capitol itself, then keeping him at an underground holding area or removing him by surface vehicle or helicopter. That option was still available, but this time there would be an escape chute that would take him to the cars below in, literally, three seconds. The Secret Service had arranged for a veritable flotilla of vehicles—high-speed "extraction," it was called in class at Beltsville—to be waiting beneath the floor, vehicles that would be used if it appeared a threat against him was specifically and irrevocably focused on the building and not just on the general area. In other words, the chute would be employed if, in the sole judgment of the Secret Service, the chief executive would be better off being far removed from Capitol Hill.

Vance remembered something else they hammered in at Beltsville: The mission of the Secret Service was to ensure the safety and security of the president, and that meant getting him out of harm's way regardless of the circumstances, number of attackers, or method of attack. It was not the Service's duty to go after someone attempting an assault on the president. At least not immediately. That was the job of the local law enforcement personnel.

Vance alternated his weight from one foot to the other. He was standing in the middle of one of the two artificial causeways that extended to the walls of the underground facility, in the direction of the Mall. They were temporary heavy-gauge steel-grid carpets, anchored deep in the concrete terrace at the base of the building itself, and designed and tested to allow the jet cars to accelerate from zero to 100 m.p.h. in less than six seconds. The maximum speed necessary for an emergency evacuation of the president had been computer-determined to be seventy-three m.p.h. Vance stepped to one of the two exit sections of the underground room. Extending from the ceiling to the floor were scored sheets of plywood. He tapped his knuckles against the unpainted surface and concluded that the walls would quickly yield to fast-moving automobiles, whether they were the jet cars or the slower limousines.

There would be three chronologically separate convoys. The first would consist of two armor-plated presidential limousines, one pointing northwest, the other southwest. Behind each car, ready to follow at its bumper, would be one of the Service's black GMC Suburban protective vans. On Inauguration Day, all four vehicles would be manned and ready, should the president be threatened and a surface getaway be ordered. Positioned on cleared walkways outside both the northwest and southwest departure points of the emplacement would be squad cars and motorcycles of the Metropolitan Police and the U.S. Park Police. Their role, if required, was to lead the first two departing motorcades through the crowds and off the Capitol grounds.

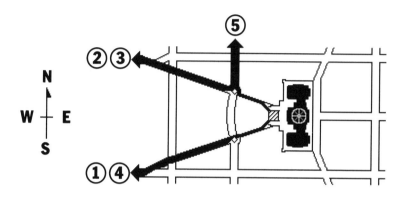

LAUNCH SEQUENCE, DIRECTIONS

If the surface escape program was activated, the first limousine and its follow-up van would roar away toward the southwest, in the direction of Maryland Avenue, picking up their already-moving police escort. Ten seconds later the other two cars, limousine and follow-up, would accelerate to the northwest. Of course, both initial processions would only be decoys, intended to draw hostile fire, especially from portable rocket launchers. Vance remembered that the well-photographed boxy limousines were scheduled to be inserted into the covered structure early Wednesday morning. Then, depending on actual terrorist actions as the lookalike presidential motorcades were exposed to attack, a second line of cars could be dispatched. It would comprise two regular black limousines with smoked windows, both with presidential seals on the doors, and their leading and trailing escorts. These limousines would also be decoys, to draw fire and to identify more precisely any terrorist positions. Also, the Service had decided, terrorists might figure that the first salvo of limousines in two different directions was a decoy and hold their fire until the second group was launched.

However, if after two separately launched processions involving four decoy limousines it was determined that the president still must leave the grounds, possibly because of a major attack on the Capitol itself, the Secret Service's third try should be a charm: the jet cars—the two sleek, hand-made $11 million Chrysler turbine automobiles weighing 12,000 pounds each and boasting up to eight inches of steel-alloy shell and the absolute latest in armament. Vance thought that if ever reality touched fantasy, these identical-looking vehicles were right out of a James Bond novel.

"What's *your* guess?"

Vance turned and saw his cohort Rick Hayes.

"My *guess?*"

"Yeah, what they might try on Wednesday. So far, the opinion's running eight-to-one airplanes over missiles. Because of the simulator found in the bunker, and all."

Vance shrugged. "For all we know, it was a missile-launch simulator. But what difference does it make? Either way, we'll probably have to use the Batmobiles."

Hayes nodded and looked at the space where the sophisticated cars would be offloaded after being concealed and delivered inside an eighteen-wheeler tractor-trailer combination.

"Nothing like the old days, is it?" he posed. "When the president could take regular 7-a.m. constitutionals on the streets of Washington, as Truman did."

"Speaking of Truman," Vance pointed at his partner, "remember the account of the Air Force's practice bombing run during the parade at his second inauguration?"

"When the B-36s came up from Carswell at Fort Worth and zeroed in on the White House at barely more than treetop level?" Hayes made a face and shook his head. "I can imagine our people. I'll bet they just about *shit.*"

"Yeah, hell of an example for the Air Force to set for someone with the wrong intentions. Took forty-six years for that wacko to copy it, when he crashed his Cessna next to the South Portico. No, we don't need role models like that."

"Maybe déjà vu for Wednesday?"

Vance didn't say anything for a minute.

"You know, it really seemed like the threats were simpler in the past. I reread the report of Eisenhower's inaugural parade in 1953—when that cowboy on horseback rode up to the reviewing stand and lassoed the president. Every agent there knew in his gut that the horse was going to bolt and Ike would be yanked off the reviewing stand and pulled down the street. Probably killed by the fall alone. Vance kicked at a congealed lump of cement. "But then I guess he'd have been just as dead as he would have been in a sophisticated attack."

"You're wondering if we're excluding other possibilities?" Hayes proposed with raised eyebrows. "Viable, *simpler* possibilities?"

Vance shrugged his shoulders.

"Maybe. After all, there *are* opportunities other than the inauguration itself."

Hayes nodded. "You may be right. Don't forget the two other successful simulated attacks on the White House . . . by the boys at the U.S. Army Chemical and Biological Warfare Research Center. First, when their operatives placed canisters in the air conditioning system and released substances that could have been germs or nerve gas. Then, second, when their group of mock tourists, some of whom had artificial limbs made of plastic explosive, got past the metal detectors inside the East Gate and made it to within fifty feet of the Man. Had those clowns in either incident been real terrorists, the president probably would have died. We picked up a lot of facial egg over those incursions."

Vance stared into space. "Times have changed."

His partner was quiet for a second. "You still think we're overlooking something?"

"Well, let's just say I'm not quite ready to give up worrying . . . or praying."

Tulsa
12:11 a.m.

"Connect the dots," Jack ordered himself while he pushed up the right-turn blinker. "Can't get any simpler than that, old man."

He'd reached the turn for the main entrance of United States Simulation Systems two minutes after five o'clock the previous afternoon. On an ordinary weekday, he would have passed a hundred workers on their way home. As he drove onto the property this time, he had the road to himself.

USSS was located within a large office and industrial park in the southeastern part of Tulsa, near where FlightSafety and other major simulator manufacturers had assembly operations. Simulation, as everyone called the company, was a complex of five interconnected buildings on twenty acres of rolling landscape. The physical work of putting together the sophisticated electronic units took place in four three-story structures in a row. The administration building sat apart in front. Jack stopped at the guardhouse and lowered his window. The white-haired uniformed man inside the booth smiled as he slid the glass aside.

"Good to see you again, Mr. Stroud. Our thoughts have been with you, sir. I, uh ... about your little Rachel ... "

"Thanks, Carl." Jack nodded. "I hope it won't be much longer."

The man pressed a lever, and the security gate rose from its housing. Jack rolled up the window and directed the car around a corner to his reserved parking space in back.

"Three steps. So simple."

It had all fallen together on the way. Jack killed the engine and slipped out of the car. "First, they had a simulator in the bunker." He continued to talk to himself as he walked to the door for employees only. "Second, they kidnapped Rachel to keep me from my office because, third, I might discover that we *manufactured* that simulator." Jack found his building access card and slipped it into the slot. The door buzzed, and he pulled it open. "If I learned what they're flying, I just might be able to gum up their plans." He headed down the empty corridor toward his office.

Jack inserted the key in the lock and made his way into the darkened reception area. He noticed the pleasant scent almost immediately. His secretary insisted on having freshly cut flowers around the office, regardless of the season. "Try telling a rosebud it's a cold and dreary day," she'd said. With an upward motion of his index finger, he flipped on the lights.

He crossed the room into his private office and continued his previous line of thinking. Without the accidental intervention and discovery by Lester Graham, there'd be little or no reason to connect the bunker at Beggs with a simulator from here.

Oh, that's why they took her, all right. Otherwise the kidnapping didn't make any sense. And if they hadn't taken her when they did, they damn sure would have after Graham got away a day or so later. They'd realize the old farmer would tell the authorities about a big white box on stilts with wires and hoses coming out of it and going into a wall. The Feds would have figured what it was in a New York minute.

"Nice and neat," he sighed.

He sat in the soft leather chair, pulled himself to the desk, and activated the terminal, which was connected to the company's mainframe computer.

"Of course, they didn't figure on needing to do all this in the first place, because I was supposed to be out of the way."

As the screen came to life, he lost his concentration for a moment. He hoped it would always be this way, that he'd be only a thought away at any time from seeing the faces of his wife and son. He drew a deep breath ... and let them go. Temporarily.

"Now if I can just find out what kind of simulator we sold them. And find out who 'them' is, while I'm at it." He squinted at the data choices that glowed at him. Where to begin?

Jack first accessed the list of active clients. There were 843, counting both those who had ever bought a simulator and those who'd bought parts since 1989. He scrolled down the long list for a moment before stopping abruptly.

"This is *not* going to work."

He punched in a request to narrow the selections to simulator purchasers only. Seconds later, 389 names came up, listed alphabetically. Jack tapped the keyboard and watched as the information rose on the screen, line by line. Not one of the names jumped out at him or even looked suspicious. He recognized most of them as bona fide companies.

Twenty-six minutes after he started, he'd scanned the entire list. He shook his head after he read the last entry. "If there's an oddball in the pack, I sure as hell don't see it."

He started over again, this time putting a computerized checkmark next to any names he couldn't positively identify or had any questions about. When he finished, after another hour, there were sixty-seven entries on the new list. Over the years, according to the data, Simulation had sold these particular firms thirty-one different types of simulators. Jack switched gears and requested the background data file. When it came up, he chose the first of the sixty-seven companies, AeroMetro, S.A., a new Venezuelan commuter airline. When the computer disgorged eight pages of information, Jack began at the top and read it all.

"Slow going," he said in a low voice when he finished, "but what choice do I have?"

He tapped up another name.

Jack read the last line of the last entry, then checked his watch. He jerked upright.

"Good God. It's after midnight."

He reached for the telephone and punched 664-3300. He sat back and waited for the connection to be made.

"Hope he's still there."

The FBI number rang once, and Jack recognized the voice on the other end.

"Corley, I don't see anything that looks out of line." He stood up. "I'm faxing the list to you as soon as I get off the phone. I hope your efforts are more productive."

FBI Office, Tulsa
7:02 a.m.

"Seven confirmations already from Europe."

Brand held open the office door for Jack. "Got three 'no-answers' we'll check through our counterparts in France and Italy." He pointed down the hall. "Second door on the right. They've moved me."

As they walked for his office, Brand continued the enumeration.

"We've started calling the U.S. numbers in the Eastern time zone. It's turning out to be a little early, since it's a Sunday morning. I think you gave us four for South America, a couple in Mexico. Won't get to those for another hour or so. All in all, though, a good start."

"Sounds to me like a good start in finding simulators we don't need to find."

The two men sat down on the padded metal chairs in front of the desk.

"Yeah, well, kiss a lot of frogs, et cetera, et cetera." Brand slid a manila folder from the side of the desk and opened it.

Jack extended his legs and exhaled. "Sorry, Corley, I'm wearing a little thin."

Brand leaned toward him. "Hey, who do you think you are, Superman?" He winked. "We're all zombies, Jackson." He tapped at the top sheet in the folder. "Let's get down to business." He peered at the page. "OK, we're going for the basics when we make the calls: Did they buy a simulator from USSS? If so, what kind is it, and do they still have it? If they don't, what did they do with it? Meet with your approval?"

Jack nodded. "How about verification?"

"Oh, we're doing that." Brand pointed to the sheet. "The second question includes a request for a serial or business property tax number." He sat back. "Right now that's the best we can do short of a physical inspection."

"Got to find that simulator, Corley. I'm convinced it's the key."

"Well, we'll keep pursuing your list. In the meantime, we're recommending that the FAA ban all Washington-area air traffic, out to at least fifty miles, for a four-hour time frame on Wednesday. Two hours before noon, two hours afterwards. Back it up with the Air Force. We may not know what they intend to fly, but if we ground everything it won't make any difference."

Jack changed the subject. "That bitch who took Rachel . . . Rima Ameen, or whatever her real name was . . . didn't someone say she was never more than five minutes from her brother?"

Brand nodded. "The Syrians passed that along to the president last Tuesday." He rubbed his face. "Why?"

"And there's something else I've been wondering about." Jack turned toward Brand. "Norman's Christian Cavalcade was supposed to hold its big camp meeting in Seattle today, with some 50,000 people in attendance. The trip had been planned for a year and a half. Anyone been keeping an eye on matters out there?"

"I'm ahead of you on that score," Brand replied. "Remember when you got curious about the missing buses on Thursday, and I asked Jerry Reynolds to have Seattle checked out? Well, we still have no idea where Norman is, but our local boys went over the Seattle International Hotel with a fine-tooth comb, and they reported that they found one of those buses abandoned at the very bottom level of the parking garage. According to the firm that operates the garage, there were three others there, same type, but they left Wednesday."

"And they were found in northern California on Thursday?"

"Exactly. The license-plate number of the bus left behind in Seattle matches those found on the buses at Vallejo. Four buses, the same phony number on all of them."

"Anything found in the bus?"

"Nothing interesting. But I've got one more item for you."

Brand closed the file folder.

"Yesterday afternoon the president notified the director that the Syrians say there's a good chance another team's in the country. A heavy-duty, supposedly 'former' KGB operation, worse than Kuttab's, but maybe working with Kuttab toward the same objective. The word is, this second group won't show itself unless and until the first group has failed. That's why the president is going through with the outdoor ceremony on Wednesday, to flush them out. It's risky business, señor, but that's the way he wants it. Needless to say, the pressure's been ratcheted off the graph at both the Bureau and the Secret Service."

Jack looked at his friend. "Corley, it's an extremely dangerous gamble, to sit like fucking stool pigeons." He paused. "But I agree that those groups have to be lured out into the open, then eliminated. Consider the horrors just one of them has produced in less than three weeks." He slapped the top of the desk with his open palm. "We've *got* to figure out what kind of simulator they practiced on. That might be the one thing that will enable us to flush out both groups before they commit wholesale murder again."

"I totally agree."

Brand rose and started toward the door.

"I'm going to have Washington make calls for us, too."

He turned and pointed at Jack as he stepped into the hall.

"Any goddamned no-answers from any purchaser will get an on-site visit. Back in a minute."

Washington, D.C.
10:00 a.m.

The honor of your presence

is requested at the ceremonies attending the

Inauguration of the President of the United States.

That's how 165,000 official invitations read. By themselves, the engraved cardstock documents didn't have any value, other than as collectors' pieces for the later sharing of memories with children and grandchildren. It was what came *with* the invitations, or at least some of them, that really counted: the appropriate tickets to the balls and other exclusive functions. These priceless passes had been allocated to members of the three branches of government and other dignitaries for placement into the hands of those who would most likely show their appreciation by a reciprocal offering of a substantial check. Another 2.2 million "replicates" of the invitations made it into thrilled homes across the country during the first seven days of the new year. Wide-eyed recipients were more than willing to send in the requested $35 as their contribution to the making of history.

The inauguration of a president was the closest thing America had to the coronation of a potentate. Ever since George Washington stepped forward and raised his right hand at Federal Hall in New York, this electrifying and unifying event had made most citizens feel as if they belonged to something important, almost mystical. Without question, it made them proud. The five-day extravaganza, which started on Saturday, would peak at the Inaugural on Wednesday. Then, inevitably at the stroke of midnight, the quadrennial cycle would begin all over again.

According to a preliminary report prepared by the General Accounting Office, more than $32 million had been allocated for all the festivities. The Presidential Inaugural Committee, the private but official operator of the event, refused comment, announcing that the actual numbers would be made public later. In truth, however, the PIC had ultimate authority over everything and answered only to the president. The GAO's estimate would probably stand.

The money poured in. In addition to the millions for the right tickets, there were loans and guarantees from America's biggest corporations and income from frenetic sales of official souvenirs and other memorabilia. The customs and traditions dictated that there be something for everyone, so Inauguration Week included speeches and fireworks and parties and parades. According to the promises, the president and the First Lady would visit twelve official balls the evening of the inauguration. Most of the standing-room-only functions would be held in major hotels within a few miles of the White House. On the circuit was the Watergate, then the Westin, the Mayflower, and the Washington Hilton . . . all the way east to the Sheraton Grand on Capitol Hill. The stops for the First Couple would include a gala at the Smithsonian Institution's National Air and Space Museum thirty minutes before they entered the Washington Convention Center for the final, and televised, celebration of the occasion.

The logistics for it all rivaled a major military adventure, and those responsible for their respective parts labored for uncounted hours. The Joint Congressional Committee on Inaugural Ceremonies was in full swing overseeing the details of the swearing-in ceremony at the Capitol. The group coordinated its activities with the Armed Forces Inaugural Committee, which knew how to secure such critical things as bullhorns and portable toilets. Thousands of government operatives dashed back and forth between the General Services Administration, the District of Columbia's offices, the Secret Service, and the Department of the Interior.

It was reported that 9,250 military personnel were involved this time. Most people would see the military presence only in the role of drivers, ushers, assistants, and aides for governors and other state representatives. Some 3,000 soldiers were assigned to the parade alone, but that was the usual size of the traffic-control contingent. However, *The Washington Post* reported that because of the "lingering threat" of a terrorist incident, an additional 4,600 troops had been moved to within a thirty-mile radius of the capital and were on full alert.

There were the inevitable complaints from homeless and consumer-advocacy groups. For years they had grumbled that the whole affair had gotten out of hand, that all the Constitution required was that the president recite a thirty-five-word oath, yet no one really tried to rein in the juggernaut. It was too much Washington, too many opportunities to make the right contacts. It was, in short, too much fun.

And even the weatherman promised a good day. A frigid day, for sure, but one on which most could see the Capitol from hundreds of prime vantage points within five miles of the pomp and circumstance at the West

Front. Since the first inaugural in 1789, clear skies had predominated two to one over rain or snow. This one looked like it would be clear but bitterly cold . . . around nineteen degrees by noon.

Already people were arriving by the thousands. Worsted wool pinstripes and fur coats disembarked at National and Dulles and Baltimore-Washington International, while windbreakers and earmuffs stepped from Amtrak runs at Union Station. Then there were the cars and vans and buses. Lots of buses.

The White House
4:04 p.m.

Sitting on the edge of his desk in the Oval Office, the president waved off assistant press secretary Jim Collins and a speechwriter and continued his telephone conversation with the director of the FBI.

"That's right, when I go on the air tonight it'll be to assure the nation that you've put an end to the threat. And I'll be *very* convincing."

He shook his head and stood up.

"No, let me make it crystal clear. I am *not* expecting any surprises on Wednesday. It's your job to get those bastards before then." The president held the cord with his free hand and circled back to his chair. "And I do *not* want anything to happen before the inaugural either. No terrorist incidents anywhere else in the country. Understand? Pull all the stops, but keep the peace!"

He sat down in the large leather chair and continued his monologue.

"I've been able to keep a gag on Homer Jenkins and the others in Congress who've been screaming ever since all this started, but if something blows up before Wednesday, there'll be such a stink I'd be hard-pressed not to cancel the outdoor function. That would jeopardize whatever decent chance we have of intercepting those killers in one place. And if I refuse or drag out my decision, Jenkins and his cohorts would call attention to my reticence, which just might alert the second group that we're laying a trap for them with the public ceremony. It would also feed his fervor to hold hearings about my decision to establish martial law."

The president rubbed at his forehead.

"Impeachment proceedings aren't exactly what I had in mind after what I've gone through for the past three weeks. No, I want peace and quiet across the country, and you *will* get those groups before Wednesday noon."

He hung up abruptly, turned around in his chair, and stared out at the long shadows on the south lawn. The only sound was a faint tick-tock from the brass clock on the mantel.

Tulsa
11:36 p.m.

For the first time in days, Jack had gotten to bed at a reasonable hour. He was brushing away the remnants of consciousness when the telephone rang. At first the sound didn't register. Then he rolled to one side and reached for the receiver.

"Hello?"

"Mr. John Stroud?"

Jack frowned. Only boiler-room salesmen called him John. All of a sudden he opened his eyes and sat up in the darkness. He recognized the accented voice.

"Speaking."

"Mr. Stroud, this is Aleksandr Voronov. Please do not ask any questions."

Jack found the light switch. The voice went on in its monotone cadence.

"I believe you have a personal interest in someone I have learned about. You must listen carefully if there is to be no further harm to that person. I have instructions. Are you ready?"

Oh, my God, he's talking about Rachel. "Yes, *yes,*" Jack exclaimed as he pulled open the drawer of the bedside table. His fingers found the pencil and pad. "Go ahead, please."

"First, only you must come. You are not to be followed. Otherwise, there *will* be further harm, and I think you know what that means."

Jack clenched his jaw.

"OK."

"Follow U.S. 64 south, through Bixby, to the town of Leonard. There's an all-night convenience store on the right side of the highway, just as you enter the town. Look for the outdoor pay phone in the parking lot. It will ring at exactly five minutes past midnight. Be there."

With a click, Voronov was gone.

Jack checked his watch. "It's 11:40? *Damn.*"

He touched the face of his wife in the photograph at his bedside. "Laura, I'm going to get her!" He threw back the covers and ran for his closet. As he pulled open the double doors, he saw the polished wood box on top of the dresser inside. He moved closer and lifted the hinged lid. There, just as he'd left it, was the new .45-caliber automatic Brand had given him. He considered the weapon for a moment. Then he reached for it.

"You're going with me."

Leonard Mountain
Monday, January 18, 12:01 a.m.

Jack accelerated through the deserted residential streets of his secluded neighborhood and headed for U.S. 64, where he turned south. A sense of foreboding alternated with a growing anger. Just how much more did Rachel have to suffer?

He stared at the concrete ribbon ahead and swore to settle the score, particularly with one individual, even if it took the rest of his life.

Although his was the only vehicle at the intersections along the way, he'd gotten a red light at every one of them. He kept an eye on the dashboard clock. If there was a genuine danger of being late, he decided he'd run a red light. Otherwise, he'd bear his frustration at the empty crossings in order to avoid a traffic cop's intrusion. It was going to be close as it was, and having to stop to explain the situation might push his arrival in Leonard beyond the time for the call ... and, perhaps, beyond making a difference in the life of his daughter.

It was sixteen miles from Jack's house to the city limits of Leonard. At this hour of the night, the small rural community was a very dark place—with the one exception of the twenty-four-hour convenience store and its lighted parking lot, just ahead. His clock indicated 12:04 as he slowed at the roadside marquee announcing the town. He left the narrow highway and headed for the red-on-silver telephone booth at the far end of the lot. Jack could hear the ringing before he turned off the engine. He ran to the booth and pushed open the flimsy door.

"Hello?"

The cold wind whined as it knifed through cracks in the glass of the battered box. He pressed the receiver tightly against his ear and cupped a hand over his other ear.

"Mr. Stroud?" It was Voronov's detached voice again. "Do you know how to get to the top of Leonard Mountain?"

"Leonard *Mountain?*" he questioned out loud.

"You're on Highway 64," the monotone went on. "Go one block further east, turn right, and go ten blocks south." Jack was sure the man was reading the message. "Turn left and drive one mile up the steep hill. At the top on the left is a one-story stone house, surrounded by a white wrought-iron fence. The house fronts . . . "

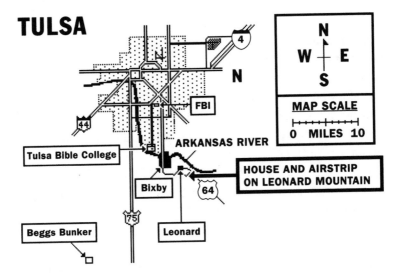

"Hold it, hold it," Jack protested. "You're going too fast. Please repeat what you said. I'm not familiar with this area at all."

Voronov cleared his throat and restated the instructions more slowly. He continued, "There is an airstrip on Leonard Mountain. The house fronts on it, but don't go that far. Stop at the driveway. The gate will open for you."

Airstrip? Jack wondered if he was being toyed with after all. He'd never heard of either the so-called mountain or its airstrip. He started to say something, but the Russian wasn't finished.

"You will pull up to the garage. Enter the house by the door next to it." There was a hollow click as Voronov disconnected.

Jack held the receiver for a moment before replacing it. As he turned and gazed out at the empty parking lot, he patted his left side and felt the holstered automatic. He pulled open the door of the telephone booth and returned to his car.

The drive to the top of the ridge took eight minutes. Just as Voronov had said, there was a house on the left, surrounded by a five-foot-high metal fence. He braked. The road continued for what appeared to be another hundred feet before it widened and disappeared into the black-ness. Must be the airstrip, he thought. Suddenly there was a clanking sound, and the heavy driveway gate began to swing inward. He waited until it had completely cleared the pavement before he pressed the accelerator and drove onto the property. In his rearview mirror he watched the gate close.

As his car advanced across the smooth asphalt at a slow roll, Jack peered ahead and to both sides. There wasn't a light in the house that he could see. His headlights were the only illumination on this part of Leonard Mountain. The garage was fifty yards from the gate. Jack stopped the car, turned off the engine, and listened. The only sound was the wind.

The house was a ranch-style dwelling common to the southwest, the exterior a combination of painted wood and sandstone. Curtains and blinds covered the windows. To Jack's immediate left was the entry door Voronov had mentioned.

"Moment of truth," he told himself under his breath as he punched off the headlights, pulled the keys from the ignition, and got out. He stood in the cold for a few seconds and rubbed his hands together. As he did so, he sensed the butt of the .45 against his elbow. After a moment's consideration he decided against drawing the weapon until he knew what he was up against. Jack stepped the remaining ten feet and gripped the doorknob. It turned easily, and he pushed the door open into a black void.

Almost immediately he recoiled at an overwhelming odor. It was thoroughly repulsive, a burnt smell that watered his eyes and made him think of decaying bacon. All of a sudden a light clicked on in the next room. There, framed by the doorway, gagged and secured to a chair, sat Aleksandr Voronov. The older man's eyes were wide with terror. Standing behind the Russian, weaving and wearing a simpering grin, was Norman Gentry.

"Hello, Jack," he purred. Norman's puffy face shone with sweat. He contemplated his prey in the chair. "We've been expecting you, haven't we, professor?"

Strands of thin hair fell in a half-dozen directions from the top of Norman's head and disclosed the paths the perspiration had coursed down his face. He was dressed in one of the flashy double-breasted white suits that had become his trademark to millions of worshipers around the world. Today, however, the high-style outfit was thoroughly wrinkled, and it was soiled with generous smears of reds and browns. Norman wore no tie. The bloated evangelist looked twenty years older in the stark light. His acne scars, usually well hidden by makeup, stood out as irregular pockmarks against his greasy, milk-white complexion.

"Yes, yes," Norman continued as he smoothed his prisoner's hair, "we've really looked forward to this." His oversize diamond pinkie ring sparkled with the back-and-forth movement of his hand.

Jack's remaining apprehension gave way to disgust and propelled him through the door of the second room. "What the *shit* are you doing?" he yelled as he advanced.

"Don't come any closer," Norman warned in an ice-cold voice. Jack saw that his former brother-in-law held something against Voronov's ear. It looked like a ballpoint pen. "You want this man to live, don't you?" His smile was gone. "This is a dart pistol, Jack," he indicated with a nod at the cylinder in his hand. "It fires an explosive needle into the brain. He'll never know what hit him."

Jack stopped in the middle of the room.

"All right. Don't hurt him. This is between you and me."

He watched the younger man's eyes and wondered where his usual bodyguards were. Perhaps they were nearby, monitoring all of this with weapons drawn.

"Where's Rachel?" he demanded.

Norman bobbed his head from side to side and started to laugh.

"That's right, try to stay in charge." Then he mocked in falsetto, "'Where's Rachel? Where's Rachel?'" His eyes contracted to slits, and he shrieked, "I'm running things now, not *you!*" His tongue darted back and forth between his lips. "Reuben's not here to roll out the fucking red carpet anymore, so you're going to have to listen to what *I* have to say for once."

Jack didn't move. Norman ranted on.

"No, this is my turn, Jack. Understand? *My* turn."

The fleshy man pointed with his free hand.

"Sit over there and keep your goddamned mouth shut while I tell *you* a few things."

Jack moved his eyes without turning his head. A metal chair was positioned at a forty-five-degree angle in a corner of the room.

"Go on!" Norman ordered.

Jack weighed his chances in the corner versus where he was. Just how was he going to gain the upper hand with that penlike weapon virtually in Voronov's ear? Being farther away would only add to the difficulty.

"Look, I don't know why . . . "

"Now!" Norman screamed. His entire body shook.

Jack stepped to the chair and wondered what combination of drugs and alcohol held sway over the disturbed man this time. As he sat down, he discerned an inappropriate tinge of sweetness to the foul air. It now smelled as if maple syrup had been poured over a putrid animal concoction while it smoldered.

"Oh, there're so many things to cover, aren't there, Jack?"

Large beads of sweat ran down Norman's face and into his mouth.

"It's been *so* long since we've had a nice family chat."

"Where's Rachel?" Jack asked again, this time in a dispassionate voice.

"When I'm good and ready, you shit." Norman waved his hand. "First I need to go over a few matters that are far more important. Starting with my beloved sister, who's better off dead."

Jack felt a surge of adrenalin, and he was about to propel himself out of the chair and across the room.

"No, no, no," Norman chided. "You must restrain yourself, Mr. Fucking Bigshot. Otherwise . . . " He inclined his head toward Voronov. "I'll have to fix you up like him." Then his smile came back. "Oh, I'm grieving for Laura all right. But she brought it on herself, marrying a Catholic. And an uppity one at that."

It was all Jack could do to hold onto his chair.

"Where's my daughter, you son of a bitch? And that cunt who took her?"

Norman ignored him.

"Yes, Laura got herself in a lot of trouble because of it. Dragged everyone else down, too." He paused, then shook his head. "No, they were right. It had to happen the way it did."

"*Who* was right?"

Norman checked his fingernails before he replied. "Bunny . . . and her friends." He smiled. "And friends of her friends."

"What the hell does Bunny have to do with this?"

Norman remained silent, with a smirk on his face. He kept looking at his fingernails.

"Did Bunny's 'friends' build the place at Beggs?" Jack probed.

Norman looked toward the ceiling for a few seconds. He licked his lips.

"Why, yes. How did you guess?"

Jack shifted to the edge of the chair. "Just how many of these 'friends' does she have?"

Norman didn't respond.

Jack seethed with anger.

"Eight people left that property a week ago in a helicopter. Was Rachel one of them?"

Norman popped open his eyes. He nodded. "I believe so."

"God damn it, where is she now?"

Norman leaned forward and looked at him.

"Yes, indeed, they took away your precious little shit, didn't they?"

Jack glared. "Where did they *go*, Norman?"

After a few seconds, Norman's face contorted again and he shouted. "*You* shut up. I told you I'm in charge here." There was a surrealistic quality to his hot-and-cold rhetoric. "I'll tell you what I *want* to tell you. And I'll ask the questions, too."

Jack abandoned the confrontational tone. He held up his hands. "OK, fine with me," he replied quietly. "You can say anything, ask anything." He crafted as he went. "Of *course* you're in charge. I'm very interested in what you have to say. Forgive me."

Norman chewed on his lower lip while he considered the conciliatory statement. Finally he shrugged his shoulders.

"They didn't tell me where they were going." His voice sounded distant. He looked up at the light. "I even asked them."

It seemed like a new opening, and Jack decided to press ahead.

"Did they take the helicopter all the way?"

"All the way?" Norman cocked his head. "No, they took an airplane from here."

"They were *here?*"

Without replying, Norman squatted behind Voronov and picked up an open liter of Wild Turkey. He fitted his full lips over the orifice and swung the half-empty bottle upward. As he drained the amber liquid in rhythmic gulps, Jack thought again about his gun. He concluded he was making sufficient headway without it.

Norman leaned down and placed the bottle on the floor, then rose again behind Voronov. Jack noticed that the ballpoint pen never moved more than six inches from the Russian's ear.

"Yes, they were here," Norman sighed as he wiped his mouth with his sleeve. He seemed to enjoy the cat-and-mouse game.

Jack restated Norman's earlier answer. "And you don't know where they went?"

"No."

"Do you know what kind of airplane it was?"

Norman stared at him. He tucked his chin against his chest and burped.

"No, again."

"Must have been propeller-driven, though, to get in and out of here. Right?"

"What?"

"It was a small plane with a propeller. Not a jet."

Norman shook his head. "No, it was a big plane with a propeller."

Jack frowned. "One propeller?"

"Uh-huh."

Jack wondered if Norman was accurately describing the aircraft. It definitely made a difference. He returned to the bigger picture.

"Will you tell me about Beggs?"

Norman stared across the room and pursed his lips. His head bobbed, then stopped, and his upper body shook as if he were attempting to disgorge something unpleasant. Jack sensed that a psychic battle was under way. He knew that the first one to speak would lose.

"It all happened so fast," Norman finally began. "I mean, who would have thought they would have caused so much . . . " He stopped and touched his hand to his temple. "I couldn't have known, you know." Jack didn't move. He had obviously pulled the right string.

"They got involved there two or three years ago."

Norman's delivery now sounded more matter-of-fact, but Jack knew it resulted from a delicate balancing between competing demons.

"Bunny never talked with me about anything after that. I had to do my own snooping. But I guess they built the building first, followed by the underground place."

Norman stopped and seemed to consider what to say next. Jack led him on with a question.

"There were a lot of buses, weren't there?"

Norman made an exaggerated nod.

"How many?"

"I don't know. Twenty . . . thirty. Maybe more."

"They brought in a flight simulator, didn't they?"

Norman shook his head. "Not with the buses."

"In a truck?"

"I think so."

"What kind of flight simulator was it, Norman?"

"I don't know."

"Was it for the type of plane they flew here?"

Norman shrugged. "Probably, but they never told me. I never asked, either."

"Where are the buses now?"

"All over, I think."

"All over the country?"

Norman nodded.

"Why?"

"I don't know."

"What about that information on the foreign bank accounts?"

"Those files you got into on the PC in the office?" Norman grinned and wrinkled his nose. "Those weren't mine. They were Bunny's."

Jack squinted. "How did you know I got into the files?"

"Oh, her friends watched you every second. Watched you leave, too. Also, you left tracks when you logged on. They didn't like your rubbernecking one bit. Gave you a scar on the head for your trouble, didn't they?"

"Who *are* Bunny's friends?"

Norman shook his head and remained quiet.

"Why did they take Rachel?"

Norman's tongue played between his lips. Nearly a minute passed. Jack couldn't tell if he was going to get an answer or not.

"A few reasons," Norman ventured at last. "But the only one that counts, I guess, is that Bunny wants to make sure you suffer. This is her opportunity to put you in your place. But I don't know what she has in mind. It'll be a nice surprise, I'm sure."

Jack looked at the floor, then rubbed his palms back and forth. In the relatively short time he had known Bunny, she had always been an enigma. Ever since Norman brought her into the family, he'd had questions about her and her background. She seemed hollow, a shell . . . or maybe a tightly constructed façade. She didn't mix socially at all. In short, she seemed to be the perfect companion for a reclusive husband. Reclusive offstage, that is. Jack raised his head and stared at Norman.

"What's her role in all of this?" he asked calmly.

Norman blinked his eyes. "*Now* I know what you're trying to do." He laughed. When he spoke, he slurred his words. "They told me it was for my own good not to know too much. So, Mister Smart Ass, you can't get that from me, because I . . . don't . . . know. Boy, they're really brilliant. I might have told everything, too."

"Why wouldn't you tell me if you knew?" Jack questioned. The latest infusion of alcohol combined with whatever pills Norman had taken earlier appeared to be having an effect. Jack decided to be blunt. "Norman, you've been used, and you're still being used. Bunny and her friends are gone, but you're still here, left behind to answer questions and to face the consequences. And, believe me, there are a lot of both."

Norman watched him in silence. Again, Jack thought, some sort of mental struggle was taking place. He hoped to influence it, and quickly.

"Why don't you put down that pen and the two of us can have a heart-to-heart talk?"

For the first time in eighteen years, Jack felt a degree of empathy for his former brother-in-law. The man had spiraled to the bottom under someone's diabolical scheme. Jack thought of what might have been averted had he attempted to reach out to Norman even once over the years.

"I'd like to open up," Jack suggested. "Wouldn't you?"

Norman ran his hand over his wet face. Then he fixed his attention on the weapon he was holding.

"I . . . I don't know."

Jack sensed that time was running out. He had to keep Norman engaged in conversation.

"Hey, how about letting me have some of that Wild Turkey," he proposed. "I could bring my chair a little closer." He pointed to the Russian. "You don't have to keep that at Aleksandr's ear, either. I know *he'd* feel better if he weren't under the gun, so to speak."

"It's too late, Jack." Norman's voice was close to a whisper.

Jack forced a laugh. "You mean Wild Turkey's too precious to waste on a pompous ass like me?"

Norman stared at the top of Voronov's head.

"They always called me a loner, didn't they? That's what *you* called me, too, Jack."

He touched the Russian's hair and seemed to ponder.

"I haven't *always* been a loner. At least, I haven't always wanted to be."

Norman looked around the room.

"Reuben—my own father—called me strange, even when I told him I wanted to be a part of his ministry. He said he didn't believe me, that I didn't belong. From right after college, when I went to Europe and the Holy Land, I tried to do what I thought he wanted. I gave up my plans, everything, so I wouldn't embarrass him and the ministry."

Jack watched as Norman pleaded his case to a judge somewhere beyond.

"But it all started unraveling two years ago, when they started crowding me."

His delivery became jerky.

"I *had* to drink to put out the fires. Anyone with any sensitivity would have reacted the same way."

Jack attempted to say something, but Norman went on.

"I could see what was coming, but I couldn't stop them. They had me right where they wanted me. They would have ruined the ministry."

He looked at Jack.

"I suppose I could have said something to you, but it probably wouldn't have made any difference. They really knew what they wanted, and they were going to get it."

Norman turned his head aside.

"I'll never forget Dad's eyes the night before he died, when he complained about something that Bunny was doing. Arranging the new shipments from the port, I think. She told him to shut up. 'Shut up, you worthless fool,' is exactly how she put it. He didn't yell back or anything. He just reached out and touched her face." Norman bit his lip. "Those were the kindest eyes I've ever seen, filled with love . . . along with his tears. But she slapped his hand away. He knew then what was coming."

It was Bunny? Jack's heart pounded. He remembered Reuben's words that night on the telephone: "I have touched the face of Death." He shook his head almost imperceptibly. It was also the first time he had ever heard Norman call his father Dad.

"Oh, she thought what she'd put in his dinner would kill him, but he was one tough old coot. It really surprised her to find him still alive the next morning, so she dosed him again. Actually held his mouth open and poured it down his throat. I'm sure his brain was already gone by that time, but his heart kept beating. The second dose stopped it."

Norman established eye contact.

"I have to tell you something else, Jack. I could never keep it from you. Bunny went to Dallas and drove the killers to Laura's plane."

Jack closed his eyes.

"They were to have killed you and Laura and the twins. Killing the Treasury Secretary was a lucky break for them, because it diverted attention for a while. But they didn't figure you'd stay behind. They didn't know Dad had called you the night before."

Norman's panting was the only sound in the room. Suddenly his expression froze, and he looked around. "Everything's my fault." He started sobbing. "I should confess to the entire world, but there's no time. I didn't mean for this to happen, believe me. I'm the prodigal son who's returned home to beg forgiveness. But my father's not here to receive me."

Resolve flared in Norman's tear-filled eyes.

"So I must go find him. Tell everyone I'm sorry."

In a blur, Norman brought the ballpoint pen to his mouth and slammed his open palm against the plunger. There was a white flash and a sharp crack as the dart detonated inside his mouth. Shattered teeth and pieces of tongue blew across the room. Norman's body fell first to its knees, then forward to the floor. As his head hit the hard surface with a thump, it settled sideways. Blood poured from the ragged opening that had been his mouth. Most of his face was a tangle of flesh and muscle, and both eyes had been ejected from their sockets. A blubbering sound came from the corpse as the lungs exhaled for the final time. Jack bolted from his chair.

Blood and shreds of Norman's face had splattered across Voronov's back and down his left side. Jack reached for the cloth gag that covered the Russian's mouth.

"Flat on the floor, asshole!"

Jack froze at the voice of Rima Ameen. Out of the corner of his eye, he saw the woman, dressed in black and standing in the open doorway behind him. He thought he recognized a cellular telephone strapped to her hip. She leveled an automatic weapon at his midsection. It appeared to be an Uzi with a silencer attached.

"Well, I should have known you were here," he replied as he started to lower himself to the ground. "I *thought* this place smelled like shit."

Suddenly a burst of bullets perforated the wood floor in a ragged line between the tethered Russian's chair and Jack's left hand. Splinters sprayed in their wake and sprinkled over Norman's body. Jack dropped to a spread-eagle position on his stomach.

"Open your mouth again," the terrorist snarled, "and I'll cut out your tongue from here."

She advanced a few feet inside the room.

"It'd be really too bad if you died before learning about your precious little Rachel." The woman laughed. "Her life is in your hands, yet you seem to keep trying to get her killed. We've kept her alive only because there are a few things you can still do for us."

Jack thought about the simulators. She probably meant, a few things I might not do *to* them.

"In any event, your troublemaking days are finished. Just forty-eight more hours, and it will all be over."

The woman leaned forward, although she never got closer than eight or nine feet.

"You might even be able to celebrate our victory with your little bitch." She laughed again. "But everything has to go according to plan, so don't try playing hero. One more slip-up on your part, and she dies."

If the whore would just step within range of my arm, Jack thought. But the woman stood her ground. Worse, a second later, she took a step backwards, putting herself further out of reach.

"You were so easy, Stroud. All teary-eyed about your poor wife and son. It's amazing how a little pussy can make a man forget what's really important to him." Her laughter this time reeked of derision. "You traded your daughter for a piece of ass. At least Judas got thirty pieces of silver."

Jack clenched his jaw.

The woman moved to the only window in the room. She slipped a finger between the opaque curtain and the glass and eased the covering back a half inch, then peered through the separation.

Who else might be coming? Jack wondered.

The woman stepped back to her previous position in the middle of the room.

"The girl's long gone, if that's what's on your mind. But you're going to be our guest for a while."

The woman shifted to her left, toward a door in the opposite wall.

"It's time for you to go to your room. Get up on your hands and knees ... very slowly."

Jack drew himself up as ordered. The woman reached back with her free hand, twisted the knob on the door, and pulled it open. She took three steps and stood equidistant between Jack and the opened door.

"Crawl!" she ordered. "Do not look at me, just at your hands."

Jack started in slow motion. All of a sudden, he heard loud popping sounds and muffled thuds. He looked up and saw the woman buckle forward, then crumble at Voronov's feet. The back of her jumpsuit was torn open in a dozen places, and blood poured from most of them.

Jack turned at the sound of voices coming from the adjacent room, which opened to the outside. A man's head poked through the doorway. It was Corley Brand. He peered at Jack.

"You OK?"

Right behind him was Don Evans. Both FBI agents wielded 10mm automatics.

"How'd you ever get here?" Jack asked as he got up unsteadily and moved toward the woman. He leaned over and put his fingers against her neck to confirm that she was dead.

"Fortunately for you, I never called off the marshals." Brand walked in and slid his pistol into its holster. "Colyers saw you take off and radioed us. We've been outside about as long as you've been inside. Heard everything with an acoustic cup against the window."

Jack stood up, peeled off the tape covering the Russian's mouth, and began to untie the cords. Voronov spat out a Ping-Pong ball and slumped against the restraints. "Thank God," he mumbled. "But it's probably too late."

Brand stopped with his toes against Norman's body. "Jesus Christ, pizza with everything." He looked over at the woman. "Lots of tomato topping there, too." He motioned toward Evans, who was inspecting the room. "Don called the county mounties before we scaled the fence. They ought to be here shortly. What *is* this stinking place anyway?"

Jack threw aside the remaining cords and helped Voronov stand up. "Some sort of a safe house," he responded. He looked at the Russian. "What do you mean it's probably too late?"

"The government man."

"Who?"

Voronov pointed to the side door that the woman had opened barely a minute earlier.

"The basement. That's where they put him. With any luck, he might still be alive."

Brand frowned. "Who might still be alive?"

"That FBI man."

Brand looked at Jack, and they ran for the door. Evans reached in and flipped the light switch. The four men pounded down the dusty wooden steps, with Brand in the lead.

The room was approximately thirty feet by twenty feet. Its walls and floor were bare concrete, and there were shipping crates of various sizes in one corner. Standing alone in the middle was a black oil drum, which had been used as a trash receptacle. Otherwise the basement was empty. The choking smell was now almost a thick fog.

Voronov pointed. "In there."

Brand unlatched and pulled open a narrow door in the wall. It creaked on its hinges as it swung outward. He felt for a switch. Just as he clicked on the light, a voice whispered from one side of the cubicle.

"I knew you'd come."

The men turned and saw a completely burned man lying in a cast-iron bathtub. His blackened arms were crossed over his midsection. Because of the layers of discolored and cracked covering of his body, it was impossible to tell whether or not he had clothes on. The small room reeked of organic decomposition.

"Might be hard to recognize me, gentlemen. Out of uniform, so to speak." He slowly extended an arm. "Special Agent Charlie Carmichael, at your service." He tried to position the limb for a salute, but he couldn't make the tight angle.

"Shit, Don," Brand yelled, "call St. Francis. Get a medevac helicopter out here immediately!"

"Oh, nooo, Charlie," Evans moaned at the hideous sight of his friend. He moved closer and bent over the form in the tub. "What happened, man?"

Brand tapped Evans on the shoulder. "OK, keep him company. I'll call the hospital." He ran from the room. Jack and Voronov drew in behind Evans. Carmichael acknowledged them with a blink of his swollen blue eyes.

"Propane blowtorches," he enunciated in a hoarse voice. "Made me a sight, didn't they?" His head jerked sideward, then recovered. "I read up on some third-degree burn victims once. The good news is that there's no sensation after the nerve endings are melted away. There's the initial shock, of course, but no pain afterward. And I'm as lucid as the day I joined the Bureau." He paused, and the men could hear his rasping attempt to breathe. "The bad news is that, well, I'll be like this for three, maybe five hours. Then it's hello, St. Peter."

Tears streamed down Evans's face as he reached out and cradled Carmichael's seared head to protect it from the hard porcelain.

"Jesus, Charlie."

Jack stared at the mortally wounded agent. He shook his head at the charred husk with the shining eyes, which had once been a vibrant human being.

"Who did this to you?"

Carmichael had to suppress a cough before responding. He forced his hand to show two fingers. "That 'nurse' and a man. Just before he left in an airplane."

Voronov nodded. "I could hear him scream. It was worse than Soviet prison."

"We got the woman, Charlie," Jack stated. "Shot her upstairs, but the man . . . "

"When?" Evans whispered. "Charlie, *when* did they do this?"

As Carmichael answered, Jack noticed that the agent's lips didn't move. They were only slits in a mostly carbon shell.

"Oh, I'd guess it's been a couple of hours now." He angled his head so he could face Evans directly. "Do you think your old buddy could have some water? Often I had to drink my own urine. Bunny's orders."

Jack made fists and shook them in frustration.

"I'll get the water." Voronov moved quickly out of the small room.

Jack noticed that Carmichael's legs appeared to be in slightly better condition than the rest of his body. The limbs were black and brown in places, but most of the surface was translucent, even clear. He could see streaks of coagulated veins under the sheen.

"So where's the little evangelist?" Carmichael's gaze was piercing.

Jack caught his breath. The sight before him was overwhelming.

"Uh, he killed himself upstairs just before we found you."

The wounded man sighed. "This whole matter's been bizarre from the very beginning, hasn't it? Who would have believed a ministry . . . " He held the thought for a breath.

Brand reentered the room. "There'll be a helicopter here within ten minutes."

"What's the rush, Corley?" Carmichael chided. "You know I'd rather be with you guys anyway. Plus, I've got a lot to tell you."

"Pain?" Brand's face looked skeptical.

Carmichael moved his head slowly from side to side. "No . . . feel fine. I'm almost on a high."

Voronov returned with a glass of water and a tablespoon. He dipped the spoon into the liquid and leaned over and extended it toward Carmichael's mouth. He tipped the spoon, and the water trickled into the opening on the burned man's face.

"Should have asked for a beer," Carmichael kidded after swallowing the tepid offering. Both Jack and Brand wiped their eyes.

"The man who did this," Voronov spoke while continuing to relay the water, "I have seen him twice before. Once in my prison cell at Leningrad and once on the TBC campus. Evil man. I am sure he is former East German Stasi."

"There was . . . another man here . . . who spoke German," Carmichael observed between sips. "One of the two guys who took me from Jack's house. The one who was dressed like a priest. But he left before Aleksandr arrived."

Brand crossed his arms. "Charlie, we're almost certain that man was the same person who tried to get Jack at the hospital, as 'Father Arnold.' Could you tell us what he looked like?"

Carmichael's eyes moved to focus on Brand again. "Tall, maybe 6-3. Medium complexion. Dark brown hair." His verbal sketch was matter-of-fact. "I think he works out . . . good build. Early, mid-fifties. Really splashes on the Aqua Velva. Wears that clerical outfit half the time. I've never seen eyes like his, though. Absolutely ice cold."

"That fits the description we got from St. Francis, when he was looking for Jack. Except possibly for the eyes. But then, he was trying to be the kindly priest."

"*I* know who you are talking about." Voronov shook the spoon for emphasis. "He was one of the worst while I was in prison. I saw him also on the campus. I'd know that face anywhere. I was very afraid after seeing that man again after Leningrad. He looked right at me. I knew he recognized me. I met with Mr. Brand shortly afterwards. Then I was taken and brought here."

"Corley," Carmichael offered with a raised finger, "there *is* one word that man used on three or four occasions. It was 'Lux.' Everyone seemed to know exactly what he was talking about."

"Lux?" Brand looked surprised. "How did he use the word?"

"Like…a code for something. For example, I heard 'Countdown to Lux.'"

"Did he elaborate?"

"No."

Brand took a deep breath.

"At the end of last month, two of our informants tapped into a viciously anti-American cell of revolutionaries in Mexico City. They reported hearing that word, too. It was always used in the context that there was, quote, more to come, unquote."

No one said anything for a few seconds.

"He also talked a lot about a guy named Graham," Carmichael added.

"Lester Graham? The Beggs farmer?" Brand shook his head. "Oh, that's right, you missed that whole episode."

"In any event," Carmichael went on, "it seems they couldn't figure out who Graham was or what he was up to. They thought he might be FBI or an informant. They still weren't sure about him when they captured him, so they kept him rather than killing him, just to be safe. If no one showed up looking for him, they'd get rid of him. They finally decided to kill him sometime after our people went to interview Norman in Albuquerque, but he got away."

"Does anyone know who this Aqua Velva guy really is?" Brand asked. "It sounds like he's one of the honchos. I don't like the fact that we're just now learning that there may be another bad apple out there. A big one."

No one responded.

"Did you find out anything else, Charlie?"

"Nothing more from him," Carmichael whispered, "but I did hear two other men discussing some of the tools they've been preparing: exploding cigarette packs, hand grenades to be inserted inside loaves of bread, fire extinguishers filled with gasoline, birthday cards with plastique, remote-control drones, newspaper-wrapped bombs. It's like they're planning to be around for a while."

Brand whistled. "I sincerely hope not. But they've had a gold mine with the Tulsa port. Contraband comes in regularly without any trouble whatsoever. I'm going to see that we review our surveillance at these inland ports. Everyone concentrates on the biggies—New York, Houston—and bad stuff just pours in at places like this. Sloppy labeling of those cylinders should have gotten someone caught along the line, but they took off scot-free."

Jack squatted down next to the tub.

"Charlie, did you hear anything about my daughter, Rachel? Norman said they took her out of here in a plane."

Carmichael struggled to breathe. "Yes, Jack," the burned man panted. "From what I overheard, I figured they kidnapped her a week after they got me. Kept her somewhere else for a day. Had me tied up down here, but I heard her voice after the helicopter arrived late Sunday night, the tenth. I knew what day it was by keeping track of my meals, such as they were. Anyway, they called Rachel by name. She asked a lot of questions ... sounded like a chip off the old block, if you know what I mean. Then they took her away."

"Charlie, one more question: who were 'they,' the people with her?"

Carmichael didn't respond immediately. Jack saw the agent's chest rise and fall rapidly. Finally he blurted out, "Bunny ... and two men whose voices I've heard before." He stopped to inhale again. "But I didn't get to see them. That so-called priest was with them, too, but, as I said, he ... he didn't leave ... until a day later."

Jack and the others sensed the end was at hand. Brand lowered himself alongside the tub. The four men watched as Carmichael tried to maintain consciousness. His limbs shook, and his breathing became rapid and shallow. His eyes darted from face to face, as if bidding goodbye to each man individually. Finally there was a prolonged sound of air escaping from his chest. His eyes remained open, but they gradually lost their blue sparkle. In the distance, the whine of a helicopter could be heard over the night wind. His chest didn't rise again.

A telephone rang. Brand jerked his head upward. "What the ... ?"

Upstairs, the telephone sounded again.

"Phone line's been cut. I saw it myself." He wiped at his eyes.

"It's hers!" Jack shouted and ran toward the door. "The bitch was wearing a cellular phone!" He glanced over his shoulder. Brand was close behind.

The telephone rang a third time. Both men dashed up the staircase. They reached the woman's body as a fourth electronic ring chimed. The cellular unit was still attached to her belt.

"Now what?" Jack yelled.

Brand seized his arm. "Let it go! We sure as hell can't answer *that* phone."

Jack pulled his arm free at the fifth ring. He dropped down, grabbed the handset, and activated it. Brand lunged for Jack's wrist but missed.

"I have Rima Ameen, you cocksuckers," Jack screamed into the telephone. "And I'll personally peel off every fucking square inch of her skin with a razor if you harm my daughter! Do you hear me, you filthy pieces of shit!"

There was a momentary pause before the connection was broken.

Jack threw the handset at the dead woman's head.

"They heard me." Jack gripped the arm of the chair Voronov had been strapped to and stood up. "Oh, they sure as hell did."

Brand stopped near the covered window. He spun around. His eyes blazed.

"When you fuck up, you do it in style!" he spat out. "We need every break, and you do something as stupid as that. Any hope of communicating with those sons of bitches is gone."

"I had to, God damn it," Jack interjected.

"Shut up!" Brand crossed the room and shook his fist under Jack's nose. "Because of that selfish and irresponsible tirade, you have just jeopardized the lives of everyone involved. Your daughter is probably dead meat as we speak, you bastard."

Jack's fist smashed upwards into the underside of Brand's jaw. Jack swung a second time, but the FBI man had staggered backwards, out of range. He plunged after Brand and tackled him at the door to the basement. The two men nearly fell down the steps as each tried to punch and overpower the other.

Evans ran up the staircase, his gun drawn. Voronov followed.

"Shit, what is this all about?"

Evans tucked his pistol away and grabbed for Brand's hands. He gripped them tightly and pulled. "I can't believe my eyes." He dragged Brand aside. "Well?"

"My fault." Jack sat up and rested his forehead on his knees. He sighed. "It all just got to me. Something snapped. Sorry."

Brand touched his fingers along the edge of his jaw. He licked at the blood that coated his teeth and turned to face Jack. "OK, what I said about Rachel was uncalled for, but you really pissed me off."

Jack flexed his fingers. His knuckles were bruised. "Corley, it was a long shot. I figured if I hadn't answered, they'd have reached some conclusion. I just wanted to influence their thinking."

Brand wiped at his mouth. "And?"

"Insurance. They've got Rachel. I've got Rima. Maybe we can use her as a hostage."

Brand leaned closer. "But the woman's dead, Jack."

"They don't know that."

Brand rose and put his hands on his hips. "Well, that certainly puts us in an interesting spot."

Jack nodded. "I know. We can't let them find out."

Brand reached down and helped Jack up. He winced and touched his chin again. "Hell of a right hook, Jackson."

Leonard Mountain
Monday, January 18, 1:59 a.m.

A turbine helicopter from St. Francis pulled away into the night with the bodies of Charlie Carmichael and Rima Ameen. Don Evans accompanied their remains. His principal job was to ensure that no official record was made of the death of the terrorist. Almost immediately, a hearse summoned by the Tulsa County Sheriff's Department arrived to pick up Norman Gentry's corpse.

Jack and Brand stood outside the house and watched the final procedures in silence. Elsewhere, other FBI and sheriff's department personnel searched and secured the premises. Two men in business suits guided a covered gurney across the driveway to the hearse and lifted it aboard. They shut the rear door and walked around to the front.

"Again, I'm sorry, Corley . . . "

"Forget it," Brand responded. "The more I think about it, the more I agree with what you did." He turned toward Jack and rubbed his chin. "Not the jawbreaker part, though."

The engine of the black Cadillac started and the lights came on.

"We're still a long step behind," Jack observed as the car moved toward the gate.

"Yeah." Brand nodded. He turned for the house. "I'm going to tell them I'll be at the office making a formal report."

Jack watched the fading taillights of the hearse for a second before following Brand.

"Whatever they're planning can only be hours away now," he added as he stepped alongside the FBI man. "We need to stir the pot . . . more than what I did on the telephone."

"Any ideas?"

"First, I want to review the disk that got Carmichael kidnapped." They walked past the sheriff department's cars. "It's got to be important, beyond the obvious. Is the original still in the office?"

"In the safe." Brand looked at Jack. "You know, I'm convinced that we have more pieces to the puzzle than we realize. They're battening down the hatches in D.C., in anticipation of Wednesday, but if we could just get a handle on what I know are real clues, such as the 'Lux' matter . . . "

The garage door of the house was open. Jack saw that two FBI agents were inspecting a seven-passenger, white Lincoln Town Car. It was the lead automobile of a fleet of seventeen, the "sacred cows." He recognized the smoked windows, the gold-plated wire wheel covers, and the personalized Oklahoma license plate bearing the exhortation PRAISE. Reuben Gentry had loved that car.

J. Edgar Hoover Building, Washington, D.C.
7:09 a.m.

It was the third Monday in January, Martin Luther King, Jr., Day, and a federal holiday. Half of the FBI headquarters building was empty. The other half was very busy.

Jerry Reynolds had been in his office since 4:30. He cradled the telephone receiver against his shoulder and talked with Brand for the second time in an hour.

"I just spoke with the director about Rima Ameen. At first he was outraged at Jack Stroud's message to the terrorists. Then he wondered if they'd actually gotten it . . . if anyone was really on the line. Finally he agreed with you that we may have a trump card, of sorts."

"Let's hope," Brand interrupted. Reynolds moved forward.

"He's notifying the SACs about Carmichael. He'll issue a formal statement later. We're not going to associate his death with the ministry or the rest of all this." Reynolds leaned back in his chair. "Did you know the guy was engaged?"

"Yes, I knew," Brand replied. "His fiancée has been in the Tulsa office a number of times."

"Corley, what kind of bastards could have torched a fellow human being like that?"

"The same type of people who've killed thousands over the past three weeks, in cold blood. And who have more murders on their agenda."

Reynolds sighed. "Well, the Secret Service has gone to their highest security level short of sequestering the president. He continues to insist on luring the groups out, for us to intercept. We're still operating in the dark, though. Is Stroud with you?"

"On the line, Jerry," came Jack's voice.

"I guess you heard, we're a little leery of your 'hostage' role for the dead terrorist," the deputy director remarked.

"Jerry, I understand, but we can't be any worse off than if I hadn't answered the call. Either way, they'd have concluded the woman had been compromised or captured. At least now they might think she's still alive, and worth something."

"Do you have anything else?"

"I'm not ready to give up here yet. We're overlooking something, Jerry—in the disk, the simulator orders, somewhere—and I'm going to find it."

"I hope to God you do. OK, you two, listen to this."

Reynolds opened a file folder.

"This is the latest communication from the Syrian prime minister. It may not tell us what's coming up, but it sure as hell helps explain how we got here."

He picked up the document.

"The Syrians assembled the picture from their own operatives and from a couple of former East German Stasi agents who worked hand-in-glove with the old KGB. Damn thing reads like a novel. Norman had plenty to atone for. Here goes, and I quote."

During the summer of 1973, amid the confusion in the United States attendant with the Watergate affair, operatives within the First Directorate of the KGB formulated a concept for what they called the "American incursion." Although the meaning of the term was not precisely defined at first, it always stood for some sort of major destabilizing action that would be carried out within the borders of the continental United States. To them, the Watergate matter highlighted the fragility of control that held America together politically. This proposal was given the approval of Leonid Brezhnev. Twelve months later, the KGB narrowed the possible action to four choices, one of which was the infiltration of a U.S. evangelical Christian organization as a cover. By 1975, the Gentry Ministries was a possible target, and Gentry's son Norman was of particular interest because of his unorthodox personal habits.

Upon his graduation from Tulsa Bible College in May 1976, Norman was sent by his parents to the Holy Land for the summer. At that time, a major role for him in the ministry was only a distant hope. The KGB arranged for Norman, then 22, to meet a young woman, Basilah Walid, who was 17 and already a member of the PLO. Basilah was physically striking, and she was fluent in Eng-

*lish. She posed as a convert to Christianity who admired Nor-
man's father and his work. Norman had trouble pronouncing her
name, so she told him her nickname was "Bunny." She unsuc-
cessfully attempted to seduce him, and she reported to her superiors that Norman evidenced disgust at her advances. On more
than one occasion, he called her "filthy." This development
heightened the KGB's interest in the Gentry Ministries, and it
indicated a way by which the organization might be compromised.*

*Basilah patched up the relationship by placing it on a clearly pla-
tonic plane. She maintained a discreet correspondence with Norman between 1976 and 1981. During that time, the KGB intensified its efforts to obtain more information on his sexual prefer-
ences. They succeeded beyond their wildest dreams in 1981 when
agents were able to obtain several photographs and videotapes of
Norman engaging in oral and anal sex with a succession of boys,
ranging in age from six to ten.*

"Oh, for Christ's sake." It was Jack's voice. Reynolds continued reading.

*The newly elected Mikhail Gorbachev shelved the program in
1985, citing his efforts to obtain credits and other forms of assistance from the West. The KGB reinstituted the program on its
own in early 1987, when it was evident that Gorbachev's activities might result in the loss of Eastern Europe, which, in turn,
would mean the loss of a honed cadre of East German operatives nominally associated with the Stasi secret police. The KGB
wanted the Germans for the American incursion. Further, what
the KGB envisioned as a possible outcome of Gorbachev's poli-
cies of perestroika and glasnost was an unraveling of the entire
Soviet Union as they knew it. Accordingly, they decided to seize
the opportunity while it was still theirs, and that meant arranging
financing through their gold-bullion accounts in Zurich and
making the overt moves to take over the ministry. It was their
conclusion that if Gorbachev failed in his balancing act and the
country fractured, they would be prepared to carry out their last
attack against the nation that had caused their demise. If they
were really successful, they might even bring America down, too.
They acted slightly out of order with their plan when Norman*

participated in his father's European camp meeting in Belgium in the summer of 1987. Basilah, still posing as a demure Christian convert, wrote to him and told him that she planned to attend the sessions in Brussels. She met with him under the guise of introducing him to her older brother, Jamie. The three had dinner where "Jamie" informed Norman that he had an extensive collection of artwork that he knew the sensitive young man would find of interest. They went to an apartment after dinner, and Norman saw that the walls of four rooms were covered with Jamie's collection of some 3,000 color photographs and a bookshelf filled with nearly 100 videotapes, all showing Norman in various deviant sex acts with boys. It was obvious that if this evidence were made public it would result in a scandal that would ruin his father. Norman was told there was only one way to avoid such an eventuality, and that was for him to marry Bunny. He asked what purpose this so-called marriage might serve the woman and her brother, but he was not given an answer, and he was in no position to object. He agreed and was assured he would not have to engage in sexual relations with his wife. He was visibly relieved when he was told there wouldn't be any public ceremony. Norman and Bunny were married in 1987. Their announcement shocked his parents, for they felt their son would never marry any woman, let alone such a beautiful one. Norman and Bunny quickly fitted into the atmosphere of the ministry. Bunny played the demure wife of a man rapidly growing in his father's footsteps. By 1989, Norman was actively assisting his father publicly. He had his own television program beginning in 1990.

"Jerry, it's Jack again. Pardon the interruption, but the family overlooked all sorts of strange signals because we were so pleased that Norman had gotten married in the first place. But we never heard anything about her family or friends. There just weren't any ties to the past. A beautiful woman like that without a history? School? Admirers? Lovers? It was as if she were created out of thin air. Which," he paused, "I guess she was."

Reynolds went on.

The first outsiders introduced themselves to Norman during the summer of 1993. They said they were friends of Bunny's brother and that they brought warm greetings from him. Norman hadn't had any personal contact with "Jamie" since the encounter in Bel-

gium six years earlier. But there were letters. About ten in all. All alluded to or outright mentioned Jamie's "interest in seeing the marriage work." Now a half-dozen men with German accents made themselves at home in Norman's life. Bunny remained mostly quiet about the new arrivals. Only once, when he got drunk and threw a glass at her, did she smile and say that everything would soon be explained. According to her report, he was infuriated by her attitude. Later she calmed him down by arranging a tête-à-tête with one of the little boys, who were always available.

The 1991 upheaval in the Soviet Union posed no problem for the KGB, since all of the funding and most of the training had already been accomplished. The secret base was about to be constructed, and their "American incursion" was well under way.

Reynolds laid the papers down and closed the folder. "End of report."

"Well, there's our confirmation of the KGB tie," Brand declared. "There're no amateurs at the top, Jerry. They didn't come over just to bomb things and kill a few people. They're here to . . . what'd it say? . . . 'bring America down.' Find out everything you can about that woman, ASAP," he boomed. "Mark my words, Bunny's background contains the names and faces of real people who are here to finish off the country. Under your very nose, Jerry."

The deputy director nodded. "There's supposed to be even more from Damascus this morning on the KGB's involvement. I'll ask the Syrians to expedite any information on Bunny's background, and I'll push our people in the Middle East. Europe, too. I'll call you back."

Reynolds punched in the interoffice number for the Strategic Information Operations Center. He started speaking as soon as he recognized Lew Bittker's voice.

"Open up an area for an emergency ID search. Be ready to access Kommissar and every other such data base. I'll be down in three minutes."

FBI Office, Tulsa
10:35 a.m.

"OK, let's go over this once more." Jack tapped the return key. Brand stood behind him. "Third time's supposed to be the charm. Nine banks, nine pages." The screen filled again with the data. "There they are, just like last time . . . Banco de México, Banque Nationale de Paris, Credit Suisse in Zurich, Frankfurt's Deutsche Bank, Barclays in London, et cetera, et cetera. It was $21.5 million in KGB funds that mysteriously and simultaneously moved to the same numbered account at Credit Suisse in Zurich on January eleventh." Jack squinted at the information. "Probably a dozen clues right there in front of us, yet I can't fathom a thing."

Don Evans entered the room and pointed to the telephone.

"Reynolds is back. Line four."

Brand motioned for Jack to join him on a separate phone.

"Nothing yet on Bunny," the deputy director reported, "but here's an additional slice of intelligence from the Syrians. Seems that one of the individuals we're looking for was trained in the Crimea, at a place called Saki."

"Shit!" Brand exclaimed. "There goes the neighborhood. Jerry, that's where the best of the worst were trained before the breakup of the Soviet Union. Didn't tell us who the guy is, did they?"

"No. Just that he's apparently in charge."

"Of course he's in charge!" Brand snapped. "Sorry, didn't mean to bite your head off. It's just that I know what the product of that place is. Whoever's here from Saki is the general of generals. I'll work with Jack for a few more hours, then I'm coming back to Washington. We may have to make a personal plea to the president to cancel the public inaugural."

4:56 p.m.

Brand was positioned next to the desk with his arms crossed.

"Nothing on the disk and nothing from the search of Simulation's files. Are you going to stay with it?"

Jack looked at his FBI friend. "No, I'm going out to visit with Lester Graham. They're dismissing him from the hospital in the morning. I want to pick his brain one more time. After that, I don't know."

"Well, I've got to go. My flight to Washington leaves in an hour." He patted Jack on the shoulder and started for the door. "I'll call you when I get there."

St. Francis Hospital, Tulsa
5:33 p.m.

"What do you mean he's gone?"

"Checked out, sir," an attractive nurse advised. "About an hour ago."

"But I understood he'd be staying one more night."

"All I know is, the doctor said there wasn't any reason to keep him." She made a gesture of helplessness. "So they left. As I said, about an hour ago."

"*They?*"

"Why, yes. Mr. Graham and a woman."

Damascus, Syria
Tuesday, January 19, 12:13 a.m.

"The Americans don't need any more bad news."

Hassan Kadry held a sheet of paper and paced across his quiet office. The only other sound in the ornate room was the faint tick-tock of an old brass clock on the mantel. The Prime Minister peered through his reading glasses and shook his head at the latest piece of intelligence.

"This will put them into shock."

The geography books told only half the story, he mused. Al-jamhouriya al Arabia as-Souriya, otherwise known as the Syrian Arab Republic, covered 71,000 square miles, an area slightly larger than Oklahoma. For decades, the country had been infamous for its role in sheltering and encouraging international terrorists. Participating in the United Nations' war against Iraq was the first conspicuous break with that past. Kadry intended to complete the epic transformation, regardless of the political perils.

He picked up a manila envelope and slid the piece of paper inside. Just a week ago, he'd sent seven pages concerning the training bases in the Bekaa Valley of Lebanon. Then there was the specific information on Jamil Nasir's facility, where Abu Kuttab and his men received their fine tuning before going to America to "sever the head of the pharaoh." Finally he'd forwarded the dossier on Rima Ameen, Kuttab's sister, along with her fingerprints.

Kadry sighed.

Jamil Nasir was considered one of the world's most vicious terrorists-for-hire. Even before the recent outbreak of violence, he was actively being sought by sixteen nations, including the United States, for his behind-the-scenes involvement in the murder of at least 1,700 innocent men, women, and children. From a background of religious zealotry, Nasir had evolved into an amoral killer, almost a diabolical robot, to whom the sanctity of human life meant absolutely nothing. The Israeli Mossad credited him with setting up the most sophisticated training operation in the Bekaa Valley, although they never saw him there. Most of the world's police and intelligence organizations had not spotted him in at least eight years.

Angels of death, Kadry thought. All of them. "The other information will have to go to the American president separately." He pressed the button on his desk. "No need to dilute the impact of this revelation."

His secretary opened the door and stepped across the heavy carpet toward his outstretched hand. She took the envelope and departed. Kadry removed his reading glasses and thought again about the two-sentence message the woman would send to Washington. He closed his eyes, pinched the bridge of his nose, and tried to imagine the reaction of the Americans when they read the words. He himself would have trouble ever forgetting them.

"EXTREMELY URGENT: Purported brother 'Jamie' verified as sole sibling of Basilah Walid, alias Bunny Gentry, and positively identified as fugitive Jamil Nasir. Subject left for U.S. approximately seven months before departure on 30 December of Abu Kuttab and five comrades and is presumed to be leader of second attack group."

United States Simulation Systems, Tulsa
12:43 a.m.

Jack arrived at U.S. Simulation Systems scarcely more than twenty minutes after the urgent telephone call from Brand. He'd been surprised and relieved when he returned home from St. Francis and found Lester Graham ensconced at the kitchen table, being served a sumptuous country dinner by Flora. His determined housekeeper had ridden city buses through two transfers to rescue the Beggs farmer from, as she put it, "all those needles and nurses."

"Mr. Stroud, I talked to the doctor myself," she chattered while he took off his coat, as if a defense were really necessary, "and he saw no reason why Mister G. had to stay another night in that place." She contemplated her special guest and beamed. "You can see for yourself. Don't he look much happier?"

Mister G., is it? Jack smiled at the man with the full mouth.

"Oh, certainly, Flora, he looks just great. You did the right thing."

Jack hung his coat in the front closet and returned to the kitchen to take a seat. Graham was chewing earnestly on a plump ear of corn, which he held in both of his callused hands.

Jack sat down at the table. "May I call you Lester?"

The older man nodded as he swallowed. "Sure thing." He advised he'd be more than happy to answer questions, too. That is, as long as there was plenty of room in between for more mouthfuls of fried chicken, mashed potatoes and gravy, green beans, and the rest.

"Three 'n' two," the farmer verified as he smoothed butter across a steaming homemade biscuit. "Like I told that FBI fella, the buses was forty-five-footers. Three arrived first, just after midnight, then two more would come the next afternoon." He picked up the puffy biscuit and appraised it at eye level. "A few nights later, all five of 'em would leave together. They did that over and over, at least twelve times." He pushed the dripping offering into his mouth.

"The same buses each time?"

Graham kept chewing. Jack noticed that Flora had extracted two apple pies from the oven. Her face radiated satisfaction with the results. Jack inhaled the enticing scent.

"No tellin'," Graham offered finally. "Maybe the same ones . . . maybe not. All had smoked windows, though."

"But there could have been as many as sixty buses, right?"

Graham picked up a fat drumstick. "You bet."

Jack leaned back and crossed his arms. "Do you know what kind they were? The make?"

The farmer crunched into the piece of chicken and answered as he chewed. "Nope." A fragment of crust adhered to his chin.

"Any idea where they were going?"

Graham shook his head. His jaw worked up and down in an oval motion.

Jack thought about the simulator. "Did you see any trucks out there?"

"Yes, sir." The farmer worked his tongue between his upper lip and his teeth in a clearing motion. "The night I took off—I guess that was the eleventh—there was three of 'em."

"Tractor-trailers? You know, eighteen-wheelers?"

Graham frowned. "They didn't sound that big, but I never did see much of them. Just their headlights, really." He felt and flicked off the fragment of crust. " 'Fraid I'd get caught, so I ducked back inside that basement before they stopped outside and the drivers hightailed it into the house."

"How about *before* that night?"

The older man poked his fork at a pile of green beans. "Once."

"When?"

"Couple days before Thanksgiving, a year ago." Graham swung the utensil toward his mouth. "Three eighteen-wheelers came on the property 'bout sunset." He pulled off the beans and began to chew.

Jack was impatient. "And?"

"They left the next morning."

"How'd you remember it was at Thanksgiving?"

Graham swallowed and grinned. "I figured someone must be bringing a lot of turkeys to a lot of turkeys."

Jack smiled. Norman had confirmed that the box on stilts Graham had seen was indeed a flight simulator. Such an object would have been nearly impossible to remove intact, unless it had been taken away inside a large truck. Jack took a deep breath. The FBI was probably right. The simulator had been destroyed in the last explosion.

"Tell me about the metal cylinders."

Graham put down his fork and squinted at the ceiling. "Well, they kept haulin' them out of the metal building and goin' to a helicopter."

Jack leaned forward. "How often?"

"Saw it done once before they captured me, then I heard it being done ten or fifteen more times while I was stuck in the basement."

"Lester, which way did the helicopter depart?"

The farmer pointed. "Came in from the northeast. Went back that way. Every time."

The telephone call from Brand had interrupted the interview. Jack prayed that there wouldn't be any more bad news about his daughter. Finding out she was also threatened by an animal like Jamil Nasir hit him in the stomach like a cannonball.

"God damn it, Corley," he'd stressed to his FBI friend, "something *has* to be on my office computer, and those holding Rachel know it. I'm going back to find it. I'll call you as soon as I do."

As he waited for the screen to come up, Jack wished he could have dialed into the computer from home. It would have saved precious seconds. For security reasons, however, the mainframe wasn't accessible from outside the building.

He decided to start where he'd left off earlier, after narrowing the field of simulator purchasers from 289 to 91 because of Norman's statement that the terrorists flew "a big plane with one propeller." He'd entered a command for the computer to sift through its memory and extract only those customers who had purchased a simulator for single-engine aircraft. Nothing suspicious had jumped out that first time, but a new hunch now motivated him. It would still be an agonizingly slow process, for each entry in the computer's memory comprised dozens of pages of data, with sometimes as many as a hundred single-space lines per page. Yet somewhere, Jack thought as he started with the first list of words he'd concocted for this second effort, there *had* to be a clue. Perhaps hidden in a description of a customer's business. He entered "Jamil Nasir" and stared at the screen. As he waited to see if a match existed, an unaccustomed sense of dread crawled across his chest and down his arms. He noticed his gold wedding ring.

"Oh, Laura," he spoke out loud and touched the heavy band. "I've lost you—and Jeff—and now . . . maybe our daughter, too." The closest I've come to Rachel so far has been twelve hours. I can't seem to get any closer. He slammed his fist against the top of the desk.

"God damn it, what in the hell am I doing wrong?"

After nearly five hours of searching, there was no match. From "Jamil Nasir" and "Bunny" to "Lux" and "Pedophile," the sought-after connection just wasn't made. However, there were three curious entries—all for Cessna Caravans, a "big plane with one propeller," as Norman had mentioned. In each case, two simulators were ordered for shipment to different brokers in El Paso. The three separate orders were placed within a week of each other, and delivery of the six simulators was effected on the same day.

"And all consigned to the same freight-forwarding outfit at the Tulsa airport."

The telephone rang. He found the handset without looking away from the screen.

"Jack, it's Corley," the voice boomed. "Here's a new clue we just got from the Syrians. It's that fictitious name that was on the FAA registration certificate for the Sabreliner that blew up at Cape Canaveral. Does 'Sánchez y Vega' ring a bell?"

Jack jumped up from his chair.

"Shit, Brand, that may be the *key*. I just saw that name on a purchase order for two Caravan simulators."

J. Edgar Hoover Building, Washington, D.C.
1:55 a.m.

The four veteran FBI officials sat at the cluttered conference room table in the Strategic Information Operations Center. Jerry Reynolds positioned himself and his bulky briefcase next to Lew Bittker and faced Corley Brand and Tex Follett. All but Brand had been in the building since the previous morning. His flight from Tulsa had arrived at National at 10 p.m., and he'd come directly from the airport. The tight cubicle reeked of stale coffee.

The alarming information from Syria concerning Jamil Nasir had raised the stakes of the potential threat tenfold. Everything known about the terrorist meant bad news, and the fact that he might be personally in charge of a second attack unit was far and away the Bureau's nightmare of nightmares. Reynolds placed a telephone console on the table and punched a flashing plastic button.

"Don, can you hear us?" He twisted the volume knob on the speaker unit.

"Loud and clear," came agent Don Evans's voice from Tulsa.

"All right, we're going to include Jack Stroud as soon as he calls back. As you know, he's at his office, tracking down the Sánchez y Vega tie-in with a flight-simulator purchase."

"Jerry, if I may," Evans began, "let me give you a new piece of information."

"Go ahead." The deputy director drummed his fingers against the polished tabletop.

"OK, Stroud called his former secretary at the ministry about an hour ago. She told him she felt terrible about how she treated him when he tried to go back to his office at Tulsa Bible College on the seventh. Of course, she was only acting on Norman Gentry's orders. Anyway, the lady's one hundred percent cooperative now, and she informed him that the ministry has nine of those so-called 'express' buses, all of which were reconditioned and customized by some outfit in this area. She's checking for the name of the place now."

Follett raised his eyebrows.

Evans continued. "With as many as fifty-five or sixty of them gone from whatever they were doing at the bunker, Jack's convinced they're all slated for more trouble."

Brand turned and faced Follett. "What do you think?"

"Since Nasir's involved, we'd better damn sure find out exactly how many buses there are and locate every one of them. That reconditioning place is worth a check for leads. Yeah, I agree with Stroud completely."

Reynolds and Bittker watched Follett for a moment. Everyone knew he felt personally responsible for the fiasco at Beggs. Reynolds had asked him to attend this meeting in order to keep him in the middle of the action. The deputy director's psychological strategy seemed to be working.

"As a matter of fact," Follett continued, "*no* buses should be allowed within ten blocks of the Capitol tomorrow. I don't know if the Secret Service has changed any plans because of this Nasir information, but Metropolitan and Park Police can start at midnight, clearing and tagging. It'd be a low-key effort that shouldn't alert the media, but it could be very effective."

Evans's voice came over the speaker again. "Once we find out where that customizing place is, Jack and I plan to pay them a visit. It's a long shot, but we might get lucky."

Brand nodded. "If you do get lucky, Don, spread some of it this way." He picked up a pencil and tapped its eraser on the table. "What about the woman's body?"

"St. Francis morgue. Tagged as a local domestic dispute victim for right now. No one's made any inquiries . . . yet."

"Good. OK, let's move on." Reynolds peered at his notes on a legal pad, then looked around the room. "The director has to brief the president at 10:30 this morning. I want all the current developments, what we're looking at based on what's happened, the impact of the Syrian input, and what we should recommend for the twenty-four-hour period beginning at midnight tonight."

Reynolds tapped his pen at the top paragraph of the yellow sheet.

"To date, over 16,000 people dead, $10 billion in damages, and now we find out that the terrormaster himself has been in the United States for months and is probably in charge of some sort of follow-up attack squad." He glanced across the table. "Brand's felt all along there haven't been more than a hundred operatives involved in the entire hidden-base effort, from the very beginning." He let the effect of his statement sink in. "One hundred individuals who've caused unprecedented death and destruction inside our borders." He waited another few seconds. "Now, considering the number of terrorists killed at the bunker, and if Corley's right, we're still looking at better than eighty percent of them remaining and preparing to strike again." Reynolds stabbed his index finger at his notes. "There's no more *time*, gentlemen. Let's take the significant activities of the past few days, starting with the raid, and extrapolate to what may be coming. We're down to the short strokes. We need good ideas fast!"

Reynolds nodded at the man across the table. "Tex, before you begin, let me say that none of us would have done anything any differently. You have our complete respect and admiration for putting together the effort that resulted in the destruction of the base."

Follett drew himself to the table. "I appreciate that, Jerry, but I wouldn't be honest if I didn't say that I have a score to settle, some avenging to do." Follett considered his notes and cleared his throat. "Quick review. There was no unexploded RDX found in the bunker. That is, there were no stores of cylinders left behind, contrary to what we'd expected. Further, there were no stockpiled Stingers, only the launchers they used to detonate the RDX supplies at the ends of the tunnels. Finally, there was no Gellex-4 left, either. So if that farmer was right about what he saw, they took the stuff away by chopper before we got there."

Brand exhaled. "Not to mention by buses, trucks, et cetera, et cetera."

Follett raised his eyebrows. "Yeah, right."

Evans added to the report. "As you know, we found the bodies of eleven terrorists during the first sweep and five more when we did the inch-by-inch search."

"Purely a suicide mission, it appears," Follett grunted.

Bittker joined the discussion. "Well, we've managed the media coverage pretty well, thanks to the president's good words about us on television."

"Media never really picked up on Carmichael's death," Brand added. "Didn't connect it with the rest. Wish we could have said more ourselves, but we've kept the lid on pretty well. That ought to please the president."

Reynolds faced the telephone unit. "Don, what's the latest on that safe house?"

"It was purchased by the ministry in the '70s, Jerry, and it was used primarily by Reuben Gentry to pray and collect his thoughts before a crusade. They housed VIPs there a few times. Norman's had control of it only during the past year."

"How about the autopsy on Norman's body?"

"No surprises, really. Alcohol and tranquilizers were his favorite recreational drugs, and he was full of both. Other than those, no abnormal pathology."

"Anything more on that Father Arnold character?" The deputy director looked around the table.

Brand shook his head.

"Zero . . . zip," Reynolds grumbled. "Hell of a note, isn't it?" He stared at Brand. "Who do *you* think he is?"

Brand placed his hands on the table. "I don't like what I'm piecing together. He's obviously one of the higher-ups, but apparently not high enough to have attracted the attention of the Syrians . . . or the Israelis. Unless, of course . . . "

"Unless he's their 'deep black' agent," Follett completed Brand's sentence. "Maybe even their trainer. Or, how about . . . their *leader?*"

Reynolds glanced at the ceiling. "Shit, Tex, that's all I need to hear."

Brand gestured at Follett. "Let me make an observation about suicide squads, like the ones you encountered at the bunker." The terrorism chief swung his chair sideways. "Suicide squads are extremely important to these people, and they're usually very successful. They've been used by Palestinians against Israel, Iran against Iraq. But there's one thing that *never* happens . . . they never sacrifice their own organizers and leaders. The higher-ups do not intend to die, and they don't . . . voluntarily. The peons, yes, but not the honchos. My point, is the eighty-plus percent massing out there against us contains those top people, one step behind the front lines. And we've got to get them. It's my opinion that whatever's going to come at us in the next day or so, suicide squads or whatever, will be the awful product of terrible—and terribly brilliant—minds. Whatever we do, whatever it takes, we've got to eliminate those behind the attacks at the same time."

A man pushed open the door of the conference room. "Jack Stroud's calling." He pointed. "Punch the blue button and you'll be able to talk with both Stroud and Evans."

Reynolds leaned forward and activated the connection. "Jack?"

"Listen to this, Jerry. One 'Arturo Sánchez y Vega' of the Sanga Corporation in El Paso, Texas, signed the purchase order for two of our Cessna Caravan flight simulators for delivery a year ago November 26, two days before Thanksgiving, via Texoma Freight Systems here in Tulsa. I just hung up from talking with Texoma's night dispatcher, who checked their files. Get this . . . there's *no* record of the simulators ever being flown anywhere. We loaded the two crates into a truck and signed off on the shipment. We did the same thing twice more that day for two other El Paso outfits. All three trucks, with the six simulators, were to go to the Tulsa airport, to the Texoma dock. Not one made it. And later that same day, Lester Graham saw three identical trucks crossing the bunker property."

"Good job, Jackson," Brand boomed and slapped the table. "The Cessna plane's *it!*" He looked across at Reynolds. "Jerry, we've got to get to every public and private airport within a fifty-mile radius. Maybe even a hundred. Those planes are potential goddamn kamikazes." Brand turned and spoke to the telephone unit. "Jack, can you fax us a picture of a Caravan?"

"Just did. Check your machine."

The White House
Tuesday, January 19, 6:17 a.m.

"I do *not* trust the FBI to find either man before the inauguration."

Secret Service director Stan Davidson glowered at the fifteen men and women seated around the polished table. Twelve other agents of the Presidential Protective Division stood along the walls of the West Wing basement command post. Ray Shaffer, chief of the White House detail, Tim Vance, and Rick Hayes sat closest to Davidson.

"Abu Kuttab himself," the big man explained as he tapped an organization chart drawn on a white marker board at the end of the table, "has killed more than a thousand people over the past ten years. God only knows what his boss, Jamil Nasir, is capable of. The Bureau credits Nasir with at least 1,700 murders. These counts, I remind you, do not include any of the deaths from what's gone on across America during the past three weeks. Thousands of anonymous killings since 28 December and not one single, solitary captured terrorist who might be able to shed some light on what they've still got in store for us."

He turned and faced his audience.

"No, the FBI got fixated on that goddamned bunker in Oklahoma, and when it all blew up in their faces, they didn't have a clue what to do next. Shaffer's said it before, and I've become an unqualified convert. Stopping Kuttab, and now Nasir, is going to be solely up to us."

He pushed back on his sleeve and eyed his wristwatch.

"I'm going to meet with the president in four hours. This time I think he'll listen and call off tomorrow's public ceremony. He himself knows how dangerous Nasir is. It couldn't have been lost on him that the Syrians sent the information directly to him and not to State."

The Secret Service leader pointed to Shaffer. "Ray, your review, please."

Shaffer rose, stood at his place, and referred to a one-page duty list. "All shift leaders and assistant shift leaders of today's second and third shifts and all three of tomorrow's are here, right?" He looked around the room and nodded at the acknowledgments. "Good. Follow along on your assignment sheets, if you would. Today there are four preinaugural meetings, two business receptions, one diplomatic reception, and then, tonight, the White House dinner for the congressional leadership and the Supreme Court justices. Fortunately these are all inside functions. Of course, as our policy's been since President Reagan was shot, we're not making available a complete and detailed schedule to the media, even for such so-called 'safe' functions as these. The electronic and print people have been happy to show up to tape or televise individual events or to write general feature pieces anyway." He turned the page over. "OK. Tomorrow it's church for the First Family, then . . . " Shaffer glanced at Davidson as a slight smile developed, "some sort of inaugural ceremony."

"Listen, everyone," Davidson proclaimed from his chair, "if I have my way, they'll conduct it in the Capitol Rotunda. Great television, because everything's set up for the building anyway. Just severely reduced opportunity for Nasir and his assassins. I'm going to do my best at ten o'clock to change the president's mind."

Shaffer pointed at one of the representatives of the Technical Development Division. "I don't think we need to make any changes in the arrangement for the Batmobiles. We probably won't need the chute if the president stays inside the Capitol, but who knows what could still transpire, especially if he insists on the open ceremony."

"He won't," Davidson predicted in a lowered voice. The TDD man gave Shaffer a thumbs-up.

Shaffer picked up a briefing manual. He opened it at a red tab. "First, assuming an emergency removal will be required from the Capitol tomorrow, we'll bring the Man here to the White House, then, if necessary, to Raven Rock, with a helicopter follow from the South Lawn. There'll be motorcycles and thirteen vehicles in the convoy, in addition to the two jet cars. Of course if we opt for Raven Rock, we'll have Air Force cover all the way." Shaffer waited until the note-taking ended and everyone glanced up again. "Second, we've brought in an additional 477 agents from the field, a hundred from the New York office alone. We'll have the White House bunker, Raven Rock, Mount Weather, and Camp David fully staffed. Third, all four National Emergency Airborne Command Post aircraft will be flying from 9 a.m. tomorrow. There's a remote possibility we'll want to change our original destination from the White House to Andrews and get the president up in Air Force One, but there'd have to be a major, generalized attack across the area for that to be seriously considered. But we can make that decision anytime after launching from the Bat Cave. Finally, fourth, we're keeping the Telenet satellite links open and monitored with all the field offices, with the thought that one sliver of a clue might pop up somewhere else, which could have a major impact on what we do here." Shaffer closed the manual and pushed his hands into his pockets. "Questions?"

"Ray?" Tim Vance requested the floor.

Shaffer nodded. "Go."

Vance placed his elbows on the table and rubbed his hands together. "Until the mid-'80s, the only perimeter protection at the White House was the fence, a thin contingent from the Uniformed Division, a few sound- and pressure-activated bells and whistles, and bulletproof windows all around. I've always been concerned that some nutcake might jam on the brakes and stop his flatbed truck at the Southwest Entrance, rip the tarp off a rocket launcher, and devastate the Oval Office before anyone could react. We had no realistic pursuit capability. Now we've added a few things, including full-time radar observers and the roof contingent with their anti-aircraft missile launchers. An improvement, certainly, but it gives me goose bumps when I think about how vulnerable this place still is. I don't need to remind anyone about the plane crash in '94."

He stared directly at Shaffer.

"All these special escape procedures we've been discussing are for the inauguration itself and have a start time of, at the earliest, nine tomorrow morning. Aren't there any new procedures for the time between now and then?"

Shaffer raised his eyebrows. "For here at the White House?"

Vance nodded. The room was totally silent.

"No."

Bristow, Oklahoma
8:06 a.m.

The dark blue Ford LTD left the Turner Turnpike and eased into the light city traffic. The drive from Tulsa had taken twenty-five minutes.

"Should be in the second block." Jack looked up from the address Dolores Hopkins, his former secretary at the Gentry ministries, had provided. "There it is," he pointed. "Shamrock Customizers." He faced Don Evans. "What's the guy's name again?"

"Shannon Kelly," the FBI agent replied as he twisted the steering wheel and their car rumbled onto a wide gravel parking lot. "He's the president of the outfit, and he said he'd pull the relevant records before we got here." Evans braked to a stop near the front door of a large metal building. "Sounds like a friendly type, too."

A wooden sign above the door proudly presented "Shamrock Customizers" in bright green letters. On each end of the establishment's name was a large stylized shamrock. At the front window, a heavyset, ruddy-faced man watched the two men get out of their car. He smiled as he opened the front door and extended a hand to Jack and Evans.

"Shannon Kelly. Come on in and have some hot coffee." His grin revealed a gold cap on a front tooth. Jack noted that the man's name, stitched above the pocket of his western shirt, was about the only obvious Irish thing about him. Cowboy boots, a string tie, and a heavy Oklahoma twang meant he had to be at least two generations removed from the Emerald Isle.

Kelly got right to the point as he directed the visitors toward his office. "Yes, sir, we did all nine of the ministry's buses. Fixed 'em up real nice. You know, special suspension, windows, air-conditioning, even a bathtub in two of them." He winked at Evans. "Lined those two bathrooms with gen-you-wine Italian marble."

"RoadCruisers?" Jack asked as he followed into a small windowless room. A battered metal desk in the center of the fifteen-by-fifteen space was surrounded by old filing cabinets and piles of papers, folders, and boxes. Three rickety metal chairs framed the dusty desk.

"Yep. Forty-five feet long, eight feet wide, 38,000 pounds empty— before we redid them. When they're configured for intercity passenger service, they usually have eleven rows of seats, four abreast." He pointed to the chairs. "Take a load off your feet."

"Do you do a lot of those?" Jack kept his overcoat on and sat down.

"RoadCruisers?" Kelly patted his cluttered desk top for the appropriate document. He nodded. "Sure do. Usually for rock stars and the like."

Evans extracted a notepad. "Any suspicious jobs? Strange requests?"

Kelly found the file he was looking for. He frowned at the new question. "You mean, like someone wanted us to do something illegal?"

Evans shook his head. "No. Maybe a different type of customizing. Something worth a conversation around town over coffee."

"Damn!" Kelly snapped his fingers. "That's right, I forgot your coffee." He started to stand up. "Cream or sugar?"

Evans held up his hand. "Nothing for me." Jack shook his head. "Me neither."

Kelly scooted his chair back in. "Well, now that you ask, probably the most curious order we ever got was for a fleet of buses we had to strip out the seats and put in smoked windows. New halogen headlights, too. We also installed layers of a thick plastic liner where the seats were. Sealed it in with heat."

Jack and Evans looked at each other. Jack turned back toward Kelly and squinted. "Did you paint the buses?"

"No, sir. Course, we *did* wash them."

Evans scribbled the information. "When was this job?"

"Did it over the past year and a half. A few at a time. Last bus went out of here about a month ago. Actually, I think two of them left at the same time."

"Who'd you do the work for?"

Kelly didn't hesitate. "An outfit called Sanga Corporation."

Jack sat bolt upright. "El Paso, Texas?"

"Yeah, right! Know 'em?"

Evans stared across. "How many buses did you do for Sanga, Mr. Kelly?"

"Uh, let me check the records." The man turned and pulled open a file drawer in his desk. After a few seconds, he lifted a thick folder. He laid it on top of the ministry file and opened it. "Let's see . . . we removed all the seats in . . . here it is, 172, and we removed . . . "

"Hold it!" Jack was at the edge of his chair. "You took the seats out of 172 buses?"

Kelly looked surprised by the reaction. "Yes, uh, *all* the seats in those. Then we removed the last six rows of seats in another thirty-three buses."

"That's over 200 buses, Mr. Kelly. Two hundred RoadCruisers?"

"Oh, no." The man perused the sheet. "The actual total was 121 Road-Cruisers."

"And the rest?"

"Plain old city transit buses, school buses." Kelly smiled. "Nothing out of the ordinary."

Jack sat back and exhaled loudly.

Evans inclined his head. "May I see one of the service orders?"

"Sure." Kelly pulled out five pages stapled together.

Evans studied the top sheet, then offered the papers to Jack. On the right side, opposite Kelly's signature and the typed name of his company, was the same for the other party to the contract. Jack couldn't mistake the signature under Sanga Corporation: "A. Sánchez y Vega."

8:46 a.m.

"When he mentioned the number of buses, it clicked." Jack slapped the dashboard as they returned to Tulsa. "There's no other possibility, Don."

The FBI agent glanced to his side. "But why in the hell would they want six simulators in that bunker? Actually, six *more* simulators, since they already had one. If they wanted to transport them someplace else, as they apparently did because the units weren't left behind, why didn't they take them from your plant to wherever they wanted them in the first place?"

"That's just it! The bunker *was* where they wanted them, because they were going to fit them into the buses there."

Evans's mouth opened slowly, and a worried look formed on his face as Jack continued.

"Eight feet wide . . . that's the outside dimension of the buses. The maximum outside dimension of a Caravan simulator with the boxy enclosure we fit around it is also eight feet, but if you don't need the shell, like if you're going to put the guts of a simulator inside a bus, the necessary clearance is then only seven feet. Don't you see, Don? They've installed those simulators inside the buses. Six buses, six simulators."

"But why would they do a thing like that?" Evans's natural skepticism showed through again. "Get real, Jack. Mobile training facilities?"

"No, it's so obvious now: to fly the airplanes from the ground! That way they don't have to sacrifice their pilots. Look, to operate a simulator, all you do is fly a picture. If that picture's coming from a camera in an airplane's nose, you can fly that airplane. Fly the picture to the target, fly the airplane to the target. Damn it, Don, we've got to find those buses!"

Evans didn't take his eyes off the highway.

"OK, suppose you're right. All we have to do then is to find six garden-variety buses among literally thousands in Washington for the inauguration . . . and all before noon tomorrow."

He looked at Jack and laughed.

"Gooood luck."

The White House
10:30 a.m.

"I'm canceling tomorrow's ceremony on the West Front."

Arms crossed, the president stood next to his desk in the Oval Office with his back to the windows overlooking the barren South Lawn. The directors of the FBI and the Secret Service had entered the room together in silence. "Please be seated." The president motioned them to one of the two couches facing each other in the center arrangement of furniture. Already sitting there was Defense Secretary Stephen McConnell.

"But I'm not going to announce it until a half-hour before, if then."

The president walked across the pale gold carpet. "It's time for us to have a little talk, gentlemen," he declared. The chief executive sat down next to McConnell and looked across at the FBI and Secret Service leaders.

"First, let me say that for years, Steve McConnell has been concerned that someday a well-financed and committed group of terrorists might worm its way into the anonymity of our society. Then, over time and without leaving any trails, it could fester and grow and ready itself for the day when it could attack." The president put his hand on the defense secretary's shoulder. "In open meetings and privately, I was pretty tough on Steve. At the outset, at least. But there were two good reasons. One, there was no indication or proof of any such activity, and, two, I wanted him to keep building his case. Then came the very real possibility that we'd have to attack terrorist training sites in Lebanon and maybe even the protective Syrian forces around them, and I wanted a plan we could implement on short notice. By the time the Syrians started delivering their helpful intelligence to us, just a few weeks ago, the joint chiefs had put together the appropriate details for an assault from the Mediterranean and had positioned a battle group there. We were definitely ready to go in."

The president leaned forward.

"When Treasury Secretary David Rowland was killed in the SST explosion last month, he was reported to have been on his way to Paris to meet with the European Community's finance ministers. That purpose, however, was a cover for a critical secret meeting with the Syrians—specifically with their new prime minister, Hassan Kadry, who had passed word to us that he was extremely concerned at the rapid and sophisticated development of two particular training bases in Lebanon. It had become evident that those two installations were beyond the control of the Syrians, and they actually decided to ask for our help in destroying them. Of course," the president looked at each man and went on, "we now know that time had just about run out. Within days, both bases were abandoned. The training was over, and the terrorists had been dispatched to their assignments."

The president sat up straight and paused. When he spoke again, his voice was softer, in the tone he used frequently and successfully to summarize a larger issue, to bring people quickly to his point of view.

"Keep the bigger picture in mind. For the past twenty years, we have watched as various governments masterminded and sponsored transnational terrorist groups. Iran, Syria, Libya, and Iraq have been the four countries most often involved, although Iraq's activity was not as extensive and didn't span as long a time. Behind all of these programs, however, was the Soviet Union—the major participant in the planning, training, and financing of groups that have been slaughtering people around the world for decades. Until mid-1991, the Kremlin was deeply involved in efforts to destabilize legitimately elected governments, while posing as an innocent observer. They even publicly condemned terrorism."

His three guests nodded.

"We now know that as Gorbachev's so-called reforms failed and the prospect grew for a collapse of the entire system, the KGB took the final steps to assemble a cadre of international terrorists who had as their singular goal the violent overthrow of the government of the United States. The leadership of this group was forged and honed at their secret training center on the Black Sea. This effort was meant to be launched at America whether or not changes were carried out in the Soviet Union and whether or not Gorbachev survived. It was a calculated decision and an unprecedented opportunity by the hard-liners in the Kremlin, who were horrified at the loss of Eastern Europe and the subsequent Iraqi fiasco. This plan, they thought, might be their only remaining opportunity to destroy America."

The president stood and walked slowly toward the windows. He continued talking.

"For years we feared an uncontrolled unraveling of the Soviet Union. Some of our DIA analysts felt that before the *nomenklatura* would release its grip on Soviet society and yield to democracy and the loss of all of their privileges, the elite group would take the necessary steps to attack America. Conventional wisdom was that this meant a nuclear strike before the power to dispatch such weapons would be gone forever. Now, of course, we know that some members of the dying regime opted to launch a surrogate attack by using some of the finest of those who wish to destroy us, using conventional means and operating from American soil."

He turned and made eye contact with each man.

"With direct control over nearly a thousand metric tons of gold on deposit in Switzerland, indeed sufficient resources to build a hundred U.S. bases, the KGB backed and sent forth a group known as the Brotherhood of the Ultimate Ijima, comprising the best of the worst who originated from the shadowy terrorist-for-hire business in the Middle East. First Kuttab. Then Nasir." The president singled out the FBI director. "You haven't been able to locate and apprehend either man, so you're not going to like the Syrians' latest message." He stepped to his desk and picked up and fitted on his reading glasses. "This arrived less than thirty minutes ago." He pulled a folded piece of yellow paper from his coat pocket and opened it. "Have incontrovertible evidence that Josef Gunter, a/k/a Arturo Sánchez y Vega, is the natural father of Jamil Nasir and Basilah Walid and is with his children."

McConnell was half out of his seat. "Just who the hell is *that?*"

"Do *you* know who he is?" the president inquired of the two men on the other couch. Both directors shook their heads.

The FBI chief shifted forward. "We *have* been chasing the Sánchez y Vega name ever since the Sabreliner explosion in Florida, but this is the first I've ever heard of a 'Josef Gunter' or that he's the father."

The president refolded the paper. "In other words, you don't have a goddamned clue."

J. Edgar Hoover Building, Washington, D.C.
11:20 a.m.

"Brand."

The chief of the FBI's Counterterrorism Section answered the telephone and positioned one foot on the upholstered seat of a corner chair in the SIOC conference room.

"Mr. Brand," the unidentified male voice began, "one of those buses you've been interested in is parked a few blocks from your office. It's on Pennsylvania Avenue in front of the National Gallery of Art East Building, facing the Capitol."

There was an electronic click, and the caller was gone.

"What the *fuck* are they up to?"

Corley Brand stabbed his index finger against a plastic button on the telephone console.

"Only *one* bus?" He winced.

"And *now?*"

He punched in the classified number for the newly activated Metro-Line, a single-call central emergency system that connected key law-enforcement entities in the Washington, D.C., area. Messages traveled by secure fiber-optic cable and simultaneously linked the FBI, the Metropolitan Police Department, the United States Park Police, Capitol police, U.S. Marshals, the Bureau of Alcohol, Tobacco, and Firearms, the Secret Service, and a dozen other security services protecting various individuals, government buildings, and departments. Brand was one of seven FBI superiors authorized to use the MetroLine's Direct Dispatch feature. Once his voice and ID number were computer verified, his message would be fed live to the other agencies for immediate broadcast. Three tones sounded in his ear. He identified himself and began.

"Brand, FBI, 02-02-325. An anonymous caller just reported a passenger bus parked on the Pennsylvania Avenue side of the National Gallery of Art East Building. No other description was given, but the vehicle may be— I repeat, may be—one of the interstate express buses sought in connection with the recent national acts of terrorism. We want a sighting report only. No radios within two hundred yards. Landlines only. Use extreme caution. . . . There may be explosives on board. Any patrol in the vicinity, please advise."

Officer Robert Donelley of the U.S. Park Police was the first to spot the bus. He'd just turned his white Ford Crown Victoria onto Pennsylvania from Constitution Avenue and was southeastbound when a dispatcher reported the suspicious vehicle, now only a block ahead. Snow grains began to tap at his windshield, and Donelley made a face. The forecast called for the temperature to fall during the day from a morning high of twenty-seven degrees.

Light frozen precipitation was expected to yield to moderate snow by sunset, with accumulations of more than seven inches in the District anticipated during the night. That in itself was going to cause enough trouble for the inauguration. No need for an assist from any lingering terrorist threat.

He hunched over the steering wheel and frowned at the sight. There was a bus parked next to the modern glass-and-concrete building, all right, but it was only a standard white Metrobus, with its red and blue stripes.

"Since when is a D.C. transit bus one of the FBI's Ten Most Wanted?" Donelley chuckled to himself. For an instant he felt better.

Just before he drew alongside the vehicle he noticed puffs of condensation from its exhaust. Engine's still running, he observed. However, as Donelley eased his patrol car past the bus, he did a double take. The driver was slumped over the wheel, his arms dangling. The policeman turned into a space in front of the bus and ignored the FBI's radio ban.

"Got only a city Metrobus here," he reported to his dispatcher. "Number 9407. But the driver appears incapacitated. Doors shut, engine running. No passengers visible."

Brand shook his head as the news was relayed by the Park Police.

"OK, stand by." He hit "hold," then the button for the FBI operator.

"This is Brand in SIOC conference. Would you get me Leo Bracken with the Washington Metropolitan Area Transit Authority?"

Brand held the handset to his ear as the woman used the FBI name to thread her way quickly to the division manager of the bus company. He and Bracken had gotten to know each other during various spy chases around town in the late '70s. A lot of intercepts and arrests were made on city buses as certain *personae non grata* attempted to fit in with the common folk. He checked his watch as he heard an extension ring. If you had a question about anything concerning the bus operation, Bracken was your man. He was a font of minutiae. The number rang again, and a secretary put her boss on the line.

"Leo, it's Corley," Brand interrupted Bracken's salutation. He eyed his notes. "You got a bus numbered 9407?"

"9407? Hold on a second, comrade. Let me punch up my list of rolling stock."

Brand could hear tapping on a computer keyboard. There were two electronic beeps.

"Yeah, here it is . . . 9407 is one of our lift-equipped Flxibles. Delivered in 1990."

"Leo, something strange is going on. I just got an anonymous call that one of the terrorist vehicles we're looking for was parked outside the

National Gallery of Art East Building. Instead, a park policeman found your 9407, with the driver slumped over the wheel."

"Why, that can't be, Corley." There was more tapping on the keyboard before Bracken spoke again. "Whatever's out there must be somebody's idea of a joke, because 9407's been in major maintenance since noon yesterday and won't be back on the street until Monday."

"Shit!" Brand exclaimed. "Leo, I'm going to need a couple dozen of your buses to block streets around that whole area." He looked at his watch again. "Don't hang up. I'll get back with you." As Brand put the call on hold he suddenly remembered that Jack Stroud had said some transit buses were worked on by a customizing place in Oklahoma.

"That's all we need, lookalike Washington transit buses . . . 1,800 more goddamn places to search for explosives before tomorrow."

Brand punched back the Park Police dispatcher.

"FBI again. That's no Metrobus. Notify everyone that we consider the vehicle to be extremely dangerous. And I emphasize: *no* radios or cellular phones near the damn thing. Landlines only for all communications. We can't take a chance on an errant transmission triggering a detonation of explosives. I'll arrange for the Metropolitan Police to evacuate all buildings within two hundred yards. Could double or triple the distance if conditions warrant. Appreciate your complete cooperation."

Brand then raised the deputy police chief.

"I suggest you initially cordon off a square, about a third of a mile on each side, bounded by C Street on the north, Third Street on the east, Jefferson Drive on the south, and Seventh Street on the west. In addition, close Pennsylvania into the Capitol grounds, and we'll evacuate the Labor Department building. Then," he poked at a city map on the wall, "block Constitution at least over to First. Gallery security and the marshals will get everyone out of the East Building and the U.S. Court House across the street."

Brand nodded as the chief read back the arrangements. He remembered the Bureau of Alcohol, Tobacco, and Firearms had said that a standard-size bus could carry enough nonnuclear explosives to destroy virtually everything within a hundred yards and blow out windows five miles away. If it's a good quantity of RDX, he figured, that one bus at a distance of less than half a mile from the Capitol would make the magnificent building look worse than it did after the British torched it in 1814. The Murrah building in Oklahoma City would look partially damaged by comparison.

Brand stared at the map. "Chief, how long will it take you to block the area?" He shook his head. "No, an hour's out of the question. I've got to get the whole place cleared within fifteen minutes. If that bus goes, thousands could be killed, and time's definitely not on our side." He nodded. "I *know* about the crowds in town." He listened for a few more seconds. "Great . . . OK, place your men at the intersections first. I'll have the transit authority supply enough buses—say thirty—to allow your men to roam and to remove everyone within the perimeter. How's that sound?" He nodded again. "Thanks, chief. I'll see you there."

He dialed Tex Follett's number from memory.

"Gone, sir, about a minute ago," the Hostage Rescue Team leader's secretary offered. "He heard you on the MetroLine and called Quantico for the APC. Then he rocketed out of here."

Brand hit the switchhook, then depressed the flashing button.

"Leo, I need thirty buses. Bring them up Seventh to the Mall. I'll tell the cops they're coming."

"Jeez, Corley, with all the extra runs because of the inauguration, there's no . . . "

"Damn it, Leo, I don't care what you have to do, just *do* it." Brand broke the connection before Bracken could respond.

WRC-TV, Washington, D.C.
11:22 a.m.

Saul Gilbert had been news director of NBC's Washington affiliate for six years. He'd gotten the post following network stints in Los Angeles and New York. He sipped at a Diet Coke and reached for the stylized door handle of the conference room. Never once in twenty-five years in the business had he felt as sure about a hunch as he did today. Or as concerned. And Zak Prosser's story in this morning's *Post* only impelled him forward.

"But damn it, Saul, that staging place out in Oklahoma was blown up," executive producer Ernie Simons posed in a loud voice as Gilbert entered the paneled conference room. "Say what you want about the original threat to the extravaganza tomorrow, the feds now have them on the run. No attacks that we know of since the DC-10 crash at Disneyland twelve days ago." He tapped his knuckles against the tabletop. "Knock on wood, of course, but the G-men should keep the remaining terrorists off guard and pick 'em up one by one. And just in time for 'Ruffles and Flourishes' at noon tomorrow. Fear not. You'll see."

Gilbert took his seat. He drained the rest of the soft drink and lobbed the can into a corner wastebasket. Around the polished wood table, in addition to Simons, were two assistant news directors, a producer, and an assignment editor. Gilbert looked at his watch just as the door opened and Zachary Taylor Prosser walked in.

"God, what's this, the ready room for test pilots at the Preparation H factory?" The smirking *Washington Post* reporter walked past somber expressions and found an empty chair.

"Not *moi,*" Simons announced, then pointed toward the end of the table. "It's Gilbert and the rest of these guys who have a problem."

Prosser slipped into a sculptured seat next to the news director and surveyed his audience.

"My column was that bad, huh?"

"Hope not." Gilbert retrieved a copy of the *Post* from the middle of the table. He pointed to the ballpoint-underlined type. "But you did raise some points that have been bothering a few of us around here."

Prosser raised his eyebrows. "The 'too quiet' part?"

" 'Too quiet' and 'too pat.' Look, maybe I'm really a believer in pre-destination, and nothing can stop what's coming tomorrow. Maybe that's why they're acting the way they are at the White House. Fellow believers, if you will."

"Like waiting for the proverbial second shoe to drop?"

"Yeah." Gilbert clasped his hands together and faced Prosser. "As you pointed out in your story, things have calmed down around the country, but since the president lifted martial law last Saturday, there's been a marked elevation of testiness at the White House. We've noticed it, too. Kevin Howard's answering our questions about the continuing threat, but I feel he's giving us 'iceberg' answers." He contemplated the newspaper in front of him. "There's just too much that's not being said. All of our requests for the bigger picture get short responses from the administration, as if we were asking unimportant questions about the appointment of some assistant secretary. If we pursue the matter, tempers get short and a wall goes up. If everything's hunky-dory, Zak, why the evasion?"

"Well, everything *isn't* hunky-dory. That was my point in the article." Prosser sat back in his chair. "Martial law seemed to work, by calming everybody down, but it only masked something from the American people. Something big. Yes, there's more going on at 1600 Pennsylvania Avenue than just apprehension about tomorrow."

"Something that goes beyond simple fear," Gilbert suggested. "We talked with the House Speaker about it yesterday. He gave us his standard blast at the president, the impeachment stuff, but the old man is very perceptive. I saw something in his eyes. I saw an awareness that he wasn't ready to talk about."

Prosser smiled. "For Homer Jenkins not to talk about what's on his mind is a major story in itself."

Gilbert stared at the reporter. "So what's your gut tell you?"

"I guess what I'm saying is that the White House knows there's more to come. They may be sitting on the story of the century."

"You know something else that's been bothering me?" Gilbert didn't wait for an answer. "That FBI guy who was burned by the terrorists. The Bureau has capped that story like it was a defense secret."

"Maybe it is," Prosser responded.

"Then let's lay out what we know." Gilbert looked around the table. "Maybe we already have the answers. We just have to ask the right questions."

The executive producer went first.

"How much of the terrorists' explosives blew up in the Oklahoma raid, and how much was taken away earlier by buses and helicopters?"

No one responded.

"All right," Simons went on, "how many buses and helicopters were there?"

The others present only shook their heads.

"Shit, guys," Simons exploded. "We don't know an awful lot, do we?"

"Let's try it another way," Gilbert proposed. "Let's say there really *is* something else coming. When?"

Prosser stabbed the table. "Everything points to the inauguration tomorrow, right? I mean, get all three branches of government exposed in the bright sunlight on the West Front of the Capitol, then blow 'em up. Makes perfect sense, doesn't it?"

Gilbert squinted, "Except ... "

Prosser pressed ahead. "I checked at the Pentagon, and the Air Force is going to police the area within twenty-five miles of the Capitol from 10 a.m. until 2 p.m. The FAA's already issued a ban on *all* flights, airliners included, starting at nine in the morning. I think it'll be a fifty-mile radius of the Capitol, from the surface up to 50,000 feet. That would seem to be an effective seal against an aerial attack."

Simons nodded. "So much so that the president seems comfortable going through with the outdoor ceremony. Now, it's supposed to snow a lot tonight. ... "

Gilbert leaned forward. "The city's full of people, yet I'm convinced the White House is gearing up for something tomorrow. Two questions: What kind of danger are they anticipating, and how much risk are they willing to expose people to?"

Prosser turned toward Gilbert. "Saul, I interrupted you a minute ago. I said something about the inauguration's being the perfect target, and you said, 'Except.' "

"Yeah, I was just wondering. One can make the case that the inauguration's too obvious. Don't you think if *you* were planning an attack, you might figure that everyone else would know that's what you'd choose? I mean, why pick the most heavily defended place and time?"

The room was completely silent. Suddenly a man burst through the door.

"FBI's got a terrorist bus located near the Capitol. They're blocking off a huge area, emptying buildings, the whole nine yards. Everybody with a badge is heading down there."

The men in the conference room jumped up. As Gilbert went for the door, Prosser grabbed his arm.

"Hey, Television, it's good to know a real pro."

"Finish the word, Newspaper," Gilbert yelled over his shoulder. "Not pro . . . *prophet.*"

J. Edgar Hoover Building, Washington, D.C.
11:35 a.m.

Brand looked through the thick glass, shook his head, and mouthed, "No, I'm walking." Jerry Reynolds stood outside the SIOC conference room and nodded. Brand reached for the Kevlar body armor jacket and slipped his arms into the openings. The special material of the coat was designed to protect him from the blunt impact of bullets but offered limited defense against sharp objects such as knives and ice picks. Not that he expected the use of such weapons. "If only this damn thing were concussion resistant," he muttered as he adjusted the underarm trauma cups and fastened the front.

The eight-room Strategic Information Operations Center was packed with 172 men and women, a third of whom displayed blue-steel 10mm Smith & Wesson handguns in shoulder holsters. Their forces would grow by another fifty-five operatives between noon and three o'clock this afternoon, as additional worldwide listening posts were established in advance of tomorrow's inaugural event. Half of those present sat at desks on tiers in the two main rooms facing color video screens and communicated with other specialists around the globe.

Brand pulled on his overcoat and went for the door. Reynolds joined him in the corridor. Three men from the Counterterrorism Section followed.

"The Secret Service will want to run everything from now through tomorrow, including this bus incident," the deputy director warned. "Ray Shaffer will meet you at the site. He's bringing Tim Vance and maybe some others from the White House detail."

"I figured as much." Brand and his entourage moved toward the main door. "They've had us on their shit list ever since we were slow to tell them about that one helicopter departure in Oklahoma."

Reynolds rubbed his neck. "The fiasco at the bunker down there didn't build Brownie points either." The deputy director put his hand on Brand's shoulder. "Davidson himself is supposed to be with Shaffer. Get ready for his song and dance that this is a direct threat against the president, so it's unquestionably their ball game."

Brand looked at his boss. "Well, I don't give a healthy crap. This is terrorism, we've got the responsibility under the law, and I'm running the show." Brand smiled thinly. "Don't worry, Jerry. I took the industrial-strength version of the Dale Carnegie course. Taught me how to be a mean son of a bitch when all else fails."

Reynolds signaled for the door to be opened.

"Well, you're probably going to need old Dale himself for this one."

As the thick seal swung outward into the brightly lit corridor of the Criminal Investigative Division floor, Brand made a curt salute. "Stay away from windows."

Reynolds pointed at him. "If there's any explosion, it'd better be only Davidson, blowing his top at you."

Brand responded with a thumbs-up.

During the ride down the elevator with his contingent of three agents, the counterterrorism chief rehearsed a short, let's-work-together-under-me exhortation. There'd probably be at least a three-way battle for control of this incident. It would take all of his interpersonal skills to come out on top. "A smooth operation, please," he concluded out loud. His men understood and nodded in agreement. Brand tucked his hands into his overcoat pockets. "Maybe this will turn out to be a real break for us, gentlemen." The elevator door opened, and Brand continued his line of thinking. "If we're lucky, we can keep going like this, pick off the bad guys one by one without blowing up the city and upsetting the president's original plans for tomorrow." Then he remembered Tim Vance's growing doubts, as relayed by Shaffer, about the FBI's ability to prevent further violence.

"In *spite* of Vance," he spoke firmly to a puzzled guard as they left the building.

Tulsa
11:36 a.m.

"Eighteen?" Jack was incredulous. "Pete, you sold them *eighteen* new Caravans?"

Jack had called Peter Albans, a longtime friend and vice president at Cessna Aircraft in Wichita.

"Yes, sir, eighteen of our model 208B, the Grand Caravan. It has a bigger useful load than virtually any other single-engine turboprop utility aircraft in production." Albans hesitated for a moment. "According to our net sheets, it looks like we cut them a deal right at a million dollars each. Usually, with the avionics they got, it would have run them nearly $1.12 million per plane."

Jack was stunned.

Albans took advantage of the momentary silence. "Yeah, two at a time, over a ten-month period, and all FAF El Paso. They all went to a Mexican firm in Monterrey by the name of MagiCo., S.A. de C.V., and the paperwork was signed by that name you mentioned, Arturo Sánchez y Vega. We flew the planes to El Paso, where they were picked up by the other company's pilots. What's the deal? Our good news is somehow your bad news?"

"That outfit may be a cover for terrorists. Now they've got my simulators, your airplanes, plenty of explosives, and tomorrow's the inauguration."

"Je-sus Christ."

"Pete, I've got to know the specifications and performance—dimensions, useful load, cruise speed—anything that can help us stop them."

Jack could hear his friend take a deep breath.

"OK, the plane holds 340 cubic feet of cargo, which computes out at 2,458 pounds of payload. It's got a ground roll on takeoff of 1,365 feet, or 2,420 over a fifty-foot obstacle. Enough fuel for six hours and thirty-six minutes at 157 knots, but it'll do 182 knots level at an altitude of ten grand."

"Potentially over a ton of explosives," Jack whispered. Albans heard him.

"Uh, yeah, I guess that's one way of looking at it."

Jack was convinced he now knew what the plan was. The terrorists were going to use the eighteen planes in the attack.

"What are you going to do now, Jack?" Albans asked.

Jack held the telephone and stared across his office as he answered. "Pray." Then he remembered something. "What was that you said about the avionics?"

"They wanted a bunch of connectors added. Said they might need them so they could add testing or measuring equipment. For some of the rough airstrips they'll fly into."

"Have you ever had a request like that before?"

"Not that I remember."

"Does it even make sense?"

"No, not really."

Jack felt a twitch across his scalp, as if an electric prod had touched where his wound was. He'd been right. "But it makes a hell of a lot of sense if they're going to hook up radio-control units. Bye."

Jack found Brand's direct number.

"Sorry, Mr. Stroud," the FBI man's secretary apologized, "but he's not here. He received an anonymous call that a terrorist bus was parked near the Capitol. He's had the area blocked off. That's where he is now."

"Does he have his cellular with him?"

"No, sir. There're no phones or radios in use. Because of . . . "

"Yeah, explosives. Please get this message to him as soon as possible." Jack repeated what he had learned from Pete Albans. "And tell him not to waste his time on the bus. It's just a ruse. It'll only consume valuable time and personnel when the real effort ought to be in finding the airplanes . . . and their control buses."

"But sir, he said . . . "

"Damn it, remind him the terrorists haven't screwed up yet. There's no way they could unintentionally afford to lose a bus now, at such a critical moment in their planning."

"Yes, sir, I'll tell him. He's going to call in on a landline in the next half hour."

"Does he have people out looking for the Caravans?"

"Yes, sir," the woman replied. "There are forty or fifty agents checking airports in Maryland and Virginia right now."

Jack sighed. "At least that's a start. Tell him he should triple that number. And get helicopters out. No telling where we'll find those planes."

"Yes, sir."

"I'm on my way to the airport now. Got a flight to National in a half hour. Hold on." He checked his notes. "American 1571. Arrives at 5:13 this afternoon."

"I'll tell him, Mr. Stroud. And someone will pick you up at National."

"Thanks." Jack clicked off and noticed the man standing in his office. "Ready?"

Don Evans waved his car keys. "Right out in front."

Washington, D.C.
11:59 a.m.

Brand and his three men stepped out of the FBI building into a light snow and saw the beginnings of the blockade almost the moment they started down the sidewalk. The Metropolitan Police had already barricaded Pennsylvania Avenue at Seventh Street. As Brand approached what appeared to be a checkpoint, he could see that the cordon was tightening to the south, in the direction of Jefferson Drive, the southern boundary of the Mall.

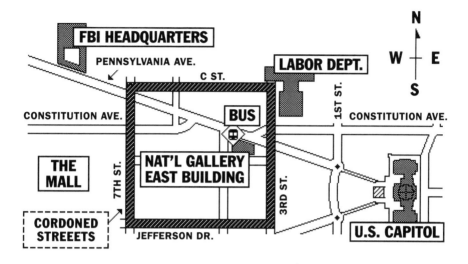

At Seventh Street they encountered two city policemen who'd taken up a position at the northwest corner of the square being cordoned off. Brand identified himself. One of the officers pointed. The bus stood a third of a mile away, right where the caller had said it was.

Pennsylvania Avenue from this point was completely clear of its usual midday traffic. Brand sensed the eerie quality of the scene. No cars or people. It reminded him of one of the old science fiction movies, when Washington was under attack. "Now we finally have the real thing," he mused out loud. Then he heard the roar of vehicles. He turned to his right and saw a procession of Metrobuses coming up Seventh. Within the next fifteen minutes this armada would take up perimeter positions and relieve the police of their stationary guard duty.

Brand thanked the uniformed officers, and he and the other agents continued along the north side of Pennsylvania Avenue. He surveyed the buildings and figured most of them had already been evacuated. Or at least people were hurrying for exits that didn't front on Pennsylvania. He was pleased at the rapid response by the police. He checked the time. If Follett had given a damn-the-torpedoes order to the materiel office at Quantico, the Bureau's specially designed armored personnel carrier would be here momentarily. The vehicle had been built in 1993 with the needs of the HRT team in mind. Even with its double-strength hull, the APC was fast and maneuverable, with a number of customized features that would be needed today.

As the four members of the Counterterrorism Section approached the point opposite the turn-in of Constitution Avenue, they encountered two of Follett's HRT specialists. Both men were wearing belt transceivers and headsets.

"No way." Brand drew his finger across his neck. "Cut the transmissions."

One of the men pointed to a wire that snaked into a building. "We're on a landline."

Brand eyed the line, then nodded. "All right, good."

"Follett warned us about the danger of an explosion, sir. There are fourteen of us here right now, at seven locations inside the cordoned-off area, and we'll maintain our vigil until 'J. Edgar' arrives. It was en route within three minutes of the boss's call to Quantico. Army and Marines are standing by to assist, but Tex wants this one for himself. He's still pissed about the outcome in Oklahoma."

Brand had forgotten that Follett's men had irreverently dubbed the APC "J. Edgar." "Cut the crap, call for a Hoover," was their leader's off-the-record slogan.

"Where *is* Tex?"

"In front of the Smithsonian, sir, waiting for the truck with the APC."

"OK. If you talk with him before I do, tell him I'm here."

"Righto."

Brand and his men crossed to the south side of Pennsylvania Avenue. Less than seven hundred feet from the bus, they met their first contingent of Alcohol, Tobacco, and Firearms agents.

"It's all yours," one of the ATF men called out as he recognized Brand. "Lehman told us this is primarily an FBI matter. But we're ready to help."

"Thanks." Good sign, Brand thought. Harold Lehman, the director of the ATF, regarded the FBI's counterterrorism chief as the epitome of professionalism. Brand hoped he could receive the same respect from the Secret Service, but he didn't really expect it. "We'll see what Follett sniffs out with the APC."

The ATF men nodded.

Ray Shaffer and Tim Vance of the Presidential Protective Division stood a hundred feet beyond. As Brand approached the Secret Service agents, Shaffer pulled off his glove and extended his hand.

"Whose ass is it going to be if there's another fuck-up?"

Brand put on a smile. "Believe it or not, Ray, I'd like for it to be mine."

"I won't keep you in suspense, Corley. Davidson's already been here, and just before he left, he said it was your ball game."

"Oh? Well, I'll take that as a compliment."

"Don't let it go to your head. It's not an endorsement."

Brand ignored the frosty tone. "OK, I'd like for Tex Follett to determine just what we have here. The APC's on the way, so we'll have the right equipment pretty quick."

"We have our own APC at Beltsville, you know."

"Are you intending to bring it here?" Brand questioned.

Shaffer's grin broke through. "Nah, I told Davidson to let Follett have all the fun."

Brand put his hand on the Secret Service man's shoulder.

"Ray, I need your help. I've chased these SOBs around the country for three weeks, and *I* need to resolve this bus matter. Depending on what goes on here, let's get together before the meeting and allocate tomorrow's duties."

"Why not do it now?"

Brand was surprised. "I'd love that. How about your being responsible for everything within a quarter-mile radius of the White House? And, of course, anything concerning the president's person. The Bureau will take the rest."

Shaffer smiled. "Done."

The two men shook hands.

"Gotta tell you, Corley," Shaffer added, "that was Davidson's exact proposal."

"Why, you son of a bitch!" He popped the back of his hand against the Secret Service agent's shoulder. "You let me think I was in for a major turf battle."

"Seriously, though," Shaffer continued, "Davidson's going to be tough on you guys at the meeting. You'd better have your ducks in a row."

From the northwest came a throaty diesel roar.

Tim Vance turned. "Here's J. Edgar now."

The men watched as the FBI's rolling bunker approached at a steady fifteen miles an hour. Right behind it was a smaller armored vehicle. Three wires bobbed between the two units. The APC and its companion rolled past and headed for the bus, a hundred yards beyond. The APC slowed and steered to the side of the street opposite its quarry.

"What's his plan?" Shaffer asked.

Brand crossed his arms. "The procedure is to maneuver for a look, then turn around and pull onto the sidewalk next to the building where it's parked. Follett will try to block the doors of the bus if he can so there won't be any surprises—terrorists jumping out, that sort of thing. Then he'll activate sensors to see if there are explosives on board. After that, he'll inspect the underside of the bus with a remote arm and camera. Finally we'll have to decide how he'll breach the thing."

Vance turned toward Brand. "What's the little chase tank for?"

"Communications. He'll plug in a line so we can talk with Follett directly."

The men remained silent as the strange courting ritual began, precisely as Brand had predicted. The APC eased around the front of the bus and slowly rolled into position next to it. The smaller vehicle maintained its fifty-foot separation. From their vantage point, it appeared to the men that the APC wasn't more than two inches from the side of the bus.

Brand looked around. "Excuse me, I've got to get to the telephone connection."

The landline hookup was behind a building and within two hundred feet of the APC. Brand nodded at the SIOC specialist who'd set up the equipment.

"Got him yet?"

"No, sir. Another minute or so. But here, it's your office."

Brand took the handset.

"I have a message from Mr. Stroud," his secretary reported. She relayed Jack's conclusion about the bus and his concerns about the threatening aircraft.

"Thanks. We'll see." He handed the telephone back to the man.

"Sir, you'll want to keep that. I think we've made contact with the APC."

Brand brought the handset back to his ear and listened.

"Holy shit, sports fans," came Follett's agitated voice. "The sniffer's about to be asphyxiated. There're more explosives inside that bus than this machine was calibrated for. The numbers hit the top and they're just flashing."

"Tex, it's Corley. Can you hear me?"

"Five by five," returned Follett. "Can't tell what they've got in there, señor, but it's more than I've ever encountered from such a small space. Could be leaking, too. That would run the ambient concentration up."

"What about the driver?"

"Looks dead as a doornail. We've got to get inside to see if it's set to go off. No way we could haul this thing out of town without risking a big boom. I think we should forget its doors and consider the windows. Probably one of the front ones."

"You got the equipment?"

"Sure do. A modified glass cutter, and it's already mounted on a remote arm. I'll have to back up first, but I think I can do the whole thing in minutes. Suction-hold the glass and slice around the edges."

"What about the shock of the cutting?"

"Keep your fingers crossed, ol' buddy, but I'm hoping to cause less motion than the shaking the bus is already getting from its engine, which is still running."

"OK, go for it."

Brand listened as the APC noise grew louder. After two minutes, Follett was back.

"Bringing out the cutter now . . . got to make sure I don't smash the glass when I swing the arm around."

"God, I hope you don't," Brand found himself saying out loud.

There was no further communication from Follett for three minutes. Brand checked the surroundings while he waited. Police and government agents stood along the side streets, at least a hundred of them that he could see. No one was moving.

"Here goes." There was a warble in Follett's voice. Brand heard clunking, mechanical sounds, then a high-pitched whine. "So far, so good," the HRT chief reported in a whisper. "Got the top of it." Another minute passed. "Down one side. The driver hasn't moved." The procedure continued. "Through the bottom now. Lookin' good."

Brand realized his mouth was pasty. He ran his tongue around and tried to generate saliva, but it didn't work. He patted the pocket of his coat for a stick of gum.

"Done!" Follett sounded ecstatic. "I'm through it, Corley, and now I'll move the glass out of the way."

Brand kept quiet.

"Here we go," Follett went on. "Off to the side with this thing. Driver still hasn't moved a muscle. Hold it, hold it. Christ, there are two more bodies inside. On the floor. And there must be ten . . . yeah, ten big cylinders in the back. In a stack."

"Tex?"

"Go."

"Are the cylinders attached to anything? Like a detonator?"

"Can't tell from here. A lot of shadows in there."

"OK, where's the front window?"

"Still holding it right above the ground. I'm going to keep it attached as I back away."

"Then what?"

"I'm going to extend a remote camera inside the bus first. Take a look around. Then two of my men will go in. Too bad we didn't have time to hook up the video connections so you could watch," Follett grumbled. "Not enough time. Anyway, here we go with the camera."

An interminable number of minutes passed before he reported again.

"Those are big fuckers, all right. Foot and a half in diameter, they look like. Actual count of the cylinders . . . eleven. And three apparently dead men. But there are no obvious detonators. Just looks like they had those tanks stored there, or were transporting them somewhere. My men are about to position an access ladder and go in."

As Brand waited for the HRT specialists to enter the bus, he wondered again what it all meant. Were the terrorists really in the process of moving the explosives into position for tomorrow? It certainly sounded logical. Or was Jack right? Another minute passed.

"Corley, those three guys are dead all right. We'll remove their bodies. Probably be good to do an expedited autopsy. As for the cylinders, my men can't see a triggering mechanism."

"Tex?"

"Hold on. They've found something else." There was a pause. "One of the dead men had something in his mouth. Piece of paper, half chewed, like he was trying to swallow it. We'll get it to you."

Brand took a deep breath and noticed that his face was wet. As he reached for a handkerchief he became aware that his clothes were stuck to his body. Hell, he realized, he was sweating as if he were in the tropics.

"Corley, it looks like a map of some kind. We're bringing it to you now."

Within seconds, an agent wearing a one-piece black Nomex suit, a ballistic vest, and an antiflash balaclava hood dashed around the corner of the building. He held out a small piece of paper. It was wrinkled, and it displayed teeth marks. Brand thanked him.

He studied the document, and his heart pounded. He had to hold the paper with both hands to steady it.

"Good God, if this means what I think it does, they're planning not one but *three* attacks on the inauguration."

En route to Washington
12:00 noon

Jack and FBI agent Don Evans jogged toward the security checkpoint at the Tulsa airport.

"Damn it, Don, I *know* I'm right. They've never broadcast their intentions before. That bus is nothing but a way to consume our dwindling time and resources. Brand had better get more troops in the field looking for those planes." He thought for a second. "There's no way he can search every bus that might potentially house a simulator or explosives. Not with the whole city full of them for the inauguration! Now even the local transit buses are suspects. No, their bus ploy was brilliant, but we don't have to fall for the whole phony scheme."

Jack realized that Evans had remained silent ever since he'd parked the car. The FBI agent extracted his American Airlines ticket envelope, the handgun transit declaration, and his identification folder and held them out to an unsmiling policeman as they stopped.

"Weapon?"

Evans nodded and touched under his left arm. "Nine millimeter."

The officer handed back the materials and looked at Jack. "FBI also?"

"No, Navy, and I'm not armed. But I do have an unloaded .45 in a checked suitcase."

The policeman motioned the two men to follow him. The procession moved briskly to the departure lounge. The policeman approached a female gate agent. "Armed FBI," he advised with a nod toward Evans. "I'll take them on board."

"OK," the woman responded and glanced at a clock on the wall. "We'll start boarding passengers in about six minutes." She smiled at Jack as he passed.

The policeman led the men down the Jetway and into a Boeing 757. The captain stood at the door of the aircraft. He took off his cap, stepped back inside, and positioned himself in the doorway to the cockpit.

"I don't see cuffs on anyone's wrists, so you all must be good guys," he joked as the three men trudged onto the plane. The officer nodded in Evans's direction. "FBI. The other man's Navy. FBI's armed."

The captain extended his hand. "Good to have you on board, gentlemen." He eyed his passengers. "Chicago?"

"Washington."

The captain nodded. "I'll be leaving you at O'Hare, but there's a nice snowstorm rolling toward the capital. Hope it won't delay you. Going up for the big day tomorrow?"

Jack smiled. "You might say that."

A flight attendant approached to see what the special boarding procedure was all about.

The captain gestured toward the two men. "Linda, these guys are going to National." He faced Jack. "Coach?"

"Right." Jack reached for his ticket folder. "I think we're in row twenty."

"Well ... " The pilot sounded conspiratorial. "How about sitting in the forward cabin, where you can talk without having six rows of passengers hanging on your every word?"

Jack tucked his ticket inside his jacket. "Got room today?"

"Yes, sir," the flight attendant beamed. "We're lighter than I'd figure we'd be the day before the inauguration. I guess everyone's already there."

Jack didn't miss the unintended second meaning to her statement. He and Evans thanked the captain and went for the first-class seats the flight attendant offered. They handed her their coats and sat down. Jack continued his argument.

"There's something else I've been thinking about: that word 'Lux,' Latin meaning 'light.' If there's an attack coming during the inauguration, why would it be called 'Lux'?"

Evans secured his seat belt. "An explosion bigger than the sun?"

"I wonder. Anyway, after talking with Pete Albans at Cessna, I've tried to find fault with my general reasoning, but the more I think about it, the more I'm convinced they're planning to fly those Caravans from the simulators in the buses."

"Well, keep trying to find holes in your thinking," Evans suggested. "You've got a few hours to put my mind at ease."

"That's not likely to happen, Don. Remember during the Gulf war we successfully used what they called unmanned aerial vehicles? UAVs?"

Evans frowned. "I think so."

"For surveillance, even bombing? The technology is ridiculously simple. A rudimentary cockpit on the ground, and a camera in the plane . . . that's all it takes. These terrorists, however, have far better flight controls than the military did, because with my simulator they have what amounts to the actual cockpit of the damn plane. Or *eighteen* planes, to be precise."

"Look, Jack, think about what you're saying. Eighteen planes being flown by one simulator? Get real!"

"Two. That Sánchez y Vega guy bought at least *two* simulators. Maybe six, if all of those we delivered to the airport went to his people."

"Oh, for Christ's sake, Stroud, even so they'd have to have eighteen simulators to fly eighteen planes. Right?"

"Wrong. It's theoretically possible to fly all of them with just one simulator. Get the planes airborne, one after the other, and adjust the cameras, and it's a done deal."

"Come *on*."

"Don, I'm telling you they can *do* it."

The other passengers began filing aboard. Jack noticed Evans grip the armrests and close his eyes. "Going to say your prayers?" he whispered to his FBI seatmate.

"Yeah, well, you'd better catch up on your own on the way. If what you say is really possible, we're up the proverbial excrement tributary."

"Is that an official FBI definition?"

Evans kept his eyes closed. "Please." He smiled weakly. "I'm trying to make myself believe this is all a dream."

Jack leaned closer. "Nightmare, honcho. The proper term is 'nightmare.' "

The White House
Tuesday, January 19, 2:35 p.m.

Ray Shaffer and Tim Vance returned directly to the White House from the site of the terrorist bus encounter. They took off their overcoats inside the Secret Service's command post. Shaffer removed his suit coat, revealing a standard Uzi in a leather "grab and shoot" body holster. Nearby, five other agents wearing Smith & Wesson Model 19 .357-caliber pistols in shoulder holsters monitored high-resolution color video screens, which produced pictures from dozens of maneuverable cameras throughout the Executive Mansion.

"So you still aren't a believer?"

Shaffer tucked in part of his shirt that had ballooned out next to his submachine gun.

"Nope," Vance answered, "and I'm going to suggest that we rearrange a few things."

"Like what?"

"The jet cars."

Shaffer held up his hand.

"Whoa, man. Everything's safe and secure at the Capitol for tomorrow . . . likewise here for tonight. Your imagination's in overdrive. There's no reason to rip up our plans just because the note smells."

"*Smells?* Ray, that's the worst piece of 'planted' evidence I've ever seen. How in the hell could a sophisticated terrorist operation be so stupid as to risk giving away their plans by distributing to foot soldiers the actual map for their attack?"

Shaffer shrugged. "Stranger things have happened."

"Oh, give me a break. They wouldn't even use that in a novel. I'm telling you, the whole episode today was phony, just to keep our concentration on the inauguration." Vance shook his head. "I think you agree with me, yet you're playing the goddamn party line. I expected more of you."

"Hey, mister." Shaffer pointed his finger at Vance's face. "Don't assume *anything* about my beliefs. I didn't get to be the head of the White House detail by being a fucking idiot. I've heard you out, and I'm telling you there's no valid reason to change our plans." He stepped back and put his hands in his pockets. His tone was lighter. "We've got a coordination meeting with the FBI at six this evening. Bring up your concerns then. Maybe you'll win converts."

Vance wasn't finished. "Just how did we decide to concentrate on the inauguration anyway?"

"Meeting tonight, Tim. Please."

"Davidson's still pissed off at the FBI for its blind focus on that Oklahoma bunker. Well, we just may have the same myopia about tomorrow."

"Vance!"

Washington National Airport
5:13 p.m.

"Remember me?" A man with a familiar face extended his hand as Jack stepped into the terminal after the flight from Tulsa. "Scott Collister, Jack. I interviewed you at the Dallas–Fort Worth airport on that terrible day. I never had a chance to tell you how sorry I am about your loss."

Jack smiled. "I remember you, Scott. Thanks for your thoughts. It was the worst day of my life." He nodded toward his escort. "Do you know your fellow agent, Don Evans?"

"Talked to him on the telephone." Collister grinned. "How ya doing, Don?"

"Not so well after all the horror stories Stroud's been telling me on the way," Evans grumbled. "Is the meeting still set for six?"

"Yes, but I'm afraid I'm going to add to the gloom. Jack, your friend at Cessna called an hour or so ago about the number of Caravans they sold to that outfit in Mexico."

"Right, the eighteen?"

"Try thirty-six."

"What?" Jack again felt an electric tingle across his scalp.

"There was another order, which didn't show up when he checked the first time. So welcome to Washington."

Jack bolted ahead. "Come on. There's practically no time."

Culpeper, Virginia
5:57 p.m.

Snowfall across the central Atlantic states increased almost immediately after sunset. The rate of accumulation was more than an inch an hour. FBI special agent Frank Crowdus braked and turned off U.S. 29 at a lighted sign advertising the "Culpeper Winter Fly-in." He was one of fifty-two agents who had been dispatched across Maryland and Virginia by Corley Brand.

Culpeper Field was a new private airport west of town that was built and owned by a Virginia pilots group. Since the facility had promoted its annual event widely, Crowdus hoped there would be a concentration of aviators available who might be able to help him locate one or more of the Cessna Caravans. He stopped at a small, one-story wood building with a "Welcome—Office" sign over the door and got out of his car.

"Special Agent Crowdus, FBI," he introduced himself inside to a heavyset, middle-aged man in a green flannel shirt who stood behind the counter.

The older man regarded the visitor and his credentials warily. "Stolen plane?"

Crowdus pushed his identification folder into his pocket. "Have a minute?"

The man crossed his arms. "Shoot."

"You're ... "

"Bill Baysinger. I'm in charge of this event."

"Mr. Baysinger, I *am* looking for an airplane or two. Cessna Caravans. Are there any here today?"

"Caravans? Hell, no. Those are big utility planes. Our pilots fly small aircraft. Two- and four-place. Piper Cherokees, Cessna 152s, 172s. Those kinds of planes." He uncrossed his arms. "Nothing as big as a Caravan comes in here for anything. Well, we did have a guy in an MU-2 once. Emergency landing. Bad engine, as I remember."

Another man entered the building. He pushed the door shut against the wintry night and rubbed his hands together.

"Damn snowstorm's picking up steam, Bill. I had to play tag with the gunk all the way from Williamsburg. Probably even punched into a cloud or two when the sun went down. Ceiling came down with it."

"We should have the NDB approach approved by next summer, Tolly. Surely will make it easier on everyone."

Baysinger looked back at the FBI agent. "So no Caravans around here, Mr., uh ... "

"Crowdus."

Baysinger shook his head. "Sorry I can't be more help to you."

"Caravans?" The other man approached the desk. "*Cessna* Caravans?"

Crowdus turned around. "That's right."

"I thought we were the only ones crazy enough to schedule a fly-in this time of the year. But somebody else apparently has the same idea. Goofy, if you ask me. All Caravans, too."

Crowdus peered at the man. "What do you mean?"

"Well, when I was zigzagging over here, trying like hell to stay VFR while there was still some light, I saw a whole bunch of Caravans."

"Where?"

"In a field, about fifteen miles east of Fredericksburg. There must have been, oh, eight, nine of them. Lined up, too, pointing into the wind."

Crowdus shrugged. "Sorry, but I'm not a pilot. Which direction would that be?"

"They were pointing north. Toward Washington."

Crowdus displayed his credentials again. "Sir, I'm with the FBI, and I'm *looking* for Cessna Caravans. Is there a map you could use to show me exactly where you saw them?"

"Here." Baysinger pointed to the wall.

The new arrival walked to the chart. He rubbed his chin, then put his finger on a spot.

"That's the Williamsburg-Jamestown airport where I left. Then I flew ... " He moved his finger to the northwest. "Uh, right along here, best I can remember." He stabbed his finger at the map. "There's where they were. I was at 4,500 feet on Victor 286, an aerial highway. Saw the planes right before I crossed U.S. 301 north of the little town of Port Royal."

"How far is that from, say, the Washington Monument?"

"Tell you in a second," the man replied. He positioned a piece of marked string that extended from a hole on the map at the location of the Culpeper airport. "Looks like right at forty-three nautical miles, which would be, I'm guessing, about fifty statute miles."

Crowdus turned to Baysinger. "Could I use your telephone?"

J. Edgar Hoover Building, Washington, D.C.
5:59 p.m.

On the coldest days of winter, seventy-five-degree humidified air was pumped through the wall registers of the narrow conference room of the Strategic Information Operations Center. Today, however, at the director's instructions, the thermostat was set ten degrees lower. "It's going to get hot enough in there without any outside help," the FBI leader had observed.

In attendance for the Bureau at this special interagency meeting and already seated at the heavy mahogany table were deputy director Jerry Reynolds; Doug Redding, assistant director of the Criminal Division; William Colquitt, AD of the National Security Division; Loren Turner, assistant director of the Laboratory Division; Corley Brand, chief of the

Counterterrorism Section; Lewis Bittker, SIOC's chief; and Paul Simpson, an intelligence research specialist in the Terrorist Research and Analytical Center. Expected shortly was special agent Scott Collister, who was bringing Don Evans and Jack Stroud from the airport. An agent stood at the soundproof door in anticipation of the FBI director's imminent arrival.

Also present and heading the contingent from the Secret Service was its 6-foot-6 director, Stan Davidson. With him were Ray Shaffer, chief of the White House detail, and special agents Tim Vance and Rick Hayes. Others from the Secret Service included one man each from the Technical Security Division, the Technical Development Division, the Intelligence Division, Protective Research, and the Visual Intelligence Branch.

The instant the digital timepiece on the wall flashed six o'clock, the FBI chief stepped around the corner and entered the room. The agent quickly shut the door, and the meeting was under way.

The director stood at the end of the table and welcomed the outside visitors. The atmosphere inside the cubicle was restless.

"I had planned to start with a step-by-step analysis of our joint plans and responsibilities for tomorrow. However, because of today's bus incident, I'm going to ask Corley Brand to begin with that and review what transpired."

Brand rose and summarized the events that had begun with the anonymous morning telephone call.

"Because of the president's quick public statement of praise for how we handled this incident, the professional media hysterics were generally muted, and they're still on hold. But I know they're not sold on his conclusion that the bus was a lone aberration, the last dying act of this terrorist group. Reporters for *The Washington Post* and WRC-TV, in particular, brushed it aside with comments ranging from 'ploy' to 'cover-up.' Speaker Jenkins and a number of senators have already met with the president, but I haven't heard yet what was discussed. I'm sure they'll have something to say about the meeting on the news tonight."

Brand paced as he spoke.

"According to the ATF report, the bus had enough explosives in it to level everything within a hundred-yard radius. The substance was RDX. They've used it a lot over the past three weeks."

He paused for a second.

"We think the three men were on their way to another position near the Capitol when they became incapacitated. The driver pulled over rather than lose control."

Davidson drummed his fingers on the table. "So what killed them?"

"Carbon monoxide," Brand replied. "Most probably from a loose connection we discovered in the exhaust system. Intentional? We can't say. The autopsy report showed that the concentration in their blood averaged eighty-four percent, definitely lethal. If the break in the hose occurred before they started the engine and closed the doors, we think it would have taken less than ten minutes for the driver to feel sufficiently incapacitated to stop the bus. For about four or five minutes before that, the men probably felt the growing effects of the gas—dizziness, headache, heart palpitation, and nausea."

Brand moved to an easel and lifted the cover sheet.

"This is an enlargement of a piece of paper taken from the mouth of one of the men found in the bus. It seems he was attempting to swallow it, but he became unconscious before he was able to do so."

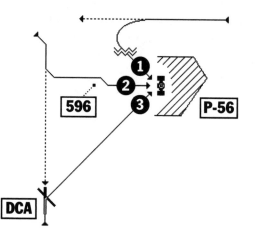

Brand picked up a collapsed metal pointer in the tray. He extended it and touched the point to a small square on the sheet. "Let's start at the '596' here in the middle. I'm told that's the elevation above sea level of the top of the Washington Monument." He lowered the pointer to the "DCA." "This is the three-letter designator for National Airport." He then moved up to the right portion of the chart and stopped on "P-56." "That's the official Federal Aviation Administration designation for the prohibited airspace from the Lincoln Memorial to the Capitol, which includes the White House. And, finally . . . " he tapped at the target of the three arrows, "the Capitol itself."

The door of the conference room opened and Scott Collister stepped inside, followed by Don Evans and Jack Stroud. Brand introduced the newcomers as they filed along the wall for seats in the back, then continued his review.

"It's our opinion that this map portrays some sort of aerial attack plan against the Capitol. We say 'aerial' because of the three obvious aviation references on it." He positioned the tip of his pointer on the chart again. "This one arrow, number three, appears to show a flight path into National Airport from the south, followed by a veering off to the Capitol, something unlikely to be carried out in a land vehicle because of the Potomac River in between."

"Corley?" It was Jack.

Brand raised his eyebrows.

"Pardon the break in the protocol, but that whole bus thing is irrelevant. I've just learned that Cessna sold not eighteen but thirty-six Caravans to the Mexican outfit. The *planes* are the real threat."

"Captain Stroud," Brand sighed, "that just happens to be what we're talking about."

Jack overlooked the rebuke.

"Corley, I know I haven't been able to talk with you personally about these latest developments, but I'm convinced the bus was only a ruse. Therefore, so is that map. Someone wanted you to conclude precisely what you did . . . that the Capitol is their target. That's why the bus was parked where it was. Frankly, I think those men were sacrificed to the lie."

Brand put aside the pointer and crossed his arms.

"All right, Jack, if their target isn't the Capitol, what *is?*"

"How the hell should I know? It *could* be the Capitol, but we can't afford the luxury of putting all of our defense eggs in one basket. We can't get fixated on one target. Their whole effort depends on those planes. We've *got* to find them before it's too late."

"Jack, Jack." Brand made a time-out "T" signal with his hands. "We have more than fifty agents checking out places in two states right now. As of an hour ago, they'd visited most public and private airports within fifty miles of here. So we're not exactly sitting on our butts."

"I'd like to add something, if I may." It was Tim Vance.

Looking exasperated, Brand stepped away from the easel. "Hey, take the whole floor, if you want."

"No, I just want to say that I, too, have been concerned that we've focused on the inauguration to the exclusion of other possibilities. The president will be at more than a dozen functions over the next twenty-four hours. I agree with Stroud. We can't be caught flatfooted watching only one place at one particular time. That's why I want to move our turbine cars to the White House immediately. It's a better location, given the president's itinerary."

"You want to do *what?*" Secret Service director Davidson stared at Vance. Shaffer looked at the ceiling.

"Corley?" A specialist stood in the doorway with a note.

Brand took it and read it. He lifted his head.

"Gentlemen, we just interviewed a private pilot at an airport in Culpeper who thinks he saw eight or nine Cessna Caravans fifty miles south of Washington about an hour ago. They were all in a line, pointing north."

The FBI director turned toward Jack. "You really think those planes are likely to be flown by your simulators, probably hidden in buses?"

"Yes, sir. It's easily done, too. The operators can use cameras to follow the terrain, and this storm won't hinder them at all. One thing I remember from my aviation meteorology is that vertical visibility is usually excellent in a snowstorm. Even a heavy one."

Davidson hit the table with his fist. "That's enough for me. The president can order Apache helicopters to go down there. They can locate and destroy targets in zero visibility."

Jerry Reynolds moved his hand back and forth in a wait-a-second gesture.

"Jack, tell us a little more about the radio control of those planes."

Jack stood up. "The transmitters are probably in the buses, because of their self-contained power supplies. And as long as the transmitters remain within line of sight, the planes can be controlled all the way to their targets. No operator has to be able to see the planes visually in order to guide them, just that the radio transmissions have to follow a straight line to the receivers in the planes."

Reynolds nodded. "What frequency would they use?"

"No telling, Jerry. They'll probably have to use more than one to handle the complex flight control orders."

"Maybe we can help." Ray Shaffer turned in his chair. "We have three mobile scanners, which we call 'FAST' units. That stands for 'Frequency Analysis Sweep Triangulator.' Our 'roadrunners,' the guys who check out areas in advance of a presidential visit, use them to look for frequencies that shouldn't be in operation at a particular time, like cellular telephone transmissions where no one's supposed to be, unauthorized use of police frequencies, that kind of stuff. The units can be programmed to disregard the usual transmissions, like radio stations, and they can even pick out special-band use or erratically timed bursts. Each unit has two receivers on top. Once a suspicious transmission is detected, we can find the location almost instantly by triangulation." Shaffer paused. "So far, they've worked flawlessly."

Jack placed his hands on the table. "How many of your FAST units are available?"

"All three."

He looked at Davidson. "Can we have them?"

"They're yours."

"Thanks." Jack stood up straight again. "Two suggestions. First, your men should report anything whatsoever out of the ordinary. We may be lucky enough to pick up a test transmission tonight. Second, there were only eight or nine Caravans reported by that pilot. That means there are still twenty-seven or twenty-eight planes unaccounted for. They may be at one or more other locations, so there's no need to waste a FAST unit on that place south of town. If we can get the planes, it doesn't matter where the buses are."

Brand went back to the easel. "I've asked for current satellite pictures and interpretations from the NSA, covering both Maryland and Virginia. If those other planes are out in the open, we might be able to spot them." He checked his watch. "The package should be here any minute."

The FBI director stood up. "I'll call the president for the helicopters. Corley, you coordinate the FAST units with Ray. Jerry, I want a hundred more agents out checking potential launching sites. Let's locate the buses, if possible, but let's damn sure find those planes." He turned toward Davidson. "Stan, I appreciate your cooperation." He adjusted his suit coat. "Anything else?"

Jack crossed his arms. "Time for a gut feeling?"

The FBI chief nodded. "Let's hear it."

"It concerns that word 'Lux' which keeps coming up. Your informants in Mexico reported it some time ago. Charlie Carmichael, minutes before he died, said he'd heard it mentioned by some of the terrorists. It means 'light' in Latin." Jack hesitated. "Maybe I have an overactive imagination, but I've been thinking . . . just when do you need light anyway?"

"When it's dark," Brand and Vance said in unison.

The director closed his eyes. "Good God."

The White House
7:00 p.m.

On the hour, a procession of limousines entered the grounds of the White House and began its measured advance toward the South Portico. The black automobiles, spaced forty feet apart, glistened in the lights of the driveway in spite of the steady snowfall. Nature's alabaster blanket covered and softened and produced a scene reminiscent of a nineteenth-century print. Its soothing effect was especially welcome this evening. One by one the cars rolled to a smooth stop, and attendants with protective umbrellas opened doors. Four Secret Service agents verified by sight that each was who he or she was supposed to be.

The guests were received by the president and the First Lady inside the handsome Diplomatic Reception Room. It was the president's hope that tonight's gathering would warm and solidify relationships as he began a second four-year term. He looked forward to being with his friends and their spouses for a momentary respite from the cares outside.

As Speaker and Mrs. Jenkins hurried in from the cold and dusted themselves off, the president stepped forward. He extended his hand. "I'm glad you were able to make it home and back so quickly after our meeting, Homer." The chief executive smiled as he greeted Carla Jenkins. The House leader extricated himself from his overcoat and handed it to a steward.

"You'd better not be bullshitting me again," the older man growled. Mrs. Jenkins glared at her husband.

At the North Portico of the White House and flanked by a dozen Secret Service agents, an unmarked truck arrived from the Capitol bearing the two armor-plated turbine cars.

West of Washington, D.C.
Tuesday, January 19, 7:07 p.m.

The winter storm continued to intensify. White curtains of snow descended over the hills and valleys of the Old Dominion, at times reducing visibility to near zero. Three inches had fallen during the past two hours, and the revised forecast called for half a foot more before sunrise.

Corley Brand squinted into the Virginia night and attempted to keep his trailing FBI van within two hundred feet of the Secret Service FAST unit as they proceeded westward from the capital on Interstate 66. The Bureau's vehicle, dubbed "Snoopy," was the mobile command center of the search for the Cessna Caravans. Eleven radio transceivers were secured to metal racks behind the front seat. Both Brand and Jack Stroud wore fly-weight headsets with boom microphones. A floor console displayed the active frequencies in glowing red numerals.

Jack steadied himself in the swaying van with a grip on the padded dashboard. He turned toward his friend.

"Why the hell isn't the military crawling all over town?"

Brand felt for a switch and increased the speed of the windshield wipers. He kept his eyes on the road.

"If they're not, they damn sure will be after the director notifies the president of the planes and your suppositions. The Pentagon's been itching for a conspicuous role in all of this ever since it started."

Jack stared at the deteriorating environment outside.

"Yeah, but with all the indications pointing toward an imminent attack, why didn't Washington, days ago, look like a scene from 'The Day the Earth Stood Still'? Jeeps at intersections, things like that."

" 'Humvees,' they're now called, my good man." Brand looked over. "Until a couple of hours ago, the almost exclusive emphasis was on the inauguration. You heard the preparations for tomorrow: the FAA, the Air Force. Also, plenty of Marines at Quantico. Army's ready, too. Anyway, don't forget the president's expectation that we'll find the terrorists in time."

Jack watched the wipers toss the heavy snow left and right.

"Great weather for a scavenger hunt."

Brand smirked. "Keep the faith, baby."

The Secret Service's three Frequency Analysis Sweep Triangulator units were dispatched to the west, north, and east, in line with Jack's appraisal that the sighting to the south probably located only a fourth of the Caravans. Logic dictated that the other planes would be dispersed in the remaining quadrants of the metropolitan area, possibly a similar distance away. Tex Follett's men and the Secret Service's HRT agents went after the planes spotted earlier.

Brand flipped the heater fan to high. He noticed Jack's face.

"You got a hunch about something?"

Jack rubbed his forehead. "Have you considered the possibility of a second base?"

Brand didn't answer.

"Corley, that Beggs facility seemed more like a storage area than a training or staging facility, even with the large metal building they destroyed." He faced his FBI driver. "For example, there were no signs of a major communications setup." He paused and looked out the windshield again. "Although I suppose they could have had it in one of their buses."

Brand exhaled audibly. "I've got to tell you something. There were *two* messages on that note I received at the meeting. The second one said the Syrians believe there may indeed be a second bunker." Jack watched him. Brand continued. "We've learned that at the time of the upheaval in the Soviet Union the training of operatives for use by the KGB's First Chief Directorate had been stepped up at its sprawling center outside Moscow. Then that base was relocated. We don't know where. Apparently they didn't go to Lebanon. Maybe North Korea. But the Syrians now think they came here."

Jack shook his head. "That's all we need."

Brand pointed. "Would you get the pictures?"

Jack lifted a briefcase and extracted a manila envelope. He reached up and punched on the map light. The thick envelope bore the seal of the National Security Agency.

Brand glanced at his partner. "Take another look at the six sites the analysts suggested. We're getting close to one of them."

Jack broke the seal and pulled out a collection of visual and infrared photographs. The top one, in black and white, encompassed a thousand square miles, with Washington in the center. The main highways were highlighted by thin strips of yellow adhesive tape. Marked with numbered red circles were seventeen areas of interest, six west of the capital. All of the sites showed at least one Cessna Caravan on the ground.

Brand directed his attention.

"Check the one southwest of Gainesville on U.S. 29. We're almost at that turnoff."

Jack studied the area within the circle, then found the corresponding picture, which displayed the site in greater detail. There, sitting in a field, was a distinctive shape. "Got it. Definitely a Caravan. A large barn, too."

"Big enough to house aircraft?"

Jack compared the image of the plane with that of the barn. "At least three."

Brand glanced over. "Enough room for them to take off?"

"Well, it looks like there's a field about a half-mile square. No trees on one side, so no problem that way, even with a full load of cargo."

Brand keyed the microphone. "Haystack One, what's your opinion of Gainesville?"

"Worth a look-see," came a deep voice over the van's speaker. "We're in the constant analysis mode, scanning up and down simultaneously, but so far, nobody's talking out of school. Only the usual radio noise plus transmissions from Dulles, off to our right. By the way, National just went below minimums, so Dulles will probably be getting a lot busier unless it has to shut down also."

The two-vehicle procession continued into the surging snowstorm. A minute later they found the exit for U.S. 29. Brand turned his head. "Where are we in relation to that mental checklist of yours?"

"Funny you'd ask," Jack replied. "I was just thinking about it. I'm having a hard time deciding. In some ways, I feel we're separated from them by an impenetrable wall."

"What's your reliable gut tell you?"

Jack sighed. "That we're awfully close . . . and we're going to cross paths very soon."

"Thinking about Rachel?"

"Always."

The vehicles slowed, left the main highway, and followed a snow-covered two-lane road back toward the east.

"They're reading that photo pretty well up there," Brand commented as he watched the taillights of the FAST unit.

A mile later, the convoy pulled to the side of the road and stopped. To the left, fifty yards away and barely visible in the blizzard, was a large barn. It looked abandoned. Sitting next to it was a Cessna Caravan, rapidly accumulating a thick coat of snow.

"What do you think?" It was the voice from the FAST unit.

Brand depressed the push-to-talk button. "We'll have the NSA keep an eye-in-the-sky on the place, but I don't think anyone's going to be lifting off from *that* field tonight."

Suddenly a radio crackled on the FBI channel. It was Tex Follett.

"Snoopy, this is Port Royal. We can see them now, about a hundred yards away. I count nine Caravans on the ground, and there are at least twenty men around them."

The White House
7:45 p.m.

The president, with the First Lady on his arm, led the vice president, most members of the Cabinet, the leadership of Congress, and all nine justices of the Supreme Court up the stairs and into the elegant State Dining Room. Thirty-three of America's most powerful political figures, together with their spouses, moved across the soft green-and-brown rug to find their marked places at the tables. A gilded chandelier hung from the ceiling of the spacious room, and golden silk-damask draperies framed five tall windows facing the south and west. Eleven round tables were set with white Lenox china with a raised gold Presidential seal, vermeil flatware, and lead-crystal stemmed glassware, with centerpiece arrangements of fresh flowers.

Absent from tonight's gathering were the acting Treasury secretary and the attorney general. Because of their respective responsibilities over the Secret Service and the FBI, they felt it advisable at this time of national apprehension to remain on duty in their offices. Regardless, they would not have been permitted to attend in any event. The Secret Service prohibited the assemblage in one place of all those in the Constitutional line of succession.

The Service twice attempted to defer the dinner and the later musical entertainment in the East Room, but the president insisted on going ahead. Because of his unyielding stance, agents arranged a color-coded method of identifying and separating the individuals to be protected. The tablecloths were in the three patriotic colors of red, white, and blue. If, for some reason, it became necessary to move the guests to safer quarters, the president, the vice president, and the House Speaker would be in three different groups.

Stan Davidson, the Secret Service's director, stepped into the room and caught the president's eye. He walked over before the chief executive could sit down.

"Sir," he whispered, "our agents and the FBI are tracking down a fleet of airplanes that appears to be part of a plot to attack the ceremony tomorrow. There's no assurance we'll find all of the planes. We feel there's a risk to you even now, and I urge you to reconsider tonight's plans."

The president shook his head. "I've already dispatched Apaches. They should take care of your problem." He waved Davidson away.

Seated with their spouses at tables with red damask coverings were the Speaker of the House, the secretaries of Defense, Commerce, HUD, and Education, the Senate majority whip, the House majority leader, the House minority whip, and three associate justices of the Supreme Court. At the white tables were the vice president, the secretaries of State, Agriculture, Health and Human Services, and Energy, the Senate majority leader, the Senate minority whip, the House minority leader, and three associate justices. The tables with the blue tablecloths were for the president, the Senate president pro tem, the secretaries of Interior, Labor, and Veterans Affairs, the acting Transportation secretary, the Senate minority leader, the House majority whip, the chief justice, and two associate justices.

House Speaker Homer Jenkins made a face when he stopped at a red table and saw his name in script on the heavy place card. "Their goddamned fire-engine color certainly matches my mood," he fumed. Jenkins had wanted a complete personal briefing from the president on today's bus incident, but he'd received little more than platitudes. "Outright lies is what they really were," he grumbled loud enough for people to hear. Well, we'll see, he told himself as he pulled out his chair. Time was fast running out on this fancy cover-up.

As his guests were seated, the president remembered the words of John Adams that were carved into the mantel on the west wall: "I pray heaven to bestow the best blessings on this house and on all that shall hereafter inhabit it. May none but honest and wise men ever rule under this roof." The president hoped he merited inclusion in Adams's prayer.

Two hundred feet away, outside the North Entrance, a dozen Secret Service agents moved purposefully under a white bulletproof tent. In the middle of the temporary enclosure was a long, unmarked tractor-trailer combination, its closed rear doors facing Pennsylvania Avenue.

Port Royal, Virginia
8:19 p.m.

"I'll be a son of a bitch," exclaimed an FBI Hostage Rescue Team man. In the snowy night, he and his partner crouched behind a split-rail fence and looked through passive night-vision infrared viewers. Immediately ahead and down a gradual incline lay a wide clearing, bordered on the west and south by thick groves of trees. Nearby, Tex Follett and nineteen other FBI men waited in the covering of the west side, while eleven Secret Service HRT agents fanned out across the southern border of the property. Nine Cessna Caravans in a north-south file were visible to the south. At least a dozen figures in white clothing continued to work in and around the planes. Beams from their flashlights stabbed in multiple directions. "Can you believe it?" the FBI man whispered to his partner. "Those assholes are getting ready to start the engines!"

Closed-circuit thermal-imaging television cameras had been placed clandestinely in three positions and recorded the scene. Also aimed at the planes were two directional microphones with laser infraometers to pick up speech from vibrations.

Each HRT man carried a special antipersonnel Mossberg pump shotgun loaded with powerful slugs. The patterning efficiency of the weapon extended beyond three hundred feet. The FBI men waited until their Secret Service compatriots made their way into positions along the southern boundary. At last a red laser light signaled that everyone was ready. Thirty-three men rose slowly and began their advance. At fifty yards, Follett raised a bullhorn to his mouth.

"FBI ... *freeze*. Nobody move!"

Almost in unison, the figures in the field turned and fired automatic weapons at the agents. From behind one of the Caravans a man rose and dispatched a missile. The projectile flashed out of its launch tube, screamed over the heads of the FBI agents, and homed in on one of their vans. Its fragmentation warhead impacted on the engine compartment and destroyed the vehicle in a massive orb of white, which produced a temporary silhouette of some of the government men. A loud boom shook the ground a millisecond later. Half the figures in the field fired in the direction of the agents who'd been outlined by the explosion. Two FBI men toppled into the snow. Other FBI agents returned the gunfire with rapid salvos from their shotguns. From the south, the Secret Service HRT members augmented the attack with multiple blasts from their own weapons.

Suddenly the turboprop engines of the Caravans flamed to life. Their piercing whines reverberated across the cold expanse, and the planes shuddered and began to move. A dozen agents directed their fire at the planes. The HRT slugs found their targets, producing a series of loud impacts. Smoke boiled out of the eighth plane, and an orange glow shone through its windshield. The accelerating aircraft followed in line for another moment, then jerked and exploded in a violent ball of fire that almost immediately detonated the cargo in the ninth plane. One of the terrorists running alongside the last plane was hurled fifty feet, head over heels, by the second explosion. He didn't get up. The tail of the seventh Caravan lifted for a second in the burst, but the plane wobbled back into the departing procession.

A new sound emerged through the white veil of snow. At first it mingled with the noise of the Caravans. The FBI and Secret Service agents then recognized the high-pitched roar of the first attack helicopters as they approached from the northeast. Five Army AH-64A Apaches had been dispatched for the central-Virginia encounter. Each carried sixteen AGM-114A laser-designated Hellfire missiles and a 1,200-round, 625-per-minute, 30-mm M230 Chain Gun slaved to the crew's integrated helmet and display sighting system. With their forward-looking infrared systems, which could detect even camouflaged ground targets at night, the Apaches were perfectly suited for the occasion. The helicopters hovered a half mile from the northeast corner of the property and surveyed the scene. The Caravans continued their takeoff roll.

"Aircraft departing," Follett shouted into a microphone, both to the HRT men and the Army helicopter pilots. "Get them!" The agents on the ground continued shooting at the moving planes.

The first Caravan lifted off into the snowy night. As it cleared the trees, gunfire sheared off a two-foot section of its left wing. The plane banked slightly but continued climbing. Right behind it came the second, then another until seven of the planes were airborne.

The Apaches had the Caravans in their sights and began the engagement process by assigning one "kill zone" per helicopter. The squadron commander didn't want two or more Apaches to waste any time by firing at the same target. The five helicopters positively identified and separately lased the first five Caravans. Their range varied from just under 1,000 yards to 1,700 yards. The point-target missiles were locked on. Each 5.4-foot-long, ninety-five-pound Hellfire missile contained fourteen pounds of explosives surrounding a cone of copper. The warhead and two plates were set to implode upon impact, closing the arming circuit. The resulting detonation was designed to produce a narrow jet of molten metal that penetrated at supersonic speed and devastated the interior of the target.

"Fire!"

Five Hellfire missiles screamed away at the ignition of their solid rocket motors. Almost instantaneously, a massive explosion lit the sky north of the property, followed by four more in quick succession. Two of the Apaches lased the remaining Caravans and launched two more missiles.

As if cued by the Hellfire encounters, the FBI and Secret Service men ran forward, firing at the scurrying apparitions in the field. Seconds later, there were two more flashes in the milky sky to the north. Their shattering booms followed. The agents downed five fleeing figures. As the men reached the prostrate terrorists, they kicked away AK-47s and Uzis with forty-round magazines.

Suddenly an injured man rose from the ground with a combat knife in his hand and lunged at a Secret Service agent. They struggled for a moment before another agent with a submachine gun yelled for his partner to disengage.

"Enough of this interpersonal confrontation shit," he called out as he fired a quick burst into the terrorist.

One of the FBI agents moved to the body of the man who'd been catapulted across the snow by the explosion of the ninth Caravan. His front was blown open, and everything within five inches of a line from his Adam's apple to his groin lay exposed. The dead man's partially severed neck sported a length of whitish-pink intestine. With the muzzle of his shotgun, the FBI man lifted the bloody chin of the corpse for a better look.

"Hey, Tex," he called to his commander. "Isn't this the guy in the photograph?"

Follett jogged over and pulled out a folded piece of paper. He scanned the black-and-white picture, then peered at the body at his feet.

"Jesus Christ, that's Abu Kuttab."

Markham, Virginia
8:34 p.m.

Brand couldn't believe his ears. "Holy *shit,* they've launched planes from Port Royal!" He stared at his friend. Jack started to say something, but Brand groaned and continued. "All the Apaches are down *there,* and we don't have the AWACS." He pounded the steering wheel. "We're fucking *blind* if they launch from any other sites tonight!"

Brand quickly explained that the Air Force reported earlier its Boeing E-3C wouldn't be airworthy until six the following morning.

"A goddamned mechanical problem, but it didn't seem like a big deal at the time." He hit the steering wheel again.

"Hold on, Corley," Jack offered. "We'll rely on the NSA."

Brand spun around. "Do you know what our chances are if . . . "

"Haystack One to Snoopy," a deep voice boomed from the nearby FAST unit. "We're getting something, gentlemen. Stand by."

Jack knew what the message would be.

Brand gritted his teeth and keyed the FBI frequency for SIOC.

"Has the White House been notified about Port Royal?"

"Yes, sir," came the immediate reply from the duty officer. "The Secret Service did that the instant the planes started to move."

"Snoopy, we've definitely got a fix." It was the FAST unit again. "I repeat, a fix. Someone's sending out a digital code on 121.45 megahertz."

"Hold on, SIOC." Brand returned to the Secret Service agent. "Where's that transmission coming from?"

"Coordinates put it ... four statute miles west northwest of the town of Marshall, about halfway to Markham. Not more than twenty miles away."

Jack frowned and activated his microphone. "What was that frequency again?"

"One two one point four five," came the reply.

He looked at Brand. "*All* the Apaches are down south?"

Another voice broke in. "This is Haystack Three. We're getting strange signals, too."

Brand leaned forward. "Where are you?"

"Halfway between Washington and Annapolis. The signals are coming from across Chesapeake Bay, over near Easton, Maryland. To be precise, it's a mile north of a place called Tunis Mills."

"What's the frequency they're using, Haystack Three?"

"There was only one burst, about two seconds long, but we locked onto it. It's 121.525."

"What the hell?" Jack exclaimed.

"Haystack Two with a similar report," snapped the radio. "Ours is showing a steady transmission on 121.475."

Brand rolled his eyes. "Position?"

"We're west of Baltimore on Interstate 70. The source is six miles west of Westminster and a little less than two miles north of the little town of New Windsor."

Jack attempted to pinpoint the locations on the NSA photograph. "Hell, Corley, they're all about fifty miles out. North, east, and west. Same distance as the Port Royal position."

"Just great." Brand rubbed his face. "Far enough away for us not to notice their launch preparations, probably camouflaged, but too close in for the Navy at Norfolk to get here in time." He dropped his head to the steering wheel. "Well, I'll call 'em anyway. They're our only chance."

"Forget the goddamned Navy!" Jack snapped. "We've got the Apaches at Port Royal."

Haystack One reported in. "We did pick up weak signals from down south."

Jack cocked his head. "Frequency?"

"We got parts of two bursts on 121.55. A second and a half each time."

"Good God."

Brand peered across. "Good God *what?*"

"Corley, 121.5 is the universal clear channel frequency for emergency use by aircraft in distress. One hundred kilohertz protection is provided to 121.5, so no one should be using the nearby frequencies. Yet they are."

Brand held his gaze. "So?"

"Pure genius," Jack sighed. "No one would figure they'd use anything in that protected zone. No one would even *look*. Air-traffic control wouldn't be alerted because their alarms are precisely tuned to 121.5."

"Go on."

"They've got twenty-five kilohertz separation with what they're using." Jack thought for a moment. "Yeah, there's a real pro out there. Those planes have to be controlled on three axes . . . rudder for pitch, ailerons for roll, and rudder for yaw. Then there's the throttle. Maybe even the gear and flaps. Usually it takes a separate frequency to operate the servos for each one of those, but someone seems to have been able to code the instructions in rapid digital form so that everything is handled with just one frequency."

"All right, God damn it, what's that mean to us?"

"There are only three frequencies controlling as many as twenty-seven airplanes. Probably one frequency per nine planes."

"Keep going."

"Give me a minute. I'm thinking."

"For Christ's sake, Stroud, we can't afford a minute!"

"Hey, Mister Counterterrorism Genius, why don't you do something constructive while you're waiting? Like call the NSA."

The White House
8:37 p.m.

The instant the warning flashed to the Secret Service, it was radioed to agents outside the doors to the State Dining Room. Eight men and two women quickly filed into the elegant chamber. Nine of them fanned out along the west wall by the fireplace and collected into groups of three. Ray Shaffer, head of the White House detail, dashed for the president and whispered into his ear. The chief executive grimaced and stood up.

"Ladies and gentlemen," he began, "may I have your attention?" The guests looked at the agents, then faced their host.

"I regret to inform you that we must interrupt our dinner and follow these people. Those of you at tables with red tablecloths will follow the first group of Secret Service agents. White tablecloths with the second group, and," he pointed, "blue tablecloths with this group over here. An agent in each group is holding a card with your color on it."

The room was abuzz. The president took a deep breath. "An attack has been threatened on the White House." His guests now stared at him in total silence. "You will be escorted downstairs, where you'll remain until it is completely safe. I am sorry."

Shaffer led the president and the First Lady from the room. As they departed, he discreetly touched the chief executive's waist and felt for the personal locator-transmitter the president was to carry at all times. It was there.

"What the hell's going on?" House Speaker Homer Jenkins tossed his napkin onto the table. "I demand an explanation right here and now." A Secret Service agent motioned for him to comply without delay.

Immediately outside the door, four other Secret Service agents formed a loose diamond around the First Couple and stepped briskly down the corridor. Shaffer followed a few feet behind. As the party rounded a corner, a waiting agent punched a code into a panel. A partition in the wall slid open, and the group entered a small room. At the far wall were the open stainless-steel doors of an elevator. The president, the First Lady, two agents, and Ray Shaffer stepped into the forty-nine-square-foot enclosure. The doors closed silently, and the elevator began its rapid, angled descent to a secret steel-and-reinforced concrete shelter 290 feet below and 170 yards southwest of the Executive Mansion.

Markham, Virginia
8:41 p.m.

Jack balanced his briefcase on his lap and drew lines on the NSA photograph to approximate the ground paths as reported by the Secret Service FAST units.

"Corley, they've launched planes simultaneously from the three sites! And all of them are heading straight for Washington!"

Brand held up his hand. He had already turned the van around and was on the radio, ordering a satellite monitor from the National Security Agency. "Damn it, colonel, we have the AWACS for tomorrow. The attack planes are on their way *now*. We need real-time information immediately!" He nodded. "Within thirty seconds? I'll keep this line open."

Brand then activated the frequency for the Army's Apache helicopter dispatch center and quickly filled in the battalion commander. "That's right," he confirmed, "the Caravans are in the air from three other sites, and their target is probably the White House."

Jack waved his hand in front of Brand's face. The FBI man kept talking to the Army commander. "We're S.O.L. without the helicopters, honcho. You've *got* to stop them."

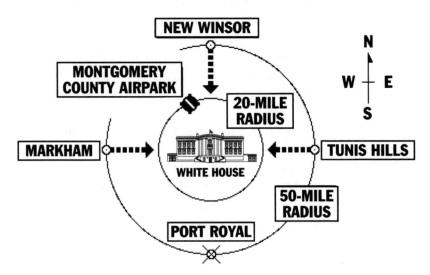

Jack hit the dashboard. "Damn it, Corley, if they shoot them down over the city, there'll be massive destruction on the ground. Maybe thousands killed."

"I don't give a shit," Brand growled.

"But the president's safe!" Jack yelled.

"Hold on a second," Brand barked into the microphone. He glared at Jack. "That doesn't make any difference, captain. Those planes have to be stopped." Brand keyed the microphone again. "Track 'em and kill every last one of them."

Jack's mind raced. He knew that some of the Caravans would get through regardless. The Apaches were good, but there was a real risk they wouldn't find all of the planes. Even if they did, there probably wouldn't be enough of the helicopters to finish the job in time. Think! he ordered his brain. He braced himself against the dash and tried to piece together an alternative plan. The planes were being controlled by radio transmissions from the buses. We don't know where the buses are, but we *do* know which frequencies they're using.

"Listen to me, Corley," he demanded. "It's a long shot, but if we can override their controlling transmissions, they won't be able to dive the planes at the last second."

Brand wrestled with the steering wheel of the van. He spoke without taking his eyes off the slick highway on their way back to the city.

"And just how in the hell are we going to do *that?*"

Jack spoke deliberately. "Washington National's closed because of the weather. It has plenty of radio transmitters, which are now available. The Apaches have transmitters. So does the White House. If we key the three frequencies being used to fly the planes, and our signals are stronger, we'll override. We'll block the digital information from the buses, and the planes will simply fly on past their target."

Brand looked to his right. "Cut off their flight data?" He shook his head. "They'll go out of control and crash for sure."

"I don't think so. They ought to continue straight and level for a while."

Brand frowned. "How long is 'a while'?"

"Under ideal conditions, until they run out of fuel."

"What about tonight?"

Jack quickly considered the weather outside.

"I don't think there's enough wind to move them too far off course. And based on this steady vertical snowfall, there couldn't be much turbulence that could bounce a wing up or down and start a turn. I'd say we can count on thirty seconds. Maybe a minute."

"A *minute?*" Brand laughed. "You want us to coordinate simultaneous radio transmissions for the last *sixty seconds* before they hit their target?" He checked the time. "And we may have a grand total of three or four minutes to arrange the whole crazy scheme? Which probably won't even work in the first place?" He turned. "What if the buses are closer than our transmitters? Give me a break, Jackson! Pray for the Army brats in their whirlybirds."

Jack glowered at his longtime friend. "Where the *shit* is the Corley Brand I used to work with? The man who always saw opportunities when others saw only obstacles. The man who hammered it into me that a hunch, well thought out, was worth a dozen textbooks."

Brand scratched the back of his head. "For crying out loud, Jack...."

"Damn it, I'm not finished. You've reverted to rookie thinking: When in doubt, shoot the bastards."

"Oh, come on...."

Jack seized Brand's arm. "Look, the Apaches will probably get some of the planes, and we could have the White House and whole city blocks on fire as a result. My plan should *prevent* all of that. There's no acceptable alternative."

The FBI counterterrorism chief stared back. "You know something, Stroud? You haven't changed a bit. You're an arrogant son of a bitch." After a moment he tapped at his chin. "And you've got a mean uppercut." He grinned. "OK, let's do it."

Jack converted his grip to an open hand and slapped the agent's shoulder.

"Hallelujah, I knew you were in there somewhere. All right, how many Apaches are airborne?"

"Maybe a half dozen," Brand answered. "Another seven in the next few minutes."

Jack nodded. "OK, they've got to follow the planes but not fire on them." He tapped his index finger at the center of the NSA photograph. "Let's get the Apaches as close to downtown as possible. They can start following the Caravans from that point. Then the NSA's got to tell us when the first planes are six miles out. At their probable speed, that should be about two minutes from the target. Shortly afterwards, we'll attempt the overrides."

Brand placed his index finger over the communications button for the Army. "Say your prayers. . . . Here goes." He winked at Jack. "It's showtime!"

While the FBI man relayed the new program to the Apache commander, Jack sat back and considered the timing. If we cut off the data flow too early, he thought, the planes could veer one way or the other too soon. Or, worse, dive for the ground, and we couldn't control them at all. No, better wait until the last possible moment.

Brand grabbed the cellular telephone and punched in Lew Bittker's special number at the Strategic Information Operations Center. The director himself answered. Brand quickly explained Jack's strategy and his own support for it.

"It's better than any suggestion we've come up with," the FBI chief's voice boomed over the speaker. He went on. "I'll follow up for you with the Apaches. The president's given us carte blanche to do whatever is necessary. So *do* it."

Brand smiled. "Yes, *sir.* Is Bittker there?"

"Coming in the door."

As soon as the SIOC chief answered, Brand gave him a summary of the situation, then the three frequencies that were controlling the planes.

"Lew, I want you to tie me in to National Airport, the Army Apaches in the air, and the Secret Service at the White House. We'll keep this line open. I'll give the order when the planes are about a minute out, OK?"

"Got it," came the reply. "But have you told this to the Service yet?"

"Just about to do it." Brand's finger was poised over the next button on the console.

"Well, *good* luck. It's in those boys' genes to block an attack on the White House."

"Yeah, I know."

"Let me handle it." Jack pushed the button. A Secret Service supervisor answered.

"This is Jack Stroud. I'm in the mobile command unit with Corley Brand. Here's what we're going to do. It has the blessing of the FBI director, in line with the president's orders."

Jack started to spell out the plan and its sequence of events.

"Bullshit!" the Secret Service agent interrupted. "We're not going to play ground zero for another of the FBI's harebrained schemes. Our men are fanning out right now with shoulder-launched Stingers and Redeyes. We'll stop those SOBs before they're within a mile of this place."

"No!" Jack yelled. "I'm telling you this will work. There are thousands of people packed into hotels and apartments all around the city. If just one of those planes . . . "

"Read my lips, Stroud. . . . Fuck you." The man disconnected.

Jack spun around. "How do I reach Stan Davidson?"

Brand thought for a second. "Try the Service's emergency frequency. It's the last button on the top row."

Jack located it and stabbed his finger into it. "Davidson!" he demanded when a man answered.

"He's here, but . . . "

"Presidential orders," Jack cut him off. It was the only thing he could think of saying, but it worked.

"This is Davidson," a calm voice replied a few seconds later.

"Sir, it's Jack Stroud. We don't have much time. I need your immediate help. A lot of lives depend on your decision." Jack pleaded his case as rationally as he could. Davidson didn't say anything. "So it's absolutely critical that your men hold their fire. I know this will work."

"You *know?*" the Secret Service leader challenged. "You've tried it before?"

"No, but . . . "

"I like you, Stroud," Davidson replied. "You have good instincts, but every ounce of my training, and that of my PPD agents, has been to protect the executive mansion. Particularly its occupant. We're not swayed by theories. Especially last-minute ones."

"Sixteen miles," a voice on the NSA channel called out. "The bogeys are tracking directly toward the zero milestone in downtown Washington. Speed 160 knots."

Jack searched his brain for another angle. Something persuasive. What flashed into his consciousness was a long shot, but it was all he had. He keyed the microphone again. "Sir, there might be chemical or biological weapons in those planes."

Davidson remained silent.

"Sir, we don't have *time!*"

"Stroud," the Secret Service director finally responded, "my head tells me to shoot them down. But my gut says you might be right." There was a pause. "I'll order my men to hold their fire."

Jack slumped backwards. "Thank you, sir."

Davidson stayed on the line. "Well, what do you want us to do with *our* transmitters?"

"Oh, set them on the VHF frequencies of 121.45, 121.475, and 121.525. And stand by. When we give the signal, key all three."

Davidson confirmed the numbers and added, "You'd better get on your knees, Stroud. I think this is going to take a miracle from You Know Who."

"Fourteen miles," came the report.

Jack turned. "One hundred and sixty knots is, uh, about 180 miles an hour. *Damn,* that's three miles a minute."

Brand nodded. "Yeah, they're bookin'. OK, the Apaches have their new orders, and SIOC's gotten National Airport in line." He smiled at his friend. "Good job convincing Stan the Man."

"Thanks. How's the FAA going to handle it at the airport?"

"They just told me they normally use a dozen VHF frequencies. All of those will be changed to the three the terrorists are using." Brand checked his notes. "Clearance delivery and ground will be on 121.45, tower and helicopter on 121.475, and the east and west departure frequencies on 121.525. The Washington VORTAC will transmit, too."

"Bogeys now at twelve miles." It was the NSA voice again.

Jack took a deep breath. "Four minutes."

"We're ten minutes out ourselves," Brand observed. He looked down and saw that SIOC's frequency was set on his transceiver. "I'd better pull over and get ready."

The FBI van steered onto a cleared section of the shoulder. Haystack One followed.

Brand pressed the push-to-talk switch. "SIOC ready?"

"SIOC's ready," Bittker's voice returned.

"Apaches?"

A background hum came through the speaker first, then, "Apaches five and a half miles out, tracking and ready."

"How many of the Caravans do you see?" Jack asked the helicopter commander.

"We've got . . . three flights of nine each. All about the same distance away. Lookin' like right at nine miles."

"Nine miles," the NSA confirmed.

"Secret Service ready?"

There was a delay.

"Yes." The voice sounded hostile.

Brand wanted positive identification. "Is that the Secret Service?"

A few seconds passed.

"Yes, this is the Secret Service." There was another pause. "We're ready."

"Eight miles," the NSA voice intoned.

"National Airport ready?"

"DCA's ready."

"OK, everyone," Brand directed, "double-check frequencies. Key your microphones on my mark."

"Seven miles."

"Stand by."

A few cars passed the FBI van. Snow billowed in their wakes.

"The first planes just crossed the six-mile radius," the NSA man reported.

"That's two minutes," Jack announced to Brand. "Please, if you would, hold for another full sixty seconds."

The FBI agent bowed his head and cupped his hands around his nose and mouth, as if in prayer. He nodded and waited. Jack saw that his friend's eyes were on the digital clock on the dashboard. Finally Brand looked out into the wintry darkness and pressed the microphone switch.

"Five . . . four . . . three . . . two . . . one," he broadcast. *"Mark!"*

The Ellipse
8:43 p.m.

Forty-five Secret Service agents had positioned themselves within a half-mile perimeter of the White House. Most of the men were concentrated in three quadrants, west, north, and east. A few agents fanned out to the south in case some of the planes diverted for an attack from that direction. Nine men supported General Dynamics FIM-92A Stinger missile systems on their shoulders. Nine others balanced bazooka launchers containing GD MIM-43A Redeye missiles. The rest wielded Remington 870 shotguns with long-distance, Teflon-coated armor-penetrating rounds. All wore headsets and waistband transceivers.

Two agents with shotguns waited in the middle of the snow-covered Ellipse, halfway between the White House and the Washington Monument. They faced north.

"Those fuckers had better not start a dive from around here," one man warned. "I don't give a shit what Davidson says, I'll bring 'em down."

His partner jogged in place to keep warm.

The first agent continued. "No poison gas or chemicals when the planes were blown up at Port Royal." He spat. "This whole thing smells like another goddamn FBI screw-up."

A slight wind ceased, and the snow fell vertically. The men stared into the cold night.

All of a sudden, from the west, whines of turboprop engines cut through the soft effect of the storm. The sounds grew in intensity. A few seconds later, similar sounds came from the opposite direction.

"Holy shit, here they come."

The two men raised their faces and looked back and forth. Snowflakes settled onto their cheeks and foreheads.

The second agent pointed to the west, in the direction of the General Services Administration building.

"There they are!"

Like an apparition from another world, the Cessna Caravans loomed out of the overcast in a single file and continued toward the White House. From the east another line of planes appeared. It was at a slightly higher altitude than the first. The two aerial processions closed on their target. None of the planes displayed running lights. The first man aimed his weapon at the lead plane of the formation from the west. He moved his sights slightly ahead of the aircraft.

"Piece of cake if I had a Stinger."

"Look!" his partner yelled. The agent raised his head above the shotgun and saw the third attack group coming from the north, directly toward them. The last group was at the highest altitude of the three. He re-aimed his gun and curled his finger around the trigger.

"Jesus Christ," the second man exclaimed. "They're flying right over the White House!"

The first man looked up and opened his mouth. Like ghostly trains passing in the night, the two formations of Caravans whined past each other in opposite directions. The third group flew over the White House a moment later.

"A fucking miracle!" the first agent exclaimed.

Seconds later they gazed in awe at the undersides of nine forty-one-foot-long, four-ton Caravans as the third formation roared directly overhead and disappeared southbound into the ragged whiteness beyond the Washington Monument.

The second man lowered his weapon. "I think you're going to have to drop the 'goddamn' when you say 'FBI' from now on."

The first agent continued to look toward the south. "Yeah," he finally replied. "This'll sure ruin the Bureau's reputation around the office."

A new sound caught the men's attention. It was the roar of Apache helicopters.

Falls Church, Virginia
9:09 p.m.

"You *did* it!" Brand shouted. He reached over and slapped Jack on the shoulder. "Man, you were goddamned right. They just kept going!"

Jack felt completely drained. He leaned back against the headrest. His clothes stuck to his body.

"Holy Mother of God," Brand continued. "You saved the White House . . . and probably half the city, for that matter." He shook his friend. "Do you realize that?"

Jack closed his eyes. "Corley, I've got a confession to make."

"Hey, save it for church. Right now you're a twenty-four-karat hero."

"It hit me the second Davidson agreed with me," Jack sighed.

"OK, if you gotta tell me, tell me."

Jack sat up. "There could have been pilots on those planes."

"What?"

"They could have planned a kamikaze finish, just in case something went wrong. Like, if we tried what we did."

Brand laughed. "Well, you've been living right, señor. I'm glad you didn't tell me that earlier." He leaned down, tuned the FBI frequency, and requested an update.

"All twenty-seven of the Caravans passed within a hundred feet of the center of the White House," a SIOC agent reported. "They were followed by U.S. Army Apaches and are to be shot down after they pass from the heavily populated metropolitan area. Confirmation of the latter is expected momentarily."

Brand watched a passing truck negotiate the ruts of ice and snow on the pavement.

"Damn weather turned out to be a worse threat than the planes."

He frowned and turned toward Jack.

"I just thought of something. When the Sabreliner blew up in Florida on New Year's Day, we checked with the FAA and found out it was registered to that 'Sánchez y Vega.' "

"So?"

"This morning the Syrians sent a message to the president, which said that a guy named Josef Gunter was the father of Jamil Nasir and Basilah Walid . . . and that he used the pseudonym of 'Arturo Sánchez y Vega.' "

Jack nodded. "Keep going."

"Well, we never asked for a search to see if any other planes were registered in that name."

Jack hit the dashboard. "You're right! Does Bittker have the emergency number of the FAA in Oklahoma City?"

"He does."

"Then let's see if there's something else hiding behind that name."

Brand had already keyed the SIOC number into the secure cellular telephone. He raised Bittker and asked for the FAA's telephone number. He waited.

"Great, Lew. Would you dial it for me?" He bent forward. "Hello? Yeah, this is Brand with the FBI in Washington. I need some aircraft registration information. It's an emergency." He motioned for Jack to be ready with a notepad while the appropriate person was put on the line. "Corley Brand, FBI. Would you check to see what's registered in the name of Arturo Sánchez y Vega." He spelled the name for the woman. "Thanks, I'll hold." A few seconds later, Brand shook his head. "No, we already have the information on the Sabreliner." Then he grimaced. "*Two* Sabreliners?" He nodded. "OK, OK, would you repeat that?" He relayed her findings.

"A second plane . . . a Sabreliner 75A . . . in that name, out of Monterrey, Mexico. It shows a home base of El Paso, just like the first one, which was registered in his name in March of 1990. The second one was put on the records last summer. It's . . . 'November One Sierra Victor.' " He smiled. "Got it. Thanks."

Jack stabbed at the sheet with his pencil. "Let's check with the air route traffic control center at Leesburg. It's a long shot, but we have nothing to lose."

Brand hit "1," then "411."

"I'm a believer in your long shots now, captain. Leesburg, Virginia? Yes, the number for the FAA's air route traffic control center, please." As the automated system delivered the numerals, Brand punched them in.

"Give me a supervisor, please," he barked when the connection was made. He flipped the switch for the overhead speaker and rested his arm on the steering wheel.

"Weiss speaking," a man answered.

"Brand here, FBI. I'm head of the counterterrorism section. Need your help."

"What the hell's going on out there?" the man demanded. "Dozens of violations of prohibited airspace, TCA incursions, then military pursuit."

Brand shook his head. "No time to explain. National security. You guys work a Sabreliner today with the 'N' number of 'One Sierra Victor'?"

"Let me check," the FAA man replied immediately. They heard him ask someone to pull up the aircraft handled since midnight. "You're in luck, Mr. Brand. We worked that plane tonight. Handed it off to Baltimore Approach. I understand it landed about fifteen minutes ago at Montgomery County Airpark near Gaithersburg, right before all the fireworks. The only IFR into that airport since, uh, six o'clock. Apparently barely made it in, because of the weather. RNAV approach, it shows here."

Jack and Brand look at one another. The FAA supervisor continued.

"Matter of fact, I *remember* that plane. One of our controllers thought the pilot was saying 'One Zero Victor.' The pilot had an accent, like German, and his 'Sierra Victor' sounded like 'Zero Victor.' "

Sierra Victor. SV . . . Sánchez y Vega. Jack's heart pounded. "Corley, don't forget there's supposed to be a backup group, in case the first one fails!"

"You've made our day, Mr. Weiss," Brand yelled as he jammed his foot against the accelerator and disconnected.

"I'm calling the Secret Service," Jack announced. "This thing may not be over by a long shot."

Montgomery County Airpark, Maryland
Tuesday, January 19, 10:06 p.m.

They tried to reach the suburban city of Gaithersburg at the normal speed limit, but the accumulation of snow on the road held them to forty-five miles an hour. The Secret Service's Haystack One withdrew from the convoy northwest of Washington and returned to Beltsville.

Brand eyed the night outside as he reached for the cellular telephone. The snowfall was lighter, but the ceiling still hovered between 1,000 and 1,500 feet. He dialed Bittker.

"Lew, we're heading north on Interstate 270. The FAA says they haven't received a departure instrument flight plan for the Sabreliner, and nobody's going anywhere in this weather without one." He hesitated. "Legally, that is. We'll need that back-up ASAP. No telling what we're going to find. We've already called the Secret Service."

"Help's on the way," Bittker advised. "Don't get too far out in front. Let 'em catch up with you."

"I want to get there quick," Brand pointed out. "In case that plane tries to leave."

"Hold on, Corley, here's the latest," Bittker continued. "The Apaches blew every one of those Caravans out of the sky. The only damage reports we have so far are two ground fires in Maryland, one east of Kettering, where debris hit an apartment complex, and the other south of Pomfret. A lumberyard. No one killed in either, though."

"Fan-tastic! Speaking of the Apaches, Lew, point a couple our way. The Sabreliner might be part of Jamil Nasir's 'second wave,' which we heard about earlier."

"Wilco. I'll keep you advised. Hey, let me talk to Stroud."

"Righto." Brand handed the phone to Jack.

"Yes, sir?"

"You redeemed us, man." Bittker's voice was enthusiastic. "I understand the president wants to thank you personally."

Jack looked at his driver. "It was really only a lucky hunch, Lew, but we're not out of the woods yet. Hey, thanks again." Jack fitted the handset into the cradle on the console.

Brand looked over. "They got all the Caravans. Minor damage on the ground."

Jack didn't react. He crossed his arms.

"Abu Kuttab was killed at the one site. He came to the United States only three weeks ago, when he murdered the Interpol guy on the plane. Makes me wonder."

Brand turned. "Like, where's his boss, Jamil Nasir?—who was supposed to have entered the country last May or June. And why did that abominable sister of his stay behind in Tulsa? And who the hell's this 'Josef Gunter,' their father?"

Jack looked out the window. "And is Rachel alive . . . ?"

Brand raised his eyebrows. "Yeah."

Jack turned toward Brand. "You called Voronov the key and Graham the smoking gun. Maybe this 'Gunter' character is the real triggerman. Maybe he's on the Sabreliner."

"Maybe," Brand replied. "Whatever, somewhere a Mister Big knows we got his Caravans, and he's one pissed-off terrorist. Phase Two may already be under way."

Jack watched the light traffic. Maybe someone's finally ready to play the hostage card. How are we going to do that with a dead hostage? Two . . . ? He closed his eyes.

The FBI van continued past Rockville and exited on the outskirts of Gaithersburg. Brand steered right and accelerated carefully on the narrow pavement.

"I've been here twice in the past year to meet with agents who flew in on private planes. Picked up Bittker at his Rockville condo for a session in one of the hangars." The counterterrorism chief felt his side for the extra magazines of ammunition. "The place is probably unattended on a night like this, so we shouldn't have to worry about any danger to others."

The van angled left at the airport sign and started down a two-lane access road. Brand killed the lights before they entered a paved apron. He stopped the van and turned toward Jack.

"Got your .45?"

Jack patted under his left arm.

Brand pointed. "I'll head to the left to check those four hangars. You go to the building and the hangar on the right. Let's meet back here in . . . " He referred to his watch. "Ten minutes."

Jack looked at his own watch. "OK, let's go."

They opened the doors and stepped into the frigid night. Three outside lights on poles a hundred yards apart provided enough illumination for the men to proceed without flashlights.

As Brand jogged in a southeasterly direction, he remembered he hadn't worn his body armor. No need for it, he'd rationalized after the SIOC meeting, because it was only "office work" he was going to perform in the van this evening. "Some office work," he huffed when he stopped at the first hangar. The square building didn't look large enough to house a Sabreliner, but someone might be inside who might have seen it land. The heavy doors were closed and padlocked. Brand looked at the five inches of snow on the ground. No tracks from a landing gear. He trotted to the next hangar. It was at least twice as large. Again, a closed building and no indication that a plane had taxied in. He looked ahead at the other two hangars. In the reflection of an outdoor light between the second and third buildings, he noticed something in the snow a few feet to his right. He walked closer.

Footprints. It was evident that as many as three people had walked in the opposite direction not too long ago. There was only a thin coating of new snow on the impressions. He leaned closer. It looked like someone had scuffed his prints. Or had walked back.

Brand drew his pistol and advanced on the third hangar. It, too, was secure and abandoned. However, three ruts came from the direction of the runway and ended at the closed doors of the fourth hangar. Definitely caused by an aircraft, he decided. He looked over at the line of footprints. They, too, extended from the fourth hangar. He moved forward.

10:14 p.m.

Jack loped to the corner of a small portable building that sat at the edge of the apron. Cinder blocks supported the structure, and metal skirts had been attached along most of its bottom to cover the open space. A twenty-foot transmitter tower was bolted to the side of the building and anchored in concrete. The place looked as if it had been built as a temporary facility, but, with time, it had acquired numerous additions of permanence.

Jack crouched and moved under a large window next to the front door. The word "Office" was painted on the glass. He listened. Other than the faint barking of a dog a mile or so away, there were no sounds. He rose slowly and peered into the window. The interior of the building was pitch black. Then he saw something. Perhaps it was only a reflection from the outdoor light across the way. He concentrated on it. Without a doubt, there was a thin horizontal glow at floor level inside. He lowered himself beneath the window. That light's coming from under a closed door, he concluded. There must be a back room to the place. And Rachel might be in there. He'd have to be very careful.

Jack stayed low and made it past the office structure to a large hangar alongside. He discerned that the two buildings were connected by a covered passageway. He maneuvered forward to the heavy doors of the hangar. They were locked. Jack turned the corner of the hulking metal building and shook his head. There was no access from the side. He kept going. In back, he saw a door. He approached and tried the handle. It turned.

10:17 p.m.

Brand stepped carefully into a dark, ten-foot space between the third and fourth hangars. There was no side door to the fourth building. He proceeded along the snow-covered corridor to the back of the hangar. No rear door either. His feet crunched against a ragged furrow of ice as he rounded the turn. He stared. A light shone through several cracks in the frame of a battered sheet-metal door on the far side of the hangar. Brand moved closer and held his pistol out in the braced-ready position. Almost immediately he noticed footprints in the snow, which led from the door toward the front of the building. He eased next to the door, reached for the knob, and twisted it. The door was unlocked.

Brand moved to the side opposite the hinges. He twisted the knob again and held his breath. The door yielded with a faint creak. He opened it a half inch and moved his face closer for a better view. Twenty-five feet inside, reflecting the weak illumination of a lone overhead fixture, stood a Sabreliner, its nose pointing toward the front of the hangar. On the side of its fuselage was the identification "N1SV."

Other than the aircraft, the building appeared empty. Brand opened the door further and, turning his head warily from side to side, stepped into the quiet building. He pulled the door shut and listened. There was no sign of anyone. All of a sudden, a muffled spitting noise erupted from the shadows in the corner to his right. Almost instantaneously, metallic sounds exploded around him, and something stabbed into his left shoulder.

"Shit!" he yelled as he spun to the floor. The machine-gun bursts continued a second time. Brand rolled behind a large metal trash barrel near the door and reached for his painful shoulder. His jacket was ripped open three inches from his neck. Brand touched bare skin and felt a sticky liquid. He winced. There was a third fusillade. The bullets slammed against the barrel and ricocheted. Where in the hell did that son of a bitch come from? There was no one there ten seconds earlier. Brand pointed his semiautomatic around the barrel and aimed it in the direction of the corner. He pulled the trigger twice. The loud reports echoed in the cavernous room. He had to buy time, if not a little respect.

Suddenly the overhead light went out. The hangar was now in total darkness. Brand realized he hadn't incapacitated his attacker, but he hoped the two of them were on a more level playing field without the light. Still, he noticed a bad taste in his mouth. He didn't like surprises. He fired again toward the corner. No response. He listened. To his horror, the submachine gun erupted behind him, from the direction of the hangar doors. He rolled on his back and returned the fire blindly. An instant later, slugs ripped into his abdomen, and he slumped against the trash barrel.

10:22 p.m.

With one hand, Jack felt his way along the back wall of the dark hangar. The rough corrugated metal was interrupted every five or six feet by vertical two-by-four wood studs. He couldn't see if there were any airplanes housed in the large structure, but he smelled solvents used during the overhaul of aircraft engines. He guessed the corner lay just ahead. A few seconds later, he found it with his open palm. Another fifty or so feet along the next wall and he hoped he'd discover access to the covered passageway and the adjacent office building. He moved slowly in the blackness and finally located a door. There were no sounds coming from beyond. He carefully turned the knob and pulled.

Jack stared into a narrow hallway that extended ten feet to another door. A faint glow from the outside came through three plexiglass portholes in the ceiling. He stepped tentatively into the corridor. The floor was covered by a frayed strip of cheap carpeting. Dust and crumpled pieces of paper littered the corners. He moved silently to the other end. On a pock-marked aluminum door was a stick-on plastic strip that read "Office." He drew his .45. There were six cartridges in the magazine and one ready in the chamber. He thumbed off the safety. Jack reached for the knob and crouched. He yanked the door open and leveled his weapon.

The lighted room beyond was twenty-five feet long and fifteen feet wide. There were two other doors to the cubicle, one to his right and one on the left which apparently opened to the outdoors behind the building. Two gray metal desks and chairs stood on either side of the rear door, and a filing cabinet was positioned against the far wall. The linoleum floor was spotted with patches of melted snow. Along the front wall were a padded recliner chair and a cheap-looking couch. Lying on the couch, bound at the wrists, her mouth taped and her eyes closed, was Rachel. Behind her on the chair, leaning forward and holding something near the girl's eyes, was Basi-lah Walid . . . the woman Jack had known as Bunny Gentry, his onetime sis-ter-in-law. She stared at him.

"You're just in time, Jack," she hissed. "It's going to be a double exe-cution after all." Basilah peered at his gun. "With two fingers, put it on the floor, then kick it over here," she ordered. "If you fuck up, I'll fire this and blow your daughter's brains out her ears." The woman's thumb was poised over the plunger of what looked like a large ballpoint pen. Jack glanced at Rachel. Her face was pale, and she was barely breathing. He bent down and placed the semiautomatic on the floor. He stood up slowly, put his foot against the gun, and shoved it in the woman's direction. The .45 skidded to a stop just beyond her chair.

"You . . . cunt." His voice was a whisper.

"Save your breath, asshole." She pointed to his left. "Sit over there and don't move a goddamned muscle. Otherwise she's a headless corpse."

Jack moved past the first desk and lowered himself into a metal chair, gripping its arms. He kept his eyes on Rachel.

"Oh, the little slut's alive," Basilah observed with a sneer. "It's up to you if she dies sooner than scheduled."

Jack looked back at the woman. What a change from the dressy cham-pagne blond with long fingernails. Tonight she wore a black tactical jump-suit, with leg zippers from her ankles to her knees, and leather boots. Her hair was pulled back into a tight bun. Her fingernails were clipped, and there was no polish. Her features were severe without makeup.

"Why did you take her?"

She glared at him. "Because I despise you and everything you stand for. You Americans and your Zionist scum have subjugated and expropri-ated long enough. We're going to crush you for the millions of innocents you have destroyed." She leaned toward him. "I have hated you ever since I was a child. I just didn't have a face to go with my nightmares until I met you." She laughed. "The past few weeks of killing your contemptible kind have been very satisfying."

Jack slammed his fist against the armrest. "Don't talk to *me* about 'innocents,' you worthless hypocrite. You and your unwashed thugs have snuffed out the lives of 17,000 human beings in your criminal orgies. So cut the bullshit propaganda. You didn't kill for religion or any other lofty cause. You killed for cold cash."

The woman ignored his outburst. "We were so sorry your precious Laura and Jeff had to feed the maggots." She laughed. "But I'm sure it was a square-mile feast."

Jack started out of the chair.

The woman moved her thumb against the plunger. "One step and Rachel dies."

Jack saw the hatred in her eyes. He tightened his lips and sat back down.

"That day Laura left?" Basilah looked at the ceiling and smirked. "It was *so* cold in Texas."

"Skip the history. I already know you drove their killers to the airport."

"We wanted *you* that morning," she snarled, "but you slipped away and sent your wife and son to their deaths." She glanced at the inert figure on the couch. "Failed to get you twice more, so you forced us to take the little bitch, to get you to see things our way." She laughed again. "I have to admit I almost lost it when I saw that video. I wish I could have seen your face when you heard the screams."

"You won't get away . . . "

"Hey, shithead," she interrupted. Her eyes were on fire. "This isn't a cowboy flick where the good guys win in the end."

Jack had never before seen such blind fury.

"I heard you killed Kuttab," she commented after a moment. She shook her head. "Doesn't matter. He had already performed gloriously in avenging the deaths of his parents in 1967."

"Why did you kill Reuben?"

"That worthless old fool just wouldn't die like he was supposed to."

Jack closed his eyes for a second.

"Then there was poor Norman," she went on. "He was one fucked-up pervert. When we were 'dating,' I told him he could eat me, but he threw up. Pathetic. But he sure loved those taut little boys."

"Why did you have to torch the FBI agent? If you were going to kill him, why didn't you just do it? Instead of *that?*"

The woman shook with laughter. "I played with him before I told Rima to fry him. Kept him blindfolded and made him drink his own piss." She smirked. "When some fucking idiot landed his plane on our property earlier, I shot him myself and cut off his penis. We cooked it, and I tried to get that FBI agent to eat it. He couldn't see what it was, and he was so hungry he actually tried to. Not a lot of meat on it. I almost laughed my ass off."

Jack stared at the woman. His mind raced.

"I've got Rima, and I'm willing to swap her for my daughter."

Basilah's expression hardened. "Too late, Stroud. Rima's finished her work, but little Rachel has a big ride ahead of her."

Suddenly Rachel's eyes popped open. She recognized her father and struggled to sit up. Her action caught the woman by surprise.

"What the fuck are you doing?" Basilah yelled. She tried to restrain the teenager by grabbing her around the neck with both arms.

Jack saw the dart pen move out of position momentarily. He had one chance. He thrust his hand inside his coat for the extra ammunition magazine, and he threw the heavy, fully loaded pack as hard as he could. The steel projectile, filled with six .45-caliber bullets, smashed into the bridge of the woman's nose and ripped open a gash upwards across her left eyelid. She screamed, and the explosive pen spun away from her grip. Jack lunged and was on her in an instant. They tumbled over the back of the recliner chair and crashed into the corner. Basilah, squirming, yanked a stubby double-edged serrated knife from her sleeve and jabbed at him. It penetrated Jack's coat and sliced into his upper arm. He felt no pain. He grabbed her wrist with both hands and slammed her hand against the hard floor while he jammed his knee into her abdomen.

"Drop it! Drop it!"

He pounded her hand down again, and the knife burst free. With a curse, the woman raised her knees and propelled him to the side. She twisted out from underneath and scrambled for the dart pen. Jack fell on his back and groaned when he hit something hard. His gun! Basilah grabbed the dart pistol and jumped to her feet. She dove over the arm of the couch and positioned the weapon against Rachel's ear. Jack fired twice. The dart pistol dropped out of Basilah's hand. Her mouth opened, but no sound came out. Jack was ready to fire again, but he saw it wasn't necessary. The impact of the bullets had torn open the woman's back at two places between the shoulder blades. Bright red blood oozed from both entry points. Basilah's body slid backwards off the couch and crumpled next to his feet. A look of shock was frozen on her face.

Jack rose and rushed to Rachel's side. His daughter's eyes were wide with panic.

"It's all right, precious." He laid the gun aside and gently removed the tape from her mouth.

"Daddy! Daddy!" she cried out. "I can't believe you're here!"

Jack leaned over and kissed her. "I'm here, sweetheart. You're going to be just fine."

He found the end of the tape restraining her hands and peeled it off.

"Can you stand up?"

"I . . . I think so."

Rachel haltingly extended her legs over the edge of the couch. She smiled at her father. Then her eyes widened, and she screamed.

Jack jerked back.

"Do you hurt?"

"Not yet," came an accented voice from behind him. Jack spun around. A man stood in the back doorway wielding a submachine gun.

"Looks like I got here just in time."

Jack stared. It was Norman's bus driver.

"You're both going to pay for killing my sister," the man growled.

"Jamil Nasir!"

"Get up."

Jack eyed his .45, barely two feet away. He rose and faced the terrorist.

"She can't walk."

"Then pick her up, you piece of shit." He started to laugh. "Isn't that what you called me on the phone yesterday? Actually, as I remember, it was 'filthy' piece of shit. Pick her up!"

Jack saw that Rachel was nearly in shock. Her eyes were half open, and her mouth quivered.

"Honey, I'm going to carry you. Just relax."

He bent over and slipped his arms under her shoulders and knees. He carefully lifted her off the couch.

Nasir pushed the door open and stepped down the cinder-block steps outside. He kept the muzzle of his automatic weapon pointed at Jack.

"Move!" he commanded. "You two are going for the ride of your lives."

Jack watched Nasir's fierce eyes as he carried Rachel toward the door.

Suddenly the room exploded in gunshots. Nasir was blown backwards. Jack spun to his left.

"Don Evans!" he yelled. "Thank God!"

The FBI agent ran into the room from the side door. He kept his gun aimed where Nasir had stood. "Brand asked for backup, so here I am. Where *is* he anyway?"

Jack carried Rachel back to the couch.

"Checking out the other hangars. How'd you find me?"

Evans didn't answer for a few seconds. He moved toward the open back door. "I've called an ambulance. Stay with your daughter. I'll check on this guy, then I'll track down Brand." Evans led with his pistol. He stopped and stared. There was a patch of blood on the snow outside, and a trail of red splotches that extended around the corner of the building.

"The son of a bitch is gone!"

10:33 p.m.

A shrill turbine whine rolled across the snowy tarmac as Evans ran from the office building. The FBI agent turned the corner and stared into the winter darkness. Bright lights shone from the open doors of the last hangar. He bounded across the apron. Bloody footprints lay ahead of him.

The Sabreliner roared out of the hangar and turned for the runway. It braked, skidded, and accelerated down the snow-covered pavement. Evans stopped in front of the open hangar and watched as the jet lifted off and banked left, toward the south. Within seconds it disappeared into the low overcast.

He pulled out his cellular telephone and punched in the SIOC number.

"Jamil Nasir's headed for Washington in a Sabreliner! I wounded him—I think in the shoulder—but he'll probably be able to make it to the White House. God only knows what kind of explosives he's got on that plane."

"Don, there's only one Apache between him and the city. The rest of them followed the Caravans to the east, west, and south."

"Then send it after him, God damn it! This guy means business. Whatever it takes, destroy the bastard!"

"The helicopter's on frequency now. We'll tell 'em."

Evans knew that virtually every square inch of terrain from Gaithersburg to the south was heavily populated. Somebody on the ground was certain to suffer from an aerial engagement. But there was no other choice. He dashed to the hangar where the Sabreliner had been and spotted a figure crumpled face-down in a corner.

"Corley!"

Brand struggled to lift himself. Blood had pooled and congealed in a crimson oval from rips in his abdomen.

"Don't move, man, please. It's Don Evans. You'll be all right."

Evans attempted to determine the extent of Brand's injuries. He didn't know if a bullet had penetrated the man's spine.

Brand mouthed something. Evans leaned closer.

"Hurts."

"Right. Save your energy by remaining completely still." Evans pulled off his coat and covered Brand's back to help maintain warmth. He decided against rolling the man over. Brand's body weight would act as a crude tourniquet against the punctures.

"Nasir did this," Brand whispered.

"I figured. I had the pleasure of shooting him after he shot you. I intended to kill the son of a bitch, but ... " He made a calming gesture with his hand. "Just don't move. Ambulance's coming."

"He's going for the White House, Don." Brand spoke between erratic breaths.

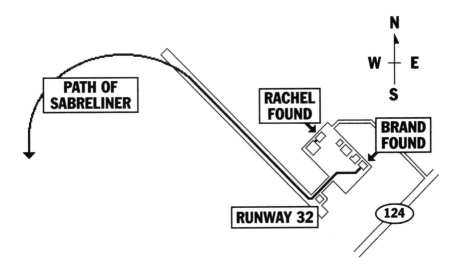

"I know. SIOC's alerted an Apache." Evans placed the palm of his hand on Brand's shoulders. "Now, stay still and don't worry."

"Not . . . much . . . time."

"Will you shut up!"

Brand raised an eyebrow. "Stroud?"

Evans shook his head at his irrepressible patient.

"Two hangars down, with his daughter."

"He found Rachel?" Brand tried to lift his head. "How is she?"

"A hell of a lot better than you are, you obstinate son of a bitch."

In the distance, the growing wail of an ambulance rose and fell. Moments later, the apron outside was bathed in alternating red, blue, and white lights.

The White House
10:39 p.m.

The president brushed past Tim Vance and moved quickly to his chair in the Oval Office.

"This is where I belong, damn it. When will the camera be set up?"

The agitated Secret Service agent looked at his watch. "Two minutes, sir, but, *please,* we don't have that long. You can broadcast from the bunker. If that Sabreliner gets through . . . "

"No." The president shook his head. "Nothing could be worse than what we just experienced. Besides, the Army can handle one airplane, and the American people deserve to hear from me *right now.* In this setting."

Arlington, Virginia
10:41 p.m.

An AH-64A Apache crossed over the Potomac near Georgetown and headed north. The helicopter pilot had acquired his target. The renegade Sabreliner was traveling at a ground speed of 292 miles an hour as it passed Somerset, Maryland, 1,550 feet above the ground. It was 5.6 miles from the White House. One minute and nine seconds away.

"Kill the transmitter," the Apache pilot yelled into his microphone. "He's on a radial, navigating direct to the Washington VORTAC."

At National Airport a supervisor pressed a switch that deactivated the navigation transmitter on the airport property.

"It's off."

The pilot watched. The Sabreliner continued on course.

"For Christ's sake, the guy's got GPS. He doesn't need the VOR!"

The helicopter's copilot gunner could see the target on a television-type display through a square-inch monocle. He double-checked. The Hellfire missile was ready to follow the laser designator.

"Don't you have him?" the pilot shouted into the microphone.

"Here goes."

The copilot gunner pressed the button, and the missile whooshed away from its modular launcher on the starboard side. The CPG fixed the laser on the target and watched. The missile homed in. Six seconds later, it hit. He saw a puff of white iridescence on his green screen. The intercept took place directly over the National Cathedral. He was sure it was a successful engagement.

"Aircraft terminated," he reported confidently.

"Like hell!" a voice cracked in the pilots' ears. It was a radar controller at National Airport. "He's still heading for the White House!"

Both Apache crew members stared at their screens in disbelief. A large object corkscrewed out of the Hellfire explosion and careened onward toward the Executive Mansion, now less than 16,000 feet away.

"Holy shit," the pilot whispered. "We must have blown off his tail."

It was too late to fire another missile. He keyed his microphone.

"White House . . . White House, you on frequency?"

There was no reply.

"God damn it, Secret Service, you've got an out-of-control Sabreliner coming at you! Do you read?"

The White House
10:42 p.m.

"Get out!" Tim Vance yelled as he grabbed the chief executive under the arms. "Now, sir, *now!*"

The television broadcast had just begun, and technicians stared in disbelief as the Secret Service agent yanked the president out of his chair in front of a worldwide audience of three billion.

"The Batmobiles?" another agent bellowed from the door to the Oval Office.

"No time." Vance shook his head. "They're pointed north anyway, where the plane's coming from. The bunker!"

A contingent of a dozen agents led the way. Vance alternately pushed and pulled the president along as they jogged for the special elevator.

Over Connecticut Avenue and L Street
10:43 p.m.

Suddenly a flash illuminated the cockpit of the Apache. To the right, a blinding-white orb held for a second at their altitude, then blinked out. The percussion of the explosion rocked the helicopter a moment later. The pilot gripped the stick to maintain control. A message snapped in his headset.

"God almighty, it's falling all around us."

"Say again?" the pilot requested.

"I got him! I got the fucker!"

The voice finally identified itself.

"Patterson, Secret Service," a man yelled. "I'm in the middle of Lafayette Park. Hit him dead on with a Redeye. Crap's burning everywhere. A few pieces hit the North Portico, but the White House itself is safe. Repeat, he did *not* make it to the White House!"

The Apache pilot closed his eyes.

Montgomery County Airpark, Maryland
11:01 p.m.

The paramedics completed their work in eleven minutes. Corley Brand was given emergency treatment for his gunshot wounds and secured with an IV inside the boxy vehicle. Rachel was next. Jack's injury was deemed sufficiently minor to merit attention only after the ambulance departed for Bethesda Naval Medical Center.

Don Evans followed in his car. As the entourage swung onto the highway, he heard a bulletin that an airplane had exploded just north of the White House. There were numerous fires. Evans shook his head and said a prayer.

The report continued with a statement from the White House that the public inaugural ceremony tomorrow on the West Front of the Capitol had been canceled.

48

Bethesda Naval Medical Center
Wednesday, January 20, 8:53 a.m.

Jack lay on the couch and watched Rachel sleep. The hospital had offered him a separate room, but he'd insisted on staying close to his daughter. She had awakened twice during the night and cried out for her mother and then for him. Both times, he'd held her and told her that he loved her and that she was safe at last. Both times, she'd called him "Dad" and whispered that she loved him, too. The nightmare was finally over. Jack could be her full-time father once again.

"Hello?" a voice whispered from the door. Jack turned and recognized the face of Tim Vance. The Secret Service agent raised his eyebrows and inclined his head toward the sleeping figure in bed. Jack smiled and motioned for him to come in. Vance stepped inside the room and pushed the door shut.

"Just talked to the doc," the agent advised in a low voice. "He says she'll be completely fine in a day or so. Physically, anyway."

"Thanks for coming by, Tim. Did he tell you what I should expect afterward?"

Vance shook his head. "Nothing specific. Just that she'll probably need intensive counseling . . . and months of TLC."

"I owe you a lot," Jack said. "Things might not have worked out, and I might not have gotten her back at all, if you hadn't been at that meeting yesterday and seconded my suppositions."

Vance grinned. "Hey, hotshot, you would have searched heaven and hell until you found her. Anyway, I'm here on official business."

Jack checked his watch and realized that their special visitor would arrive in less than an hour. "Oh, right, the president."

Vance glanced at Rachel. "He wants to tell her himself how much he appreciates you and what you've done." The agent squinted at Jack's arm. "How's the wound?"

Jack raised and lowered his arm slowly.

"That woman was lousy with an edged weapon."

"Not what I heard. She was supposed to be a hand-to-hand combat expert."

Jack shrugged. "Yeah, supposed to be." Then he peered at the Secret Service man.

"Corley?"

Vance thrust his hands into his overcoat. "Took five hits. One in the shoulder and four in the gut. Only a miracle the bullets didn't sever an artery, but a slug did crack his hip. They had him in surgery until about four this morning. But he'll make it. His veins are full of piss and vinegar, you know. Probably be stuck here for six weeks, though. They had to do a colostomy. Won't be repaired for another two months. He'll love that."

"Can I see him?"

"Possibly this afternoon. I've heard the FBI director is planning to be here at three."

"Well, when the smoke clears, I'd like for him to take some time off and come down for a little R and R."

Vance laughed. "I'll bet Brand won't want to get any closer to Tulsa than 37,000 feet over it with a double scotch securely in his hand."

"Dad?"

The men turned and saw Rachel peering at them.

"Good morning, precious." Jack moved to her side. "How do you feel?"

"Sleepy."

"Any pain?"

She shook her head. She considered the visitor. For a moment, fear clouded her gaze.

"Tim Vance, Rachel," the agent spoke softly. "I'm a friend of your dad."

The teenager nodded sluggishly, then smiled.

Vance walked closer and reached into the pocket of his overcoat. He withdrew a small box with a pink ribbon. "I was passing a store a few minutes ago, and, well . . ." He handed her the box. Rachel suddenly drew back, as if the object were a threat. Then she leaned forward hesitantly.

"For *me?*" Her eyes were wide. Accepting the gift, she slid off the ribbon and removed the glossy white wrapping. She looked at her father before she lifted the top.

"Do *you* know what it is?"

Jack shook his head. "Haven't a clue, sweetie. After all, Tim *is* with the *Secret* Service."

Rachel peeked beneath a pad inside the box. "Ooh, he's beautiful."

She laid the cotton aside and extracted a silver representation of an Arabian horse. She held it up. Tears welled in her eyes, then sobs shook her.

Vance looked on helplessly. Jack immediately put his hand on Rachel's head to smooth her hair and calm her. After a moment, her sobs abated, and she lifted the bed sheet to dry her face.

"I'm sorry. I don't know what's wrong with me." She considered the horse. "I *love* him. He'll stand right next to the one my brother gave me." She again wiped at her eyes with the sheet and opened her arms. "This deserves a hug, Mr. Vance."

"You're a brave young lady, Rachel." Vance leaned over and returned the embrace tightly. "God bless you."

The agent stood back and fumbled for his handkerchief. "Hey, I'm supposed to be on duty." He turned and feigned blowing his nose. "Gotta stay detached and unemotional in this job, you know." Vance completed his grooming and faced her again. "And I have another surprise for you. The president himself will be here to see you in about forty-five minutes."

"The president?" Rachel looked at her father.

"That's right." Jack smiled back. She seemed only a little different than usual. At least she was alive. That was all that counted for now.

"I'd better go," Vance said. He stepped toward the door. "Be back shortly."

"Mr. Vance?"

Vance stopped and turned at Rachel's voice. She smiled. "Thank you so much. He's perfect." The Secret Service agent delivered a modified salute, and a wink, and left.

Jack reached for a nearby chair and moved closer to Rachel's bed. She held the horse and stroked it. He heard her humming softly.

"Know something?" Jack roughed her hair and sat down and looked at her. "Sometimes you sound just like your mom."

Rachel's eyes met his. Her voice was controlled. "I've thought a lot about her. Jeff, too." She looked back at her gift. "I talk to them a lot." She continued humming to the tiny silver horse.

Jack took a deep breath. "So do I, sweetie." He looked at his watch. "Hey, how about something to eat? Still time before the president gets here."

She smiled. "OK."

Rachel reached up and pressed the call button. A woman's voice responded from an overhead speaker. "Yes, Miss Stroud?"

Rachel looked toward the speaker. "May I have my breakfast, please?"

"You certainly may," the woman replied. "Be about fifteen minutes."

Rachel returned to her new acquisition, and her private thoughts.

Jack tried to keep his worries at bay. Just act natural, he told himself. Get her back into her regular routine—and life—as smoothly as possible.

"Let's call Flora while we're waiting."

Rachel rolled to her side. "Oh, could we?"

Jack picked up the telephone and tapped in his home number in Tulsa. When he heard it ring, he handed the phone to Rachel. She positioned herself on her elbow.

"Flora? It's me, Rachel!"

Jack watched his daughter's assorted facial expressions as she told the housekeeper some of the horrors she had experienced. He hadn't wanted her to relive what she had suffered, at least not so soon. As she spoke, he shook away the thoughts of her ordeal. Maybe, he decided, it was better for her to express her feelings. Maybe, in truth, it was better for him also.

"I love you, too, Flora. Oh, please don't cry. I'm going to be all right. And I can hardly wait to see you. Dad and I will be home . . . " She questioned Jack with her expression.

"Friday," he replied.

"Friday," she exclaimed. "Isn't that great! Say, Flora, did I get any calls?"

Jack laughed. "Hey, Rach, you can resume your social life when you get home." He was pleased with her display of curiosity about her telephone calls. Maybe she would recover as fast as he hoped. He reached for the phone. "Here, let me talk to her."

Rachel cupped her hand over the mouthpiece. "I'll call you later. He hasn't changed a bit. Still thinks the telephone belongs to him." She handed him the handset and put on her best pout.

Jack rolled his eyes.

"Hello, Flora."

"Mr. Stroud, everyone is talking about you and Miss Rachel. Every time we turn on the television they say that you are a hero, that you . . . "

"Every time *we* turn on the television?" he interrupted.

"Why, Mister G and me."

Jack lifted his head. "Oh, of course. Lester Graham."

Flora continued. "He don't have a place to live yet, Mr. Stroud, so I fixed him up in the guest room. I told him you would want it that way."

"Yes, that's fine, Flora. I'd like a chance to talk to him when I get back." He winked at Rachel. "So I'm on TV?"

"Yes, sir. They say the president is going to give you an award or something."

"Really?" It was a surprise to Jack.

"I don't remember what's it's called, but we're so happy for you."

"Well, thanks, Flora. I'll let you know what happens. And give my best to Lester."

Rachel reached for his hand as he hung up.

"I love you, Dad."

"I love you, too, precious."

"I just wish Mom and Jeff were here . . . " Her voice trailed off. Tears welled in her eyes.

"Me, too, sweetie." Jack squeezed her hand. "Me, too."

Outside the White House
9:15 a.m.

The White House had announced ten hours earlier that the formal ceremony at the Capitol would not be held. Instead, the president would take the oath of office in the East Room of the executive mansion. The world would be present through television, and it was expected that the president would make his most important address ever.

Outside, crowds waited in the cold, listening to radios and watching portable television sets. Ministers mingled with their parishioners and led them in prayer for the spiritual rebuilding of the nation.

At the southwest entrance to the White House, uniformed guards opened the heavy security gates. A procession of Secret Service cars and vans and a heavy limousine with red lights flashing through its grille eased forward, met a police escort, and pulled into the street, which had been cleared of crowds.

"Why, it's the president!" a woman shrieked and waved.

The distinctive boxy limousine was the fifth car in the procession. Three follow-up vehicles maintained close separation, and the motorcade roared away.

Bethesda Naval Medical Center
9:45 a.m.

Jack stood before a mirror. He concluded that he didn't look exactly distinguished in his hospital robe, but he didn't have any other choice. His shirt and undershirt had been sliced open by Basilah's knife and had been disposed of by the emergency room personnel when they'd stitched his wound. He opened the closet and saw the coat and pants he'd worn in the struggle the previous evening. It was the midnight-blue worsted wool suit Laura had given him on Christmas Eve. He bit his lip as he surveyed the fine pinstripes in the soft material. He felt for and found the cut on the inside of the sleeve. He closed the door and touched at the still-sensitive spot on his skull.

"All ready!" His daughter emerged from the bathroom in her robe. Jack studied the beautiful young woman before him, with her auburn hair and aquamarine eyes. She was a living memory of Laura. He put his arms around her.

Rachel padded for the table next to the window and the radio. She punched the "on" button and twisted the dial. Most of the selections were news programs about the attack on the White House. She finally found a station playing patriotic music. She set the volume at a background level.

"How's this, Dad?"

Jack nodded. "Perfect."

There was a knock on the door. Jack noticed a hunted look on Rachel's face. It disappeared as quickly as it had appeared.

"Mr. Stroud?" A big man poked his head into the room. He wore a dark business suit and had a fitted earpiece with a coiled wire extending under his collar. Four other men were with him, all wearing identical lapel pins. Rachel slowly moved to a position behind her father, as if for protection from intruders.

"Sir, John Braddock, Secret Service. There are three of us from the White House detail." He indicated with his hand. "I think you already know Tim Vance. Plus the White House photographer and a video cameraman."

"Please come in, gentlemen," Jack motioned. He grinned at Vance.

"The White House press corps won't intrude today," Braddock advised as he stepped inside. "The president's on his way." He put his hand to his ear. "He'll be here in . . . seven seconds."

Jack motioned for Rachel to stand alongside him. "Quick!" He took a deep breath and tightened the belt of his robe.

The president, wearing his unmistakable grin, walked briskly around the corner and extended his right hand. "Captain Stroud, this is an honor for me."

Jack shook the president's hand. "Thank you, sir." He turned. "This is my daughter, Rachel."

The president reached for the teenager's hand. "What a beautiful name," he observed as he cupped her hand in his. He looked at her with the eyes Americans had overwhelmingly decided mirrored a good soul. "Did you know that Rachel was my mother's name?"

The pretty sixteen-year-old blushed.

"No, sir, but did you know I'm awfully proud of my Dad?"

The president laughed. "Well, we are, too, Rachel."

Jack extended his arm in the direction of the three chairs and a couch.

"Mr. President, would you care to be seated?"

The president took a chair. Jack and his daughter sat down on the couch. The president rubbed his hands together.

"Jack, as you may know, I canceled the formal inaugural ceremony on the West Front of the Capitol. Under the circumstances, I thought it best. If you don't mind, I'd like to tell you what I know about the assault on America that took the lives of your wife and son . . . and so many others. It might help you put some personal feelings into perspective."

"Please. I need to do that." Jack looked at Rachel. "We both do."

"All right, let me give you a brief review, starting with its genesis in the disintegration of the Soviet Union. Much of this information we owe to Hassan Kadry, the new Syrian prime minister, and others in the government of his country."

The president shifted to the edge of his chair.

"We used to think that the leaders of the former Soviet Union would eventually act in any way, including war, to destroy capitalism in general and the United States in particular. However, their economic system was a mockery, which many in our intelligence community realized as early as the 1950s. Unfortunately the CIA didn't get the message until four decades later, after their inflated economic evaluations and growth predictions missed reality by miles. That was when Gorbachev, through *glasnost,* was finally forced to reveal the truth. Then the operative strategy in the Kremlin became the simple survival of their political and economic system. But the leaders could see the end of all that they and their forebears had worked to establish. That's why Gorbachev, in effect, was 'created.' He was their best hope to secure from the West the needed support while the internal changes were attempted in an atmosphere protective of the system. Unfortunately for them, they were overwhelmed, and everything fell apart."

The president sat back.

"Certain elements of the KGB had feared just such an outcome, and, as far back as 1980, they made plans to take a 'stabilizing' action on their own. The specific program that led to the horrors we've suffered over the past three and a half weeks was devised in 1987, and the go-ahead to source the newly developed terrorist group in the heartland of America was given a few years ago. While we don't know for certain if Gorbachev was aware of their final plans for the 'American incursion,' as they called it, it is fairly safe to say that he would not have opposed it. In the last analysis, we know that his fondest hope in early 1991 was to maintain the elite *nomenklatura* by yielding, if necessary, some control to the populace. He seemed to believe that, given time, he could do enough to change the lot of the ordinary Soviet citizen so that the pressures for further change would subside and control by the Communist Party could be maintained. Of course, it didn't work out that way."

The president looked at Rachel. She was listening intently. He continued.

"One thing that had fascinated the KGB was the political power and influence of the extreme elements of the religious evangelical movement. Over the years, respected elected members of both American political parties paid a lot more than lip service to the leaders of the various televangelist organizations. They attended their services, and they actively sought their support and that of their congregations. The KGB easily saw the connection between the goals of some of these ministries and their own. On the surface, to the unsophisticated, it looked like an incongruous marriage. Underneath, it was a natural. 'Made in hell,' as it turned out."

Jack shook his head slowly.

"KGB strategists discussed the vulnerability of certain financially troubled televangelists who vigorously—some say violently—opposed the direction America seemed to be taking. Terrorism in the name of religion had become de rigueur around the world, from Beirut and Belfast to Bogotá. The KGB concluded that its operations under the cover of the righteousness of a widely known ministry in the heart of America would be well concealed and Constitutionally protected, at least long enough for them to carry out their objectives.

"It took them nearly five years of analysis before the ministry of Reuben Gentry was selected. His son, Norman . . . " The president paused and looked at Jack and Rachel. Both appeared resigned to his message. He took a deep breath. "Jack, your former brother-in-law had shown . . . uh . . . deviant interests, and a thorough investigation through the KGB's network of informants in the United States had produced incontrovertible proof of his tastes. So, having decided upon their target, all that was necessary then was funding, training, and implementation."

The president went on.

"It was an unholy trio: The KGB hard-liners who had access to the equivalent of $9 billion in Soviet gold on deposit in Zurich, the best North Korean trainers to perfect killing skills, and religious fundamentalists who were willing to die in martyrdom because of their hatred for America. The unraveling of Eastern Europe was the last straw. The transfer of the terrorist operatives to America began shortly thereafter. Even the possibility of a return to authoritarian rule after Yeltsin didn't dissuade them."

The president gripped the armrests of his chair. "We should have recognized the World Trade Center bombing as their first full-scale test, but we didn't. Oklahoma City was 'homegrown,' so we didn't pay attention to the warning signs. Then came the Hamas incidents around the country. We still couldn't imagine a U.S.-based operation."

He looked Jack squarely in the eye.

"I have thought about and prayed for your wife and son a hundred times. I have done the same for you and your daughter. Your family has suffered beyond any human ability to make recompense. But I have to tell you that without your help, we wouldn't have defeated this diabolical plan. The United States will forever be in your debt."

Rachel beamed at her father.

"Jack," the president went on, "I cannot thank you enough for what you've done. You stayed the course when you had every right to ask to be left alone with your grief. But I can express the gratitude of the nation, however little that may be in relation to the price you have paid."

The president nodded toward the White House photographer and the cameraman.

"These gentlemen are here to record for all Americans what I am about to do now."

He rose. "Jack, please join me." The president smiled at Rachel. "Would you like to be with your dad for this?"

Rachel nodded and moved to her father's side. As the video man positioned and adjusted the camera, she took her father's hand and held it tightly. When the cameraman signaled his readiness, the president began.

"This is an occasion that happens so infrequently that a separate ceremony and award have been prepared as a testimony to its significance. America has many heroes and heroines of whom she is proud. But only once in a great while does an individual do something unique which must be acknowledged by the nation as a whole. We are fortunate today to be able to express our gratitude to just such a person. John Harrington Stroud, with a single-mindedness of purpose, risked his life to uncover and help defeat a terrible plan by international outlaws to bring about the destruction of the United States of America. Nearly a month ago, he lost his beloved wife, their son, and his father-in-law to these evil people. During the ensuing and agonizing days of attempting to comprehend why, he nearly lost his own life and that of his precious daughter, Rachel. Today she stands proudly next to him."

The president opened a box that the photographer had handed him.

"It is time to thank one of our fellow countrymen who represents the highest aspirations of the human spirit. Speaking from my heart and as the representative of the citizens of the United States, I am honored to present the Presidential Medal of Freedom to a true American hero, Jack Stroud."

10:31 a.m.

Jack stood at the window with Rachel. The sky was a cobalt blue, and branches of the bare trees outside shifted back and forth in a cold breeze. Eight inches of snow coated the nearby buildings and sparkled in the sunlight. Two stories below, a procession of police cars, Secret Service vans, and the presidential limousine waited in the cleared driveway.

Jack reached into his pocket and drew out a small velvet pouch. He took his daughter's left hand and placed a heavy gold object into it.

"Rachel, there's no better time for me to give you this St. Christopher medal. I gave it to your mom when we were married. Just before she boarded the plane, she returned it to me, because she was worried about me. I've carried it ever since. The inscription on the back reads, 'To protect you for me wherever you may be.' I want you to have it as a remembrance of your mother and of her love."

Rachel's eyes filled.

"Your mother . . . " Jack hesitated and then continued in a whisper, "your mother was the most wonderful human being I've ever known." He stopped again. "And I want you, her beautiful daughter, to have this, to protect you, with my love." Tears streamed down his face.

Rachel accepted the medal and held it tightly. She started to cry.

"Oh, Daddy, I will cherish this every day for the rest of my life. Maybe this will help me get over everything I've been through."

"I hope so, Rach." Jack pulled her close. He was glad she had started calling him "Daddy" again. Maybe things would return to normal after all. "We'll help each other get over our fears."

"I . . . I'm still scared, Daddy." Her eyes darted toward the door, then to Jack, and her head bobbed nervously.

Jack sat down with his daughter. "That makes two of us, sweetie. We'll never be able to forget what we've gone through, but we need to work through it and get past our grief." He looked into her eyes.

"Let's make a deal."

Rachel reached for a Kleenex and frowned. Jack continued. "I'll help you if you'll help me. That way we can get back to living. OK?"

Rachel tightened her lips for a second. Then she smiled and hugged him. "It's a deal." After a moment, she popped backwards. "Hey, I want to watch him leave."

"What?"

"I hope I'm not too late."

Rachel dashed to the window. Below, the president had stopped next to the open door of his limousine. He turned, looked up, and smiled at her. She watched as he touched the tip of his hand to his lips and blew her a kiss.

Outside the main entrance to the Bethesda complex, half a hundred individuals stood in the cold stillness and waved as the presidential motor-cade coursed swiftly from the hospital grounds and headed down Wisconsin Avenue. When the last Secret Service chase car rounded the corner, a tall man in a gray cashmere overcoat with silver-flecked brown, razor-cropped hair and a clipped moustache stepped closer and smiled benignly at two young women. He wore expensive sunglasses.

"Pardon me, ladies. Do you have the time?"

"Mm, sure," one woman replied. She pressed a gloved finger against her coat and moved the cuff back to expose her wristwatch.

"Ten thirty-seven," she returned with a smile.

The man nodded. "Thank you very much." He walked south, toward Washington.

When he was beyond earshot, the woman turned to her friend.

"Ooo-eee! Good looking guy, even if he *is* middle-aged. Sounded British . . . or maybe even . . . " she rolled her head, "a rich German." She kept her gaze on the man.

"And, wow, what a wardrobe."

Her friend wrinkled her nose. "But a little too much aftershave."

"Yeah," the first woman observed, almost as an afterthought. "Aqua Velva. I didn't think anyone wore that stuff anymore."

THE END